THE GOODING GIRL

'The baby's father. Who is the baby's father?' Hettie repeated dully, her eyes on the ground that separated them. She glanced up. 'If you lie to me,' she said calmly, 'and I find out, I'll kill you.'

Agnes's blue eyes widened fearfully and she took a step backwards. 'Kill me? You wouldn't dare! You're mad!' she whispered.

'It's George, isn't it?'

Agnes was backing slowly towards the comparative safety of the front door, considering how best to protect herself and her child. She would slam the front door and lock it and then run through to bar the back door.

'The baby's father – it's George, isn't it?' Hettie continued to stare at the ground in front of her. 'I shall not leave here until you tell me the truth.'

Agnes opened her mouth to shout, 'No, it's not!' but shouted, 'Yes, it is!' instead. Let her know then, she thought, since she's so determined . . .

Pamela Oldfield

THE GOODING GIRL

WARNER BOOKS

For Joseph Portsmouth
who gave me the original idea, with my love

A *Warner* Book

First published in Great Britain
by Century Hutchinson Ltd in 1985
Published by Arrow in 1986
This edition published by Warner Books in 1993
Reprinted 1998

A CIP catalogue record for this book is
available from the British Library.

ISBN 0 7515 0131 X

Printed in England by Clays Ltd, St Ives plc

Warner Books
A Division of
Little, Brown and Company (UK)
Brettenham House
Lancaster Place
London WC2E 7EN

CHAPTER ONE

In retrospect, it was generally accepted that Henrietta Coulsden –
called Hettie by everyone – went into labour at the most inconvenient time possible although no one, not even Cicely, went so
far as to suggest that she did so deliberately. The first contraction
came at 3.20 a.m. on Thursday 18 July, 1910, and Hettie's
immediate reaction was one of disbelief. The child was not due
for another two weeks and, before departing for his summer
holiday, the doctor had assured her that all was in order and her
third pregnancy now proceeding satisfactorily. Earlier on she had
suffered from anaemia and excessive sickness, which in turn had
resulted in acute anxiety symptoms. Hettie, normally so robust,
was apparently not designed for childbearing. Each of her two
earlier attempts to give George an heir had resulted in a mis-
carriage – one at three months, the other at five – and now she
stood with both hands clasped protectively over her abdomen and
uttered a hasty but fervent prayer that *this* baby would survive.
Was eight-and-a-half months long enough for the child to take a
firm grasp on life? Hettie appealed to God's generous nature and
asked that it should be; then she remained quite still and waited to
see if the sharp knife-thrust would come again.

When it did she consoled herself that it was not as bad as she
had expected and that if it became no worse, she would certainly
be able to endure the pain with dignity. There would be no
inelegant writhing and no biting on leather straps as Cicely had
suggested. Her beautiful sister-in-law, Hettie reflected scornfully, was the delicate orchid type who went through life accord-
ingly, wilting with indecent haste whenever an opportunity
presented itself. How the delicate Cicely had survived the births
of her three children remained a mystery to everyone who knew
her. Hettie saw herself more as a sturdy marigold.

With the third contraction Hettie decided to make herself a pot
of tea while she considered what to do next. The arrangements
for the confinement had never been quite finalised, although it

was generally understood that at the due time her mother would
be with her until the midwife arrived. But her widowed mother
was at King's Lynn, helping a friend through a bereavement, and
was not expected back until the end of the week. Sarah Coulsden,
her mother-in-law, always spent Thursdays in Hastings visiting
Jane and Stanley. Hettie sighed. It would have to be Cicely then,
she thought, renewing her determination not to exhibit any signs
of weakness or give way to any kind of panic or hysteria.

'No fuss,' she muttered as she waited for the water in the kettle
to boil. She would *not* give Cicely anything to gloat over and
certainly no chance to say, 'I told you so.' There would be no
delicious details for Cicely to pass around the rest of the family.
Spooning tea into the pot, she added the boiling water and then
found a cup, saucer and spoon. The sugar and milk were still on
the table – uncovered, she noted with a sigh.

'That foolish girl!' said Hettie.

Being Thursday, it was of course Mrs Mack's day off, and as
luck would have it the housekeeper had been given permission to
spend the night with relatives and was not expected back until
early on Friday morning. Eunice, the new daily help, had been for
her customary two hours and then gone home again. Hettie
crossed to look in the mirror which Mrs Mack had hung on the
back of the door.

The face that stared back at her was much plainer than she had
hoped. It seemed that going into labour did not enhance a
woman's appearance. Her hair was just as mousy and she looked
exactly the same as usual, apart from a wariness in the usually
calm brown eyes and a sudden tightening of the small mouth as
another pain shot through her. George Coulsden – as everyone
knew – had married her for the money her parents would leave
her. In fact the union had met with disapproval from both sides.
Hettie's father was a prosperous grocer and also a sidesman at the
church; the idea of their only child marrying into the local fishing
community did not please her parents at all and they had made it
clear to her that she could and should make a much better match
for herself. Hettie, hopelessly in love with her 'rough diamond',
pleaded so tearfully and so persistently that, against their better
judgement, they finally consented.

On George's side, his parents objected to the match on very
different grounds. They found Hettie 'full of airs and graces' and
advised him to choose a wife from among his own kind. George,

however, impressed by Hettie's background, insisted that he would rather marry her while he could do so decently and not wait until it became a shotgun affair. The threat implied in these words sparked off a family row, but the Coulsdens had survived many such clashes – in fact they seemed to thrive on them – and eventually George got his own way. To everyone's surprise, the union was not the disaster that was prophesied and the only shadow blighting the young couple's happiness was lack of a family. Hettie was content. She was married, she had a home of her own and when she presented her husband with a son she believed he would be well-satisfied.

Now she carried her tea to the front window and stood looking down on the familiar scene. The cliff, covered with grass and shrubs, fell steeply to another road which curved towards the Strand Quay in one direction and towards Camber in the other. Beyond the road the flat grassy area known as 'The Salts' lay dry and browning in the warm sun which glistened on the broad ribbon of water which was the Rother. The nearest bank of the river was partly obscured by a row of wooden huts. From some of these the women sold the fish their menfolk had landed; others contained gear and tackle belonging to the fishermen. The boats were still moored alongside and Hettie put up a hand to shade her eyes as she searched among the fishermen for the familiar figure of her husband. As she did so a fierce contraction made her gasp and then curse under her breath as the tea-cup toppled from its saucer and fell on to the carpet, splashing tea on to the hem of her long skirt as it went down. So the pains *were* going to get worse, she reflected uneasily and offered up another prayer that she would be able to endure the ordeal, however severe, with some semblance of self-respect. Perhaps it was time to get in touch with her sister-in-law, she thought, bending awkwardly to pick up the cup. She had not had so much as a sip of tea, but now decided not to bother. No doubt Cicely would make one when she arrived. With an involuntary sigh she again scanned the doll-like figures that moved on and around the boats, still hoping to see George. If she did, then she would ask her neighbour's son to bicycle down with a message asking him to fetch Cicely in the dog-cart.

For the last two months George had spent most of his spare time at his brother Jack's boatyard; since he was now needed rather urgently, probably he would be in Hastings with his other brother Stanley and not so readily available.

'How typical,' she said, referring not to her husband but to the awkward vagaries of fate.

The moored boats rocked very slightly in the breeze and the sound of gruff voices came faintly to her ears, followed by a spurt of childish laughter. Hettie's expression softened suddenly; God willing, she and George would soon have a child of their own.

'Oh God!' She gritted her teeth and doubled up in agony as the muscles of her womb contracted once more. She tried to visualise the child beginning his journey into the bright world and told him with a faint smile, 'You're *hurting* me, you know that?'

But by that time the pain had faded almost as suddenly as it had come. Now she must act quickly, she decided. Soon she was going to need help, but already she wanted reassurance. She wanted her mother, but that she knew was out of the question. Hurrying into the hall, she picked up the telephone with hands that trembled and, when the operator answered, asked him to make the connection as quickly as possible.

*

Cicely Coulsden prided herself on the fact that, despite being five feet eleven inches tall, she did not stoop, neither was she round-shouldered. She sat at her desk straight-backed and with head erect, fully aware that to the woman opposite she gave the impression of a person with whom it would be unwise to trifle. She stared across the desk at Miss Marjory Mills, a small fat woman in her late thirties with button eyes that almost disappeared into the fleshy folds of her face. Cicely, beautiful and willowy, had taken an instant dislike to her. She did not like people who were smaller than she was because they made her feel taller than ever and such feelings undermined her confidence on the few occasions when it was at a low ebb.

'And how long were you with your previous employer?' she asked.

'Seven years.'

Cicely would have preferred her to add the word 'ma'am', but nowadays it seemed unfashionable to expect these courtesies from servants. The problem was becoming increasingly difficult and sometimes Cicely envied Hettie the devoted Mrs Mack.

'Seven?' Cicely raised her eyebrows and read from the letter which she held in her hand. 'Let me see . . . ah, yes . . .' She quoted from the letter, ' "Miss Mills has been in our employ for six and a half years ..." ' Cicely smiled charmingly at the puddingy Miss Mills.

Miss Mills shrugged. 'Well, nearly seven years,' she said. 'Near enough seven.'

'Six months short of seven,' Cicely corrected her. 'You might equally say it was "nearly six".'

Already Cicely had made up her mind that Marjory Mills was the only suitable applicant, but saw no point in telling her so just yet. Cicely enjoyed interviewing people and had therefore convinced herself that too brief an interview would be an insult; she prided herself on a clear understanding of what was and was not the correct way to behave towards those she chose to consider as 'the lower classes'. She believed that she had gone up in the world by marrying one of the Coulsden boys because the Coulsden family owned a boatyard, two fishing boats and a house called South View in nearby Appledore. Her own family owned nothing at all and were usually three or four weeks behind with the rent. Her uncle had been cowman to the farmer whose land adjoined South View and she had grown up as a gawky child with a secret passion for all three Coulsden boys. Jack had hardly been aware of her existence until she had suddenly blossomed into a beauty at the age of fifteen. By that time Stanley, the oldest boy, had already married and moved back to Hastings. George, the youngest, did not even like her, so she had no alternative but to turn her attention towards Jack with immediate success. As Jack's wife, Cicely tried hard to be a lady; her extravagant tastes had been more than once the subject of bitter quarrels between herself and her husband.

Ignoring the sulky look which now darkened Miss Mills's face, Cicely said, 'You only looked after one child, I see, with your previous employer. I have two young children – Leonard and little Benjamin. My daughter Winifred is fourteen, so you would only have charge of the boys. Do you think you could cope with two boys?'

'Yes, Mrs Coulsden,' said Miss Mills. 'I had four to look after at my first place – twin girls and two older boys. I was only twenty then.'

Cicely smiled again because she knew that her smile was attractive. 'Did you really?' she said. 'But then of course you were much younger. We all had more energy when we were twenty.'

She softened the comment by adding, 'I wish *I* had the energy now that I had then.'

'But they were a real handful,' Miss Mills insisted rashly, whereupon Cicely allowed her expression to change to one of alarm.

'Oh, dear! You found them a handful, did you?'

Miss Mills was beginning to have second thoughts about her prospective employer. At first she had been awed by the gracious manner and undoubted beauty and elegance of the mother of Winifred, Leonard and little Benjamin. Now she began to see flaws in the beauty (for one thing, the neck was rather too long) and to suspect that a mean streak was concealed beneath the gracious manner.

'They were a handful,' she said firmly, 'but I was quite able to cope with them.'

'You were? I see.'

In spite of her rapidly cooling feelings towards her potential employer, Miss Mills envied her her looks – a pale complexion, large blue-green eyes and luxuriant auburn hair – and would cheerfully have overlooked the sprinkling of freckles which were not entirely masked by the light dusting of powder. Miss Mills had suspected for many years that God was not always fair and to give Mrs Coulsden good looks *and* a husband convinced her that her suspicions were well-founded. However, she herself had no looks, no husband and no money and she desperately needed a job. As nannying was all she knew, she made an effort to concentrate on what Mrs Coulsden was saying, making a mental note that if the interview *was* successful she would astonish her employer by her determination, hard work and undisguised devotion to the two boys.

'The boys are very young, you know,' Cicely told her. 'Leonard will be six just before Christmas and little Benjamin – we never abbreviate any of their names – will be two years old on the third of October. He is still not much more than a baby. I'm afraid all three were quite devoted to Miss Jay, their last nanny who was *so* good with them; it was a delight to see them all together, but with the death of her father she has to return home to nurse her invalid mother. That's the way it goes, I'm afraid, these days. Find a good nanny and after a year or so, off she goes for some reason or another. Are your parents in good health, Miss Mills?'

'Yes, they are and so are my maternal grandparents,' Miss

Mills told her eagerly. 'We're a long-living family, my mother says. *Her* mother was well over sixty when she died and her grandmother lived into her *seventies*, with good health up to the very last minute when she suddenly dropped dead. She –'

'Yes, thank you. I see. That's quite splendid.'

Cicely nodded to show that she had heard enough. Garrulous, she noticed. A pity, for she did not like garrulous women; she always maintained that a garrulous woman was a time-waster and no one could deny it. But the other three applicants had proved unsuitable for various reasons and had even fewer redeeming features. One was much too attractive, one was too young and the third spoke with a strong Irish accent which was hard to understand. Marjory Mills was far from ideal, but she would have to do; in spite of her appearance, she spoke well and seemed surprisingly well-educated.

At that moment the telephone rang in the hall, then there was a knock at the study door and the housekeeper came into the room.

'Yes?' said Cicely, frowning at the interruption.

'It's Mrs Coulsden, madam,' Mrs Matthews told her.

'Oh, really! Isn't it always the way!' Cicely's smile was brittle. 'I can't talk to her now. Say that I will ring her back later.'

The housekeeper hesitated. 'She did sound a bit upset, madam.'

'Upset? In what way "upset"?'

'Well, madam – first she said it was urgent and then she said it wasn't. I told her you were engaged with someone and then she said—' She looked embarrassed and glanced towards Miss Mills.

Sensing that something was wrong, Cicely rose to her feet. 'You will please excuse me a moment, Miss Mills,' she said and followed Mrs Matthews outside into the passage.

'Said what?' she asked.

'She said, "I can't . . ." and then "Oh God!" and then there was a long silence and she made a sort of groaning noise and then she said, "Just tell her." Her voice was all funny, madam. Sort of odd.'

'Oh, Lord!' said Cicely. 'Surely it's not the baby already? I suppose I ought to have a word with her.' She hurried along the hall to the telephone, muttering irritably to herself.

'Hettie, is that you?' she asked. 'What is all this about? I can't make head or tail of what Mrs Matthews tells me.'

'Yes, it's me,' said Hettie. 'Do you know where George is? I can't see him on the river bank or I'd send my neighbour's boy down there, but he might be at the boatyard with Jack. I think I'm starting the baby and I'd like him to come home as quickly as possible. Someone will have to – ah!'

There was a long pause, then Cicely said, 'Hettie, are you still there?'

'Yes,' Hettie gasped. 'It's all right, really it is. It's just that I'm having the pains and there's no one in the house. It's Mrs Mack's day off and Eunice has gone home.'

'Well firstly, dear, *don't* panic!' said Cicely. 'It all takes positively ages, I can assure you.'

'I'm *not* panicking.'

'Good girl! Have you sent word to your mother?'

'She's in King's Lynn and George's mother is in Hastings.'

'Oh, this is quite ridiculous!' said Cicely. 'The doctor, then?'

'I thought George could fetch the midwife. Dr Jamieson's on holiday.'

'Hm . . . I see what you mean. No one is where they should be. Poor Hettie! Well, look, dear, I'm in the middle of interviewing nannies, but I'll send someone down to the yard at once to find George and send him home. Then as soon as I'm through here, I'll come right over . . . Hettie, did you hear me?'

'Yes.'

'You'll be fine, Hettie dear, so don't start to worry. There's no rush at all. Try not to upset yourself.'

'I'm *not* upset!' cried Hettie.

'That's marvellous. Look dear, walk about a little in between the pains. It helps. I don't remember why, but I do know it helps.'

'Thank you. I'll try it – and will you please tell George to hurry?'

'Of course I will and I'll be with you myself as soon as I can.'

Cicely hung up. 'We all go through it, dear,' she muttered to her absent sister-in-law, 'and I'm afraid it's no picnic!'

She instructed Mrs Matthews to find a lad and send him down to the boatyard to deliver Hettie's message. Then, with a sigh of impatience, she straightened her back, patted her hair into place and returned to Miss Mills.

*

Jack Coulsden, Cicely's husband, stood on the slipway with his hands on his hips. His swarthy head was tilted well back on his thick neck and his dark eyes were half-closed against the bright July sunshine.

'Watch what you're doing with that bloody paint, Tom!' he bellowed. 'It's going all over the place.'

'Sorry, Mr Coulsden.'

Tommy Bird dabbed at a thin trickle of red paint. The rest of the boat's hull had been tarred but George Coulsden, the owner, wanted a red band three strakes wide just below deck level, and since he was paying for it, he would get just that. Jack Coulsden did not intend to give his brother any chance to find fault with the latest craft to leave his yard. It was a matter of family pride. Coulsdens had been building boats in Rye for over a century; their well-deserved reputation for quality and craftsmanship had been hard-won over the years and would not be lightly relinquished. The yard had been started in 1806 by their grandfather, Joseph Coulsden, and in 1837 had passed to his only child, Stephen who, although in his forties, was still a bachelor when he died suddenly five years later. Having no family of his own, he left the business and the house at Appledore to his cousin, Harold. Harold's branch of the family was based in Hastings but he willingly moved to South View, hoping to impress the parents of his young wife Sarah. Her father was an estate agent, well-to-do and highly respected in the town of Hastings, and their daughter's husband was not at all to their liking.

The boatyard covered a small area on the north side of the Rock Channel, a stretch of the river which linked the Fishmarket and the Strand Quay. The new boat now on the stocks was 27 feet long and fully decked, and was their largest craft to date. Both George and Jack were justly proud of it. It was of traditional construction, clinker-built of elm and oak with a pine deck. Baltic fir would be used for most of the spars – which would be added later – and the whole boat had been built 'by eye'.

Tommy Bird glanced down from his perch on the steps, brush raised above the paint-pot which he held in his other hand.

'Nice name,' he said slyly. '*Silver Sprite*. I like that.'

'Well, I bloody don't!' said Jack scornfully. 'It's not meant to be spritely, for God's sake! She's broad and beamy and there's nothing spritely about her. A boat should have a real name – "Enterprise" or "Industry". Names that mean something. *Silver bloody Sprite!*' he snorted. 'That's Hettie's doing, I'll bet. Just the sort of name she would come up with. George should never have let her choose it; he's only got himself to blame.'

The boat certainly was broad-bottomed, but there was a reason for that. For most of the year she would fish in Rye Bay between Dungeness and Hastings and harbours were few and far between along that stretch of coast. If at any time she could not put in at Rye she would probably have to be 'beached' when, with the aid of a few wooden blocks, she would sit comfortably upright on the shingle.

Shaking his head at his brother's folly, Jack left Tommy to get on with his work and went back to the boat-shed. It was a large L-shaped room with a raftered ceiling below which various lengths of planking were suspended. The whitewashed walls – covered with a fine layer of dust which showed up every irregularity in the rough brickwork – were hung with a selection of tools, some well-oiled and obviously in daily use, others rusting and dull. Beyond a coil of wire and a tangle of rope lay an old lifebelt painted white and bearing the name *Miranda* in crude red lettering. A half-completed boat filled most of the centre of the shed, and a pair of discarded overalls had been thrown over the side of it. The earth floor was deep in sawdust and wood shavings, but beyond the boat the rough floor gave way to a broad platform of wooden decking below a bench. Above this was a shelf bearing cans of paint, turpentine and old rags. Three large machines stood at this end of the shed – a circular saw, a planer and a band saw. Light coming in through grimy windows fell on to a man hunched over a wooden name board, chipping away industriously with a small curved chisel and humming tunelessly to himself. Born Alfred Hall, he had answered to the name of 'Ratty' for most of his fifty-two years.

'How's it going then, Ratty?' Jack asked him.

The man grinned to himself as he looked up. Ants in his pants, he thought. The guv'nor was always the same when a boat was nigh-on finished – couldn't leave well alone, but had to be snooping round, popping his head over everyone's shoulders and making them all jumpy.

'Not bad, guv'nor,' he said. 'Not bad at all.' He straightened up reluctantly to reveal his handiwork. The first four letters of 'SILVER' had been carved into the elm; the 'E' was half-completed.

'Pretty name,' he said innocently, for like everyone else in the yard, he knew Jack Coulsden's view. But Jack, running his fingers

over the carved lettering, did not rise to the bait as Ratty had
hoped, contenting himself with a bleak shake of the head.

'Tomorrow's the day, then,' said Ratty, changing his tactics
and deciding to humour him. 'I reckoned your brother would be
around today. I would, in his shoes, I can tell you.'

Realising for the first time that George was *not* around, Jack
frowned. 'Hasn't he been in?' he asked.

Ratty shook his head. 'And tomorrow's the day,' he repeated.

'He'll be by,' said Jack curtly, reflecting calmly that tomorrow
was indeed 'the day'. The official launch of the *Silver Sprite* was
planned for midday and hopefully would be attended by a good
crowd of noteworthy people – the Mayor and his wife and one or
two councillors had been invited; the harbour master too, and
representatives from Customs and Excise and Trinity House – all
had been informed of the occasion and, barring accidents, Jack
knew many of them would put in an appearance. All the Coulsden
family would be there, of course, and George had arranged for a
few members of the town band to play the new lugger into the
water after Hettie had broken a bottle of champagne over her
black bows. As usual, the *Sussex Express and County Herald* would
send a reporter to cover the event and Jack hoped that the
prolonged spell of fine weather would continue for another
twenty-four hours. Coulsdens had seen many launches, but this
one held greater significance for the family than most others; it
was well-known amongst the fishing fraternity that the building of
the boat had healed a two-year-old rift between George Coulsden and his two brothers.

George and his father, Harold, had never seen eye to eye and
the boatyard had frequently been the scene of violent quarrels
between the two men. Father and son were very alike, both
showing a great weakness for women and drink, yet each despis-
ing in the other the faults they condoned in themselves. Since
they shared the same choleric disposition, minor disagreements
between them rapidly developed into full-scale rows; these gave
them both the opportunity to work out their aggression and
neither attached too much importance to the flare-ups which
were usually resolved almost as quickly as they arose. On one
occasion, however, when Harold was goading his son, he went too
far and punched him in the chest. George, losing his self-control,
retaliated by striking him in the face and knocking him down. The
fight that followed made local history. Stanley, the oldest of the

three brothers, lived to regret his decision to intervene, for he lost a couple of teeth in the ensuing battle.

George and his father never spoke to each other again since four days later, only two days before his birthday, the old man collapsed and died. Two days previously he had altered his will so that George received nothing at all. The boatyard and the old man's motor car went to Jack and the two fishing punts to Stanley. The family home was left to his widow, Sarah. When she had recovered from the shock and grief of her husband's death, she stopped blaming George for Harold's collapse and set about 'putting matters to rights'. Being a forceful woman, she set out to end the bitterness that her husband's will had engendered. Sarah knew that she held a trump card, for the value of the house in Appledore was greater than either the boatyard or the two boats, and she let it be clearly understood that if Stan and Jack did not cooperate in her plan, she would leave the house to George and he would thus eventually get the lion's share of the family wealth. In view of this, Stan was at last persuaded to sell one of the punts and the money went to buy the necessary timber for a larger boat for George. Jack's contribution was to build it at the yard free of charge. For a few months George, smarting under a deep sense of injustice, insisted that he would have nothing to do with the scheme; however, his mother's bullying, Hettie's entreaties and his own common sense finally won him over to a grudging accept-ance. The news that Hettie was once again pregnant came at an appropriate time; it lifted George's spirits sufficiently for him to take an active interest in the boat's construction, and to Sarah's relief, the feud between her three sons was resolved. The bitter-ness faded and the relationship between the three men recovered a little of its earlier warmth. Now the Coulsden family once more presented a united front and the launching of the new boat was being given maximum publicity.

Ratty had just completed the letter 'R' and was brushing away the tiny curls of surplus elm, when a young boy rode furiously into the yard on a bicycle demonstrably too big for him. He braked with a squeal of tyres which raised the dust and scattered a few loose stones, then balanced himself precariously on the toes of his shoes as the two men stared at him.

'Message for Mr Coulsden,' he declared loudly swinging up his arm into a crisp salute. 'He's wanted at home and it's urgent!'

'Urgent, is it?' demanded Jack, unperturbed. 'What's urgent

about it? And who are you – and take off your cap when you speak to your elders.'

The boy did as he was told. 'I'm Billy Saunders,' he said indignantly, for his aunt Mrs Matthews had been housekeeper to Jack Coulsden for many years.

'Good God!' said Jack. 'Young Billy, is it? Didn't recognise you, lad! You've shot up over the last few months. What's your Ma feeding you on, eh? And what's so urgent that I'm wanted at home?'

'Not you, Mr Coulsden,' said the boy. 'It's the other Mr Coulsden. His wife's getting a baby.'

'We know that.' He turned to Ratty. 'This is my housekeeper's nephew. Shot up overnight, he has; I didn't recognise him.'

'I mean, she's getting it *now*,' Billy insisted. '*Your* Mrs Coulsden sent me to find the *other* Mrs Coulsden's husband, to tell him to get home as fast as he can because she's getting it now and there's no one home.'

As his words sank in, an angry red flush darkened Jack's weatherbeaten face. 'Getting it *now*!' he roared. 'She's no business to be getting it now, damn her! We've got the launch tomorrow. Christ Almighty!' He appealed helplessly to Ratty, who shrugged his shoulders in sympathy but decided it would be wise to make no comment. He reckoned that Jack, though not as fiery as George, could be just as nasty if you got on the wrong side of him.

'Is he here, then?' asked Billy, glancing round the yard.

'Is who here?' said Jack, his mind already busy with the problems of tomorrow's launch.

'The *other* Mr Coulsden.'

Jack glared at him. 'No, he's not here! You can see that for yourself, can't you? He never is where he's supposed to be. And don't ask me *where* he is, as I don't know. Am I his bloody keeper or something?'

'No, sir.'

'Well, hop it then!'

'But where to?' the boy stammered. 'I mean, where is he? No,' he amended hastily, 'I mean, where shall I look now? She said it was urgent.'

'Oh God!' muttered Jack, running an agitated hand through his hair. 'I've told you, I don't know where he is, unless he's in Hastings with Stan. Oh Hettie, Hettie!' he sighed deeply. 'Why do you do this to me? Today of all days!'

Ratty, meeting his harassed stare, shrugged again and ventured, 'That's women for you.'

'Women?' Jack's voice rose. 'You mean, that's *Hettie* for you. The day before the launch and she has to bloody well give birth. Can't get anything right, that boot-faced—' He bit back the last word in case it ever reached George's ears. He had never forgiven George for marrying a woman with money. Cicely was a beauty, indeed she was a 'catch', but she had come from poor stock and brought no money with her.

Ratty said, 'He'll never bike to Hastings in time.'

'Of course he won't. I'll have to go and fetch him.'

'In the motor?' asked Ratty, who longed for a ride in the motor car. Ever since Harold had bought it after a wildly successful flutter on the Derby, Ratty had been trying to wangle a ride in it. It would be something to boast about in the Pipemakers' Arms.

Jack hesitated. He did enjoy driving the motor and he enjoyed being seen driving it; moreover, a run to Hastings was always very pleasant. He turned back to Billy.

'Tell Mrs Coulsden – that's *my* Mrs Coulsden – that he's not here so he must be with Stan and I'm on my way to Hastings to fetch him. She'll pass the message on to Hettie. Here!' He tossed the boy a coin and strode away in the direction of his office, shouting his decision to Tommy Bird as he passed. Billy pocketed the money, remounted his bicycle and rode out of the yard.

*

As Sarah Coulsden's youngest son laboured over the prostrate form of Agnes Dengate, the sweat broke on his skin and he silently cursed the hot July weather. The loft at the top of the net shop was stiflingly hot and the familiar smell of cotton rope, creosote and cork found its way up from the three floors below. Air came in from a crack in the wooden walls, but it brought with it the smell of the Hastings seashore – a combination of salt, fish, seaweed and warm shingle.

'Hurry it up, George!' Agnes giggled. 'I haven't got all day, you know. I've got a living to earn.'

George grinned. 'You talk too much – and stop wriggling!'

'If you had a bit of straw up your back, *you'd* wriggle,' she protested. 'Or an ant or something. It's all right for you, you're always on top. It's always me what gets filthy!'

He kissed her mouth to silence her, fearful of losing his concentration. Agnes wriggled again, then put out her tongue and licked the sweat from his upper lip. George rose and fell, but it was becoming an effort and Agnes's idle chatter did nothing to help. He thrust his tongue between her teeth and obligingly she sucked it into her mouth and felt his rhythm improve. With a last determined effort, he reached a quick shuddering release and she heard the familiar gruff sound that was half a gasp and half a satisfied groan. Immediately he slid down to lie beside her, panting hard but secretly congratulating himself that his reputation as the most handsome and randiest of the three Coulsden boys was still intact. Not that he had been very randy since his marriage to Hettie, except on the occasions of her pregnancies when she suffered from day-long sickness for weeks on end. Any husband, he assured himself, could be expected to stray under such circumstances. Now he reached for his thick serge trousers and wriggled into them. He was heavily built, with thick black hair that waved naturally and framed large, heavy-lidded eyes, a strong nose and firm mouth. When he smiled his teeth were firm and well-shaped; his smile was his fortune. Buttoning his flies, he grinned at her.

'Well?' she demanded, sitting up but making no effort to fasten her blouse.

'Well what?'

'Don't I get a thank you, then?'

'You just had it!' he laughed. 'Think yourself lucky! Lots of girls would give their eye-teeth to be where you are now.' He pulled on his boots and began to lace them up. 'Come on then, Ag. Do yourself up. Stan'll be wondering where you are. Hurry it up!'

She gave him a cool look. 'I'm not in any hurry, George Coulsden,' she said, 'because I've got something to say to you.'

'Well, make it quick, love.' He stood up and fastened his belt buckle.

Agnes hesitated and then took a deep breath. 'I've decided I want to change my job,' she announced. 'Go up in the world. You know?'

'No, I don't know,' he said impatiently. 'Now, on your feet, girl, or I'm going to leave you here. I've got things to do. Launching the boat tomorrow and everyone's going to be there. Big day.'

Still she made no effort to get up from the pile of sacks on which they had been lying but with deliberately slow movements straightened her skirt. She wore no underwear in the hot weather.

'I fancy something respectable and clean,' she said. 'I'm sick of all this.'

With a vague wave of her hand, she managed to indicate not only the net shop but all of the surrounding seashore. For Agnes Dengate worked on the nets – repairing old ones and making new – from eight in the morning until six at night, and in a good week she was lucky to earn thirteen shillings. The work was hot in summer and cold in winter and the coarse tarred ropes and thick cotton mesh tore her hands to pieces. She had thought nothing of this until she took up with Stan's brother George. Her plump twenty-year-old body was shapely, her dishevelled brown curls were a delight and her willing ways had endeared her to George Coulsden. She was quite content to be of service whenever his wife was with child, for George was a generous man and the extra money came in very handy, but recently she had been doing some serious thinking.

George slicked back his hair, pulled on his jacket and looked at Agnes uneasily. There was something about her studied reluctance to stand up that disturbed him.

'You chose the work,' he reminded her. 'Everyone know it's men's work, but you would do it. Nobody made you.'

'So what? I just wanted to show 'em I *could* do it. Prove I'm as good as they are.'

'Well, you did,' said George. 'So why moan about it now?'

Agnes twisted her mouth into a dissatisfied line. 'It's not ladylike,' she muttered. 'Because I'm sick of it now. Sick of ripping my hands to bits. Sick of stinking of fish. I'm sick of it and that's all there is to it. I've had enough!'

George was rapidly losing interest. The Dolphin would be open and he was looking forward to a lunchtime drink. 'Well, do something else,' he said. 'No one's stopping you. Work in a shop or take in washing.'

'Thanks *very* much!' said Agnes.

She watched the fingers of her right hand as they tweaked at a crease in her cotton skirt.

'I thought I might get a job as a daily help,' she remarked. 'Why can't you give me a job in your house?'

George Coulsden's mouth fell open with shock at the girl's effrontery.

'Give you a job in . . .' He left the sentence unfinished and shook his head. 'You must be going off your rocker, girl,' he told her and held out a hand. 'Come on! Up! I've got things to do.'

Ignoring his proffered hand, Agnes tossed her head, drew up her legs and hugged them defiantly. 'I told you, I'm not ready to go,' she stated. 'Like I said, I want to talk about you getting me a better job. Why *can't* you let me work at your house? Aren't I good enough?'

'Course you are,' said George, 'but it's just out of the question. You should stick with what you do best. That's only common sense. You've always worked on the nets and you're good at it. You're a fast worker too, according to Stan.' Improvising rashly, he added, 'He thinks a lot of you, Stan does; he told me so. You're thought of pretty high, you know. Stan wouldn't want to let you go.'

'Can't stop me, can he?' she argued cheerfully. 'Not if you say you're giving me a job. You said yourself that that Eunice is daft as a brush. Why not give me a chance? It could be very handy . . .' she winked. 'Know what I mean?'

George swallowed hard. He knew exactly what she meant and the idea was at once terrifying and a definite temptation. To have Agnes on hand to oblige him, when Hettie's back was turned . . . But no! He pulled himself up short. It was utter madness even to consider it. The risks were enormous and if Hettie ever rumbled their game there would be hell to pay. She'd make his life a misery. And Hettie was a good enough wife, in her own way; he'd no complaints. No, it was out of the question.

'The answer's "No",' he said firmly. 'Now, will you get up or do I leave you to the rats?'

With a shrill squeal Agnes scrambled to her feet and looked round with anxious eyes. 'Where?' she demanded. 'I can't see any rats. You're lying, George. I've never seen a rat here.'

He scowled. 'Don't keep calling me George!' he snapped. 'How many times have I told you? It'll slip out one of these days and then there'll be some explaining to do. It's "Mr Coulsden" to you.'

At least she was on her feet at last, he thought thankfully, but he did not like the sullen way her mouth drooped.

'So are you coming or not?' he asked.

'*Not*!' she said and to prove it, she picked her way over the accumulation of debris to peer down through the crack in the wall. Below her she could see Stan Coulsden arguing with Ernie from the Fishmarket, wagging his finger aggressively in front of Ernie's eyes. She wondered if Stan really *had* said she was a good worker.

'There's your big brother down there,' she remarked. 'If I called, he'd look up. He'd wonder what was going on up here.' She turned and smiled, a smile loaded with meaning which made a knot form in George's stomach.

'You wouldn't dare,' he said. 'You little bitch! You wouldn't.'

'He'd tell your wife,' said Agnes.

They glared at each other across the tiny loft and George felt a trickle of sweat run down his back. He clenched his fist, feeling a great urge to punch her, and had to struggle to stay calm. Whoever would have thought that soft little Agnes, with her sense of fun and a fancy for 'what men had to offer', would turn out so calculating. He was impressed in spite of himself.

'Listen,' he said, trying to conceal his anger. 'It would be your word against mine and who's going to believe you?'

'Your wife might,' she said, her tone no more than conversational.

His eyes narrowed. 'If you told Hettie anything about us I'd—'

'You'd what?'

'I'd break every bone in your stupid body!' he shouted, losing control momentarily.

Agnes laughed. 'Then they wouldn't wonder no more!' she taunted. 'That would be all the proof they needed. I mean, if you had nothing to hide it wouldn't bother you, would it?' She moved towards him and her face softened. 'Look, don't let's quarrel, George – sorry – *Mr Coulsden*.' Her tone was mocking. 'I'm only asking you to think about it, that's all. Honestly, it could be a lot of fun – me in the house and no one knowing about us. A whole lot of fun.'

She reached up to put her arms round his neck and he made no effort to stop her. This soft wheedling was more like the Agnes he knew, he thought with relief. For the time being it might be best to keep her sweet, for she certainly *could* make life very difficult for him if she wanted to. But the idea of having her in the house! Even as he rejected it as pure folly, he could still see the attractions in the idea. He looked into her eager blue eyes and noted the firm rosy flesh of her cheeks and the curve of her full lips as she smiled, showing her teeth which were small and well-shaped.

'I really love you, you know,' she told him with a little sigh. 'Do you love me? I mean, even a little bit? Don't I mean anything to you after all this time? For nearly three years now I've given you what you wanted, haven't I? And never asked no questions. Never made no fuss, have I? I only want a proper job – a nice respectable job. You could get rid of Eunice if you wanted to. I'd be ever so grateful!'

Agnes clung to him, burying her face in his chest. As he looked down on the tousled curls still flattened and dusty from the sacks and tried to imagine her in a starched white apron and cap, the vision made him feel weak at the knees.

'How could I?' he hedged, feeling his resolve weaken. 'Eunice *is* a bit slow, but she does her job and it was Hettie took her on.'

'Say she's cheeked you or something,' Agnes suggested. 'Getting uppity. *You* know.'

'No. I don't know, Ag!' George was shocked at her easy duplicity.

She shrugged, opening her eyes wider. 'You'll think of something; you could get rid of her if you really wanted to. Listen, just promise me you'll think about it. It would be such fun and we could do it on a real bed, instead of up here.'

'I don't know . . .' he began, but she reached up on her toes and muffled his words with a flurry of kisses.

'You and me stark naked in a bed!' she whispered. 'Oh, George!' This time he did not notice the slip and Agnes knew immediately that she had a chance.

'I'll *think* about it,' he told her, 'but no promises, mind.'

'No,' she said demurely. 'But, oh George, I swear you'd *never* regret it. When I think of all the things we could do . . .'

Her eyes sparkled and her mouth twitched mischievously and George finally relaxed enough to grin. His hands gently slid down to grasp large handfuls of her plump buttocks and he began to imagine the two of them naked on the bed while Hettie was otherwise engaged – shopping or visiting Cicely, perhaps.

'You're thinking wicked thoughts!' she whispered. 'I can feel you coming up again! George Coulsden! Don't tell me you want to—'

Before he could tell her that, yes, he *did* want to, they heard a motor car approaching and when it stopped Jack Coulsden's voice rang out.

'Stan! Where the hell's George? It's Hettie's time; she's

started. I thought he'd be here with you.'

George gasped and pushing Agnes aside, he stumbled over to the window and squinted down. Oh God! Hettie had started her pains! This time it could be a live child – his son. Hettie was giving birth to *his son*!

'Christ!' he muttered as below his brothers conversed, their voices agitated. 'I've got to go.'

'But George—'

'And don't keep calling me George!' he snapped.

Agnes bit back an angry retort. 'Hettie's time?' she repeated. 'Already? I bet it's not.'

'What d'you know about it?' said George. 'Christ Almighty!' He looked terrified.

They heard Stanley's voice in answer. 'He must be about here somewhere, Jack. I saw him not half an hour since.'

'But where?' cried Jack. 'I've come to fetch him back. Hettie will be getting in a right state. Doctor's on holiday or some such.'

'Oh God!' cried George, looking helplessly at Agnes. 'I'll have to go.'

'Well, go then,' she told him crossly. 'I'm not stopping you. Get yourself downstairs before they start looking for you.'

He stared at her as though she spoke a foreign language.

'George Coulsden,' she hissed, 'get downstairs, for Pete's sake! D'you want them to come looking and find us together? What's up with you?'

'Right,' he said. 'Right.' And without another word, he turned and clambered down the ladder.

Agnes watched him go, shaking her head in exasperation. Men! Great babies, the lot of them. Mention childbirth and they fell apart. If *they* had to give birth the human race would have come to an end long ago. She peered through the crack until he appeared below, strolling casually across to where his two brothers still debated his whereabouts. Despite his attempt at a jaunty air, his guilty conscience lent a certain stiffness to his movements. After a quick exchange, Agnes saw him climb into the car with Jack.

'George Coulsden,' she said, 'I really love you. God knows why, but I do.' She sighed. 'And I want to be a daily help, George,' she muttered. 'So don't you forget it.'

She counted to a hundred as usual, then made her way carefully down the ladder and out into the sunlight where the inevitable net – stretched out across the shingle to dry – awaited her attention. George had spoken truthfully, she reflected wearily, for she had flown in the face of convention in order to take up the trade that was traditionally men's work. However, she had done so after a row with her father in which he assured her she would not last a month and although she had come to detest the work after only one week, pride would not allow her to admit that he was right. So she had made the most of a bad job and struggled to master the skills and techniques required. These were many and complex for the long nets were massive affairs, heavy and un-wieldy after their submersion in the salt water for so many hours and sometimes shiny with weed, fish scales or old herring roes. After each trip there were repairs to be made, some minor, others major. A slit in the net of maybe a yard and a half would take several hours to mend and occasionally she would spend days or even a week making good a ragged net which had been ruined by the sharp teeth of dogfish.

Eventually, with sheer determination, she had become as good as some of the men and better than one or two, for her hands were small and thus more nimble; but the soft flesh suffered accord-ingly until it formed callouses to protect itself from the rough hemp of which the nets were made.

As Agnes moved over the beach she glanced back towards the road in time to see Jack Coulsden's car roar away, taking her lover back to Rye. Back to his wife and long-awaited child, she thought, her mouth twisting enviously at the prospect of their shared happiness, but after a moment or two her cheerful nature re-asserted itself and she settled down to her net, intent on making up for lost time.

'George Coulsden,' she muttered as her thread drew together the ragged edges of a small tear, 'you're as daft as the next man, but if you take me away from all this I'll make you the happiest man on this earth, and that's a promise!'

*

As soon as George arrived home, Jack was dispatched again to fetch the midwife. In the bedroom Hettie lay on the bed ex-hausted and fearful, clinging to her husband's large hand. Unable to bear the sight of his wife's distress, George knelt on the floor beside the bed and bent his head. The obvious agony which seized her at rapidly decreasing intervals frightened him so much that his clumsy attempts at reassurance convinced neither of them. Hettie had bitten her lower lip in an effort to stifle her screams of pain and it was swollen and bruised.

'Oh, Hettie!' he gasped. 'I'm sorry. I'm so sorry. What can I do? I just don't know, dear. She'll be here soon, the midwife I mean. Jack will find her. Don't worry. Just you hang on and they'll be back. Or I could telephone Cis again.' He raised his head hopefully, grasping at any excuse to leave the bedroom and escape from this awful scene. 'Shall I do that, Hettie? Shall I ring Cicely?'

Hettie shook her head. 'She's got interviews,' she told him jerkily. 'She said she'd come when she'd finished them; she only had one more to see.'

'But she must have finished by now! I could hurry her up—'

'No! Please don't leave me, George,' Hettie begged. 'I'm so frightened. I think something's wrong, don't you? It shouldn't be like this, should it? So terribly painful? It's tearing me apart. I can't bear it, George, if I lose this baby. I can't!'

Her voice rose and he hastily buried his face against the bedclothes, unwilling to meet her frantic eyes and show to any greater degree the fear which had already made a child of him. Her thin high-pitched scream filled his ears.

'Don't!' he shouted, snatching his hands from hers and covering his ears. 'Stop it, Hettie! Stop it! It'll do no good. Don't scream like that, for God's sake. Where is that bloody midwife? Jack must have found her by now.'

He huddled against the bed, his face averted from the writhing form of his wife as she arched her back in a futile attempt to reduce the pain. Then another thought struck him. 'Some tea, Hettie? Some milk? Brandy? Would you like a drink?'

The prospect of a nip of brandy rallied him slightly but before Hettie could answer her waters broke and she was distracted by the flow of liquid which saturated her clothes.

Horribly startled, George scrambled back to a safe distance with panic in his eyes.

'It's all right,' Hettie assured him. 'It's called the waters breaking. The doctor told me it would happen. Really, it's all right, George. Now it's the next part – the bearing down bit. Oh, I *wish* they'd hurry. It's getting so *near*, George, and I'm not sure what I have to do. I'm so frightened and tired, I can't remember what he told me. He was supposed to *be* here. Someone should be with me.'

'The bed!' he whispered. 'And your skirt . . .'

'It doesn't matter, George,' she told him. 'Oh! Now the pain *is* changing. It feels different somehow, it's the pushing down. I remember now, but I don't think I should do that yet. I think I have to wait for the doctor to tell me when . . . or the midwife. Where is the stupid woman! Is she never coming? Go and look, George, will you? Out of the window. See if they're coming.'

She began to breathe very rapidly, her mouth wide open. Perspiration glistened on her face and she wiped it away with a handful of the white linen sheet as George scrambled thankfully to his feet and backed away from her.

'We'd hear the motor,' he said from the comparative safety of the window, 'but there's no sign of them. No sign of anyone. The road's deserted.'

He wondered what he would do if no one came before the child was born. He knew he would never be able to bring Hettie through safely – that she would die, or the child would die, or both! His son and his wife would die and everyone would blame him. He began to tremble. Please, God, they *must* come. They *must*!

'George?'

'Yes.'

'I will have that brandy. It might help.'

'Brandy? Yes, of course. That brandy . . . Good idea.'

He almost ran from the room. The whole episode was taking on the proportions of a nightmare. If only Eunice or Mrs Mack would turn up! He would run next door for help if the baby was going to be born. He simply could not face it alone. He dare not. They would die and he would have lost his wife and his baby son. 'Oh God,' he prayed as he poured two generous measures of brandy with hands that shook. 'Don't let my son die. Don't let Hettie die!' Remembering with deep guilt that barely an hour ago he had lain with Agnes, he thought briefly of her soft, untroubled body and then scolded himself for his infidelity. Perhaps this nightmare was God's punishment. 'If they live,' he vowed, 'I'll never speak to another woman as long as I live. I swear by Almighty God and the Holy Ghost . . .' His imagination failed him. Like most of the fishermen he was not a devout man and only went to church for the annual ceremony of 'Blessing the Sea'. This ceremony took place on the beach at Hastings and was always attended by the entire Coulsden family, for Sarah Coulsden would not have it any other way. She knew that the sea ruled their lives – that it gave the fishermen a living but exacted a high price in return. It had claimed many victims and was not to be treated lightly. Any man hoping to survive the perils of the sea needed all the help his prayers could enlist.

However, prayer did not come as easily to George's lips as to his mother's, and after this amateurish attempt he drank one of the brandies, refilled the glass and went back into the bedroom. Hettie had struggled into a sitting position, her legs parted inelegantly beneath the sodden skirt. Her collar was undone, her bodice unfastened half-way to the waist; her hair had slipped free of its pins and framed her face untidily.

'I'm sorry,' she apologised, reading his expression as he handed her the glass.

'It doesn't matter,' he comforted awkwardly.

With a quick toss of his head he gulped down his second brandy, breathing deeply as the fiery spirit warmed his terrified soul and thawed his frozen mind. 'It's going to be all right,' he told her.

She nodded, nervously gripping the glass of amber liquid. 'I'm sorry,' she repeated helplessly.

George thought she resembled an abandoned doll slumped awkwardly against the pillows, her head resting uncomfortably against the brass bedhead. With her bulging body and dishevelled appearance, she looked of no significance and George felt a rush of resentment towards the doctor, the midwife, Jack and Cicely who by their non-appearance had reduced his wife to such a state. He watched her finish the brandy and was on the point of offering her another when they heard a car making its way along the road, the horn sounding.

'It's them!' he cried and saw the wild relief in her eyes as he gave her a brief smile before hurrying downstairs to open the front door. The midwife, Mrs Swain, was sitting beside Jack.

'You'll have to be quick,' George told her urgently as she heaved her large body out of the car and headed for the front door. 'The waters happened,' he told her as he followed her up the stairs, 'and she wants to start the next part – the pushing. You'll have to help her – the pain's very bad. The waters—'

She stopped so abruptly that he nearly cannoned into her back. 'Hot water, Mr Coulsden,' she said, 'and clean towels—'

'Yes, yes, of course.'

'Something to wrap the baby in—'

'Yes.'

'A pot of tea would go down very well . . .'

'Yes, of course.'

'And don't try to tell me my job, Mr Coulsden—'

'No, but she's—'

'I've never lost a mother yet, nor a child.'

'Yes, I mean no . . .' he stammered.

'Or a father,' she smiled. 'So it's hot water, and clean towels—'

Hettie screamed. 'She said she wants to push—' said George.

'Mr Coulsden, *please!*'

'Yes. Right . . .'

Mrs Swain made her way into the bedroom and closed the door firmly behind her. George, harassed but relieved, ran a hand through his hair and turned to stare at his brother who was waiting at the bottom of the stairs.

'Christ!' he said shakily. 'Is it always like this?'

'Pretty much,' said Jack. 'You'd best do what she says. Hot water and clean towels. You look like a ghost,' he grinned as George stumbled down the stairs. 'It'll be OK. She'll come through. They do, you know.' He put a hand briefly on his brother's shoulder. 'They're so tough, women; it's amazing, it really is. Even Cicely.'

'I could with another drink,' said George. 'D'you fancy a brandy?' Jack nodded and followed him into the parlour; the hot water and towels, the pot of tea were already forgotten. A moment later they raised their glasses.

'So tough, women,' Jack marvelled. 'So bloody tough! Here's to them. Here's to women, God bless 'em!'

Five minutes later Cicely arrived and soon had hot water and clean towels ready for the midwife. She warned them not to drink too much, but an hour later when Hettie's triumphant gasp mingled with her new daughter's lusty cry the two Coulsden brothers were almost too drunk to care.

CHAPTER TWO

At seven o'clock the following morning Mrs Mack returned to the house and let herself in by the back door. She took off her coat and hat and was on her way through to the hall to hang them up when she discovered George and Jack still sprawled in their respective armchairs, snoring heavily. She stood astonished, clutching her coat and hat to her as George grunted heavily and opened his eyes. For a moment they regarded each other in silence.

Mrs Mack was the least surprised of the two. Not one to gossip, she had nevertheless 'heard things' and was well aware that the brothers were not angels. Old Harold Coulsden had taught them well. Now *there* was a wild drinker, but he was dead and gone now and she was not a woman to think ill of the dead. So she was not too surprised to find the master of the house and his brother the worse for drink, but she did wonder what had provoked it. She waited for George to gather his wits.

'Good morning, sir,' she said at last. 'Can I get you anything?'

With an effort, George straightened his body into a more acceptable position and put a hand to his throbbing head. 'Brandy,' he said slowly. 'Too much bloody brandy!'

As his eyes focused more clearly he saw his brother's ungainly form and frowned. Then suddenly his gaze widened as memory flooded back.

'The baby!' he cried, making an unsteady effort to pull himself out of the chair. 'It's happened, Mrs Mack! That was it.' A large grin spread over his face and suddenly she saw the young George Coulsden as she had first known him. Her mother had taken the job as cook to Harold and Sarah Coulsden when young George was only thirteen and his lean body had not yet thickened into manhood. He was the least handsome of the three boys until he smiled, but then his heavy features lit up, his eyes glowed with a kind of excitement and an unexpected warmth of spirit shone through. Mrs Mack, twenty-three at the time, had nevertheless fallen under his youthful spell and when he grew up and married Henrietta Lovatt she had immediately become housekeeper to the newlyweds.

'The baby's born,' he told her now. 'We've got a daughter, Mrs Mack. A little girl. Hey, Jacko! Wake up, can't you?' He shook Jack roughly by the arm. 'I've got a daughter, remember? Jack, wake up, I tell you!'

Mrs Mack's face registered shock, then indignation. Having shared the family's previous disappointments, she had been looking forward wholeheartedly to the baby's birth with all its attendant thrills and alarms, and now it appeared it had happened on her day off and she had missed it all.

'Born already!' she exclaimed. 'And nobody told me a word?'

Jack opened his eyes, belched loudly and then closed them again. George shrugged and left him to his stupor. He rubbed his own face clumsily and grinned again.

'She took us all by surprise,' he told the housekeeper. 'Come on upstairs and take a look at my new daughter. Yes, *now*, Mrs Mack. Come on!'

She hesitated. 'Should we disturb the mistress?' she asked. 'If she's tired, she'll want to sleep on . . .'

But George had taken her arm and was urging her towards the stairs. When they reached the bedroom door he leaned against it for a moment, gathering his wits, while downstairs Jack began to cough.

'A little girl!' said Mrs Mack, patting her hair into place. 'And both doing well?'

'Both well.'

'But the doctor – isn't he on holiday—' she began, dismayed.

'The midwife came – and my sister-in-law.'

'Ah.' She beamed at George and said, 'I wanted it to be a girl, though I didn't dare say.'

Just as George reached for the door handle, the spare room door opened and Cicely stood there, tying the cord of her dressing-gown and glaring at George.

'Oh, you've sobered up, have you?' she said sharply, ignoring the housekeeper. 'We must thank the Lord for small mercies. A lot of good you were last night—'

'But a daughter, madam!' exclaimed Mrs Mack hastily, not wanting Jack's wife to spoil the great moment. 'What a surprise – a little girl!'

Cicely was not to be diverted however and gave Mrs Mack a withering look which put the housekeeper in her place instantly and discouraged her from making any further comment.

'Oh, you slept here, did you, Cis?' asked George.

'It certainly looks like it!' she snapped. 'It was a case of *having* to, since I could hardly go home and leave Hettie and a new baby in your care. You were scarcely able to look after yourself, let alone a wife and child. As for Jack, I shall have a few words to say to him when finally he gets home. Now, if you'll excuse me' – she gave the dressing-gown cord an extra tug – 'I'm on my way to the bathroom. I do hope you are not intending to wake Hettie; I'm sure that after what she went through yesterday she deserves a little consideration. And for your information, George – since you don't have the courtesy to ask – I did not sleep well, I never do in a strange bed. The window wouldn't open and it was terribly stuffy. So if you intend to have any more children, I hope you will do me the kindness of staying sober while they're being brought into the world!'

She swept past him, went into the bathroom, closed the door and immediately opened it again. 'And my name is Cicely, *not* Cis!' The door closed once more.

George looked at Mrs Mack with a sheepish expression on his face.

'Take no notice, sir,' she whispered. 'She doesn't mean it, it's just her way.'

He leaned forward and said confidentially, 'She can be a real cow, that one. Poor old Jack! Come on.'

For some reason that he didn't understand George tapped on his own bedroom door and they heard Hettie calling to them to come in. She was already propped up in bed with the sleeping child in her arms and she smiled radiantly at them.

George hurried forward. 'Oh, Hettie!' he began. 'I'm sorry – that is, about last night. I didn't – me and Jack, we were so . . .' He stopped and Hettie smiled.

'It doesn't matter,' she said. 'Here, you take her, George, and show her to Mrs Mack. Our little girl! No, go on. Take her in your arms, she won't break. She slept right round to just after five o'clock and I fed her and she went to sleep again. She's got your mother's hair, see? There, let her head rest in the crook of your arm. That's it.'

George stood awkwardly beside the bed with the baby in his arms, lost for words.

Mrs Mack came forward eagerly. 'Oh ma'am, it was such a shock,' she began, 'when I came in this morning and the master told me. I must have a peep – oh, what a little pet! Just look at her lying there, good as gold. Slept right through the night, did she? What a little lamb. Oh, she's lovely, sir! Lovely, ma'am!'

Lightly wrapped in a shawl, George's first-born was sturdy with long limbs and a smooth pale face. Her neat head was covered with a dense layer of silvery-white hair which lay flat to the skull like a close-fitting cap. Her eyes and mouth were closed and her expression was tranquil.

George met Hettie's eyes in mute gratitude while Mrs Mack clucked admiringly over the child in his arms. 'She's lovely, Hettie,' he said humbly. 'She's beautiful. Just perfect. You are a clever girl.'

'You helped too, sir,' said the housekeeper with a saucy wink and saw that he was pleased.

When George looked at Hettie again he was vaguely aware that motherhood had changed his wife somehow. There was a warm colour in her cheeks and a new confidence in her eyes which suited her homely features.

'You must send a telegram to King's Lynn, to my mother,' she said. 'She'll be so thrilled. She won't forgive us if we don't tell her right away.'

George nodded and looked again at the sleeping child. 'My little girl,' he said softly. 'My little lady.'

Mrs Mack went on talking. 'She's bonny, ma'am . . . and that hair! Like silver – like her grandmother, as you say. She's a Gooding right enough. Oh, what a thrill for the grandmothers! But so sad the grandfathers won't see her. Still, another grand-child! Oh ma'am, she's so – so . . .'

Suddenly overcome with emotion, she fumbled in her pocket for a handkerchief and blew her nose loudly, just as the door opened again to admit Cicely. Still in her dressing-gown, she had washed her face and cleaned her teeth. She took in the scene at one glance and was immediately irritated on several counts. For one thing, George did not appear to be out of favour with Hettie, as she considered he most certainly ought to be; further, Mrs Mack was being treated with undue familiarity considering she was only a servant; and moreover Hettie, and not Cicely herself, was the centre of attention.

'Thank you, Mrs Mack,' she said briskly. 'I think we would all enjoy a cup of tea if you wouldn't mind. George, I'd like you to speak to Jack as soon as you get downstairs. *I* certainly don't want to talk to him after his behaviour last night. Send him home, please, and say I will be home later when I'm no longer needed here.'

Mrs Mack was already on her way to the door but George, his head still bent over his daughter, ignored Cicely's homily.

'I shall get dressed,' Cicely told Hettie, 'and then I'll be right back to get you organised. Mrs Swain is calling back about ten, remember. George, you did hear what I said, did you?'

At that moment there was a crash from the room below and Cicely's mouth tightened into a thin, exasperated line.

'George!' she said again. 'For heaven's sake go down and see to your brother. It's your fault that he's in that state; it really is *quite* disgusting!'

She waited, but once more it seemed that her words had fallen on deaf ears.

George finally tore his gaze from the baby in his arms to look at Hettie. '*Silver Lady!*' he exclaimed. 'How about that, Hettie? The boat, I mean. Not *Sprite. Lady*. After our little girl?'

'I don't mind, George,' said Hettie. 'Anything you say.'

'*Silver Lady*,' said George again. 'What do you think of that for the boat, Cicely?'

Cicely felt a surge of jealousy. None of her children had had a boat named after them. 'There's hardly time to change it,' she pointed out. 'Ratty will have finished it by now.'

But no one was listening to her.

'It's up to you, Hettie,' said George. 'I said you could choose the name for the boat and *Silver Sprite* is all right with me. I just thought . . .'

The baby murmured and Hettie smiled and held out her hands.

'*Silver Lady* sounds fine,' she said, taking her daughter once more into her arms. 'Look, George, she's opening her eyes. She's looking at you!'

George thought he had never seen anything as wonderful as the blue eyes which now turned vaguely towards him and he held his breath, afraid to dispel the magic.

Cicely said, 'They can't focus, of course, at this age. She can't see you, George. It's your voice; she can hear your voice.'

'My little silver lady,' said George softly.

Hettie, aware of Cicely's mood, felt suddenly magnanimous towards her beautiful sister-in-law who was so accustomed to the limelight and was obviously finding it hard to adjust to the new situation.

'Perhaps Cicely could take my place,' she suggested generously. 'At today's launching, I mean?'

George slapped his forehead. 'Christ Almighty! The launching – it's gone clean out of my mind!'

Cicely's eyes widened. 'Me?' she cried, a hand fluttering up to her chest. 'Launch the boat? Oh goodness! I suppose I could. Someone will have to do it and obviously it won't be poor Hettie. Oh Hettie, I'd do my best. Would you mind awfully? Will you be *too* disappointed? Honestly, of all the days for the baby to arrive . . .' She was already working out in her own mind that she could wear the new blue suit originally made for the Easter garden fête. She had been ill with a migraine on the day and had never worn it. 'What do you think, Hettie?' she cried. 'I'll do it if it will help.'

'Oh, please do,' Hettie urged. 'You're so good at things like that, Cis. You'll do it much better than I could.'

'What do you think, George?' Cicely asked. 'Are you happy about me taking Hettie's place?'

George nodded vigorously. 'That's settled then,' he said and rushed to the door. 'I'll get Jack sobered up and then dash over to find Ratty. If he can't carve another name board in time, he'll have to paint it just for today. *Silver Lady!* It sounds good, that!'

And then he had gone from the room, slamming the door behind him. The baby, startled, whimpered uneasily but resumed her sleep.

Cicely, realising how much *she* had to do to prepare herself for the launching, hastily made her excuses and rushed off to get dressed. Hettie, left alone with her child, felt blissfully at peace with the world and everyone in it.

'Let them go and launch their silly old boat,' she whispered. 'We don't care, do we, little one? I've got you and you've got me and that's enough for us.'

With gentle fingers she smoothed the silver hair. 'Your papa is a good man,' she said. 'He's got his faults, but so have we all. He's a big clumsy bear of a man but he means well – and I am sure he

loves us. He'll be a good father, you'll see. I expect he'll spoil you.'
She sighed, a deep sigh of contentment, then smiled suddenly.
'You've knocked him for six, little one. He didn't even remember
to kiss me, but never mind. He will!'

*

The weather held fine to the great relief of all concerned in the
launching ceremony and by five minutes past twelve most of the
guests had arrived. Only the Customs and Excise officer was
missing, having been called away unexpectedly to investigate the
matter of a French fishing boat suspected of smuggling. After
delaying the start for another ten minutes in the hope that he
would arrive, Jack decided to go ahead without him. Coloured
bunting and a Union Jack had been draped along the sides of the
boat. The spars would be added later, round at the Strand Quay
where there was a crane available to lift the heavy masts and
capstan into their positions on the deck. Apart from Coulsdens'
modest workforce and the guests, there were plenty of family and
friends present – most of whom, resplendent in Sunday-best
clothes, were clustered behind the rows of chairs on which the
dignitaries sat. To one side, six members of the town's band
waited to provide a musical background to the occasion – two
drums, a euphonium, a trumpet and two clarinets. Feeling rather
exposed without the rest of the band, they grinned at each other
sheepishly while they waited and studied their music with unaccustomed earnestness.

A temporary and rather unsteady dais had been constructed as
usual from tar barrels and some planking and amid loud cheers
Jack climbed on to it and settled his feet carefully. He waited until
the noise had died away and then nervously thrust his hands into
his pockets. Catching Cicely's eye, however, he hastily pulled
them out again and put them behind him. Changing his mind
once more, he folded his arms over his chest and grinned self-
consciously. 'Unaccustomed as I am . . .' he began, 'and all that –
it is my great pleasure here today – this morning – to say a few
words.'

Here a wag in the crowd called out, 'Not too many!'

Cicely turned her head disapprovingly and a few people
shushed him.

Jack continued unabashed. 'A few brief words about our latest
boat and then I'll be handing you over to my brother George, her

new owner and skipper. Well, I reckon the men have done a real good job on her and she's a bonny little boat – not so little either, because at twenty-seven feet and fully decked, she's our biggest yet.'

Loud applause and a few whistles came from the audience while Jack glanced at the reporter to see if he was getting down all the salient facts. He waited until the man had finished writing and then continued.

'So I want to say thanks to all my men for their hard work and they're all invited afterwards to the George for a bit of a do – and I'll now hand you over to my brother.'

Cheers and good-natured cat-calls ensued as the brothers exchanged places; then George thrust his hands into his pockets and, ignoring Cicely's disapproval, began his speech.

'Today's a very good day for me,' he said. 'It's a big occasion for two reasons. One is the launching of my boat – and I'd like to say a big "thank you" to my family because they've made it all possible. As for the boat, well, I've watched her grow and by God, she's a real beauty! Second is the reason why my wife Hettie isn't here today to do the launching, but she had a baby instead and I'm the proud father – at least, I hope I am!'

There were exclamations of surprise, shouts of laughter and loud congratulations and the reporter's eye gleamed with excitement as he realised that his copy would get a bigger spread than usual and maybe even his name would be used.

'It's a girl,' George told them, 'a proper little blondie and I'm told she takes after her grandmother.' Sarah smiled and, nudged by Cicely, stood up briefly and then sat down again. 'I'll tell you this, she's a real cracker! Seven pounds two ounces. Mother, daughter and father all doing well!'

There was an appreciative roar of laughter. 'A boy next time then, George!' someone shouted and George nodded, grinning and thoroughly enjoying himself.

'So,' he went on, 'I'm naming the boat after my little girl and I now call upon Jack's lovely lady-wife, who's been kind enough to step in and do the honours instead of Hettie.'

Cicely stepped up on to the dais; she looked the part and knew that she did. The blue suit fitted her perfectly and she wore a cream-coloured boater with a blue silk rose at the front and blue ribbons at the back. To everyone's surprise, she took from her purse two folded sheets of paper on which she had prepared some notes. Cicely had decided to give the event a little lift by making a speech of her own. She was confident that she could lend a little graciousness to the occasion and smiled round at the upturned faces, clearing her throat discreetly.

'Ladies and gentlemen,' she began, 'I am greatly honoured to be invited here today to launch my brother-in-law's new boat. As you know, the Coulsden family has been engaged in the fishing industry in one way or another for a very long time—'

She glanced at the bent head of the reporter and hoped that he could write shorthand. Perhaps she would offer to lend him the speech afterwards so that he would not leave anything out.

'I think it is fair to say,' she continued, 'that Rye and the Coulsdens and the fishing community are indivisible.'

She paused until someone took the hint and cried, 'Hear, hear!'

'Where would Rye be without her fishermen?' she asked. 'Since time immemorial our little town has seen a succession of vessels come and go. Boats of all shapes and sizes – fishing boats, pleasure craft, merchant ships, barges, brigantines and –' here she turned the page – 'and sloops.' She paused again and gazed round her at the audience who were listening with increasing amazement. 'Once the sea lapped at our very cliffs,' she went on, 'but then it receded and has left us high and dry. But we still have our river and while we have that our boats will continue to ply to and fro maintaining that heritage of which we are so justly proud. The sea is a cruel master, but while we have vessels like this we need have no fear.'

As she turned the next page there were one or two giggles and a hastily muffled groan, but if Cicely was aware of them she gave no sign and continued smoothly, 'This boat will ply the bay in search of fish – plaice, mackerel, sprats, herring – as other boats have done before her. Its crew will be part of that brotherhood of men who put their lives at risk so that we can be fed. The Coulsdens, like all the other fishing families, have the sea in their blood. Harold Coulsden was a builder of fine craft, but he also served his time on a boat in Hastings before he took over the firm. And his father worked as a boy – ashore on the Hastings stade. I feel quite sure that so long as boats fish in the bay, the Coulsdens will play their part. This new boat, the reason for us being here today, is proof of that!'

That was the end of the written speech, but Cicely suddenly

felt confident enough to extend her homily. Folding up the paper, she raised her voice and cried out dramatically, 'Come wind and weather, the fishermen of England will go down to the sea in ships. I know I speak for the whole family when I say, hand on my heart, that we are proud to build and sail these ships.'

There was heartfelt applause, not so much for the speech as for the fact that it was over.

'I name this boat *Silver Lady*,' Cicely declared loudly. 'And may God preserve all who sail in her.'

They all watched as she turned to take hold of the champagne bottle. Her arm swung back and then forward and they saw the brief glint of sunlight on the bottle before it smashed against the black hull of George's new boat.

A second round of applause broke out as the depleted town band burst into a lively rendering of 'Sussex by the Sea' and the photographer, crouched behind his tripod, buried himself hastily beneath the black cloth and recorded the moment for posterity. The 'shore-dogs' were pulled clear from beneath the boat; then, at a shout from Jack, a dozen young boys who waited on deck now began to run together from side to side across the boat so that the regular shifting of their weight rocked it and helped to ease the keel free from the mud of the river bank. Almost soundlessly *Silver Lady* began to slide stern first into the muddy water of the river, to rousing cheers from the men who had worked on her and enthusiastic clapping from all the guests.

George sprang up on to the dais. 'You did us proud, love,' he told Cicely, landing a smacking kiss on the left side of her face and almost knocking her hat off. 'I didn't know you could spout like that.'

'She certainly did well,' Jack agreed. 'Hettie herself couldn't have done it better.'

Couldn't have done it half as well, thought Cicely smugly, nor looked so attractive. She bestowed a gracious smile in the direction of the photographer, who was calling to them to 'keep absolutely still'. The baby's early arrival had proved highly fortuitous, after all, she reflected with satisfaction, even if it had interrupted her interviews with prospective nannies.

'Well done, Cis!' shouted Stan. 'Isn't she a beauty, eh? A real beauty!'

'She is indeed,' said Cicely. She hated being called 'Cis',

particularly in public, but forced a smile none the less. 'A beautiful sight!'

'All credit to you and your men,' cried the Mayor, then Jack was being slapped on the back and the crowd was pushing forward to the water's edge to admire the boat as she rocked gently, checked in mid-stream by her mooring ropes.

George turned to his mother. 'Isn't she a sight for sore eyes, Ma?' he demanded, giving her a fierce hug.

'Get off, George,' she protested. 'You're breaking my ribs!'

'Sorry!'

'Yes, she's a lovely boat. She'll do you a treat, George.'

She spoke with sincerity, but in fact her thoughts were elsewhere – at the top of Hilders Cliff with Hettie and the new granddaughter she had yet to see. It had all been such a scramble, she thought. Nothing ever seemed to go according to plan in her experience and even Hettie's child had proved no exception. George had set his heart on a boy, she knew, but he seemed pleased enough. A boy next time, he had whispered.

Sarah sat down gingerly on the rickety chair provided for her and wondered why Jack had not had the sense to hire a dozen decent seats. So like Jack to think the Mayor's wife and other ladies would make do on a few dusty chairs taken from the office. No attention to detail. No appreciation of the finer things of life. Jack had always been scatterbrained and he was not likely to change now.

Jane, Stan's wife, leaned across to her. She was a 'plain Jane' with uninspired colouring, a large mouth and no redeeming features. When Stanley had married Jane – a widow with a son named Ernest – the match had not pleased Sarah who considered Jane to be a 'gold-digger', but she had been unable to dissuade her son from the marriage and was forced to keep her feelings to herself.

'Have you seen the baby yet, Ma?'

'Not yet,' said Sarah, 'but I intend to as soon as this is over.'

Jane nodded. 'Are you feeling all right?'

Sarah nodded although in fact her legs ached, as they often did. They said the new baby took after her side of the family, and if that were so, then she would give thanks. The Gooding girls were well-known in their day for their beauty and charm. Sarah was the last of the three famous sisters; the other two had succumbed to the ravages of tuberculosis in their late teens and only Sarah had

survived to produce a family. To her deep regret she had borne
three sons and no daughters and had looked to her boys to
produce another Gooding girl. This they had failed to do – until
now. Now Hettie had given birth to a girl with silver hair and she
was, so they said, the image of her grandmother. Another Gooding girl. So be it! Now Sarah could view her wrinkled skin and
thinning hair with equanimity and could allow her granddaughter
to take her place on the stage.

'She's got the Gooding looks, I hear,' said Jane. 'Blonde and
beautiful!'

Sarah smiled, pleased that this was a talking point. She had
been secretly disappointed when Cicely's daughter had not taken
after her side of the family. Blonde and beautiful, Jane had said –
but Jane, Sarah knew, was 'buttering her up' and she also understood why. When Sarah grew too old to live alone, she would
move in with one of her sons; South View would be sold and the
lion's share would go to the couple with whom she lived. Jane
hoped that Sarah would choose to live with them and Sarah
intended to let her go on hoping, for it was nice to be 'buttered up'
and therefore she told no one that she had already made up her
mind. Jack had always been her favourite and Cicely, although a
snob, managed house and children with skill and a certain
amount of grace, and would make Sarah's remaining years very
comfortable. True, their house on the Winchelsea Road, almost
opposite the approach to Rye Harbour, was not in the best part
of the town but it was roomy and Sarah would be quite near to
George and Hettie. Stan and Jane would be disappointed of
course, but Sarah would pretend she did not wish to return to
Hastings. In fact she did not like Jane, nor could she contemplate
sharing a house with fifteen-year-old Ernest who, in Sarah's
view, was wilful and disobedient. She had brought up her own
three boys and that was quite enough for one lifetime. It would be
Jack and there would be no argument.

Blonde and beautiful, thought Sarah with a wistful sigh. Yes,
she had enjoyed the good things of life that came with being an
attractive and desirable woman, but she was an old lady now and
the bloom had long faded. Her once slight figure was now brittle
and birdlike and her skin had mottled. Still, now there was
another Gooding beauty to take her place and for that small mercy
she was truly thankful. Fancy Hettie, her homely daughter-in-
law, producing another Gooding girl! Life was full of surprises.

Jane leaned across again. 'Is the sun troubling you?' she asked. 'I could fetch a parasol from the car if you wish.'

Sarah regarded her with growing irritation. Jane simpered and she could not bear simpering women.

'It *is* hot,' she replied, 'but they can't be much longer. I think it's all over bar the shouting and I shall go straight to see Hettie.'

Jane's eyes opened wide. 'But the luncheon,' she protested. 'Aren't you coming to the luncheon?'

'No, not this time,' said Sarah. 'I've seen enough launchings in my time and they're all the same Everyone eats and drinks too much and my stomach won't take it any more. I'd rather see the new baby and have a quiet bite to eat with Hettie. Mrs Mack will get us something light.'

She saw a protest forming on Jane's lips. 'No – don't try to talk me out of it, for I'm old enough to know my own mind and awkward enough to insist on getting it!'

Sarah chuckled and then held out her hand to shake that of the Mayor as he bent forward to congratulate her on both the boat and her new granddaughter. He and his wife were on their way to another engagement and he must be off, he explained. She watched him go without regret.

The crowd was breaking up now and Sarah waved good-bye to various people whom she knew by sight – the men from the neighbouring boatyards and tradesmen from the town.

The photographer came up to shake her hand. 'Another fine boat, Mrs Coulsden! You must be very proud.'

'I am. Yes, I am,' she agreed. 'My son makes boats to last. I hope you've got some good photographs for your newspaper?'

'So do I!' he laughed. 'It'll be the sack for me if I haven't.'

'Are you invited to the "do"?' she asked him.

He shook his head.

'Well, you go along to the George,' she told him, 'and eat my share. Tell them I sent you.'

His eyes lit up. 'Gosh, that is kind! I'd love to. Thank you very much.'

As she watched him making his way out of the yard she was suddenly aware of a young woman standing nearby. 'Lovely boat!' the woman said eagerly.

Sarah nodded distantly, not recognising her and wanting only to be on her way.

'I had to come,' the woman went on, 'when Mr Coulsden told

us. About the launch, I mean. *That* Mr Coulsden,' she pointed to Stan, who had his back to them. 'I work for him sometimes on the nets.'

'Do you?'

'I suddenly thought, I'd love to see a launching so why not go along. I just took the day off. I'll lose a day's pay, but it was worth it. Mr Coulsden didn't mind a bit. He's ever so nice. He said it was up to me, so I got a lift here off a chap I know who was bringing some gear over. Creosote and that. He's a good guv'nor, Mr Coulsden.'

'Stanley Coulsden is my son,' remarked Sarah.

The woman clapped a hand to her mouth. 'Ooh, he's not, is he? Oh dear, hope I haven't spoke out of turn.'

Sarah thought, 'The woman's lying. She knows quite well who I am.' Aloud she said, 'Not at all, I'm glad you enjoyed it.'

'I did. Ever so. But when that champagne smashed!' She laughed. 'I thought what a waste, although I know it's not really. Must do it properly and all that. But crikey, champagne! I shall have to buy a paper and read about it.'

Sarah wondered why the young woman kept glancing over her shoulder.

'Are you looking for someone?' she asked.

'No!'

The word came out rather quickly and Sarah looked at her suspiciously.

'What's your name?' she enquired.

'Agnes. Agnes Dengate.'

Sarah nodded by way of answer. There was something about the girl's manner that made her uneasy. Suddenly she saw George, Jack and Stanley walking towards them, deep in conversation. Stanley, her eldest son, was taller than his two brothers and less attractive to women, lacking their arrogance and aware of the long thin nose which spoilt his looks. He caught sight of Agnes and smiled. 'Oh, you came then,' he said. 'Did you enjoy it?'

'Oh, *yes*, sir,' said Agnes. 'It was really lovely. Really exciting. When that champagne smashed . . .' She laughed again and her brown curls danced. 'I'll never forget it.' She turned to George and Sarah noticed that at the sight of her he was suddenly silent, all the animation fading from his face. 'It's a lovely boat, sir,' said Agnes. 'I bet you're ever so proud.'

Stanley slapped George on the back. 'Of course he's proud.

Proudest bloody man in Rye this morning, I'll tell you! She's a fine little craft, a bloody fine craft.'

'Yes,' agreed George, not looking at Agnes. 'Yes, she is.'

Sarah gave him a sharp look, immediately aware that something was wrong.

'*Silver Lady*,' said Agnes. 'Pretty name for a boat.'

Stanley grinned. 'Named it after his daughter.' He jerked his head in George's direction. 'There stands a man on whom the sun shines. Yesterday a new daughter. Today a new boat! He's a jammy bugger, is George!'

Sarah began to ease herself up from the chair. 'If you're going to swear, Stanley, then I shall leave,' she said. 'You know how I hate it. Jack, you can take me up to Hettie's before you go to lunch.' She unhooked her walking stick from the back of the chair, taking care not to look at George or the girl.

To cover his confusion Stanley turned to Agnes. 'Well, it's all over now,' he said. 'Glad you enjoyed it.'

Agnes hesitated, also put out by the old woman's words, while George mumbled, 'I can take you up home, Mother,' and took hold of Sarah's arm.

'No, thank you, George. I have asked Jack,' she said firmly. She hobbled along slowly while Jack slowed his normal stride to keep pace with her.

Agnes, Stanley and George watched them go. 'What on earth was all that about?' asked Stan. 'How come you're out of favour, George?'

George shrugged and said nothing.

'My ma hates me swearing,' said Agnes quickly. 'I have to be real careful what I say even now and God, what a clout I used to get when I was a kid! Even "damn" was enough. Wallop! It's a wonder I'm not stone deaf, the clouts I used to get; right round the ear too.'

Jack ignored her, while Stanley stared uneasily after his mother. Jane came up and, giving Agnes a frosty look, slipped an arm through Stanley's. 'Are you ready to go?' she asked. 'I'm starving. I had no breakfast at all.'

'We're waiting for Jacko,' he replied. 'He's taking Mother up to Hettie's to see the baby; she doesn't want any lunch.'

Agnes turned to Jane and said brightly, 'Lovely launching, wasn't it?' Jane pretended not to hear but Stanley nodded. Then Cicely appeared and they explained why they were waiting.

'But what's the point in waiting here?' she argued. 'Jack will probably go straight to the George. That's where I'm going.'

Jane agreed eagerly and the four of them moved towards the road, leaving Agnes standing alone, staring after them.

'I hope your chickens die!' she said bitterly, making a rude gesture. She had hoped that if either Stanley or George had been in a generous mood, she might have been invited to the George Hotel, but Cicely had effectively put paid to that hope.

'Miserable lot,' Agnes remarked to nobody in particular. She remembered the shocked look on George's face when he saw her and laughed.

'Remember, Georgie Porgie,' she whispered, 'I want to be a daily help, so get that into your head once and for all. You owe me, George Coulsden, and I'm collecting!'

She glanced down hopefully at her calloused hands; she had been working on them for several days with a mixture of glycerine and honey and there did seem to be a slight improvement, she thought. Slowly she made her way across the boatyard; the crowd had already thinned and only a few small groups remained. She wondered if she could get a lift back to Hastings; it was a long walk otherwise. 'That old woman *knew*!' she said to herself with reluctant admiration for George's mother. 'She only had to look at us and she *knew*.' But what if she did? She could hardly blame a girl for trying to better herself. Agnes Dengate was going to be a daily help and the old woman could scowl all she liked. If she didn't want her son to be a naughty boy, she should have brought him up better! 'I want to go up in the world,' Agnes reminded herself, 'and I've got to start somewhere. That somewhere is George Coulsden and if the old girl doesn't like it, she can damn well lump it!'

*

The day after the launching of *Silver Lady* Hettie developed a severe fever and was confined to bed for more than five weeks. During the latter part of this period she became very depressed and Mrs Mack, reluctant to worry her, kept to herself the knowledge that certain small objects of some value had disappeared. However, on Hettie's first morning downstairs the housekeeper suddenly found she could no longer keep the news to herself.

'I'm ever so sorry, ma'am,' she began breathlessly, 'but I've something quite dreadful to tell you and I don't know how to start.

I've waited until now – you being so poorly and everything – but I can't go on like this, ma'am, really I can't!'

Hettie glanced up at her in alarm as the housekeeper tucked the rug securely over her legs. 'Like what, Mrs Mack? I don't know what you mean.'

'Why ma'am, it's this stealing,' cried Mrs Mack. 'Things just disappearing! First the silver sugar tongs and then the apostle spoon. She's never done anything like this before, ma'am, and you know what a good reference she had from the school when she came here—'

'Who?' asked Hettie. 'Who had a good reference?' Weakly she put a hand to her head and wished that she had stayed in bed.

'Why, Eunice, ma'am. Who else could I mean? I mean, it's not me that's taking the stuff and it can't be you or the master. Who else *is* there?'

Hettie stared at her in horror. 'Mrs Mack! Oh, surely you don't think Eunice is stealing from us? But why ever should she? There must be some mistake. Surely she wouldn't do such a thing. Not Eunice!'

Mrs Mack kneaded her hands together anxiously. 'I know, ma'am, but what else am I to make of it? How on earth she expects to get away with it, I don't know, because she knows what a stickler I am for checking and counting. You know me, ma'am, I check and double-check. I'm too careful, I am, and she knows it. So how can she expect to fool anyone, least of all me? It's almost as though she wants me to find out. It's beyond me, ma'am, and that's the truth.'

'Poor Mrs Mack,' said Hettie. 'Look, please sit down.' She pointed to a chair. 'Do try not to upset yourself. You look quite ill.'

The colour had receded from the housekeeper's face, leaving her as white as a sheet. Gratefully she sank on to the chair and stared helplessly at her mistress.

'I suppose I shall have to talk to her about it,' said Hettie reluctantly. 'Though really I don't feel up to it. Perhaps George . . . Oh no! That's not fair; the servants are my concern.'

'It's not very nice for you, ma'am,' said Mrs Mack, 'and I'm that sorry to have to upset you, but I didn't know what else to do. It's been worrying me for weeks now. It seems like for ever!'

Hettie managed a faint smile. 'I'm sure it does,' she said. 'Now just tell me again what she has taken – or rather,' she amended hastily, 'what is missing.'

Mrs Mack began to count on the fingers of her left hand. 'There's the sugar tongs. They went first and then the apostle spoon – I mean, you've only to look in the box to see it's gone!' She shook her head in amazement. 'And two of the silver napkin rings that you had as a wedding present. Oh, that I should live to see the day when such a thing should be happening under my very nose!'

Hettie sighed and then a sudden thought struck her. 'Has she got a young man at all, do you know?'

'A young man? Not to my knowledge. I can't see Eunice with a young man, somehow. No, I don't think she has. Why do you ask?'

'I just wondered,' Hettie shrugged. 'Maybe she has met someone who's led her astray. Someone taking advantage of her trusting nature, perhaps. Persuading her against her will . . .' Her voice trailed off. 'It was just a thought. You haven't seen her with anyone, then? Talking to a young man in the street, perhaps?'

'No, ma'am. Not Eunice. She's too shy, like. Not the sort to go after young men, nor them after her. She's too . . . well, ma'am, you know what I mean. She's not dim, just a bit on the slow side.'

'Yes, I know,' Hettie sighed. She still felt very weak and quite unprepared for a problem of such magnitude. A trusted servant stealing the silver! It was quite terrible.

'There's no one else it could be, I suppose,' said Hettie. 'I should hate to accuse her unjustly.'

Mrs Mack shook her head. 'I don't see who,' she said. 'It's not me – and if it's not her, then it would have to be you or the master stealing your own things! There's no one else here!'

Hettie sighed again. 'I suppose so. Yes, I see that. Well, it's a very sad thing to happen, but I must ask my husband what we should do. He'll know what's best, I'm sure.'

Mrs Mack stood up slowly. 'Please, ma'am,' she began, 'it won't mean the police, will it? I really don't think I could go into court and all that. And Eunice – I don't defend her, ma'am, and I know she's done wrong, but I wouldn't like her to be sent to prison or anything. I'd have it on my conscience for ever, I know I would. Whatever she's done, ma'am, I wouldn't like to think—'

Hettie interrupted her. 'Yes, Mrs Mack, I understand,' she said. 'No, of course we wouldn't involve the police, but she'll have to go, I suppose, unless she promises not to do anything of the kind again.' She brightened a little. 'Perhaps if she returns what she's taken, I could let her stay on. Oh dear! I really don't know what to do for the best. How could we give her a reference? Yet how will she ever find another job without one?'

She covered her face with her hands and tried to think logic-
ally. Concern lined Mrs Mack's face. 'Are you all right, Mrs
Coulsden? It's been a shock for you, I'm afraid.'

'Yes, it has,' said Hettie. 'I'm feeling rather exhausted. Perhaps
you could bring me a cup of tea and a biscuit, Mrs Mack, while I
try to decide what's best to be done.'

*

At five minutes to ten the next morning Hettie stood beside the
window in the front parlour, twisting her fingers nervously, waiting for Eunice to appear. Mrs Mack had orders to send her in as
soon as she had taken off her coat. Hettie gave a little gasp of
nervousness as Eunice came into the room looking remarkably
unconcerned.

'You wanted to see me, ma'am?'

Hettie had rehearsed her opening words, so they were not too
difficult.

'Yes, Eunice,' she said. 'I have something rather serious to say
to you and I think perhaps you know what it is?'

This would alert the girl to the fact that her thefts had been
discovered, thought Hettie; then she could begin to defend herself. She prayed that there would be sufficient mitigating circumstances for the girl's behaviour to enable her to overlook the lapse
and give her another chance.

'No, ma'am.' Eunice looked at her in surprise.

'Please think hard, Eunice,' prompted Hettie, taken aback by
the girl's expression. There was not a trace of guilt on the plain
face.

'I don't know what you mean, ma'am,' said Eunice. 'What shall
I think *about*?'

Hettie hesitated. 'About yourself,' she said at last, 'and about
something you have done which has shocked me.'

'Me, ma'am?' Eunice frowned. 'I haven't done nothing shock-
ing, leastways not as I know of.'

Hettie groaned inwardly. 'It's no good pretending, Eunice,' she
said sharply. 'We know what you have done and are very upset and
angry, but I want to hear your explanation. I think the least we can
do is give you a chance to speak in your own defence. My husband
agrees.'

'Defence, ma'am? Why, what have I done?'

Hettie shook her head in amazement; the wretched girl seemed determined to make it as difficult as possible for her. She took a deep breath and went on, 'You have taken some things which don't belong to you. Oh yes, we know all about it . . .' She faltered as a succession of expressions crossed the girl's face – shock, what looked like anger and, lastly, fear.

'Mrs Coulsden!' The maid's eyes widened with horror. 'What are you saying? That I *pinched* something?'

Again Hettie hesitated, reluctant to put the accusation into words.

'Because I never have!' Eunice stammered. '*Never* would I do such a thing, ma'am. Never! However could you think it of me?'

'I don't know,' Hettie began. 'That is, of course I hate to believe such a thing but, well . . . things are missing and of course it is not Mrs Mack. It was she who reported the thefts after all – an apostle spoon, the sugar tongs, napkin rings—'

She stopped as Eunice flung out her arms and cried dramatically, 'Then *search* me, ma'am. No, *search* me! I mean it. You won't find nothing.'

'For goodness' sake!' cried Hettie. 'Do stop it, Eunice; you are being ridiculous. Search you, indeed! Of course I shall do no such thing. No, I shall—'

But Eunice – cheeks now tinged with a bright flush – interrupted her. 'Yes, *search* me!' she cried. ' 'Cos I've taken nothing, nothing at all. Not the spoon, nor the tongs. Not none of them. It must be Mrs Mack although . . . no, it can't be – she wouldn't . . .'

Hettie shook her head. 'Of course it isn't Mrs Mack, she's been with us for years. I'm afraid it can only be you, Eunice, and since I cannot imagine why you should do such a thing, I have persuaded my husband to agree that we should give you this one chance. If the items are returned, we will say no more about it and trust you never to do anything so dreadful ever again.'

'But I never took *nothing*,' Eunice insisted desperately. 'How can I put them back if I haven't got them? Oh, ma'am, you *must* believe me!'

To Hettie's dismay she covered her face with her hands and burst into hysterical weeping, while still protesting her innocence. Resisting the impulse to put a comforting arm around Eunice's shoulders, Hettie told herself firmly that the girl was a thief after all, and it was only right that she should suffer some remorse for her misdeeds.

Suddenly Eunice uncovered her tear-stained face. 'A burglar, ma'am!' she gasped. 'It could have been a burglar; it *must* have been!'

Hettie hardened her heart. She had so wanted to forgive and forget, but obviously the stupid girl was not going to take the opportunity to save herself from dismissal. If she persisted in these lies, there would be nothing for it but to sack her, nothing at all. George had been adamant on the matter.

'There was no burglar, Eunice,' she told her wearily. 'There were no broken windows, no forced locks. Nothing at all. You really are extremely unwise to persist in these denials.' A new thought struck her. 'Have you pawned the things? Is that it? We could always get them back. Eunice, if only you tell me the truth, I promise you the police will not be involved and I won't bring charges against you or anything dreadful like that. Have you pawned them, Eunice? Or sold them, perhaps?'

If she had sold them, thought Hettie, the problem would be more serious. She could perhaps stop the money from the girl's wages over a long period ... Eunice, never an attractive young woman, now looked positively frightful with reddened eyes and nose and tear-streaked cheeks. Hettie wished she had taken up George's offer to deal with the matter himself, but the servants really were her province and she had insisted on speaking to Eunice personally. Having confidently expected a confession of guilt and a proper show of genuine contrition, she was quite unprepared for this determined denial. She was still weak from the prolonged fever and now felt quite exhausted. Her patience with the girl was fast running out and she stood up abruptly.

'This has gone quite far enough,' she declared with more confidence than she actually felt. '*I* know you have taken the things and so do you. There is no one else who could have done so. Just admit it, tell me you are truly sorry and I promise I will talk to Mr Coulsden about keeping you on. If you do not admit it, there is nothing I can do for you and you will have to go.'

Eunice's face puckered once more and tears rolled down her cheeks. Her nose was beginning to run and while she fumbled in her apron pocket she sniffed frantically.

'Oh, ma'am, you can't sack me. You *can't*! My Pa will half kill me if I tell him I've lost my job. He'll have to know why and then he'll think I *did* pinch the stuff. He'll be that mad with me, ma'am – but how can I say I pinched them things when I *didn't*?'

'Oh, this is too much!' cried Hettie, her patience now entirely at an end. 'You really are insufferable, you stupid, ungrateful girl! I'm beginning to think my husband was right; he said you would try to lie your way out of it. You don't deserve to be helped if you won't even help yourself. Now I do not intend to talk to you any longer. I will give you until tomorrow morning to come and tell me where my silver is. If not, then you have only yourself to blame.'

'But, ma'am!' wailed Eunice.

Hettie, unrelenting, pointed to the door. 'Please go home at once. We have nothing more to say to each other. No! I mean it. Put on your coat and go before I say something I shall regret. You have until this time tomorrow to tell the truth. If I have not received a reasonable explanation by then, you will no longer be in our employ. I warn you, Eunice. There will be no second chance.'

*

To George's secret relief, Eunice did not appear the next day and the missing items (hidden by him in the garden shed) were not recovered. The girl was assumed guilty of the theft and a note was sent to her home to the effect that her employment was terminated.

However, the wretched affair preyed on Hettie's mind. She confided her doubts to Cicely, who assured her repeatedly that she had behaved quite properly, even generously, but insisted that no one could be expected to keep on a dishonest servant. Sarah, also consulted, agreed wih Cicely and encouraged Hettie to put the entire matter out of her mind for good. George and Mrs Mack added their entreaties that Hettie should forget about it and concentrate on recovering her health. Dr Jamieson was also concerned and several weeks later he took George on one side and spoke to him about it.

'Your wife is letting this unfortunate business prey on her mind,' he said. 'It's quite unhealthy and she must be persuaded to forget it. I'm very much afraid her depression is becoming more acute, not less. She blames herself for letting such a thing happen and is morbidly interested in the wretched girl's fate. She keeps asking me what has become of her and talks of nothing else. I suggest you spend as much time as you can with her; it will leave her less time to brood. I really am becoming seriously concerned about your wife's mental health; it is quite delicately balanced at present and we must do all we can to help her throw off this depression.'

*

One evening a few weeks later, George came home and gave Hettie his usual kiss by way of greeting. Then he grinned – the particular boyish grin which he knew could always melt her heart.

'Surprise!' he said. 'I've found someone to take Eunice's place – at least, I think I have,' he amended quickly.

'George!' cried Hettie. 'Found someone else, already? But how on earth could you? I mean . . . so soon. Where on earth did you find her?'

George took her hands and kissed them. 'I used my loaf, didn't I?' he told her, tapping his head. 'It's not sawdust in here, you know, Hettie, it's the old grey matter.'

'But so quickly!' she protested. 'Oh, George, suppose I don't like her?'

'Then we don't have her,' he assured her. 'But you *will* like her, Hettie. She's from Hastings – used to do a bit of work for Stan on the nets and that sort of thing. A bit rough and ready, Stan says, but very willing to learn. He thinks very highly of her, says she's not afraid of hard work.'

Hettie did not know what to say. It was all so sudden and she did prefer to engage her own servants, but George was obviously eager to help and she had no wish to appear ungrateful. Nor, if the truth were known, did she feel up to the effort necessary to begin the long process of finding a girl of her own choice, for although she struggled to hide what she considered to be weakness, everyone was aware of the extent of her depression.

'You say Stan recommended her?' she asked doubtfully.

George nodded. 'She was at the launching,' he said. 'That's how I met her. Really thrilled too, she was; came specially to see the launch. Pretty name for a boat, she said. She was thrilled about our little girl too – asked me all about her.'

Immediately Hettie warmed to the girl, just as George had guessed she would, but then she frowned slightly. 'But how did she know about me and the baby?'

'Everyone was asking where you were,' he explained. 'Seeing Cis there instead of you.'

'Oh, I see – and you told the girl about the baby?'

'Yes, and she was really delighted. She loves kids apparently, and she's set her heart on coming – still, if you don't want her, Hettie, you've only to say so.'

'I didn't *say* that, George,' Hettie protested. 'I only said—'

'But if you don't want her, you must say so and then I'll leave it to you to find someone.'

'I expect I will like her,' said Hettie.

George grinned. 'I've got my own silver lady, I told her,' he said. '*And* a clever wife who's going to give me a boy next year.'

'George!' Hettie blushed. 'You didn't say *that*!'

'Didn't I?' He kissed her. 'Well, I must get down to the Strand. We've got to step the mast and stow all that gear that turned up yesterday. I ask you! Half-past bloody six it came, when everyone had gone home. I was tempted to send it back.'

Hettie held up her face to his.

'So,' he said, 'I'll tell her you will see her, shall I? This girl of Stan's?'

'Yes, you can tell her. But make it early next week, George. I just don't feel up to it at the moment.'

'Leave it to me. Oh, and Hettie – I registered the baby's birth this morning.' He grinned again. 'Do you want to know her name?'

Hettie stared at him in alarm. 'Know her name? Oh my God! It's Julia, I hope. George, you haven't called her something else? We decided on Julia. We *agreed*.'

'It *is* Julia, Hettie. We agreed her first name is Julia. But her second name is Lady.'

She looked up at him blankly. 'Lady? What do you mean, George? That's not a name.'

'It is now. Julia Lady Coulsden,' he recited with satisfaction.

'Oh, no! George, you're not serious!'

George laughed. 'Oh, but I am, Hettie. Our daughter is named Julia Lady Coulsden, so don't let's have an argument about it. The man was very uppity, so I put him in his place good and proper. It's to go with the boat, you see. *Silver Lady.*'

'Oh, George!' Hettie wailed. 'I don't want our little girl named after a boat – and whatever will people say? They'll think we're mad!' She looked at him with a sinking heart as she saw the sullen expression settle over his face.

'To hell with people!' cried George. 'They can say what they bloody well like. And so can you, Hettie. She's my daughter and

I'm entitled to choose a name for her without all this hoo-ha. You chose Julia and I chose Lady.'

He glared at her and Hettie felt a sudden sympathy for her mother-in-law. How on earth had she managed with three of them, she wondered.

'All right, George,' she said wearily. 'It's done now. I won't say any more.'

'I should bloody well hope not,' he snapped and went out, slamming the door behind him so loudly that upstairs Julia Lady Coulsden woke up and began to cry.

CHAPTER THREE

Sam Bligh and his grandson, Frank, moved over the short springy turf, heads bent, their eyes searching the grass. Sam walked slowly. His bowed legs were now afflicted with rheumatism but his feet in their old but well-oiled boots carried him steadily over the grass where hopefully the precious mushrooms were concealed. The old man and the boy were dwarfed by the broad flat areas of Romney Marsh which spread about them on all sides, cool and untroubled in the early morning sun. The marsh fields were dotted with grey sheep and bordered with dykes darkened with weed, as yet unruffled by the breeze which would later ripple the water and bend the tall brown sedges that sheltered heron and wild swan from prying eyes.

Ahead of them the crumbling walls of Camber Castle rose from land reclaimed from the sea in preceding centuries, its rock walls greened with ivy, its squat irregular outline stark against the cloudless blue of early autumn.

As they walked away from the small village of Rye Harbour the sun, rising behind them, cast long thin shadows across the grass. Over his arm Sam carried a shapeless bag in which to collect the mushrooms, but so far it was empty. Four-year-old Frank jumped on to his grandfather's shadow with shrill cries of excitement, his dark hair a mass of curls, his currant-brown eyes shining with mischief.

'Got you!' he cried. 'I've jumped on your shadow, so you're dead!'

Sam sidestepped neatly and the little boy sprang after the elusive shadow which was removed once more and returned to its original course.

'Grandad! Stop it. I got you!'

'Is that so?' The old man moved again, this time to the other side, and Frank squealed indignantly.

'Don't, Grandad!'

'What am I doing, then?' the old man protested innocently.

'You're moving!' cried Frank. 'I don't want you to move. I want to get you.'

Sam shook his head. 'It's not my doing,' he asserted solemnly. 'I'm just walking along. It's this darned tricky shadow. Won't behave itself nohow. Real devil, it is. Will it go where I tell it? Of course it won't. Jumps about like nobody's business. Whoops! There it goes again.'

'Grandad! It *is* you. *You're* doing it. I don't want you to.'

'It's not a case of what you want in this old world,' Sam told him. 'It's what you get, lad. And I'm stuck with this darned shadow that won't behave itself.'

For a moment the boy was half convinced by this story and he dropped back and trotted along thoughtfully beside his grandfather.

Frank Bligh's mother had died a few days after his birth and his father, Luke, had moved back to live with his parents, taking the motherless child with him. Now the four of them shared the tiny ramshackle cottage which Sam Bligh had built forty years earlier for his young bride, Alice.

'Stop!' Sam cried suddenly and the little boy froze in mid-step, his eyes gleaming. 'I smell a mushroom,' Sam told him. 'Now, who's going to find it, you or me?'

'Me! I'm going to find it. I am.'

Sam, who had seen the pearl-white shape in the grass, made a pretence of searching in the wrong place so that eventually Frank was able to discover it.

'Well, I never,' marvelled the old man. 'Not one but two. Now remember. Never pull them. Cut them. Then another will grow. Now where's my old knife? Ah, here we are!'

They knelt together as Sam's blade sliced diagonally through the yielding stem of the mushrooms. He handed each one to Frank who, with elaborate care, placed them in the bag. The greengrocer's shop in the High Street in Rye would pay sixpence a plate for clean mushrooms, but they needed to be fresh and firm and wholesome to look at. These two were highly eligible.

'That's a good start, that is,' said Sam as he eased himself back into a standing position. 'Now, no more larking about. It's eyes skinned from now on and we'll see who finds the most.'

The first lark of the morning sprang suddenly skyward and Sam paused in his searching to point it out to his grandson.

'Climbing up to heaven, that there bird,' he told him. 'Going to have a word in God's ear.'

'What about, Grandad?'

'About good boys, I shouldn't wonder. Good boys, and naughty boys.'

'About me, Grandad? Am I good? I am, aren't I, Grandad?'

The boy stared up into the old man's face, concerned, and Sam nodded. 'Aye, you're a good young 'un,' he admitted. 'Most of the time, that is. But you don't always eat up your greens, do you? Your Pa has to get on to you, doesn't he? You're a good young 'un except for the greens.'

Frank, chastened, glanced skyward and muttered a promise that he would eat them up. Sam grinned at him and ruffled the boy's untidy brown hair.

'Well, see that you do,' he said. 'I ate my greens and look what it's done for me!' He laughed wheezily and began to cough and the boy regarded him with some doubt. 'Well, let's get on with it, lad,' said Sam. 'We won't find any mushrooms standing here, that's for sure. They won't come looking for *us*.'

They walked on in silence for a while and were rewarded by the discovery of several more large mushrooms. Two platefuls would buy an ounce of Nut Brown tobacco for Sam's pipe, with threepence left over and a halfpenny that would be for Frank to spend next time they walked into Rye. As always, he would buy a square of bread pudding from the little baker's below the Landgate.

Sam Bligh's sixty years rested heavily on his bent shoulders. His life had been long and hard and he did not expect to live much beyond seventy, but he had few regrets. The world was changing fast and he had no wish to change with it. King Edward VII had died a few months earlier and eventually his son George would be crowned – the fifth George to sit on England's throne. The world was always changing, but not for the better, in Sam's opinion. For one thing there were too many people after too few jobs – *and* there were too few horses. Trams were ruining the roads and the newfangled motor cars were filling the air with unhealthy fumes. In Westminster the politicians had been wrangling over something called the 'People's Budget'. The so-called Lords had thrown it out, but Lloyd George and the Liberals were back in power and God only knew what would happen next. Sam didn't really care, although he argued the toss with his son willingly enough just for the sake of bandying words until Alice put a stop to it with a few sharp words of her own.

'Your grandma's a tough old bird,' Sam remarked.

Frank looked up briefly and said, 'Is she?'

'She is that. Women can be the very devil if you let 'em.' They were demanding the vote now! Once let them get the vote, thought Sam, and who knew where it would all end? Alice would make a good suffragette. The corners of his mouth twisted upwards in the wry smile that the young Alice had found so endearing many years ago.

'Yes, she's a tough 'un, is your grandma,' he told the boy. 'Funny things, women. You've got to keep a sharp eye on them. Specially nowadays. Everything's gone haywire, if you ask me. Quite haywire. Mad. They do this rag-time, you know,' he went on, 'and they tango. Always has to be something new for some folks. Old ways aren't good enough, seemingly. I don't know where it's all leading. I don't know at all.'

'I don't know, too,' Frank assured him earnestly, trying to lengthen his stride to keep in step with his grandfather. He enjoyed these outings, for the old man told him things that no one else did. 'What is tango?' he asked.

'Blessed if I know, lad, except it's a dance. Aye, that's it – a dance or some such.'

The old man did not speak of the growing threat of war, for he preferred not to think about the Kaiser and his rapidly expanding navy.

'Your mother was a good woman, though, bless her,' said Sam. 'You've got her eyes, you know. Lovely brown eyes, she had, poor soul – *and* she always ate up her greens! Oh yes, always ate up her greens, your mother.'

When he paused, putting a hand to his back and trying to straighten up, Frank did the same.

'They want the vote, women do,' said Sam, 'and they're getting all het-up about it. The papers are full of their antics. See, that's women for you, that is. But they won't get it. Not in a million years! You know how many a million is, do you?'

Frank shook his head.

'Well, it's a heck of a lot.'

'A *heck* of a lot,' Frank repeated, enjoying the words. 'A *heck* of a *lot*.'

'And you mind, young Frank, when you're a man. You watch out for women, else they'll tie you in knots before you can blink an eyelid.' Sam chuckled as his grandson nodded, his eyes large, his expression suitably earnest.

Neither of them knew that less than five miles away a girl lay asleep in her cot – a girl who would one day dominate Frank's thoughts and bring back a long-forgotten echo of his grandfather's warning.

*

Launching the lifeboat – whether as a practice drill, or major exercise or in answer to a real distress call – involved exactly the same amount of effort from its crew and launchers. The lifeboat station was a mile and a half from Rye Harbour village and was reached by a cinder track edged with white stones that ran through grass, sand and shingle wastes. As soon as crew and launchers were alerted (Tommy Bird was one of the latter), they ran as fast as they could to meet up at the shed where the boat was housed and as soon as they were inside, began to struggle into their equipment – sou'westers, yellow oilskins and the brown cork life-jackets on which their lives would depend in an emergency. They were cheerful but mainly silent, so intent were they on improving the time it took them to get the boat manned, fully operational and into the sea.

The huge surf boat was nearly 40 feet long and weighed more than four tons; it was heavy work to haul her down the sloping shingle beach. Once in the water she relied on her helmsman, her sail and the strength of her twelve oarsmen to force a passage through the pounding waves. Today was a practice launch and no lives rested in the hands of the seventeen-man crew. Next time it might be very different. The craft was launched into the rising tide in a flurry of breaking waves and frothing spray, then Tommy and the rest of the launchers watched and waited as the various life-saving manoeuvres were thoroughly rehearsed. After that the boat was painstakingly winched back into the shed where it was the responsibility of the honorary bosun, a shore-based member of the team, to see that it was restored to a state of full readiness for the next time. Tommy joined in the friendly banter which ensued, enjoying the companionship of the crew, but when it was time to go he gave them a curt 'Cheerio' and struck out along the beach alone while the others went back to the village. Tommy's

home was a solitary, somewhat derelict bungalow, set back a few
hundred yards from the high-water mark. Here he had been born
and bred and now, with his parents dead, he remained alone with
the roar of the sea forever in his ears. He was a carefree, un-
reliable and uninhibited man of forty-seven years, but looked
older. The bungalow was his and his day-to-day needs were few,
for he had no wife or children to support and worked at the
boatyard as little as possible – only when he needed a few extra
shillings for a pair of boots or coal for his fire. The lifeboat was his
main reason for living.

As he crunched his way over the beach he kept his head well
down and searched among the shingle for 'blue boulders' – the
blue-grey pebbles, large as turkey's eggs, which were needed in
Staffordshire, so they said, to glaze pottery. Three shillings and
sixpence was all he got for a ton of 'boulders', but as he frequently
assured himself, that was 'better than nothing and a whole lot
better than a kick in the teeth'. Tommy would leave the stones
in piles at predetermined spots along the beach to await collection
by the one-eyed owner of the *Merry*, the little gaff-rigged work
boat which fortnightly nosed out of the harbour on an ebb tide and
returned on the flood with its cargo. Tommy Bird would have
given his own right eye to own the *Merry* but it was not to be.
Sometimes he went down to the jetty at the harbour and watched
the blue boulders reloaded on to *Runcorn*, the West Country
schooner which took them on the last stage of their journey.
Sometimes a French ship would be moored there also – in from
Cherbourg with a load of flints for the construction of Sussex
roads. Once he had worked his passage on a boat called *L'Oiseau*,
but France had been a bitter disappointment to him with heavy
rain, an impossible language and no decent beer.

Now Tommy glanced up briefly, assessing the weather. High
above him the south-west wind had blown the clouds into fall-
streaks, while a strong breeze blew on to his back from the east.
The wind was rising; it might make force eight, he thought, and
would almost certainly bring rain within the next few hours. As he
lowered his head, his eye caught a slight movement on the beach
ahead of him and he squinted into the setting sun, muttering,
'Looks like Ratty Hall's girl, with a young 'un tagged along.'

He had seen her a few times walking on the beach, and had
managed to avoid her. Today, however, Ratty's dog had spotted
him and came bounding towards him, barking an ecstatic wel-

come as though they were old friends instead of sworn enemies, since the dog had killed Tommy's only chicken two years earlier. Not that the hen had laid any eggs – it was far too old – but that was not the point. It had escaped the pot merely because Tommy had been too lazy to wring its neck and he certainly had not fancied it after Ratty's dog had mauled it into a mass of blood-stained feathers. Ratty had offered him a measly sum in compensation and Tommy had refused.

Eunice Hall now recognised Tommy and raised her hand briefly. She was dragging along a sack, into which she put pieces of driftwood. The child ran towards him, shouting a greeting. Damnation, thought Tommy. Too late now to make a getaway.

'Hullo there, young 'un,' he said, surprised to see that the boy was Luke Bligh's son, Frank.

'Mr Bird!' shouted Frank. 'It's my birthday tomorrow. I'll be five years old and I'm having a present. It's a jig-saw puzzle, but it's going to be a surprise. I'm four years and eleven months, and thirty days, but tomorrow I'll be five!'

He hopped from one foot to the other in his excitement and Tommy grinned down into the brown eyes under the untidy mop of brown hair.

'Five, eh?' he said. 'Well, bless me. I can't remember being five. Maybe I never was . . .' He scratched his ear and looked very puzzled. 'I remember being four and then bang! All of a sudden I was six. Yes, that was the way of it. I never was five.'

Frank stared at him, a frown darkening his face as he tried to see the logic of what Tommy had told him.

'Hullo, Eunice,' said Tommy. He was embarrassed to be face to face with her after what he had heard.

Eunice tossed her head and her dark eyes flashed. 'Oh, you needn't pretend,' she said. 'I know you know. You work at Coulsdens' yard so you must have heard. Everyone has. Why don't you ask me, then?'

'Ask you what?' he mumbled, wishing he had seen her in time to avoid her.

'Whether it's true or not. Whether I'm a thief.' She swallowed hard. 'Go on, Tommy Bird! You're dying to know why I lost my job.'

'It's none of my business,' he began, reluctantly looking her straight in the eye. 'I don't expect you did nothing wrong. Your father brought you up proper. You—'

'You don't *expect*!' she cried, her eyes smouldering. 'But you don't know, do you? I just might have pinched them things, eh? You're not sure, are you, Tommy? Nobody's sure. Everyone thinks I just *might* be guilty. Everyone . . .'

To his dismay her lips trembled and suddenly she burst into loud sobs. Tommy and Frank watched her helplessly for a moment, making no move to comfort her, then exchanged rueful looks.

'Women!' muttered Tommy.

When her tears showed no sign of drying up, Tommy said loudly, ' 'Course no one reckons you stole them things. 'Course they don't!' He snatched up a scrap of driftwood to fiddle with in case he should be tempted to pat her on the shoulder or make any other rash gesture of sympathy.

Young Frank stared at his patched boots and then at a nearby strand of seaweed. 'Grown-ups' were not supposed to cry and he didn't know what to do. He teased the dry brown bladderwrack with the toe of his boot and cast a sly glance at Eunice out of the corner of his eye. She was mopping her eyes with a grubby handkerchief and sniffing and hiccupping. Frank was glad he was a boy and didn't have to make those awful noises. Boys don't cry; his grandmother had told him that, so he knew it was true.

Tommy Bird shuffled his feet and threw another glance upwards. Yes, it was definitely going to rain before nightfall.

'Well,' said Eunice, 'I didn't take 'em, so I don't care what you think. Or anyone else. I don't know who it was done it, but it wasn't me and you can all go to hell 'cos I never took nothing. Never!' She twisted her damp handkerchief into a shapeless ball. 'What would I want with all that soppy stuff?'

' 'Course you wouldn't,' said Tommy lamely. He felt sorry for her, in spite of himself. She looked terrible with her reddened eyes and blotched face and that poor little trembling mouth. Suddenly he wanted to say the right thing – but he couldn't for the life of him decide what the right thing might be. ' 'Course you wouldn't pinch nothing,' he repeated.

To his horror, her eyes filled with tears once more. 'For Christ's sake!' he said. 'Don't start that again.'

She only shook her head in mute desperation and before he knew it – to his own intense surprise – he had thrown down the piece of driftwood and put his arms round her shoulders, pulling her closer so that eventually her head rested on his chest. Over the top of her head Tommy Bird caught Frank's surprised eyes and they regarded each other wordlessly.

'Tomorrow,' said Frank, feeling he ought to say something to end the silence, 'I'll be five.'

Tommy Bird nodded. 'And you're having a jig-saw puzzle,' he said casually, as though the woman sobbing in his arms was nothing to do with him.

Frank nodded in turn and then looked at Eunice. 'She keeps *on* crying,' he said.

'Aye, she does,' Tommy agreed.

Awkwardly he began to pat Eunice on the back and finally, with a supreme effort, she stopped crying for the second time and blew her nose on the damp handkerchief.

'I'm sorry,' she gasped.

He let his arms drop and she stepped back away from him; but then Tommy stepped forward, pulled her awkwardly into his arms and kissed her. Frank's gaze went from one to the other, astonished.

A few seconds passed and then it was Tommy's turn to say, 'I'm sorry,' as he released Eunice and looked at Frank.

'Five, eh?' he said. 'I was never five, leastways I don't reckon so.'

Frank looked at Eunice who laughed tremulously, over-whelmed by the speed of events.

'Don't believe him, Frank,' she said. 'He's having you on!'

'Are you?' the boy asked.

'Maybe,' said Tommy. 'Maybe not.' He looked at Eunice. 'You not got another job then?'

'No,' she said. 'Who'd take me with no reference? It's not fair, Tommy. I really didn't take those things.'

He nodded and she went on, 'I may be a bit slow on the uptake, but I'm not daft, Tommy. I think there was something funny going on — but I'm blessed if I know what. I've thought and thought until my head spins.' She gave a slight shrug. 'Still, I'm out of work and that's that. Old Alice Bligh's giving me a few coppers, bless her, to fetch her some driftwood, and me Pa's feeding me for the time being, but it's a fine old mess.' She shrugged. 'Why did you kiss me just now?' she asked curiously.

'I don't know.'

'Oh. Where've you been? Coulsdens?'

'Boat drill,' he said laconically.

'Oh.' She sighed deeply. 'They've got a new girl already for my job. Some fish girl who used to work on the nets at Hastings. Didn't take them long to find someone else.'

'No, it didn't. Real quick, that was.'

They both watched Frank as, losing interest in the two adults, he made his way among the debris which had been carried in on the last tide.

'Look, Eunice!' he shouted, holding up a starfish.

'Lovely!' called Eunice. 'He's a nice kid,' she said wistfully. 'I sometimes wonder . . .' She broke off.

'What, then?'

'Nothing.'

'Tell me,' he insisted.

'It doesn't matter. I must find some more wood and get on back, or young Frank'll be late for his tea.'

Tommy caught hold of her hand. 'Tell me what you wonder.'

She looked at her small hand held in his large rough one. 'I wonder if I'll ever have any of my own. Kids, I mean. Now I must go.'

Frank ran up with a handful of shells. 'Look, Eunice, look! I'm taking these home for Grandma.'

'Lovely,' said Eunice. 'She'll like them.'

Frank forced the shells into his already bulging pockets and then took Eunice's free hand.

'I must go,' she said again and suddenly felt Tommy Bird's hand tighten over hers.

He gave a surprised smile. 'I'll walk you back,' he heard himself say.

*

A very fine rain was falling as Cicely, underneath her umbrella, made her way distastefully between yesterday's puddles, aware that her flimsy shoes were not suitable for such terrain. They were buttoned and pale grey to match her dress and jacket and her hat was grey straw with coral satin roses. She was on her way to collect 'the books' from what Jack laughingly described as the office – a small corner of one of the benches in which a rusting spike held all the invoices and an ancient ledger contained details of the orders for new boats and repairs to the old; these were all written in Jack's sprawled and indecipherable handwriting. For the purposes of income tax, Cicely was officially on the payroll as a clerk, a word she detested, but Jack had laughed when she suggested 'secretary' as a more fitting title. She did not enjoy being considered one of her husband's employees, but there was nobody else able to deal with the paper work, Jack being notoriously muddle-headed when it came to figures. It was therefore necessary for her to visit the yard and collect the relevant material for a check-up at least once a month. When she did this, Cicely liked to feel that she was making a call on the firm as wife to the proprietor rather than looking in as a clerk to collect the books. She therefore dressed accordingly, secretly hoping that the men appreciated the rare vision of loveliness which appeared to brighten their grim days amid what she considered to be squalid surroundings. It did not occur to her that the men might enjoy their rugged environment, and be content to spend their days in their working clothes amidst a clutter of boats and tackle, exposed most of the time to the vagaries of the elements and sharing occasional crude jokes.

She paused to take stock of the yard and its inhabitants before she went in. The shingle roof of the boat-shed would soon need replacing, she thought, and the firm could afford it. Business was looking up, with an order for a new fishing punt and enough repairs to last them five weeks or more. She made a mental note to speak to Jack about the roof, knowing how much he hated her to interfere but, as she repeatedly told his mother, 'the place would fall down around his ears' if she, Cicely, did not take an interest.

Beyond the shed the bow of the *Mona Lisa* loomed high, set on blocks at the top of the slipway; she could see Ratty Hall crouching on the deck. Ratty! A ridiculous name, she had always thought, and she therefore made a point of calling him 'Mr Hall'. Tommy was 'Mr Bird' and Cicely believed that the two men appreciated her courtesy and respected her accordingly. Not that she had ever felt the same about Ratty since his daughter Eunice had stolen Hettie's silver.

Ratty, perched on the *Mona Lisa*'s deck, was renewing the rotten frames of the hatch covers. Although he had seen Cicely making her way along the path, he now pretended to be unaware of her presence and kept his head well down as he screwed on one of the hinges.

'Good morning, Mr Hall.'

He glanced round in pretended surprise, then came to the boat's rail, looked down and tugged a lock of his hair with exaggerated humility.

'Morning, Mrs Coulsden, ma'am.'

She eyed him suspiciously. Was he mocking her, or was he going out of his way to show her the respect she was entitled to expect from one of her husband's employees? She could never tell with Mr Hall.

'Keeping busy, are you?' she asked.

'Oh very busy, Mrs Coulsden, ma'am.'

Cicely felt she should show an interest in their work, so she said, 'What exactly are you doing, Mr Hall?'

' 'Atch cover, ma'am.'

'Ah, I see.' She smiled encouragingly, imagining herself as he saw her, aware how well the grey umbrella framed her auburn head for she had tried out the effect in the bedroom before leaving the house.

'You're making a good job of it, I'm sure,' she said, at a loss for further topics of conversation. She could not enquire after his wife who was dead, or his daughter who was a thief, and she could hardly ask after his dog. As far as she knew he had nothing else in the world.

'I'm doing me best, thank you, ma'am, like I always do,' he told her sharply. 'Never had no complaints so far.'

'That's really splendid.'

His features contracted into a slight frown. 'Leastways,' he added, 'no one's complained to my face, put it like that. If the guv'nor had any complaints about my work, he'd tell me straight.'

'I'm sure he hasn't,' she said slowly, twirling the umbrella.

'So if he had any complaints about my work I'd be the first to hear about it,' Ratty told her, warming to his theme. 'Oh yes, there'd be—'

'Mr Hall!' Cicely interrupted him. 'No one has suggested that you do not do a good job of work. I'm quite sure my husband is perfectly satisfied with you.'

But Ratty, touched on a sensitive subject and gaining momentum, had straightened up now and towered above her. 'I've always done a decent day's work,' he said, 'and so has all my family no matter what's been said. My girl's always done a decent day's work, same as what I do.'

Cicely began to say, 'I'm sure she has' and then realised she could not do so without suggesting that Eunice had been wrongfully dismissed. She felt at a great disadvantage dwarfed by the *Mona Lisa*'s hull, with her head tilted backwards at an uncomfortable angle. Drat the man, she thought irritably. She must not allow herself to become embroiled in an ugly squabble over his wretched daughter.

'We are not discussing your daughter, Mr Hall,' she began in her coldest tone. 'I have come to collect the books and speak to my husband. Is he around?'

'No, he's not,' said Ratty, his tone sulky. 'And my Eunice has sworn to me on her mother's grave that she never took nothing.'

'I have just told you we are not discussing—'

'Well, *I* am!' he shouted. 'She's my daughter and she's done nothing wrong and your brother-in-law had no right ...' He broke off, aware that he was losing his temper and possibly putting his own job in jeopardy.

Cicely was trembling with anger and disappointment. The stupid little man was spoiling her visit. Who did he think he was to shout at her and adopt that surly attitude? She drew herself up to her full height.

'I think you've said quite enough, Mr Hall,' she said as firmly as she could. 'In fact, I think you have said too much. I am not interested in your daughter and I don't wish to hear her mentioned again.'

Unfortunately, instead of putting an end to the matter, her words provoked him to a further rash outburst.

'Oh yes! That's right!' he cried furiously. 'That's just like you Coulsdens! Take away her good name and then it's "Oh, we don't want to mention her." Bloody marvellous, that is! Typical of your sort. Think you're little gods, you Coulsdens.'

Cicely's composure faltered. 'Mr Hall!' she stammered. 'I – I won't hear another word!'

'Oh yes you will,' he shouted, throwing caution to the wind. '*You* can hear it and all bloody *Rye* can hear it as well, for all I care. It's about time somebody put you in your place – coming down here like Lady Muck and calling my daughter a thief.'

'It was my brother-in-law!' cried Cicely wildly. 'It was George, not Jack, who sacked your stupid daughter!'

'Well, my daughter is *not* stupid. That's where you make a big mistake.'

To Cicely's dismay he leaped down from the boat's hull to stand beside her and shake a fist in front of her face. 'My daughter was sacked for something she didn't do and all you can do is call her names. Well, that's what I think of your brother-in-law!' He thrust two fingers into the air in a rude gesture and Cicely shrank back in horror.

'Don't you *dare* . . .' she began hoarsely, but her throat was dry and her heart was racing. In desperation she turned away from Ratty's contorted face and stumbled blindly towards the boat-shed. As she fled her toe caught on a length of timber concealed in the long grass and with a shriek she fell headlong on to the ground, her umbrella rolling away and coming to rest beside the door of the shed.

For a moment Cicely lay full-length in the damp grass, breath-less and almost sobbing with rage and mortification. Her second-best suit would be completely ruined; she could imagine how pathetic she would look when she stood up – crumpled and dishevelled – and she knew full well how that wretched little man would crow over her misfortune. She felt she could hardly bear it and wished she could lie there and die. As she wondered if anyone else had witnessed her quite literal downfall, tears of self-pity trickled from her eyes to mingle with the wet grass. No doubt her hat was askew – she would look like a scarecrow!

The sound of Jack's motor reached her ears at the same moment that she heard footsteps. She closed her eyes quickly, then opened them a fraction to see who had approached her.

'Mrs Coulsden, ma'am, are you all right?'

She closed her eyes again. It was that hateful Ratty and he sounded very frightened. Good, she thought vindictively. Let him think she was injured. Let him worry! It came to her suddenly that a woman who had tripped over and *injured* herself was no longer a figure of fun and she moaned faintly. Then she heard the car stop and Jack shouted, 'What's up then?'

'It's Mrs Coulsden,' cried Ratty. 'She's . . . she's fallen down.'

'Fallen down? Cicely?'

Then Jack was crouching beside her and Cicely moaned again. 'Christ, Cis!' He tried to lift her head, failed and attempted to roll her over. Cicely decided that this would be undignified, so she opened her eyes and said 'Jack?' in a faint voice and then looked slowly round her as though she was not sure where she was.

Ratty, eyeing her, was obviously in a state of great trepidation, she noticed. Serve him damned well right!

'Cis! What happened?' Jack asked. 'Are you hurt, love? Can you talk, Cis?'

Cicely allowed her tearful gaze to rest on the terrified Ratty and for a long moment she let him suffer.

'Whatever happened, love?' asked Jack again, helping her to sit up. 'Did you faint or something? Oh! Look at the state of you!'

Cicely put a hand to her head and murmured faintly, 'I want to go home, Jack. Please take me home.'

'Can you stand, Cis? Here, let me help you. Give us a hand, Ratty.'

Cicely opened her eyes in horror. 'No!' she gasped. 'Not that man!'

Ratty, who had moved forward, now took a hurried step back, his face scarlet as Jack stared from him to Cicely.

'What the hell's been going on here?' he demanded.

Before Ratty could answer, Cicely swayed suddenly, letting herself fall into Jack's arms.

'Take me home,' she whispered.

With a muttered curse, Jack picked her up in his arms and carried her towards the car where he laid her in the back seat, arranging her as comfortably as he could.

'The books . . .' she muttered. 'I came for the books.'

He ran back to the shed, seized the books and invoices and hurried back to the car.

'I'll talk to you later!' he shouted to Ratty as the car reversed. 'So you'd better *be* here.'

*

Ratty, cursing his bad luck, watched them go with despair in his heart. It would be his turn now to be unemployed and all because of that stupid cow. God Almighty, but he wouldn't be in Jack Coulsden's shoes, married to a woman like her! He returned to the hatch cover and crouched beside it, but could not bring himself to put in another screw. He might as well give up now, he told himself, because it would be a week's wages, if he was lucky, and good-bye to the job he had held down for the best part of nine years. He looked around for Tommy, but the boatyard appeared to be deserted.

'Tom?' he called, but the only sign of life apart from himself was a small, scruffy-looking dog which found its way into the yard on various occasions.

Ratty, his mood worsening, threw a piece of wood at it, but although he missed, it was near enough to frighten the animal which gave a surprised yelp and looked around, puzzled, not seeing Ratty who was still on board the *Mona Lisa*.

'Hop it!' cried Ratty and the dog took to its heels and dis-appeared. Ratty threw down the screwdriver, then picked it up again. It was *his*. His bag of tools was in the shed on the bench next to the out-of-date calendar and the clock that no longer worked. He sighed mournfully, abandoned his work and jumped down from the *Mona Lisa*. Should he bother to wait, he wondered. It would make no difference to the outcome. Jack Coulsden was a decent guv'nor, but that bitch of a wife would have the last word and that word would be 'Go'. Habit dies hard, however, and he had been told to wait.

He wandered to the end of the slipway and stared down at the retreating tide which had exposed several yards of creamy evil-smelling mud as well as the weed-encrusted timbers of the ramshackle 'jetty'. Bloody Coulsdens! They were all tarred with the same brush; nothing to choose between them. Stan had a temper when he was drunk – or so he'd heard from a reliable source – and George was as crooked as they come. Yes, George had done for Eunice and now Jack would do for him.

He looked left along the river bank towards the Fishmarket, to the familiar tangle of catwalks, jetties and black huts. He had been part of that cheerful crowd, he thought with a rush of self-pity. Now he would be out of work and outside it all. Maybe he'd get a job crewing, although he hated and feared the sea and would rather stay on land. His uncle had drowned at sea in a storm which washed him off the deck and delivered his body to the beach at Dengemarsh. Ratty was seasick, too, as soon as his feet left dry land. Damn and blast Cicely Coulsden, he thought. And damn his own stupidity. Why hadn't he kept his mouth shut?

At the far end of the yard, half in and half out of the water, a dilapidated dinghy lay upside down in the mud, her planks sprung apart, her paint peeling like dandruff. Further up on the bank there was the familiar pile of old fenders – knotted ropes and corks to hang over a boat's side to distance and protect her hull from obstacles which otherwise might damage her. There was an ancient lifebelt from the old *Anne-Marie* which Fred Leggett's father used to sail out of Hastings before he went funny in the head and had to give up. Everything in the yard held memories and Ratty would miss it all more than he would ever admit.

Slowly he walked across the grass and into the shed, where he collected his personal belongings – the black waterproof apron he wore when he was painting and the thigh-boots he donned when they were launching or careening a boat.

For the next twenty minutes he sat in the boat-shed, breathing in the smell of the wood shavings, creosote and oily rags and staring at the 'No Smoking' sign. As a last act of defiance he rolled a cigarette and lit it, but when he heard Jack's car pull in to the yard his courage failed him and he hastily trod it out before his employer stormed in.

'So let's hear your story, you idiot,' he roared. 'Not that it'll make a blind bit of difference, but I won't kick you out without giving you your say. Well, don't just gawp at me, man, get on with it!'

Ratty stammered out his version of the incident and Jack groaned and slapped his forehead. 'You're a bloody fool, Ratty!' he said. 'What's between George and Eunice is no concern of mine and you know it. You picked on the wrong one when you tangled with Cis and she wants your head on a plate with gravy. Here . . .'

He pulled a wad of notes from his pocket and peeled some off. 'Take this and think yourself damned lucky. It's two weeks' wages and more than you deserve. Now get out of my sight, man, before I change my mind.'

Ratty, muttering his thanks, took up his belongings and stumbled out of the yard in a state of shock, heading for the nearest pub.

*

The public bar of the Pipemakers' Arms was a cheerful bustling place. Every seat was taken and more fishermen stood at the bar, foaming mugs of dark beer or stout in their hands as they shouted greetings to their fellows through the thick tobacco-rich haze which shrouded them all and made the barmaid's eyes run; she knew better than to complain, however, for Will's Woodbine cigarettes and Old Holborn pipe tobacco were part of the pub's stock in trade and the more the fishermen smoked, the better it was for the landlord's pocket. They talked in loud voices, laughed uproariously and downed pint after pint. There were a few women sitting at the tables with their husbands or men friends, but they were greatly outnumbered and mainly ignored by the rest of the men.

The room itself was lit by two flaming gas-lights on each wall and the decor – a serviceable dark brown – was not particularly inspiring but nobody even noticed it, so great was their enthusiasm for the company they found there and the chance to forget for a few hours the rigours of life at sea. Marje, the barmaid, was the landlord's niece and had served behind the bar for six years, ever since leaving school; she was used to the clamour and pretended not to hear the earthy jokes which were bandied about. She had also grown accustomed to the smell of salt, sweat and fish, the shuffle of boots in the sawdust and the sound of the spittoon being used.

At the far end of the bar and furthest from the door, Ratty leaned his elbows on the counter and stared moodily into his half-empty mug of bitter. He had been out of work for three whole days now and was not enjoying the experience. Earnest enquiries after alternative work had come to nothing and his mood swung between maudlin self-pity and a fierce hatred towards each and every member of the Coulsden family. Occasionally he blamed Eunice for his predicament; once or twice he considered whether or not he himself was to blame, but since that suspicion merely increased his gloom the Coulsdens had to shoulder most of the responsibility.

The door swung open and Tommy Bird came in to cries of 'Hi, Tommy!' and 'How goes it, then?' Tommy, grinning, ducked a playful swipe from the skipper of the *Mona Lisa*, slapped the back of one of his many cousins and winked at his sister-in-law, but he was searching the crowd for Ratty and, when he found him, elbowed a space for himself beside the other man.

'How goes it, then?' he asked, after ordering two more drinks.

Ratty sighed. 'Good question,' he said. 'Rotten answer.'

'I heard,' said Tommy. 'Eunice told me. I wondered when I didn't see you about. A new chap started, Ned something-or-other, but the guv'nor never said a word.'

'Sod *him*,' said Ratty.

Marje produced two more bitters and gave Ratty a smile. 'Cheer up, love,' she said. 'It may never happen!'

'It already *has*,' he told her. 'Too bloody right it has.'

'Oh dear! I am sorry, whatever it is.'

'Thanks, Marje.'

She left them to it and they drank in silence for a while. Then Ratty said, 'He fixed Eunice, you know, somehow. God knows how, but he did. George Coulsden, I mean.'

'Must have,' agreed Tommy, 'but how? We'll never know.'

'My girl swears she never did it. I threatened to thrash her if she was lying but she wasn't, I could tell. Broke her heart, it did.'

Tommy nodded sympathetically. 'You had to stick up for her,' he said. 'Your own flesh and blood. I'd have done the same. Mrs Jack had it coming anyway, silly cow. I wish I'd seen her, flat on her face.'

Ratty's face relaxed briefly into a reluctant grin. 'Smack, she went,' he said. 'Wallop! I thought she'd knocked herself out. She just lay there, like she was dead.'

'Yes?'

'I didn't see the funny side of it then, I was that rattled – but then her old man turned up. She was moaning and groaning.'

'Stuck-up prune!' commented Tommy.

'I tell you what,' said Ratty, lowering his voice, 'I wouldn't half like to wipe the smile off their smug faces. I've been thinking . . .'

Marje, hovering nearby, could hear nothing of what followed. She had heard about Ratty's dismissal, as indeed she heard about everything else that went on, but she had learned to keep her mouth firmly shut and to all intents and purposes was profoundly innocent of any knowledge of the nefarious activities regularly indulged in by many of the pub's regulars. The police had long ago learned that when a man was beaten up, or fishing tackle stolen, Marje at the Pipemakers' Arms could tell them nothing.

*

One evening a week after Tommy and Ratty's meeting, Jack was hunched over the table doing the accounts because he and Cicely had quarrelled over the incident in the boatyard. He had insisted that Cicely must have said something to upset Ratty, while she hotly denied his allegation and in turn suggested that maybe George *had* dismissed Eunice unfairly. Jack had then defended George and forbidden Cicely to ask him outright what exactly had happened. When she had threatened to ask Eunice, Jack had forbidden her to do so and Cicely had then refused to go near the yard or touch the accounts ever again. Ratty, of course, had been sacked on the spot. Cicely, however, was not mollified by this and now sat in an easy chair, knitting herself a bed-jacket, her eyes gleaming with unexpressed triumph.

Jack licked the pencil and wrote carefully, 'Brett . . . £62-5s-2d.'

'Brett's bill,' he said. 'It's been owing two months.'

'I'm fully aware of that, Jack.' She came to the end of a row, changed the needles round and tugged another length of pale green wool from the linen wool-bag at her feet.

'Shouldn't he have a reminder, then?'

'He's had two already. The copies are there.'

'I can't see them.'

'That doesn't alter the fact that they are *there*,' said Cicely smugly.

Jack searched among the mass of papers and finally found them with a pile of other reminders, neatly clipped together.

'We'd best send him another, then?' he suggested.

'Is that a statement or a question?'

'It's a bloody question, of course,' he snapped. 'Shall we or shan't we?'

'Don't ask *me*, Jack,' said Cicely sweetly. 'I'm just "a bloody interfering old bag". Remember?'

Defeated, Jack put the offending invoice to one side. Since he hated putting pen to paper he would have to send Ned round to Brett's in the morning and remind him verbally. He sighed deeply, wondering how it was that, throughout his entire married life, Cicely always managed to defeat him.

'Knit two together, wool over the needle . . .' murmured Cicely. 'This is making up into a very pretty pattern. Even better than the picture.'

He ignored her and wrote down two more figures, then totalled them. The answer looked unlikely, so he tried again and got a different answer. Neither looked right, but he could not be bothered to make a third attempt. Turning his attention to the rest of the invoices, he sorted them carefully and matched them with the stubs in the firm's cheque book. It all seemed to add up to a very healthy financial situation – in fact, the best for at least four years. The business did seem to be flourishing, he concluded cautiously, almost afraid to admit the fact in case an unkind fate should overhear and punish him for their success. He wanted to share his findings with Cicely, but obviously she was in no mood to enthuse.

Turning his attention to the ledger, he scrutinised the list of work in hand – they were recaulking the deck of the *Integrity* and replacing her wheelhouse; the *Bonny Blue* was in for new port-side shrouds and forestay; George's *Silver Lady* had a torn mainsail and Bob Harris's boat was coming in for an engine overhaul. There was also a half-finished dinghy on the stocks for rich Mr Plater's son, but the lad's sixteenth birthday had been and gone and Lord knows when they'd have time to finish it. Still, he had warned them the working boats must come first – a boat that supported a family would always take preference over a birthday present, at Coulsdens at any rate.

He closed the ledger with a snap and a feeling of well-being lightened his mood. Impulsively, he swung round in his chair.

'Well, love,' he said cheerfully, 'things are really looking up at last. It all appears very promising. Very good indeed.'

Cicely's eyes did not leave her knitting. 'Slip one, purl one, knit two together,' she murmured. 'What's that you say, Jack?'

'I said it's all looking very good. Very promising.'

'I should hope it is, Jack.'

'Well, it is.'

'Good.'

He persevered in the face of her pretended lack of interest, wanting to share the moment. Times had not always been good for Coulsdens' yard, with the old man gone and Ben and Leo too young to share the load. If George had come in with him it might have been easier, but Jack had inherited the yard and Cicely had insisted they keep it to themselves – 'for the boys', as she had put it. Probably the right decision, anyway, Jack reflected, because he and his brother could never see eye to eye for long and George was better off with *Silver Lady*. For Jack, though, it had been a long hard haul as all the skilled work fell to him; although Ratty and Tommy were useful men in their way, he would be glad when he could take his sons into the business.

Remembering that now he had Ned Price instead of Ratty, he sighed. A lot of fuss over nothing, in his opinion, but after the way Ratty had behaved there was no way Cicely would have been satisfied by anything less than dismissal. 'Ratty, you're a fool,' he told him silently, but then returned to the more pressing problem of Cicely.

'Suppose we celebrate,' he suggested hopefully. 'Suppose we go out to The Flushing and I treat you to a slap-up meal, eh? How would you like that?' He waited, but she was apparently concentrating on the intricacies of her knitting once more. Inspiration came to him. 'What about that new hat you took a shine to, in the shop up the hill? You pointed it out about a week ago when we were coming back from church – with the white flowers?'

Slowly Cicely raised her head, tempted beyond measure. 'But that was so expensive, Jack!' she said. 'Could we *possibly* afford it?'

Hope surged through Jack's heart. 'Why not?' he said recklessly. 'If it'll cheer you up, Cis, then you shall have it.' Impulsively he left the table and crouched beside her. 'We're doing well, love, after all these years, and it's about time we spoiled ourselves. You shall have the hat and we'll go out for a meal and you can wear it.'

Cicely's knitting lay in her lap, forgotten. 'Oh, but Jack, I've no gloves to wear with it—'

'Gloves as well!' he cried.

'Oh, Jack!'

'And we're friends again, aren't we?'

'Of course we are, Jack—'

The telephone rang just then and Jack reached out to answer it. Cicely's joy turned to apprehension as she saw his expression change.

'What's that? I can't hear you properly. Yes, of course I'm Jack Coulsden – it's what? On fire? Did you say *on fire*? Christ Almighty! I'm on my – what's that? – oh God! I'm on my way!'

Slamming down the instrument he stared at Cicely, wide-eyed and fearful. 'It's the yard – there's a fire! That was the police. Oh God Almighty!'

And he ran out of the room leaving Cicely stunned with shock. 'A fire?' she whispered. 'Oh God, they must save it!'

She jumped up from the chair, spilling the knitting on to the carpet. 'I'm coming with you, Jack!' she shouted, but by the time she reached the front door his motor was out of sight.

*

A crowd had already gathered on the path behind the yard as Jack leaped from the car. There was no sign of the fire-engine.

'Let me through, for Christ's sake!' he shouted, elbowing a way through the gaping onlookers. 'Get out of the bloody way!'

The sight that met his eyes made his stomach churn with a terrible fear. The boat-shed was ablaze, the inside lit with a bright orange glow; already part of the wooden roof had fallen in and flames leaped towards the sky, competing in colour with the crimson sunset. A solitary policeman, who was urging the fascinated crowd to keep back, recognised Jack as he rushed forward but held out his arms to bar the way.

'I'm sorry, sir,' he said. 'You can't go in there. There's nothing we can do. We're expecting the fire-engine at any moment.'

'Nothing we can *do*?' shouted Jack wildly. 'There must be! There's a river full of water. We could make a chain. There's a bucket – we've got buckets.' He stared around him. 'Oh Christ, most of them are inside. I can't believe this is happening!'

A few of the crowd pressed forward and as the policeman shouted another warning the windows of the shed exploded outwards and broken glass rained down. The crowd panicked and someone fell to the ground screaming with pain.

'She's hurt!'

'Her face is cut!'

The policeman left Jack and hurried to attend the injured woman. Jack stood appalled, watching speechlessly, his mind unable to function.

'The machines!' he muttered helplessly. 'I must save the machines.'

But now flames were licking from the windows. With a strangled cry, he ran round to the far end of the shed, but there was no hope of an entry there. In fact the flames were worse, if anything, for a light breeze was blowing in from the sea. The lurid colours of the fire were reflected in the placid water and the sound and smell of bursting timbers and the sight of the glittering sparks circling within the rolling smoke would haunt Jack until his dying day.

The interior of the boat-shed was bright as day and Jack could clearly see Mr Plater's dinghy, the once beautiful mahogany hull blackened and distorted by the flames. He watched with a feeling of such agony of spirit that his body ached with grief as the questions flooded his mind. How did it start? Had they left a machine on? Was the wiring at fault? Had someone left a cigarette smouldering?

'Christ!' he whispered, weak with panic as a new thought struck him. Had they kept up the insurance? Yes, yes. Cicely had reminded him countless times, but had he done anything about it? Had *she*? And was everything else safe? The other boats?

'Cis!' he whispered. 'Oh Cis, I'm sorry. I'm sorry!'

The policeman appeared suddenly at his side. 'You'd best come back, sir,' he suggested. 'There's really nothing you can do; it's got such a hold.' He put a hand on Jack's arm, but Jack pushed him aside and ran to inspect the other boats. A spark could start another fire. The *Integrity* was safe so far and the *Bonny Blue* was moored on the water. *Silver Lady* was still at her mooring in the Fishmarket, thank God, and Bob Harris's boat was not due in until tomorrow.

'Jack!'

He turned to see George running towards him, panting desperately and clutching his side. 'Oh Christ, Jack! I'm so sorry,' he cried and for a brief moment the brothers clung together, united by disaster. Tears rose suddenly in Jack's eyes as he felt George's arms close round him. Once, very many years before when his mouse had died, George had hugged him in the same way – a sudden demonstration of love that caught them both unawares. Jack had cried then, too.

'I came as soon as I heard,' cried George, releasing him and turning to watch the blaze. 'Did you get anything out?'

Jack shook his head. 'I've only just got here,' he said. 'I was too late; it's hopeless.' His tears, reflecting the flames, glowed like rubies on his cheeks and his eyes were wide with unspoken horrors.

'Was anyone hurt?' asked George. 'I mean, was anybody in there?'

Jack shook his head, too choked to speak. Where was the bloody fire-engine, he wondered dully.

The clanging of the bell answered him and a cheer went up from the waiting crowd but at that moment, with a terrible rending sound, the whole roof of the shed collapsed and a fresh shower of sparks and flames flew skyward.

'You're too late,' said Jack, as two firemen with a hose raced past him towards the river. 'It's all gone, lads. The lot!'

George tried to comfort him as they stood quietly together, watching as the firemen began to extinguish the blaze. They both knew what the intense heat would have done to the machinery – motors burnt out, ruined beyond all hope of repair – and the timbers stored in the roof of the shed – the paint, tools, ropes and other chandlery. No words of George's, however well-meant, could minimise the extent of the calamity for either of them. Coulsdens' yard could survive – it *must* – but both men knew that the fight back to prosperity would be long and hard.

*

The cause of the fire was never established, although suspicion inevitably fell on Ratty Hall. However, he was able to establish that he had been with Tommy Bird at the time the fire started and extensive enquiries by the police could not prove otherwise. For a few weeks the incident remained a source of speculation, but eventually interest faded. Fortunately for Jack Coulsden, his wife had paid the premiums which he had consistently forgotten – although the amount of the compensation, when finally awarded after months of argument, proved to be disappointingly low. Work was lost due to the delays and long-standing customers were forced to take their boats elsewhere.

Inevitably, some never returned.

The boat-shed was rebuilt and new machines ordered to replace those lost . . . slowly, imperceptibly, life at the boatyard returned to normal.

CHAPTER FOUR

By the time *Silver Lady* was a year old, change was in the air.
The Edwardian era was at an end and 1911 would be remembered not only for the Coronation of George V but also for the
glorious summer. Unrest continued in Ireland and there was still
the possibility of a war in Europe provoked by the activities of
Germany's Kaiser Wilhelm. The latter problem was reflected in
Rye in the construction of a Drill Hall and Armoury, which now
went ahead at a great pace to the satisfaction of all concerned.
Rye's harbour meanwhile was enjoying a period of comparative
prosperity, so far undisturbed by outside alarms. Stone from
Fairlight was being used to improve the harbour and, hopefully,
to hold back the accumulations of shingle driven relentlessly
across the harbour mouth by the currents prevailing in the bay. A
large number of boats and ships used the harbour facilities, either
at the harbour village or in Rye itself. Nearly fifty fishing vessels
plied to and fro, unloading their catch at the Fishmarket below
the cliff; the boatyards were kept busy supplying fishing boats to
Hastings, Lowestoft and other towns around the south and east
coasts. *Silver Lady* earned her keep along with the rest of the fleet
with rich hauls of fish – sprats at the beginning of the year,
mackerel and flat fish throughout the summer and herring in the
autumn. There was a friendly rivalry between George and Stan
with regard to profits and an unspoken envy of Jack who, in the
boatyard, was becoming too prosperous.

One morning, while Hettie and young Julia were at South View
visiting Sarah, George and Agnes spent an enjoyable lunchtime
in bed. When the lovemaking was concluded, Agnes dropped her
bombshell.

George stared at her, slack-jawed with shock.

'Pregnant! What d'you mean, *pregnant?*' he demanded, rolling
out of bed. 'I don't believe it! You never are.'

He stood glaring down at Agnes, who in the space of ten
seconds had suddenly become ugly in his eyes. Ugly, careless and

expendable. Since filling the vacancy left by Eunice, she had proved her worth in many ways and a happy complacency had developed between them. It was all made very easy for them by Hettie's continuing depression. The doctor did not want her to be left alone for long periods, so she made regular visits to Cicely and to Sarah, taking the baby with her. Her absences from the house made it possible for George to slip home to share an hour with Agnes in the large double bed where the gleaming brass of the bedhead frequently reflected their passion.

'Well, I am, so there!' Agnes rolled her eyes and patted her stomach. 'Little Georgie Coulsden's in there somewhere. Say hullo to your pa, Georgie.' She had had plenty of time to accustom herself to the idea, for although she had not intended the pregnancy, she now had every intention of playing her trump card.

'I thought you wanted a son, George,' she said with a look of gentle reproof. 'At least, that's what you told me. All I want is a son, you said. Well then, I'm giving you one. You might at least give me a "thank you". Homely Hettie only managed a daughter.'

Her shrewd nickname for George's wife, which he usually enjoyed, now grated on him as he stuffed his shirt back into his trousers with clumsy haste.

'You *can't* be,' he repeated, playing for time. What the hell was the silly bitch up to, frightening him like this? 'If this is one of your jokes . . .' he began.

Agnes looked hurt. '*Joke?* Joke, you call it, George Coulsden? I'm stuck with a kid and you call it a joke! Well, I'm not laughing, Georgie. It's no laughing matter. I'm telling you, gospel, cross my heart and hope to die. I'm having a baby and you're its father, like it or lump it!'

George uttered a stifled groan. Why, *why*, he thought, did he always pay so heavily for his pleasures? Other men got away with much worse. Someone up there had a grudge against him. He stared at her as she sat up in bed (on Hettie's side, that had always amused him) hugging her knees; gradually her ugliness faded and her blowsy good looks reasserted themselves. Christ, he thought, if it wasn't for his daughter and Hettie he'd *marry* the girl! A man could do a lot worse than Agnes Dengate. A lot worse. But he had got Hettie and she had given him a silver-haired daughter. Agnes pregnant – oh, the silly cow!

Agnes pursed her lips and blew him a kiss. 'A son, Georgie.

Think of that now! Wouldn't that be nice? He'd go out on the boat with you when he's older. You could show him the ropes and teach him all you know. I expect he'd take after you – a chip off the old block.'

'No!' he cried. 'For Christ's sake, are you mad? Look, get out of that bloody bed. Time's getting on and Mrs Mack will be back from shopping. Get out!'

As she made no move he leaned forward, seized her arms and pulled her towards him across the bed. She smelt tangy and warm and her eyes glinted with mischief.

'George! You don't know your own strength!' she complained when she stood naked on the floor beside him. She rubbed her wrists. 'You hurt my wrists. There's no need to be so rough. What have I done?'

'What have you done?' cried George. 'What kind of bloody silly question is that? What have you *done*? You've got yourself pregnant, that's what you've done! God Almighty!' He picked up her discarded clothes and flung them on to the bed. 'Get dressed, for Christ's sake. Pregnant! Hell and damnation, Ag, do you want to ruin me?'

Agnes wriggled into her skirt. 'It's me what's ruined, Georgie, not you. You're not going to produce a bawling infant in five months' time—'

'Five months! Jesus wept!' He strode wildly about the room.

'And don't keep glaring at *me*, Georgie. I didn't get myself pregnant. I may be smart, but I can't do miracles. *You* got me pregnant and you know it – so don't have any rash ideas about pretending it was someone else.'

He turned away so that she would not see the tell-tale look in his eyes, for the idea had just crossed his mind. Hastily he abandoned it.

'Five months!' he said helplessly. 'Oh my God!'

He watched her buttoning her blouse. Usually he liked to delay her, standing behind her with his hands cupping her full breasts. Today he thought her fingers would never be finished.

For a while neither of them spoke. George was silent while his thoughts tumbled darkly; Agnes was instinctively allowing him time to think. When at last she was fully dressed she began to remake the bed, while George regarded her resentfully.

'What are we supposed to do now, then?' he asked. 'If I give you some money, will you get rid of it? Is it money you're after?'

She shook her head, carefully plumping the pillows back into shape, drawing up the sheet and folding and smoothing the top edge. She picked Hettie's nightgown from the floor, folded it and replaced it under the pillow.

'What, then?'

He looked, she thought with a quick glance at his face, like a sulky schoolboy.

'It's far too late for that,' she said firmly. 'Much too late.' She pulled up the blanket and moved round to arrange the other side of the bed.

'I want a home, George, for me and the boy. Nothing grand. Just a—'

'A home!' he spluttered, while all the colour in his face drained away. 'Nothing grand? Christ Almighty! What do you take me for? A bloody millionaire? It's all I can do to keep *this* home going. You need your brains tested, that's what you need. A home? You'll be lucky. You can put that idea right out of your head. Get that straight right now.' He mimicked her voice. ' "A home for me and the boy" – you must think I'm made of money!'

She gave him a brief smile, the smile a nurse gives to a fractious patient.

'You're doing all right, George. You can afford it. Don't let that side of it worry you.' He gaped soundlessly. 'I've found a little place, just a shack, down at Winchelsea Beach; Marsh Cottage, it's called, and it will do us fine. Three shillings a week, that's all. Only needs a few repairs and a lick of paint inside and we'll have to have a few sticks of furniture.' She kept her eyes averted as she rattled on, knowing she had to take him by surprise; it was the only way. She knew George Coulsden better than he knew himself. 'At the end of Sea Road it is, along towards Pett. Nice and private, see. You'll be able to come and visit without no one knowing. It'll be a hideaway for you and me and the boy will always be waiting for you. Poor Hettie'll never know a thing about it. We'll have some fun, George. You really do deserve some fun, d'you know that? You do, honestly. What sort of life is it, with a miserable wife like you've got?'

'Hettie can't help it,' said George. 'She's ill. Leave her out of it.'

'Leave her out of it? But how can I?' Agnes protested. 'She's part of the problem, isn't she? It seems to me she's getting worse, not better. Be honest now, George. Granted she can't help it, but she's not much of a wife to you, is she, the way she is? Funny in the head and—'

'She's not funny in the head.'

'George, my love, she *is*,' said Agnes, her tone gentle. 'That home did her no good at all and you know it.'

George sat down on the edge of the bed and shook his head. 'I've told you before – it wasn't a home, it was a holiday. She went to Bognor for two weeks' holiday. A rest, if you like.'

'She went to a *nursing* home for two weeks, George. You know it. I know it. Why keep pretending? She can't snap out of this depression because her mind's gone funny and you are having a pretty rotten time of it, one way and another. With me in a home of my own, we could put all that right. It would be something for you to look forward to – a bit of fun to brighten things up. Every man deserves that much and she'd never find out, George. Honest she wouldn't. How could she? She never goes to Winchelsea Beach. Look, three shillings for the rent and something for our food. I'll bring in a bit of extra cash somehow—'

'Hang on,' said George. 'Of course she'll know. She'll have to know why you're leaving, won't she?'

Again the nurse's smile. 'She won't know it's yours though, will she, George? It won't be born with a label round its neck saying "George Coulsden".'

She noted with satisfaction that he had not actually rejected the idea of providing her with a home of her own, but was merely reassuring himself that his own role in the affair would not come to light. George Coulsden, she thought gleefully, you're already hooked! Men were such fools. With a final pat for the ordered bed, she went over to him and slid her arms round his neck.

'Tell me you're not cross, George,' she wheedled. 'Tell me you love me. I didn't mean it, but you do want a son. It will be fun, George, even more fun than me being here. And you'll be one up on Jack and Stan. Two homes! Just think of it, Georgie. Hettie here and me there. Talk about lucky! And me not making a bit of fuss or demanding money or threatening to tell anyone. I could make trouble for you, George. Lots of women would, but I'm not lots of women. I'm me. *And* I love you, George.'

He returned her kisses absent-mindedly, trying to imagine life without her. Hettie's mental state still gave cause for anxiety, although Dr Jamieson assured him that depression often followed the birth of a child. The two weeks in the nursing home had done her no good, but the doctor still insisted that it was merely a matter of time before she would be well again and that patience and understanding were the order of the day. But now it was August and as time passed George saw no improvement in Hettie's condition and turned more frequently towards Agnes.

'Three shillings . . .' he began.

Agnes drew back. 'Look at it like the club man,' she told him. 'So much a week, see? A bit on the side for so much a week! I mean, if I was to just go off and have the baby and not see you again it'd be hundreds of pounds you'd have to give me, to see me through. This way it's only a few bob a week and you've still got me *and* all your fun like before *and* a son at long last. It's only a poor little shack, George, but we could do it up a bit. Maybe later on you could buy it. Fancy owning a bit of property, do you? Proper tycoon, you could be, in time. I'd love to see old Jacko and Stan when you're a blinking tycoon and they're nothing. A man's got to start somewhere, after all!'

Before Hettie returned from South View, George had recovered from the shock of impending paternity and agreed to install Agnes in the home she had found. They had also planned how they would break the news about Agnes's departure to Hettie. She might be sympathetic to Agnes's plight, but in that case George would have to insist that Agnes be sent packing.

'Two dailies in two years!' Agnes giggled. 'They'll be saying the Coulsdens can't keep their staff. Oh Georgie, you are a wicked man but I really do love you!'

*

It was the middle of June 1912 and George Coulsden – having a quiet pipe on *Silver Lady* – was looking back over the events of the last six months or so.

The boats in the bay had been drifting for three weeks, searching for the shoals of summer mackerel now moving eastward along the coast. Later the shoals would return westward and after that the trawling would begin. Today eleven boats had put out from Rye, eight smacks and three luggers. These had been joined by a dozen or more fishing punts from Hastings and beyond them, close in against Dengemarsh, the Dungeness boats were in position and waiting for dark. These last were small craft, few longer than 18 feet and mostly built in the Rye yards. The relationship between the men from the various areas was uneasy at best and sometimes arguments broke out. Ribald comments carried across the water as one by one the boats took up their sea berths and waited for sunset. The fishermen waited for dusk because if the nets were lowered too early into the clear water the mackerel would see them and take fright. No greetings, however – ribald or otherwise – were extended to the eight French boats a mile or so further out, for these were a long-standing source of ill-feeling among the English fishermen.

The boats would drift all night with the tide and in the morning would haul their nets aboard before setting sail for their respective harbours. The Dungeness boats would run up on their own beach. The Rye skippers had a choice between Rye or Hastings. The Hastings men would land their catches at Hastings itself, where a daily auction was held. It was during one of these auctions that George had first met Agnes Dengate, who had been there with her father Alec, a man George despised. To annoy Alec, George had flirted with his teenage daughter and the friendship had developed from there. Now, sprawled on a pile of ropes at the stern of *Silver Lady*, he reflected on his folly as he sucked at a pipe which would not stay alight and gazed up into the clear sky. Agnes, cosily installed in her own home at his expense, had given birth to a girl on the first of December. He could and did blame her for this aberration but the child, Emily by name, was healthy enough and Agnes had promised him a son 'next time round', whatever that might mean. He could not deny that she was a good mother and a hard worker, earning a shilling wherever she could. She collected blue boulders and she made rabbit nets for the local poachers. She kept a goat for its milk and a few chickens which scratched amongst the shingly soil. She had even coaxed some ragged vegetables from the unresponsive ground which a few centuries ago had still been part of the sea-bed. In all weathers she searched the beach for driftwood, coconut shells and anything else that would serve as fuel for the fire. Occasionally she met but did not recognise Eunice, who was now Mrs Tommy Bird – much to everyone's surprise – and a relatively near neighbour.

Eunice recognised *her*, however, for she had made it her business to see the woman who had supplanted her at the Coulsden house and it was not long before she discovered that George was a regular visitor to Marsh Cottage.

When the child was born Eunice felt intuitively that the relationship between Agnes and George had been connected with

her own dismissal from the Coulsden household. There was no
way now that she could get her old job back – indeed she did not
want it, for Tommy was a fair enough husband and would be a
good father to their own child which she expected in August – but
somehow she knew that between them George and Agnes had
stolen her job and her good name. *They* were the thieves, not her.
Ideas of revenge began to fill her waking hours and at last, on the
same afternoon when George lay back awaiting dusk and con-
templating the ironies of fate, Eunice Bird took matters into her
own hands.

*

That evening Mrs Mack picked up a letter from the mat long after
the postman had made his last delivery. She turned over the
rather scruffy envelope and saw 'Mrs Coulsden' pencilled in
uneven letters and underlined heavily.

'Now what on earth . . .?' she wondered aloud as she carried
the letter into the garden where Hettie was relaxing in a blue-
and-white striped deck-chair. Young Julia, her head encased in
an elaborately frilled bonnet, sat in the wicker pram which Hettie's parents had bought for them. Dr Jamieson had ordered rest,
fresh air and sunshine for Hettie – and insisted that she was not to
be worried unnecessarily. She was very thin in spite of the nourishing additions to her normal diet which he had prescribed –
beef tea three times a day and calves' foot jelly last thing at night.

'This letter's come, by hand seemingly,' Mrs Mack told her.
She gave it a disapproving glance as she handed it over and then
delayed her return to the house by shaking Julia's rattle for her
while she waited for her mistress to open and read the letter.

She turned as she heard Hettie gasp and saw her staring at the
letter, ashen-faced, while she held the paper at arm's length as
though afraid of contamination.

'Ma'am? Mrs Coulsden? What is it? Are you all right?'

Hettie managed a nod. 'Yes, I'm fine. It's nothing.'

Reluctantly, the housekeeper left her and Hettie read and
re-read the scrawled message:

Dear Mrs Coulsden,
    Go to Marsh Cottage at Winchelsea Beach.
    Do not tell your husband.
                                        Well-wisher.

At first she told herself it was a mistake, that the letter must be intended for someone else, but at last she was forced to admit that she *was* Mrs Coulsden and a mistake was most unlikely. George was somehow involved; she felt a wave of panic rising within her. What had George to do with Marsh Cottage? She looked at Julia.

'What has he done?' she whispered. 'Your Papa – what on earth has he done?'

And where exactly would she find Marsh Cottage if she decided to follow the urgings of the writer of this scribbled note? No, she thought, she would show it to George and he would laugh in his boisterous way and dispel her fears. It was a poison pen letter – malicious, nothing more. She would throw it away. George was her husband and she loved and trusted him. This scrap of paper could not alter that. Nothing could. Yet she knew all the time that she would *not* show him the note and she *would* go to Marsh Cottage.

Abruptly she stood up. 'I'll go now,' she told the child. 'I'm going to Marsh Cottage, but I won't be long. I'll tell Mrs Mack to keep an eye on you.' She leaned down and kissed the child. 'Julia,' she whispered with tears blurring her eyes. 'Oh Julia, I'm so frightened!'

*

Hettie felt unclean as she made her way along the track which ran behind the wooden sea wall from Winchelsea Beach to Pett Level. She had given her maiden name to the carrier who had brought her as far as Dog's Hill, although deceit did not come naturally to her. She had lied to Mrs Mack too, explaining that 'a friend needs me urgently' and promising to be back within an hour or so.

It had taken several local enquiries to elicit the whereabouts of Marsh Cottage, but now that she saw it Hettie approached warily, like a dog sensing danger. It was very small, ugly and squat – dirty white pebble-dash walls under a tiled roof orange with lichen. It had been crudely extended on one side by means of half an upturned boat supported by planks of driftwood, and this was also painted white to match the rest of the building. There seemed to be no real boundary to the property but a nanny-goat, tethered to a post, tugged on a chain in an effort to reach a nearby plant. There were a few chickens around and a very young child cried lustily from somewhere inside. For a moment Hettie's courage deserted her and she struggled to overcome an urge to turn and run from whatever awaited her. Tearing her eyes from the little shack, she took in the broad expanse of marsh which surrounded it, reaching to Winchelsea on the hill and westward to the rising ground of Fairlight. The cliffs themselves were hidden from her view by the sea wall on her left.

Suddenly she remembered that she had paid the carrier for the return journey and that he now waited further back along the beach, no doubt slumped in his seat and dozing in the June sunshine. She envied him. Looking once more towards Marsh Cottage, Hettie saw that the front door was now open and that a woman had come out and was pegging clothes on to the line. Unnoticed, Hettie watched as each garment was shaken into shape and fastened with pegs. There were no men's garments amongst them, not even a pair of socks. Hettie swallowed and breathed deeply. She felt very strange, almost light-headed, as though the bizarre adventure was happening to someone else. There was something very familiar about the woman's back. The child was still crying as Hettie moved forward, and when her feet crunched on the shingle, the woman turned sharply in her direction.

'Agnes Dengate!'

Hettie thought it must be someone else who spoke, but the unfamiliar voice was her own.

Agnes recovered from the shock first and after a moment's hesitation, said brightly, 'Mrs Coulsden – well, what a nice surprise!'

'Is it?' Hettie asked.

Agnes picked up the laundry basket and wedged it against her hip. 'Yes – I mean, shouldn't it be?'

'I had a letter,' said Hettie. 'Someone sent me a letter. A well-wisher.'

'Oh?' Agnes did not immediately grasp the significance of what Hettie was telling her.

'Your baby?' Hettie indicated the sound with a small movement of her head.

'Yes, that's my Emily,' said Agnes, deciding to brazen it out. 'Six months old and always hungry, bless her!'

They eyed each other: Hettie stupefied, her wits slow and erratic, Agnes successfully hiding her surprise. At last, to break the silence Agnes asked, 'How's Julia Lady Coulsden?' The

mockery in her tone was barely perceptible, but Hettie recognised
it at once and frowned as her daughter's name registered in her
mind. That ridiculous name for which George was entirely to
blame! Hettie felt that her lungs were failing her and took a great
gulp of air. Surely her lungs could function without her attention,
she thought irritably.

'Well,' said Agnes as Hettie made no sign of having heard the
previous question, 'perhaps you'd like a cup of tea?'

It occurred to her that Hettie's presence on her doorstep might
not be as disastrous as she at first suspected. Had George sent
her, in some mad moment? Was it his idea of a joke? After all,
Hettie did not know the name of the baby's father. Agnes hesitated, some of her boldness deserting her in the face of Hettie's
strange manner.

'No, thank you,' said Hettie slowly. 'I won't have any tea.'

'Please yourself!' said Agnes with a shrug of her shoulders.

'That baby,' said Hettie.

'What of it?' She was immediately on the defensive. 'What
d'you mean – that baby? What sort of remark is that?'

'The baby's father. Who is the baby's father?'

Agnes tightened her lips. 'That's my business. You've no right
to ask me such a thing.'

'The baby's father,' Hettie repeated dully, her eyes on the
ground that separated them. She glanced up. 'If you lie to me,'
she said calmly, 'and I find out, I'll kill you.'

Agnes's blue eyes widened fearfully and she took a step backwards. 'Kill me? You wouldn't dare! You're mad!' she whispered.
'You're off your head. Kill me? You're crazy!'

'It's George, isn't it?'

Agnes was backing slowly towards the comparative safety of the
front door, considering how best to protect herself and her child.
She would slam the front door and lock it and then run through to
bar the back door.

'The baby's father – it's George, isn't it?' Hettie continued to
stare at the ground in front of her. 'I shall not leave here until you
tell me the truth.'

Agnes opened her mouth to shout, 'No, it's not!' but shouted,
'Yes, it is!' instead. Let her know then, she thought, since she's so
determined. If she knows the truth she might go away. Nevertheless she didn't like the tone of Hettie's voice or the strange look in
her eyes. Maybe she *was* funny in the head . . . or even mad.

Agnes darted inside and slammed the door and Hettie heard the bolt being rammed home. After a while she turned and walked wearily away without a backward glance. By the time Agnes had secured all the doors and windows Hettie was on her way home.

*

George did not return home next day. The mackerel catch was a good one and most of the fishermen decided to stay out for another night. The Dungeness boats landed their first catch in the west bay, whence it would go by cart to Lydd and from there by rail to London. George, Stan and the rest of the Rye and Hastings fleet landed theirs at Hastings. Stan's lugger nosed in on to the beach and the net was stretched out along the shingle and picked clean of fish. Then it was washed in the sea, dried and stowed on board again for the turn-around trip. George's boat had remained off-shore. The nets were picked clean on deck and then the catch was ferried to the shore in the small ship's boat. By early afternoon, they were all sailing back to take up their positions once more. It would be time to rest when the fish failed to appear.

Hettie waited until four o'clock and then asked Mrs Mack to take round a letter to Cicely.

'Perhaps you would take Julia with you?' she suggested. 'I don't feel up to pushing the pram today, but she does so enjoy a trip through the town.'

Mrs Mack agreed at once. The prospect of a walk through Rye with the baby delighted her, for she knew she would be stopped many times so that George Coulsden's beautiful daughter could be duly admired and fussed over. Hettie had returned from the previous day's outing in a quiet mood, but seemed otherwise undisturbed by whatever was in the letter and the housekeeper reminded herself that it was not up to her to interfere or poke her nose in where it was not wanted. If Mrs Coulsden did not choose to confide in her about the contents of the letter, then so be it, but she did wish Mr Coulsden was at home more with the poor mistress the way she was. Mrs Mack and Julia having left the house, Hettie sat down to write another letter. When it was done, she put it into the envelope, added a stamp and walked along to the post-box in the High Street. Next, she visited the family solicitor and then called in at Ashbee's for a pound of best braising steak.

She made the casserole with her usual care, perhaps a little more, adding a finely chopped onion, thinly sliced carrots and a few fresh herbs from the garden. As she put it into the oven her hands trembled slightly.

'You're not to worry,' she told herself gently. 'Please don't worry.'

When she had taken off her apron, she went upstairs to the bathroom to find the laudanum bottle. There was not as much in it as she had hoped, but after a search she found a small amount in another bottle which she added to the first. On further reflection, she decided that she would follow it with some brandy, which would surely help the poison to act and might even speed up its action. She congratulated herself wordlessly on solving the problem with so little bother.

After washing her hands and face, she took off her shoes and lay down on the bed. Beside her on the table were a bottle of brandy, a medicine bottle three-quarters full of laudanum and a large glass. She poured and drank a glass of brandy, then drank all the laudanum straight from the bottle and washed it down with another glass of brandy to take away the taste. Almost immediately there was a great warmth in her stomach which engendered a very positive feeling of well-being. She drank a third brandy, then leaned over and hid the bottle under the bed. The laudanum bottle and the tumbler followed it. 'Out of sight, out of mind,' she whispered and then repeated the phrase, finding the repetition soothing.

'Out of sight, out of mind . . .'

She lay back and closed her eyes. Now if Mrs Mack glanced in she would think she was sleeping. Hettie did not want to be found before she was dead. Sighing deeply and smiling contentedly, she arranged her body and limbs more comfortably on the bed. The late afternoon sun, shining through the heavy net curtains, speckled the ceiling with spots of bright light which soon began to blur together.

'Julia Lady Coulsden,' she muttered and suddenly the name did not seem so very dreadful, rather humorous really. Her smile broadened as the warm feeling inside her spread over her entire body. She thought she was laughing, but did not hear anything. The spots on the ceiling blurred again and then began to slide across the ceiling. Very pretty! She turned her head slightly towards the window and saw that it too had blurred. Two or three bright rectangles now danced together on the wall.

'Very, *very* pretty!' she said.

A clock chimed the quarter-hour somewhere in the distance. 'Quarter boys,' said Hettie, seeing in her mind's eye the tiny figures on the church clock, their arms upraised in readiness to announce to a wondering world that a quarter of an hour had passed. Old Harold Coulsden had told her once that there was a similar striking clock on the church in Calais – two little figures on horseback charging towards each other, the clash of their lances being the clock's chime. This suddenly seemed a very important item of knowledge and Hettie felt inordinately grateful to George's father for passing it on to her and wished she had seen the clock for herself. Still, it was too late now to look at clocks.

'The quarter boys,' she repeated and the words had a wonderful clarity that she had never heard in her voice before. When she said, 'Very, very pretty,' that also sounded marvellously clear. Sleepily she closed her eyes and let the image of the quarter boys slip away. She wanted to repeat Julia's name but that, too, seemed suddenly unimportant. She did not think about George or Agnes or Emily once. Not once. Gradually her thoughts faded into a gentle confusion of sensations – and dimly heard sounds. It really was, she thought, quite a pleasant way to die.

*

After the funeral the chastened family gathered at South View, where Hettie's body had lain in its coffin prior to the burial. It was all in accordance with her last wishes, expressed in the letter to her mother-in-law.

Later there would be salad and cold meats and fruits in season, but first there was the will to read. The family sat round the large oval table, saying little, as Mr Dawson opened his case and began to rustle papers. Sarah Coulsden sat bolt upright in her black suit and veiled hat at the head of the table. Her expression was grim as she fixed each member of the family with a steely eye. In her last letter, Hettie had explained quite simply why she was going to kill herself. Sarah let it be known that although George was obviously the chief culprit, in her opinion the rest of them were also at fault for not being aware of what was happening. Someone, she insisted, must have suspected something and she swept aside their fervent denials as of no consequence.

George, utterly demoralised and guilt-ridden, sat half-way

down the table with his jaw set, his right elbow on the table, his broad calloused hands masking his eyes. Next to him on his right was Stanley, who fiddled with a new fountain pen. On his left sat Stanley's wife Jane, staring fixedly at her hands which were clasped on the table in front of her. Jack Coulsden faced George across the table, his rugged face creased into a scowl; he felt hot and uncomfortable in the new dark suit Cicely had insisted he buy for the occasion. Cicely, between Jack and Sarah, was happily aware that her pale and delicate colouring was shown to great effect by the new black silk coat and the broad hat decorated with tiny black feathers. Ernest Brett, Jane's son, sat on Mr Dawson's right hand while Winifred, Jack's daughter, was on the solicitor's left. Aged seventeen and sixteen respectively, they had been included at Sarah's request – for the specific purpose, she had told George pointedly, of 'learning from the mistakes of those who should know better'.

Once or twice Winifred and Ernest exchanged conspiratorial looks across the table, which went largely unnoticed by their elders who were engrossed with their own problems.

Ben, Leo and Julia were in the garden, jointly supervised by Mrs Mack and Miss Mills who, to judge by the subdued mutter of voices from the lawn below the study window, were ruling their little flock with the proverbial iron rods.

Mr Dawson picked up the will, cleared his throat and stood, all faces turning obediently towards him. Only Sarah was not surprised by its contents, which the solicitor read in the lugubrious tone which he reserved for such occasions. Briefly, Hettie referred to George's infidelity with Agnes and the existence of a child. All her money and the few stocks and shares she owned were left to her daughter. George owned the *Silver Lady*, but apart from his boat he had nothing in the world; the house was rented. Sarah watched with grim satisfaction as reality dawned in the eyes of her youngest son. Serve him right, she thought vindictively, for bringing such a scandal on the family name. She was very disappointed in him. Wilful and headstrong he had always been, rebellious even and he had played truant from school more than once; his reports from that establishment were notoriously bad, but she had never considered him stupid. Her eyes glittered with spite as she watched him.

'I'll be buggered!' said Stan.

He caught his mother's baleful eye, but continued to shake his

head in disbelief. So Hettie had done George in the eye, after all.
God! Poor old George! But he had only himself to blame. And
that sly little Aggie with her flouncing ways! No wonder she was
always hanging round the net shops when George came over to
Hastings. Not that he hadn't wondered once or twice about that,
but he never really thought there could be anything in it. Not
young George! He didn't think his brother had it in him to be so
cunning. Years it had been going on, it seemed. Not months, but
years! The young fool! George would always be 'young' to Stanley, for he had been fourteen when his youngest brother was born,
red and screaming, in the small back room in the shabby house in
Claremont Passage. That was before the old boy died and they all
moved back to Appledore to the house in which they now sat,
silent and ashamed. They were drawn together in a shared guilt
for somewhere, as Sarah said, somehow, someone should have
saved Hettie. But who would have thought that young George
would go and find himself a mistress? Naughty George. Lucky
sod! And who would have thought Hettie would kill herself!

'If there are any questions . . .' said Mr Dawson when he had
finished.

'Is that will legal?' demanded Jack. 'Surely she wasn't in her
right mind when she made it?'

'Of course it's legal,' snapped Sarah. 'Mr Dawson knows what
he's doing.'

'Well, I hope he does,' said Jack, 'because that will, if it's legal,
is enough to ruin the man.'

Sarah glared at him. 'George has ruined himself by his behaviour. You will understand it better when you have heard poor
Hettie's letter. She was only safeguarding the future of her
daughter.'

'But George is Julia's father. He can safeguard the girl's future,
can't he?'

Jack was not at all sure of his ground, but he felt that as a
brother he should at least be seen to be on George's side. Poor old
George looked as sick as a dog – and who wouldn't, with a dead
wife and everyone blaming him for what happened.

'Hettie obviously did *not* think him a suitable person,' snapped
Sarah. 'She wanted to make sure that George did not take
advantage of her death to marry Agnes Dengate.'

Jack, ignoring a warning look from Cicely, said, 'Well, someone's got to look after Julia.'

He knew immediately that he had gone too far, as there were shocked gasps from Cicely and Jane, and Sarah rose to her feet.

'If you mean what I think you mean, Jack, you will leave this room at once,' she hissed. 'If you think for one moment that it's appropriate for a nasty little slut like Agnes Dengate to take Hettie's place, then I advise you to think again! While I live, that woman will never set foot in Hettie's house, or—'

'Or mine!' cried Cicely.

'Or mine!' echoed Jane, giving Stan a warning look in case he should try to argue with her.

'I didn't mean . . .' Jack began helplessly, but George came wearily to his rescue.

'I have never ever *thought* of such a thing,' he said, 'so you can all stop carping about it.'

'*Carping*, George?' cried Sarah. 'I hope you are not suggesting that I am *carping*? I am trying to salvage some shred of decency from this sordid business, so that at least we can hold up our heads when we walk down the streets. There must be no squabbling among the family; we must stand together on this.' There were nods of agreement and George groaned.

'What am I supposed to do about Agnes and the kid, then?' George demanded. 'Let them starve?'

'What a good idea!' said Cicely sweetly. 'Yes, I second that. Let the bitch starve. Her bastard, too!'

'Cicely Coulsden!' screamed Sarah. 'I will not have that sort of language in my house, and at a time like this.'

Mr Dawson rustled his papers frantically and closed and opened the lid of his briefcase. 'Please, ladies and gentlemen, *please*!' he begged. 'Let us keep our tempers. Let us remember, as Mrs Coulsden reminds us, that this is a sad and solemn day.'

As Sarah subsided, Mr Dawson took advantage of the lull to answer Jack's original query.

'It most certainly is a lawful document,' he explained. 'When poor Mrs Coulsden visited our offices on the day before her demise, we judged her to be perfectly sane and to be behaving quite rationally. There is no doubt in my mind and there are two witnesses, myself and Mr Winter, to testify to her sanity.'

During the ensuing silence Ernest stretched out his leg under cover of the table and touched Winifred's knee. At the same time he slowly closed his left eye in a wink, watching in delight as a pink flush of excitement darkened her cheeks. If only Mr Dawson knew what was going on right under his nose, she thought! She lowered her eyes and waited until Ernest had withdrawn his shoe and then tried to reach *his* knee with her own foot. Not being so long in the leg as Ernest, she found this impossible until she allowed herself to slide down in the chair a little. She watched as his expression changed and then she saw the corners of his mouth twitch suddenly. As she straightened up, she turned her head towards Mr Dawson who was explaining another point of law in answer to a question from Stanley. From the corner of her eye, Winifred saw Ernest take up a pencil and fiddle with it absent-mindedly. Then she heard it clatter to the floor and her heart began to thump wildly as she guessed what would happen next. With a muttered apology for his carelessness, Ernest bent to retrieve it, ducking below the table top. Seconds later she felt his hand on her ankle – firm and warm, fleeting as a kiss – and clapped a hand to her mouth to hide her confusion. Mr Dawson gave her a brief glance to reassure himself that the family conflicts were not proving too much for a girl of such tender years, then continued. When at last Winifred stole another look at Ernest's face he was apparently attending to the solicitor's words with sober interest, but suddenly he turned to her with a look of such intensity that she felt quite weak with longing for another touch of his hand.

When Mr Dawson's business was finished, Stanley showed him out of the room and delivered him into the capable hands of Mrs Tooks, Sarah's housekeeper, who took him into the dining-room for a glass of sherry and told him to help himself to the cold collation.

Sarah rose to her feet as soon as Stanley was back in his seat, a letter in her hand.

'This,' she told them, 'is poor dear Hettie's last letter which, as most of you know, she wrote to me just before she died. I intend to read it and abide by it *to the last word*. There will be no questions. When I have read it we shall adjourn to the dining-room.' She cleared her throat and began: ' "Dear Mother-in-law, Forgive this hasty scrawl, but by the time you read it you will understand. I have discovered that George has set up home with Agnes Dengate and has had a child by her. She and Emily are living at Winchelsea Beach—'

With Mr Dawson's exit there was no longer any risk of discovery and Ernest's toe once more explored the space below the table, to discover Winifred's leg outstretched towards his own. By careful manoeuvring, he was able to push back her long skirt as far as the knee before she suddenly gasped, jumped up and ran from the room, spluttering into her hands.

'Oh, the poor child!' cried Jane, misunderstanding the emotion which had caused the outburst. 'Do go after her, Ernest, there's a dear, and see if she's all right. I did wonder if it was wise for her to listen to these sordid details. I expect it's all been rather a strain for her.'

Sarah continued to read the letter aloud as Ernest hurried out in search of Winifred, who was nowhere to be seen. She was not in the bathroom, nor was she downstairs in the dining-room where Mr Dawson sat at the table in solitary splendour with a white napkin tucked under his chin. The housekeeper had not seen her either, but after a further search he found her in the conservatory, wiping her eyes and trying to control a fit of the giggles.

'Oh, that was awful of you!' she greeted him. 'Are they very cross with me? I just had to get out. I knew I was going to laugh. I bet Mama will be simply furious and it's all because of you, Ernest Brett! You're a thoroughly hateful beast – you meant to get me into trouble.'

She was talking breathlessly, meaning very little of what she said, aware that for the first time in her life she was alone with a young man who had aroused in her the very first stirrings of desire she had ever experienced. And Ernest, of all people! Ernest, her half-cousin, whom she had known all her life. Ernest had *wanted* to flirt with her! He had chosen deliberately to provoke a response, but did he guess how successful he had been? It was rumoured that already he had known two girls in Hastings *intimately*. Winifred nearly swooned with excitement. She had heard her parents discussing him on more than one occasion and invariably Cicely had forecast 'a bad end' for him, while Jack defended him as a bit wild but insisted that he would likely grow out of it in time. Now she faced him across a tray of geranium cuttings, aware that only the wooden bench separated their two bodies.

Ernest looked at her as she faced him, her head framed by the greenery that towered behind her, her sharp features softened by the green film that covered the glass roof. So this, he thought, was his Aunt Cicely's precious daughter Winifred, who must never be called Win or Winnie. 'Skinny Winnie', he used to call her when

they were younger, and her face would go so red with rage that the
freckles were lost in the flame of her cheeks. This was Winifred
who taught Sunday School and who never used bad language or
went without stockings even in the hot weather.

'Well,' he grinned, 'if it isn't skinny Winnie!'

Laughing, she picked up a flower pot and pretended to throw
it, excitement robbing her of speech.

'Don't call me that,' she managed at last, desperately trying to
imagine what exactly might have happened between this handsome young man and the two girls. He smiled but said nothing
and self-consciously she replaced the flower pot.

'I'm coming round there,' said Ernest, 'and if you run away I
shall not run after you.'

She tried to say, 'I won't run away', but could only give a slight
shake of her head, watching the gleaming head with its smooth
dark hair as he made his way between the plants. When he
reached her they stood in a wondering silence; helpless under the
spell of his dark eyes, she allowed him to put his arms lightly
around her shoulders, then to pull her forward until she was
pressed close against him. Winifred thought she would die of
disappointment if he did not kiss her, but at last he did. She never
forgot the smell of geraniums or the feel of the sun on the back of
her neck as Ernest's mouth closed over hers for the first time.

*

The following day George went to Marsh Cottage to explain his
protracted absence. Since Hettie's death, he had been unable to
find an opportunity to visit Agnes, but he suspected rightly that
the news of the tragedy would have reached her. After the initial
greetings had been exchanged, he threw himself down into the
only easy chair and took Emily on to his lap. He cuddled her
absent-mindedly and Agnes noted how drawn he looked – like a
soft toy with all the stuffing knocked out of it, she thought.

'You look ill,' she said. 'Was it so terrible?'

He shook his head without comment.

'I heard what happened,' said Agnes, 'from the woman at the
store. I don't know what to say, George. It wasn't my fault. I didn't
ask her to come out here; someone told her.'

'*You* told her,' said George dully. 'She said in the note. She left
a note, you know.'

Agnes swallowed; she remained standing as though poised for

flight. 'I mean someone told her at the beginning. Someone sent her a letter. A well-wisher, she said. Who was it, George?'

'I don't know.'

'It's *her* fault, George – whoever sent the letter. So don't you go blaming it on to me.'

'You told her the baby was mine,' said George. 'No one knew that. Why did you have to tell her that, for God's sake?'

It was Agnes's turn to be silent. Emily, sensing her father's disinterest, began to whimper and George held her out for Agnes to take.

Agnes's mouth hardened as she took Emily from her father. 'And don't take it out on Em,' she said sharply. 'It's not the kid's fault.' She comforted her daughter. 'I only told Hettie the truth. Why shouldn't I? Why should I be ashamed of my own daughter? You *are* her father and I'm not ashamed.'

'Well, you should be.'

'Well, I'm not,' Agnes snapped. 'Are you? Are you ashamed of us? You never said you were before this happened, so how come? Just because your wife . . . did this thing . . . well, why does that make you ashamed of us, all of a sudden? We haven't changed, have we? It's bloody unfair, George, and you know it.'

George appeared not to have heard the little outburst, but stared at his boots with an expression of defeat.

'George!'

'What?'

'Well, say something, for Christ's sake!'

'There's nothing *to* say.'

Agnes bit her lip and tried to suppress the anger rising within her. She felt ill-used and wondered fleetingly why she had ever become involved with the Coulsden family. She sat down, but almost immediately stood up again.

'Look, George,' she began again, 'how can it be our fault, or your fault? Or anybody's fault except hers. It's Hettie's fault, she did it. Anyone would think *we'd* killed her. She killed herself, the way I heard it.'

'How *did* you hear it?' asked George. 'What are people saying?'

'That she killed herself with poison.'

He nodded.

'What sort of poison, George?' she asked, her curiosity getting the better of her.

'Does it matter?'

'No.'

'Well then, drop it, will you?'

Agnes regarded him helplessly. In this mood she had no idea how best to attack and felt herself hopelessly on the defensive.

'Look, George, however you may feel about things,' she said at last, 'it's happened and it's no good blaming anyone because what good will that do? Blaming someone won't bring her back. She wanted to die, George, or she wouldn't have done it. You know how depressed she was; most likely she would have done it anyway. People do when their minds go funny. She'd been in that home and they couldn't—'

'It was a holiday,' said George, 'and her mind was not funny; she was just depressed after having Julia.'

'What, *two years* after having her? Talk sense, George.'

There was a long silence. Emily smiled disarmingly at George and held out plump arms.

'She's growing so fast now,' said Agnes, as George took back the baby and kissed her. 'More than a fortnight since you've seen her – I thought you was never coming again.'

'Oh, don't talk so daft, Ag; I've had things to do. You've no idea. It's been a nightmare, a bloody nightmare. Police, newspapermen, post-mortem, inquest – the whole bloody shooting match! Nightmare's not half of it! Oh God, Ag!' His voice was choked and he blinked back tears of misery. 'How could she do this to me?' he complained. 'How *could* she? What I've gone through these past weeks is nobody's business. And my mother! Hettie left a note, naming you.'

Agnes drew in her breath sharply. 'She never!'

He nodded.

'Christ!' gasped Agnes.

'That's not all.'

'What?'

'All the money. It's all gone to Julia.'

Agnes's mouth dropped open and, without taking her eyes from George's face, she groped for the nearest chair and sat down heavily.

'But . . . I mean how . . . I mean, can she do it?'

'It was her money, from her family,' said George. 'From her grandmother. Oh yes, she can do it all right.'

'Left it all to bloody Julia? Oh, George. She certainly did hate you.'

'Us,' George corrected her, eyes narrowed. 'She said she wanted to make sure *you* didn't benefit from her death. You can't blame her, really.'

'Whose side are you on, George?'

'My own!'

'Oh, that's very nice to hear!' cried Agnes furiously. 'Pull up the ladder, George Coulsden! That's charming, that is. Well, you can just leave us out of it – me and Em. *I'm* not married to Hettie and she's not done the dirty on me. Me and Em have just lived here quietly, minding our own business. She's your wife, George, not ours; she's nothing to do with us, so don't go dragging us into it.'

George lifted his head and looked at her with something approaching loathing. 'It's all because of you,' he reminded her. 'All because you wanted to come and be our daily. You wanted to go up in the world! Remember? Or has *your* mind gone "funny" too? And who was it insisted on a place to live in?'

'Did she leave much money?' asked Agnes, ignoring his remarks.

'A fair bit.'

'Have you got to get out of that house? You could come here, George.'

'You must be mad! My mother would half kill me.'

'Your mother? Oh, for Pete's sake, George. You're not scared of an old woman!'

'And Hettie's mother. Not to mention Stan's Jane and Cicely – all carrying on as though I murdered Hettie. Forget it, Ag, because there's no way. Anyway, I don't have to get out; the house is rented. The furniture's Julia's, though, and the horse and trap and the building society money. Hettie went to the solicitor before she died and sorted it all out, tied it up good and proper. Hettie was no fool. All I own now is *Silver Lady*.'

Agnes looked a little more cheerful. 'Well, then, you've still got a roof over your head and you can earn your own living. It might be worse.'

Emily was tugging at George's collar and giggling. He looked down at her and smiled. 'Who's a clever girl, eh? You want to have a crawl, do you?'

He put her down on the floor where she promptly sat hard on her bottom, grinning widely, delighted to have George's attention.

While he played with the baby, Agnes made a pot of tea. When it was brewing she said, 'Perhaps we could move in with you . . . in time?'

George rolled his eyes despairingly. 'You really don't understand, do you?' he asked. 'You have no idea. My wife has poisoned herself because of you: it's in all the papers; my family are down on me like a ton of bricks and I can't show my bloody face in the pub without it goes deathly quiet – and you think you could move in with me! Honestly, Ag, I thought you had *some* sense!'

Emily, sitting on the floor, was alarmed by his raised voice and began to cry. George pointed a slim finger at her. 'And you can pipe down, too,' he added.

'Leave her alone,' said Agnes.

'Bloody kids! Bloody women! I'm sick of the lot of you!' George put his head in his hands and Agnes watched him dispassionately.

'So,' she said, 'who's going to look after Julia?'

'She's gone to South View, to my mother. Mother insisted.'

'Why not to Cicely or Jane?'

'They offered, but Mother wouldn't hear of it. She says she's going to make a lady out of her. A real Gooding girl.'

'So, you'll be all on your own. Who's going to look after *you*?'

'Mrs Mack will cook for me; I can just about keep her if I cut down her hours.'

'I can cook for you,' said Agnes jealously. 'You can spend a bit more time with us.'

'Oh, yes. You'd like that!'

'Of course I would. I've been bloody Cinderella too long, George Coulsden. It wears a bit thin, you know, being hidden away here like a skeleton in a cupboard.'

'Well, I shan't be spending more time with you, not just yet. I've got to let things blow over, let the dust settle. I don't want fingers pointing every time I set foot outside the door.'

'Oh, don't you, George?' she said, her voice heavy with sarcasm. 'Then how do you think I shall feel? Don't you think fingers will point at *me*? You are a selfish bastard, George. You're so busy being sorry for yourself that you don't give a damn about us.'

George gave her a spiteful look. 'Watch your tongue, Ag,' he warned. 'I've had about all I can take without you piling on the agony. I could walk out on you tomorrow and no one would lift a finger, d'you know that? They'd say it served you right, that you got what you deserved. I've got nothing to lose now, the way I see it. I could—'

'You wouldn't dare!' stammered Agnes, shocked by his abrupt attack.

'Wouldn't I? Well, go on like you are doing and you'll find out if I dare,' he told her. 'What you ought to do is play your cards right, Agnes Dengate, and mind your manners, because it's all out in the open now and you've got no hold over me. I'm a single man now and I might – I just *might* – find myself someone else!'

Agnes nearly choked with a mixture of impotent rage and fear and George watched her with malicious satisfaction as she closed her eyes to hide her chagrin.

'So,' said George grimly, 'let's have no more carping, Ag. Just pour me a cup of tea.'

CHAPTER FIVE

In 1914 Winifred and Ernest became engaged, after much heart-searching on the part of their parents who considered them too young. At just eighteen Winifred had grown taller than was considered elegant and her freckles were a source of secret dismay. Only her hair, rich auburn curls, saved her from being labelled 'plain'. She worked part-time as companion to an elderly lady, but chafed at the dullness of her existence and had already joined the local branch of the Red Cross where she spent two hours each week rolling bandages, knitting khaki socks and learning how to splint broken limbs. When she daydreamed, her fantasies revolved around her forthcoming marriage to Ernest and she was very content with her lot.

It was the August Bank Holiday weekend and Winifred had obtained permission from Sarah to take Julia to Hastings on the train, to meet Ernest and share the fun of the bustling sea-front in all its summer glory. There was plenty to see and do in 1914 for Hastings, with its broad shingle beach, was already a popular holiday resort. The town had developed during the previous century, when the coming of the railways brought wealthy visitors to the area to enjoy a holiday or recover their health.

Julia squealed with excitement each time her feet left the ground, which they did about every twenty paces. Ernest would give the warning cry of 'Up she goes!' and he and Winifred would swing her up and Hastings sea-front would suddenly whirl delightfully in front of her eyes. In 1914 four-year-old Julia was not the 'lady' of her name, and not at all how her grandmother felt a Gooding girl should be. Sarah blamed George for her granddaughter's boisterous ways, because he frequently took her down to the Fishmarket with him, to play on *Silver Lady*, and brought her home filthy and smelling of fish.

Julia was in a seventh heaven, for to her Hastings was a magical place. Sometimes her father brought her over to see Uncle Stan and Aunt Jane and then she was allowed to play among the boats drawn up on the foreshore. To them she was the solitary orphan child and the tragedy in her past imbued her with a certain glamour.

'Look, Ju, horsey!' said Winifred now, pointing.

They stopped to watch a bathing machine on its way down the beach, pulled on large iron wheels by an apparently tireless horse. Further along there were stationary huts with long mats which ran right down to the edge of the sea, to save the feet of the bathers from the worst rigours of the pebbles.

'I want a horsey,' said Julia.

'One day,' said Winifred cheerfully. This was her stock answer to Julia's frequent demands.

They jumped down on to the beach and made their way between the groups of holiday-makers to where a young sand artist was hard at work with a 'comb' on a sketch of Dover Castle. Ernest handed Julia a halfpenny to drop into his waiting cap and he gave her a hearty, 'Thank you kindly, Missy' to encourage further donations from his little circle of spectators. There was so much to see on that last bright day before war began. The *Albertine*, a large pleasure boat, was drawn up on the beach and a queue of holiday-makers waited to climb the ladder on to her deck while a performing dog entertained them. A young lady sat sketching, her paints and brushes in the care of the young man who sat beside her, admiring each stroke of the brush. An elderly lady sold cakes from a basket covered with a cloth and, to wash it down, tea was poured from a large metal urn into white china cups. The beach photographer was doing a roaring trade and later Winifred would regret the fact that they could not afford a photograph. Two young boys were playing in the shallow water with a toy yacht, but Julia suddenly spotted a line of donkeys trekking to and fro and Ernest was persuaded to expend a further coin on a ride for all three of them. When it was over, Ernest asked Julia if she had enjoyed it and the little girl nodded enthusiastically.

'You didn't!' Winifred teased her. 'How could you enjoy it? You had your eyes tight shut. I saw you. You thought you were going to fall off!'

'But I liked it,' Julia protested. 'I did. I *did*!'

To Ernest the beach was home, for he had grown up in the old town and knew the shoreline like the back of his own hand. He had swum from the beach and dived from the old harbour wall. In search of adventure, he had scrambled up the rugged cliffs which rose at the eastern end of the town behind Rock-a-Nore and had wandered over the Fire Hills, hopefully bent on any mischief that might present itself among the blazing yellow gorse that clothed the cliff-top. His own escapades had been numerous and sometimes terrible, but he had survived his moody rebellious youth to acquire a more generous view of the world around him and Winifred's mellowing influence had made itself felt over the last two years.

'Punch and *Judy*!' cried Julia, catching sight of the tall theatre, gaily striped in red and orange.

'I was afraid of that,' laughed Winifred. 'I suppose you want to watch? Come on, then. I suppose I can bear it.'

They found her a place in the front and retired to the back of the crowd where the parents clustered together, pretending to be too old to enjoy the antics of Mr Punch and the long-suffering Judy. As Winifred and Ernest stood together hand in hand, they gradually became aware of an intrusive clamour further along the sea-front. Winifred's heart sank, for she knew they would have to pass the recruitment stand on their way to the old town and it was becoming increasingly difficult to keep Ernest's thoughts on their forthcoming wedding and away from the enticing prospect of a uniform and Kitchener's Army.

The Punch and Judy show ended and inevitably they found themselves on the edge of the crowd that stood before the recruiting platform. All eyes were on the speaker, a large woman in a suit of navy blue bombasine trimmed with red and white braid; her face was shaded by a broad-brimmed straw hat also in navy blue, decorated with red and white silk roses.

'. . . your children ask it, your womenfolk ask it,' she continued in strident tones, 'and last but not least, your country asks it. We ask, gentlemen, for your loyalty, for your courage and for your devotion to duty! Today we ask for one man to enlist, or ten, or a hundred. But if war comes we shall ask for tens of hundreds—' She pointed at random, stabbing a fierce finger towards the crowd. 'We need *you* and *you* and *you*! The security of this precious island may soon depend on every man among you. It rests on the shoulders of every able-bodied man here today. We ask for your allegiance to this flag!' She swung round to the huge Union Jack which formed a back-drop to the small group on the Army transport wagon that served as a platform. 'Austria is threatening the peace of Europe, and God knows who will be next. France? Belgium? England? Only the Channel stands between us and the tramp of marching feet – the tramp of jackboots, the rumble of guns and the dreadful flutter of a foreign flag over our country. We ask for your help –' here she dropped her voice dramatically, so that the audience strained their ears to catch her words, ' – to keep our own flag flying over the land of the free! The land we call England. The land of our fathers which we are proud to call home!'

There was an enthusiastic burst of applause as the drum began to throb, ending in a crescendo of sound as the bugler raised his bugle and sounded the call to arms.

'Take the King's shilling!' cried the large woman whom Winifred was beginning to hate. 'Wear the King's Colours! Join the King's Army and take the path that leads to glory. Are we afraid to fight if we have to?'

'No!' roared the crowds, revelling in the mounting excitement.

'Are we free to follow the dictates of our hearts?'

'Yes!'

'Do we want the German hordes to crush us underfoot?'

'No!'

'Never!'

'Then who will be the first to step up here and sign on in the greatest army the world has ever known? Fight for King and country. Step up! Step up! That's the way, young man. A big hand for the brave young gentleman here – come up, young man, and let me shake you by the hand. I will be proud and grateful to do so.'

The young man in question blushed as he grinned sheepishly from beneath his large, greasy cap. As he went up the makeshift steps the recruiting officer stepped forward, resplendent in his uniform, moustache waxed to perfection, boots and belt gleaming with polish. A very young soldier knelt beside a portable gramophone which stood at one end of the wagon and seizing the handle, wound it up. Seconds later a rousing march blared tinnily through the horn-shaped speaker.

Winifred, clutching Ernest's right arm, felt the muscles tighten beneath her fingers and was seized by a sense of foreboding.

'Come on,' she urged. 'We've heard it all before.'

Julia cried, 'Lift me up, Ernest. I can't see. Lift me up!'

He swung her on to his shoulders and she perched there, her

small hands held securely in his, her large eyes wide, her soft silvery hair blown by the breeze. On the platform the young man was signing his name in a book that stood on the small table and the recruiting officer slapped him on the back. Later he would present himself for a cursory medical examination and, if he passed that, would take the oath and receive his token shilling.

'Waste of time,' muttered Winifred. 'They say it will last only a few months, when it does start. *If* it starts. It's a waste of time if you ask me.'

She kept her voice low and for Ernest's ears alone, since she knew that her view was not shared by most of the people around her. They were fired by the mood of growing patriotism which was sweeping the country as Austrian forces threatened Serbia, and Russia began to mobilise along her own borders. The British Home Fleet had been ordered to sea and was on its way to Scapa Flow to show itself in force, while last-minute efforts were being made to set up a meeting, in a desperate attempt to save a rapidly worsening situation.

Three more men mounted the steps. 'Christ!' exclaimed Ernest. 'It's Wally Doyle! Look! Just going up the steps. Wally Doyle of all people, with *his* eyes! He's blind as a bat behind those specs.' He released one of Julia's hands in order to wave to his friend while Julia, fearful of falling, screeched for him to take hold of it again.

'Wally! Come down from there, you daft sod! You'll never even see the bloody enemy!' cried Ernest.

'Ernest!' Scandalised by his language, Winifred tried to silence him but it was too late. Wally Doyle was peering short-sightedly in their direction.

'Wally! It's me, Ernie Brett. Come down from there!'

Several people in the crowd turned disapproving looks in Ernest's direction.

'You let him be,' cried an elderly man with campaign ribbons pinned to a threadbare jacket. 'The lad's got guts, which is more'n what you've got, by the look of it.'

Wally, catching sight of Ernest, beckoned him up to the steps with extravagant jerks of his arm.

'Come on, Ernie! Let's see what you're made of,' he yelled. 'Show your girl what you're made of!'

'You dare, Ernest Brett!' hissed Winifred. 'You just *dare*, that's all!'

The queue to climb the steps was growing slowly but surely as Wally continued to call for Ernest while Winifred, trying to hide her fears, did her best to stop him from committing himself.

The march came to an end and another record was put on. Strains of 'The British Grenadiers' drifted on the summer air and the woman on the platform began to sing in a resonant voice which throbbed with emotion.

'Let's go,' said Winifred desperately. 'Ju wants some ice cream, don't you, Ju?'

But Julia was not listening. Her ears were filled with the music and she had eyes only for the small drama being enacted on the stage before her. Young as she was, she responded to the charged atmosphere and laughed aloud, her eyes shining. She wriggled with excitement and Ernest warned, 'Steady on! You're nearly strangling me.'

'Right, who's for some ice cream?' Winifred repeated more loudly and at last caught Julia's attention.

'Me! I want some,' she cried.

'You hear that, Ernie?' demanded Winifred. 'Ju wants some ice cream. Oh, do come away, Ernie. Wally can sign on without your help.'

He turned to her and as she saw his expression, her heart sank.

'Here,' he told her, 'take hold of little 'un for a minute.' He unseated Julia from his shoulders and set her down on the ground. 'Hold Win's hand,' he said, 'and when I've signed on we'll—'

'Ernest, you *dare*!' cried Winifred. 'Are you mad? Uncle Stan will half kill you. What about the boat? He needs you, you know he does.'

'Oh, bugger the boat!' Ernest grinned at her and she thought he had never looked so handsome or so infinitely desirable. Somehow she resisted the urge to throw her arms round him and restrain him bodily.

'But Ernie—'

Julia, scowling, began to complain that she could not see and that she wanted some ice cream. To her surprise, her doting cousins ignored her.

'I must, Win,' said Ernest, his tone quiet but firm. 'If poor old Wally can sign on, then so can I.'

'You'll listen to him and not me, then?' she demanded. 'I don't matter any more, I suppose. If *Wally* says sign, you'll sign. Well, that puts me in my place, doesn't it, Ernest Brett!'

'Don't talk so daft, love . . .' he began, taken aback by the unexpected attack. 'It's nothing to do with you or Wally. It's to do with me and how I feel about things.'

'Oh no, it's not!' snapped Winifred. 'It's to do with that stupid fat cow on the platform up there and your friend "four-eyes". I thought at least *you* had the sense to think for yourself.'

'I *am* thinking for myself!'

'Well, you certainly aren't thinking for me, Ernest Brett, because I don't want you to sign on. We aren't even at war yet, for Pete's sake!'

'But we will be – it could come at any moment. This week, next week—'

'OK then. Sign on next week,' she agreed. 'Sign on when it starts.'

His expression was hardening, but she went on recklessly, 'Sign on when England declares war on Germany – if she ever does – and then I'll give you my blessing.'

'I'm signing on now!' Ernest's tone was final.

Julia tugged at Winifred's skirt. 'I want some ice cream,' she insisted. 'I do. I want—'

'Oh shut up, you!'

Winifred gave the child a furious push and Julia, caught off-balance, fell over backwards and a woman inadvertently stepped on her hand. Julia screamed with rage and pain and Winifred, full of remorse, knelt to help her up and comfort her. Seizing his chance, Ernest slipped away through the crowd and by the time Winifred had pacified her small cousin, her fiancé was on the platform and putting pencil to paper.

'Oh, my God!' whispered Winifred. 'Now look what you've done, Ju.'

As Ernest stood in the line with his arm round Wally's thin shoulders, he caught Winifred's eye and received a look that brimmed with resentment; the next moment she had turned on her heel and was pushing a way through the crowd, towing Julia ignominiously behind her. He watched her until she was lost to view among the teeming crowd and Julia's shrill screams had faded. Then there was back-slapping and hand-shaking and the large woman was kissing them amid swelling cheers from the crowd. Ernest felt a glow of satisfaction; in spite of all Winifred's efforts, he had done the right thing.

Two days later, after Germany had invaded Belgium, the German ambassador received the British government's ultimatum, and within hours Britain was at war.

*

Heavy autumn rain lashed the windows of Cicely's front room, drumming against the glass with such ferocity that Sarah looked up from her stitching and gave the weather one of her more intimidating frowns. She was edging a pillowcase, part of a set of bed linen which would be her wedding present to Winifred and Ernest. Sitting opposite her, Cicely shook her head.

'What must it be like in the trenches,' she said, 'if the weather over there is as bad as this? Those greatcoats are thick, I grant you, but they're not waterproof.'

Winifred looked up eagerly as the topic once more reverted to a subject on which she prided herself she knew more than anyone else in the family.

'Oh, but they have their capes,' she told her mother, 'and they're waterproof. Ernest says that the—'

She broke off suddenly as a burst of hastily subdued giggles came from her two brothers who sat on the floor behind the sofa. They had each been given a volume of the *Children's Encyclopaedia* to read, with dire warnings from Cicely of what would happen to them if they stopped reading and made a nuisance of themselves during their grandmother's Sunday visit. Leonard, nearly ten years old, was like his father – of stocky build with dark hair and brown eyes. Benjamin, four years younger, was like Cicely – tall and thin, but with lighter auburn hair and blue eyes.

Now Leonard leaned over to his brother and whispered, 'Ernest says! Ernest says!' Cicely's sharp ears caught the whispers though not the words, but Winifred guessed and coloured faintly. Sarah, a little deaf, heard neither.

'That will do, you two!' said Cicely. 'Remember what I said.'

'Ernest says what, dear?' prompted Sarah. She stuck the needle into the velvet pad on her wrist and bit off a thread. Reaching into her small work-basket for more white silk, she nodded encouragingly to Winifred.

'Nothing,' she said. 'It doesn't matter.'

Cicely turned her attention to her daughter. 'What kind of answer is that?' she demanded irritably. 'You know better than to leave a sentence unfinished. Tell your grandmother what Ernest said in his letter.'

There was another explosive sound from behind the sofa, but Cicely chose to ignore it. Recently the boys' behaviour had not been at all satisfactory and she made up her mind to have another talk with Miss Mills. She had long acknowledged that discipline was not the nanny's strong point, but kept her on for her other virtues. She was a well-educated woman and coached the boys in English and arithmetic for two hours each weekend, which Cicely considered necessary if Leonard was to attend a preparatory school. None of the Coulsden males had ever attended a private school, but Cicely had set her heart on it and only her husband remained to be persuaded. Miss Mills was worth her weight in gold as far as Cicely was concerned, for it did not occur to her that the standards Leonard reached might not be high enough. Nor did it prick her conscience that Miss Mills was grossly underpaid for her work. Cicely was a snob, although she would have repudiated the suggestion. Now that she and Jack were comfortably off she had only one regret – that fishing had such a poor public image. If her children were to move up in the world, as she hoped they would, she was determined that the humble origins of the Coulsden family must be overcome in some way and education seemed to be the most obvious answer. Winifred's engagement to Ernest had been a terrible disappointment to her, although she dared not say so. Ernest was a Brett and there was nothing very creditable known of his dead father. Ernest had no money and he was a fisherman. Cicely had hoped for something better for her only daughter, but her reservations on the matter had been brushed aside amidst the general family approval.

'Ernest says they are stoutly clad,' said Winifred, 'but that their boots . . . shall I read you his latest letter from Salisbury?'

Sarah nodded and Winifred flew upstairs to fetch it.

'Poor girl,' Cicely told Sarah, 'she lives for the postman. It's quite ridiculous, of course, but what can I say? If there's no letter she is plunged into gloom. When there is a letter, she locks herself away in her room with it. She is so moody, it really is quite wearing to be in her company. Whatever will she do if he gets sent abroad?'

Sarah shrugged. 'She has her Red Cross work. That's something – a distraction, if nothing else.'

Cicely sighed. 'I suppose so, although it all seems rather pointless. They say it will all be over by Christmas, although I don't quite see how. Jack says the Germans are stronger than anyone expected and it won't be long before Belgium collapses. He's gone down to the harbour today. There's a rumour that a lot of Belgian refugees will be putting in there later.'

'Putting in to Rye, you mean? But why?'

'Nowhere else suitable for them to tie up, apparently. The harbour master got word that a lot of boats are on their way from Ostend, full of refugees. They will be dropped off in Folkestone – security checks, I suppose – and then the boats and their crews will come on to Rye.'

'But where will they put them all?' Sarah protested. 'There's surely no room on the Strand Quay.'

'Up behind the railway quay down at Rye Harbour,' Cicely told her. 'At least, that's what Jack reckons. Plenty of room there without blocking the main channel.'

'Poor souls,' said Sarah.

Leonard's head appeared suddenly above the back of the sofa. 'They might be spies!' he said. 'They might be Germans sent to spy on us and they'll go back and tell the Kaiser—'

'Tell him what?' laughed Cicely. 'And how will they get back to the Kaiser if their boats are laid up? You get on with your reading. Spies, indeed!'

Winifred came in at that moment with Ernest's letter and Cicely decided she could not face hearing the contents yet again.

'If you will excuse me,' she murmured, rising quickly to her feet, 'I'll see how lunch is progressing.'

When she had gone, Winifred opened the folded letter reverently and began to read self-consciously.

' "My dearest Winnie. . ." '

'Oh, how sweet! That's nice,' said Sarah, smiling.

'He knows I hate being called that,' Winifred explained. 'It's his joke.'

Leonard made a loud whinnying noise and both boys began to giggle.

'He thinks you're a horse!' said Leonard, bolder now that his mother had left the room. 'Horses whinny!'

Winifred put out her tongue in his direction.

'Wini*fred*!' cried Sarah. 'You are a young lady now, not a hoyden. Whatever next! Just read the letter, dear, and take no notice of the boys.'

' "My dearest Winnie," ' Winifred read, ' "I got your letter yesterday and my thanks. We have had rifle drill with blank ammo, also a route march. Twelve hours and heavy boots. Not much fun I can tell you. Also early morning parade and pack drill. Wish Wally was here . . ." ' She broke off to explain that Ernest's friend had finally been rejected on medical grounds because of his poor eyesight, then continued:

But I have met a chap called Alf White. We call him Chalky. He comes from Fairlight and is a tram driver in Civvy Street. We share a few laughs. Out here we are all in the same boat and who you are does not matter. There's another man called Ian. A bit of a toff, I suppose, but good fun. He has bright red hair, so of course we call him Ginger. His father is a surgeon. Still no news of embarkation, but rumours we shall go to India. We all hope not, wanting to be where the real war is on the other side of the Channel. Life in a tent is OK but draughty. I miss you.

Your loving Ernest

Sarah nodded her approval. 'Well, he seems cheerful enough,' she said, 'but I must say he'd be better off in India than stuck in a muddy trench. At least the sun shines in India and he's not likely to get trench fever. Really, I don't know where it will all end. I'm glad Harold isn't alive to see what a mess we've got ourselves into. That Ian he mentions sounds nice enough. I'm glad he's made a few friends. He always was a bit of a loner, Ernest. I suppose his father dying and him having a stepfather is always difficult, although I know Stan does his best for him.'

She bit off another thread and began to fold up her sewing. Leonard stood up and said, 'I'm tired of reading. Why can't Julia come to lunch? I want to show her my rabbit.'

'She's got a nasty cough,' said Sarah, 'so I thought she should not come in case you and Ben catch it. You'll see her by and by, don't you worry. Her father's taking her to see her other grandmother.' She stood up with some difficulty and Winifred hurried to help her. 'Poor soul,' said Sarah, referring to Henrietta's mother. 'She's never recovered from Hettie's death and most likely never will. It's over two years now and the doctors are not at all hopeful. Shock can do terrible things to the mind, terrible things! George says her mind is quite gone at times and she talks as though Hettie were still alive. Terrible!'

'Poor Aunt Hettie,' said Winifred. 'It's dreadful to think that she's dead and that awful Agnes and her brat are still . . .'

She stopped, remembering Leonard and Benjamin who had emerged from behind the sofa and were listening with undisguised interest.

'Little pitchers have big ears,' reminded Sarah.

Downstairs the gong sounded for lunch, and while the boys cheered, Sarah sniffed at this latest proof of Cicely's aspirations towards gentility.

'George has bought Julia a tricycle,' she told Winifred. 'It's much too big for her and I've warned him she could have a fall, but will he listen to me? No. He never did as a boy and I don't suppose he's going to start now.'

In the dining-room they gathered at the table, standing behind the chairs while Cicely said grace. As they sat down, the food was carried in.

'That looks a nice piece of beef,' Sarah remarked, brightening a little. 'I think I shall do justice to my lunch today.'

*

Julia sat on the seat next to her father, her short legs in their buttoned boots sticking out in front of her. She did not lean back on the wooden seat, because Mama Sarah had told her it was not ladylike to slump. Ahead of her the horse's rump and creamy tail swayed to and fro and she could see right along its broad back to the creamy mane and nodding head with pointed ears and jingling harness. Out through Rye they went, past the river where a timber boat was unloading on to the bank. George, holding the reins, glanced at her once or twice but said nothing and a sense of unease filled her. Why wasn't Papa speaking to her? Why weren't they on *Silver Lady*? Where were they going in the dog-cart? She clung to the edge of the seat with plump fingers and tried not to fall off, because the ground was a long way down and she knew she would hurt herself. From under her long pale lashes Julia cast a surreptitious look at her father, although his grim expression did nothing to reassure her. But she must not ask. Little girls should be seen and not heard. 'Speak when you are spoken to', Mama Sarah said, and when Julia was with her in the big house she did what she was told because she did not want Mama Sarah to go to Heaven as well as her mother. When she was with her father she laughed a lot because he teased her and tickled her under her chin and pulled funny faces. When she was with Leo and Ben she did whatever Leo told her to do and was often led astray, but Aunt

Cicely 'made allowances' for her because her mother was dead.

As they sped along the road towards Winchelsea, Julia stared thoughtfully at her boots, her large eyes dark with apprehension. Something bad was going to happen, she felt sure. That was why Papa had not spoken to her and why he didn't call her 'my silver lady'.

They turned left as they left the bridge behind, running along between the flat fields dotted with sheep. Suddenly George smiled at her and she returned his smile wonderingly.

'We're going to see someone,' he told her. 'You'll like her – them, I mean. Her name's Agnes and she's got a little girl.'

Julia frowned in puzzlement. Her mouth puckered and her anxious eyes were fixed on George's face.

'It will be a nice surprise for her,' said George. 'You'll like Agnes. She's very nice, very kind.'

He swallowed hard as he said this and glanced away. Julia's eyes missed nothing and her anxiety grew throughout the long silence which followed.

'You give her a nice kiss,' said George, 'and then she'll like you. You want her to like you, don't you? You want to be friends? Julia? I said, you want to be friends?'

'Yes, Papa.'

Julia now knew for certain that this outing with her father was quite different from any other. They were riding in the dog-cart, going to see Agnes, and there would be no teasing and no tickles.

'I hope you will remember your manners,' he said. 'I want you to be a good girl and behave nicely.'

Agnes. The name was familiar, but Julia could not recall exactly where or when she had heard it before. Had Mama Sarah spoken of an Agnes? Was it the same Agnes?

George smiled at her again and now she could see that he was not really happy behind the smiling mouth. His eyes looked funny, as though he was afraid. Perhaps he was afraid of Agnes?

'Agnes's little girl is called Emily,' he told her. 'That's a nice name, isn't it?'

'Yes, Papa.'

'You can play with her – two little girls playing together like two little sisters. Won't that be fun, Ju?'

He wanted her to say 'Yes' so she said it and he smiled again and put an arm around her shoulder.

'That's my girl,' he said heartily.

Julia regarded her boots while another silence developed. It was not over, she knew, and she did not want to see his eyes when he told her the rest of it . . . whatever it was. Her boots were comfortingly familiar, her father's expression was not.

'Julia . . .' he began slowly, 'I want this to be our secret, this visit to Agnes. Just you and me having a secret. Would you like that?'

She scowled at her boots and said nothing.

'Julia? You'd like a secret, wouldn't you – just you and me?'

'Yes, Papa.'

'Then you mustn't tell anyone about Agnes. Not Mama Sarah and not Aunt Cicely.'

'Can I tell Leo?'

'No!' he cried. 'For God's sake don't tell that little brat or it will be all over Rye. Proper chatterbox, he is.'

'Ben?'

'No. Not Ben, not anybody. Do you see, Julia? If you tell *anyone*, you've spoilt our secret.'

She nodded miserably.

'Look at me, Ju,' he said, slowing the horse to a walk. 'We're nearly there now, so I want you to remember. Be a good girl. D'you understand?'

'Like two little sisters,' she repeated.

'Yes.'

'What is a sister?'

'What is a – oh, for God's sake, Julia! It's like Winifred and the boys. Winifred is Ben's sister and she's Leo's sister. See? Uncle Jack is my brother, you see, and so is Uncle Stan. Brothers and sisters. You see now?'

She nodded dutifully, understanding nothing, but her mouth tightened as she recognised the exasperation in his tone. She did not want to see Agnes or Emily. Suddenly she wanted quite desperately to go home.

*

Agnes Dengate was rolling out pastry for the rabbit pie when George arrived. She straightened up as she heard his voice and pushed back a stray lock of hair with floury fingers.

'In here, Georgie,' she called, wondering how it was he always seemed to come when she was looking her worst – either black-leading the ancient stove, scrubbing the floor or rolling pastry.

She heard him speak to Emily who sat playing in the tiny hallway, then looked up to see him holding Julia by the hand. Shocked, Agnes stared at her speechlessly, then finally found her voice.

'What the hell are you up to, George Coulsden?' she said. 'You've got a nerve, you have, bringing *her* here! Damn it, George, I've told you before, I don't want her here.'

'It's OK,' said George. 'I had to bring her. I'm supposed to be with Hettie's mother, but ten minutes is all I can stand of her these days. It was either that or lunch with Cis and she gets on my wick with her high-falutin' ways. Christ, Ag, there's no need to stare at her as though she's a freak or something; she's only my daughter.'

'So is that!' Agnes, stung by his remark, jerked her thumb in the direction of her own daughter.

'I know. I know. God, you do go on!'

He sat down heavily and Agnes said sarcastically, 'Do sit down and make yourself at home, Mr Coulsden. And her ladyship, of course. What am I supposed to do, curtsey?'

'Cut it out, Ag, will you? I'm in no mood for a row.'

Agnes opened her mouth, closed it again, draped the pastry over the pie and slashed angrily at the surplus with the knife. It took her a moment or two to calm down.

'Don't I get a kiss, then?' she asked him at last.

George glanced at Julia who stood beside him, examining the untidy room with obvious interest.

'Better not,' he said.

'Oh, charming!' She rolled out the pastry scraps and cut them into leaves. As she decorated the pie, her fingers trembled noticeably.

'I'm sorry,' said George. 'I suppose it was stupid to bring her, but I wanted to see you and it's so bloody difficult. My mother's got eyes in the back of her head!'

'You should tell her about us. Talk to her about Em, her grandchild. She'll get used to the idea.'

'When pigs fly she will!'

'Won't *she* say anything?' said Agnes, referring to Julia. 'I mean, if she's going to open her big mouth as soon as she gets back home, there'll be no need for you to tell anyone.'

'She won't,' said George. 'She's a good kid. I've told her it's a secret between us.'

'Hmm.' Agnes was far from reassured. 'Well, it's rabbit pie, so you timed it well.'

'Rabbit?' asked George as she opened the door in the front of the stove and pushed the pie into the oven. 'Where did you get that?'

She grinned. 'Wouldn't you like to know, George Coulsden? Perhaps I've got an admirer. Ever thought of that, have you? Maybe you shouldn't leave me on my own for days on end. Weeks sometimes. I'm not a nun, you know, and I'm still a bit of a looker.'

'I never said you weren't,' said George defensively.

'You both staying for something to eat?'

'Wouldn't say no.'

'I'll have to do a few more spuds, then.'

From the hall, Emily began to cry and George went out to her. Agnes and Julia regarded each other curiously.

'You're getting a big girl then,' said Agnes, reluctantly comparing George's two daughters. Julia's hair had been brushed by the devoted Mrs Mack until it shone and it hung neatly from beneath a small felt hat with an upturned brim. Her warm coat was trimmed with a narrow band of fur and she wore long buttoned boots and suede gloves. Emily's curly hair would be tousled and her face had not been washed. Her legs and feet were bare and her worn dress, bought at a jumble sale, had lost its collar. Julia regarded Agnes steadily without answering, her eyes wide and unafraid.

'Lost your tongue, have you?'

Still eliciting no response from the little girl, Agnes began to peel a large potato, savagely attacking the eyes with the point of her knife as though she bore it a personal grudge.

When George returned he was carrying Emily and Julia's eyes widened in surprise.

'Not missing much!' warned Agnes with a nod towards Julia.

George smiled. He sat down and Emily turned herself round to kneel on his lap and wrap her small arms round his neck.

'Say "hullo" to Emily,' George suggested.

'Hullo,' said Julia dutifully.

'You're a fool, George,' Agnes told him. 'She's taking it all in, I'm telling you. She'll say something when she gets home.'

George sighed heavily. 'If she does, she does. I've weathered worse storms.'

'Not on land, you haven't! If your Ma gets a whiff of all this she'll eat you for breakfast, George Coulsden, and spit out the bones!'

'So, who gave you the rabbit?'

She grinned. 'Oh, you're jealous! Georgie Porgie's jealous!'

'Who was it? Tommy Bird?'

'It was Luke Bligh, if you must know.' Agnes saw his eyes narrow. 'Real nice, he was. He asked me to make him a little purse net for when he goes ferreting, so I did and next day he popped by to give me a couple of rabbits. He goes rabbiting up the sand dunes. He says I can sell the pelts, too, to a chap who farms just below the Winchelsea cliffs. I forget his name, but Luke's promised to tell him about me and he says I might get a bit of work later in the year thistle spudding. He's going to tell his mates that I make and mend nets too. He reckons some of them will give me a bit of work, skim nets and stuff like that. His mother smokes fish and he says he'll give me a pair of bloaters next time he's by this way *and* he's going to show me how to catch prawns.'

She stopped at last, out of breath, and there was a pause while George – lips pursed and with a thoughtful expression on his face – jogged Emily up and down on his knee.

Suddenly reckless, Agnes added, 'I think he's lonely since his wife died, and he's got this boy of eight called Frank. They live with Luke's folks.'

'I know they do,' said George irritably. 'I've known him for years.'

'Sorry, I'm sure,' said Agnes, delighted with his reaction. 'How am I supposed to know who you know and don't know? There's no need to get arsey with me, just because some fellow takes a bit of an interest and tries to help. Me and Em can't live on air, you know. If someone's offering, then I'm taking.' She tossed her head defiantly and the dark curls bobbed around her flushed face. 'Two mouths I've got to feed, and no man of my own—'

'You've got me. I do my best.' His tone was sulky and he avoided her eyes.

'Have I? Do you? I sometimes wonder,' Agnes said bitterly. 'Twice you've been here in the last three weeks. Oh, don't shake your head. I've kept a special note, written down. I can prove it. I don't think you give a toss for us, George Coulsden. You've got your precious Julia – Julia *Lady*, I should say. Julia Lady? God, George, you make me sick, you know that? You've got Lady Muck here and your nice house and all your family and friends – and me and Em have got sod-all! No money, no family to speak of and stuck in this God-forsaken place day after day—'

This tirade was interrupted suddenly by Julia, who without warning stepped forward and sank her teeth into Emily's bare arm, causing her to utter a piercing scream. Julia stepped back and wiped her mouth with the back of her hand, her blue eyes glittering with satisfaction now that she had hurt the child who sat so carelessly on her father's lap. *Julia's* father, she told herself, and *Julia's* father's lap.

Everyone stared at the neat circle of tooth-marks which showed up white on Emily's arm, but before George could collect his thoughts Agnes dealt Julia a stinging blow to the side of her face and then snatched Emily from his knee.

'Bloody little wild-cat!' she cried. 'There, there, then, Ma's got you now.' She patted Emily's back and rocked her to and fro. 'She won't hurt you again. Christ, George, that's a bloody spiteful kid you've got there. Just look at those marks! I mean, biting her poor little arm like that. Well, I'm damn glad she's not mine, I'm telling you. Real vicious streak, that is. There now, my pretty, don't you cry! Let's wipe those poor little tears away.'

George was silent, stunned by the speed of what had happened and dismayed by Julia's uncharacteristic behaviour. He swallowed hard.

'Come here, Julia,' he said, 'and say you're sorry. Do you hear me? Say you're sorry to Emily.' He tried to pull her towards him, but she evaded his outstretched arms.

'I won't,' she said, her voice cold and distant. A broad red mark was appearing across the side of her face where she had been struck and George glared at Agnes. 'Christ, Ag!' he exclaimed, pointing to the mark. 'Look at that! Julia's only a child, but *you* should know better. She'll have bruises by tomorrow. You can see the fingermarks. How am I supposed to explain how she got them, eh? Nice mess this is!'

'Serves her right,' responded Agnes. 'Who asked you to bring her here anyway, flaunting her buttoned boots and her fancy clothes? Emily's your daughter too, you know. You should be ashamed of yourself when you see the two of them together, and Emily without so much as a decent pair of shoes to her feet. Poor little mite, she's never done you no harm, but you bring that spiteful, stuck-up Julia along and she bites her. If Julia's got bruises on her precious little face, she's got no one to blame but herself for having such a nasty nature. She got what was coming to her. You can take her away, George Coulsden. That kid's not welcome here and come to that, nor are you.'

To her relief, he made no attempt to take her at her word but sat with his head bowed, staring miserably at the threadbare carpet. Emily, her tears over, turned in Agnes's arms and held out her own to George.

'Ah, bless her!' Agnes said. 'She wants to go to her Pa. Take her a minute, George. These potatoes have got to go on or we'll never eat today.'

George took his younger daughter into his arms and felt a lump in his throat. 'Look,' he said, 'I'm sorry, Ag. I can't say more than that. I don't know what got into her; she's never done that before.'

'Jealousy,' said Agnes, recovering a little. 'That's plain enough. Only natural in a way, I suppose. I bet she's been spoilt rotten by your mother. But that's not to say she should get away with it and she's had a smack for being spiteful. So let that be an end to it. I'm not going to say I'm sorry, 'cos I'm not!'

'But the mark,' said George. 'Someone might think *I* did it. That I hit my own child.'

Agnes snorted. 'And someone might think I bit Emily's arm. Tit for tat, isn't it, George!'

She busied herself at the sink, lifting the potato peelings into an old saucepan in which she would cook up the chickens' food later. Then she spread a cloth over the kitchen table and began to set the cutlery.

'If she's eating with us,' said Agnes, glancing over at Julia who remained staring into space with her jaw clenched, 'she's got to say sorry to Emily.'

And she held back a knife and fork to show that she meant business.

George looked hopefully towards Julia. 'Say you're sorry to Emily.'

Julia shook her head and pressed her lips together as though to prevent the word escaping accidentally.

'Little wotsit!' exclaimed Agnes with a faint and reluctant stirring of admiration for what she considered to be the girl's pluck. 'Say you're sorry, Julia, or you'll get no dinner – see? Here's your knife and fork. Shall I put them back in the drawer or on the table? You going to say you're sorry?'

Julia opened her mouth, said, 'No', and closed it again.

George groaned, but at that moment Emily inexplicably held out her arms to Julia and smiled winningly.

Julia, taken by surprise, had smiled back before she realised what was happening. Softening towards her, Agnes said, 'Well, I'll be damned. Look at that! Emily wants to be friends, bless her heart. See that, Julia? You bit her arm, but still she wants to be friends. Give her a little hug. Go on!'

Startled, Julia looked at her father who smiled and nodded. She stepped cautiously forward and Emily's arms closed round her neck, knocking her hat crooked in the process.

Agnes, her own resentment forgotten, beamed at George. 'Look at that!' she marvelled. 'Well, I'm blowed. Mind you, Emily's a loving little soul.' She smiled at Julia. 'I think she's taken to you, Julia. She's very loving. Quite taken with Luke Bligh, she was, too. Kissing him and laughing – you know how she does.'

Catching sight of George's face, she decided not to pursue that particular subject and to overlook Julia's refusal to apologise. It was a matter, she reflected, of playing your hand right. With another cheerful smile at George, she set a knife and fork for Julia and turned back to the stove. Everything comes to them that waits, she told herself. She took a quick look at the rabbit pie and thought that if she used one of the rabbit skins to trim Emily's coat, the other one might make her a little fur hat.

CHAPTER SIX

Alice Bligh was tall and angular, with broad hips and shoulders to match. Her straggly hair was piled on top of her head and anchored with a dozen large grips beneath a large flat cap, but neither the grips nor the cap succeeded in restraining the long grey locks. Her eyes were small, her mouth a thin line and her cheeks and nose were criss-crossed with tiny broken blood vessels.

She stood now at the kitchen sink, swearing and pushing back a lock of hair with salty fingers, hardly aware that she did so for the habit was so much a part of her daily life. One by one she plunged the salted herrings into a tubful of water, washed them, rubbed off the scales and left them to drain. As she crossed the yard to the lean-to fuel store to fetch kindling and oak chips, she thought about the war and argued aloud against Luke's suggestion that he should enlist in the Army.

'If you're off to the war, who's to care for the boy? Don't ask me because I've got my hands full already with this little lot.'

By 'this little lot' she meant the house, the garden, the cleaning she did for the vicar's wife down at the rectory, the herrings she smoked, young Frankie – bless him – and Sam, her husband. Not to mention occasionally rowing the boat across the harbour when a fare turned up and both Luke and her husband had nipped down to the William the Conqueror for a quick pint.

'Damn you, get up there,' she muttered, as her fingers lifted once more to deal with her recalcitrant hair. She bent down and tugged a bag of oak chips into her arms, straightening up awkwardly with it and then staggering to the small garden shed which served as a 'herring hang'.

'Like as not get yourself killed,' she went on, haranguing the absent Luke, 'and then the boy'll have no one but us and we won't live for ever . . . and what's to become of him when we're gone? Let them others go as have got no young 'uns to care for and you stick to your ferrying, Luke Bligh. That way you get to keep your head on your shoulders and we shall all be a lot better off. They can win the war without you, so make up your mind to it.'

She had only Luke, Sam and Frank in the whole world, she thought – except for Ellen, her younger sister who lived a few miles further along the coast at Pett Level in a tiny shack of a home tucked into the side of the hill. Married to a no-good man named Alf Bittens, known as Bitty to all who knew him – a man she met at a fairground – a feckless man who scratched a living from the sea *when* he was sober. Still, to give him his due he did let Alice have fish on the cheap and she could make a bit of profit on the bloaters, a shilling some weeks, getting the fuel for nothing. Well, not for nothing exactly, but for the labour of sweeping it all up from the floor of Coulsdens' workshop.

She dumped the bag with a soft gasp of relief and straightened up. Fumbling for a hair-grip, she pulled it out and jabbed it back in again, muttering impatiently as she did so. Then she returned to the kitchen and the waiting fish. With practised fingers, she threaded a pointed wooden rod through the gills of each fish, taking care to keep each one a few inches apart from its neighbour so that the smoke could circulate freely. When she had threaded them – sixty in all – she carried them out into the hang and wedged the rods across from wall to wall at a height of seven feet. This was not really high enough – the experts hung theirs from eight feet and upward – but Alice's hang was what she termed 'a make-do', and although both Sam and Luke had promised repeatedly over the years to raise the roof another two feet, it had never been done and she knew it never would. She was resigned to the fact and only occasionally raised the matter when she wanted something to nag about.

She started the fire with shavings, coughing in the thick resinous smoke, and waited until she was satisfied with its progress. The oak must not be allowed to burn, only to smoulder if the herrings were to be properly cured. When at last the smouldering wood met with her approval, she nodded her head and warned, 'Now keep at it, damn you!' before escaping into the fresh air. Closing the shed door behind her, she wiped her streaming eyes on the corner of her apron.

Back in the kitchen Alice paused with hands on hips surveying the mess of fish scales, salt and spilt water which waited to be cleaned up as she checked off in her mind the whereabouts of the rest of her family. Frankie was with Eunice Bird, playing with their little Charlie. Alice approved of Eunice in spite of what she had heard, although she thought Tommy Bird a strange man to choose for a husband, having been a bachelor so many years. Still, the boy was a nice little lad, and even though Frank was older than him, they seemed to have taken to one another. Frank was a gentle soul with a loving heart, and when Alice allowed herself a glimpse into the future, she feared that women might take advantage of her grandson's kindness and foresaw for him a great deal of heartache. She sighed.

And where was that son of hers? She glanced out of the window and saw the light in the rough wooden shelter which Sam's father had made beside the jetty where the ferry-boat was moored. Sam Bligh had been ferryman before Luke, and Sam's father had done the job before Sam. The same boat, the *Lucy*, had been rowed across the river by three generations of Blighs and presumably Frank would be the fourth. To some folks, she reflected, it might seem a funny way to earn a living, sitting beside the river all day waiting for passengers, but it wasn't all waiting and there were busy times. Morning and evening, the men came across from Camber to work in the unsightly chemical factory half-way between Rye Harbour and the Hastings road. There were frequently harbour officials to be carried and in the summer a few holiday-makers who lingered to watch the fishing boats come in. But when the small fleet was at sea and the tide was out, nothing remained but a vast expanse of mud and the criss-crossed beams of the jetties. Rye Harbour was a bleak and uncompromising place and it bred a community of reserved women, taciturn men and self-reliant children. The harbour folk, isolated by their position, kept very much to themselves, looking no further afield for husbands or wives but choosing from amongst their own number. They were a separate people cut off from Rye, remote in their 'island' bounded by marsh and water; there was no love lost between the harbour fishermen and the 'Ryers'. The crews of Rye boats passing Rye Harbour received no more than a nod of recognition, sometimes not that. It was not unknown for jeers and taunts to be exchanged as the boats sailed past the village, and now and then the village children threw stones.

Once out in the bay the Rye Harbour men eyed the others warily, ever on the alert for sharp practice. The Hastings men, they said, would cut your nets as soon as look at you. The 'Dunge men' from Dungeness had nothing but a lighthouse to their credit

and were to be trusted no more than the French. Nor were the
Rye men above reproach, for under cover of darkness they might
let their boats drift in too close by way of guiding another boat's
fish into their own nets. Certainly the Rye Harbour men knew
that no man dared relax his vigil. Fishing was not a living for the
faint-hearted and a trusting nature was a great disadvantage.

So, thought Alice, Frank and his father were accounted for and
Sam was round at Arnold's having his only boots patched and no
doubt talking about the old days. But he would be back shortly.
She hooked a strand of hair into a hair-grip with a curt, 'Stay
there,' and decided to make the most of her brief respite by
making herself a cup of tea.

*

That night the Belgian fishing boats sailed in on the high autumn
tide. The harbour lights had been extinguished with the outbreak
of war and the unfamiliar channel was intensely dark. They nosed
in cautiously, nine in number and varying in length from 35 to 70
feet. The majority of them were powered by small motor engines
which over the preceding years had been added to many of the
sailing boats on both sides of the Channel. Most of them accomplished the feat successfully but one of the larger craft, misjudging
the entrance to the harbour mouth and deceived by the excep-
tionally high tide, sailed up the wrong side of the eastern harbour
wall and ran aground on the sands of Jury's Gap.

Eventually, however, all the crews were safely landed and after
being welcomed by the Mayor and the Harbour Commissioner,
were escorted to Rye. There, further official preliminaries kept
the weary crews and their families from the hospitable towns-
people who had volunteered to help them through their first night
on English soil. One small boat, they reported, had disappeared
during the escape from Ostend. No one knew what had happened
to it or whether it had finally reached England, but the coastguards
were alerted to keep a watch for an unidentified sailing boat.

When the last of the Belgians had left the harbour, Luke – after
a few words with the harbour master – rowed himself back across
the river. Quietly he let himself into the silent house, undressed
and fell into bed. Beside him his young son slept deeply, one arm
thrown protectively across his face, snoring softly. Luke did not
glance at him but lay for a long time, wide awake, thinking over
the events of the past few hours. One of the Belgians who was able

to speak English had described the dread with which his country faced the prospect of occupation, the atrocities allegedly committed by the approaching German army – women raped, children bayoneted – and the shame they all felt because their efforts to stop the Germans' advance had proved so disastrously inadequate. 'Help us,' his wife had repeated, again and again, the only English she knew. What did she mean, Luke wondered. Help her and her family or help all of her countrymen? As he tossed and turned, Luke's imagination played horrible tricks: he saw his son stabbed to death, his parents subjected to indignities and torture; he heard the sound of marching feet in the streets where he had played as a boy and saw the village of Rye Harbour in flames. 'Help us,' the woman had begged and Luke, usually so passive, had been stirred by her desperation. She had looked into his eyes, *his*, and had begged for help. It was an appeal he could not ignore. If he ignored her plea and if the Germans did come, where would *he* turn for help? Where would the Blighs sail to, in *their* desperate need? There would be no one and nowhere.

Luke did not put all these feelings into words; in fact he did not think coherently at all, but the emotions and ideas drifted and tangled in his consciousness until at last he knew what he had to do. His instincts had been right all along and he should never have allowed his mother to persuade him against his better judgement. Young Frank would be well cared for, he knew, and he made up his mind. Tomorrow he would go.

*

Two mornings later, soon after daybreak, the coastguard at Galloways saw a small craft appear through the sea mist, drifting slowly and erratically towards the shore, her sail ripped to shreds, one lonely figure at the helm. The craft, an undecked fishing boat, was escorted into Rye Harbour where the body of the helmsman's father was found to be on board. He had been killed by one of a hail of machine-gun bullets which had also destroyed the sail and damaged the motor engine. Jean Dessin, the blond fifteen-year-old son, had miraculously escaped their pursuers under cover of a timely fog and, more by luck than good management, had guided the ship on to the English coast. The boy was badly shocked and very hungry. His gold hair was matted with salt water and there were dark shadows beneath his blue eyes. Interviewed by the police and then the military authorities, he finally satisfied them that he was not a spy and gratefully accepted their offer of a bed for the night. He was taken to the home of Sam and Alice Bligh, who gave him the bed vacated by their son Luke the previous day. After a shy smile at young Frank, Jean Dessin fell thankfully into bed and slept for twenty-one hours without stirring.

*

Across the Channel, the war raged on over the following months until soon no one believed any more that it would 'soon be over'. Thousands of men were dying from thousands of wounds. Winifred had joined a unit of the Voluntary Aid Detachment and was sent overseas. On 16 December 1915, she wrote home from a hospital unit on the Somme:

> I'm sorry I have not had time to write but every minute off duty is so precious. All we want to do is SLEEP. We are now five miles behind the front line and the casualties pour in. Some die even before they are examined. It is so terrible. A nightmare. Last week a soldier came in with shrapnel in his back. He was here for two days before I realised it was Luke Bligh, who used to be ferryman at the harbour. Do you remember him? I spoke to him a few times, but then he was moved on to another hospital unit. I didn't get a chance to say good-bye to him, but they removed the shrapnel and he is going to be well enough to go back to the front. Poor lad. Like all the others he probably hoped for 'a Blighty one', that is a wound so bad he would be sent back to England to recover. He was in great pain but very brave. There are so many boys dying, it would break your heart. Thank you for your letters. Thank God, too, for the letter you forwarded from Ernest. He is, or was, alive and well. But for how long? Forgive me. I get very depressed whenever I have time to think, which luckily is not often . . .

Three months later Luke Bligh was shot in the head by a sniper's bullet and died instantly. He was one of the lucky ones, they said.

The following day the war came closer still when a fishing trawler struck a mine and sank in Rye Bay, six of the crew being killed. The fishing fleet itself was sadly diminished; many of the fishermen had enlisted and their boats lay idle, stranded at low tide on the Rother mud like beached whales. The harbour itself, now so little used, suffered from lack of revenue and dire neglect, and the harbour mouth began inevitably to silt up yet again. *Silver Lady* was among the Rye boats which still operated in the restricted area of the bay which had not been mined. Alice and Sam shared the job that Luke had left vacant, but saw very little river traffic apart from the usual fishing boats, barges carrying pitch or boulders and the occasional patrol boat on government business of one kind or another. Shipbuilding, too, was almost at a standstill and Jack Coulsden built only one boat – a small fishing punt for a Hastings fisherman, a friend of his brother Stan. For the fishing community, as for everyone else, the war years were a time of decay and yet, in spite of everything, a cautious optimism persisted throughout the country as life and the war continued hand in hand.

*

In the midsummer of 1916 Sarah Coulsden experienced a sudden and virulent attack of 'flu and agreed reluctantly that Julia, now almost six years old, should rejoin her father in the house above Hilders Cliff, much to Mrs Mack's delight. This was the first time since her mother's death that Julia had been home, for Sarah had not allowed it. She suspected that George might take Agnes to the house and was adamant that Julia and 'that woman' should never come face to face, but George was welcome at South View and visited his daughter frequently. Mrs Mack also visited occasionally at the old Appledore house, but to have five-year-old Julia all to herself at Hilders Cliff for a few weeks was an unexpected bonus for her. She led Julia into the house, holding her by the hand.

'Here we are,' she said brightly. 'Home again, home again, jiggety jig! Do you remember that? Your mother used to say that rhyme to you while you sat on her knees and she'd jiggle you up and down, as though you were riding a horse.'

Julia looked at her blankly.

'Don't you remember?' the housekeeper persisted. ' "To market, to market, to buy a fat pig. Home again, home again, jiggety jig." '

The child shook her head. 'Oh well, never mind,' said Mrs Mack. 'I suppose to you four years is a long time.'

Julia was experiencing a bewildering range of emotions as she stared round at the house which had once been her home. She had left it at the age of two, but vague impressions had stayed with her. To her young eyes it was strangely familiar, yet the joy of rediscovery was overshadowed by dimly remembered grief. The

hall with its patterned tiled floor looked smaller than she remembered and the steeply rising stairway less lofty. She said very little
as Mrs Mack led her upstairs and into her parents' bedroom,
which was still a magical place with softly draped curtains of
cream lace and pale fluffy rugs. The smell of lilies of the valley –
Hettie's favourite perfume – brought a lump to the little girl's
throat which she did not understand. To Julia, her dead mother
was a photograph, a distant voice, a reason for tears and recriminations. 'Hettie' was a name to be spoken with hushed voices and
accompanied by a certain look – a shameful memory with which
her grandmother could and frequently did berate her father.
Julia's long-dead mother was 'poor dear Hettie'. Nothing more.
Over the past four years Julia had heard and understood much
more than the concerned adults realised and the whispered
comments or shouted accusations had confused her. On one
occasion, she had asked her cousin Leo about her mother.

'She was funny here,' he had told her, pointing a podgy finger
at his forehead. He added solemnly, 'She was a tragedy.'

'What is a tragedy?' asked Julia, but the young Leo did not
know.

Julia's own bedroom had remained exactly as it was when she
moved to South View, although most of her toys had moved with
her. She looked at the pink gingham curtains which matched the
bedspread; the small brown wardrobe and matching chest of
drawers; the rug beside the small bed. She knew them all and yet
they meant nothing. Only the light in the middle of the ceiling
stirred a chord in her mind – she had lain in her cot and later her
bed, looking up at the pink lace with its dangling white fringe.
When the window was open, the wind would sometimes rustle the
fringe . . . as it did now. The little girl's cautious expression
relaxed into a smile and she pointed to it.

'I remember that,' she told Mrs Mack.

The old lady was delighted. 'Do you now? Well, isn't that nice?
After all these years! Your mother made that lampshade with her
own hands – very clever she was with a needle and thread. I expect
you'll be clever, like her.'

'Mama Sarah shows me how to hem,' Julia told her earnestly,
'and I can do cross-stich and satin stitch and chain stitch and
blanket stitch.'

'Well, you are a clever girl!' the housekeeper praised her. 'Your
mother would have been proud of you.'

When they had completed their tour of the house, Mrs Mack took her into the back garden. A large ginger cat leaped over the fence as they walked along the path.

'Do you remember the cat – old Toodles?' Mrs Mack asked Julia. 'You used to call him "Doodle" because you couldn't say "Toodles". A big black cat. He got run over, poor thing; right under the horses' hooves he went, just like that. Jet-black fur – a lovely old cat, he was. Don't you remember Toodles?'

Julia shook her head. She stood in the middle of the lawn and stared round, remembering the rockery with its profusion of purple flowers, the slim and twisted trunk of the elderly lilac, the glossy leaves of the laurel tree and . . . she pointed suddenly to a spiky clump of lavender.

'It smells!' she whispered. 'I remember. It smells so good!'

Mrs Mack beamed at her, feeling that they had achieved another success. 'Well, I never. Fancy you remembering that, after all these years. Do you remember what it's called, this plant?'

'Lavender,' said Julia.

'Clever girl!'

The housekeeper pointed to a shady corner of the garden. 'You used to sit here in your pram and your ma used to sit beside you, doing her crochet, God rest her soul! I used to watch the pair of you from the kitchen window and think how lovely you looked. Every now and then she'd reach out and rock the pram to keep you happy – to let you know she was still beside you.'

Mrs Mack's expression changed and her voice faltered; Julia recognised the familiar transposition.

'Poor soul,' the housekeeper went on, 'she used to look so troubled towards the end. That's the only word I can think of that described it: troubled. As though she had all the cares of the world instead of a nice home and a nice husband – well,' she amended, 'we thought he was then – and a lovely little daughter.'

Julia put a finger to her temple. 'Was she funny here?' she asked. 'Leo said she was.'

Mrs Mack was shocked. 'Leo had no right to say that,' she exclaimed. 'He's a bad boy, don't you listen to him. Funny, indeed! No, Mrs Coulsden was not funny. She was troubled and that's not the same thing at all. Troubled is worried and unhappy. Your mother was a lovely lady, Julia, and she adored you. You remember that.'

The child regarded her calmly. 'What *is* poison?' she asked.

Mrs Mack put a hand to her heart. 'What a question!' she hedged. 'Now where on earth did you hear *that*?'

'But what is it?'

'It's bad stuff that you drink and it makes you ill and then you die. Don't think about it, Julia.' She found Julia's manner disconcerting and it flustered her.

'See that swing?' she said quickly, trying to change the subject. 'Your father made that for you, but you were too young for it really. You had to be held on it; Mrs Coulsden was so sure you'd fall off. Your father used to push you and you'd squeal with excitement.'

'Is Mama Sarah going to die?' Julia asked. 'Will she be a ragedy too?'

'Certainly not!' Mrs Mack shook her head to reinforce the statement. 'She's got the 'flu. Influenza, that's what's the matter with her. The doctor's going to make her better.'

'Why didn't he make Mama better?' Julia looked up at the housekeeper with large, innocent eyes.

'Because . . . well, I suppose he couldn't.'

'*Why* couldn't he?'

'I don't know, Julia,' said Mrs Mack. 'Didn't Mama Sarah tell you all about it? Didn't you ever ask her?'

Julia shook her head. She had never asked the adults, only Leo.

Sometimes adults could not be trusted; they said things and then later on you found out that they weren't true. But here with Mrs Mack in the home she had once shared with her mother and father, she felt she would learn the truth.

Mrs Mack hesitated. She had no wish to hide the truth from this child, but would it be wise? Was she, the housekeeper, the right person to tell her?

'Your mother drank the bad stuff,' she said at last, 'and then she got ill and when they found her it was too late. She was dead. The doctor came, but he couldn't make her alive again. That's all.' She waited for Julia's comment, but none was forthcoming. 'Now then, would you like a glass of my best lemonade and a biscuit? Julia, did you hear me?'

At last Julia nodded and Mrs Mack, relieved, hurried back into the house, thinking how very quiet the child was. Too quiet by half, she thought. And a little too old for her years, with all these questions and that serious expression. If only that terrible thing had never happened – how happy they would all be together. She sighed. Instead, the little girl spent all her days with an elderly lady. What sort of life was that for a growing girl? Nearly six now and with no companions of her own age. If only Mr Coulsden could keep her at home . . . but the old lady would not allow it. If only a lot of things were different! With another sigh, she reached for the small kitchen knife and began to slice the lemons.

Julia meanwhile had explored the garden and now opened the rickety door of the garden shed, the interior of which was quite unfamiliar. She stared round curiously at the assembled iron-ware: a lawn mower, several baskets and a large watering-can. Behind these was a pile of folded sacks and several wooden boxes and behind these again a roll of badly-cracked linoleum and a large number of flower pots. A selection of tools hung on the wall and Julia put up a hand to unhook a pair of secateurs; she would ask Mrs Mack if she could cut off the dead roses, for she had done the task at South View to Mama Sarah's satisfaction.

She tutted suddenly as the secateurs somehow slipped from her grasp and fell down out of sight behind the linoleum. Julia wondered whether she dare leave them there and say nothing, but her conscience smote her and she decided to retrieve them. Stepping gingerly over boxes and sacks, she steadied herself precariously with one hand against the wall and leaned down, running her hand carefully along the gap. Her fingers closed around something interesting which felt like an object wrapped in paper and she drew out a small package tied with string. The paper had become brittle with age and it disintegrated in her hands to reveal a glimpse of tarnished metal. To Julia's dismay a small spoon fell out. She picked it up guiltily and tried to push it back into the wrapping, but the paper crumbled.

'Julia! Where are you, dear?'

Mrs Mack appeared in the doorway, holding a jug of lemonade and two glasses on a small bamboo tray.

'I'm sorry,' stammered Julia, holding out the package. 'I wanted the cutters, they dropped down the back there. This spoon fell out—'

She stopped abruptly as Mrs Mack's face registered shock and an emotion the child was too young to appreciate.

'Show me that!' the old lady gasped, putting down the tray on the nearby garden table with hands that trembled. 'Give them to me, Julia. No, I'm not cross, dear,' she said, seeing her alarm. 'I'm just . . . well, I don't know what I am. The apostle spoon! Oh,

Lordy! And what else?' From the tattered package, she drew out a pair of silver tongs and a napkin ring. A second ring fell on to the grass and Julia picked it up.

'Oh, my Lord!' whispered Mrs Mack. 'After all this time! Now, how on earth did they get there? If Eunice had put them there she would have found them again easily and she never would have got the sack.' She shook her head in bewilderment. 'And look at the state of them all!'

'What is it?' asked Julia.

'Nothing. At least, yes, it's something,' Mrs Mack told her. 'But nothing for you to worry your head about.'

'I'm sorry,' said Julia. It seemed that finding the package was a bad thing to have done. 'I didn't mean it.'

Seeing her dismay, the housekeeper pulled herself together and managed a smile. 'Don't look so gloomy,' she teased. 'It will all come out in the wash, as my mother used to say. There's no harm done, but I tell you what we'll do – we'll keep it a secret, shall we? Just between you and me?'

'Shall we tell Papa?' asked Julia.

Mrs Mack's smile faltered a little. 'No, I don't think we will,' she replied. 'We won't tell anyone; it will be our very own secret. You like secrets, don't you?'

Her mind was busy with possibilities as Julia nodded. 'That's settled, then,' said the housekeeper thankfully. 'Now, come out into the sunshine and sit yourself up at the table and I'll pour the lemonade. Do you know how to make lemonade and barley water?'

Julia shook her head.

'Then I'll teach you my own very special recipe. "Mrs Mack's speciality", that's what your mother used to call it. She loved my barley water, your mother did. Specially when she was poorly after she had that dreadful fever.'

The more she considered how the package of missing silver had found its way into the shed, the more convinced she became that only one person could have put it there. If it wasn't Eunice or Mrs Coulsden, or herself, it had to be Mr Coulsden. And with the benefit of hindsight Mrs Mack was beginning to understand why he might have done it. By the time she had poured out two drinks she was convinced that she knew who had hidden the things and why. Everything fell into place – poor Eunice's denials and Agnes Dengate's prompt arrival on the scene.

Absorbed in her thoughts, she temporarily forgot the small girl sitting opposite her. 'Oh, you wicked man!' she whispered.

'Who's wicked?' Julia's sharp ears had caught the words and Mrs Mack hurriedly jerked her thoughts back to the present.

'No one you know,' she told her firmly. 'So you just drink up and eat your biscuit while I take these bits and bobs back into the house. We don't want anyone else to see them or they won't be a secret any more. Then, if you're a good girl, we'll walk down to the Salts and see if we can find *Silver Lady*. Your father tells me you haven't been down to the Fishmarket for some time. Is that right?'

Julia nodded, although she had no idea how long it was since her visits to her father's boat had ceased.

'Then you'll enjoy that,' said Mrs Mack, slipping the items of silver into her apron pocket and making her way back to the house. Her face wore an unnaturally cheerful expression, but her thoughts were grim.

*

Mrs Mack decided to do nothing about the silver until Sarah had fully recovered and Julia had returned to South View, but she lost a great deal of sleep wondering what exactly she should do then. There seemed to be four possible courses of action. She could do nothing at all – and that had its advantages. Or she could take her information to Sarah Coulsden and let her deal with the matter. That might be the best solution; at least it would be the simplest, although if Sarah refused to believe her son capable of such deception, she might well resent Mrs Mack's suggestion. Another way would be to tackle George Coulsden and see his reactions for herself. But then, if he were guilty, George might turn against her; he might even sack her. She had no proof of his involvement – only her intuition. A fourth possibility – that of taking the information to Eunice – worried her, for she believed that it was Eunice who had sent the fateful letter to Hettie Coulsden. A woman as vengeful as that might well create further havoc and the housekeeper wanted to ensure that whatever happened, little Julia would not suffer in any way. There must be no unpleasant repercussions.

Julia had been back at South View for ten days when yet another idea presented itself to Mrs Mack – an idea so simple that she wanted to shout with triumph, and she lost no time in putting it into action.

George came in for his supper in an unusually genial mood that evening. The catch had been a good one and they had managed to get the fish on to the 6.33 pm train to London. He had had a few 'jars' with Jack at the Pipemakers', had worked up a good appetite and now he could smell roast lamb. After a quick wash, he settled himself down at the dining-room table and began to read the front page of the newspaper, without bothering to unfold it fully.

'I see we're on the move,' he called out. 'Start of a great attack! It's the Somme at last.'

'Oh yes?' Mrs Mack called back. It was George's habit to discuss the day's headlines with her and he always assumed she had not read them. In fact she read the paper for herself while he was out, unfolding and then refolding it with great care to preserve its pristine appearance. 'Oh yes?' was her stock answer to his comments.

'About time, too,' he shouted. 'Give the Huns a bit of their own medicine.'

'That's right, sir,' she agreed.

The housekeeper brought in the joint and then returned with peas and roast potatoes. George noticed vaguely that the table setting seemed more elaborate than usual – milk jug and sugar bowl, cup, saucer and spoon – but he paid no real attention.

'Smells good,' he remarked.

'Thank you, sir. I know you like a bit of lamb. Nice lean shoulder. I'll just fetch the mint sauce.'

She came in with the sauce and a gravy boat. Then she went to the sideboard drawer, took out a white napkin rolled in a silver ring and laid it beside his plate.

'Might as well do the thing properly,' she remarked and left the room, resisting the urge to run.

Once safely back in the kitchen, she put a hand to her thumping heart and wished she had confided in Sarah Coulsden instead of taking matters into her own hands.

George cut three generous slices of meat and heaped the plate with peas and potatoes; he added gravy and put a large forkful into his mouth. When he caught sight of the table napkins he grinned. Mrs Mack was a queer old bird; he hadn't bothered with such niceties since Hettie's death, but now he unrolled the white linen square and laid it across his knees. A forkful of vegetables followed the lamb into his mouth. So, they were beginning a new offensive. If the Tommies could take the Somme . . .

Something – he would never know exactly what – made him lay down his knife and pick up the napkin ring. It had been recently polished, he could see. Frowning a little, he peered at the initials: H.M.C.

The food he was swallowing went down the wrong way and he began to cough and splutter, gasping for air. It *couldn't* be! A cold surge of adrenalin swept through him, followed by a moment of deadly exhaustion. He felt on the point of collapse and his hand shook as he studied the slim silver band, hoping to reassure himself that he was mistaken.

But there was no mistake.

'It's *hers*!' he muttered. 'But how?'

The fork fell into the plate, splashing gravy on to the tablecloth. A terrible suspicion filled his mind, robbing him of breath. Reluctantly, he let his eyes move to the sugar bowl and recognised the tongs. The spoon in the saucer *had* to be the missing apostle!

'Jesus!' he thought. He tried to think coherently, but his mind was paralysed. How? Who had done it? Hell! He took a great gulp of air. Mrs Mack – she had laid the table – had *she* found them? Had she guessed? Could she *know*? Listening, he was aware of the absence of clatter from the kitchen. She was listening! Waiting. George swallowed painfully because his throat was dry. Acting on impulse, he called, 'Mrs Mack. Come in here, would you?'

When the housekeeper entered the room he tried to discern from her expression how much she had guessed, but she kept her eyes on a point immediately below his chin and he found it impossible to read them. Her mouth was set in a firm line and she folded her arms across her chest as always.

He picked up the sugar tongs. 'Aren't these the tongs that disappeared?' he asked innocently.

'Yes, sir. They did, sir.'

'And the napkin ring and the spoon. When did they turn up?'

'A few weeks ago, sir. Julia found them in the garden shed.'

'How very odd.'

'Yes, sir. That's what I thought.'

Her gaze did not waver and only an almost imperceptible tremor in her voice revealed her anxiety.

'In the garden shed,' he repeated. 'I wonder how they got there?'

'I don't know, I'm sure, sir,' said Mrs Mack. 'They were wrapped in brown paper. Someone had made a little parcel of them and stuffed it down behind the old linoleum.'

George decided to risk a confrontation. 'Eunice, I suppose,' he said. 'That silly girl. Whatever made her do such a stupid thing?'

There was a long pause, during which the housekeeper stared woodenly at the carpet between them.

'Do you think it was Eunice?' he persisted.

'It's not my place to say what I think,' she answered.

'But *do* you?'

'No, sir. I don't believe it was Eunice.'

He took a few deep breaths to calm himself, aware that whatever he said now might prove crucial.

'Well, it's too late to do much about it now,' he said at last. 'Least said, soonest mended.'

She raised her eyes suddenly and looked at him directly. 'I told Julia it was to be our secret,' she said calmly.

'Oh, did you? Good! I think you did the right thing, Mrs Mack. We don't want to go upsetting people, do we? Mrs Coulsden's dead and we can't bring her to life again with a silver spoon and a napkin ring.'

'No, sir,' agreed the housekeeper.

'Well, all's well that ends well. That's what they say.' He managed a shaky smile.

'They *say* that, sir,' said Mrs Mack in the tone of one who chose to disagree with the axiom.

George hesitated. 'Don't you think so?' he asked.

'Not my place to say, sir.'

'No, it isn't.' A great weight was lifting from his shoulders and George felt like a drowning man grasping an outstretched hand. He picked up the knife and fork and cut off a piece of meat.

'Nice bit of lamb, this,' he said.

'Their meat's always reliable. Poor Mrs Coulsden wouldn't shop anywhere else.'

'No. Well, that will be all, thank you, Mrs Mack.'

'Yes, sir.'

She went out, closing the door behind her with exaggerated care. George laid down his knife and fork and let out his breath slowly.

'Agnes bloody Dengate!' he muttered. 'Sometimes I wish to God I'd never set eyes on you and that's the truth!'

CHAPTER SEVEN

When Julia was seven, her grandmother arranged a small birthday party for her to be held at South View. Invitations were sent to Leo, aged twelve, and Ben, now nearly eight, and to Mrs Mack who had also been asked to make the birthday cake. This was a large round sponge filled with jam and cream, covered with deep pink icing on which 'JULIA 7' were picked out in tiny silver balls. Mrs Mack came in person to deliver it half-way through the morning of the birthday and Julia, her grandmother and the housekeeper were in the process of exclaiming over it when George arrived unexpectedly. He appeared agitated and, after a few polite but unenthusiastic words about the birthday cake, told his mother that he had some news for her and wanted to talk in private.

'News for me?' Sarah repeated, immediately apprehensive.

Mrs Mack, who had overheard him, tightened her lips. 'Well, I can take myself off now,' she said. 'I've brought the cake and if that's all that's required of me . . .'

'Oh, no!' cried Sarah. 'Won't you stay a little? I'm sure Julia would like to show you her new dolls' house, wouldn't you, Julia?'

Julia nodded.

'There, you see? We can't let you go just yet.' Sarah forced a smile although her mind was racing. 'Take Mrs Mack up to your room, Julia,' she suggested, 'while I talk to your papa for a moment.'

When they were gone, she turned to George who looked distinctly ill at ease and her heart sank.

'Look, mother,' said George. 'Why don't you sit down?'

'I'm perfectly all right standing up.'

'But I just think you'd be better . . . look, we can both sit down.'

To her surprise he threw himself into the nearest armchair and waited for her to do the same. Sarah's misgivings grew. 'Just tell me, George,' she said. 'What is it?'

'When you're sitting down, mother. Please!'

'Oh, for heaven's sake! What nonsense!' She sat down on an upright chair. 'There. Now tell me!'

Immediately she had sat down her son leapt to his feet and whirled to face the window.

'I want to get married, mother,' he said, speaking very rapidly, 'and I'd like your approval. You may not like her, but that can't be helped. A hell of a lot of tongues will wag, but I don't care. I've made up my mind—'

'You want to marry again!'

Hearing the tremor in his mother's voice, George swung round to face her. She was very pale and the hand that covered her mouth trembled slightly.

'Yes.' He swallowed and gabbled on, 'I've been thinking about it for some time now and Julia needs a mother. Not that you aren't good to her – I don't mean that. Of course you are, but I can't go on any longer with this thing hanging over me.'

'Which thing?' asked Sarah. 'Don't gabble on so, George. I've been telling you not to gabble since you were a boy. You're not making any sense, George, and I don't know what you're talking about. Stop prowling about and explain this "thing".'

George's expression puzzled her. How, she wondered, does a mother lose touch with her children? She read guilt, fear and defiance in his eyes . . . and there was something else, an emotion she could not identify. Seeing his distress gave her courage and she clasped her hands in her lap and waited for him to speak.

'George!' she said again when he gave no answer. 'Who is this woman you want to marry and why do you think I shall disapprove of her?'

'Because you will,' he told her. 'You will all disapprove, but it won't make any difference. I want to marry her. I *must*!'

'Must?' She pounced on the word. 'There's no *must* about it.'

He threw himself down into the recently vacated chair and groaned.

'George? Are you all right?' she demanded.

'Yes, Mother. It's Agnes Dengate, she's with child again.'

Closing his eyes to avoid seeing her expression, he heard the rustle of her clothes as she rose to her feet and knew that she stood glowering down at him.

'Agnes Dengate?' she cried. 'The one who killed poor Hettie? Now, just you listen to me, George. If you intend to take that creature into your home – Hettie's home – and think you're going

to share it with Julia, you are very much mistaken. Julia does not
need that kind of woman to be her stepmother, nor does she need
a brood of illegitimate half-sisters or stepchildren or whatever you
call them. Hettie's money was left to Julia. The poor soul would
turn in her grave at the very idea of this upstart Agnes stepping
into *her* shoes and enjoying *her* money!'

George jumped to his feet and faced her. 'You can't stop me!'
he cried.

'I can try,' she told him, 'and don't think I won't. Why, it would
be all over Rye! Think of the scandal and what it would do to Julia.
If you put this cheap woman and her children above your own
flesh and blood, then—'

'Mother, Emily *is* my flesh and blood!' shouted George. 'Emily
is my daughter and Agnes is right; she deserves a father. It's
bloody ridiculous. Julia's with you, Emily and Agnes are stuck out
there and I live at Hilders Cliff with Mrs Mack! I think it's time
we got together and made a new start.'

'My God, George,' said Sarah, 'you astonish me! Agnes and
her brats sharing a home with Julia? It's a disgusting idea. If your
father was alive, he'd beat some sense into you.'

'He could try!' cried George, 'but he didn't have much luck the
last time he pushed me around.' He had gone too far this time and
his mother slapped him resoundingly across the face.

'Don't you speak that way of the dead, George Coulsden!' she
warned him furiously. 'You would have done better not to remind
me of that. When I think of all I've done for you! Maybe Harold
was right and maybe you don't deserve a share of his money.
Maybe you don't deserve *Silver Lady*. No, don't you dare interrupt me. I shall have my say and then you can get out of my house.
If you hadn't fooled around with Agnes, Hettie would be alive
today. I hold the pair of you entirely responsible. And before you
decide to defy me, George, let me remind you that I am the
executor of Hettie's will and I can make things very difficult for
you if I so wish.'

He faced her, his eyes wild, his voice loud and ugly with rage.

'But you can't keep my daughter away from me!' he shouted.
'You can't keep Julia from me. I could take her to live with Agnes
at Winchelsea Beach – think of the scandal then! Oh yes! Think
how you would all like *that*! You and Cicely and that bloody
sanctimonious Jane! You'd all get together and tear me to shreds,
but I could do it if I wanted to. If you drive me hard enough. If you

force me into a corner!' His voice broke suddenly. 'Oh, for God's sake, Mother, what else am I to do? Agnes is not a bad woman; she's put up with a hell of a lot and now she's having another kid. It might be a boy, you see. A son. I would want a son to have my name. There's no reason to leave them stuck out there in that God-forsaken place when I've a home for them. Julia has no mother and you're not going to live for ever – then what will happen to Julia? They'd get on, the two girls. Emily likes her and they would soon—'

'Emily *likes* her?' cried Sarah. 'You mean they've met? Julia and this . . . this Emily?' She choked on the word.

'Yes, they've met.' He had not meant to tell her that, but now it was said.

Sarah put a hand to her heart suddenly and bowed her head.

'Mother? Are you all right?' he asked anxiously.

'Let me sit down, George. Help me. Quickly!'

He guided her into the chair and watched helplessly as she struggled to regain control of her wildly beating heart.

'Mother?' he repeated.

'I'm all right, George,' she said at last, 'but no thanks to you. I just felt dizzy for a minute.'

'But shall I call someone?'

'No, George. Don't fuss. I tell you I'm all right, it was probably just the shock. Don't look at me like that. I'm not dead yet; far from it. It will take more than a shock to get rid of me, George, and God only knows I've had enough shocks in my time. You boys have not been . . .' She stopped abruptly, aware that she was wandering from the matter at hand, and fixed him with a stern look which at least reassured him of her recovered health. 'Does Stan know about all this? About this second child? And this scheme of yours? And Jack? Who else knows?'

'I've told no one. I wanted to—'

'Well, more's the pity, then. One of them might have knocked some sense into you. Oh George, you always were so headstrong, but this is going too far and I can't let it go on. No, I have made up my mind: that woman is *not* going to move into Hettie's shoes.'

'But you can't stop us living together,' he repeated wearily. 'You can't stop us from marrying either. We're both free.'

'She's responsible for Hettie's death! I could stand up in church and say so!'

'You wouldn't dare!' he gasped.

'Try me, George,' said Sarah, her voice low and even. 'I still know right from wrong and it is not right for that woman to profit in any way from Hettie's death.'

'Hettie didn't have to die!' he shouted, ashen-faced. 'She chose to. She could have lived with it . . . could have fought it. It wouldn't be the first time or the last that a woman has known her husband has another woman. It happens all the time and you know it. You just want to punish us!'

George was losing the battle and they both knew it. Once his mother made up her mind she was quite implacable. She had decided in his favour over the matter of Harold's will and she had won. But this time she was against him and he knew, despite his blustering denials, that she would win again.

'Damn and blast you!' he cried through gritted teeth. 'Why can't you give her a chance? Why can't you give *me* a chance? It's all bloody Hettie, but she's dead and I'm still here. What about me and my life? Don't you give a damn about me? Do I have to stay alone for the rest of my life because Hettie's dead?'

'You could find a *decent* woman, George,' said Sarah. 'We would all be delighted for you if you did.'

'How can I?' he shouted, falling into the trap. 'How can I ask any other woman to marry me, eh? What do I say? "Look here, I've got a mistress and two illegitimate children, but I'd like you to marry me and we'll pretend they don't exist." Who the hell would marry me on those terms?'

'There is no need to raise your voice, George,' she told him coldly. 'Maybe you are right. Maybe no decent woman would want a man like you. But that is no excuse for marrying Agnes. I don't want her for a daughter-in-law, thank you, George. No one in the family wants her.'

He opened his mouth to speak, but his mother held up an imperative hand.

'Listen to me, George,' she said, her voice ominously quiet, 'this argument has gone on long enough. It's Julia's birthday and I don't intend to let you or anyone else spoil it for her. My mind is made up. I do not approve of you setting up house with Agnes Dengate. If you do marry her, then she makes an enemy of me – a dangerous enemy, I may say – and she will not be welcome in my house. No, please don't bother to argue with me; I have made myself quite clear. Now as regards Julia, I shall continue to bring her up at South View because I am sure Hettie would have wished it. While I live Julia is my concern, George, and I shall protect her interests for Hettie's sake so long as I am able. I warn you that I shall fight you in court if you try to take her away. Now, please go home and think over what I have said and you will realise it's for your own good. I will *never* approve of women like Agnes Dengate!'

They stared at each other for a moment in silence. George felt crushed, defeated – but he had never really expected anything else. For Sarah's part she was exhausted, upset and afraid that he *would* defy her and marry the wretched Agnes. She had spoken with more confidence than she felt for, ever since he was a child, George had defied her. Twice he had run away from home and twice Harold had gone after him, hauling him back by the scruff of the neck or the seat of his pants! Yet for all his wild ways he was dear to her. When *he* won, she found it in her heart to forgive him and when *she* won, her victories were tinged with regret. Poor foolish George, she thought. But then she hardened her heart. She would not allow a scheming servant to make a fool of one of her sons.

But even as Sarah fixed him with a look of steely determination, a corner of her heart ached for him. 'Go home, George,' she said coldly. 'You do *not* have my approval. There is nothing more to be said.'

'Look—' he began.

'Go *home*, George. You will not marry that wretched Agnes and that's an end to it.'

He uttered a strangled oath and left the room, slamming the door behind him.

*

Julia looked very attractive in her new blue party frock and Sarah watched her with satisfaction. As predicted at her birth, George's daughter had inherited the Gooding looks. Though less sturdy in build and with narrow frame, she had long legs. Young Julia, thought Sarah, was as fair as any Gooding before her, with dark blue eyes and long silvery lashes. Her pale hair was fine and straight and there was a delicacy about her appearance that was at odds with her behaviour – which on occasions was more boisterous than Sarah thought seemly. Sarah had already made up her mind that Julia would be her success story. God willing, she would see to it that the child married well, perhaps a professional man. Winifred had been so foolish to take Ernest as a husband. She did not have Julia's looks, of course, but she could have chosen better for herself. Sarah blamed Cicely for allowing that friendship to develop. True, the young couple seemed happy enough but that was not the point; she could have been just as happy with someone more suitable.

Mrs Mack lit the candles on the birthday cake and beamed round the table at the children's faces.

'There now!' she said, standing back to admire her handiwork. 'What do you all think of that, eh? Our little Julia's seventh birthday!' She turned to Sarah who stood behind the chairs, watching. 'Seven years old! I can't believe it. Where have the years gone, ma'am? I'm sure I don't know!'

'I don't either,' agreed Sarah.

Sarah's housekeeper came in with a second jug of lemonade. Although unmarried, she was known as Mrs Tooks and had been with Sarah for nearly forty years.

'Oh, that's a lovely cake!' she cried. 'Really pretty. Oh, Mrs Mack, you are clever!'

'Now then, Julia,' said Cicely. 'You'll have to take a deep breath and see if you can blow out the candles in one puff.'

'*I* can!' cried Ben, 'because I'm bigger than Julia! I'm nine. I'll blow them out for you, Ju.'

'No, thank you, Ben,' said Sarah. 'You must let Julia blow them out because it's her birthday.'

'And don't scowl so, Ben,' his mother chided him. 'You will have a turn to blow out candles when it's your own birthday,'

'But that's not until December!' he wailed, his mouth puckering.

'Good heavens, you're not going to cry, I hope?' said Cicely. 'A big boy like you?'

Julia stared round-eyed at the glowing candles.

In spite of the new party dress, the cake and the presents, she felt a deep sense of loss. Her beloved Papa was not at the party and she wanted him there. Mama Sarah loved her and so did Mrs Mack, but they did not *belong* to her like Papa. Aunt Cicely was pretty and always made a fuss of her, but Julia did not like her tinkly way of laughing and *she* did not belong either. Leo was just Leo and could do no wrong in Julia's eyes and when she was grown-up she knew she would marry him. Ben was good fun and he played 'Snakes and Ladders' with her and nearly always let her win, although he was cleverer. The guests at her party were the wrong people, she decided sadly, and the whole birthday was spoilt.

Tears pricked her eyelids, but she lowered her head and blinked them back. She was seven and that was a tremendous age to be. Girls of seven, Julia was sure, should not cry. She looked around her at all the faces turned expectantly towards her. Why was it, she wondered, that nobody realised that all she needed to make her birthday was her beloved Papa . . . and Emily. Since her one and only visit to her father's other family, Julia had been obsessed with the idea of her 'sister' and thought about her constantly. She plied her father with questions and thus learned a great deal about Emily, although her requests to visit them again had met with reluctant refusals. According to her father, Agnes suffered from headaches and that made it impossible for visitors to call. Julia found it all very mystifying. But according to Papa, Emily always sent her love to Julia and sometimes she sent little messages too: 'Tell Julia I'm longing to see her again' or 'Tell Julia I can write my name.' Julia treasured these messages and repeated them again and again each night before she went to sleep. She had taken the absent baby sister to her heart and so Emily too 'belonged'. Papa and Emily were Julia's family and she wanted to share the birthday party with them. Without them she felt cheated and at odds with the world. Why did no one understand? She could ask for Papa, she knew, but she could never ask for Emily because Emily was a secret.

'Where's Papa?' she asked at last. 'I want Papa to help me blow them out.'

Sarah's heart sank. 'He's at sea, Julia,' she said. 'I've told you that already. He's away at sea catching some fish and he'll come and see you when he gets back. Now, you must blow out the candles like a clever girl or no one can have a slice of cake!'

She glanced hastily at Cicely, who earlier had expressed surprise at George's absence and had obviously disbelieved Sarah's hastily improvised explanation. Sarah had said nothing to anyone about her conversation with George, because she did not know what to do for the best. Possibly Jack and Stan might come down heavily on George's side and in favour of the marriage, although she knew the wives would not. George had not returned to the house after his furious departure earlier and she could only surmise that he had gone back to Agnes to make his report.

Julia frowned. 'I want Papa,' she insisted.

'She idolises that man,' said Cicely, her tone disapproving. None of Cicely's children adored Jack the way Julia adored George, but that was only to be expected, she thought resentfully, for Jack had less and less time for them as the years went by and the boatyard absorbed more of his time and energy.

Julia pressed her lips tightly together and stared around defiantly. 'I want *Papa*,' she insisted once more.

'You'll have to hurry up,' coaxed Mrs Mack. 'Look, all the wax is running down into the icing and soon there will be no candles left for you to blow out.'

Julia swung her foot and kicked the table from underneath, making the cutlery jump and clattering the crockery.

'Julia!' cried Sarah, aghast. 'Is that the proper way to behave? After all I've told you!'

Mrs Mack saw disaster looming and said hurriedly, 'Now do be a good girl, Julia. You're a *birthday* girl, remember?'

'I want Papa,' Julia repeated doggedly.

'He's never missed her birthday before,' said Cicely. 'I wonder what's got into him?'

Sarah hardened her heart. 'If he doesn't choose to come, that's his business,' she said. 'I don't want to discuss it. Now if you won't blow out the candles, Julia, I shall ask someone else to do it for you.'

'Me!' cried Ben and Leo together.

'Well, Julia?'

Julia glanced at her grandmother and Sarah thought, 'She may have the Gooding looks, but she also has their obstinacy!'

Cicely tutted disapprovingly and Mrs Tooks said suddenly, 'I've got a good idea.' She looked at Sarah. 'Why don't they all blow together? One giant puff!'

'Oh yes, that would be great fun!' Sarah agreed.

Julia, however, shook her head stubbornly, but at that moment there were footsteps on the path and the door-bell jangled.

'Papa!' cried Julia, her expression changing at once.

'He wouldn't ring the bell,' said Cicely, puzzled, as Mrs Tooks hurried to the front door. They heard a scuffle and the housekeeper's voice saying, 'Here! Who said you could – you come back!' Then the dining-room door flew open and Agnes Dengate stood before them, clutching a whimpering Emily by the hand.

Trembling violently, Sarah rose slowly to her feet as the rest of the party stared in astonishment at the intruders.

'Oh, don't get up!' cried Agnes sarcastically. She glanced at Sarah. 'It's only that pregnant slut Agnes and her bastard Emily – no need for you lot to show any respect. I'm just George's bit on the side.' She glared round at everyone, hushing her daughter who, awed by the tension in the room, had begun to cry. 'I thought I'd bring the birthday girl a little surprise – you might call it a birthday present.'

Sarah found her voice. 'Get out of here at once!' she cried furiously. 'Get out of my house!'

Cicely was utterly bewildered. 'It's . . . it's Agnes Dengate,' she stammered. 'The one—'

Mrs Mack said, 'Agnes! What do you think you're doing, barging in like this? Have you lost your wits, girl?'

Agnes rounded on her. 'Don't you "girl" me, Mrs Mack,' she hissed. 'Don't try that la-di-da stuff on me 'cos I won't wear it. As soon as I'm mistress you'll be out on your ear, see, and you'll go so fast your feet won't touch the ground!'

'How dare you?' Mrs Mack was outraged.

Sarah said, 'Stop this, Agnes. I demand that you leave this house at once.'

Cicely turned to her mother-in-law. 'But what's going on? I don't see how she has the nerve to come bursting in like this.'

'No,' cried Agnes. 'None of you do, except *her*.' She stabbed a finger towards Sarah. 'That old bitch knows—'

'How dare you speak to my mother-in-law like that?' protested Cicely. 'This is disgraceful. I think we should send for a constable.'

'*Do* you? Well, before I go I have something to tell you.' Agnes shook Emily roughly. 'Stop it, Emily! There's nothing to cry about.'

'Don't!' cried Julia and slipping down from the chair, she ran towards Agnes and pummelléd her with her fists. 'Don't you hurt Emily!'

Before anyone could intervene, Agnes gave her a violent push and Julia stumbled backwards and nearly fell, but Mrs Mack caught her and held her tightly as she wriggled to free herself and renew the attack.

'Bloody little savage!' said Agnes triumphantly. 'I told George, but he wouldn't believe me. Out of hand, that's what she is. Spoilt rotten by her grandmother. Don't think I want her because I don't. Spiteful little brat!'

Mrs Tooks looked helplessly towards her mistress. 'Shall I telephone for a constable?' she enquired hopefully.

Agnes swung round on her. 'Don't bother,' she told her, 'because I'm not staying long. Just long enough to tell you what George is too scared to tell you all – that him and me are getting married. In three weeks' time. Oh yes, mother-in-law, we *are*!' She grinned at Sarah with malice. 'Three weeks from now! You may scare your son, but you don't scare me. The banns will be called. So if any one of you tries to stop us, by God, I'll make you sorry. With my bare fists, if I have to.'

Sarah had sunk back into her chair. Mrs Mack still struggled to restrain Julia who, red-faced and furious, was shouting at Agnes and threatening to tell her father. Emily was now bawling at the top of her voice and Mrs Tooks edged nervously towards the door, anticipating physical violence. Leo and Ben watched the scene with frightened eyes. Leo plucked up courage to say, 'Don't you speak to my grandmama like that,' but regretted it immediately. Agnes swung round on him as Cicely moved forward to put an arm protectively around each of her children.

'Oh, your *grandmama*, is she?' Agnes demanded. 'Well, for your information she's also grandmama to Emily and *this*.' She slapped a hand to her abdomen and Cicely gasped.

'You disgusting creature,' she cried, 'bursting into someone's house and carrying on like a mad-woman!'

'Oh dear, oh dear!' Agnes mocked, hands on hips. 'High and mighty Cicely. So you're going to be my sister-in-law. Well, that's my bad luck, you stuck-up bitch. Oh yes, don't look at me like that. I've heard all about you from Georgie Porgie! Ah, that's scared you, hasn't it? That's put the wind up your prissy sails! Yes, Georgie Porgie talks too much when he's had a few, but I expect you know that already. Coulsdens!' She spat derisively. 'You think you're the bloody cat's whiskers, the lot of you. Well, I'll have you know that I'm worth any two of you and I've as much right to be a Coulsden as anyone. *And* I will be, so help me God!'

'This is preposterous . . .' began Cicely again.

Mrs Mack thought the scene quite unsuitable for a child of tender years and pulled the still-struggling Julia out of the room as, quite undaunted, Agnes went on.

'I'm sick of being stuck in a rotten little shack and I'm sick of being hard up. I'm sick of George telling me "one day" and I'm sick of promises and precious little else. Hettie's dead. All right, I'm sorry, but I've got problems and I've got feelings. My kid wants a father and I want a husband and George Coulsden owes it to us. So you lot can like it or lump it—' Her voice broke and she struggled for a moment to regain her composure.

'Like it or lump it, George Coulsden is going to marry me. We've been to see the vicar. If you lot decide to give us a chance, all well and good. We just *might* even be friends. If you don't, by Christ, I'll fight you all the way!'

Sarah raised her head and asked shakily, 'Where is my son?'

Agnes tossed her head scornfully. 'Getting drunk. What d'you expect? You know him as well as I do. Weak as water, that son of yours. You should have brought him up to have more guts. After what happened this morning he's too scared to tell you, so I've done it for him. Now I'm going.' She pulled Emily towards her, brushed the tears from her face and turned to go.

'Oh yes,' she said, pausing at the dining-room door. 'You're all invited to the wedding!' Then she went out and they all stared at each other wide-eyed as the front door slammed violently.

There was a long, shattered silence and then everyone began to talk at the same time. Mrs Mack came back into the room with a subdued Julia and, blinking back her own tears, began to scrape the pool of sooty candles from the top of the spoiled birthday cake.

That night Julia made the first entry in her new diary:

18 July 1917
   Today I am 7. I Had prezents. I Had this diry. Agnes came and Emily crid. END

                                    *

The day of the wedding dawned bright and clear and Agnes woke with a feeling of triumph. At last George Coulsden was going to make an honest woman of her. Her son would be born in wedlock. Corny the words may be, she thought, but an honest woman was what she longed to be. She lay beside George in Marsh Cottage, trying not to wake him, savouring the knowledge that before the day was out she would be Mrs George Coulsden. The *second* Mrs George Coulsden, she amended ruefully, but that was all in the past. After much argument, George had bought her a loose-fitting cream silk dress and a matching hat which she had piled with artificial flowers. She had wanted to wear white – a long dress with a veil – but George had refused to agree. Emily was to be bridesmaid and her dress, made by Agnes's mother, was of bright pink taffeta.

Agnes and George had quarrelled about the wedding because Agnes wanted to 'show Rye what a wedding should be' – a lavish affair with all the trimmings. George was anxious to keep it as quiet as possible, although he wanted Julia to be present. Sarah resisted that idea and Agnes was torn between supporting George in order to spite his mother and keeping the beautiful Julia away from the plainer Emily. She had no wish for comparisons to be made between her daughter and Hettie's and finally added her own objections to Julia being present. Nobody asked Julia what *she* wanted to do.

Invitations to the wedding were sent out to all the Coulsdens, but they all declined to attend. Sarah wrote a scathing letter by way of reply; Jack and Cicely ignored the invitation altogether; Jane wrote a polite letter saying they were unable to be present. Later, however, George persuaded Stanley to act as best man and this caused another family rift – Jack, Cicely, Jane and Sarah uniting against him and declaring that he had let down the family. Stanley however insisted that, as George's older brother, he should set aside his personal feelings and stand by him on this one occasion.

So, thought Agnes, she was going to be married!

'And about time, too,' she muttered. She would be Mrs Coulsden, a respectable married woman, and people would have to show proper respect whatever they might think of her. She would live in the house above Hilders Cliff and she would not have to mend nets or go out in all weathers to gather driftwood. George would come home in between fishing trips and when the boy was born the four of them would go out into the town and be seen together. No more skulking in dark corners. If Julia wanted to come to tea occasionally, Agnes thought she would allow it, but obviously Julia would not see her father as often as before because his new family would come first. She turned her head to look at the man beside her. 'Yes, George,' she thought, 'you've had it all your own way long enough. Now it's my turn.'

She gave him a nudge with her elbow. 'Hey! Wake up, Georgie Coulsden. We're getting married, remember? Today's the day!'

As he opened his eyes, she planted a quick kiss on his stubbly cheek and slid out of bed.

*

'Dearly beloved, We are gathered together here in the sight of God and in the face of this congregation to join together this man and this woman in holy matrimony . . .'

Julia, Leo and Ben tiptoed into the church and crouched down out of sight behind the last pew at the back. Breathless from running, they exchanged conspiratorial glances. They were supposed to be at the barber's where the boys were due to have their hair trimmed and Julia, spending the day with Cicely, had begged to go with them. Twelve-year-old Leo had suggested they sneak in and watch the wedding. No heads turned their way and the three children eyed each other gleefully. Attendance at the wedding was strictly forbidden them, but as Leo had argued, George *was* Julia's father and surely she had a right to see her own father married, even if it was to 'that woman'. The backs of the small congregation were towards them as the children peered over the top of the pew. Only the vicar faced them, but his eyes were on the book in front of him. No one was aware of the children's presence.

The vicar continued, '. . . And therefore is not by any, to be enterprised nor taken in hand unadvisedly, lightly or wantonly . . .'

The last words stirred an echo in Leo's mind. Wanton. That's what Cicely had called Agnes. Julia's father was marrying a wanton woman!

'I hate her,' Julia told Leo in a whisper. 'I do!'

'She's *evil*,' he whispered back. 'She's an evil, wanton woman.'

Ben said, 'Look at her stupid *hat*.' They all took another peep and giggled.

'She looks stupid all over,' said Leo. 'Uncle George is stupid to marry her.'

'He is not stupid,' hissed Julia. 'My father is *not* stupid!'

'All right, then, he's not,' said Leo. 'But keep your voice down, can't you?'

'. . . If any man can show any just cause why they may not lawfully be joined together, let him now speak or else hereafter forever hold his peace.'

'Emily looks stupid, too,' whispered Ben, to please Julia. 'She looks like a fat pink pig.'

Nervously, Julia smothered another giggle. She wished they had not come to the wedding because she knew that if they were discovered there would be trouble, but Leo had suggested it and he was her adored cousin. Leo's word was law. Ben was now nearly eight and she loved him, too, but her feelings for him paled into insignificance beside her adoration of Leo, whom she would have followed to the ends of the earth.

Taking another look, she saw the plump back of Emily in the pink dress and tried to imagine herself in Emily's place. If her father had married anyone else *she* could have been the brides-maid. Sighing, she visualised herself in a buttercup yellow dress with a posy of rosebuds and a circle of flowers in her hair. If only her father had married someone else, someone who was not 'that woman' and who was not wanton or evil. Julia found herself wishing that she' and Emily could have been bridesmaids to-gether. She frequently imagined herself and Emily as sisters, sharing secrets, laughing together, although she knew she could never have admitted the fantasy. She pitied Emily her terrible mother.

The vicar's voice rose and fell and all eyes were on George and Agnes. Julia saw Uncle Stan – unfamiliar in his dark suit – and recognised most of the fishermen. Jean Dessin was there too. Soon they would all go back to the house on Hilders Cliff, where they would have beer to drink and wonderful things to eat and everyone would make a fuss of Agnes Dengate with her stupid hat and her stupid bobbly curls and she would smile at everyone and maybe kiss Julia's father. They would be married for ever and ever.

'. . . So many as are coupled together otherwise than by God's word doth allow are not joined together by God, neither is their matrimony lawful . . .'

Leo turned his head to whisper in Julia's ear and her eyes widened as she listened. She shook her head, but he nodded. Suddenly she scrambled to her feet and, evading Ben's out-stretched hand, ran out into the central aisle. At the sound of her footsteps, the vicar stopped speaking and all heads turned to-wards her.

'Agnes Dengate is wanton!' she shouted. 'And she killed my mother! It's true! Ask Mama Sarah. Ask Aunt Cicely. She might kill my father, too.'

Charged with emotion, her voice rang out in the hollow air of the lofty roof and Julia was aware of a buzz of dismay. She saw her father's shocked face and beside him Agnes Dengate, her face scarlet with rage and embarrassment. The vicar was blinking his eyes as though in disbelief. Julia looked round her. Jean Dessin was laughing, but from behind her she heard Ben's frantic plea, 'Come back here, you little idiot!' She ignored him. Now that the words were out and everyone was looking at her, she felt a deep sadness. It would make no difference, she knew. She was only a little girl and grown-up people never listened to little girls. But she had said it. Agnes Dengate had killed her mother. Now no one could blame Julia if Agnes Dengate killed her father too.

Suddenly she caught sight of Emily and saw the tears gathering. Emily, six years old, knew only that her father's other daughter had interrupted the wedding and had spoiled her own and her mother's big day. With a cry of anguish she hurled the first thing that came to hand – which was her posy – straight at Julia and then burst into tears. Julia had a confused impression of raised voices, some smothered laughter, loud threats and tears as she stooped to pick up the flowers.

'Leave them!' hissed Ben. 'Julia! Leave them and come on out!' As her father approached, his face like thunder, she dropped the posy and ran back to where loyal Ben waited; then they fled from the scene and ran to the barber's shop. Leo, having masterminded the débâcle, had made good his escape and was already sitting in the barber's chair having his hair cut. Julia stood speechlessly while both boys had their hair cut, then they walked home together. On the way Julia said, 'Poor Emily!' but neither boy answered her and apart from those two words no reference was ever made to what had taken place.

For days they waited for retribution but none came. George assumed rightly that the children would not tell their parents what had happened and he had no wish to give the rest of his family the satisfaction of knowing that Julia had ruined the occasion. Even to Julia he said nothing, not knowing what to say and not wishing to drive a further wedge between himself and his daughter. Stanley did not tell Jane because he knew she would gloat. Only the second Mrs Coulsden spoke of the affair and she did that often and with devastating effect; she would, she vowed, never forgive or forget.

*

The marriage which began so ingloriously continued in the same way. Mrs Mack had given in her notice and had left George in order to take up a new position as companion to an elderly friend of Cicely's. Agnes interviewed the only applicant for her job and was deeply mortified when, having been offered the position, the girl declined it. After that rebuff, she declared herself 'hale and hearty enough' to do her own housework and George wisely let the matter rest there. He insisted that Julia come to tea with them once a fortnight, but these visits were not successful – everyone concerned felt ill at ease and only Emily looked forward to them, a fact she kept strictly to herself for fear of her mother's disapproval.

Agnes awaited the birth of her second child with a touching eagerness. She had convinced herself that it would be a boy and that in some miraculous way his birth would put right all that was wrong in her life with George. She had vague but rosy dreams about a wonderfully happy and united family and generously included Julia in this picture. Once she had given George the son he longed for, she felt sure that Julia would take second if not third place in his affections and then she, Agnes, would feel more kindly disposed towards the child. Her favourite daydream was one in which she magnanimously appealed to George on Julia's behalf, begging him not to neglect the girl.

All these dreams were rudely shattered however when, two weeks late, she finally went into a prolonged and difficult labour and gave birth to a silent, breathless son. *Stillborn.* The terrible black word echoed inside her head as she lay back on the pillows, weak and exhausted, and saw the compassion in the midwife's eyes.

'Give him to me,' she had insisted. 'Let me hold him. I won't let him be dead.'

But the small frail body which she cradled in her arms had not been warmed into life by her frantic kisses and her grief was total. The loss of her long-awaited son affected her spirits and resulted in a deterioration in her relations with George; moreover, her previous resentment of Julia crystallised into hostility. George was forced to put a stop to Julia's visits and *Silver Lady* became their rendezvous, these meetings being very happy times for the little girl.

*

One day in October Julia, Jean Dessin and young Charles Bird –
now known as Chick – were sitting together on a pile of coiled
ropes on *Silver Lady*, which rocked gently in the wake of the
Mona Lisa as she passed them on her way in. Jean raised his hand
in friendly salute as the old lugger skipper, Billy Dann, called out
'It's cushy for some folk!' and shook his head, grinning. *Silver
Lady* had been first back into harbour and her catch had already
been unloaded and boxed; now it was waiting on the jetty to be
collected. The orange-brown net, washed clean, was draped over
the side to dry in the sunshine and the deck had already been
scrubbed. Julia, Jean and Chick sat amidships, looking towards
the hatch cover, mast and cable chain. Behind them, the deck
stretched towards the lute stern.

'After the war,' Jean told them, 'we will have fun. We will go to
places. I will go back to Belgium.'

'Why will you?' asked Julia. 'I don't want you to go. I want you to
stay here.'

He grinned and shrugged his shoulders. 'Belgium is my home.
My mother and my grandparents are there and I have a little sister
like you.'

'Won't you come back?' she said. 'Not ever?'

'Perhaps I will one day.'

Julia let her gaze roam over the newly scrubbed planking of the
deck as she listened to the metallic music of the halyards overhead. She breathed in the tangy smell of fish, wood, iron and
sunshine. On *Silver Lady* she felt content and safe, that she
belonged, that the time spent aboard was precious to her. Aboard
the boat she felt secure, able to deal with the small world that
stretched from side to side and from end to end of the familiar
deck. Over the years she had explored every inch of it and had
crawled into every nook and cranny at one time or another. She
knew where the ropes were stowed, where the water tank was
housed; she knew all the names.

'Ask me,' she begged Jean, wanting to impress young Chick
with her cleverness. 'Ask me!' she cried. 'You listen, Chick.'

Jean grinned and his dark eyes regarded her humorously. He
was a handsome young man, slimly built with silky blond hair
and delicate features. Lazily he pointed and the well-loved ritual
began.

'Jib boom!' chanted Julia gleefully. 'Bowsprit! Mizzen mast!'

'*I* can say them,' Chick protested, not wanting to be outdone by a mere girl. 'Mizzen mast! Bowsprit—'

'But I just *told* you,' said Julia crossly. 'You didn't know them before I told you. You *didn't*. Oh Jean, he really didn't!'

Jean lifted his shoulders in a light shrug and said, 'He is learning, Julia. You are his teacher.'

Julia looked from Jean to Chick, who smiled at her nervously. Eunice's son, just five years old, was a stolid child with short legs and a plump round face. His light brown hair waved untidily around his head and he had odd eyes, one brown and one almost yellow. His mother's often expressed anxiety over this defect had given him an apologetic manner.

'Well, then,' Julia said cheerfully, 'I'll say them, Chick, then you copy me. Do you see? Because I know all the names. Now, listen carefully.'

She pointed. 'Mast case—'

Before he could repeat the words, there was a shout from the jetty. 'Charlie Bird! Come down from there at once. How many times have I told you?'

They turned to see Eunice approaching, picking her way carefully round the boxes of fish and along the rough wooden catwalk that linked jetty and boat. Chick jumped to his feet guiltily and threw an appealing look at Jean.

'What is wrong?' Jean asked. 'The boy is doing no harm.'

Eunice halted at the end of the catwalk and glared at Julia.

'That's for me to say,' she told them. 'No son of mine is going to set foot on George Coulsden's boat. I've told the boy time and again. Chick Bird! You come off there at once.'

'But we let him come,' said Julia innocently, misunderstanding the reason for Eunice's anger. 'We said he could come and Papa doesn't mind.'

'Papa! Huh!' She snorted. 'Don't talk to me about your papa, the way he's carried on. I'm particular who my son talks to. Did you hear me, Charlie Bird? I said come off there and I meant it.'

'I was only learning the names . . .' he began, scrambling hastily over the side of the boat.

'I don't care what you were doing. You're to stay off that man's boat.' She seized his arm as soon as he was near enough and slapped the backs of his legs. 'That's for going on George Coulsden's boat!' she told him loudly for the benefit of Jean and Julia and the curious passers-by.

Chick began to cry and Julia ran to the side of the boat, her face flushed with anger.

'You're a mean old cat!' she shouted. 'He wasn't doing anything.' She shook off Jean's restraining hand from her shoulder. 'I'm glad you're not *my* mother, because—'

'*I'm* glad I'm not your mother!' snapped Eunice. 'Your poor mother's well out of it all, if you ask me. If *I* was married to George Coulsden I'd have . . .'

Suddenly Eunice became aware of a shadow across the catwalk and whirled to see George Coulsden standing not a yard away.

'You'd have what?' he asked.

She swallowed. '*I'd* have killed myself,' she told him defiantly.

Julia began to explain to her father that she was only teaching Chick names, but he was not listening to her.

'I'm sorry,' said George to Eunice.

Startled, Eunice looked closely at him and noted the haggard eyes and puffy face. He looks haunted and ill, she thought, with a moment's compassion.

'Sorry for what?' she asked, her voice low.

'Just sorry. For everything. The whole bloody mess.'

'So you should be.'

'He's a nice lad,' said George, glancing at Charlie. He looked into her face for a long minute and then sighed deeply. 'I lost my son,' he whispered.

His breath smelled of whisky. He's a broken man, thought Eunice, but suddenly the thought gave her no satisfaction.

'I heard,' she said. 'It was bad luck.'

'Let him stay.'

'No!' She was not going to let him win *her* over with his persuasive tongue. George Coulsden was jinxed, everyone said so. He couldn't put a foot right and was not to be trusted. She had tried to revenge her own humiliation with her letter to Hettie, but Hettie had died. It was all George's fault, she reminded herself, determined to take none of the blame. His and *hers*, for Agnes must take some of the blame. If their son had died, then maybe that was God's judgement and George Coulsden was suffering now for his wickedness; he was being justly punished for his sins.

She bent down and shook her tearful son. 'D'you hear me, now?' she repeated. 'You stay away from his boat. I won't tell you again. If ever I find you on *Silver Lady* again I'll tell your pa and you'll get a good hiding. *Silver Lady!* Huh! You just stay away,

Charles Bird.' With one last look that encompassed George, Jean and Julia, she stalked away, dragging a still-protesting Charlie behind her.

George watched her go, his shoulders sagging dispiritedly, then he turned to look at Julia. She thought he was going to speak to her, but instead he swung on his heel and strode away. Her mouth trembled and her eyes filled with tears, but then Jean's arm was around her.

'I have my dinner to eat yet,' he reminded her. 'You will share my cheese and bread? I may find an apple also.'

'But Papa—' she began.

Sometimes her father took her up into the town to a café and bought her sausages and mashed potato with thick brown gravy. At weekends or after school when the tide was right, Sarah allowed George to collect his daughter from South View and to keep her for a few hours. Usually they spent the time together on the boat, which either had just returned from or was being prepared for another fishing trip. With so many young men away at the war, *Silver Lady*'s crew now consisted of two old fishermen dragged back from retirement and young Jean Dessin who, forced by circumstances to sell his father's boat, had gratefully taken the job George offered. Every other week, George took Julia to see Emily, but she always resented sharing her father's time, especially there.

Jean shook his head kindly. 'I think your Papa has gone back to the Pipemakers',' he said shrewdly. 'He has business with his friends, eh? We eat together, you and me.'

Julia nodded and five minutes later she was once more sitting with Jean on the coiled rope enjoying the November sunshine, the unpleasantness with Eunice and her father forgotten. She had a square of Cheddar cheese in one hand and a crusty chunk of fresh bread in the other. The feeling of security was slowly returning as the familiar motion of the boat calmed her body and soothed her soul. Around them, the other fishermen unloaded their catch, the river sparkled in the sunshine and the Fishmarket bustled around them.

'Good cheese?' asked Jean, smiling at the silver-haired girl beside him.

'It smells,' she told him, wrinkling her nose, 'but it's good,' she added tactfully. She nibbled at it delicately, having discovered that a large mouthful of bread smothered the strong flavour of the cheese and made it palatable. 'Tell me again, Jean,' she prompted him. 'Tell me again about after the war.'

*

Jack stood back and surveyed the boat's skeleton with narrowed eyes and was amused to see that his young niece did the same, holding her head at a similar angle to his own and pursing her lips in concentration. He nodded his head approvingly and Julia's small head nodded also.

'That's about it,' he said.

'That's about it,' she repeated earnestly.

Keeping his face straight, Jack patted the stern post and Julia, at the far end, patted the stem post. Eighteen feet of keel stretched between the two posts and this was steadied by three rough timber props nailed to an overhead beam. A half-mould wedged against the middle prop indicated the shape to be taken by the side strakes, which would form the boat's hull. Jack had no plans from which to work and blueprints were unknown to him – his years of experience and a 'good eye' would serve him instead. The lowest strake, or garboard, was already in position and with the help of his young assistant he had added two further planks, which were already held in position with copper rivets.

'Right then,' he told her. 'Here we go again.'

The next shaped plank had been coaxed into position, over-lapping the previous one and now held in place with wooden grips. Jack drilled a row of holes and then held out his hand. 'Ten, please,' he demanded and Julia's small fingers scrabbled eagerly in the chest for the two-inch copper fastenings which would hold the planks together. She was counting these into her uncle's hand when Sarah Coulsden came into the shed and set down her basket.

'That foolish man,' she grumbled, seizing a cloth and dusting off a stool. 'Calls himself a butcher and can't tell one piece of fillet from another. He gave Mrs Tooks quite the wrong cut and I have had to take it back *personally*. Poor Mrs Tooks is positively fright-ened of him, it's quite ridiculous.' She sat down on the stool and smiled at Julia. 'Has Julia been a good girl?' she asked.

Jack looked at Julia and feigned surprise. 'A girl? Is that Julia?' he asked. 'Good Lord, I thought it was my new assistant. Well I'm blowed. You're right. I can see now – it *is* Julia.'

Julia beamed at the compliment and looked at her grandmother

to see the effect her uncle's comments had had. She wished her
father could be here also to hear Uncle Jack call her a 'new
assistant'. Perhaps Mama Sarah would tell him later and then
perhaps Papa would tell Emily. Emily might be *living* with Papa
while Julia had to make do with Mama Sarah, but Emily was *never*
Uncle Jack's assistant in the boatyard and Emily would *never*
understand about stern posts and stem posts, Julia consoled
herself. Papa's other daughter would *never* be able to count out
the copper fastenings and having an Uncle Jack was almost as
good as having a father – at least Julia liked to think so. She had
often wondered if Emily was allowed on *Silver Lady* and rather
unkindly hoped she was not.

Sarah started to speak as Jack began to hammer and Julia,
laughing, put her hands over her ears.

'Jack!'

He stopped with hammer poised and looked at his mother
enquiringly.

'I'm talking to you, Jack,' she said crossly.

'I'm listening.'

'I said I've just been talking to Cicely.'

'Oh, yes?'

'And I am very concerned.'

Jack took another rivet and began to hammer it into place.

'Jack!' cried Sarah. 'Will you stop that noise and listen to me? I
want your full attention.'

With an exaggerated sigh he turned from his work, the hammer
still held in his hand.

'And you can put that down,' his mother told him sharply. 'I
want to talk to you about Cicely and about the yard.'

Julia sensed her uncle's unease and felt a surge of resentment
towards her grandmother for interrupting their fun. As Jack laid
down the hammer she threw the remaining rivets back into the
chest with a petulant gesture which her grandmother ignored.

'Cicely seems to know absolutely nothing about the yard,' said
Sarah. 'I simply couldn't believe my ears. I asked her a few simple
questions—'

'You should have asked me,' said Jack. 'Not her.'

'But she's your wife,' Sarah argued. '*I* used to know precisely
what was going on when your father was running the yard. I
understood the accounts and I knew the work that was in hand
and what else was expected to come in. Cicely knows nothing at

all, if I'm to believe what she says, and what is more she doesn't want to know.'

Jack shrugged. 'It's up to her. If she asked me I'd tell her.'

'But she used to know,' insisted Sarah. 'What on earth is wrong, Jack? She's your wife and she *ought* to know. She ought to *care.*'

Jack glanced apprehensively at Julia, but intuitively his young niece was looking at her boots, apparently absorbed in fastening a button.

'I know she should and I wish she would,' he said, 'but since the fire she's been touchy about things. She won't talk about the yard and won't listen if I talk. I don't know what's wrong.' He shrugged again. 'I just give up,' he finished.

Sarah was silent for a moment, digesting this information. 'How d'you mean?' she asked at last. 'That fire was a long time ago now; it's history.'

He hesitated. 'She blames herself,' he said reluctantly, 'because of Ratty. Because they had words, the two of them. She kept saying that if she'd stayed away from the yard it would never have happened.'

Sarah made no attempt to dispute this. 'And so she stopped doing the accounts,' she said. 'Is that what you're saying?'

'That's about it.'

'And *you* do them?'

He nodded.

'Oh dear,' said Sarah. 'You never could add two twos to make four. Oh, poor Cicely! It's guilt, is it?'

'I reckon so, but she won't talk about it. Hasn't for a long time now. "You sort it out, Jack." That's all I get out of her.'

Sarah snorted. 'I'd like to sort *her* out,' she said.

Jack looked up in alarm. 'Now don't you start on her,' he said defensively. 'You'll only make matters worse. Leave it be, Mother, for heaven's sake. It's just the way she is, I'm afraid, and you won't change her now.'

'Maybe, maybe not,' muttered Sarah. 'A ridiculous way to carry on. She ought to know better at her age.'

He coughed suddenly. 'Little pitchers . . . !' he murmured warningly, but Julia seemed to be engrossed in the infinite variety of screws and nails in the old chest.

'So,' said Sarah, 'I'll have to ask you — how are things?'

After a painful silence Jack replied, 'Not good.'

'This boat here?' She nodded towards it.

'For a chap in Hastings,' he told her. 'One of Jane's cousins. But there's precious little else. A couple of minor repairs. A name board. Nothing substantial.'

'Does George know?'

He shook his head. 'What could George do?' he asked. 'What can anyone do? Bloody war drags on—'

'Please watch your language, Jack!'

'Enemy mines in the bay and restrictions on this and that,' he went on. 'Not to mention the harbour mouth! According to George, it's hell's delight getting in and out, it's that choked up with shingle. Talk about neglect – but what can they do? There's no money for dredging because there are no harbour dues. No money for anything. George is not going to admit it, but it's bloody—'

'Jack! I won't tell you again!'

'Sorry, sorry.' He held up his hands placatingly. 'I'm just fed up with it all,' he told her. 'This war – life is never going to be the same again, Mother. Do you realise that? Never. Not for the fishing industry.' He sighed heavily. 'By the time it ends and they do something about the harbour, it's going to be too late for us. We'll all be finished.'

'Don't talk so daft, Jack.' Sarah's sharp tone did not disguise her fear. 'Of course we won't be finished. Coulsdens' yard has been here for more than a century and will still be here another century from now – and don't shake your head at me, Jack.'

'But I'm telling you, Mother,' he said patiently, 'that times are hard and they'll get a darned sight harder. A lot of good men will go under.'

'A lot of good men are dead, Jack,' she told him angrily. 'A great deal of blood has been spilled to keep us free and that sort of talk is unpatriotic. That kind of attitude helps the enemy.'

Jack was slowly shaking his head. 'It's no good, Mother,' he said gently. 'I know how you feel, but you can't change the way things are by refusing to admit what's happening. Whether we like it or not, Coulsdens could go under—'

'*No*, Jack!' she broke in.

'George might go under. Stan might.'

'No!' she cried again. 'I won't listen to this kind of talk.'

'It's not talk,' he said wearily, 'it's facts. You asked me how things are and I'm telling you: they're bad. And as long as the war goes on it will get worse.'

As the silence lengthened Julia turned to face them. 'Uncle Jack, am I still your new assistant?' she asked.

He nodded absent-mindedly, his eyes dark.

'Then why can't we put some more nails in the boat?'

Jack glanced at his mother and after a moment she nodded. 'Just for five more minutes, then,' she told her granddaughter. 'And then we must go home. Mrs Tooks will be wondering where we are.'

Five minutes later she stood up and obediently Julia handed Jack the last of the rivets. 'Can I be your assistant another day?' she asked hopefully.

He gave her nose a playful tweak. 'Of course you can. I can't finish the boat without you, can I?'

'What about Mr Bird?' she asked. 'He helps you.'

Jack leaned forward, drew her into the circle of his arms and whispered, 'You're my number one assistant, but don't tell Tommy – it would only upset him. Understand?'

As Julia nodded he gave her a quick hug and a kiss and she flung her arms round his neck and closed her eyes. With her eyes shut Uncle Jack smelt very much like her adored Papa.

CHAPTER EIGHT

The war ended at last. A cease-fire was ordered and the Armistice was signed on 11 November 1918.

Sarah Coulsden decided to take Julia to visit all the members of the family by way of celebration, and after seeing Cicely and Jack, they set off in the dog-cart to Hastings to visit Stan and Jane. As they passed through Winchelsea, Icklesham and Ore, people greeted them enthusiastically and, overcome with emotion, Sarah thought the journey the happiest she had ever undertaken. When they eventually reached the old part of Hastings, she went first to the foreshore; there she reined in Bram, her elderly horse, and waited, hoping to see Bill Breed, an old family friend. Sure enough, less than a minute later a burly man in his fifties detached himself from the boisterous crowd and limped across to her, touching his cap respectfully. She leaned down from the cart and he clasped her hand.

'Mrs Coulsden, ma'am, and young Julia!'

'Mr Breed!' Sarah smiled down at him. 'After all these years.'

'It's a wonderful day, ma'am,' he grinned. 'A bloody wonderful day! Peace at last. It's over. A bloody wonderful bloody day, if you'll pardon the expression. I've got two boys left, ma'am, but one's still over there.'

'Poor Mr Breed,' said Sarah. 'I heard the news a few weeks ago and I wanted to tell you how sorry I am that you lost your youngest boy.'

'Aye, God rest him! Albert, that was. Enlisted in the September and he were dead in the January. Terrible time, that was. First the telegram, like, from the Army: "Regret to inform you . . ." They always put that. "Private Albert Breed badly wounded." Mind you, we were lucky really, because we were able to go to France and see him in hospital, the missus and me that is. We got there just in time. He was still alive and he knew us, ma'am; he knew we were there beside him, but there was no hope – the sister had told us that. Gangrene in both legs and they'd have to amputate.

Albert looked at us and he grinned. He had a rare grin, did Albert! Then he closed his eyes and died. Just gave a bit of a sigh and died. He was best off dead, that's what the missus reckons.'

'Oh, Mr Breed. How terrible for you!'

'The missus took it hard, but you couldn't blame her. They gave him a wonderful funeral. The coffin was covered with a Union Jack and then there was a military salute. Full military honours, you see, ma'am.'

'Yes, I see. You must have been very proud.'

'And the "Last Post". They played that, too. He was buried with honours, ma'am. We like to think on that, you know. Makes us feel better, like, about losing him.'

'I'm sure it does.'

'Doesn't bring him back, though. He was a good boy, young Albert. Oh yes, they did him proud, the Army, but it doesn't bring them back. But what can you do, ma'am? We're all in the same bloody boat. My brother's boy's gone; we've all lost someone.' He shook his head. 'Still, it's no good grieving. They did their duty, God bless 'em! We must thank our lucky stars the others are saved and cheer them all when they come home.' He turned to Julia. 'So this is young Julia? She's a fine little lass.'

Sarah nudged her granddaughter and said, 'Say "hullo" to Mr Breed.'

'Hullo, Mr Breed,' said Julia serenely. 'I'm eight years and three months.'

The man laughed. 'Eight and three months! Well, I'm blessed. Not so little, then?'

'I'll be nine in nine more months,' she told him.

'Oh dear,' said Sarah. 'Why do the young always want to be older?'

Mr Breed shook his head. 'Beats me. I'd be glad to shed a few years, but that's the way it goes. Still, today's a milestone, like, in all our lives. That's what my missus says – a milestone. She's good with words. It's a meaningful day. No more killing. No more dying.'

'Peace,' said Sarah simply.

'Aye. Peace,' he nodded. 'On your way to Stan's then, are you? I'd best not keep you.'

They said good-byes and soon Sarah and Julia had tethered the horse and were making their way along the path to the door of No. 17. Lifting the Union Jack which hung there, Sarah found the knocker and beat a sharp tattoo with it. Jane opened the door and the two women flung their arms around each other.

'It's over!' cried Jane. 'I still can't believe it; I've only just heard the news – a few minutes ago.' She knelt down to hug Julia, then straightened up again. 'They say everyone's gone wild with joy in London. It's all over and Ernest will be coming home – he will, won't he?'

'Of course he will,' said Sarah. 'You must thank God, Jane. There are so many poor souls with nothing to celebrate. No husbands or sons to come home. It's been terrible. I've just been talking to Bill Breed, poor man. He lost his youngest boy. So terrible – it's hard to believe it's over at last.'

Jane smiled at Julia. 'The war is over, Ju,' she said. 'Isn't that lovely? Do you know what that means? All the brave soldier boys will be coming home again. We've beaten the horrid old Huns.'

Julia nodded cautiously and Jane laughed. 'I don't suppose she can remember a time when we weren't at war. But come on in, both of you.' She led them along the passage and into the kitchen, where Sarah sank down in to a chair with a sigh of exhaustion.

'Put the kettle on, Jane, please dear,' she said. 'I'm parched. The ride out here took so long. And the church bells ringing everywhere. Bram was terrified, poor creature, and there are so many people about, the roads are crowded in spite of the cold and everyone singing and cheering – and half of them drunk, if the truth be known. I was so afraid of running someone down.'

Jane said, 'God has heard our prayers; I knew he would.'

Sarah sniffed. 'Well, it's a pity he didn't hear them a bit earlier,' she said. 'Then a lot of mothers would have seen their sons again.' She glanced round and her mouth tightened. 'Where's Stanley?'

'On the stade,' said his wife grimly. 'He's putting out on the next tide. You know Stan – he won't let something like winning the war interrupt his fishing!'

Jane and Stanley had never been reconciled over what Jane considered his dereliction of duty with regard to George's marriage to Agnes. Stan's insistence that one of George's brothers should act as best man had annoyed her, but when Jack declined and it was obvious that Stan himself would do it, she was positively outraged. It put her in an invidious position with Cicely and Sarah, as she told her husband, for in the eyes of the world it would appear as though Stan was condoning the wretched affair. In fact, of course, he *was*, for Stanley maintained that George should be allowed to live his own life – he had made his bed and he should damn well be allowed to lie on it, no matter how uncomfortable it might be. All Jane's prayers, tears, pleas and recriminations failed to dissuade him. Time had passed now, of course, but the situation had scarcely changed. George and Jack rarely saw one another but George and Stan, partners in the 'crime', met frequently to drown their sorrows in drink, which further incensed Jane. Sarah remained inflexible, refusing to make any contact with Agnes, who declared herself quite un-moved by the family's rejection of her and her daughter but was actually bitterly disappointed at their continued hostility. George had prophesied a gradual improvement in family relationships, but so long as Sarah remained adamant the rest of the women followed her lead.

Sarah nodded now and as Jane began to fill the kettle said, 'Perhaps tea is a poor sort of drink to celebrate the end of the war! What about a nip of something stronger while we wait for the kettle to boil? I refused a sherry at Cicely's because I wanted a clear head to drive over here.'

Jane, a little tight-lipped, replied, 'You're welcome, of course, but you won't mind if I stick to tea? It's a bit early for me to start drinking.'

'Please yourself entirely, dear,' said her mother-in-law, 'but we don't win a war every day,' and as Jane went into the front parlour to find something suitable Sarah wondered why Stanley had married such a kill-joy.

'Ah, thank you, dear.' She took the glass and sniffed. 'What is it?'

'A little brandy we had left from Stan's birthday.'

'Cheers!' said Sarah, taking the first sip. 'Here's to peace.'

She watched her daughter-in-law as she poured boiling water into the tea-pot. A stringy woman, she thought. Stringy, cold, lacking imagination. She never has to ask forgiveness because she never does anything that He would not approve of. Throughout the entire war she had 'done her bit' as exhorted by the posters. She had grown vegetables in what had once been the rose-bed; had knitted comforts for the boys at the front; had 'made do' with patched and faded clothes. If she had owned a dachshund, Sarah was sure she would have followed the fashion and surrendered it to the vet to be put down.

Jane poured Julia a glass of milk.

'Cheers!' said Julia and the women laughed.

'I second that,' said Sarah. 'Let this be the war to end all wars, please God!' She wondered why 'good' women were so boring and wondered if Stan ever regretted marrying the widow.

'I daresay Winifred and Ernest will be wanting to find their own place now,' she remarked. 'Though Cicely's going to miss her and the baby. A pity they had such a quiet wedding without all the trimmings, but there – the war seemed to be dragging on so and you couldn't blame them for not wanting to wait any longer.'

'No,' agreed Jane, 'war alters everything, doesn't it? I know Cicely and Jack hoped they would wait and have a proper wedding when things were back to normal, but it must have been a great relief to them to have her safely home again. And fancy, Ernest is twenty-four. It seems impossible; he's a grown man. We haven't seen him for nearly a year.'

Ernest had been home on leave three times, the last occasion in the December of 1917 before returning to France three days before Christmas. It was then that he and Winifred had managed to get leave together and decided to get married. Winifred had become pregnant straight away and their first baby had been born in the following September. In July Ernest had been wounded in the shoulder, but it was not 'a Blighty one' and they had nursed him back to health and returned him to the front where two months later he had been wounded in the leg. He was still recovering and would always limp, he had told them in his letter, but the doctors had saved his leg and he was a great deal luckier than many others.

'Well,' Jane turned to Julia, 'you're not saying much. The dreadful war's come to an end at last. What do you think of that?'

Julia took a deep breath. 'It's four years and a hundred days exactly,' she said. 'Mama Sarah told me.' She screwed up her face in concentration. 'And it's the eleventh day of the eleventh month and the Armistice was signed at the eleventh hour! All elevens! And there's going to be a party in the streets one day.'

'My,' said Jane, 'you certainly found your tongue at last.' She turned back to Sarah and lowered her voice. 'Have you seen anything of *her* lately? Any news?'

'I don't care to ask,' replied Sarah. 'I refuse to take any interest at all.'

She finished her brandy and drank her tea, then she stood up. 'Well, we came to share the day with you so we'll go and have a word with Stan if we can catch him. We should have had a family party or something but,' she shrugged, 'that woman is not going to set foot in my house and George won't come without her. It makes it very awkward.'

'You asked him, then?' Jane asked curiously. 'About the party?'

'I said I was thinking of having a get-together and would he like to come and he said not without the other two. So I thought, well, if we can't all get together at least Julia and I can go round and see everyone. Are you ready, Julia? You've finished your milk? Good girl! Well, say good-bye to your Aunt Jane and we'll go and find Uncle Stan.'

They set off a few moments later and made their way on foot down All Saints towards Rock-a-Nore, where they found Stanley in a hurry to catch the tide which was on the turn. Sarah expressed her delight at the signing of the Armistice.

'Aye, and about bloody time too,' commented Stan.

It appeared that his ill-humour was due to two of his crew members who, reasonably enough, had expected the day to be exclusively devoted to celebration. They had not turned up for work and Stanley had decided to take the boat out with just the boy as crew.

After a few more words Sarah and Julia returned to the dog-cart and climbed back in. Sarah tapped Bram, who began to pick his leisurely way back through the crowds of excited revellers.

*

South View had been built in the seventeenth century, wooden-framed with plaster under a thatched roof, but the latter had been badly damaged by fire in 1882 and replaced by a new tiled roof. From its vantage point on the hillside it faced south-east across the broad marshland towards Dymchurch, Romney, Lydd and Dungeness. To Mrs Tooks, the housekeeper, South View was home and she took as much pride in it as if it were her own and not merely her responsibility to dust and polish. The heavy work was done by seventeen-year-old Amy, the daughter of a neighbouring farmer.

After Sarah had left South View in the dog-cart to go visiting, Mrs Tooks found herself alone in the house and free to celebrate the wonderful news in any way she chose. The first thing she did was to clap her hands, close her eyes and whisper, 'Hallelujah!' Not because she was a religious woman – she was not – but because it was the only word she could think of with the dignity, weight and power which she considered suitable for the occasion. Mrs Tooks had lost no one to the German guns, for she had no one to lose. After she had said 'Hallelujah!' again, she went into the kitchen and finished the washing-up while she wondered how else she could express her feelings about the signing of the Armistice. Silky the cat, a sleek tortoiseshell, slept in a chair; Mrs Tooks touched one ear lightly so that it woke up.

'It's over,' Mrs Tooks declared. 'The war's over! Not that it means much to you, but it is, thank God. At least I did my bit.' She nodded with satisfaction as she stroked the cat, which uncurled lazily and stood up, arching its back to her caress. Four pairs of khaki socks, two pairs of gloves and three scarves had gone to grateful hands, feet and necks and with Julia's eager assistance she had also made eighty-six lavender bags from the lavender in the garden, which had been sold to raise money to buy cigarettes for the 'lads'. She thought somewhat wistfully of the camaraderie of the knitting circle and the sense of unity which came with sharing a common enemy. Presumably that was all over now. She sighed.

'You can celebrate, too,' she told Silky. 'Come on, I'll give you some milk – no, some cream off the top! How's that, eh? You are a lucky girl, aren't you?' She poured out the top two inches from yesterday's milk and watched the cat settle beside it, tongue flicking in and out.

'Ah, purring, are you? Well, that's a special treat for a special occasion. The war is over.'

It sounded odd, the words unfamiliar. 'No more "war effort",' she said. 'No more "make do and mend". No more bad news and all those terrible telegrams. Well, thank goodness. That's all I can say. D'you hear me, Silky? Thank goodness!'

She felt the need to shout or sing a patriotic song and began hesitantly, 'Pack up your troubles in your old kit-bag and—' and then stopped, feeling foolish. If she had had a flag she could wave it. Or a whistle. She wanted to blow a whistle or shake a rattle.

'I don't know what to do,' she whispered, suddenly tearful. 'It's over and I don't know what to do.' She sat down and put her hands over her face. 'Don't be so silly, Maudie Tooks,' she told herself sternly. 'Pull yourself together. There's nothing to cry for, the dreadful war is over.'

But she cried just the same . . .

Much later, she heard the clip-clop of hooves on the road outside and crossed to the window. It was certainly Sarah Coulsden's dog-cart, but to the housekeeper's astonishment Julia was sitting with the reins in her hands and there was no sign of her grandmother. The horse reached his usual stopping place outside the gate, slowed to a halt and shook his head.

'Now, what on earth—?' said Mrs Tooks. 'Where's the mistress got to? She's never let that child come home on her own! What on earth is happening?'

Bram put his head down and snatched a mouthful of grass and Mrs Tooks put a hand to her heart with a sudden premonition.

'She's never been thrown out! Oh, my godfathers!'

She opened the front door and ran down the path. Before she reached the gate the horse moved on a few paces to tug at a hawthorn hedge and the large wheels of the dog-cart rolled on.

'I drove Bram home,' shouted Julia excitedly. 'Mama Sarah has gone to sleep. She felt funny and then she went to sleep and fell off the seat.'

'Went to sleep?'

'I couldn't wake her up,' said Julia, 'but Bram was very good and let me drive him. He wasn't naughty at all. I held the reins and he just went on and on.'

Mrs Tooks, her heart beating wildly, held the horse steady as Julia scrambled down, then she put a foot on the nearside step and heaved herself up so that she could see inside the cart.

'Oh no! Please God, no!' she gasped as she saw Sarah's crumpled body in the bottom of the cart. With a supreme effort of will she clung there, until the wave of faintness passed.

Julia was chattering on about all the people who were singing and dancing in the streets, but she faltered to a stop when she saw the expression on the housekeeper's face.

'What is it?' she asked. 'What's the matter?'

'Your grandmother is poorly,' she told Julia. 'Very poorly. You must run over to the farm for help. Go now – go quickly.'

As soon as help arrived, they carried Sarah into the front room while Mrs Tooks telephoned Dr Jamieson. When he arrived, he confirmed what they had already guessed: that Sarah Coulsden was dead. A heart attack, he told them, mercifully quick. She wouldn't have known much about it, not for long anyway. A tragic thing to happen on such a triumphant day, he said. Probably the excitement had been too much for her. A very sad thing. He would send someone to lay her out.

Jack was notified of the tragedy and he arrived with Cicely and George. The latter was determined to take his daughter home with him, but Julia refused point-blank. She also refused to go home with Jack and Cicely, or in fact to leave the house at all. She wanted to stay at South View with Mrs Tooks and at last it was agreed that she could remain where she was for the time being.

That night, between sobs, she wrote in her diary:

> Mama Sarah is ded but I don't want her to die. The war is over but I am so sad. Bram was a very good hors to let me drive him hom.

She thought about her grandmother, lying so still in the next room with a tall white candle burning beside her bed. At Julia's own insistence, Mrs Tooks had taken her in to say a last 'good-bye' to her grandmother, but now Julia wished she had taken the housekeeper's advice to 'best remember her how she was'. But it was too late now. She lay awake for a long time but eventually, exhausted by the day's events, fell into a dreamless sleep.

*

At the graveside, Julia stood between George and Mrs Tooks and watched silently as her grandmother's coffin was lowered into the ground. She knew that Mama Sarah was inside the long polished box, because she had seen her. She knew also that her mother had been laid to rest in a similar box, because Leo had told her so. Leo had explained that dead people never did wake up again, but floated up to the sky and from there to Heaven. Julia had asked him about Heaven.

'It's full of clouds and angels,' he told her, 'and they all sing hymns and everyone is happy and nobody ever gets a good hiding in Heaven, because nobody ever tells lies or says rude words.'

Julia thought Mama Sarah would enjoy being there. She tried to imagine her floating up through the lid of the box when the family had all gone home, and was glad that her grandmother would never get a good hiding.

Meanwhile the vicar's voice droned on and Julia glanced round at all her uncles and aunts. Her other grandparents were also present, but since Hettie's death she had seen them so rarely that they were almost strangers. Mrs Mack was sobbing and so was Ben, but Leo was stabbing the toe of his right shoe into the grass and appeared quite unmoved by the solemnity of the occasion. Julia wished she could cry. The tears were pressing heavily against her eyes and yet they would not flow.

Mrs Tooks had said that only good people go to Heaven but, of course, Mama Sarah *was* good. Bad people went to Hell, where it was very hot and everyone was thirsty but no one was ever given a drink of water. There were only bad people to talk to in Hell, so you could never have a nice friend there. Julia was glad that her grandmother was a good person and would float up to Heaven. People did not float down to Hell, according to Leo – they fell like a stone out of the bottom of the coffin, right through the earth and into the fire. Suddenly Julia wished that Ernest would hurry up and come home to join Winifred.

Then it all seemed to be over. Her father's hand tightened over hers and she saw that the vicar was leading the way to the church gate. A bell began to toll eerily in the still air and several birds fluttered from the church tower and headed for the safety of the nearby trees. Looking up at her father, Julia saw that his face was drawn into a frown and his eyes were dark.

'She was a good woman,' said Jane, appearing beside them. 'A very good woman.'

George nodded.

'It was a lovely service,' Jane went on. 'The vicar does these things so well.'

'It's his job,' said George tersely.

Jane smiled at Julia. 'That was your grandmother's favourite hymn, the one we sang. She chose it for your grandfather's funeral, so I knew she would want it at her own. I think she would have approved. And all these lovely flowers!'

Jack, Cicely and Stanley joined them and Cicely looked at Julia with red-rimmed eyes. 'Poor soul,' she said. 'But it was a good way to go: quick and merciful, as the doctor said. She knew nothing about it.'

'She did,' said Julia. 'She said she felt funny.'

'But she didn't know she was dying,' explained Cicely. 'I expect she thought she was just overtired from all the excitement.'

'But to go on Armistice Day,' said Jack.

'We all have to go sometime,' said Stanley.

Someone was tugging at Julia's free hand and she turned to see Leo grinning at her.

'Coming?' he asked.

'Where to?'

He shrugged. 'With me and Ben.'

'But where?'

'Play kiss-chase?'

'I don't want to,' she said.

Cicely had heard Leo's whispered words and now she seized him by the arm and gave him a little shake.

'You will not play anything, Leonard Coulsden!' she exclaimed. 'The very idea! You stay right here with me and behave yourself.'

Julia wondered if kiss-chase among the gravestones was bad enough to send you to Hell.

Then they were all moving towards the gate where the carriages waited. The funeral breakfast had been prepared by Cicely, but it had been agreed that it should be served at Sarah's home. It would be the last such gathering held there, for South View would now be sold, but by tacit agreement no one spoke of that. Only George dreaded the disclosure of the contents of Sarah's will, for he had defied her wishes in the matter of Agnes Dengate and did not doubt that her vengeance would be terrible. She had spoken to him since the wedding, but Agnes had never been allowed at South View and George had not dared to bring her to the funeral in spite of her entreaties. Agnes's motives were purely malicious – she knew that Sarah would not have approved – yet as George's wife she felt entitled to attend and secretly was convinced that on such an occasion no one would raise any audible objections to her presence. She also insisted that Emily ought to attend her grandmother's funeral, but to her dismay George remained adamant on that score also and they were both left at home. However, Agnes was a force to be reckoned with and when the family left the churchyard, they saw her standing with Emily on the opposite pavement. Both wore black armbands which Agnes had hastily stitched from a yard of newly purchased ribbon. Emily seemed not to understand what was happening, but when she saw Julia a smile of recognition lit up her face.

'Well!' cried Cicely, deeply affronted by their appearance. 'That woman! How dare she show her face here!'

George gave an exclamation of annoyance and hurried over to them, still holding his daughter's right hand, but Cicely caught hold of her left and briefly Julia found herself tugged in two directions until George released her and Cicely hurried her into the waiting car with Leo and Ben.

Julia understood now why Agnes was not approved of by the
Coulsdens. Her grandmother had been at pains to explain the
reason and she knew that her mother had loved and trusted her
husband but that he had 'taken up' with Agnes. The truth had
come to light and her mother had 'died of grief'. Sarah's modified
version of the facts had been filled out by Leo's garbled account of
the poison. Julia knew that Agnes was Emily's mother and that
Emily was a half-sister, because they both had the same father.
Now, in the short encounter outside the church, Julia looked for a
likeness between her father and Emily and found none. Emily
looked like Agnes, but with fair hair instead of brown.

As soon as the mourners reached South View, Mrs Tooks
busied herself with the refreshments. Mr Dawson, the family
solicitor, was unable to attend so the reading of the will had been
postponed for a week.

Julia, Leo and Ben sat at one end of the long table. Leo was
sulking because Cicely had refused to allow him to sample the
wine, but Ben and Julia chatted together and ate their way
through a large number of salmon and cucumber sandwiches and
chocolate cake and biscuits. Suddenly Leo leaned forward, bent
on mischief.

'I know what they do,' he told them. 'To get babies. I know how
they do it!'

'You don't,' said Ben.

'I *do*.'

Julia regarded him blankly. 'Do what?' she asked.

'You know,' said Leo. 'I asked Miss Mills. At first she said she
wouldn't tell me, but I said I'd tell on her if she didn't so she had
to. She went all funny when she said it.'

Ben stared at his brother, shocked. 'But Mama said you
weren't to ask! She said you weren't old enough.'

Leo grinned. ' "All in good time, Leo," ' he mimicked his
mother. ' "There's no hurry." '

'Did she really tell you?' asked Ben. 'Miss Mills, I mean. I bet
she didn't.'

'She did, then! Because she had to – because I saw her kiss
Eddie Fitch and Mama doesn't allow that.'

'How do they, then?' Julia asked him. 'How do they get the
babies?'

'Wouldn't you like to know!'

Ben and Julia exchanged looks. 'He doesn't know,' said Ben.

'He's just pretending. Miss Mills wouldn't tell him.'

'Well, she did then!' cried Leo.

Julia looked at him. 'Aren't you going to tell us?'

Leo leaned forward, one plump finger pressed to his lips to emphasise the need for discretion. Julia and Ben leaned towards him with ears strained. 'They get into bed together,' he whispered, 'under the blankets – and then it just happens. There isn't any stork.'

Julia reached for another biscuit. 'In bed?' she repeated. 'Are you sure?'

'Cross my heart and hope to die.'

'Did you see Miss Mills get into bed with Eddie Fitch?' asked Ben.

'Of course not, stupid, but I saw them kissing. They kiss first and then they get into bed and it happens.'

Julia tried to picture her father getting into bed with Agnes, but the image was a hazy one.

Suddenly Mrs Tooks loomed beside them to enquire if they were being good children and having enough to eat.

Leo tried again. 'Can I have a glass of wine, please?' he demanded. 'I am nearly fourteen.'

'A glass of wine? Good gracious me, no!' said Mrs Tooks and hurried away before he could argue the point.

George came up a moment later and told Julia he wanted to talk about something. He led her upstairs into the spare bedroom where all the coats and wraps had been laid across the bed; then he sat down on a pale green wicker chair and drew her towards him. He seemed nervous, Julia thought, and his large hands felt damp.

'I want you to listen carefully,' he began. 'It's about where you should live now that Mama Sarah is dead. You can't stay at South View, because it will have to be sold. You could live with your Aunt Cicely and Uncle Jack, or you could go to Uncle Stan's at Hastings. They have all offered to have you live with them.'

Julia felt a coldness sweep over her. She did not want to live with *any* of them. At times she felt that Aunt Cicely did not like her very much – and Hastings was a long way away. Her large blue eyes filled with tears and her mouth trembled. Seeing this, George put an arm around her shoulders and gave her a quick hug.

'You don't have to go, love,' he told her. 'I'm just telling you that they're willing to take you. You could come with me, Julia. I think that might be best, don't you?'

She had opened her mouth to say, 'Yes,' when a thought struck her.

'Just you and me, Papa?'

'No, Julia.' She could see the perspiration on his forehead. 'There's Agnes and Emily too. You like Emily, don't you?'

She looked at him with stricken eyes. 'I don't like Agnes,' she stammered. 'She's bad, she killed Mama.'

'No, Julia; she did no such thing,' her father protested. 'It wasn't like that at all. Ag wouldn't kill anybody, of course she wouldn't. She's a good person at heart.'

He didn't tell his daughter of the prolonged row which had followed his suggestion that Julia should move in with them.

Julia shook her head. 'She hates me,' she said in a low voice, 'because of the wedding.'

'No, she doesn't. That's all over and done with. All forgotten. I really would like you to come with us, Julia,' George assured her. 'Now that Mama Sarah and your Mama have gone you only have me and I want us to stay together. Don't shake your head, dear. I want you to try to think differently about Agnes. Forget what everyone else tells you about her and listen to me. I know she doesn't hate you. No, love, don't cry. Here's a hanky. I wouldn't lie to you, would I? Eh? Would I lie to you?'

'I . . . don't . . . know,' sobbed Julia.

'Of course I wouldn't! Now, you pay attention to what I say. Agnes is a good person and she's my wife. We were properly married in a church. The vicar would never have let us marry in church if Ag was a bad person, would he? But he married us in his church and we're very happy together. Well, happy enough, anyway,' he amended. 'And Emily's happy too. She calls me Papa and I'm her father, the same as I'm yours. I want us all to be happy together and so does Agnes.'

A sudden memory flooded back. 'She hit me,' said Julia. 'Agnes hit me in the face!'

George was taken aback. 'Good God! That was years ago! She only smacked you because you were naughty,' he told her. 'You bit poor little Emily.'

Julia stared at him. '*I* bit Emily?'

'Yes, you did. You made her squeal.'

Unaccountably Julia giggled. She was in a state of great con-

fusion, half hysterical with the shock of her grandmother's death
and the threatened upheaval in her way of life.

'I bit Emily?' she repeated, as her laughter grew.

'Yes, you did,' said George, smiling with her, 'but Emily still
loves you and she's longing to have a sister. She keeps asking if
you'll come to live with us. Would you like a sister?'

Julia controlled herself with a conscious effort of will. 'I don't
know,' she said soberly. 'I've got Leo and Ben.'

'They're only cousins.'

'And Winifred – and Ernest when he comes home.'

'They're cousins too, but Emily is a sister. Well, a half-sister.
You two girls would have a lot of fun.'

A new and awful thought struck Julia. 'But nobody speaks to
them,' she protested. 'No one's allowed to talk to them. They
won't talk to *me* if I live with you and Agnes!'

George's mouth hardened. 'Uncle Stan speaks to them, Julia,'
he told her. 'The others didn't speak to Ag and Emily because of
Mama Sarah,' he explained. 'She had strong feelings about it and
everyone took notice of her. Everyone will talk to you just the
same as before. Of course they will.'

He would make damn sure they did, he resolved grimly, or die
in the attempt.

Julia was weakening. She did not want to live with Agnes, but
neither could she entertain the other options open to her.

George put a finger under her chin and tilted up her face.
'Come with us,' he said. 'You're my little Julia Lady and I love
you. We'll have lots of good times. Say you'll come, eh?'

Looking at her father, Julia was astonished to recognise the
pleading in his voice. Suddenly she felt years older than him and
she wanted to make him happy. The glimpse of Emily with her
fair curls and the black armband has also awoken a great curiosity in her.

'I'll come, Papa,' she said and then squealed in mock alarm as a
delighted George leapt to his feet, lifted her from the ground and
hugged her.

When at last he put her down, he straightened up and his
expression changed. Persuading Julia had been the easy part.
Now he had to persuade Agnes.

*

As usual, Sarah Coulsden had the last word. In her will she

stipulated that South View be sold at once and that the money should be divided equally between her four legitimate grand-children. Winifred's quarter was to go to her immediately, Leo and Ben's shares were to be put in trust for them when they came of age at twenty-one. The remaining quarter of the money would be at Julia's disposal when she too reached the age of twenty-one, but could be released earlier in any emergency or special circum-stances with Mr Dawson's approval. Five hundred pounds was left to Ernest as a gesture of Sarah's goodwill.

Almost every aspect of the will aroused resentment in some-one. Stanley objected to the fact that Ernest did not receive a full share and Jane blamed Stanley for acting as best man at George's wedding in defiance of Sarah's express wish to the contrary. George was mortified to learn that his mother entrusted Julia's share of the inheritance to Mr Dawson rather than to him. Agnes was furious that Emily was left nothing although she was George's natural daughter and Ernest was only Stanley's 'adopted' son. The only bequest which met with universal approval was that Mrs Tooks received a small pension.

South View was put on the market and the housekeeper showed a succession of people over the house. Julia was still there for George had not yet managed to persuade Agnes to give her a home, although Julia was unaware of this fact and assumed she was being allowed to stay on at South View until it passed into new hands. At first she went round the house in the wake of the prospective buyers and listened to the estate agent extolling its virtues. She did not want anyone else to live in South View, but Mrs Tooks had told her it was always the way 'when folks died'. An acceptable offer was eventually made for the property and the sale was agreed. Solicitors exchanged letters, Mrs Tooks left to live with her sister in Dorset and George and Julia watched the removal men take out the furniture which was going to the auction room to await the monthly sale. Colonel and Mrs Cornwell took possession of South View on 3 March 1919 and George and Julia drove to the house on Hilders Cliff which Agnes had finally agreed would once again be Julia's home.

*

'Well,' said Agnes, with an attempt at a smile. 'So here you are, Julia!' She left George to help Julia take off her coat and hat. 'Nothing to say for yourself, then?' asked Agnes. 'No "hullo"?'

Julia stared beseechingly at her father and George gave his wife a warning glance. 'We saw the furniture out,' he told her. 'They were very quick really, took just over an hour. The place looked terrible when it had gone. So empty.'

'What time are the new people moving in?'

'About three. They've a fair way to come.'

Without her coat and hat Julia felt very vulnerable and her heart ached for South View. Her father was wrong, she thought. The house had looked sad, not terrible, without Mama Sarah's furniture. There were patches on the walls where the furniture had protected the paper from the sun. Without curtains, the windows let in too much light and the only shadows were cast by the open doors; moreover it was clear that the windows needed cleaning. Julia sighed and tried not to think about South View. Instead, she looked round the home where her mother had once cared for her. She wanted Mrs Mack to bustle in with her cheerful grin, a jug of her special barley water or lemonade in her hands. But Mrs Mack had gone, too. It seemed that everyone she loved had gone.

Agnes was regarding her coldly. 'What's the matter with you? Cat got your tongue, has it? Politeness costs nothing.'

George said, 'Say "hullo", Julia.'

She stared fixedly at the floor. 'Hullo,' she said tonelessly.

'At last,' said Agnes. 'Not exactly chatty, are we, but never mind. Well, cheer up for goodness' sake! No one's going to bite you.'

George put a protective hand on Julia's shoulder. 'Where's Emily?' he asked. 'Doesn't she want to say "hullo" to Julia?'

'Why should she?'

'Why shouldn't she?' George snapped.

Julia stood forlornly in the middle of the room and wished herself dead. Yes, she would like to be with Mama Sarah and her mother in Heaven. Except that she had done that terrible thing at Papa's wedding and maybe now she might have to go to Hell. Straight down like a stone, she thought wearily and wondered . . . if she did one very good deed, would it cancel out the one very bad thing? She would have to ask Leo when she saw him again. If she ever did! For the first time the realisation struck her that now she was living with 'the enemy'. Would she really be allowed to see Leo and Ben? Would they want to see her? Would she ever see Winifred again? And Ernest? And would Uncle Jack and Aunt Cicely ever visit?

George was trying not to lose his temper, although he could read Agnes like a book and knew that Emily was being kept out of the way so as to make Julia's arrival as unwelcoming as possible.

'I sent her to her room,' said Agnes, 'to tidy it up. It's so cramped now that she has to share it. The other bed takes up so much room. I told you that old furniture wasn't suitable, but you would insist. They'll hardly be able to move up there.'

Julia's heart leaped at the reminder. Her father had allowed her to bring from South View her roomy bed with its heavily carved elm headboard. The old oak chest from the hall had also been saved from the ignominy of the auction and contained her clothes and a few prized possessions. The bed and the chest were all that remained of that other life.

George moved to the stairs and called up, 'Emily, Julia is here.'

'I told her to stay there,' said Agnes, 'until *I* tell her to come down.'

'Then you'd better tell her,' said George.

Agnes hesitated and Julia waited with a sick feeling in her stomach. Aware that Agnes was looking at her, she was determined not to cry. She would not give 'that woman' the satisfaction of knowing how empty and frightened she was. Nothing too awful would happen to her while Papa was with her, but when he next went to sea – what then? Agnes gave in as gracefully as she could and shouted up the stairs.

'Em! Is your room tidy?'

'Yes, Ma.'

'Then you can come down.'

As Julia's half-sister came into the room, the two girls exchanged a quick look. Emily wore a new green dress with a deep lace collar, the dark green colour contrasting with the fair curls which framed her plain face. She smiled shyly at Julia and said 'Hullo, Julia.'

'Hullo, Emily.'

Agnes turned to George. 'Satisfied now?'

He ignored her and crouched down to put an arm around each girl. 'Now I want you two girls to get along,' he said. 'You can have lots of fun together.'

Emily nodded earnestly and Julia's feeling of desolation lessened marginally. She tried to speak but her throat was dry and no words came; she smiled faintly.

'Em's been longing for a sister, haven't you, Em?' George prompted.

Agnes said, 'Oh, has she?' She almost added, 'That's news to me!' but didn't dare risk it. Emily *had* been looking foward to Julia's arrival in spite of Agnes's efforts to persuade her – by subtle ways and means – that she would be forced to play second fiddle to George's other daughter.

'So you two remember,' George went on. 'No squabbling! Be nice to each other and then we'll be a happy family.' For a moment his voice faltered. 'Because we can if we try. If we *all* try.'

It was Julia's turn to nod while Agnes gave a mocking laugh. 'Quite a little speech,' she said. 'Well I never!'

They all ignored her.

'Now then, Em,' said George. 'When I tucked you up last night, what did you tell me you were going to give Julia? Do you remember?'

'A hug,' whispered Emily, embarrassed by her mother's presence.

George beamed at her. 'A big hug, you told me, and a kiss! So go on, Em, you give Julia a hug to make her feel welcome.'

To Julia's surprise, Emily threw her arms round her neck in a fierce hug that nearly made her lose her balance. George laughed delightedly as Julia slowly returned the embrace and the two children clung together.

'There you are, Ag!' cried George. 'I told you it would be all right. Two little girls with not much more than a year between them – of course they'll get along!' He kissed both girls and straightened up, a broad smile on his face.

'Off you go, then!' he told them. 'Upstairs or out in the garden. Do a bit of talking, get to know each other. Two little sisters!'

His pleasure was infectious and Julia smiled shyly at Emily, who grinned back.

'Upstairs?' Emily suggested.

Julia nodded and together they went upstairs, then George and Agnes heard the bedroom door close firmly behind them.

George breathed a deep sigh of relief and turned to Agnes, who was trying to hide her disappointment that the meeting had passed off relatively well.

'Well,' she said, 'time will tell, I suppose.'

George was feeling magnanimous. He held out his hands and when she made no move, crossed the room to take her in his arms.

'They'll be all right, Ag, if you let them,' he said. 'For my sake, Ag, give it a chance, eh?'

She shrugged, not trusting herself to speak, suddenly feeling unwanted. His two daughters – they were all he really cared about, she told herself. Poor old Agnes must take second place to a couple of kids. Bitterness and self-pity welled up in her, and to her dismay, tears spilled suddenly down her cheeks and she was trembling.

'Ag! For God's sake!' cried George. 'What's up, love? There's no reason to take on like this.'

She saw the concern in his eyes but also the lack of understanding and knew there was no way she could explain how she felt. He wouldn't understand; she hardly understood herself. Shaking herself free from his arms, she muttered something about 'seeing to the dinner' and removed herself to the kitchen. Once there, she turned the key in the lock and gave way to scalding tears of frustration and fear which led to a fit of noisy coughing. George rattled the door handle and called to her in a low voice, but she could not answer. She heard him go back into the parlour, slamming the door. Upstairs she heard Emily laugh and wondered miserably how it would all end. Nothing went the way she expected, she reflected. Nobody cared about her and her feelings. Sniffing, she tied on her apron, found a handkerchief in the pocket and blew her nose. Then she splashed cold water over her face and used the teacloth as a towel.

George had got his precious little girls, but no one mentioned her poor little boy who had been born dead. The girls had each other and bloody Julia had all her mother's money plus a share of South View. She, Agnes, had got nothing, she reflected sourly, except a husband who drank too much and in-laws who hated her guts.

'Oh Christ!' she groaned. 'I'd be better off on the Hastings stade mending nets. I wish to God I'd never set eyes on George bloody Coulsden!' She took some potatoes from the basket beside the sink and snatched up the peeler. Digging out the eyes afforded her some relief and she peeled them thickly with deliberate abandon, relishing the amount she was wasting.

'Twenty-nine years old,' she muttered, 'and I might as well be sixty-nine for all the notice anyone takes of me. Fit to peel spuds and that's about all!'

Suddenly she remembered Luke Bligh. She thought he had

fancied her and if it hadn't been for George Coulsden . . . But poor Luke was dead, along with so many more. She racked her brains to think of anyone else who had found her attractive. Perhaps Stan Coulsden did, but that la-di-da Jane had got her clutches on him good and proper. Jack Coulsden? She laughed; that would set the cat among the pigeons! Cicely wouldn't be so high-faluting if Jack took a shine to her. That *would* be interesting. It would show George a thing or two, she thought, but unfortunately Jack had never given her the eye so there was not much hope there. Frowning, she began to cut the potatoes into quarters. There was that young Jean Dessin from Belgium. He was a well-built lad and very good-looking, but he couldn't be very old or else he would have gone to the war. Adding a spoonful, of salt to the potatoes, she put the pan on to the stove and lit the gas. The meat pie smelled good. She took three knives and three forks from the drawer. Oh Lordy, she must remember to lay for four now *and* cook for four. Not to mention washing and ironing. That was all she was good for, in George's eyes – housework! She was nothing but a skivvy. With a deep sigh, she began to lay the kitchen table. Then very quietly she unlocked the kitchen door.

She thought again of Jean Dessin. 'Right, George!' she said aloud. 'We'll see what we shall see.' She didn't quite know what she meant by these threatening words, but just saying them made her feel much better.

CHAPTER NINE

Winifred stood on the beach at Rock-a-Nore, rocking the pram which contained her baby daughter. At twenty-three she had retained many of her girlish charms and her auburn hair was as thick as ever, although she wore it up so that the natural wave was not shown off to best advantage and now it was mainly hidden by a hat secured by a scarf tied under her chin. Her freckles were as prominent as ever – more so perhaps, because with a young child and a husband to care for, she had less time to spend on her appearance and the daily applications of lemon juice were no more than a luxurious memory. Her figure had thickened a little, but only her eyes truly revealed the transformation from child to woman, for her experiences during the war had erased the look of youthful innocence. Her expression bore the tell-tale traces of a youth eroded by long hours of grim and unremitting work in an atmosphere of prolonged despair. Winifred and Ernest had gone to France young and full of hope. They had both returned sadder and wiser, but grateful to be alive and still deeply in love.

She had come down to the beach hoping to have a word with Ernest before they put to sea, but found the crew in the process of launching the boat and knew better than to interfere at such a time. On returning from France, her husband had taken up his place in Stan's crew on the old *Hope*, a 30-foot lugger built in 1894. Since then he was invariably to be found on the stade when he was not at sea, for he had taken to the life of a fisherman like the proverbial duck to water and had been accepted by the men who for generations had known no other master but the sea and to whom this part of the seashore was a second home. Here they exchanged news and gossip, tended their boats, mended their nets and even sold their fish, for not all the catch would go to the Fishmarket for auction, a small quantity being held back for an impromptu sale on the beach. Today the cool wind blew lowering clouds from the west with the promise of rain, giving the grey-green cliffs behind the stade a sombre appearance so that they

seemed to threaten the men and boats dwarfed below them on the
sloping beach. The wind whipped the crests of the waves as they
broke noisily along the shoreline and flung the salty spray into the
faces of the men who struggled to launch their sturdy craft into
the grey water. Three boats were already afloat and heading out to
sea in a bid to secure the best sea berths and, hopefully, the largest
hauls of fish. Six more – Stan's amongst them – were in the
process of being launched, while two others were still being
prepared for sea. Everywhere groups of dark-clad men moved
purposefully about their work, with no urgency apparent in their
movements. When the last boat had put to sea only the 'boys-
ashore' would remain – the young boys and elderly retired fishermen who would tidy up the huts and make their way home. The
beach would be littered with ropes and chains, spars, unwanted
anchors and nets awaiting repair and piles of baskets, crates and
barrels. The capstans would stand idle, the onlookers would drift
away and the cries of the seagulls wheeling overhead would go
unheard.

'He's seen us,' said Winifred, amused. She addressed herself
to the baby, for there was no one else nearby to watch the
fishermen as they struggled to propel the boat across the stretch
of shingle that separated it from the sea.

'He's seen us, your papa, but he'll not let on. He's funny like
that.' She shivered in the cool March wind which gusted erratically across the beach. It was not ideal weather for fishing, but if the
boats stayed idle whenever the weather was unkind their families
would often go hungry.

Winifred had hoped that after her marriage her father would
offer Ernest a place in the boatyard, but he had not done so and
Stanley had obviously expected his stepson to work with him as
before. She knew that when Stan died the boat would pass to
Ernest, but nevertheless regretted the fact that her husband
would put his life at risk every time they put to sea. Stern first, the
lugger moved slowly across the greased wooden trows. The
combined efforts of the four-man crew could never have made it
unaided, but there were always plenty of willing helpers – retired
fishermen who spent their days on the stade, or 'boys-ashore' who
worked on the boats while they were beached. She recognised
Sam Breed, Bill's brother, who had lost a leg years earlier when
he had been crushed between two boats.

'Chalk away!' cried Stan.

'All 'aunch!' cried one of the men.

'Oh!' roared the rest as, five to each side, they braced their backs against the hull and pushed with all their might.

Fishing was men's work and women were not welcomed on the busy stade, except when there was fish to be gutted and graded – then they could earn a shilling or two and take home a few of the fish which for various reasons were unsuitable for the market.

'All 'aunch!'

'Oh!'

With each heave, the boat moved forward a foot or so; it was slow, backbreaking work and Winifred shook her head wonderingly. It still astonished her that, after the effort of launching a boat, the crew had any energy left for the actual fishing trip. Now the boat moved faster suddenly and there was no trow in place in front of it.

'Hold-fast!' roared Stan and the man following with the anchor dug it into the shingle to hinder the boat's progress, while Sam Breed snatched up the wooden plank and limped round to the stern to wedge it in position. The anchor was removed and the launch continued.

'All 'aunch!' echoed Winifred as the commands rang out once more. 'Oh! Come on, Sukey! You can say that. Oh!'

The baby, christened Susan, laughed delightedly and jogged up and down in her pram, pursing her lips to give a fair imitation of the men's chant. Winifred laughed. 'You'll make a good fisherman one day,' she told her daughter. 'That *will* surprise your papa!'

Five minutes later, to the accompaniment of grunts of triumph from the men, the boat cleared the shingle ridge and slid into the water. At the same moment Winifred heard footsteps on the shingle behind her and turned to see a young man approaching. She guessed him to be about her own age or perhaps a little younger. He was hatless and his red hair, dishevelled by the wind, topped a pleasant face with a fine nose and large hazel eyes. As he drew nearer, she could see a scar on the left side of his face.

'Good morning,' he said, smiling ruefully. 'My hat blew into the sea and I didn't feel like going in after it! I'm looking for Ernie Brett, but not having much luck. Any idea where he might be?'

Winifred returned the smile and then pointed towards the crew of the *Hope*. 'He's one of that lot,' she told him, 'and he's my husband. I'm Winifred Brett.'

The young man's face lit up with genuine pleasure. 'You're Winnie!' he exclaimed. 'Forgive me, but I feel as though I know you. Ernie talked so much about you.' He glanced at the baby and grinned. 'I see you and Ernie have begun your family. How splendid! It was his one ambition, as I remember, after marrying you, that is!'

He held out his hand and Winifred shook it.

'I'm Ian,' he told her. 'Ian Cornwell. They used to call me "Ginger" because of this.' He touched his flaming hair. 'Perhaps your husband—'

' "Ginger" Cornwell!' she exclaimed. 'I remember now – there was "Ginger" and "Chalky" and . . . you all served in the same regiment! Oh, what a lovely surprise. Ernest will be . . . oh dear!'

'What is it?'

'They're just putting out to sea,' she explained, 'which means they'll be away for at least twenty-four hours. You'll be able to catch him before they go, but what a shame. Have you come far?'

Ian was shaking his head. 'Don't worry,' he told her. 'My grandparents have bought a house near Rye and I am visiting them; I shall probably be down again before the year's out.'

Winifred breathed a sigh of relief. 'But you can still catch him. Uncle Stan – that's my father-in-law – will be sailing shortly. Run down now and have a word with Ernest; he'll be so pleased to see you again.'

She watched him run across the beach and heard him call to Ernest who, after a moment's disbelief, shouted a delighted greeting.

'What a nice young man,' she said, giving Sukey a hug and adjusting her bonnet to give her more protection from the cold wind. 'That's a friend of Papa's,' she told her. 'He was fighting with him in those terrible trenches. He's a brave man.' She gave a little laugh. 'Ian Cornwell. Well I never, after all this time.' She put her head on one side consideringly as she saw Ernest lean down from the boat in a vain effort to shake Ian's hand. Ernest had told her Ian was 'posh'. 'I suppose he is a bit posh, but nice with it,' she said.

She shivered a little, watching as the boat moved into deeper water and the foresail was hoisted. It filled at once and the boat turned gracefully towards the fishing grounds. It always astonished Winifred that a craft so bulky on land could be so elegant when afloat. She waved as Ernest shouted, 'Cheerio!' and then waited with Ian beside her until the boat was a quarter of a mile out to sea.

Then she said, 'Well, that's all there is to see and we ought to be going home. It's cold standing about. At least have a bite to eat with us before you go?'

Ian accepted the invitation and they began to walk back across the beach towards the road, weaving their way between the capstans and the piles of nets.

'It's a hard life,' said Ian. 'Don't you worry about him?'

Winifred sighed, then nodded. 'But it's all he knows,' she said simply, 'and it's what he wants. That's good enough for me.'

*

As Winifred had predicted, Ernest had been delighted to see his friend again. The sight of Ian had revived many memories – some of which he would rather forget, others which he valued and was glad to recall – but he kept his thoughts to himself until they had reached the selected fishing ground. The herring season was well over and Stan was drift-netting for sprats, although a few of the skippers were already trawling for flat fish. The pole, or 'dan', went over the side with its flag on top to mark the end of the nets and after a few more yards of rope the long net was shot. Corks at intervals along the top edge would keep the nets upright in the water. As usual, Stan had surreptitiously inserted a sixpence into one of the corks to ensure a good catch. It was an old superstition but still respected. Next the foremast came down and the mizzen was hoisted. When it grew dark a warning light would be hung aloft.

Ernest, meanwhile, had prepared a bit of supper. On the stove below decks a large pan simmered, containing a piece of silver-side, onions and potatoes. He added dumplings, replaced the lid and gave the rest of the crew a shout to let them know the meal was as good as ready. Life on board could be tedious and the men looked forward to the food to relieve the monotony, as well as to fill empty bellies. The large seed cake which Winifred had made would serve as a pudding.

When they were all seated and eating, Stan asked, 'Who was that then, Ernie?' and Ernest explained eagerly that he and Ian had served together in France.

'No flies on our Ian,' he told them, tapping his forehead. 'Was going to be a doctor, but he was mad keen to get into the war. His folks nearly went mad – under age, too, but if the Army guessed they looked the other way. "Ginger" we called him. He got teased at first because of how he spoke, very posh and lots of big words, but he took it all in good part. He was a real dare-devil, though you wouldn't think it to look at him. And the girls loved him! I'll say they did. Those French mam'selles couldn't do enough for him. Give him anything, they would!'

'Oh yes?' Stan winked. 'Like what? The pip?'

'No. Nothing like that,' protested Ernest. 'He was a bit of an innocent and younger than me, but it was the red hair that did it. Wine, they gave him. Chocolate. Bunches of flowers!'

'You should have dyed your hair!'

'I thought of it, don't you worry!' Ernest forked a mass of dumpling and beef into his mouth and wiped the drips of gravy from his chin with the back of his hand. 'The things he got up to! And looking so innocent, no one ever blamed him. We had some laughs. He used to call himself the "food taster" because if ever we found food left by the enemy – and we often did – rumour had it that it would be poisoned. Old Ian used to taste a bit of everything, just like that. "Well, lads, I'm still hale and hearty," he'd say in that posh voice of his, and then of course we'd all tuck in. It was like a gift from heaven after our rations – four biscuits, a tin of bully and a bit of tea and sugar.'

'Did they ever?' asked Stan.

'Ever what?'

'Poison the food?'

'No, course they didn't,' said Ernest. 'We had some real feasts: chicken, wines and all that. Oh, the Huns know how to look after themselves. But Ginger was a real good sort. He could've been an officer, you know, taken a commission, because his grandfather was a general – or maybe it was a colonel, I forget. Anyway, he said he wanted to be in the thick of it so he stuck with us lot.' He helped himself to some more vegetables, then laughed. 'How he didn't get himself killed I'll never know! Talk about scrapes! I remember one night—'

There was a mocking chorus of roars and cat-calls from the rest of the crew at this point and Ernest grinned. He was the only member of the crew to have been the right age to enlist and his stories were notoriously long-winded. It was good-natured chaffing, however, which in no way implied a reluctance to hear the tale. Ernest went straight on as though he hadn't heard it. 'We'd all just finished eating a tasty bit of rabbit stew. Ginger had pinched five rabbits from a hutch, when one of our officers sent word along the trench that a local farmer had promised us all a feed of rabbit pie at seven o'clock that night. 'Course, he never did because his rabbits had all disappeared! I don't know how we kept our faces straight. And that scar on Ian's face – that was a lucky escape if ever there was one. One of our chaps got knocked out with a bullet in the leg and without a by-your-leave Ian ran out there and began to hoist him on to his back. A sniper got him right across his cheek – just grazed him. He was lucky not to be dead.'

The men finally finished the nourishing stew and Ernest produced the seed cake already cut into thick slices.

'I can see why you wed young Winifred,' laughed Stan. 'She's a fair old cook, bless her.'

'That reminds me,' Ernest began again, 'there was this cook—'

Another roar went up and one of the men pointed out that it was time for a 'cuppa' to help the cake down; reluctantly Ernest relinquished his role as story-teller and set about more mundane matters, consoling himself that before long he might well be sharing a few pints with Ian Cornwell at The Dolphin. Time enough then to reminisce about old times.

When at last the men tumbled topside with the coming of dawn they found a heavy rain falling, hissing into the sullen waves and pattering on to the deck. A thin band of light showed on the eastern horizon, but the rest of the world was cold and grey. Visibility was poor and the low, dark land mass was barely distinguishable from the heavy clouds and dull grey seas which bounded it above and below. The wind had lessened and the five-foot waves rolled sluggishly past the boat as the crew took their places at the rail and prepared to haul in the nets.

Ernest mumbled a curse as his boots slipped on the wet deck and he grabbed at the wheelhouse to steady himself. Ahead of him someone less fortunate sprawled full-length and Ernest reached out a hand to help him to his feet. Already the rain had found its way down his face and neck and his hands were chilled. An oiled rag was wrapped round each of his wrists to prevent the harsh edge of his oilskins from chafing his skin, but his hands were bare. They worked in unison, three hauls on the net and then a shake to loosen the gleaming fish which then dropped into the hold. There was no need for words; they had hauled together long enough to know each other's rhythm of work, but it was back-breaking labour. Within a few minutes of the first fish coming on board the deck was slippery with fish scales and water dripping from the nets added to the men's discomfort. In a heavier swell it would have been dangerous, for a man could lose his footing and go overboard in less time than it took his mates to shout a warning.

The hauling went on for more than an hour with no let-up, but the total catch was a good one and since the crew worked a 'share system' – each owning a proportion of the catch – there were few grumbles when finally the last net was stowed and they stood looking down into a hold full of gleaming fish. Their backs ached and their hands were raw from handling yards of coarse wet net, but their hearts glowed with a sense of achievement and the knowledge of a job well done.

The hatch cover was replaced and the exhausted men gathered below while Ernest brewed up cocoa. As he poured hot milk into the cups he looked at his hands – scratched and sore and red with cold – and wondered again what power it was that held men bound to the sea. It repaid the fishermen's dedication with hardship and danger, but when times were good it fed and clothed their families and made them independent of the rest of the world – of this they were fiercely proud.

Ernest did not put his thoughts into words, but as he handed out the steaming mugs of cocoa he felt a deep sense of achievement and knew he would never want to live his life any other way.

*

Later that year the day of the Rye Regatta dawned once more, bright and clear, and by lunch-time Rye was filled with visitors determined to enjoy the August Bank Holiday sunshine. The event, so popular before the war, had now been revived and the new organisers, enthusiastic to a man, intended to make the day an outstanding success. Posters had attracted people from all directions, the town was full of traffic and the restaurants and public houses were doing a roaring trade. The cobbled streets, where everything was usually so restrained, were bright with balloons and loud with voices as the day's festivities got under way.

The Fishmarket was the scene of frantic activity as the time of the Regatta approached. On both sides of the river the contestants worked on their boats, watched by interested spectators who urged them on with good-natured chaffing. Jean Dessin grinned broadly as he rubbed blacklead into the hull of the upturned dinghy. In the hot sunshine he wore only trousers and they were rolled up a few inches above his bare feet.

'It'll go faster,' he told an enquiring onlooker. 'Be smoother, you see, when I've polished it with blacklead.'

'Go faster?' He looked unconvinced.

'That's right.'

'You reckon?'

'I *know!*'

The man turned to his wife. 'Did you hear that?' he asked. 'He says it goes faster when it's polished.'

'Well, I never!' said his middle-aged wife. She smiled at Jean, secretly impressed by his youthful good looks. At twenty years of age he had broadened out and the soft lines of his face had strengthened. With his smooth gold hair and pale blue eyes she thought he looked delicate and somehow 'foreign'. 'You going to win, then?' she asked teasingly. 'Shall we put our money on you?'

Jean's right arm moved in steady circles until he had covered one side, then he asked the man for help and together they turned the boat over so that the other half of the hull was exposed.

'Your boat, is it?' the woman asked.

Jean shook his head. 'Belongs to my skipper,' he said, 'over there.' He pointed to where *Silver Lady* lay at anchor. 'That's his, this is just the ship's boat, to bring stuff to shore and back. I'm only crew.'

He dipped the rag into the tin of blacklead and went on applying it to the upturned hull.

'Your hands!' said the woman. 'Black as the ace of spades.' She looked round at the selection of boats in and out of the water. 'All these boats racing, then?'

He nodded. 'Dinghies race against dinghies, barges race against barges and so on.'

'Oh, that's how you do it. Well I never! We must buy a programme and see what's what.'

The man, feeling that his wife was monopolising the conversation, said, 'The ships used to go to Boulogne from Rye in the old days. My grandfather remembered that. The *Windsor Castle*, one boat was called. Oh, he was very made up with that. You could go one day, say a Saturday, stay on for a few days and then come back on, say, the Monday or Tuesday. He used to go for business, you see. Oh yes, he liked foreign parts, as he called it. Used to tell us kids all manner of tales about France. Seven shillings and sixpence it was to Boulogne in those days, and you could take your horse and carriage over with you if you wanted – but that was extra, of course.'

His wife, who had heard all this before, said to Jean, 'Ever been to France, have you?'

Jean shook his head. 'My home was in Belgium,' he said. 'That's where I came from when the Germans invaded. I went back as soon as the war ended, but I couldn't settle so I returned here.'

'Well, I never!' cried the woman triumphantly. 'I *thought* you was foreign! I mean, you speak good English but with a funny accent.'

At that moment Julia, Emily and Agnes arrived to join them and the couple reluctantly wandered away.

'Hullo, Jean,' cried Julia. Regardless of his dirty hands and her own spotless dress of white organdie, she flung herself into his arms for a hug.

'Can I help you? Can I do some polishing?' she demanded. 'Why *are* you polishing it, Jean? Are you going to win the race? Oh, you *must* win it, Jean, because Frank Bligh says *he* is going to and because I want *you* to win it!'

Jean glanced up at Agnes with ill-disguised curiosity. He had not met the threesome together before and wondered how Agnes and Julia were getting along under one roof. Julia seemed cheerful enough now, but then it was Regatta time and there was a truly festive feeling in the town as this was the first such event since the outbreak of war.

Agnes smiled at him. 'That looks like hard work,' she said. She was looking very attractive in a green-and-white checked dress and white hat with green and yellow feathers. The hat, shading her face, flattered her and gave her a youthful appearance. He wondered how old she was and guessed twenty-five.

'The sweat's pouring off me,' he agreed. 'I wish the sun would go in for a bit.' He looked at Emily, resplendent in blue. 'And how are you, miss?' he asked. 'You're looking very bonny.'

'I want Frank Bligh to win,' she told him.

'Frank Bligh!' he cried, rising deliberately to the bait. 'That scoundrel? Did you hear that, Julia? She wants Frank Bligh to win.'

Emily looked at Julia and giggled. 'I *do*,' she insisted. 'I really *do*.'

Julia stepped forward to stand beside her champion. 'Jean is going to win,' she declared, 'because he's older than Frank and bigger and stronger.'

Agnes raised her eyebrows provocatively. '*Are* you big and strong, Jean?' she asked him.

'Yes, he is,' cried Julia, but Agnes was continuing to look at Jean, waiting for his own answer.

He was both amused and flattered that his boss's wife was trying to flirt with him and decided at once to encourage her. 'Big enough and strong enough,' he answered.

Julia cried, 'I told you so!' and Jean grinned at her. 'And look at my Julia,' he said, 'in a frilly white dress.'

Julia and Emily exchanged looks and giggled.

'Supposing,' Jean suggested slyly, 'I put these hands round you two girls . . .' He left the sentence unfinished and made a sudden threatening move towards them, fingers outspread. Screaming, they took to their heels and put a distance of ten yards or so between themselves and their tormenter. Then he turned back towards Agnes and offered his black hands.

'What about you, Mrs Coulsden?' he joked. 'Suppose I was to put them round you . . .'

He saw the flicker of awareness in her eyes as she laughed. 'Would I scream and run away, you mean?'

'*Would* you?'

'I don't know. You'd have to try me!'

He inclined his head in such a way and with such an expression that Agnes knew at once how he chose to interpret her answer and she blushed slightly, which made her look even younger. Almost innocent, thought Jean. Had he not known otherwise, he would have thought her a charming and desirable woman, but he *did* know otherwise. Everyone in the town knew that she had had an illegitimate child by George Coulsden, but that now they were married. The veneer of respectability was a thin one.

Agnes was struggling with her emotions. Part of her wanted to flirt outrageously with this good-looking young man, but part of her wanted to play the desirable but unattainable married woman, a little shocked by this unduly familiar member of her husband's crew.

After a pause during which neither dared speak, Jean dropped to his knees, picked up the cloth and applied himself once more to the business of polishing. Let her make the next move, he thought. He was not foolish enough to commit himself too far . . . just yet. Agnes watched the gleaming golden head and admired the broad shoulders and tanned back. She took a step towards him, but he did not raise his head. Then she moved again, so that the skirt of her gown swung out and brushed his bare arm. Slowly he lowered the cloth and turned to look up at her, squinting into the bright sunshine.

'Will you win?' she asked softly. 'For me?'

'If you wish it, I will win,' he replied huskily. 'If *you* wish it.' The fleeting touch of her skirt had affected him as she had hoped it would.

'I do wish it,' she said.

He stood up. 'Then, Mrs Coulsden, I must win,' he promised. He sounded a little breathless, she noticed with satisfaction.

'I'll be watching,' she said softly, and held up her right hand with two fingers crossed for him. Out of the corner of her eye she noted Julia and Emily talking animatedly to old Alice Bligh while behind Jean – and thus unseen by him – George was approaching deep in conversation with Stanley. For a long moment she looked into Jean's eyes and thought, 'This is how it used to be with a lad, all excitement and teasing and not quite knowing. Him looking at me that way and me getting this certain feeling deep inside. I could have had any man I wanted and I gave it all up for George Coulsden and look where it's got me. I might just as well be invisible for all the notice he takes of me.'

Jean thought, 'So she wishes me to win. Then by God I'll make sure that I do and then we'll see how it goes from there. She could be dangerous, but she's exciting.' The knowledge that she was married to George Coulsden gave the flirtation added appeal. For Jean, taking risks was a need which his smuggling activities did not entirely satisfy.

Suddenly he felt a heavy hand on his shoulder and George Coulsden was beside him. He knew the shock showed on his face and Agnes laughed lightly. The bitch! She must have seen her husband coming. If that was how she wanted to play it, he was a match for her any day.

'Jean is going to win for us,' she told George with a smile at her brother-in-law. 'Isn't that wonderful?' She glanced around with a puzzled expression. 'Jane not with you?' she asked Stanley. 'One of her headaches, I expect.'

Her smile was sweet but there was malice in her heart. Since Sarah's death the family's attitude had softened towards her. Jack had visited them once and Cicely had spoken to her politely on three occasions when they had met in the town. Stanley had visited the house several times and had brought Winifred and the baby. Julia, Agnes now realised, was her trump card. The family were fond of George's daughter and now that she lived with George and Agnes, they must acknowledge Agnes and Emily or lose touch with their niece. Julia had a vital role to play if Agnes was finally to be accepted into the Coulsden family. Sarah's death had been the first step; Julia was the second, although Agnes had not appreciated the fact immediately. As soon as she had done so, however, her manner towards Julia had changed and Julia's life became considerably more tolerable. George, unaware of the thinking behind Agnes's behaviour, congratulated himself that his daughter's charm had wrought the magic.

To date, however, Jane had steadfastly refused to meet Agnes and Stanley, with characteristic lack of imagination, always pretended that Jane was unwell. So now when Agnes asked him whether Jane had 'one of her headaches', he mumbled, 'Afraid so,' with a resigned shrug.

At that moment Julia and Emily returned and greeted their uncle excitedly. Jean resumed his polishing and Agnes was reluctantly forced to waste her charms on her husband and his elder brother.

Further along the river bank, at the boatyard on Rock Channel, Jack and Cicely were watching Frank Bligh; he was going to row one of the dinghies for them, since this year Tommy Bird had declared himself 'past it'. Frank was also blackleading the bottom of the boat.

'There's a ten-bob note in it if you beat George's lad,' Jack told him. 'Ten bob! You think of that now, young Frank.'

Leo and Ben craned forward in order to see better.

'Leonard! Benjamin!' cried Cicely. 'How many times do I have to tell you to keep back? You'll get yourselves dirty.'

Ben stepped back obediently but Leo, with great deliberation, leaned over closer to the gleaming black keel – then Frank dabbed the cloth in his direction and he was forced to retreat.

It was a matter of family pride that one of the Coulsden boats should win the race. At the last Regatta, held the summer before the war, Jack's boat had won, rowed by a triumphant but exhausted Tommy Bird. The year before that Luke Bligh had stolen a march on them, rowing a boat belonging to one of the holiday-makers. Many years earlier George, Stanley and Jack had vied with each other in the swimming events, sharing the prizes more or less equally. The majority of the competitors were drawn from the crews of the fishing boats or were members of the boatyards.

The Regatta promised plenty of spectacle for the crowd who strolled the banks of the river in eager anticipation of the delights ahead. They admired a small boat which had been converted into a copy of a Plantagenet warship, complete with forecastle and imitation cannon. It contained real gunpowder and later in the evening the 'ship' would be towed out to a safe distance and blown up.

Further along, the bowsprit of the *Victoria* was being greased with tallow. A leg of ham would hang from the end of it and hopefuls would try to walk along the slippery spar. If they reached the end, which was unlikely, they would allow themselves to fall into the water, snatching at the ham as they went down.

When the daylight had gone and the races and competitions were all over, a procession of boats would use the last of the ebbing tide to sail along the river. They would be lit up by hundreds of flickering candles and the town band would provide a background of suitably romantic music.

Meanwhile, the programme was due to start and the drifting crowds collected round the dais on which the Mayor and several other dignitaries were waiting to make their speeches. A bugle call from one of the town bandsmen silenced the crowd.

'My Lord Mayor, ladies and gentlemen . . .'

Julia held George's right hand, Emily his left. Agnes stood beside them but alone. A strong friendship had rapidly developed between the two girls; each felt she had an ally against the unpredictability of adults and they took some comfort from their shared predicament. Agnes's frequent outbursts of irritability alienated both girls and they turned more and more to George for proof that they were cherished. Agnes, vaguely aware of their withdrawal, watched helplessly as his relationship with the girls improved and felt rejected by her husband. Now, aware of those linked hands, she felt a wave of self-pity for her apparent isolation; as she thought again of her brief exchange with Jean Dessin, the barely formed notion of an affair hardened into determination. Damn George and his precious daughters! She was not without admirers herself – she too could be loved.

As the Mayor began his speech, Julia glanced at the little group around her. Winifred was there with Ernest and baby Susan. Uncle Jack stood next to Aunt Cicely, his arm round Ben's shoulders. Catching Julia's eye, Ben dodged away from his father to come and stand beside her and his place beside Jack was taken by Leo. Uncle Stan whispered something to Cicely and Julia saw her smile. Aunt Jane would not come, Julia knew – and she knew why. The two girls often crept out of their room to sit at the top of the stairs and listen to George and Agnes talking below. According to Agnes, Jane was a 'stubborn narrow-minded bitch', but in George's estimation she was 'entitled to her opinion, same as anyone else'. So Aunt Jane disapproved of Agnes.

A burst of applause brought Julia's attention back to the Regatta and she tried to concentrate on what the Mayor was saying.

'Fellow Ryers,' he began and a roar of approval went up. 'Fellow Ryers and visitors, I welcome you here on this very special occasion – that of the first Rye Regatta to be held since Kaiser Wilhelm was foolish enough to think he could get away with murder!'

There was delighted laughter and the Mayor continued, 'We showed him that he was wrong!'

Shouts of 'Hear, hear!' followed.

'Now, thanks to our brave boys, we can relax, safe in the knowledge of a job well done. We all work hard and we deserve to play a bit and this Regatta is designed especially for that purpose.'

He lost Julia's attention again as she suddenly became aware that Ben had taken her hand and was staring at her. She stared back in astonishment, looking down at her hand clasped so firmly in his. What on earth was happening, she wondered? Her cousin had never held her hand before and had certainly never looked at her with that funny expression on his face. She tried to pull her hand free but Ben tightened his grip.

'Let go!' she hissed. 'You're hurting my fingers.'

Ben put his mouth close to her ear. 'I can't. I'm going to marry you when I grow up,' he whispered, his round face flushed with excitement.

'You are *not*!' hissed Julia, alarmed by the suddenness of Ben's proposal. 'Let me go or I'll tell.'

'I am!' He held her hand with both of his so that to extricate it would prove a painful exercise. 'Say you'll marry me.'

'No! I told you. Let *go*, Ben!'

George glanced down and shushed them because the Mayor's speech was still going on.

'Say you *will*.'

'I won't.'

Ben, distraught and furious, crushed her hand as hard as he could and Julia let out a squeal of pain and rage. Frightened, Ben released her, whereupon she pushed him as hard as she could so that he lost his balance and tumbled backwards, arms flailing wildly, to crash against Cicely's legs. She instinctively stepped back and cannoned into an elderly man who was eating an ice cream which was promptly knocked from his hand. Julia watched the ensuing disturbance with indifference. Marry Ben? The idea was impossible. She had long ago decided she would give her heart to Leo.

The race started promptly at 3.10 pm as advertised in the programme and five boats took part. They were rowed by Frank Bligh (at thirteen, the youngest competitor), Jean Dessin, a man from another boatyard, the nephew of the harbour master and one of the men who worked in the sail loft. As the starting gun went off there was a great roar from the crowds, who all yelled and cheered to urge on their favourites.

'Jean! Jean! Come on, Jean!' roared George, his large hands cupped to his mouth. 'Pull, man! Pull, dammit! Put some beef into it, man! You're losing your lead.'

As the boats sped across the water the spectators' roars increased and they edged across the banks, perilously near to the edge of the water, in an effort to see what was happening. Young Frank Bligh was doing surprisingly well. He was the image of his dead father, although as yet his body had not broadened into manhood. He had the same square face and dark brown eyes and his curly dark hair was as tousled as ever Luke's had been. He pulled on the oars as though his life depended on it, instead of glory and a ten-shilling note. To frantic cheers and deafening shouts of encouragement, he overtook the man from the sail loft and began to threaten Jean.

'*Go on*, Jean!' screamed Julia. 'You've got to beat him. Go *on*!'

George bellowed instructions to Jean while Agnes, Cicely and Winifred covered their ears as the screams of the crowd grew even louder.

'He's going to do it!' cried George, beside himself with delight. 'Jean's going to make it!'

'So he is,' thought Agnes, 'and he's doing it for me, George, not you. He's sweating his guts out to please me!'

As the shouting rose to a crescendo, Jean pulled across the finishing line a half-length ahead of Frank. But as the applause rang out, Jack frowned suddenly: 'Something's up! The lad's keeled over.'

There was consternation as the rest of the crowd realised that something was indeed wrong. Frank had fallen forward in a state of collapse and Jean, his own boat alongside, was trying to assist him.

As Jack began to run, Julia ran after him. 'Uncle Jack!' she screamed. 'I want to come too.'

Together they pushed a way through the crowd. At the finishing line they learned that Frank had been taken to the Red Cross tent and there they found him laid out on a canvas bed with a doctor and nurse in attendance. Alice Bligh was already there and she looked up as Jack and Julia entered.

'He's going to be all right,' she told them tremulously. 'It was just the heat and that.'

Jack looked at the doctor for confirmation and he nodded.

'Exhaustion, heat, too much excitement.' He shrugged and smiled. 'But he should be none the worse by the morning.'

'He rowed a damn good race!' said Jack.

Turning his back on Frank, the doctor lowered his voice. 'He was too young for that race,' he said. 'Too little stamina at that age. They outgrow their strength, but you weren't to know that.'

'Christ!' said Jack. 'I never gave it a thought. He was so keen to do it. On and on at me, he was.'

'Does he work for you?'

'No. Helps his grandmother at the harbour ferry.'

'Ah.' He turned to Alice. 'He ought to take it easy for a day or two. Don't want to strain his heart.'

'Right, doctor. I'll see to it.'

Julia had moved close to Frank and stood staring down at the pale face, still beaded with sweat. His eyes were open and he looked up at her for a moment, then with an effort he propped himself up on one elbow and wiped the sweat from his face with his forearm.

'You were very good, Frank,' she told him.

He grinned. 'Did you enjoy it, Julia? Did you see me nearly win?'

She nodded solemnly and to Frank Bligh she looked like a dainty china doll, with her cool blue eyes and long silvery hair.

'Give us a kiss, then,' he teased her. 'The winner always gets a kiss.'

Obediently she leaned forward and planted a chaste kiss on his cheek.

Then abruptly she frowned. 'But you didn't win,' she protested.

He laughed. 'Ever been had?' he asked.

'Frank Bligh, you're a beastly boy!' she told him indignantly.

Wearily, he flopped back. 'But I did nearly win,' he whispered. 'Next year I *will* win – you see if I don't.'

Alice said, 'You're to stay there and rest for an hour, Frank. Oh yes!' She pushed him back as, contrarily, he made an effort to sit up. 'Isn't that right, doctor?'

'Yes, an hour's rest,' the doctor insisted. 'Then just take it easy. No more races today – and I mean that.'

Jack plunged a hand into his waistcoat pocket and pulled out some coins. 'Here's your money, lad,' he told Frank. 'You didn't win but by God, you damn near did! No, you take it. You've ruddy well earned it. Now we must love you and leave you. Say "good-bye", Julia.'

'Good-bye, Frank,' she said dutifully and was rewarded by a large wink. As she left the tent she reconsidered her intention to marry Leo. She could always change her mind, she thought, and marry Frank Bligh instead.

CHAPTER TEN

Three weeks later Agnes stood at the window of the front parlour with the binoculars to her eyes. They were trained on the Fish-market area and she was looking for Jean Dessin's familiar figure. She could see the two girls on *Silver Lady*'s deck and George was with them. Also 'Buzz' Roberts, one of his crew – a middle-aged man with a family of nine children who worked round the clock to provide for them. When he wasn't at sea, he mended boots and shoes in his garden shed, returned the washing done by his wife and mother-in-law and helped out behind the bar at the Pipemakers'.

Agnes tutted as Jean Dessin continued to elude her. 'He must be there somewhere,' she muttered crossly.

She would be glad when tomorrow came and the new term started, then Julia and Emily would be safely out of the way in the infants school in Lion Street. Then, perhaps, she would get a chance to speak to Jean alone. She had seen him twice since the Regatta, but on one occasion the girls had been with her and on the other George had been on the boat.

Agnes had thought about little else since the idea of a flirtation had first entered her head; in her imagination, they were already madly in love and enjoying a torrid affair. She was quite certain that in spite of his youth his body would delight her, and the prospect of clandestine meetings excited in her a growing impatience. On one occasion, she had casually raised with George the question of Jean's 'attachments'.

'They're falling over themselves,' he told her, 'but none of them seem to last. No one serious. Just as well at his age – he won't settle down just yet if he's got any sense.'

Agnes had agreed with him a little too fervently, but George did not notice. Turning the binoculars now, she scrutinised the men on board the other boats in case Jean was 'visiting' but there was no sign of him. They were all unloading and the river bank was covered in the flat wooden crates holding the gleaming fish which were being examined by a variety of would-be purchasers.

She could see Dan Biddle's horse and cart which he drove round the outlying villages – Iden, Peasmarsh and Appledore. Tubby Mr Clark was there with his hand-cart and so was Charlie Bean; they delivered direct to the hotels and restaurants in the town itself. Most of the catch, however, would go to Billingsgate in London, although a small amount would be sold over the counter in the little wooden shack close by the river which served as a shop.

Agnes lowered the binoculars and rubbed her eyes. If only she could see him alone, just for a moment or two!

'Where are you, Jean Dessin?' she sighed. Turning from the window, she looked at herself in the mirror, baring her teeth to admire their whiteness and smiling roguishly at herself to see how she would appear to Jean. How long was it since George had paid her a compliment, she wondered? A sight too long. A bit of competition from a younger man would do him good . . . if he knew. It might be an idea to drop a few hints. Perhaps if Jean was not the kind to give presents – and that seemed quite likely – she could buy a little something for herself and tell George that she had done so, but in such an unconvincing way that he would suspect that she was lying. She smiled at herself in the mirror again.

'Oh yes, George Coulsden,' she said. 'I can be cleverer than you if I put my mind to it. I'll play you like a fish.'

Then the door-bell rang and reluctantly she tore herself away from her own reflection and went to answer it.

Jean Dessin was standing on the doorstep! Agnes' heart leaped as she stared at him, unable to hide her delight. He had obviously been unloading fish, for he wore a short oilskin smock over his flannel trousers and dark blue jersey. His hands were dirty and his boots glistened with fish scales, but Agnes thought he looked wonderful and was momentarily stunned by his good looks.

Jean grinned at her. 'Message, Mrs Coulsden,' he said in slightly mocking tones.

'Oh yes?'

'For the *beautiful* Mrs Coulsden!'

'That's me!' she laughed breathlessly. So he *did* still feel that way about her and she had not been mistaken.

'From your husband,' he went on. 'To say he'll send the girls home an hour earlier than he said, because he's going to Hastings with Jack to see Stan and won't be back until late.'

Agnes's dazzling smile almost faltered. Damn George! That was so like him. He would go off for the evening with his brothers and they'd all have a good time while she was left looking after his kids!

She gave a little shrug. 'How kind of him to tell me,' she said sarcastically and then, trying not to sound waspish, added hastily, 'And how kind of you to bring the message.'

'It was my pleasure,' he replied. 'Talking to the beautiful Mrs Coulsden beats swabbing down the deck any day.'

Agnes feigned indignation. 'I should jolly well hope so,' she said. 'I should hope it beats a lot of things.'

'Oh, it does,' he agreed softly. 'I think Mr Coulsden is a very lucky man.'

'Well, I wish *he* thought so!'

'Doesn't he?'

She hesitated, wanting to enlist his sympathy or a compliment or both, yet reluctant to admit that George no longer found her wildly attractive.

'He's never here,' she hedged. 'He loves that boat more than me.'

'He's a fool then, begging your pardon, ma'am. A man who neglects his wife deserves all he gets.'

'You reckon so?' Agnes shifted her weight on to one foot and put a hand on one hip.

'I reckon so,' he told her. 'I reckon another man will come along and . . . do the honours.' He looked her straight in the eye. 'Someone like me, for instance!'

'You'd do the honours, would you?'

'I would deem it a privilege,' he grinned – a charming grin which lit up his eyes and made him seem more handsome than ever.

Agnes felt weak at the knees, quite literally, and was glad she could lean against the door jamb.

'Are you going to ask me in?' he suggested. 'I have something for you.'

'For me? Something . . . ?' Startled, Agnes glanced quickly up and down the street in case anyone she knew happened to be passing. Seeing no one, she held open the door and Jean stepped inside. He gave the neat hallway a brief glance and then drew a small package from his pocket and held it up.

'What is it?'

'Perfume. From Paris.'

'Jean! Oh but – how on earth did you . . . from *Paris*?' She stammered.

He nodded and tapped the side of his nose with a grimy forefinger. 'Ask no questions,' he told her. 'I know a man who knows a man . . .'

'Was it expensive?' she asked.

'Oh yes. It will cost you a kiss.'

Careful not to embrace her for fear of leaving tell-tale fish scales, he leaned forward to kiss her cheek and put the package into her hands. Before she could speak, he had opened the door and was half-way down the street.

Agnes ran after him. 'Jean!' she called and he turned. 'Thank you for the perfume and . . . oh, Jean! I will see you again, won't I?'

'Oh yes, you will,' he said.

*

Frank lay in bed wondering about Jean Dessin and his strange disappearances over the past few weeks. He never seemed to be around when he should be, he whistled a lot and seemed to be always grinning as though he had a secret joy which he was not prepared to share. Frank tried hard not to feel hurt by this lack of trust – the two boys had been like brothers since Jean first moved into Luke's empty bed and Frank had no secrets from him.

He stared across the narrow strip of threadbare carpet that separated the two beds and considered the possibility that Jean had a lady friend. It seemed quite likely, but if that was the case why would he not confide in Frank? Unless Frank, at thirteen, was too young for such confidences – or unless she was a married woman. Frank knew it happened all the time, but he could not believe – and did not want to believe – that Jean would become involved in this way. His grandparents, he knew, would be horrified if such a suspicion should ever cross their minds and Frank was very much afraid that they might go so far as to throw Jean out of the house rather than be involved in such a scandal.

He turned over restlessly, squinted at the ancient clock on the small bedside table and saw that it was nearly midnight. He could be out smuggling with that awful Bitty, thought Frank hopefully. True, smuggling was an offence, but at least it was an acceptable crime in the eyes of Rye Harbour's inhabitants and one for which many an honourable fisherman had been prosecuted. Having an

affair with a married woman was most certainly *not* acceptable and
if Jean was caught by the woman's husband and thrashed no one
would sympathise with him. Frank wondered whether or not *he*
should sympathise. Jean was his closest friend, after all, perhaps
his only friend, and Frank felt he should support him but he knew
that would bring down his grandmother's wrath upon his head.
She had said nothing so far, but there was gossip in the village and
she would almost certainly hear it. Someone in the William the
Conqueror had linked Jean's name with George Coulsden's wife,
but Frank could not believe Jean would be that stupid. His
guv'nor's wife? It was impossible! With a deep sigh, he changed
position yet again. The bed was narrow and the flock mattress
lumpy. Jean's bed – which had once been Luke's – was marginally
more comfortable, but it had never crossed Frank's mind to claim
it for himself. Jean's father was dead too, and he was a stranger in
a foreign land. The least Frank could offer him was a superior
mattress.

A sudden noise alerted him to the fact that Jean was coming in
and he watched as the Belgian's dark frame filled the rectangle of
dim light that was the window and dropped lightly on to the floor,
closing the lower sash quietly behind him.

'You still awake, Frank?'

He asked the same question whenever he came in late.

'Yes.'

Jean sat on the edge of his bed. As he fumbled with the laces of
his boots, Frank was at once aware of an unfamiliar excitement in
his friend's movements and was filled with an overriding curiosity
to know what Jean had experienced which had brought about
such a change. As Jean leaned forward, Frank's nostrils caught a
faint but unmistakable hint of perfume.

'Been on the water?' he asked.

'No.'

'Where then?'

Jean laughed. 'Now that'd be telling, young Frank!'

'I'm near on fourteen,' said Frank. 'Who with, then?'

'Aha!'

'I bet it was a girl!'

'Do you, then?'

'Was it?'

'Wouldn't you like to know!'

'Yes, I would.'

'Well, I'm not saying.'

'Don't, then!' said Frank crossly, 'but I don't know why not. I wouldn't say anything – you know I wouldn't. And I'd tell you if it was me.'

'You wouldn't, Frank. Not if it was this special person. I couldn't, you see, because I've promised her.'

Frank's heart sank. So it *was* a married woman. Oh, Jean! He propped himself up on one elbow and stared earnestly in Jean's direction.

'Suppose I guess her name?' he suggested hopefully. 'You could just say "yes", and then you wouldn't be actually *telling* me. Surely you could say "yes"? Or nod your head? Couldn't you, Jean?'

Outside the clouds had broken up and now Jean's blond head and naked chest gleamed palely in the moonlight as he wriggled out of his trousers and Frank held his breath for the answer.

'Oh, go on then,' said Jean, tossing the trousers into a heap on the floor and easing his slim frame between the blankets. 'If you get it right, I'll tell you.'

Frank drew a deep breath because now that the moment had arrived he was scared of what he would learn. By the light from the window he could see Jean grinning at him.

'Is she pretty?' he asked.

'Oh yes, she's pretty.'

'Young?'

There was a moment's hesitation before Jean said lightly, 'Young enough.'

Frank swallowed. 'Do I know her?'

'I reckon you've seen her around,' said Jean. 'Yes, I think you know her.'

There was a long silence and Frank knew that Jean was watching him with amusement.

'Is she . . . good?' he asked.

Jean laughed aloud and Frank 'shushed' him anxiously.

'She's good for me,' said Jean.

'I meant – you know – good at it.'

'That too. Do you envy me?'

The question took Frank by surprise. *Did* he? 'I suppose so,' he mumbled.

'Your turn will come – or maybe it already has?'

'No.' His voice was muffled.

'There's no hurry, Frank.'

'I know.' He took another deep breath and said as casually as he could, 'Do you want to tell me about it, Jean? How it was? You know what I mean.'

Jean's soft laughter was kindly and not meant to offend. 'I dare not,' he said. 'If she found out, she would never forgive me.'

'Oh, Jean!' cried Frank. 'How can you bear it? If you love her and she belongs to someone else?'

'Did I say that?' Jean hedged.

'No, but I know,' said Frank. 'Everyone is talking about you. I said it was all lies but – oh Jean! She's so old!'

'Age doesn't matter,' Jean said gently. 'She is wise and generous and fun to be with. She's not mine and never will be, but she makes me so very happy.'

'But when it's over?'

'Ah, then I shall need "cheering up", as you say in England. But that won't be just yet.'

'But Jean . . .'

'Yes?'

'If *he* finds out . . .'

Jean slid down further into the bed. 'He won't,' he said. 'Don't worry, young Frank.'

Frank did not dispute the word this time. He felt very young and confused and afraid for his friend. His grandmother's upbringing had been strict and she set great store by old-fashioned virtues. In her eyes Jean was committing a sin. Adultery! The very word had a terrible ring to it. Yet Jean was a 'good person', so how was it possible to stray so far from the straight and narrow . . . and be so happy!

'I'm glad she makes you happy, Jean,' he said at last. 'But I'm sorry she belongs to someone else. For your sake, I mean.' He paused, considering the next question carefully. 'Will you take her away from her husband?'

'No.'

'If he died, would you marry her?'

'He won't die.'

'If he left her, then?'

'He won't leave her, but if he did . . . no, I think not.'

'But if he left her and she *wanted* you to marry her—'

'You ask too many questions,' Jean laughed. 'It's never as simple as it seems. Life is not easy and neither is love. You will find out one day, Frank, when you fall in love.'

'Perhaps I have already,' said Frank, racking his brains to see if he could think of anyone, in case Jean should challenge him. Unbidden and to his great surprise, the image of Julia Coulsden appeared, smiling down at him, serene and doll-like, the way she had looked in the doctor's tent at the Regatta. As he saw again the deep blue of her eyes, the pale smooth flesh of her face and neck and the silvery sheen of her hair, a great rush of tenderness swept over him at the thought of her. Julia Lady Coulsden. The daughter of Jean's guv'nor. The stepdaughter of Agnes, who was 'wise and generous and fun to be with'.

'May I go to sleep now?' Jean asked.

'Yes, of course. I'm sorry.'

The clouds had again crossed the room and the bedroom was plunged into darkness. Another thought occurred to Frank.

'Jean?'

'What now?'

'You said you would ask Mr Coulsden about me – about a place in his crew.'

'So I did.'

'And you forgot?'

'No.'

Frank sat bolt upright. 'You asked him, Jean? What did he say?'

'He said, "Probably".'

'Jean!' Frank's heart was suddenly bursting with gratitude and a wild excitement. A job on *Silver Lady* with Jean! 'That's terrific!' he cried. 'Why didn't you tell me, Jean?'

'I'm sorry, Frank. I had other things on my mind,' Jean told him. 'I would have remembered in the morning. It may be a few weeks, mind, or longer. Les Tanner will be giving up soon. His heart's bad and he can't take much more. Mr Coulsden will let you know.'

Frank smiled ecstatically into the darkness and wished it was already morning so that he could dazzle his grandparents with his prospects. A permanent job on *Silver Lady* would be something to boast about, for times were not easy and regular jobs were hard to come by.

'*Now*, may I go to sleep?' said Jean.

'Yes, Jean – and thank you a hundred times!' His conscience pricked him and he added hastily, 'I'm sorry for Les Tanner, but if his heart's all that bad . . .'

'Go to sleep, Frank,' said Jean and he turned over noisily,

determined to be alone with his memories for a few minutes before sleep claimed him. A few minutes later his fitful snores went unheeded as Frank lay wide awake in the other bed. His concern for Jean's moral welfare had been swept away by the news that he would one day be a member of *Silver Lady*'s crew and he was too excited to sleep. He wondered how his father would have received the news and knew that Luke would have been proud of his son. He rehearsed a little scene in which he thanked George Coulsden for giving him the opportunity and discovered that Julia was there as well, standing beside her father and smiling approvingly. Yes, he thought, she would certainly be impressed and once he was crewing for *Silver Lady* no one would ever again call him *young* Frank.

*

Christmas came and went. For the children it was a magical time, but for the adults the season had never been the same since Sarah died and the family no longer converged on South View.

The beginning of the year 1920 brought a cold snap as life went on in the house above Hilders Cliff. On the surface, George's household was a comparatively happy one; Agnes was much better tempered and Julia suffered less from her sharp tongue. Unaware of his wife's involvement with Jean, George was lulled into a false sense of security and began to think his troubles were over.

Of course, the affair was no secret amongst the fishing community, but no one intervened and Jack, when it came to his ears, found it just that George, the biter, should now be 'bit' and decided to pretend ignorance of what was going on. Cicely remained unaware, for now that the boys were older and less demanding of her time she was becoming more involved in a variety of leisure pursuits which brought her into contact with the kind of people she wanted to meet. Once a month, she attended a knitting circle which provided garments for the new-born babies of poor families, and occasionally she was persuaded to sing at musical evenings provided for the inmates of the Union at the top of Rye Hill. She had also joined a poetry appreciation group and was striving to improve her mind. In fact, by the middle of September the affair was still flourishing undiscovered by those closest to Agnes, although Jean's frequent absences from any of the fishermen's pubs were the source of ribald comment and of continued interest. Stanley, of course, knew nothing of the liaison and Jack left him in ignorance.

Julia was now ten years old and her friendship with Emily prospered. The two were as close as full sisters, if not closer, and they found life surprisingly pleasant. Agnes seemed content to let them out of her sight and together they roamed the streets of Rye enjoying a new-found freedom from adult supervision. They did not know why, but whenever they asked permission to go to the Salts, the cattle market or the Strand, it was invariably granted; they were not aware that their absence from the house made it possible for Jean to call, or that a half-open window in the bedroom was the signal to him that only Agnes was at home. On several occasions when it rained, the polished wood floor still glistened with drops of water when George returned home, but he dismissed this as carelessness on his wife's part and read nothing into it. Although the affair had lasted just over a year, the couple had spent relatively few hours together since, as members of the same crew, the two men were always at sea together. It was pointless for Jean even to try to find another boat, for the fleet usually put to sea and returned within a few hours of each other. So when conditions were right for *Silver Lady*, they were right for all the other boats. The times when Jean could be with Agnes were few and far between, but on two occasions he pretended ill-health and did not sail. They also met on several occasions when George and Jack had driven to Hastings to see Stanley, but when these visits coincided with the school holidays there was always the risk that Julia and Emily might take it into their heads to return home from their forays. A plan was therefore devised which served them well. Jean would walk along the road in the direction of Camber and Agnes would follow after an agreed interval in the dog-cart. She would overtake him and offer him a lift, which he always accepted with exaggerated surprise for the benefit of anyone who might be passing. Hidden among the sand dunes, they then made love with a passion which was heightened by the infrequency of their meetings.

One evening a message reached Agnes from George to say that he would be staying overnight with Stanley and Jane. Winifred's second child had been due for over a week and apparently she had just given birth to twin girls.

'Well, I hoped it would be a boy,' said Julia, when Agnes repeated the message. 'I'm sick of girl cousins.'

'So am I,' said Emily, who invariably agreed with Julia.

'They're not your cousins,' said Agnes. 'Winifred is your cousin and her children are your second cousins – or maybe it's cousins once removed. Oh, I don't know, but I *do* know they're not cousins.'

As she was speaking, her mind was racing with the possibility of a meeting with Jean now that George would not be coming back and a wild idea was taking shape. They had not met for nearly a week and she was desperate to see him.

'Are they my second cousins, too?' Emily asked.

'Of course they are,' said Julia generously. 'They're cousins to both of us.'

'But if I'm your half-sister, they might not be.'

Julia considered her objections and could see the logic behind them. 'Well, maybe they're still your second cousins,' she suggested. 'Are they, Agnes?'

It had been agreed that while Emily called her mother 'Ma', Julia would be allowed to use her Christian name, much to the relief of Agnes who did not relish the idea of Hettie's child calling her by anything so intimate as 'Ma'.

'What?' asked Agnes, who was paying very little attention to the discussion. The two girls exchanged exasperated looks. They *had* noticed and commented on the fact to each other – that Agnes seemed to be going deaf.

'Are they Em's second cousins?' Julia asked again, raising her voice considerably.

'There's no need to bellow,' said Agnes. 'I'm not deaf, Ju. I've told you before about that.'

'But *are* they?'

'Are who what?'

Emily tried. 'Are they my second half-cousins? I mean . . .'

Both girls giggled at the slip.

'Or *third* half!' mocked Julia. 'Or fourth half?' They giggled again.

Agnes regarded them irritably. Why were girls such gigglers, she wondered. If only her little boy had lived, she might one day have had someone intelligent to talk to. She became aware that both girls were looking at her expectantly.

'What?' she asked again.

'Are they Em's second cousins?' asked Julia. 'Or Em's half-cousins once removed?'

Agnes had lost the thread and hesitated.

'Half a cousin?' cried Em, breaking into peals of laughter. 'I wonder which half. I've never seen half a cousin, have you, Ju?'

As Julia joined in the hilarity, Agnes's limited patience ran out. 'Oh do stop it, the pair of you!' she snapped. 'I never heard such a load of nonsense. Giggle! Giggle! And silly talk. It's enough to try the patience of a saint!'

'Is the saint a doctor?' asked Julia rashly and the two girls laughed helplessly while Agnes stared uncomprehendingly.

'It's a joke,' cried Julia. 'Doctor, *patients*. You said "patience". Don't you get it?'

'She can't hear you!' screamed Emily hysterically. 'You'll have to speak up, Ju.'

Julia raised her voice. 'You said, "The patients of a saint",' she told Agnes. 'Patients – doctor. See?'

Agnes glared at them. 'No, I don't see,' she said. 'All I see is two silly little girls, giggling and carrying on alarming. You're laughing at nothing. So you can stop it this instant! Do you hear me? Stop it at once. I've had enough of your silly noise and I can't hear myself think.' But by now the two girls had reached the borderline between pretended and real hysterics and they found they could not stop.

'Julia! Emily!' screamed Agnes. 'I won't tell you again. *Stop it*, I say. Stop that stupid giggling or I'll – I'll stop it for you.'

When this threat failed, she finally lost her temper and, stepping forward, dealt both girls a sharp slap. She caught Julia across the jaw and Emily received a blow to her right ear. The sudden silence which followed sobered them all and Agnes stared at them as Emily burst into loud sobs and Julia gazed back white-faced and furious.

Agnes swallowed nervously. She regretted her action immediately, but it was too late now to undo it and she certainly would not apologise. All she wanted was to be left in peace with her thoughts, so that she could find a way to contact Jean.

Julia narrowed her eyes. 'I hate you, Agnes *Dengate*!' she said. 'I *hate* you. And I shall tell my father.'

Regarding her wearily, Agnes wondered if she would carry out her threat. Earlier on, before Jean came into her life, Julia had made the threat frequently but rarely carried it out. For a long time now the threat had not been uttered and Agnes cursed her own stupidity for this unnecessary confrontation.

Glancing at the clock, she saw that it was nearly quarter-past seven. Right, she decided abruptly, they could go to bed early.

'You can both get to bed now,' she said. 'And if there's any fuss you'll go to bed even earlier tomorrow, so let's not have any back-chat from either of you.'

Julia muttered something which was loud enough to be heard but not clear enough to be understood. Agnes ignored her. 'I mean it,' she insisted. 'Now shift yourselves and get up those stairs.'

'What about our supper?' wailed Emily, for they usually had a cup of milk and a slice of cake before they went to bed.

'No supper,' said Agnes. 'Now get upstairs the pair of you! I don't want to hear another word – just get out of my sight.'

The two girls went upstairs rebelliously. Emily ran up, stamping her feet, red-faced and tearful. Julia followed as slowly as she dared, her face set, outwardly calm. At any other time, Agnes would have longed to shake her, but now her mind was on the dazzling prospect of a whole night with Jean.

*

In the early hours of the following morning Julia awoke with a pain in her stomach. She did not have a large appetite and the supper-time milk normally settled her digestion for the night. Going without it meant that she had last eaten at four o'clock in the afternoon – a tea of jam and bread and biscuits – and now she was experiencing mild hunger pangs.

'Em!' she whispered into the darkness. 'Are you awake?'

There was no answer and she resisted the temptation to wake the other girl. As she held her stomach, her resentment towards Agnes grew.

'We were only laughing,' she thought. 'We were only having a bit of fun. That's just like her, the hateful old cat! She doesn't like us to be happy, she doesn't like us to have any fun. She's a mean, hateful pig! Just because *she's* too old to have fun, she doesn't want us to have any.'

For a while Julia revelled in this line of thought, giving wide rein to her imagination. 'I'd like to make *her* go without any supper,' she thought. 'Just because she's older than us, she thinks she can starve us. Well, I'm telling Papa tomorrow the minute he comes home. The very minute! I shall tell him she starved us.' Then a new thought struck her. 'I bet she did it so that she could eat our share. I bet our share of the cake has gone. I hate her, the greedy pig. I'm really going to tell Papa.'

She sat up suddenly, deciding to creep downstairs and see for herself how much of the cherry cake remained. That would be proof enough! She imagined Agnes's guilty face as she denounced her. Slipping out of bed, Julia tiptoed across the room and opened the door carefully, for there would be certain retribution if she was discovered by Agnes while her father was not present to take her part. The landing light was out, but a thin beam of moonlight shone through the window and Julia could see well enough to avoid the aspidistra in its tall stand which stood to the left of the bathroom door.

As she tiptoed past the room where Agnes was supposed to be sleeping, she suddenly froze and turned her head in disbelief. She had distinctly heard voices – not just one, but two. So Papa *was* home! He had changed his mind and come back. Julia was delighted by her discovery and her eyes gleamed. Now she need not wait until tomorrow; she would go in and complain of the terrible pain in her stomach, would say how hungry she was because she had had no supper – and then Agnes would get into trouble. Hastily she straightened her face and removed all traces of the triumphant smile. Frowning, she doubled up and, with a flash of brilliance, decided to groan loudly and stumble noisily about on the landing. *That* would bring out her father!

The long-drawn-out groan was an instant success and the voices in the bedroom stopped abruptly. Julia promptly threw herself on to the floor and cried, 'Papa!' To her surprise, nothing happened; her father did not come rushing out to see what was wrong. Instead the voices began again, but now she could detect an urgency about them. She thought it likely that Agnes was trying to prevent her father from coming to help her.

'Papa!' she called again.

The bedroom door opened and Agnes came out and closed it behind her. She wore a dressing-gown, but there was no sign of a nightdress beneath it. Her face was flushed and her manner agitated. Serve her right, thought Julia.

'I want Papa!' she wailed.

Agnes seized her by the arm and tried to pull her to her feet, but Julia gave her no assistance. As Agnes leaned forward the dressing-gown parted and Julia saw her naked legs.

'Get up!' hissed Agnes. 'What on earth is the matter with you? Julia! Get up!'

'My tummy aches,' said Julia. 'I'm hungry and *I want Papa!*' The last three words came out louder than the rest.

'Your father's not here,' said Agnes, as reluctantly Julia allowed herself to be pulled to her feet. 'You know he's not, he's staying over in Hastings because of Winifred's babies. You know that perfectly well.'

Julia's eyes widened. The wicked old witch! She was lying! Julia had heard her talking to him.

'My tummy hurts,' she cried loudly. 'I'm *hungry*!'

Agnes was looking frightened, she thought with satisfaction. Agnes *knew* she was going to get into trouble from Papa.

'I want Papa!' she cried again, trying unsuccessfully to manage a few tears. 'Papa!' She made a move towards the bedroom door.

'He's not there,' cried Agnes, seizing her arm to restrain her. 'I just told you!'

'But I *heard* him. I heard him talking.'

'No, you didn't. There's nobody in there. You imagined it, Julia.'

Agnes tried to smile, but Julia saw the expression in her eyes. Oh yes, Agnes was frightened all right.

'Now Julia,' Agnes pleaded, 'you go back to bed and I'll bring you up some milk and cake. How's that? Would you like that?'

Julia nearly said, 'Yes', because milk and cake would be very good. Almost like a midnight feast. Agnes was propelling her towards the room she shared with Emily.

'And Emily?' said Julia. 'We both want milk and cakes.'

To her surprise, Agnes agreed at once. 'Yes, some for Emily as well,' she said. 'I'll bring up some for both of you if you just get into bed and stay there like good girls.'

Julia climbed back into bed and grinned at Emily, who had been disturbed by the noise and was now sitting up looking puzzled and only half-awake.

'Now look,' said Agnes. 'You've woken poor Emily – but never mind,' she added quickly, 'I'm not cross with you, Julia. I'm not cross with either of you. I'll bring you up some milk and a nice big slice of cake each, but you *must* promise me you'll stay where you are. No more wandering about, d'you hear me?'

The two girls stared at her, surprised by her earnest manner and obvious desire to please.

'Do you *hear* me?' They nodded. 'Right then, I'll only be a minute. And you *must* stay in bed. It's cold tonight.'

Emily, smiling, held up her arms for a hug and her mother leaned forward. 'Where's your nightie?' asked Emily, shocked.

Agnes put up a hand to close the top of her dressing-gown. 'I was . . . too hot,' she stammered.

Julia said, 'But you just said it was cold!'

'It's cold *out* of bed; it's hot *in* bed,' stated Agnes. 'Stop arguing, Julia, or you won't get any cake.'

The two children watched uneasily as Agnes's expression changed yet again. Julia, more fully awake than Emily, sensed Agnes's distress and her secret jubilation was tempered by an ill-defined fear. Something was wrong – and whatever it was, was making Agnes behave in this unfamiliar way. Her stomach churned with fright. Was her father ill? Was he dead? Was Agnes keeping something from them? With an effort, she remained in the bed.

'Right now,' said Agnes, her tone once more appeasing, 'I'll only be two ticks. Would you both like cherry cake?'

They nodded as one. So, thought Julia, she hasn't eaten our share. But what was wrong with Papa? Emily and Julia looked at each other as soon as Agnes had left the room.

'Why, Ju?' whispered Emily. 'Why are we having supper, I mean?'

'I told her I was hungry and had a pain and that I wanted to see Papa.' Julia listened until she heard Agnes's footsteps going down the stairs, then she scrambled out of bed, ran to her father's bedroom and threw open the door.

'Papa!' she began. 'I've got a pain. I . . .'

A long silence followed as Jean Dessin stared back at her from the rumpled bed, then he grabbed suddenly at the bedclothes and tucked them in around his waist. For a moment Julia could not believe her eyes; she thought they *must* be playing her tricks. Her headlong flight along the landing had been noted by Agnes, who now rushed back upstairs and into the room to stare at Julia with a terrified expression.

'What did I tell you?' she gasped. 'I told you—' She turned to Jean. 'I *told* them to stay in bed. They promised!' She looked at Julia with wild eyes. 'You said you would!' she gabbled. 'I told you only if you stayed in bed! I said no cherry cake if – I said you were to . . .'

Faltering to a stop, she moved slowly across the room and sat down heavily on the bed. After a moment's hesitation, Jean tried to put an arm around her shoulders but she shook him off. Julia thought Agnes was going to cry but she turned to Jean again. 'I *told* them to stay in bed—' she began again. 'Oh, Christ!'

Her eyes were brimming with tears as she looked from Jean to Julia. 'I don't know . . .' she whispered. 'I don't know what's best. Jean?' She turned to him appealing for help, but he had none to offer.

Julia watched them and shook her head. It was a bad dream. It must be. And where was Papa? Papa should be in the bed instead of Jean.

'Papa,' she said, her voice thin with fear. 'What have you done with Papa?'

'Done with him?' echoed Agnes. 'We haven't done anything with him. I told you, he's over with Stanley. Your precious papa's quite safe.'

From the other room, Emily called, 'Ju?'

'Look, Julia,' said Jean, 'you go on back to bed before we have Em in here as well. There's nothing wrong with your pa, so just forget about everything and—'

Agnes rounded on him shrilly. 'Forget? Don't be so daft, Jean, of course she won't forget! Christ Almighty! You must be barmy if you think she'll forget. *That* one won't forget. Not her. Not that little madam!'

Julia listened and watched as they bickered in low voices over what they should do. She was frightened and now had a very real pain in her stomach. Thinking she might be sick, she clung to the door handle for support. It occurred to her that perhaps Jean was their father now and no one had told her.

'Isn't Papa coming home any more?' she asked tremulously.

Jean and Agnes stopped whispering and stared at her. 'I should bloody well hope so,' said Agnes. 'Yes, of course he is.'

'Julia, go back to bed,' Jean pleaded. 'This is nothing to do with you. Little girls don't understand about grown-up people, so why don't you go back to bed and Agnes will fetch your cake and milk? Be a good girl.'

'But when *is* Papa coming home? I want to see him.'

'Tomorrow,' he told her. 'Agnes told you that.'

'Do *you* promise, Jean?'

'I promise.'

'*He* doesn't have to promise,' said Agnes, bridling at the implication that her word was not as reliable as Jean's. 'You don't have to ask *him*.'

Julia's fear was giving way to anger. 'But you tell lies,' she said. 'You said there was nobody here and Jean's here. You're a liar!'

Agnes made a sudden lunge towards her, but Jean caught hold of her arm. 'Leave her be, Ag,' he warned. 'Just get her out of here. I want to get dressed.'

'Dressed? But why? You're not going?'

'I am. I've had enough of this; I didn't come here to squabble with a ten-year-old kid.'

'Oh, that's bloody marvellous!' screamed Agnes, losing the remaining vestiges of her shattered self-control. 'I'm in this mess and you're sodding off! Christ, Jean! I don't believe it. You can't mean it! Just up and out and leaving me to sort this out. What am I going to tell George?'

'That's up to you. He's your old man, not mine.'

Provoked beyond reason, Agnes began to pummel him with her fists, raining blows down on his head and shoulders while Julia watched with horrified fascination.

'Pack it up, Ag, or I'll clip you one,' he warned, protecting himself as best he could from the small flailing fists. 'I mean it!'

But she continued to beat him while tears of despair and rage streamed down her face, until suddenly he lashed out with the back of his hand and knocked her backwards off the bed.

Julia backed out of the doorway as Jean leaped out of bed and began to pull on his clothes, while Agnes seized hold of his legs and began to sob hysterically.

'Don't go, Jean! Don't go, my love,' she begged. 'I'm sorry, I'm truly sorry. I'll send her back to bed. Jean, please don't go! You must help me. I love you, I can't let you go like this . . .'

Julia, unable to bear it, turned and ran back to the safety of her own bed. Emily was still sitting up and she stared at Julia with large frightened eyes as both children listened to the drama which continued along the landing and then down the stairs. Finally the front door slammed and they heard Agnes moving about downstairs; at last Emily could bear the suspense no longer.

'What is it, Ju?' she asked fearfully.

'It was Jean,' said Julia. 'In Papa's bed with Agnes.'

'Oh, Ju! But why is Ma crying?'

'She's mad because Jean's gone home.'

'Oh, Ju!'

'Don't keep saying "Oh, Ju!" '

Julia hugged her knees and wondered what to do. Experience told her that in Agnes's present mood retribution was more likely than milk and cherry cake, so she slipped out of bed and turned the key in the lock.

'Why?' asked Emily, alarmed. 'Why are you locking the door?'

'Just because.'

This was one of Julia's favourite answers and Emily decided not to probe further into the whys and wherefores.

'Aren't we having cake and milk?' she asked.

'I don't think so.'

Eventually Agnes came upstairs, having fortified herself with a large amount of George's whisky. She hammered on the door, then the girls heard her stumble back into her bedroom and all was quiet again.

Much later when Emily was asleep, Julia dressed, crept downstairs and out of the house.

*

Next morning Ian Cornwell glanced up at the clock and sighed. He felt luxuriously decadent, lazy. It was nearly eight-thirty and he was still in bed. He grinned; his parents would have a fit if they knew, for idleness was a long way from godliness in his father's book. He lay back with his hands clasped behind his head while downstairs he could hear his grandmother pottering about in the kitchen, making small reassuring sounds with the crockery and cutlery. Ian knew exactly what she would be doing and he felt a rush of affection for the old lady. She was preparing a breakfast tray: a boiled egg (brown-shelled); toast (not too dark); a small glass of fresh-squeezed orange juice; tea (in the blue and white teapot his parents had given her years earlier); sugar lumps; a small jug of milk and six round pats of butter on a plate.

Only a few more days and then he would be off to London to resume his medical studies. He was glad the war had delayed him, for now he would be better able to enjoy the experience. The raw schoolboy had vanished, lost for ever in the muddy rat-infested trenches of No-Man's-Land; he had exchanged youth for manhood in the terrible battle for survival. Now it was already fading from his mind, although he had thought nothing would ever dim those dark images and had believed the trembling figures and sprawled shapes would haunt him for the rest of his life.

There was a knock at the door and he struggled to a sitting position. 'Come in!'

His grandmother entered, her face wreathed in smiles. 'Ah, good. You are awake! I wanted you to have a nice lie-in,' she told him.

Helen Cornwell was small-boned and birdlike. Ian was fond of telling her that she didn't move, she hopped, but anything Ian said was acceptable to his grandmother. He was the only child of her only child and could do no wrong.

'That looks delicious,' he exclaimed as she settled the tray across his knees and removed the teapot and milk jug to the bedside table.

'It *is* delicious,' she told him, dropping a brief kiss on the top of his head. 'Now you eat it all up.'

'Can I leave the crusts?' he teased. It was a familiar request dating back many years.

She laughed. 'Certainly not. You know what I told you when you were little – crusts make your hair curl.'

'But I've been eating them for years and my hair's as straight as ever.'

'You just keep trying,' she told him. 'And that's home-made marmalade.'

'It all looks perfect. You spoil me, Grandmother.'

'That's what grandmothers are for, Ian, to spoil their grand-sons.'

'I'm not complaining, I think it's a very good idea. I suppose Grandfather was up at the crack of dawn?'

'Oh yes,' she said with a smile. 'He's been out there since before seven. That blessed garden! He's weeding the rose-bed so that it will look its best when he gives you the guided tour. He lives for this garden, you know. I never see him these days. He gets together with Harry who does the heavy digging, and then I have to talk to myself all day.'

Ian laughed. 'And he always maintained he hated gardening.'

'That was before we had a garden. To be fair, I suppose we spent all that time in India and then three years in the London flat – really he's never had the chance to find out whether he likes it or not. Now he's discovered he has green fingers!'

'I'll go out and admire everything as soon as I'm up,' he

promised, and his grandmother patted his shoulder affection-
ately.

'Do that, dear. He's so looking forward to it. If you'd come an
hour earlier last night you could have seen it then, but I persuaded
him the light was failing and wouldn't do everything justice.'

Ian drank the orange in three quick gulps and cracked open the
egg.

'Not hard is it, dear?' she asked anxiously.

'It's just right,' he assured her.

Helen crossed the bedroom and looked down into the garden.
Then she frowned. 'What on earth . . . ? Now who's that at this
time of the morning?'

Ian looked up enquiringly, his mouth full of egg and toast.

'Your grandfather's talking to a little girl,' she exclaimed.
'Perhaps I should go down. Good gracious me! He's bringing her
into the house!' She hurried out of the room and down the stairs.

Ian, though curious, continued his breakfast, but as neither of
his grandparents came up to tell him what was happening, he
finally stuffed the last triangle of toast into his mouth and went
downstairs to find out for himself.

In the kitchen he discovered a young girl eating a bowl of bread
and milk. She was very pale and her face was blotched, apparently
from recent and prolonged tears. Her long silvery hair reached
well below her shoulders and she looked at him through large
blue eyes.

'Hullo,' he said cheerfully, but she did not answer.

His grandparents were watching her. 'Poor little soul, she's
starving,' said Helen. 'Just look at the way she's tucking into that
bread and milk!'

Henry Cornwell was every inch a military man, from the
straight back and bluff manner to the large Kitchener moustache.

'Damned queer,' he told Ian. 'Just popped up at the gate, she
did – stood there staring at me as though I'd got two heads or
something. Kept muttering something, but I couldn't catch what
she said. She looks all in, poor child.'

'But who is she?' asked Ian.

'She won't tell us,' said Helen. 'In fact she won't say anything.
Henry rang the police station, but they have no report of a missing
child and it's a complete mystery. I don't know what else we can
do except keep her here until she's claimed. The police sergeant
is going to make some enquiries. Perhaps she'd talk to you, Ian?'

Ian crouched beside the girl's chair. 'Hullo,' he said. 'My name's Ian. Ian Cornwell. Do you like that name?'

She nodded shyly.

'What's your name?'

She concentrated once more on her food, scraping the dish noisily.

'Steady on!' cried Ian. 'You'll scrape off the pattern.'

The ghost of a smile touched the child's lips, but then her eyes closed wearily. Ian stood up. 'She looks exhausted,' he said. 'Perhaps she should lie down for a bit. I wonder if she comes from Rye – if she's not local, then—'

'From Rye!' exclaimed Henry. 'Dammit, that's five miles away – a damn long walk at her age.'

Ian shrugged. 'She looks dead-beat,' he said, 'and she ought to rest.'

Helen smiled at her. 'Would you like to have a bit of—' But suddenly the girl swayed.

'Quick! She's going to faint!' cried Helen and Ian caught her as she toppled from the chair.

'That settles it,' decided Helen. 'Carry her up to the spare room, Ian, while I fill a hot-water bottle. That's always a comfort, I feel. Poor little mite! I wonder if she's run away from a school somewhere. I mean, surely no one's abandoned her? Tut! Whatever is the world coming to?'

'We ought to call a doctor,' Henry suggested. 'She may be ill, delirious or something. Lost her memory, perhaps?'

'Oh, what a good idea, Henry. Will you do it while I fill this hot-water bottle?'

Upstairs Ian laid Julia on the bed; her lips trembled and her eyes filled with tears. 'I want Mama Sarah,' she whispered.

'You want who?'

'Mama Sarah.'

'Who is Mama Sarah?' He brushed back a few stray hairs from her forehead and then stroked her hair. 'Don't cry, little one. There's nothing to cry for. Tell me who Mama Sarah is. Has she got any other names? Can you be a clever girl and tell me?'

'Mama Sarah Coulsden,' she whispered, 'but she's dead now.'

'Dead? Oh dear!' He was frowning. Coulsden? The name had a familiar ring to it.

Helen hurried into the room and found Ian with his arm around the little waif. 'Coulsden?' she echoed in reply to his question. 'Why, yes, we bought this house from the Coulsden family. Is she a Coulsden, then? Ah, light begins to dawn.'

Ian gave Julia a friendly squeeze. 'Is your name Coulsden too?'

'Julia Coulsden.' As she looked up at them with tear-filled eyes, they blurred into formless shapes. 'I want Mama Sarah,' she sobbed. 'I want Papa! I don't want to go home!'

Fortunately Dr Jamieson arrived quickly; he found her quite hysterical and suffering from shock and exhaustion after walking through the dawn to South View. He recognised her immediately: she was Sarah Coulsden's granddaughter. Once they were downstairs he briefly explained the history of the Coulsdens to the bewildered Cornwells.

'Confidentially,' he concluded, 'they are a very volatile family, the Coulsdens, but they go back a long way. Always been in this area and generally well-thought-of in spite of the occasional fireworks. Though what has provoked this little lady's walk is a mystery. I should give the police a ring and they will contact George Coulsden, her father. As for Julia, I've given her a mild sedative so that she'll sleep for a while. From what little she would tell me, I suspect there's been some friction with the stepmother.'

'Oh dear,' said kind-hearted Helen. 'I don't know what to do for the best. She looks a nice little thing, but we shall have to send her back.'

'Of course you will,' the doctor agreed. 'You mustn't fret about that; it's the way of the world I'm afraid, Mrs Cornwell, and these things blow over in time. Nothing much an outsider can—'

'Good Lord!' Ian interrupted him. 'I've just realised who she is!'

'We *know* who she is, dear,' said Helen patiently.

'No, I mean the penny's just dropped. She's related to Ernie Brett, the chap in Hastings I told you about who was in my regiment. His wife Winifred was a Coulsden and he's spoken of Julia. Good Lord! What a small world. This must have been the family home – that's really incredible.'

The doctor closed his bag with a snap. 'It's a very small world,' he said, 'but I must go now. I have surgery waiting for me. No peace for the wicked, they say, and I'm sure it's true. Don't disturb her, just let her sleep until she's ready to wake up. It's a great healer, sleep. She's obviously been through quite a lot and doesn't have a lot of stamina. Children can outstretch themselves just as adults can. Don't bother to see me out; I know the way!'

*

Much later the same day George Coulsden arrived with Jack in the latter's car to collect the runaway. He had finally been traced to Hastings, but first he had gone home to find out from Agnes exactly what had happened. By the time George arrived home with Julia, Agnes had a large purple bruise developing under her left eye; she had seen no point in lying since Julia would obviously tell all, and George's temper had got the better of him.

Jean Dessin had wisely left Rye before George returned and all George's efforts to find him failed. Someone reported seeing him at Dengemarsh, where he was apparently looking for work, but two days after the sighting he disappeared again and Agnes, bruised in body and spirit, was left to wonder about his whereabouts and pray for his return.

CHAPTER ELEVEN

At low tide the shingle at Winchelsea Beach gave way to a vast area of smooth sand and Frank Bligh now marched across it with head bent and hands thrust into his trouser pockets. He was on his way to Pett Level to collect some fish from Alice's brother-in-law, but his thoughts were on the lifeboat. He had watched the launch as usual, as it put to sea on one of its regular exercises. One day he might be a member of the crew. A place in the lifeboat crew was an honour and was greatly courted, but was usually passed on from one generation of a family to the next. Frank wanted to prove his worth, to know that his dead father would have been proud of him. A few more years and with any luck he might be in with a chance, he thought. There were no hard and fast rules, but very few men stayed on past middle age and there were a couple of crew members nearing fifty.

The beach was deserted. The few holidaymakers had gone home and, apart from the odd seagull wheeling overhead, fifteen-year-old Frank was quite alone. He stomped along in his boots, glancing back occasionally to see the line of footprints he had made as, filling with sea water, they reflected the daylight. Over his shoulder he carried an ancient bag made of sacking in which he would carry home the fish – if there were any. Alice had sent him 'on spec', as she was getting short of money. He had been helping Tommy Bird with his keddle net, but the season had ended now. If he returned from Pett empty-handed Frank decided he would put down a few baskets off the harbour wall and try for crab.

He stopped to pick up the heavy outer shell of a coconut and send it curving through the air with a well-aimed kick. He had heard there was a job going as junior caddy at the Camber Golf Course and he wondered if he should apply for it. Ninepence a round, so they said, and there might be a tip as well. Ninepence wasn't much but later, if he stuck at it, he could make double that and one shilling and sixpence was a bit more like it! It all depended on how many rounds he got and it would mean leaving his grandmother to do the ferry full-time. No, that wouldn't do, because when would she manage the cleaning at the rectory?

'Damn!' he muttered, for he rather fancied himself strolling across the golf links with a bag of clubs over his shoulder. But in that case he would never be available when the maroon went up for the lifeboat, for he could hardly drop the clubs and race back across the dunes. Even if he had a bicycle – which he didn't! He grinned at the idea. Somehow, somewhere, there *must* be a way for him to make a bit of extra money, if only he could find it. It seemed to Frank that as long as he could remember there had never been enough money to go round. If only his father had done a bit of smuggling! He sighed; that would have been exciting and they might have been rich . . . although, come to think of it, no one else was. The point was, how could you suddenly start throwing money about? The Customs men had eyes and ears everywhere and would be buzzing around like flies. Still, it *would* be exciting to row out after dark and meet your Frenchman right under the noses of the coastguards. But Luke Bligh would never touch it. Too risky, he had said. Who feeds the wife and kids while you are in jail? But he was dead now and somehow they muddled through without him. Smiling suddenly, Frank remembered the Regatta and his near-triumph. And his ten-shilling note. He didn't care what folk said about the Coulsdens, to him Jack was a decent man. He had given him the money for only coming *second* – who else would have done that? Remembering how he had lain in the Red Cross tent and how little Julia Coulsden had kissed him, he laughed aloud.

Up ahead a dog was barking – most likely Ratty's moth-eaten old dog, he thought. He heard a woman's voice scolding it: Eunice, probably. Suddenly she screamed and Frank, startled, broke into a run. As the screams continued he shouted, 'I'm coming! Hang on!'

He raced over the wet sand and stood beside her. She was dragging Ratty's dog away from a body which sprawled on the wet sand, bloated and grey with mud. A bundle of driftwood tied with cord lay where she had dropped it.

'I didn't know what it was,' she gasped. 'Oh stop it, you stupid animal!' She shook the dog angrily, but he continued to bark. 'I kept calling him and then I came . . . and saw it.'

'Here, let me hold the dog,' cried Frank. 'He'll have you over in a minute. Who is it?'

He took hold of the dog's collar and clouted him and the frantic barking gave way suddenly to a whimper.

'I don't know,' said Eunice. 'I'd only just found it when you shouted. Ugh! It's revolting, I can't bear it! What shall we do? It must have come in on the tide. The dog spotted it first. Oh, Frank, isn't it awful? A dead man!'

'Here,' said Frank. 'Give us that cord from your wood and I'll tie this wretched animal to the groyne. Shut your noise!' The unfortunate dog received another slap which set him yelping.

'Why did you hit him?' Eunice said. 'You're only making him worse, poor thing!' But Frank took no notice. He tied up the dog some distance away and when he returned they stood together staring down at the body.

'We must leave everything exactly as we found it,' said Frank. 'They always say that in detective stories.'

'Suits me,' said Eunice. 'I'm not touching him. You should respect the dead.'

'I wonder who it is? If only we could see his face.'

'Well, I don't want to, thanks very much,' exclaimed Eunice. She shuddered at the thought of a gaping mouth and black, swollen tongue. 'Just leave it, Frank. Please.'

'We'll have to tell the police,' he told her.

Her eyes widened. 'The police? Has he been murdered then?'

'I don't know. But he's dead,' Frank said, 'and we shall have to tell someone.'

'Oh God, Frank! I'm glad you came along,' she confessed. 'It's made my legs go all wobbly.'

'We're witnesses!' Frank told her. 'We may have to go into court and everything.'

'Oh no, Frank! I couldn't!'

Eunice refused to remain alone with the body, so he sent her back along the beach with the dog while he took up a position a few yards away from the shapeless grey mass which once had been a man. It dawned on him gradually that since he and Eunice would have to give evidence, they might also get their photographs in the local paper. Would he, at fifteen, be the youngest person to give evidence in a murder case, he wondered. If it *was* murder! Would the local paper pay for an exclusive story? He considered becoming a reporter or a detective. The job of a junior caddy on the Camber Golf Course had suddenly lost its appeal.

*

That evening Frank was eating plaice and boiled potatoes, which Alice had just cooked for him. He ate fish and potatoes every night and could not imagine how anyone would ever want to eat anything else. Sometimes it was herrings dusted with flour and then fried; sometimes mackerel slashed through and grilled; tiny dabs were baked whole on the bone in a covered dish; codling were cut into steaks and fried in batter. Whichever way the fish was cooked, it was always accompanied by a large quantity of boiled potatoes.

On the rare occasions when they had pudding it was invariably rice pudding, with a thick brown skin on the top which Frank would chew until, in his mind's eye, it resembled tea-leaves. Only then would he swallow it and progress to the creamy white rice beneath.

Today however there was no such luxury. Frank held hot potato in his mouth and sucked in air to help cool it.

'Must you?' asked Alice.

'It's too hot.' He swallowed, screwing up his face.

'Let it cool a minute, then.'

'I'm starving!'

'Tell me something new,' said Alice tartly. 'I never knew a day when you or your grandfather – or your father when he was alive – were not starving. All you men think about are your stomachs. Damn, now you've made me drop a stitch!'

'*I* made you?'

'Taking my mind off what I'm doing.'

'Where's the vinegar? That'll cool it down.'

'There's none left and I forgot to get some more. You can nip round to the shop if you want it.'

Frank was in an awkward mood. Finding the body was absorbing all his thoughts, but after long discussion Alice had banned the subject as 'morbid', insisting that she would rather talk about something more cheerful. Frank sighed noisily as Sam came in at the back door. Alice gave him a quick glance, but he went straight to the sink and ran some cold water into the tin bowl without a word. She made no comment on the lack of a greeting; they had all been on edge since Jean had gone off without a word to anyone and Mr Coulsden had come looking for him with a face like thunder and no proper explanation. If Frank or Sam had heard anything they had not told her, but people made odd comments and gave her sly looks and she felt in her bones that something serious had happened.

Suddenly there was a knock at the front door and Sam, drying his hands on the teacloth, turned round with a wary expression.

'Who the hell's that?' he asked.

'I can't see through the door, Sam.'

'Well, open the bloody thing, then. You, Frank – open the door, can't you!'

The knocking was repeated. It had an authoritative sound which made them exchange anxious glances.

'Frank!' cried Alice.

'All right, I'm going.'

He left what remained of his plaice and potatoes, wiped a hand over his mouth and opened the door.

'Mr Sam Bligh?'

Alice didn't recognise the voice.

'I'm his grandson. I'll fetch him.'

Sam hurried to the door and Frank returned to finish his supper. They heard him say, 'I'm Sergeant Tucker from Rye. May I come in?'

'What's it about?' Sam demanded, always belligerent in the presence of policemen. 'We've done nothing.'

'I know that, sir. There's no suggestion of that, but I would prefer to come in if I may, sir.'

Alice called out, 'Let him in, Sam. What's got into you?'

Reluctantly the old man opened the door wider and Sergeant Tucker followed him back into the kitchen. The sergeant was a burly, red-faced man with sandy crinkled hair and small blue eyes.

'What is it?' asked Alice. 'It's not bad news, is it? It's not Jean?'

'Jean Dessin? Yes, I'm afraid it is, ma'am.'

'Oh, my godfathers!' cried Alice. 'What's he been up to?'

'He hasn't done anything, ma'am. At least, nothing wrong. Not that we know of. There's been a bit of an accident, I'm afraid.'

Frank pushed the last potato into his mouth and gave the sergeant his full attention, while Alice looked at Sam fearfully.

'What sort of accident?' Sam demanded. 'Where is he? Is he hurt?'

The sergeant considered his words carefully. 'Would you know, sir, if he has any next of kin?'

Alice gave a gasp of fright. 'He's dead!' she whispered. 'He is, he's dead.' She sank on to a chair. 'Jean's dead, I know it.'

Frank and Sam stared at the sergeant.

'I'm afraid so,' he admitted. 'I'm sorry to bring bad news.' He looked at Frank. 'We have reason to suppose it was *his* body that was found this afternoon at Winchelsea Beach. We believe it to be Jean Dessin, but there's the matter of identification, I'm afraid, sir.'

'The body?' cried Frank. 'No! It can't be Jean.'

He pushed back his chair angrily and stood up.

'I'm afraid it looks that way,' maintained Sergeant Tucker.

'The body Frank told us about?' said Alice. 'But how could that be Jean? Frank said he'd drowned and Jean was a good swimmer. Oh, no, it *can't* be Jean!'

The sergeant looked apologetic. 'Of course we're not certain, but we do believe it *is* Dessin. Obviously we have to make our enquiries. If you feel up to answering a few questions, you may be able to help us.'

Sam Bligh shook his head in disbelief. 'Dead,' he said. 'Jean? Oh, God. First our Luke and now Jean.' He looked up at the sergeant. 'He was our lodger, I suppose you'd say, but he was more like a son and we were right fond of him. He's been with us ever since the beginning of the war, when he escaped from Belgium.'

The sergeant shook his head. 'It's a terrible thing . . . may I sit down, do you think? I shall have to make a few notes.'

He took a notebook from his pocket and Sam indicated the chair next to Frank at the table.

'We can't tell you much,' said Alice. 'We haven't seen him for a while.'

'Been some trouble, has there?' The sergeant's tone was casual, but Sam gave Alice a warning glance.

'No!' Alice spoke quickly.

'Alice, let me deal with this,' said Sam. 'Trouble? Not that we know about – put it like that, inspector.'

'*Sergeant* Tucker, sir.'

'Sergeant, then.'

'You say you haven't seen him for some time. Did he tell you where he was going?'

'Well, not exactly, no.'

'Was that usual, sir?'

'Not really. He never went anywhere usually.'

'You didn't know, then, if he'd had a quarrel with Mr Coulsden – Mr George Coulsden?'

Alice shook her head, but Sam averted his eyes.

'No, I don't,' said Sam.

Frank opened his mouth to speak, but Sam gave him a look which effectively silenced him. The police sergeant looked at Frank. 'You heard anything, sir?'

'Nothing. Just like Grandpa said. I didn't hear anything about a quarrel.'

'Oh, poor Jean,' said Alice, her mouth trembling. 'I can't believe it. He was so well-liked, was Jean – and he liked Mr Coulsden – always said he was a good gaffer and a decent man to work for. George Coulsden was very good to him as far as I know. It's not true, he can't be dead.' She threw her apron over her face and rocked backwards and forwards in her chair, overcome by the shock.

The sergeant hesitated, then began to ask Sam routine questions about Jean's age, height and so on, establishing the facts concerning Jean's background and his behaviour and daily routine prior to his disappearance. This gave Alice the opportunity to pull herself together and make a pot of tea. She did not say much, but she listened shrewdly to the policeman's line of questioning and when Agnes Coulsden's name was mentioned she was finally forced to accept what she had secretly suspected for some time – that Jean and George's wife had been 'carrying on'. Now she understood, she jumped to the inevitable conclusion.

'You'd best see Mr Coulsden then,' she burst out, the teapot poised over a cup. 'Ask him what happened to Jean! If there was a row and now Jean's dead. Ask Mr Coulsden!'

'Alice!' cried Sam in alarm. 'Whatever are you saying? You keep that sort of talk to yourself.'

'Why should I?' cried Alice. 'Nobody would have harmed the boy. Everybody liked him.'

'Alice! Nobody's saying it was anybody,' Sam insisted, rather red in the face. 'It was probably an accident, see. The inspector's told us already—'

'Sergeant,' said Frank rashly. 'He's a *sergeant*, Grandpa.'

Sam rounded on him furiously. 'I don't care what the bloody hell he is! You pipe down, Frank – it's me he's talking to, not you.'

'I only said—'

'I know what you said. And *I'm* saying keep quiet until someone asks you a question.'

'We do have another line of enquiry,' said the sergeant. 'Would you know, sir, if Dessin ever went out to sea after dark, perhaps, for any reason?'

'After dark?' said Sam. 'Smuggling? Is that what you mean?'

'Yes, sir. We do have to follow—'

'We don't know anything about that,' stated Sam firmly.

The sergeant wrote in his notebook. 'Well, I think that's all for now, then,' he said. 'As I said, I'm sorry to bring bad news and trouble you with all these questions, but we shall soon have the matter well in hand. At present there is no reason to suspect foul play, but of course we have to establish all the facts. If we have any cause to think it was not an accident, we shall very likely need to talk to you all again, but I hope it won't come to that. We shall know more after the post-mortem.'

'Post-mortem?' cried Alice. 'Oh, no! That's horrible. Let the lad alone, sergeant. He's dead – why can't you let him rest in peace?'

'We will, ma'am, of course, as soon as we are satisfied that he met his death by accident and no one else was involved. If not – and I only say *if* – you would want the villain brought to justice, wouldn't you? But as I say, we don't know yet if there is a villain so it's all hypothetical.'

Alice shrugged. 'Whatever it is, he's still dead. Our Jean – dead! I should have guessed something was wrong. He's never disappeared before like that, without saying a word to anyone.'

The policeman stood up and put notebook and pencil into the breast pocket of his tunic. 'Well, that's all for now and I hope there will be no need to trouble you further. However, we must ask you, sir,' he turned to Sam, 'if you would identify the body. Maybe tomorrow? Then there will be an inquest, of course, to hear the pathologist's report and decide if there's a case.'

'Where do I have to go?' asked Sam. 'And when?'

'I've written it all down here, sir, on this paper.'

'I see.' Sam took it nervously. 'Yes, all right then.'

'Not a very pleasant job, but we always encourage people to look upon it as the last duty you can do . . . for the departed, I mean.'

'There will have to be a funeral,' said Alice dully.

'Plenty of time to worry about that later,' Sergeant Tucker assured her. 'Let us deal with our enquiries, then if you need any help we can put someone in touch with you. Well, I must be off.'

'Frank, show the inspector out,' said Sam.

Frank opened his mouth, closed it hastily and led the way to the

front door. After it had closed behind the policeman, Alice looked
at her husband. 'Did you know?' she asked. 'About him and Mrs
Coulsden?'

Sam nodded, then amended, 'Well, I heard plenty of talk, put it
like that. I put two and two together. He should have known
better, the young fool!'

'He shouldn't have to die for it, though; it's not a crime, not in
that way. Do you think . . .' She shook her head. 'No, I can't
believe it!'

'Do I think George Coulsden killed him?' said Sam. 'I wish I
knew. Let's hope they find out at the inquest or whatever it's
called. Oh God, what a day!' He sank down on to a chair. 'Just
minding my own business and bang! This happens. It's one
bloody thing after another.'

Alice moved to stand beside him and he put his arms round
her. 'Was he smuggling, Sam, do you think?' she asked.

'He might have been, everyone's doing it. You know that, love,
but it's best to say nothing.'

'It's a bad do,' she said slowly. 'A real bad do.'

Frank stood in the middle of the room with his fists clenched.
'If Mr Coulsden killed Jean,' he began fiercely, 'then I'm going to
kill him!'

'Don't talk so daft,' Alice snapped. 'You'll do no such thing.
Keep well out of it, Frank, and let the police sort things out.
That's what they're there for. If you take the law into your own
hands, they'll be looking for you next.'

'But if he killed Jean—'

'Most likely he didn't,' said Sam. 'Your grandma's right,
Frank. Keep out of it, lad, for God's sake. It's bad enough already
without you making things worse.'

'I get the feeling,' said Alice, jerking her head skywards, 'that
someone up there has got it in for us Blighs.'

'You can say that again,' said Sam. 'And tomorrow I have to
identify his body. I could do without that, I can tell you. I could
really do without that.'

*

The following day George Coulsden spent nearly two hours with
Sergeant Tucker in a small room at the police station. He arrived
home again just before three o'clock, when Emily was still at
school and Julia was with Cicely. Relations between Julia and

Agnes had proved impossible and in desperation George had
asked Cicley to look after the child for a few days. However, after
the identification of Jean's body and the inevitable gossip, it was
tacitly understood that Julia's stay with Jack and Cicely should be
indefinitely extended.

Agnes was peeling potatoes. The bruises on her face had
turned to a dull yellow. She gave George a frightened look, but
said nothing. For a moment he watched her in silence, then he
took off his Guernsey and slumped into a chair with his legs
sprawled in front of him.

'Well, go on then. Ask me,' he said sullenly.

'I don't want to know,' said Agnes.

'Of course you bloody want to know!'

'I don't care.'

'You'd care if I was going to be arrested, wouldn't you?' he
taunted.

'How can they arrest you if you haven't done anything? You
said you didn't touch him.'

'I didn't.'

'Did they believe you?'

'So you *do* want to know,' he cried.

'You seem set on telling me,' said Agnes.

'Ask me then.'

She threw down the potato and the knife. 'Oh Christ, George.
All right then – do the police think you did it?'

'No, they don't. Do you?'

'I don't know, George.' She stared at him, trying to hide the
extent of her unease.

'Well, they believe me, so why don't you?'

'I know you better than they do.' She went on preparing the
potatoes, working mechanically without really noticing what she
was doing. 'What makes them so sure you didn't do it?' she asked
at last.

'They've had the pathologist's report and they seem fairly
certain he just drowned accidentally.

'He could swim,' said Agnes. 'Jean could swim, you know he
could!'

'He could have been drunk,' said George. 'He could have been
drunk and fallen in the water.'

'Or been drunk and then someone pushed him in.'

'It's possible.'

'But it wasn't you?'

'No.'

'The police are quite happy, then?'

'Someone else might have done something, but there's no proof. It just looks like he drowned, by accident. That means nobody else seems likely to have been involved. Make what you like of that, we have to wait for the inquest.' He sighed heavily and rubbed his eyes tiredly.

'Did they ask you about my face?' asked Agnes spitefully. 'Did they ask why you hit me?'

'Yes.'

'What did you say?'

'I told them the truth and that was OK.'

Agnes swallowed, relieved that after all she was *not* sharing a bed with a murderer. George had consistently denied harming Jean and insisted from the beginning that he had never even found him. If he *had*, he would have given Jean a thrashing and presumably – so Agnes reasoned – there would have been marks on the body and the police would know there had been foul play, as they called it. Presumably then there had been no foul play by anybody, including her husband. She decided not to let him off the hook too easily, however.

'Somebody could have got him drunk on purpose' she insisted, 'and then taken him out to sea and "*let*" him fall in!'

George gave her a withering look. 'And do you think he'd have been drinking with *me* after what happened? Two friends drinking in a pub together? Oh, don't be so bloody stupid, Ag! I'm telling you for the last time that if I'd found him, which I didn't – though God knows I looked hard enough and that's why he scarpered – *if* I'd found him I *would* have half-killed him. I'm not denying that and not one man would have raised a hand to help him against me, because he had it coming to him. You both did. I would have half-killed him, but I never would have been such a fool as to go all the way. Give me credit for *some* brains. Now, I don't want to go over and over it, so give it a rest. If he was killed, I certainly didn't do it. Maybe he had another girl friend . . . maybe you weren't the only one . . . maybe some other poor sod found he's been—'

Agnes whirled to face him. 'Stop it, George! Stop it!' she shouted. 'I won't hear those things about him. We did wrong, I'm not pretending we didn't, but you always liked him before that and if we . . . well, just because I . . . whatever, he's dead now and it's a waste of life . . .' She began to cry. 'I'm not going to hear anyone say a word against him, not even you. There was no other "poor sod", George; you can take my word on that.'

'Is that supposed to cheer me up, for God's sake?' cried George. 'You are a stupid bitch at times, Agnes. A really stupid bitch. Look, we're *still* going over it and I said it's done with. I know I didn't kill him and the police are satisfied. OK he's dead, and maybe he didn't deserve that but he is. Arguing and carrying on and accusing people won't bring him back, Ag. Nothing will. Not ever.'

Her tears fell on to the potato which she was still peeling though her sight was blurred and she had long since removed all the skin. George watched her hunched and shaking shoulders dispassionately.

'If it hadn't been for you he might be still alive—' he began and then stopped. It was all over and there was no point in destroying each other. 'Oh, pack it up, will you?' he told her. 'You'll make yourself ill if you go on like this. I'm sick of all this bloody grizzling. You should be jumping for joy that *you're* still here. Most men would have thrown you out!'

'I don't care!' she sobbed. 'Throw me out – I don't care about anything! You don't love me and you blame me because now your precious Julia's gone. Oh, I know what's really upsetting you. All I wanted was someone to love me and now he's dead. What do I care about anything?'

She ran out of the kitchen and up the stairs and he heard her coughing as the wardrobe door creaked open. Upstairs he found her packing after a fashion, wildly throwing garments into a bag, muttering and crying. Roughly he snatched a blouse from her hands and swung her round to face him.

'You're not going anywhere,' he said, 'and I do love you because if I didn't you could have gone off with young Dessin and I wouldn't have given a damn. So stop acting up – it's bloody ridiculous. I hit you because you said you loved him and that means you don't love me. So—'

'It does *not*!' cried Agnes, wriggling unsuccessfully in an effort to free her wrists from his grasp. 'It means I love you both, but you wouldn't understand that. I've always loved you, George, not that you've noticed these past few years. If I hadn't loved you I would never have put up with everything like I have. I'm not ugly, whatever you may see when you look at me. I could've married plenty of fellers and not got hidden away in that awful shack and had people whisper behind my back— Oh yes, they do even now. But I've put up with it because, for better or for worse, I *love* you!'

'But you loved *him*,' said George desperately.

'Yes, I did,' she cried defiantly, 'but in a different way. Just for a bit of excitement, for someone to notice me and make me feel pretty. I'm not making excuses; it was wrong and I'm the first to admit it. But I am trying to make you believe that I could love him and still love you— You're hurting my wrists, George, they're all red.'

'Serves you right,' he muttered, releasing her.

She stood rubbing them and looked at him wearily. 'You just say, George,' she said. 'If you love, me, I'll stay. If you've stopped loving me for any reason at all, I'll go. Me and Em will make out.'

'And I'll have no one, is that it? Julia gone. You and Em gone. Is that what you want?'

'No, it isn't, George. I've told you – I'll stay if you love me but if not, there's nothing left for us here and I'll sling my bloody hook. After all, you'd get Julia back if I was gone.'

His face crumpled suddenly. 'I want you *all*,' he whispered. 'All of us. A family. I can't stand any of this.' He sat down on the bed with tears flowing from his eyes, as he gasped painfully with the unfamiliar emotion. 'Help me, Ag! Help me,' he spluttered.

Agnes looked down at him with a heavy heart. He was forty, putting on weight and losing his hair. He drank too much, but he was a good father and he said he loved her. She thought of poor Jean with the beautiful lithe body and imagined it bloated and grey with all the joy and life gone from it. Now she could believe that George had not killed him – if anyone had. Maybe they would never know the truth about it. Jean was dead, but while he lived she *had* made him happy for a while in the only way she knew how.

Dry-eyed, she put her arms round George and sighed deeply.

'It'll turn out all right in the end,' she told him dully. 'I'm sure it will.'

*

Three days later the inquest was held at Pett Level, a mile or so beyond the spot where Jean's body had been found. Evidence was given by various people, including the coastguard from the station at Fairlight who reported a brief sighting of a small unidentified craft on the night the pathologist believed Jean to have met his death. A Customs and Excise officer then revealed that they had been watching Jean and two other unidentified men for nearly a year, believing them to be engaged in smuggling activities involving spirits and perfumes. The possibility existed that while thus engaged under cover of darkness, Jean had somehow met with a fatal accident. A verdict of death by misadventure was recorded.

CHAPTER TWELVE

On a November evening in 1921, Leo, Ben and Julia – warmly dressed against the chill, foggy air – made their way into Cinque Ports Street with Cicely's warning already fading from their minds.

'Don't go too near the bonfire,' she had told them. 'You could get pushed into it. And don't eat too many bloaters, Ben – you know what happened last year! Remember to keep an eye on Julia, Leo; you are not to let her out of your sight – George will be on us like a ton of bricks if anything happens to her. Oh, and if you see that wretched Agnes you are not to be rude. You hear me? I won't have it said that my children don't know their manners, so remember: be polite. A "good evening" will do; *don't* get into conversation if you can avoid it.'

Julia, tall for her eleven years, walked proudly between Ben and Leo. Her hair was pushed up inside a fluffy tartan beret and a long matching scarf was wound around her neck. She chattered excitedly and her eyes shone. Bonfire Night was a time of darkness, noise and bustle, of fantasy spiced with a hint of danger. Her aunt's dire warnings merely added to the sense of adventure; she felt that anything might happen on such a night – and secretly hoped it would. The pockets of her blue coat bulged with pennies, some destined for the collecting tins, the rest for the purchase of toffee apples, hot chestnuts or fudge, not forgetting the dreaded bloaters hot from the fire.

Leo at sixteen years of age was already a carbon copy of his father. His long body had broadened, he had the same short neck and moved with a slight spring on muscular legs. Ben, at twelve, was becoming less like Cicely. He was nearly as tall as his brother now, with long thin legs. His hair had lost its auburn tints and, to Cicely's secret dismay, was now fine and 'mousy'. The girl who danced along between them was well-proportioned and moved with a natural grace and a deceptively cool manner.

'Where are we going?' she enquired as Leo led them through

the gathering crowds towards the Salts.

'To the procession,' he told her, 'and don't tell Mama – she'd have a fit.'

Ben and Julia exchanged shocked glances. The procession! That meant torches and they were strictly forbidden.

'We're too young,' said Ben nervously. 'They'll never let us!'

'*I'm* not too young,' retorted Leo. 'They'll let me, so you two can walk with me.'

'And share your torch?' asked Ben, ever hopeful.

'Maybe – but not for long.'

'And me?' asked Julia.

'No, you're a girl,' said Leo.

'Then I'll tell about you,' she announced.

'Oh Christ!' said Leo.

'Leo! You're not to swear,' Julia rebuked him. ' "Christ" is swearing.'

'Christ!' said Leo loudly. 'Christ! Jesus Christ! Christ Almighty!'

Ben took hold of Julia's hand and gave it a reassuring squeeze. 'He'll be the one that goes to Hell,' he whispered. 'We won't'.

Julia hoped matters would not go that far, but there was no telling. 'Please God, forgive him,' she prayed silently. 'I'm sure he didn't mean it.'

The procession consisted of nineteen decorated 'floats' representing various groups in the town: the fire brigade, the Red Cross, the local dairy and many more. Farm carts pulled by horses were elaborately decorated with foliage, paper flowers and coloured ribbons, providing suitable backgrounds for the groups of people in fancy dress who formed the tableaux; these would be judged later and coveted prizes would be awarded. On this occasion, Julia thought them even more spectacular than usual. As the three children headed towards the pile of torches, they passed Robin Hood and his Men; Alice in Wonderland, with a man in a brown velvet suit as a rather rotund dormouse; a group of old-time 'smugglers' complete with eye-patches and pistols; and a dozen girls from the local dancing class disguised as flower fairies. Julia admired the latter tremendously and when Leo made a disparaging remark about them she defended them fiercely, making a mental note to ask Aunt Cicely if she could enrol at the dancing class in time for November the following year.

The torch-bearers were already taking up their positions

alongside the floats and soon Leo was the proud possessor of a four-foot stave with a bundle of oily rags bound to one end with loops of wire. He was told to walk beside one of the floats – a humorous seaside scene in which large men dressed in women's bathing dresses disported themselves in striped deck-chairs in front of a painted background of curling blue waves and brightly coloured fish.

At the head of the procession the town band was tuning up and a murmur of anticipation grew as the last of the daylight faded and one by one the torches were lit and the ragged yellow flames leapt up into the darkness. They cast a magical glow over the costumed figures on the floats and threw eerie shadows among the surrounding trees. A man wearing a top hat and tails went by on stilts, jangling a collection tin; Julia dropped a penny into it, while Ben, preferring to save his money until later, hastily looked the other way. The band struck up, startled horses neighed and, as the floats rocked, screams and laughter filled the air.

A familiar voice said, 'Well, if it isn't Julia Coulsden,' and she turned to see a masked figure grinning down at her. He carried a burning torch and wore a red spotted scarf tied over his head; two brass curtain rings served as earrings.

'Is it you, Frank Bligh?' she asked dubiously.

'Right first time.'

'Are you a pirate?' she enquired.

'Right again.'

George had offered Jean's job as crew member of *Silver Lady* to Frank, and after much heart-searching, Alice and Sam had agreed that he should accept it.

'Should you be here?' Frank asked her now.

'Leo is,' she hedged.

'Leo's much older than you.' He smiled to soften the reprimand. 'Well, you just mind how you go and keep back from the torches. Don't want you burned to a cinder, do we?'

As the band got into its stride, the procession with its accompanying torch-bearers moved off, Ben walking close to his brother and Julia hurrying to keep up with Frank.

'I like your hat,' he told her. 'Posh, that is!' She beamed and he leaned down to whisper, 'I just saw Emily down by the station yard.'

'And Papa?'

He nodded. 'But no 'orrible Aggie,' he told her.

Julia suppressed a giggle. Frank's nickname for Agnes had become a joke between them. Now she sighed briefly. Only to her diary did she confide the fact that she missed Emily. The boys were good to her – they teased her and occasionally spoiled her – and after a year she had begun to feel part of the family. But a boy cousin, however well-intentioned, could never enjoy the same confidences which Julia had shared with her half-sister. True she and Emily met in the playground at school, but since that terrible night there had been a certain constraint between them.

'I wonder where Agnes is,' said Julia.

'Perhaps they've had a row,' said Frank, 'and aren't speaking.'

'A row?'

'Oh, they're always rowing,' he told her. 'They go at each other hammer and tongs. I've heard them. You're well out of it, Julia, at your auntie's place. Think yourself lucky.'

'But poor Em,' said Julia, 'and poor Papa.'

'Don't you worry about them,' said Frank. 'You just worry about yourself, see? That's how to get by in this life. Now, no more about that lot – we're here to enjoy ourselves.'

As the procession wound its way through the narrow streets of the town the occasional firework sped skyward to burst in a spray of coloured light. Underfoot a few fire-crackers set the crowd shrieking and there were isolated bangs and plenty of sparklers. The pavements were packed with onlookers; women stood on the steps of the shops and children perched on the shoulders of long-suffering fathers. The bandsmen played march after march, and when they passed the public houses, men – some already the worse for drink – came out briefly to shout encouragement or derision depending on their temperament, and to dip into their pockets for the collection tins.

A huge bonfire waited on the Salts and later in the evening it would be lit. The preceding week had been reasonably dry and so the wood would burn well. A derelict fishing boat which had been well-tarred on the inside would be set alight also, but the local constabulary would be nearby to ensure that any horseplay on the part of the 'Bonfire Boys' – and they were notorious for their wild ways – was kept well within the limits of safety. As they passed the station yard, Julia looked for her father and Emily but saw no sign of them. The press of people on the pavements seemed to grow at an alarming rate and she edged closer and closer to Frank.

'Here, give us your hand,' he said at last and she took it gratefully. She turned to speak to Ben but her two cousins had disappeared, separated from her by the milling crowd. It seemed a long time before they reached the Salts, but even here there was no respite from the people who streamed down the hill and surrounded the bonfire.

'We've lost Ben and Leo,' said Julia.

Frank grinned. 'No, we haven't,' he replied. 'They've lost us.'

'But Aunt Cicely said—'

'Don't fret,' comforted Frank. 'You'll be all right with me. I can take care of you just as well as Leo. Better in fact, because he's lost you and I haven't!'

At that moment five young revellers surged towards them, cheerful but hopelessly inebriated. One of them stumbled, lurched forward and fell against Julia, sending her flying. She screamed as she fell, terrified of being trodden on, but within seconds Frank was standing beside her and pulling her to her feet. He shouted at the youth to watch what he was about and received a rude gesture by way of answer. Suddenly their good humour evaporated, and to Julia's dismay the irate exchange turned into a slanging match. It appeared that the revellers were visitors to the town and more than willing for a scrap with one of the locals. Frank found himself fighting one of the 'foreigners' and suddenly Leo appeared and they were joined by two other young fishermen who had been hoping for some fisticuffs by way of excitement for the past hour. Several others pitched in and the crowd hurriedly eased back to escape the flailing arms and legs and thudding bodies which fell and rose again in a grand mêlée. The onlookers seemed to be enjoying it and Frank and Leo were grinning cheerfully, but Julia watched horrified.

'Give it to him!' came a voice from the watching crowd.

'Land him one for me!'

'Up the Ryers!'

There was plenty of encouragement from the crowd. This added attraction to the night's events had not been expected, but they accepted the bonus gratefully.

'Watch out behind you! Oh, too late!' Loud laughter.

'Lovely one! That's the spirit!' Shrieks of delight.

'Trip him!'

'Hack him with your leg! No, not like that!'

Surely, thought Julia, Frank and Leo could never survive such a battle? Expecting at any moment to see them lifeless upon the ground and unable to bear the sight any longer, she turned and pushed her way through the spectators in a desperate bid to escape before the worst happened. As she pummelled her way through the crowd her hat was knocked off, but she dared not stop to retrieve it.

'Hang on, young lady! Not so fast.' Strong arms closed round her, preventing further flight. 'This is your hat, I believe – Good Lord, it's the little runaway! The Coulsden girl.'

She found herself looking into the amused eyes of Ian Cornwell. 'It's Frank!' she cried. 'Frank and Leo. They're all fighting and they're going to be killed.'

'Killed? Of course they won't be killed. Hey, come back here.'

But Julia was not at all convinced by Ian's reassurances and needed to put a greater distance between herself and the disaster. With a sigh of exasperation, Ian followed her erratic progress until they both emerged on the far side of the crowd and found themselves beside the river.

'Phew!' he exclaimed. 'I'm glad to be out of that mob. So, what next, young lady?'

Julia stared at him, surprised. 'How did you know my name is Lady? Who told you?'

'Lady?'

'Yes. Julia Lady Coulsden. Leo says my father was drunk when he went to the registrar. Leo says it's a silly name.'

Ian laughed. 'Leo says an awful lot, doesn't he? Well, I think it's a very nice name. Does anyone call you Lady?'

'No. It was because of the boat. Because of *Silver Lady* and my hair.'

This garbled explanation left Ian none the wiser. 'Well, I don't think your father was drunk,' he said. 'Who is this Leo?'

'My cousin. He's nearly sixteen and he knows about *everything*.'

'Does he now? Well, you take what he says with a pinch of salt, Julia Lady. Now, put your hat on again – that's it.' He helped her to push up her hair and tuck it inside the beret.

Julia pointed suddenly towards the dark river. 'There's *Silver Lady*. Do you want to see it? I was born the day before it was launched and Papa calls it my second home.'

'I'd love to see it. Would your father object?'

'No.'

They walked along the path which ran parallel to the water

until the boat loomed eerily in the darkness. The tide was ebbing and the deck was just below shore level, so it was simple enough to clamber aboard. There was scattered cloud, but for the moment the full moon shone through and by its light Julia saw a hunched figure sitting on the far side of the boat.

'Who's that?' she cried.

At first there was no reply, then the figure muttered indistinctly and when Julia and Ian moved closer she saw to her surprise that it was Agnes.

Recognising Julia, Agnes cried out, 'Get away from me! I've nothing to say. Nothing!' Swaying slightly, she raised a bottle to her lips and drank noisily from it.

'She's drunk,' whispered Ian. 'Do you know her?'

'It's Agnes. My stepmother,' said Julia reluctantly.

Ian recalled the name as soon as he heard it. George Coulsden had mentioned Agnes on the occasion of Julia's flight to South View and Ernest had spoken of her on several occasions.

'Perhaps we should leave her alone?' he suggested.

Julia was staring at the woman who had caused her so much grief in the past years. It was Agnes's fault that her mother had died; Agnes's fault that Jean was dead; Agnes's fault that Emily shared a home with her beloved Papa while she, Julia, lived with her aunt and uncle.

It seemed that everything that had gone wrong in her life was Agnes's fault, Julia reflected bitterly, and for a moment she forgot Ian's presence and the fact that Frank and Leo were fighting and Ben had disappeared. All she remembered was that she hated Agnes more than anyone else in the world.

'Get off my father's boat!' she cried. 'You've no right to be here.'

'I have every right,' Agnes answered, waving the bottle threateningly. 'I've every damned right, d'you hear me? Do you hear me, Julia bloody Coulsden? I've every right and I'm *not* moving for you or anyone else.'

Ian tried to hold Julia back, but she shook off his restraining hand and took a step forward.

'And I say you have no right,' she insisted. 'And you're drunk too. You're disgusting! Does Papa know you're here? He'd soon throw you off if he could see you – sitting there, guzzling whatever it is.' Her voice rose as the anger within her grew: anger that had lain dormant and unexpressed for as long as she could remember.

'He'd throw you off,' she shouted, 'because you're hateful and wicked! Drunk and horrible!'

'Julia! Don't!' cried Ian, shocked and embarrassed. 'Come away and leave her. You'll only upset yourself.'

She rounded on him fiercely. 'I won't come away. I won't leave her on *Silver Lady*. It's my boat, mine and Papa's!' She turned back and raised a small fist in Agnes's direction. 'If you don't get off *Silver Lady*, I'll—'

'You'll *what*?' yelled Agnes. 'You nasty spoilt brat! Yes, that's what you are! You think you're the cat's bloody whiskers, but let me tell you something, Julia *Lady* Coulsden. You're not half the girl my Emily is. Not half! And your father knows it.' She took a last mouthful of gin and tossed the bottle over the side. 'He knows it perfectly well. And if he doesn't, it's because he's too stupid! Too bloody stupid, your precious papa!'

'Don't you dare call my father names!' shrieked Julia furiously. 'I hate you, I've always hated you. Just you get off this boat. Get *off* it, I tell you!'

Alarmed by Julia's rising anger, Ian tried once more to take hold of her arm but suddenly she jerked herself free and ran towards Agnes. There was murder in her heart. It seemed to her at that moment that all the pains and miseries of her young life were directly attributable to Agnes, and since moving into Jack and Cicely's home, Leo's horror stories about her had added fuel to the flames. In that instant, she could not recall one good thing in Agnes's favour. Her mother, in death, had come to stand for everything that was good and Agnes for everything bad. Most of all, undeniably, this woman had come between Julia and her father, robbing Julia of the person who should have been her closest, dearest ally in a hostile world. Agnes deserved to die!

With a cry of fear Agnes tried to avoid the passionate figure hurtling towards her, but the gin had slowed her reactions and Julia's outstretched hands caught her full in the chest. With a strangled scream, she toppled backwards over the side of the boat and they heard a loud splash as she hit the water.

Julia whirled as Ian ran to lean over the side of the boat and peer down into the water.

'Don't help her,' she screamed. 'Leave her. Don't help her, Ian! Please don't!'

But Agnes had surfaced and, unable to swim, was thrashing desperately about in the cold dark water. The tide was moving strongly and she was being carried away from the boat.

'Oh, my God!' cried Ian. 'She can't swim, she's going to drown!'

Julia watched helplessly as he pushed her away, pulled off his shoes and jacket and plunged into the river.

'Don't save her,' she whispered, sinking to the deck, a small huddled figure; but with these words her anger evaporated, leaving her exhausted and afraid.

A large crowd which had rapidly assembled on the river bank witnessed the rescue, as Ian swam through the swirling water and struggled to bring a hysterical Agnes back to the bank where willing hands reached out to haul them both to safety.

Julia, alone on *Silver Lady*, heard the clamour and recognised her father's voice among others. She covered her ears with her hands. 'I don't care what they say,' she thought wearily. 'Or what they do to me.' She closed her eyes, but almost at once someone was beside her, patting her on the back. She opened her eyes to find Emily there.

'Don't cry, Ju,' she said. 'Please don't cry!'

'I'm not,' said Julia, 'but – oh, Em!'

Wordlessly, the two girls stared at each other until Ian joined them.

Julia looked up. 'Is Agnes drowned?' she whispered.

'No, of course not. She'll be fine. She's very wet but she's going to be OK.'

'You're all wet, too,' said Julia. 'Oh, I'm so sorry.' To her surprise she found that she *was* sorry because Agnes was Emily's mother. 'I'm sorry, Emily,' she whispered.

'What about?'

'I don't really know. About everything. I'm sorry about everything.' She shook her head in confusion.

George appeared beside them. 'I've got to get Ag home and into bed,' he said to Ian, 'and you must get out of those wet clothes. Will you come back with us for the time being? Later I'll send you home in a cab if there's one to be found on a night like this. If not, I could make you up a temporary bed and we could get a message to your grandparents somehow.'

Julia felt ridiculously proud of her father. She thought she had never heard him so calm and sensible. He had not blamed her for pushing Agnes, but perhaps that would come later.

'Leo,' she said suddenly. 'Leo's supposed to look after me.

Aunt Cicely will be cross with him.'

'And so she should be,' said George, 'but I'll let her know what's happened. Come on, you two girls. We must all get home or Ag will catch her death of cold.' He climbed back on to the river bank. 'That's all there is to see,' he told the crowd, with an attempt at humour. 'We're off home now.'

As he spoke, a cheer went up from the crowd around the bonfire as the first flames licked up into the darkness and the crackle of burning branches filled the air. Fireworks were set off and there were sporadic bursts of ragged singing as all faces turned towards the small orange glow within the heart of the fire – a glow which grew rapidly, minute by minute, as the flames spread. Sparks flew up and for a moment the guy propped at the top was outlined in the glare. The people who had been watching the Coulsden drama now hurried away towards the bonfire while George, Ian, a shivering Agnes and the two girls made their way back to the road; they skirted the crowd and were soon climbing up the hill.

*

Twenty minutes later Agnes was tucked up in bed and the rest of them were sitting in the parlour drinking cocoa. Ian wore a pair of George's pyjamas and his dressing-gown. Emily and Julia were in nightdresses. A match had been put to the fire and, sitting beside Emily on the hearth-rug, Julia was experiencing a strange and unfamiliar feeling of security. She did not acknowledge the feeling and could not have rationalised it if she had done so, but she felt relaxed, almost soporific as she looked from Ian to her father and down to Emily.

'What an evening!' said Ian with a grin. 'I had no idea that Bonfire Night in Rye would hold so many excitements!'

'It used to be a hell of a lot rougher,' George told him. 'In the last century they killed one of the constables – threw him into a burning boat for a joke, but it turned sour on them. They clamped down after that. The "Bonfire Boys" were a real wild lot. Still are, most likely, but the police keep a better eye on things nowadays.' He set down his mug and stood up. 'I'll just have a look at Ag,' he said. 'She was a bit weepy when I left her.'

They heard his footsteps on the stairs and then subdued voices. Ian caught Julia's eye and raised his eyebrows enquiringly, but Julia lowered her eyes hastily. She knew exactly what his expression meant, although he had not spoken a word. Nor had he once referred to the fact that Julia's action might have had very serious consequences.

'I know,' said Julia in a small voice. 'I'm going to tell her.'

Emily frowned. 'Tell her what?'

'Nothing. At least, I don't want to talk about it.'

Emily looked at Ian. 'What doesn't Ju want to talk about?'

Ian smiled. 'It's just something private,' he told her. 'Julia will tell you one day, I expect, but not tonight. Is that right, Julia?'

Julia could only nod. Her throat tightened with apprehension but she finished her cocoa and stood up. 'I'll go now,' she told Ian and was rewarded with a smile of such warmth that some of her nervousness left her.

Upstairs she stood on the familiar landing and hesitated outside the bedroom. With horrible clarity she saw herself a year earlier standing in the doorway, looking at Jean Dessin. Now, she heard sobs and then her father's voice . . . soothing, gentle. A great love for him welled up inside her. The constriction in her throat returned, but she knocked on the door before her courage could desert her. Without waiting, she pushed open the door and saw George sitting on the side of the bed with his arm round Agnes's shoulder. He looked large and awkward and Julia wanted to die with love for him.

'I want to speak to Agnes,' she stammered and then, seeing the wary look in her father's eyes, added, 'It's all right, Papa. Truly it is.' After a brief hesitation, he nodded and went out, closing the door quietly behind him.

Agnes looked frail and helpless alone in the double bed. Her face was puffy and her eyes were red. She twisted a damp handkerchief in her fingers and, as Julia stared at her, waved her hand in a helpless gesture.

'Nothing . . .' whispered Agnes huskily. 'Just nothing . . . ever . . .' She dabbed at her eyes, oblivious of her bedraggled appearance. 'It won't ever come right. I don't know what to do – there's nothing . . .'

'I'm sorry,' said Julia, swallowing hard. 'I want to say I'm sorry.'

Agnes seemed not to hear her as she was racked by fresh sobs. 'He won't forgive me – George. He won't ever forgive me because of you – he's lost you and he – I know it's my fault and he blames me.' She stared appealingly at Julia. 'I just want us all to be happy, but it never will happen. It's never going to come right. *Never.*'

Julia moved to one side of the bed. 'I didn't mean it,' she said. 'To push you like that. At least, I did mean it but—'

Agnes shook her head. 'What can I do? I can't leave him because he needs me. He does, Julia. He needs me . . . and I love him.'

'Do you?' Julia was genuinely surprised. She had heard from Leo how her father had beaten Agnes and even Frank said they quarrelled.

Agnes nodded. 'I want to love him, but he won't let me. It's because of you and Hettie, because of your mother. How can he forgive me for that? How can I forgive myself?' She took a deep shuddering sigh. 'If only I could turn back the clock, don't you think I would? How do you think I've lived with that all these years? Oh, Ju, it's never going to be any good. So much has happened – it'll never come right, I know it won't.'

Julia watched her and then asked abruptly, 'Did you really kill my mother?'

Agnes tried to keep her voice level. 'No, Ju, I didn't. She killed herself, but it was because of me and Em. Oh God, Ju, I *know* it was wrong but I can't undo it. I didn't mean for her to die. I had no idea she would do such a dreadful thing and now you've got no mother and . . . I think George hates me,' she whispered.

'No, he doesn't,' said Julia. 'He only hit you because of Jean. I think he was jealous.'

An odd smile touched Agnes's ravaged face and made her look almost childlike. Strangely, Julia felt older and wiser than her stepmother.

'Jealous?' echoed Agnes. 'You *think* he was jealous? Oh, he was jealous, I know. That's why he hit me. But he wanted to do it, you see. He'd been longing to hit me ever since . . . ever since Hettie died.' And she began to cry again, soundlessly, without bothering to wipe away the tears.

'When I pushed you,' said Julia, 'I did hate you then . . . but now I don't. Now I'm really sorry and I'm glad Ian pulled you out.'

'Are you?' cried Agnes. 'Well, I'm not. He should have let me drown – it would have been all over then.'

She lay back on the pillow, emotionally drained, her hands limp on the coverlet. Julia thought sadly that she looked like a broken doll.

'We could try again,' she said timidly, but Agnes only stared straight ahead. Julia took hold of the hand nearest to her and held it in her own. 'Agnes! Do you hear me? I said we could try again. All of us together here?'

Agnes shook her head. 'I don't know,' she whispered. She turned her head and stared at her hand held in Julia's. 'Do *you* think we could, Ju?'

Julia climbed up on to the bed and knelt beside her stepmother. For a long time they stared into each other's eyes, wondering, hardly daring to hope.

'*Could* we, Ju?' asked Agnes. 'Could we really?'

'I'd like to come home,' said Julia, her lips trembling and then suddenly, unbelievably, they were in each other's arms.

*

2 January 1922

Another New Year has started and I have made my resalutions. No. 1 to be kind to everyone inc. Agnes. No. 2 to work harder at Geog. and Hist. (but how I hate them). No. 3 not to swear. No. 4 to get up earlier on Sat. and Sun.

I hope A. is making a resalution to be nicer to me and E. tho' she does try and she is much better than she used to be and does not keep calling me Julia Lady, thank goodness. This year I will be 12, E. will be 11, Papa will be 41 and Agnes won't say how old she is. My mother would be 36. Sometimes E. and I go to her grave and take primroses or whatever we can find wild. E. is sorry about her.

I hope it will snow so we can use the new tobogan.

A. has a bad chest but won't go to the doctor. She coughs and then gasps and spluters. It sounds awful.

I must close now. E. is already snoring.

*

Cicely smoothed the white lace cloth over the tray and began to arrange the second-best china – white patterned with blue and pink roses, and with curly handles which looked elegant but were awkward to hold. The best tea service was reserved for Mrs Hook-Brayne's visits, but Jane was calling in for a chat some time after four o'clock, following her visit to the chiropodist, and Cicely wanted to impress her. She had therefore made a tray of Queen cakes which she had iced and these were on a matching plate beside the tea tray, covered with a smaller lace cloth. Many of these items of lace had been handed on to her when Sarah died and Cicely liked to be seen to use them as a mark of respect for her departed mother-in-law. Various table napkins and cloths had, of course, gone to Jane and the rest to Julia, while Agnes had received nothing.

Cicely prided herself that, although Stanley was the oldest of the three brothers, his home in Hastings could in no way compare with South View and that Jack's home – under her own discreet influence – was the only one of any real distinction in which Sarah's tableware could be shown to proper advantage. She wanted Jane to be aware of the difference between Jack's home and Stanley's. If only Sarah had survived long enough to move in with them, Cicely felt sure that the old lady at least would have appreciated her efforts to maintain standards and to give Jack the kind of home that befitted the owner of one of Rye's best known boatyards. It still grieved Cicely, when she allowed herself to think about it, that Winifred was *not* a Gooding and had compounded the omission by marrying a nobody like Ernest.

She had made the cakes herself because – for reasons she chose not to understand – they could no longer afford a house-keeper; but she had never referred to this fact to anyone but Ben, Leo and Jack and they were under strict orders not to speak of it to family or friends. Miss Mills had also left their employ, but this was because the boys had outgrown her usefulness and no one could argue with the logic of that.

Satisfied with the tray, Cicely hurried into the kitchen to see if the kettle was near to boiling. She did not want to prolong Jane's visit and had hinted vaguely at a prior evening engagement. In Cicely's opinion, Jane was not the wife for Stanley – he could and should have made a much better match – but now that Winifred and Ernest were married there was no way to avoid a closer relationship between their two families.

Having checked the kettle, Cicely went to the hall mirror to assure herself that she was looking her best and then back into the parlour, where she took a sheet of music from the piano stool and arranged it on the music rest. Then she sat down and began to play a simple study in C sharp minor, a piece she had practised for an occasion such as this. She played several wrong notes, tried to pick up the thread, failed and was forced to start from the beginning once more. Again she went wrong and tutted irritably to herself as she began for the third time. She had started to learn to play the piano when she was first married – the lessons had been a birthday present from Jack – but she had not progressed further than Grade Two. She did feel, however, that an elegant wife seated at a piano was an asset to any man and had discovered by discreet questioning that Jane could not play a note. It would be rather nice, thought Cicely, to be 'interrupted at the piano' by Jane's ring.

After several more unsuccessful attempts to master the piece, however, she gave up and banged down the piano lid in exasperation. Perhaps she could be singing, she thought, or rearranging the dried flowers. Or she might be seated at the table writing a letter to an old friend . . . no, a very close friend. Or knitting, perhaps? Sighing heavily, she decided that knitting would not be particularly impressive and wished she had taken up oil painting or marquetry. However, before she could make a final decision Jane was ringing the bell and, pausing only to lift up the lid of the piano again, Cicely hurried to open the door.

'Jane, my dear! How lovely to see you,' she gushed. 'And so prompt. Six minutes past four. You must have run all the way from the chiropodist. What was it, a corn?'

Jane opened her mouth to reply, but Cicely rushed on, 'Beastly things! I don't suffer from my feet at all, I'm happy to say, but I can and do sympathise with those less fortunate in that respect. Let me take your coat – that's the way. I was just practising until you arrived . . .'

'Practising what?' Jane asked and Cicely was able to give a little tinkle of delighted laughter.

'Why, the piano, of course! Jack loves to hear me play, he simply won't let me give it up. An hour a day *at least*! Some men are so funny about these things . . .'

She led the way into the parlour, noticing Jane's brief look at the elegant tray setting. 'Nothing grand,' she said. 'I thought it would just be the two of us. *A deux*, as they say.'

Jane made no answer to this comment and Cicely noticed for the first time that her sister-in-law was looking slightly agitated.

'Are you all right?' she asked. 'You look rather flushed. Do sit down.'

Jane sank into a chair and pressed one hand to her chest. 'I've just seen her!' she told Cicely excitedly. 'Nearly walked bang into her! Oh, if I had I think I would have died on the spot with shock. As it was—'

'Seen who?'

'*Her*!' Jane insisted. 'George's woman. She was walking down the High Street as bold as brass, heading straight for me. I nearly had a fit, you can imagine. Well, whether or not she saw me I'll never know, but suddenly she dived into The Apothecary's and I was able to walk right on without letting on that I'd even seen her.'

'Agnes, you mean?' Cicely had forgotten that Jane still had not spoken to George's second wife.

'Of course: Agnes! Awful jumped-up hussy! I mean, Cis, we all have—'

Cicely's smile was forced. 'Do please call me *Cicely*,' she said.

'What?'

'Cicely. My name is Cicely. I won't allow even Jack to call me Cis.'

'Oh, no, I forgot. So sorry.' But Jane was quite unperturbed by the snub. 'Yes, well . . . where was I? Oh, that's right. We all have our standards and that creature's behaviour falls so far below that of any decent woman that – well, if I've said it to Stan once I've said it a hundred times, wild horses will not drag a "Hullo, Agnes' from my lips. I just could not bring myself to say it; I think I should spit in her eye first.'

She eased off one shoe and felt her big toe gingerly. 'Twice a year I come all the way to Rye to see this Mr Robbins. It's silly really, but it was Sarah's idea that my feet needed attention and it is nice to have someone who cares – Mr Robbins I mean, not poor Sarah.' She frowned, trying to recall her original line of thought. 'Oh yes, that woman! Mind you, Stan's not with me, you know. He simply can't take a stand on the matter. Weak, that's what Stan is. I've never forgiven him for what happened at their wedding. Best man, indeed! It almost broke up *our* marriage, you know. Oh yes it did—'

Cicely interrupted her briefly. 'I'll just make the tea,' she said, but Jane followed her into the kitchen, limping.

'I thought we would have Earl Grey,' Cicely began, 'unless you prefer something more scented. We have quite a nice selection, actually. There's—'

'Oh, anything will do me,' Jane assured her, 'as long as it's dark brown and with plenty of sugar. Don't go to any trouble for me. Where was I? Oh yes, I said to Stan that he'd shamed me in front of the whole family. He didn't like that, but I told him straight. The rows we had over that wretched woman! I shall never forgive

George for marrying her. Nor Stan for what he did. I envy you your Jack, Cis, I do really. "If you were a bit more like Jack, we'd be a lot happier," I told Stan. Our marriage has never been the same since, but what can you do?'

Jane followed Cicely back into the parlour, talking non-stop while Cicely, cringing, remembered just how little she cared for Stanley's wife and was heartily thankful she had not invited her to dinner.

As she poured the tea through the silver strainer, she decided that Jane was a complete and utter peasant. She listened with only feigned interest to an account of Jane's problems, but at last a small snippet of information caught her full attention.

'Stan is what?' she asked sharply. 'Laying up one of the boats?'

'Well, he's talking about it,' replied Jane through a mouthful of iced Queen cake. 'Things are no better than they were six months ago. In fact, I reckon they're worse. Not that it's just us, is it? I mean, Lowestoft is feeling the pinch and other places further west. Stan does nothing but moan about "the state of the industry". If I hear that phrase once more, I think I'll scream. "They'll pick up," I tell him, "so don't keep moaning." But it doesn't look too good. How's the yard doing? They must be feeling it, Stan says. And George, too. We're all in the same boat, if you'll excuse the pun.'

'Are we?' said Cicely reprovingly. '*I* don't think we are.'

'Well, Stan says that—'

'Stanley knows nothing about the boatyard,' said Cicely. 'George may be finding things difficult – I really couldn't say – but I can assure you that Coulsdens' yard is thriving and you can tell your husband so from me.'

Jane looked unconvinced. 'Well, that's not what Stan reckons,' she began.

'Then Stan reckons wrong,' said Cicely firmly with a brief disregard for the niceties of grammar. 'Not that I do the books these days – I like to leave that side of the business to Jack – but I would certainly know if Coulsdens were in any kind of trouble.'

'But the fire,' said Jane. 'Stan thinks—'

'Oh, the fire!' Cicely managed another tinkly laugh. 'The fire was years ago and we *were* insured, you know!'

'But not for the proper amount, Stan says—'

Cicely stood up abruptly and, reaching for the small brass

crumb tray and brush, began to clear up the cake crumbs which Jane was scattering.

'Stan says a good deal too much,' she said sharply. 'Perhaps he should spend more time on his own affairs and less nosing into those of other people.' She straightened up and carried the offending crumbs into the kitchen to dispose of them, giving herself a few precious moments in which to calm down. She reflected angrily that if Stanley's marriage was not all it might be, she could well understand why. Taking a deep breath, she smiled determinedly and went back into the parlour.

'Quarter to five already,' she said. 'Where does the time go? Will you have a second cup of tea before you leave?'

'Before I leave?' said Jane. 'Oh dear, in all the excitement about *her*, I forgot to tell you that I bumped into Jack on my way to the chiropodist and he said to stay to supper. Wouldn't take no for an answer. You're a very lucky woman, Cis, to have a husband like Jack.'

Cicely, choking with silent rage, could cheerfully have strangled him.

CHAPTER THIRTEEN

The best part of two years passed in comparative peace and Julia's thirteenth birthday arrived. She was awake just seconds before the alarm rang on her bedside clock and was able to clamp a hand over it at the first trill so that the rest of the household need not be disturbed by it.

She woke Emily, who could sleep through anything, and together the two girls washed, dressed and crept downstairs to the kitchen. They would eat their breakfast when they returned. It was just after five o'clock when they left the house with their bicycles and rode along Cinque Ports Street and out on to the Winchelsea Road. Passing Jack and Cicely's house, they then turned left down the road which led to Rye Harbour, then almost imediately right along a track running parallel to the river and, letting themselves through a gate, came out on to the marsh proper. Ahead they saw Camber Castle grey and squat against the skyline, its crumbling walls patched with green ivy. A single lark sang overhead and a small herd of Friesian cows grazed to the left of the ruined walls. Julia eyed them apprehensively. 'I hope they don't see us,' she said. 'Frank didn't say anything about cows.'

'Or bulls.'

'Stop it, Em! They're not bulls, are they? Do you think they might be?'

'I don't know. They're too far away to see.'

'Could we cycle faster than they could run, do you think?'

'I don't know. Why have you slowed down?'

'I haven't,' Julia protested. 'I'm going at the same speed.'

'Well, suddenly I'm in front.'

'You must have speeded up.'

'I have not,' said Emily. 'You're scared!'

Julia pedalled faster, bumping unevenly over the fast disappearing track. She passed Emily and was turning to jeer when the front wheel of her bicycle failed to negotiate a grassy hummock and she found herself thrown over the handlebars. Luckily a patch of longish grass cushioned her fall, but she scrambled to her feet shaken and irritable.

'A nice way to start my birthday!' she grumbled. 'That was your fault, Em. I wouldn't have gone so fast if you hadn't kept on at me.'

Emily laid her bicycle on its side and went to Julia's assistance, brushing grass and moss from her clothes and then examining the machine to see if it was damaged in any way.

'Nothing wrong,' she said cheerfully, pretending not to notice Julia's lapse into ill-humour. 'Perhaps now you're thirteen your luck's going to change.'

'You call that luck?' cried Julia. 'How is falling off my bike good luck? Are you mad?'

'It's good luck that you didn't hurt yourself and it's good luck the wheel's not bent—'

'And if I got run down by a motor car and broke one leg, I suppose it would be good luck not to break them both?' She remounted and Emily followed suit. 'Is that how you work it out? Because, if so, you're crazy! I've always said so and now I know!' She grinned suddenly. 'Oh, come on! We're wasting time and we've still got to get the mushrooms.'

The early morning outing was more than a cycle ride out to Camber Castle. Julia's birthday project was to beautify the Castle ruins which she considered to be sadly neglected, and then to move towards the harbour mouth picking mushrooms on the way. They would call on Frank Bligh and give him some or all of the mushrooms – depending on how many they had found – and then cycle home in time for breakfast.

In Julia's saddlebag there were four packets of seeds which they planned to plant in various crevices in the Castle walls as well as other more strategic positions. Emily's saddlebag contained a large bottle of water with which to give the seeds a moist start in life. 'After that,' Julia had declared, 'they'll be on their own and must make their own way in the world.'

She had the notion that the seeds would flourish and be self-perpetuating and that year after year visitors to the Castle would marvel at the astonishing variety of unlikely flowers bursting in profusion from the walls. In fact, very few people visited Camber for it was fairly inaccessible, surrounded as it was by areas of marshland and offering little to the determined sightseer except crumbling outer walls and an inner keep. Over the centuries all the timbers had rotted and fallen in, while rocks and rubble from the collapsing walls had blurred under grass and weeds so that the original design of the interior was no longer discernible to the uninitiated.

Julia had been to the Castle on several previous occasions when much younger, accompanied by Leo and Ben. Emily had never been before. They reached the Castle without interference from the cattle and propped their bicycles against the walls.

'Leo climbed up that ivy,' said Julia, pointing, 'last time we came. I remember thinking, "Don't fall!" My heart was in my mouth.'

'Ugh!'

'You know what I mean,' said Julia. 'Suppose you saw Ben climbing up there, risking his life?'

'Why was he risking his life?' asked Emily, refusing to be impressed. 'He was just showing off!'

'No, he was *not* showing off. It was a dare: Ben dared him to, so he did. If Aunt Cicely had known she would have been furious. She always insisted that we didn't climb the walls.' She giggled. 'Of course, she meant from the *inside* – it's much easier that way. Even I did it. I'll show you.'

'Where's the moat?'

'There isn't one. Not all castles have moats.'

She opened up the saddlebag of her bike and took out the seeds. 'Now you get the water and we're ready,' she announced. 'The Birthday Expedition is about to begin!'

'I thought it had already begun.'

'Well, it hasn't. The ride out here doesn't count.'

Julia led the way inside the Castle and together they climbed the slopes of earth which had built up against the interior of the walls. It was a simple business then to clamber the remaining feet to the top. The view was spectacular: Romney Marsh stretched away on all sides and they could see for miles towards the sea wall on one side, round to Winchelsea and Rye on their respective hills and across to the harbour village.

'And we're all alone here,' said Julia gleefully. 'Come on. Let's start planting before the sun gets too hot.'

They spent the next half-hour clambering over the walls, planting seeds. Julia had chosen wallflowers and marigolds, and Emily, after long deliberation, had decided on poppies and forget-me-nots. They mixed the seeds with earth, damped it down and then pressed the resulting 'paste' into any suitable crevice in the rock surface, sharing out the seeds so that there was sufficient for each wall. When at last the task was completed, they stood inside the keep and regarded each other triumphantly as they rubbed their hands clean on the grass.

'Well, that job's jobbed, as Ma would say,' said Emily. 'I wonder how long they'll take to flower? D'you think if we come back in a few months' time?'

Julia was dubious. 'Maybe a bit longer,' she suggested. 'The trouble is, most of these should be flowering by now. July is rather late to be planting, but they might still grow this year.'

'If not,' said Emily, 'we could come back next spring and have a look. If they've been planted all winter they should have a good start.'

Julia considered this. 'I don't think it works quite like that,' she said. 'I think – oh no!' She clutched Emily's arm and together they stared in horror at half a dozen heifers which had wandered into the Castle and now blocked their retreat.

Emily gave a gasp and looked over her shoulder for an alternative way out, but even as she did so more cattle were pushing through what had once been a broad doorway but was now a large irregular gap in the fabric of the rock wall.

'We can get up to the top of the walls,' cried Julia. 'They can't climb, can they? Not like goats.'

About ten animals were now ambling about in the confined area within the walls, snatching in leisurely fashion at tufts of grass and only occasionally casting a curious glance in the girls' direction.

'You're wearing a red dress!' cried Julia. 'Bulls go for red! Why did you have to wear that?'

'Ju! How was I to know we'd meet these wretched . . . whatever they are.' She peered at the nearest animal. 'It's got no udders, so it must be a bull.'

'I don't know,' said Julia. 'It hasn't got any . . . you know, what a bull should have. At least, there's something there – oh, help!' She scrambled back a few yards as the animal turned towards her. 'They've got nasty-looking horns, whatever they are. Oh Lord, I hope we're not going to be stuck here. Suppose they won't go away – should we try shooing them, d'you think?'

'They might get angry – oh dear! Where's the farmer, I wonder? Perhaps he's due to come and have a look at them.' They scanned the surrounding fields hopefully and Emily was the one to spot a human figure making its way slowly and erratically over the grass, about half a mile away.

'There!' she cried. 'There's someone – I think it's a man or else a boy. Wandering about out there.' She raised her voice and shouted. 'Hi! Hey! You there!'

Julia joined her and to their infinite relief the man shaded his eyes and looked around him. They resumed their shouts and he finally saw them and waved. Emily groaned.

'He thinks we're just shouting "Hullo",' said Julia. 'We'll have to try again and shout something different like "Help us!". That couldn't be mistaken for "Hullo".'

'I'm not so sure,' said Emily, 'but let's try it anyway. Anything's better than sitting here surrounded by cows.'

Eventually they managed to convey that they needed assistance and the man hurried towards the Castle. A few of the heifers grazing nearby ran away as soon as he drew near and the two girls watched until suddenly Julia recognised him.

'It's Tommy Bird's son,' she said. 'Tommy Bird who works for Uncle Jack. It's Chick Bird. I've seen him at the yard once or twice. Hey, Chick! It's us, Julia and Emily.'

Chick looked up and grinned. At twelve years of age, Eunice's son had grown into a stocky boy with a shapeless mass of brown curls.

'What's up with you two then?' he shouted.

'We're trapped!' cried Julia. 'All these bulls – we can't get out.'

'They're heifers,' he said. 'They won't hurt you.'

'We don't trust them,' said Julia, 'whatever they are.'

Emily leaned over and smiled at him. 'Could you chase them out for us?'

'Why should I?' he retorted. 'You're Coulsdens, aren't you?'

'What if we are?'

'We've a bone to pick with your lot, that's what!'

The girls were intrigued.

'Look,' cried Julia, 'get us out of here and then tell us about the bone. *Please.*'

'They're only heifers, I told you. You can chase 'em out yourself.'

Emily muttered something rude under her breath and then smiled winningly. 'We'd rather you helped us,' she wheedled.

'We'd be ever so grateful. *We* haven't got any bones to pick with anybody.'

'You reckon?' he yelled back.

'I reckon!'

'I can't stand this,' Julia whispered to Emily. 'For two pins I'd drop a rock on his head. Why does he have to argue?' She laughed suddenly and whispered something to Emily, who giggled delightedly and nodded. Then she leaned over again. 'Charlie! We'll give you a reward if you rescue us. Honestly! You'll like it. Take it or leave it.'

The two girls then backed away from the edge of the wall and clung together, laughing. 'What a birthday!' gasped Julia. 'I shall remember being thirteen!'

'But don't let Ma know,' said Emily.

'Or Papa!'

'No fear!'

A sudden rumble of hooves alerted them to Chick's presence inside the Castle walls. The heifers scattered as he clapped his hands and then he watched self-consciously as the two girls scrambled down towards him.

'Oh, thank you, Chick,' said Julia. 'You really are kind.'

He thrust his hands into his pockets. 'So, what's my reward?' he asked.

'Outside,' said Emily. 'We'll give it to you when we're safe outside the Castle and these bulls – heifers, I mean – are not so near. That was awful, being stuck there. We're ever so grateful, aren't we, Ju?'

'Ever so,' Julia agreed.

They all hurried out, stumbling over the uneven ground in their haste.

'What was you doing there, anyway?' Chick demanded. 'Bit early for two girls to be—'

'Two young ladies!' Julia corrected him. 'It's my thirteenth birthday.'

'Bit early for you *girls* to be gallivanting about,' he repeated. 'I don't usually see anyone this early, 'cept sometimes Frank Bligh. Having a picnic or something?'

'It's a secret,' said Julia hastily. 'We were doing something to benefit mankind—'

'And womankind!' Emily added.

'But it's a secret, so don't ask,' said Julia. 'And we wanted to pick some mushrooms. Are there any about? We were going to pick some for Frank.'

'Not in July,' Chick told her. 'So now we've left the mad dangerous "bulls" behind, what's my reward?'

As Julia leaned forward he stepped back warily, so she was forced to grab his shoulders. She kissed him quickly on the tip of his nose and then Emily kissed his cheek.

To their amusement a deep blush swept over his face as he rubbed at the spots where the kisses had landed.

'Get off!' he cried, embarrassed. 'What d'you do that for?'

'The reward,' said Julia innocently. 'We thought you'd be pleased.'

'Well, I'm not,' he said gruffly, although secretly he was thrilled.

'Perhaps,' said Julia, 'you're too young to appreciate being kissed by two beautiful young ladies. I bet Douglas Fairbanks would appreciate us.'

'Well, I'm not him so I don't!'

'You don't want us to kiss you again, then?'

He hesitated and then said firmly, 'No, I don't.'

'Don't be cross, then,' begged Emily. 'It was only a joke and we really are grateful. Is it "Pax"?'

'If you like,' he agreed. The girls collected their bicycles and the three of them began to walk back across the marsh.

'What did you mean, a bone to pick?' asked Julia. 'Don't you like us?'

'I don't like the Coulsdens,' he told them. 'Least, my folks don't like you. Don't you know why?'

'No!' they chorused.

'Is it something awful?' Julia asked. 'It can't be.'

'Well, it is then, so that's all you know, clever dick! It's very awful and my ma never stops going on about it. Not that *you* did it, you two girls. It was your father and mother.'

'It can't be my mother,' said Julia, 'because she's dead. She died when I was a baby. I was two when—'

'It's sort of her,' interrupted Chick, 'and Agnes Dengate.'

Emily scowled. 'What's your ma got against ours, then?'

'Your father told lies about my ma and she was accused of stealing things and got the sack,' said Chick triumphantly, 'before I was born, that is. My ma worked for George and Hettie Coulsden and he got her the sack and that's the God's truth – may

He strike me dead if I'm telling a lie!' He looked up into the clear sky as though appealing for confirmation. 'See?' he added.

'See what?' asked Julia.

'I'm not struck dead, so it must be true.'

'Oh, don't be silly!' said Julia. 'He doesn't strike people dead, just like that. I've never seen anyone struck dead, have you, Em?'

'No, I haven't.'

Chick scowled. 'Well, I don't care what you've seen,' he said. 'I'm telling you the God's truth. Then my ma was out of work and met my pa and . . .' he shrugged.

'And made you,' completed Emily.

He shrugged again. 'I don't know.'

Julia said slowly, 'So that's the bone, is it, that you've got to pick with the Coulsdens? Something that you say happened before you were born, so you weren't even there and you don't know for sure.'

'I know because they told me,' he said stoutly.

'Well, I don't believe it,' said Julia. 'My father wouldn't do a thing like that.' But she spoke with more conviction than she felt. She had heard enough half-finished remarks within the Coulsden family over the years to persuade her that something unsavoury had happened. And certainly Agnes had replaced someone called Eunice, so she could believe part of the story. But had her father and Agnes really contrived Eunice's departure? Could it have been a conspiracy?

'My ma wouldn't do that,' maintained Emily.

Chick rolled his eyes and said, 'Huh! That's all you know. You don't know anything so you needn't put on airs – *and* you're scared of a few heifers!'

'We thought they were bulls,' said Emily. 'And we don't put on airs, do we, Ju?'

'I don't think so,' she answered thoughtfully. 'So, Chick, it was because your mother got the sack that she met your father – right?'

He nodded.

'Well, then,' she went on, 'you should be grateful to the Coulsdens, because if your mother hadn't got the sack she wouldn't have met your father and you wouldn't be here now.'

'So what?' he said, unsure how to react.

'Perhaps,' said Julia, 'it was God's way of making it up to your ma. *If* what you said about stealing the stuff was true. I mean, if

God knew she was innocent—'

'That's right,' broke in Emily, relieved. 'I bet that was how it happened.' She laughed suddenly. 'So you owe your life to the Coulsdens, Chick. You should be giving *us* a reward,' she said. 'Do you want to?'

'What, kiss you?'

'Yes.'

'No thanks!'

'Not even a little kiss?' Emily put her hands on her hips and tilted her head in what she imagined was a provocative angle.

'No, seriously,' said Julia. 'If Papa did do that, then it was awful of him and I'm sorry for Chick's mother.' She smiled at him. 'I expect Emily's sorry too, but you can't blame us. I was only a baby and Em wasn't even born!'

Emily smiled. 'I bet he does want to reward us – don't you, Chick?'

'*Emily*!' Julia protested. 'I'm being serious. I think we should apologise to Chick on behalf of our father and your mother. Then we could forget all about it and be friends.'

'All right then,' nodded Emily. 'Chick, d'you know your eyes don't match? Were they like that when you were born?'

Julia frowned. 'Em! That's making personal remarks,' she said. 'You should never make personal remarks. And anyway, I'm trying to sort out about Chick's mother.' She looked at him. 'If we make a formal apology, would that be all right? I mean, don't tell your parents – or maybe you could, but then they'd know you had told us.'

'I shan't tell them,' said Chick. 'But you can apologise if you want to.'

Julia laid down her bicycle and stood to attention with her right hand held palm forward, as if taking an oath.

'I, Julia Lady Coulsden, do solemnly and deeply apologise for the wrong done to members of your family by members of our family and I hereby beseech that the matter be erased from our memories. Amen.'

'It's not a prayer,' Emily objected, but Julia ignored her and turned to Chick. 'Will that do?' she asked.

'I suppose so.'

'And Emily must say it too.'

After much prompting, Emily was persuaded to repeat the impromptu 'apology'. When that was over she said, 'I wasn't being funny about your eyes, Chick. I was going to say that I like them. No, I mean it – they make you look interesting. *Most* boys look so ordinary.'

Overcome, Chick mumbled something as the colour re-appeared in his face, then suddenly Emily flung her arms round his neck and kissed him on the mouth. Thrown off-balance, he stumbled and by the time they had stopped laughing and the girls had picked up their bicycles, the unpleasant 'bone' was already a thing of the past and the present seemed rosier with each passing minute.

*

Mary Mack had put on a lot of weight. Her new employer was very fond of cakes and the two ladies would enjoy a large slice of cake with their mid-morning tea and another with their afternoon tea at four o'clock. Very often they would also indulge with their bed-time cocoa. It was a pleasant arrangement and Mrs Mack did not really mind the extra pounds. When her clothes no longer fitted her, she let out the seams or inserted a gusset, whichever was easiest, and told herself that she was not fat but 'comfortable'. Now as she squeezed her body between the table and the chair in the small tea-shop, she positively beamed at Julia.

'Fancy us meeting like this, after all this time,' she said. 'I was so surprised to receive your note. I showed it to Miss Fookes and she said, "Well, isn't that nice!" She really envied me. But what a day! I'm all of a lather, as they say. The perspiration was rolling off me before I was half-way down the hill. Thank goodness for a few trees and a bit of shade! I had to keep stopping for a rest – puffing and panting, I was, like nobody's business. Ah, that's better. They don't give you much room in these tea-shops, do they? They expect us all to be thin Lizzies but we're not. Oh dear!' She took out a handerchief and dabbed at her face. 'It must be eighty degrees at least,' she said. 'It was over ninety yesterday in our back garden; Miss Fookes showed me the thermometer. "Look at that, Mary," she said, "it's ninety-one!" And she was right!'

'It is hot,' Julia agreed. 'I'm sorry you had such a long walk. I didn't stop to think how far you had to come.'

The waitress stopped by their table, notebook in hand. 'What can I get you ladies?' she asked with a brief, professional smile.

'Oh,' said Julia, unfamiliar with the role of hostess. 'Er – a pot of tea – or should we have lemonade?'

Mrs Mack shook her head and her chins wobbled. 'Tea, dear. It's so refreshing. Miss Fookes always says that cold drinks make you hotter and it does seem that way.'

The waitress licked the pencil. 'Pot of tea for two – and any pastries?'

'That would be nice.'

'A selection?'

'Yes, please.'

When the waitress had gone, Mrs Mack began to fan herself with the menu. 'This is such a lovely idea,' she said. 'When I got your letter I said to Miss Fookes, "Why didn't we think of this before?" Meeting for a cup of tea and a pastry to catch up on all the news! And my word, you've grown so much, Julia – I hardly recognised you. "Is that her?" I said to myself. If only your mother could see you now, God rest her soul! She'd be that pleased. But how are things, dear? Are you happy? That's the main thing. As I said to Miss Fookes, "Is she happy?"'

'Yes, thank you,' said Julia. 'I am.'

'You are? Oh, thank goodness for that. Miss Fookes *will* be pleased. She takes such an interest in you because she's got no family of her own, poor soul. So you're happy. Good. Oh my! Just look at these pastries!'

The waitress placed the cake-stand in the middle of the small round table. 'We've no éclairs,' she said, 'so I've put on an apricot slice. Is that all right?'

Mrs Mack's face fell slightly, but Julia nodded.

'No éclairs!' whispered the old lady. 'How very odd!'

'Perhaps it's the heat,' said Julia. 'Maybe the fresh cream went sour in the heat.'

'Do you think so?'

'Maybe.'

When the teapot, sugar, milk and china were set out, the waitress returned to the kitchen and Julia looked across at Mrs Mack.

'Shall I pour out?' she asked nervously.

Mrs Mack nodded, and while Julia poured out the tea, she told her all about Miss Fookes's palpitations, her giddy spells and her swollen ankles. Julia thought that Miss Fookes needed a nurse rather than a companion by the sound of it.

'So, Julia, which cake would you like?' asked Mrs Mack, after taking a few sips of her tea.

'You must choose first,' said Julia, 'because you're my guest.'

Mrs Mack laughed. 'Your guest! Doesn't that sound grand? Well, then, I'll have that Eccles cake; they've always been a favourite of mine. To think that we're sitting here sharing tea and cakes – and all those years ago I used to push you out in your pram. Everyone used to stop me, you know. "Oh, the Coulsden child!" they'd say. "Isn't she like her grandmother? A real Gooding girl!" Of course I was as proud as Punch. I used to love it. Your poor mother – she was never really well again, never really well in her mind after you were born. Not that it was your fault, I don't mean that, but it happens sometimes. She was depressed and she couldn't seem to fight it, poor soul. Oh, I did love that woman, Julia; your mother was a real gem. So straight, so honest. I was proud to work for her. And if I looked a bit under the weather some days, she'd say, "Go and put your feet up, Mrs Mack." She was so considerate towards other people and she was lovely to work for. Mm, this Eccles cake is delicious, Julia. But I'm doing all the talking. You tell me all about yourself while I finish my cake, else I'll be spitting crumbs everywhere and that would never do!'

She took another bite and stared expectantly at Julia, who was feeling rather guilty because she had an ulterior motive for inviting Mrs Mack to the tea-shop.

'I am quite well,' she began, 'and I'm getting on quite well at school.'

Mrs Mack, her mouth full, nodded approval.

'I get on very well with Emily,' Julia continued. 'It's not so lonely with a sister.'

'Of course not, dear.' Mrs Mack wiped crumbs from her mouth with a handkerchief and emptied her tea-cup.

'Have another pastry,' said Julia as she refilled the empty cup.

'Thank you, dear. Miss Fookes always says the first cup just lubricates the throat. The second one always tastes better because you've quenched your thirst with the first cup. Mm, I think I'll have the apricot slice. They do very nice pastries here, I must say, and very light pastry – although why they have no éclairs I don't know. Funny, that! Still, this looks nice. Julia! You haven't eaten your first one yet. I'm leaving you behind.'

'I'm not very hungry,' Julia invented. 'I don't usually eat much in the morning.'

'Well, go on, dear, about Emily and everyone. I'm all ears. I said to Miss Fookes that I would have all the news to tell her when I came back. No family at all, poor soul and . . .' she lowered her voice, 'never been married.'

Julia nodded. 'And my father is well,' she said, 'and Agnes – I think she tries her best.'

Mrs Mack nodded. 'This is made with real apricots, you know, not just apricot jam. She tries her best, does she? I should hope so. But as long as you're happy, Julia! You certainly do look well and when you came in just now, so tall and grown-up, I could hardly believe my eyes. Thirteen years ago you were just a baby in arms. Where has the time gone to, eh? It rushes past and here we all are, thirteen years older and all in the twinkling of an eye.'

Julia talked generally for a while, but then took a deep breath. 'Mrs Mack, may I ask you something?' she said. 'It's about Eunice and those things I found in the garden shed. Do you remember? That time I came back because Mama Sarah was ill and—'

'I remember, Julia,' said Mrs Mack. 'I remember distinctly, but I wasn't going to say anything. I thought it's all over and done with, so why rake it up again? Fancy you remembering after all this time!'

'I met Charlie Bird one day last week,' said Julia carefully. 'That's Eunice's son – and he told me that his mother was sacked because Agnes and my father told lies about her. Do you know what really happened?'

The excitement faded from Mrs Mack's face as she regarded Julia anxiously, but as she hesitated Julia said, 'You don't have to tell me, but I should be grateful if you would and I think I'm old enough to be told. I'm not a child any more.'

It had long been a source of regret to Mrs Mack that the knowledge she had could not be shared with anyone else. She had often thought she would write a letter to Julia – telling the story as she saw it – and ask a solicitor or equally responsible person to deliver it to Julia in the event of her death. In that way she would avoid being blamed if there was any trouble as a result of the disclosures. Or maybe she could write a letter to Eunice. She had never quite made up her mind, but now that Julia was asking outright and demanding to know the truth, she was very willing to shed the responsibility. She finished the apricot slice and took a sip of tea.

'I will tell you, dear,' she said, flicking a few stray crumbs from the cloth, 'but what you do with the information is up to you. I don't want to cause a rumpus after all this time, but poor Eunice got the dirty end of the stick and someone should know what really happened. I'm past sixty now and I shan't live for ever. Miss Fookes says we all go when our number's called.'

'I suppose so.'

'Well, then, it was like this. Putting two and two together, I think there was something going on between your father and Agnes Dengate and then, after you were born, they must have decided that Agnes should work for your parents, because suddenly all these pieces of silver began to disappear and I had to say something, you see. What else could I do? Someone might have suspected me. So your mother said she'd talk to Mr Coulsden – and Eunice, of course – and I think if Eunice really had taken them, your mother would have forgiven her so long as she gave everything back. But of course Eunice hadn't got the things, only no one knew it then and so she had to go. Your mother was that upset. Anyway, to cut a long story short, before you could say "knife", Mr Coulsden tells her he's found someone to take Eunice's place and no one knows what's been going on. I thought the hanky-panky started *after* she moved in, but later I thought differently. You see, when you found those things there was only one way they could have got there.'

'You mean my *father* put them there?' Julia was shocked.

'Well, who else? It certainly wasn't me, and if it had been Eunice she could have given them back and stayed on.'

'I see,' said Julia slowly. 'How awful for poor Eunice!'

'Well, of course it was. It was terrible . . . and us not realising. Then suddenly Agnes is pregnant and off *she* goes, but we still didn't know it was Mr Coulsden's child. They played it all very close and no one knew anything.'

Julia frowned. 'But then how did my mother find out about Emily? Who told her?'

'An anonymous letter!'

'Good heavens!'

'My dear, you may well say "Good heavens",' said Mrs Mack, shaking her head with disapproval over the whole sorry tale. 'I think it was Eunice who sent it, though if it was she must have felt terrible – your mother killing herself like that.'

'So, if Eunice hadn't sent the letter my mother might never have known.'

'Who knows, dear? She might have found out some day. Truth

will out, that's what they say. Is there another cup in the pot? There's hot water in that jug to top it up; let me do it. Poor Eunice! I think it must have been her who sent the note, although perhaps I'm slandering the poor girl, but she was living at Winchelsea Beach so she had plenty of time and opportunity to find out what was happening. I don't know who else would have bothered.'

Julia sighed deeply and was silent for a moment, considering all the facts. 'Does my father know that *you* know – about the silver, I mean?'

'Yes, he does. I tackled him, showed him the silver to let him know. He only said, "Least said, soonest mended" or words to that effect. It was a long time after, you see – ten years, or maybe less? Yes, he knows that I'm aware of the truth, but I've kept quiet all these years, afraid of stirring up more trouble. It can't be undone and I thought it best forgotten. It was Eunice's son who told you, you say?'

Julia nodded.

'And what will you do now, dear? Now that you know?'

'I don't really know,' said Julia with a sigh. 'I suppose it's best left alone except for poor Eunice. Chick says she still talks about it, and for her sake, I suppose something should be done.'

Mrs Mack looked worried and said, 'But then it's going to throw dirt at your father and at her for sending the letter – and they're not going to be very pleased. Do think it over carefully, Julia, before you do anything rash. I should hate to spark off some new tragedy – folks are so funny, you can't tell what they'll do. Who would have thought your poor mother would kill herself? Terrible! Really terrible!'

'And poor Eunice, if it was her.'

'Or silly girl! She certainly didn't mean that to happen. I expect she just wanted to cause trouble for your father and Agnes and you can't blame her, everyone being led to believe she was a thief. But she'll have that letter on her conscience, I suppose, to the end of her days.'

'Oh, Mrs Mack! Why is life so dreadfully difficult?' cried Julia.

'Ssh! Someone will hear you.'

They had been holding their discussion in low voices, but Julia's outburst caused several heads to turn in their direction.

'What shall I *do*?' whispered Julia, seeing Mrs Mack glancing towards the clock on the wall. 'I ought to tell Eunice. I ought to make it up to her.'

Alarm showed in Mrs Mack's eyes and she began to hunt for a lost white glove.

'If you want my advice, dear, you'll do nothing,' she advised. 'Where is that glove? Oh there it is, on the floor. Can you get it for me, dear? I can't bend like I used to. Ah, thank you. Yes, Julia, do nothing at all. That's best, I'm sure. Well now, that was very pleasant. After all these years we've had a nice little get-together. We must do it again one day.' Pulling on her gloves, she began to squeeze herself out from under the table. 'I promised Miss Fookes I wouldn't be too long. so I really must go.'

Julia stood up to help steady her until she was once more upright, if a little out of breath.

'Thank you for coming, Mrs Mack,' she said. 'And for telling me. And give my best wishes to Miss Fookes.'

'I will, dear, and thank you for the tea and cakes. Most welcome – and now I've so much to tell Miss Fookes!'

She leaned forward and hugged Julia and then, with another glance at the clock, hurried out of the tea-shop. When she had gone, Julia sat down and caught the waitress's eye for the bill.

Perhaps Mrs Mack *was* right, she thought. Perhaps she *should* do nothing? Perhaps in the long run it would be wiser not to interfere. It was not a pleasant story and she could understand why Eunice still harboured a grudge, but if the whole matter was raised again then the fact that Eunice had sent the fateful letter would also come to light. And Chick was their friend and she and Emily were innocent of any malice. By the time she had paid the bill, Julia had made up her mind to do nothing – except to tell Emily, who was already involved and had a right to know the whole truth.

Later the two girls talked things over well into the night and Emily finally agreed with Julia. George and Agnes had committed the wrong and it was up to them to make amends. Hopefully at some time in the future they might do that, although Julia thought it most unlikely. Emily, however, was optimistic. They also agreed to say nothing to Chick, whom Julia thought was too young to be worried by such secrets. As she settled down to sleep, she reflected ruefully on the old adage that 'ignorance is bliss' and was fully prepared to believe it.

CHAPTER FOURTEEN

28 April 1925

Our Easter picnic was cancelled because Emily had terrible tooth-ache and had to go to the dentist. Will go tomorrow if weather stays warm. Ben came round again and E. says she is in love with him but he teases me all the time and she is so jealous. How can she be in love? She's too young. Only three more days and my beloved Leo goes back to college. How can I bear it? If ONLY he would just NOTICE me. Aunt Cicely says she thinks he has a young lady friend at the college but I don't believe it. I *won't* believe it. When he looks at me with those brown eyes I could die. *Leo. Leo. Notice me!* He is so like Uncle Jack, it's uncanny, but so much cleverer, of course. Uncle J. will *never* forgive him for not going into the boatyard. Only I defend him. B. and E. make fun of him, but he is above it all. I am nearly fifteen. But he is twenty!

One more term and I shall leave school. What shall I do? I don't know at all.

Silver Lady is at the yard waiting to be re-keeled and Papa is bad-tempered because Uncle J. won't give us priority.

Oh yes, Winifred's baby is *another* girl. It was born two days ago. That makes five girls: first Sukey, then the twins and little Rose about eighteen months ago. Poor old Ernest. Uncle Stan says he is very gloomy and I know they were all hoping for a boy this time. I shall go to see the baby after my BELOVED LEO goes back. Please God let the sun shine tomorrow . . .

*

Julia's prayer was answered and the next morning she, Emily, Ben and Leo met at the Monkbretton bridge and made their way together to the tram station, a simple building constructed of wood and corrugated iron. They greeted the other passengers who were already in the carriage – a group of fishermen and a family of early holiday-makers. Going to Camber on the tram was all part of the day's fun and they soon settled themselves on the wooden seats with their picnic baskets between them on the floor. The other carriage was first class and used almost solely by golfers.

'Still on 'bliday then, are you?' one of the fishermen asked Leo slyly. It was well-known in the town that Jack Coulsden's son was 'brainy' and had got a scholarship and was going to 'one of them colleges' in spite of his father's ranting.

Leo smiled easily. 'A few more days,' he said, 'then it's back to the grindstone.'

'Oh, they do make you work, then?' He regarded Leo humorously through faded blue eyes and rubbed a hand over his chin which was white with two days' stubble. 'A grindstone, is it?'

'Afraid so.'

Leo's voice already held the beginnings of an accent which lightly overlaid his broad Sussex speech. His manner was more relaxed and less defensive than it had been, and the old man's jibes aroused in him only good-natured amusement. All the fishermen were known to him, some well-known, for many of the boats on which they crewed had at one time or another been wedged up on Coulsdens' slipway for repairs even if they had not actually been built there. It was Ben who squirmed a little in his seat, knowing that his brother's 'defection' had called forth plenty of criticism and that only Cicely had been untouched by them. 'Envy,' she had declared, 'pure envy,' and she had continued to encourage Leo in all his aspirations. Jack's disapproval did nothing to deter her, in fact it only strengthened her resolve. Her enthusiasm for her son's career was partly for his benefit and partly for her own, since she considered her personal position in both family and community was considerably elevated by Leo's prospects. And, of course, it pleased her secretly to see the boy stand up to his father and win the day.

The old fisherman turned his attentions towards Ben. 'And what's it like to have a brainy brother?' he asked.

Emily, seeing Ben hesitate, answered for him. 'He's pleased as Punch,' she said sharply. 'We all are. Any more questions?' And she stared at him defiantly, her blue eyes wide under the straw boater with its bright red ribbon.

Julia gave her a glance of grudging admiration and vowed silently that if Leo were under attack she would spring to *his* defence. She looked at Leo and, as usual, her heart seemed to melt within her. He was a Coulsden, no doubt about that, with

dark strong features and broad shoulders over a stocky frame.
Ben had inherited Cicely's colouring, with pale freckled skin and
hair with a natural wave which he was always trying to eradicate.
His pale hazel eyes gave him a deceptively delicate look and his
body was longer and thinner than Leo's.

'Pleased as Punch, is he?' the old man persisted, ignoring
Emily's curt tone.

'Noses to the grindstone,' said Leo cheerfully. 'Shoulders to
the wheel. Backs to the wall and all that!'

Julia smothered a giggle and Emily nudged her with her
elbow.

'Oh, aye,' said the old man doubtfully and he looked at Ben,
who grinned.

'Take no notice of Leo,' Ben advised. 'All that studying's gone
to his head. Many a good man's been ruined by a bit of book-
learning!'

There were seven fishermen in the carriage – crew of two of the
boats moored at Rye Harbour who travelled each day with season
tickets. Holiday-makers paid 5d. for a day return to Camber, and
for their money would be shaken and jostled in the most delightful way along the two miles of narrow-gauge track there and back,
at a speed of ten miles per hour. The blue and yellow steam
engine would pull two carriages and two open waggons and the
latter would be brought back to Rye full of sand. However, Julia,
Emily, Leo and Ben had bought single tickets, as they intended to
return via the ferry at Rye Harbour.

One of the other fishermen now grinned at Leo. 'Going to be a
schoolteacher, I hear?'

'That's about it,' said Leo, with a wink at Julia which set her
heart beating with joy.

'Be schoolteaching at Rye then, will you?'

'I don't know yet. It's possible.'

Julia smiled sweetly at the fisherman. 'He might be teaching
your grandchildren,' she told him.

'That so?' He laughed wheezily. 'By God, I don't reckon much
on his chances. Right little buggers they are, my lot! Up to
everything. You'll have your work cut out to teach my grand-
children writing and arithmetic, but you ask 'em about fishing and
they've got it all up here.' He tapped his head. 'They'd come top
of the class for fishing!' He slapped his leg in delight and appealed
to the others to see the joke. 'Top marks for mending a net, eh!

Top of the school for gutting a herring! Ten out of ten for shooting a trawl!'

They all laughed and Julia was watching Leo in the hope that he would wink at her again, but at that moment the engine whistled and with a shuddering jolt the train was off on its first run of the day.

Julia turned her attention briefly to the other holiday-makers who were sitting together watching the scenery go by. The parents were carrying bags and a folded tartan travelling rug; the children – two young girls – were each armed with a brightly painted tin bucket and a wooden spade. The mother caught Julia's eye and smiled shyly.

'It's a lovely day,' she said. 'So warm. Fancy picnicking in April! We had no idea we'd be so lucky with the weather. Just like summer it was yesterday.'

One of the fishermen, a younger man, shook his head. 'It'll maybe not last the day,' he warned. 'See that?' He jerked a thumb skywards and everyone stared out of the little square windows.

'Mackerel sky,' he told them. 'You know what they say?' The two little girls shook their heads dutifully. ' "Mackerel sky, un-natural sky, not long wet and not long dry." See? Maybe a bit of rain, not much, then a bit of sun . . . ah, here's where some of us get off.'

The tram slowed down at the golf course to allow the golfers to alight and then it continued and stopped again almost directly opposite Rye Harbour.

'There, see that?' cried the young fisherman. 'There's our boat – over there. *Maid Marion*, that's her name, though you can't see it from here.'

'But it's the other side of the river,' one of the girls protested.

'You're right, it is, and we have to get the ferryman out of his hut to row us over.'

The young girl sighed. 'I wish I was a fisherman,' she said. 'Can girls be fishermen?'

' 'Fraid not, miss,' he told her firmly. 'Bad luck, see, a woman on a boat. Same as whistling. Whistle up a storm, that's what they say. And don't you never bring a rabbit on board – nor say the word "pig".'

'Pig?' repeated the girl, giggling.

His six companions were already jumping down on to the platform as he stood up. 'Oh, dear me, yes,' he told her. 'Very unlucky that word: pig. Our old skipper, he hates that word.

You'd be surprised. Well, have a nice time, girls. Have a paddle for me, will you, and make me a sand castle?'

The two girls nodded again, wide-eyed and giggling, but their father said 'Say "good-bye" then.'

'Good-bye,' they chorused as with a nod the fisherman clattered down on to the platform and hurried to join the others.

It was only a matter of minutes before the tram stopped for the last time at the terminus, a grand name for such a simple place. The platform was made of old sleepers and there were no buildings of any kind, but not too far away Thomson's Café promised food and shelter. Here the rest of the passengers alighted and the two little girls ran on ahead, dancing delightedly across the fine gold sand.

Julia and the others hung back to let the strangers move away. There were already a few people on the beach – a man walking his poodle and a group of children flying kites.

'D'you think it really *will* rain?' asked Julia.

'Probably,' said Ben, 'but it won't be much even if it does and it might not happen until the evening.'

After much good-natured argument, they finally found a suitable spot and thankfully dumped their baskets and rugs in a sheltered hollow before starting to shed some of their outer clothing. It was still early and there was very little power in the April sunshine – certainly it was not hot enough to brave the water and swim, but they had brought a tennis ball and they played cricket for the first hour or so with a piece of driftwood for a bat. When they were tired of that, they strolled together along the water's edge, searching among the debris brought in on the previous tide.

The poodle, now freed from his lead, ran up to them and they made a fuss of him. 'I shall have a dog when I'm married,' said Emily. 'Will you, Ben?' She spoke as casually as she could.

'It depends,' answered Ben, equally casually. 'Would you like a dog, Julia? When you're married, I mean?'

'I don't know,' said Julia. 'I've never had a dog, but I suppose they might be good fun.' She turned quickly from Ben's intense look to Leo. 'Do you like dogs, Leo? Shall you want one when you're married?'

'No, I won't,' he replied. 'They're such a tie and I want to travel a bit if I can—'

'But children are a tie anyway,' said Emily earnestly. 'So if you have children, you might as well have a dog. I'd like to have both. What about you, Ben?'

Emily, mortified, was hoping against hope that Ben would not defer to Julia again and consoled herself with the thought that Julia had not encouraged him – she had asked Leo instead. She wondered if that meant that Julia was in love with Leo? Surely he was much too old for her . . . and far too good for her with all his brains and such a sparkling future. Granted Julia was pretty in a pale sort of way, and her hair was an unusual colour, but was she the girl for Leo? She certainly wasn't the girl for Ben; Ben liked a girl with . . . there a sigh escaped her. What sort of girl *did* Ben like – and was she, Emily, anything like that girl? If only the foursome could split up into two pairs, she thought wistfully. Then she could find herself with Ben, while Leo could make do with Julia. Or perhaps – here Emily's imagination ran away with her good sense – she could get into difficulties in the sea and Ben would swim out and rescue her and then realise how much she meant to him. His eyes would be opened and he would murmur her name and that would be the beginning of his love for her . . . This was a wonderful picture, but unfortunately they were all good swimmers and anyway the water would be freezing – and the tide was well out and that would mean wading out for hundreds of yards before she was out of her depth.

Julia meanwhile threw a stick for the poodle and the dog scampered after it, barking shrilly and splashing through the water's edge. Having retrieved the stick however, it returned at once to its master, carrying the trophy proudly in its mouth. Everyone laughed as the dog shook itself and its owner hurriedly stepped backwards.

'Of all the ungrateful beasts,' laughed Julia. 'I threw the stick and he's taken it back to his master! I think I'll have a cat instead.'

'Cats are cuddly,' said Emily as they strolled on. 'If I come back to earth in another form, I shall be a cat.'

'A one-eared alley cat?' asked Ben, ducking as she lunged towards him.

'*Not* a one-eared alley cat,' she told him firmly. 'A beautiful Persian tabby or perhaps something rarer – a Siamese maybe – and I'll belong to a rich widow who dotes on me and I shall live in luxury because she'll buy me the best of everything and love me more than anything else in the world and when she dies she'll leave me all her money!'

'How boring!' said Julia. 'I'd be a wild cat living in the depths of Scotland or somewhere and I'd live off the land. I wouldn't go short of food because there would always be plenty of rabbits and birds and mice. *I* wouldn't need a doting owner.'

'You'd get no love then,' said Leo.

Julia shrugged. 'If I was a wild cat I wouldn't know anything about love, so I wouldn't miss it, would I? It wouldn't matter.'

Ben picked up a pebble and skimmed it into the water. 'Well, someone's got to be the one-eared alley cat,' he said. 'We can't have the country full of empty alleys.'

'It'll have to be you, then,' said Julia. 'Then one dark night you can lie in wait for the beautiful Persian tabby and because it will be so unworldly you'll be able to take advantage of it and then it will have lots of one-eared kittens . . .'

Leo grinned at Emily. 'And the rich widow will turn you all out into the snow, while someone plays a tune on a violin . . .'

'And she'll leave her money to a nephew in Australia!' Julia concluded. 'What a sad story! Poor Emily – are you sure you want to be a cat?'

'Maybe I'd think it was worth it,' she answered. 'Maybe it wouldn't seem so bad. I might enjoy living with an alley cat; it would all depend on who it was.' She turned to Ben. 'I think you'd make a rather nice alley cat – let's see how you look without one ear.'

She tried to cover his left ear with her hand, but he ducked again. 'I think I'd rather be in Scotland,' he said, 'with all those rabbits.'

Julia pretended not to notice the implied compliment and said, 'Well, it's up to you then, Leo. Do you fancy leaping on to a beautiful Persian tabby?'

'It might be fun,' he said, 'if Emily doesn't mind.'

'Oh, I don't mind,' she told him, hiding her disappointment. 'But you ought to be a brainy sort of cat. Maybe a valuable circus cat that does tricks?'

'Circuses don't have cats,' Ben objected. 'Performing dogs, yes, but not cats.'

Emily clapped her hands in sudden delight. 'But of course they do! They have *big* cats,' she cried. 'Tigers and *lions*. Leo would have to be a big cat. Isn't that what your name means? We could all come and watch you doing your tricks.'

'I wouldn't go,' exclaimed Julia. 'I hate to see them doing those awful things – jumping through hoops. They look so angry all the time, as though they hate to have to do it but they're scared of the whip. Leo mustn't be one of those, I won't allow it.'

'Oh really, Julia,' Emily pouted. 'You're not his keeper. If Leo wants to be in a circus—'

'He didn't say he did,' broke in Ben. 'It was you who suggested it and it was—'

Emily rounded on him. 'That's right! Side with Julia. Julia can't say anything wrong, can she?'

'I only said—' Ben protested.

'I don't care *what* you said,' cried Emily. 'It's why you said it. There are times when I hate you, Ben Coulsden!'

'I'm sorry,' he shrugged. 'I only meant—'

'I *know* what you meant,' cried Emily.

'Look, let's forget it,' interposed Julia. 'It was only a bit of fun about cats.'

But Emily had now committed herself and felt there could be no drawing back. She was angry with herself for giving way to her emotions and allowing the other three to see the extent of her feelings for Ben and, unable to cope with the situation, she now took refuge in a childish sulk. Turning abruptly, she marched off in the opposite direction, her head high, her back rigid with imagined rejection.

'Oh Lord!' said Julia. 'Now see what you've done. Go after her, Ben, there's a dear, and talk her round. It's not a very good start to the day otherwise.'

Ben hesitated. 'She takes offence too easily and I was only teasing.'

'She's only thirteen,' Julia reminded him, aware that she would be fifteen in July and thus considering herself much older than her half-sister.

'I think she's taken a fancy to you, Ben,' said Leo wickedly. 'Can't think what she sees in you, of course, but you should be grateful.'

Ben's fists clenched by his sides and Julia groaned aloud. 'Don't you two start,' she grumbled. 'If everyone's going to bicker, we might as well go home again. Do fetch her back, Ben.'

'Why can't Leo go after her?'

Ben was acutely aware that, if he went after Emily, Julia would be left with Leo, whereas if *Leo* went after Emily, *he* would be granted a few brief moments alone with her.

'Because you're the one who's upset her,' said Julia patiently. 'you know what she's like. Please go after her, Ben – just to please me?'

This put Ben in a terrible quandary and Leo saw his expression change from a willingness to please her, through realisation that he would be leaving her with Leo and dismay at his dilemma.

'Oh, damn Emily!' cried Ben and with an anguished last look at Julia, he set off at a loping run along the beach, leaving a trail of oozing footprints in the wet sand.

As soon as she had achieved her purpose, Julia felt ashamed and could not meet Leo's eyes. She was so certain he would have seen through her strategy.

'Poor old Ben!' said Leo. 'You put him on the spot and he couldn't win.'

Julia felt herself blush. 'It's all so silly,' she said. 'Why does Emily have to take it all so personally?'

'As you say, she's only thirteen.'

Julia nodded. They watched Ben and heard him call out to Emily who, on hearing him, began to run in the opposite direction.

Now that Julia had Leo all to herself, she had no idea how to proceed. How do you seduce someone you love, she wondered, vague even about the meaning of the word. What do you say or do? If she said something, would he laugh? *Had* he found himself a young lady as Aunt Cicely suspected?

'I suppose you find us all a bit dull,' she hazarded, 'after all your clever college friends?'

'No. You're never dull.'

What sort of answer was that, thought Julia. Did he mean her specifically or was he speaking of them collectively? She chanced a look at him, hoping to gain some insight from his expression but he had his hand up, shading his eyes from the sun as he watched Ben and Emily now dwindled by distance.

Leo looked down at her. 'I think she's carrying a torch for Ben. Poor little Emily!'

'Why poor?'

'*He's* carrying a torch for you, isn't he?'

All Julia could think of to say was, 'Oh dear.'

Leo put his head on one side and regarded her with amusement. 'Oh dear? Is that all you can say? Julia, you disappoint me. You can surely do better than just "Oh dear"!'

Julia's heart was hammering as she struggled to find the right words for what she wanted to say. She so wished to sound witty or clever or subtle.

'Oh dear,' he repeated in a gentle mocking voice. 'Julia Lady Coulsden is lost for words. That's a novelty!'

'I'm not lost for words,' she protested. 'At least, not exactly.'

Further along the beach she could see Emily and Ben talking together – probably arguing, she thought. Why was it all so difficult? Why couldn't people love the people who loved them? Surely it ought to be possible?

'Suppose I'm carrying a torch for someone else,' she said. 'Would that surprise you?'

She was pleased with the phrasing, which sounded intriguing and somehow challenging. Excitement roared through her body at the thought that she was flirting! Flirting with her beloved Leo.

'No, it wouldn't surprise me,' he answered. 'Is it anyone I know?'

The direct question terrified her and the excitement threatened to overwhelm her. 'Ah, that would be telling!'

'Julia! We don't have secrets from each other, do we?'

'Of course we do!' She thought that sounded rather sophisticated and allowed herself a quick glance at his face to see if he was looking impressed. 'And what about you? Who are you carrying a torch for?' she asked, as lightly as she could manage. 'There's sure to be someone.'

Leo sighed and scuffed the sand with bare toes. 'Let's just say my torch was blown out by a heartless female who shall be nameless. Luckily, we don't die of broken hearts even if we would like to.'

Julia stared at him in amazement. 'Leo!' she gasped. 'You don't mean someone turned you down? There *was* someone then – Aunt Cissie was right. Oh, how awful for you! I just don't believe it – how someone could – not *you*, Leo. She must have been mad, quite mad to turn you down. That's all I can say. Quite crazy!'

He shrugged. 'She seemed sane enough, but it doesn't matter now. Plenty more pebbles on the beach, as they say.'

Julia was appalled by the revelation and amazed to learn that a woman existed who did not find Leo utterly adorable, but she was also secretly relieved that the woman concerned *had* rejected him.

'Poor Leo,' she said. 'I'm so sorry, it must have been dreadful. Was it a girl at the college? Did you go out with her or wouldn't she? Do you mind me asking? Do you feel like talking about it? It's supposed to help to tell someone.' She looked frantically towards Ben and Emily and saw with dismay that they were beginning to move back towards them. 'You can talk to me, Leo. I'd never repeat a word, I swear it!'

Leo shrugged. 'Nothing much to tell, really. We went out together a few times, to the cinema and to a restaurant.' He hesitated. 'She wasn't a student, so we had to be careful.'

'Wasn't a student? What *do* you mean? Who was she?'

There was a long silence as he debated whether or not to tell her. Ben shouted something, but he was too far away for them to understand what he said. A few more minutes, thought Julia, then they would be back and this wonderful unexpected closeness with Leo would end.

'Please tell me,' she urged. 'Honestly, Leo, I swear to God I'll never tell a living soul.'

'It was the wife of one of the tutors.'

'Leo!' For a moment shock robbed her of further speech. A married woman! Leo had been in love with a married woman!

'She's married to a pig of a man,' Leo told her, 'who treats her like dirt. It's embarrassing to be in their company when he's in one of his moods and she's such a lovely woman—'

Julia did not want to hear that. 'How old is she?' she asked quickly.

'Thirty-one. An intelligent, attractive, affectionate . . .'

Julia swallowed hard, her mouth suddenly dry as she tried unsuccessfully to visualise her beloved Leo with an intelligent, attractive, affectionate . . . *How* affectionate, she wondered, weak with jealousy.

'Did you—' she stammered, then hastily abandoned the question that was uppermost in her mind. *Her* beloved Leo had had an affair with a married woman of thirty-one! It was quite unbelievable.

'Did you love her very much?' she substituted.

Leo nodded and shrugged again. 'Very much – and I thought she loved me, but if she did, it obviously wasn't enough. Not enough to leave him, anyway. However, it's all over now; it ended just before Christmas and we don't see each other any more.'

'Does Uncle Jack know or Aunt Cissie?'

'Of course not.'

Ben and Emily were now only a few hundred yards away and Ben waved his hand. 'The wanderer returns!' he shouted.

Leo raised a hand in acknowledgement. 'So there you have it,' he said quietly to Julia.

'What was her name?'

'Florence.'

'And it really is all over?' He nodded.

'Poor Leo,' she whispered, then blurted out, 'I love you, Leo, if that's any help.'

He gave her a quick smile, but there was no time for him to reply. She imagined she saw surprise, gratitude, sorrow, hope and perhaps even affection in the smile. Not the affection of a cousin but the affection of a lonely man for a sympathetic and warm-hearted woman. She cursed the untimely return of Ben and Emily which had interrupted the enthralling exchange of confidences, but at least she had told Leo that she loved him, although now she half regretted doing so. Perhaps she had been too hasty, but it was too late now. He must think highly of her to trust her with such a secret – he had been honest with her and she had been honest in return.

Emily smiled brightly at everyone and said, 'I'm thirsty. What about some lemonade?'

Ben was giving Leo a keen look but Julia, feeling years older than when he had left them, was able to meet his eyes without betraying the turmoil within her.

'Or champagne,' said Leo.

Emily squealed. 'Oh Leo, you *haven't* got champagne!'

'No, not really.'

'Oh, you *beast*!' she laughed. 'I thought, just for a minute, that you meant it. Or we could have an ice cream at Thomson's. I suppose our funds would run to that?'

Leo put a hand in his trouser pocket and jingled the loose coins. 'My treat,' he said. 'To celebrate!'

'Celebrate what?' Ben asked suspiciously.

'Anything you can think of,' responded Leo airily. 'The weather, Easter, the mystery of life . . .'

'If it's your treat,' said Emily, 'I shall have a *double* strawberry!'

'I'll have chocolate,' decided Julia.

Emily turned to Ben. 'What will you have, Ben? Strawberry?

It was such a simple question, yet they all knew immediately and instinctively that the success of the rest of the day depended on Ben's answer. Once again Emily had challenged him, and if he chose the same as Julia, she would sulk again.

Ben looked at Julia with such a depth of meaning in his brown eyes that she felt a great warmth for this younger brother of Leo. 'I've changed my mind,' she told him. 'I think I'll have strawberry too.'

The danger past, Ben smiled at her in unspoken gratitude and Leo, grinning, pulled out a handful of money.

'Yes, I think it will stretch to four double ices,' he told them. 'Come on, then. Race you all!'

They began to run, feet flying over the warm sand. As they went, Ben held out his hands to Emily and Julia and the three of them ran together until Julia held out her free hand and Leo took it. They arrived hot and breathless at the café where the worn wooden steps were delightfully warm to their bare feet.

*

Frank Bligh watched them as they all stood on the opposite bank of the river, his eyes narrowed in an effort to distinguish their features. Their voices, laughing and excited, carried across the intervening waters and he recognised that of Ben Coulsden. So the second boy, he presumed, was Leo Coulsden and more than likely the girls were Julia and Emily. Nice for some people, he thought, without a trace of envy. Then he heard the 'gong' which summoned the ferry, a suspended metal tube struck with a metal rod.

'Keep banging!' he grinned to himself. 'I shan't hurry.'

Lowering himself into the boat, he released the rope and took up the oars. The tide was high and he had to row strongly against the current, leaning well into the oars to keep the boat on course.

'Ahoy there!' shouted one of the girls.

He thought he recognised Julia's voice but could not be sure. A funny family, the Coulsdens. George, Jack and Stan had all gone to school with Luke Bligh, who had called them 'tearaways' with a hint of admiration in his voice which had not gone unnoticed by the young Frank.

'Oh, it's Frank Bligh!' cried Emily. 'Hullo, Frank.'

He made no answer, enjoying as he always did the motion of his own body in relation to the boat's movement: the pull on the oars, the dip of the blades in the brown water. The rhythm hypnotised him, making thought difficult. He could see them more clearly now -- Julia and Emily in their pastel dresses, their short hair wind-blown and tousled; the two boys beside them showing off, trying to skim flat pebbles across the swirling surface of the river and vying with each other for the girls' attention. Frank allowed himself a glance over his shoulder as he neared the river bank and the tug of the current grew less.

'It's us!' cried Emily.

'Oh, aye.' He tied the rope loosely through the mooring ring and said shortly, 'Get in, then.'

'Ladies first,' said Ben gallantly.

'Who'd be a mere man?' asked Leo and Julia laughed.

Frank caught the adoring look in her eyes and thought, 'She's sweet on him;' he was surprised to find how much he minded. Emily was already scrambling clumsily into the boat, which rocked alarmingly and made her scream.

Leo said, 'Oh God, he's going to drown us!' and Julia laughed again as though he had said something very witty. Frank was beginning to dislike the older Coulsden boy.

Clasping her hands together, Emily stared up at Frank. 'Oh you're not, are you, Frank?'

'Don't tempt me,' he said and Julia smiled at him. At *him*! Frank's heart gave a leap and as he held out his hands to help her into the boat he allowed a brief smile to soften his stern expression.

'Thank you, Frank,' she said quietly, waiting for him to let go of her hands so that she could take her place beside Emily. The latter, seeing the look of admiration in Frank's eyes, said crossly, 'Well, hurry up then, Ju.'

Julia's skin glowed warmly, her body was drowsy with fresh air and exercise and her love for Leo was making her beautiful. Frank knew only that she gave off a kind of radiance which touched his soul and played havoc with his body.

Hastily he released her hands and sat down, drawing in the rope as he did so.

'Hi!' called Leo. 'What about us?'

'Two's enough,' Frank said abruptly and seizing the oars he bent his head and began to row.

Emily giggled. 'He's kidnapping us!' she cried. 'Help!'

'Come back here!' Leo protested. 'You've got plenty of room for all of us!'

'Help! We're being kidnapped!' screamed Emily, delighted.

Julia, amused, caught Frank's eye. 'Are we?' she asked.

'Would you mind?' His voice was low and she shrugged, aware of something unspoken in his eyes.

'Maybe,' she said. 'Maybe not.'

Emily was shouting to Ben, urging him to swim after the boat and rescue her. Leo was cursing and Ben was laughing.

'There's plenty of room for them,' said Julia. 'Why didn't you bring them?'

'Maybe I wanted you to myself,' he said with a challenging look.

'I see.' She leaned forward and whispered, 'Suppose I said I don't mind being kidnapped. What then, Frank Bligh?'

She saw his expression change and the brown eyes darken as he struggled for a flippant answer and could not think of one.

By this time the boat was nearly in mid-stream and the two boys, left behind on the bank, had dwindled into the distance. Emily turned her attention to Frank and Julia and was at once jealous of the spark that glowed so obviously between them.

'Oh Ju, don't encourage him,' she cried. 'He's kidnapping us, remember? We might never be seen again. He's got a wicked look in his eye – you have, haven't you, Frank?'

He gave her a brief smile and resumed his rowing. Both girls watched him silently – broad shoulders moving steadily, muscles tensing in strong arms, bent head topped with untidy dark curls. They saw his hands moving the oars with deceptive ease and noted the slight gasp as he sucked in each new breath.

Aware of their scrutiny, Frank kept his eyes averted and no one spoke until they reached their destination. Then he shipped the oars, secured the rope and stepped ashore. He turned to Emily who was nearest and helped her out of the boat.

'Thank you kindly, sir,' she said with a provocative smile.

He turned back, extending a hand towards Julia. As she took it, she saw a flicker of emotion in his eyes that was almost pain.

'The boys will pay you,' Emily was saying. 'We haven't got any money left.'

He nodded as Julia sprang out of the boat to stand beside him. As she almost stumbled he steadied her and for one short moment their eyes met and held wordlessly.

'Come on, Ju!' cried Emily. 'Let's go on and hide. Frank will be ages fetching the boys over. We needn't go far – just make them think we've gone on home without them.'

Frank stepped back into the boat and Julia watched him push off from the bank, then she followed Emily along the path without a backward glance. A quarter of an hour later Leo and Ben found them and they began the long walk back into Rye.

*

As his four passengers set off to walk back to Rye, Frank watched them go – Jack's boys and George's daughters. Coulsdens, all of them, he thought. Emily was pretty enough but Julia – God! He shook his head. She was in a class of her own.

There was another shout of 'Ferry!' from the other side of the river, but at that moment his grandmother came out of the little hut.

'I'll fetch that one,' she told him. 'You get on home and see what you can do with those four loose roof-tiles. Your grandpa's had a look at them and he reckons the next high wind will have them off. Who was that last lot?'

'The Coulsdens – they've been on a picnic to Camber.'

Alice snorted. 'Funny lot,' she said with obvious disapproval. 'Which reminds me, I'm nearly out of wood chips, so you'd best get over to the boatyard when you have a moment and fetch back another couple of bags. Tomorrow will do.'

'Right,' said Frank.

Alice stared after the retreating Coulsdens. 'A real funny lot,' she repeated. 'I don't know how that Julia can bear to set eyes on Emily after what happened to her ma. Me, I'd as soon spit!'

'Maybe she doesn't know all the ins and outs of it,' he said defensively.

'Everyone else does.'

'Maybe they kept it from her.'

Alice shrugged.

'She's pretty though,' said Frank casually. 'Julia, I mean.'

'Oh, she's pretty enough,' said Alice, giving him a sharp look. 'She's a Gooding – takes after her grandma, God rest her soul. But she's a Coulsden too. So don't you go getting any fancy ideas as far as *she's* concerned.'

'Don't worry, I won't,' Frank assured her, but at her words the 'fancy idea' which had been in his mind for so long suddenly started to take on a more permanent shape.

*

That evening Frank sat on the river bank long after the sun had gone and thought seriously about Julia Coulsden, wondering exactly how old she was and whether or not she had a boy friend. Probably not, he thought, for she was still at school and her father was almost certainly strict with her in such matters. Any father with such an attractive daughter would be duty bound to protect her from the attentions of the opposite sex. Frank certainly hoped so, for in Julia's cool eyes he had seen the innocence that fades with the first experience of passion. He thought about her slender body, considering how mature or otherwise it might be. If he was going to marry her . . .

Abruptly he frowned, taken aback by the notion. He had never contemplated marriage before, but the idea did not alarm him in any way and he gave it careful consideration. If he seriously intended to marry Julia, then the question of her virginity was of greater significance. He did not relish the idea that another man might share her first venture into love-making, yet hardly dared hope that he himself might be fortunate enough to do so. He sighed. His aimless fingers found a small pebble which he tossed into the darkening water, where it fell with a brief plop into the mud. Overhead clouds obscured the moon and he knew from the feel of the air that by the morning a wind would have risen, but with any luck the shower would be of short duration. He leaned back against the bows of the old ferry boat and closed his eyes, listening contentedly to the night sounds: a distant shout, the faint hiss and clatter of the train as it left Rye Station, the lap and gurgle of water against the river bank as the tide rose and the whining of a dog as it scratched at a back door seeking admittance.

Julia Lady Coulsden. Her very name was already assuming magical proportions and he repeated it softly to himself. She was a girl to be admired, respected and loved. To be *cherished*, he corrected himself, seeing nothing old-fashioned in either the word or the idea. If he married Julia Coulsden she would bear his children and he would be proud to provide for them. She would have the best he could give her, he vowed, the very best and would want for nothing. He would work night and day if necessary to feed and clothe his family and *his* children would never go barefoot.

Damnation! It occurred to him suddenly that she was probably going to be a wealthy woman – the realisation came as a shock and the prospect hurt him. For some time his newly formed plans wavered dangerously close to the point of collapse as he struggled to come to terms with the problem, for that was how he saw it. A man provided for his wife and family – at least he had never known it any other way. His disappointment was only overcome by the thought that her father was in the prime of his life and would live for many years, so that Frank could marry Julia *before* she inherited any money. If an inheritance came to her later on in their marriage, that would be another matter. 'Julia Lady Coulsden, I love you,' he said softly and then his stern expression relaxed into a smile. He felt suddenly older and wiser and was glad he had settled his future. When the time came he would court Julia and then they would marry.

Ahead of him in the darkness he fancied he heard the soft splash of oars and screwed up his eyes trying to pierce the darkness.

'Who's there?' he called.

At once the sound stopped and Frank shrugged. Whoever it was showed no light and he knew well enough what that meant, grinning to himself as he imagined the man's curses. On his way to the sea, with the ebbing tide helping him, he dared not use his oars after hearing Frank call out. In a rush of generosity, Frank stood up noisily and made his way indoors, slamming the door behind him. Smuggling was 'a mug's game', he told himself, but none the less found himself wondering who it was who had slipped on his way so quietly in the darkness towards an illicit assignation at sea.

*

Hearing the slam of a door the boat's solitary occupant resumed his rowing, pulling steadily against the tide, dipping and raising the blades of his oars as gently as he could while his eyes probed the darkness for signs of danger. In each pocket of his jacket he carried several pebbles and a slim bundle of five-pound notes was tucked into both socks. Not that such crude precautions would save him if he was intercepted by the Customs men who might well be patrolling the beach between Rye Harbour and Fairlight. If his information was correct, however, they *should* be busy between Fairlight and Hastings, but no smuggler in his right mind relied too heavily on other people and it was not unknown for the Customs officers to put out false information in their efforts to outwit the men who so impudently pitted their wits against His Majesty's Government.

He stopped rowing after ten minutes, shipped his oars and listened again until – reassured by the silence – he began once more to ply them, confident that they would make no sound in the rowlocks for they were tightly bound with strips of rag. It was not even his own boat but had been 'borrowed' for the night's adventure; however, since he had successfully borrowed it before on numerous occasions, he saw no reason why tonight should prove more risky than any other. The money in his socks gave him a good feeling – he had obtained an excellent price for his goods and the demand for quality perfumes, tobacco and spirits showed no sign of diminishing – the money under the loose floorboard in his bedroom was proof of that. He flattered himself that he was prudent in all his dealings and would never fall into the trap of becoming too greedy, for that inevitably led to ill-feeling which was dangerous. A spiteful word from a resentful customer could spell immediate disaster and he knew that arrest and a successful conviction would mean a prison sentence. No, his only real worry was Bitty, his partner in crime who drank too much on occasions, but so far the wretch had managed to hold his tongue and their shared clandestine trips had been going on for nearly two years without any serious incidents.

Now the boat slipped past the mud-flats of Jury's Gap on his left hand and he would soon be able to pick out the outline of the wooden groyne to his right. He bent over the oars and the boat sped forward on the last water of the ebb tide. By the time the exchange was made, the tide would be on the turn and flowing up the narrow harbour and the sea would once more be his ally. He boasted that he knew the harbour entrance as well as he knew the back of his hand, and approaching always from a south-easterly direction he would nose in between the west-side groyne and east-side pier without difficulty at any time of the day or night unless there was an off-shore wind blowing. There was rarely less than eleven feet of water in the harbour entrance and the last hour of flood tide and the first hour of ebb created problems only at times of exceptional high water. Once clear of the harbour mouth, he turned west and rowed steadily. The water was fairly calm now, but the wind would rise during the night – though not in time to cause him any real problems, he hoped. Bitty would be waiting for him beside the lifeboat house and he would know the new meeting place. The contact and the pick-up point were Bitty's responsibility, while providing a dinghy to make it all possible was his own.

When at last he ran the boat ashore there was no sign of life and he cursed furiously under his breath as he took a pebble from his pocket and threw it towards the lifeboat house. There was no response, and when a second pebble was also met by silence, he stepped cautiously from the boat on to the shore. He wore dark clothes, including gloves, and had smeared his face with soot, but still he felt vulnerable and exposed, hating every moment he must spend on shore where it was almost impossible to move silently on the shifting pebbles and where the slightest sound travelled surprising distances through the still night air. Moving as carefully as he could, he made his way up the beach towards the spot where Bitty usually huddled, but tonight there was no one there. His heart began to beat faster as several unpleasant possibilities filled his mind. Suppose Bitty wasn't coming or had been delayed? Suppose he had already been caught and this was an ambush?

'Christ Almighty, Bitty!' he whispered, fighting to subdue his panic. 'Where are you?'

After what seemed an eternity, a sudden crunching of footsteps from the direction of Fairlight came clearly to his ears and he froze, lowering his head to hide the whites of his eyes. However it was not the steady tramp of official boots but the unsteady lurch of a man who has drunk too much beer. He put out a hand to steady the figure that stumbled towards him.

'Bitty! You bastard!'

'I'm fine,' mumbled Bitty. 'Just fine.'

'You fool!'

There was no time to argue. Once he had managed to elicit the rendezvous point from the befuddled man, he half-carried his partner back to the dinghy and within minutes they were on their way once more. Another half-hour's rowing brought them into the area where their French counterpart would be waiting and when at last the outline of another boat was spotted, a low but distinctive whistle provided the second of the night's signals. Quickly the two craft pulled together and one man from each crew held the boats steady while first money and then shapeless bundles wrapped in sacks were passed from hand to hand. A rapid conversation in French followed and a final handshake sealed the night's bargaining. Within minutes the two boats were drawing away from each other in the darkness – one on its way back to Rye, the other heading for a fishing smack which waited a little further out in the bay and would make similar transactions at three other prearranged points along the coast before venturing to the comparative shelter of her home port of Calais. For the men concerned it would prove a profitable night's work and they would all look forward to repeating the experience in a month's time.

*

At Hastings, the same Sunday was proving eventful in less pleasant ways for another member of the Coulsden family. Jane sniffed hard. Her handkerchief was in her apron pocket, but her hands were in a sink full of soapy water and she didn't want to stop and dry them. Her eyes were angry and her small mouth worked as she rehearsed silently what she would say to Stan when finally he showed up for his Sunday dinner. He was already forty minutes late and Jane – in an attempt to work off some of the energy which rage had engendered – had decided to wash up the various cooking utensils which she had used during the meal's preparation, instead of leaving them until afterwards.

The roast potatoes were hard and the roast lamb was overdone; the cabbage had boiled dry and stuck to the bottom of the pan – she had scraped off the best of it and transferred it to another saucepan. The gravy had simmered away to a glutinous mess and had been diluted twice with hot water. The home-made mint sauce had been accidentally knocked over and scooped back into the dish with the side of Jane's hand.

Now she sniffed again, stiffening suddenly as the back gate clicked to. Then she gasped. More than one pair of feet were treading the cinder-strewn pathway through the small, unproductive vegetable garden and Jane fought back tears of irritation and frustration. She threw the dishcloth into the greasy water and hastily dried her hands on the teacloth. He had brought someone home unannounced, but who was it? She felt sure she would swing for her husband one day! She closed her eyes and with an effort, forced herself to think more tolerantly. Turn the other cheek, the Bible said. Well, she would try but . . . she heard voices and her hands clenched into fists. Oh God, not George, surely? It was – *and* that slut Agnes was with them! Stan had dared to bring that woman into his house! Jane felt a surge of passionate anger as the back door opened and she found herself face to face with Agnes Coulsden, the first time they had met since Agnes had left George's employ some years ago.

Seeing the look in Jane's eyes, Agnes hesitated but Stan side-stepped and came into the kitchen.

'Bit of a surprise for you, love!' he said with false heartiness.

'Guess who happened to drop in at the Dolphin? The two girls have gone to Camber with Ben and Leo, so George and Ag are on the loose. Why go back to Rye, I said to them. Jane will have a bite of dinner for us and a bit of company'll make a nice change.' He pretended not to notice Jane's silence and it was obvious to her that he had drunk plenty to fortify himself for the confrontation; his face was very flushed and his eyes were bleary.

'Come on in, Ag,' he said loudly, with a nervous laugh. 'That's the ticket! And you, George. Not that you need telling. My home's your home.' He rubbed his hands together. 'Mm. Smells good, love, whatever it is! Sorry we're a bit late, but old Topper was in there, and Foxey, and we all got talking. Haven't seen old Topper for months – been laid up with a gammy leg. Terrible, the trouble he's had with that leg. Gone to ulcers, all up one side – it looks terrible. Would put me off my dinner if I wasn't so hungry.'

Jane, rooted to the spot with fury, still said nothing as they all trooped through the kitchen and into the dining-room where the table in the window was laid for two. Hearing Agnes say, 'What a cosy little room!' her stomach churned at the prospect of the trouble ahead. She heard Stan say, 'Give us your coat, Ag, and park your bum as they say.' And then Agnes's laugh, as though she was not used to such vulgarity. She covered her face with her hands. 'God give me strength,' she muttered. The effrontery of that woman, to come where she *knew* she was not welcome! Wait until she told Cicely! If only Sarah had still been alive, Stan would never have dared to do this. Never!

Stan reappeared in the kitchen just then and quickly pulled the door closed behind him, staring at her as she held her trembling hands clasped together in front of her mouth. He made a clumsy attempt to kiss her, but she shook herself free and hissed, 'Get rid of them, Stan, or I won't be responsible for the consequences! No, I mean it. I won't have her here! You *know* that.'

'It's my home, too.'

'I don't care. I won't have it – she killed Hettie!'

'That was years ago, Jane, for heaven's sake,' he protested in a fierce whisper, 'and she didn't kill anyone. Hettie killed herself.'

'It was *because* of her,' said Jane vehemently. 'Get rid of her, I tell you. George is welcome enough, but not Agnes.'

Slowly Stan raised a large fist and held it in front of her face; she could smell the beer on his breath.

'Keep your voice down,' he muttered. 'That's quite enough

from you. Now you listen to me – Ag is my brother's wife and she's *my* guest in *my* house!'

There was a burst of loud laughter from George in the dining-room as Agnes said something they did not catch.

'Get the dinner on the table, Jane,' said Stan menacingly, 'and keep a civil tongue in your head. You're not going to insult my brother's wife.'

'Don't you raise your fist to me, Stan Coulsden!' cried Jane, her anger outweighing her fear. 'You had no right to bring her here – to spring it on me like that. I've made it perfectly clear all these years – the others may let bygones be bygones but I won't. The fact that Julia accepts her now cuts no ice with me. If she's insulted, then you have only yourself to blame.'

Stan's fist still hovered threateningly as Jane turned away to the sink.

'Anyway, the dinner's ruined,' she stated. 'You're so late, nearly an hour. How do you expect me to keep a decent meal hot without it drying up? And then on top of everything else you bring two extra people – all that work and it's ruined!'

The door opened and Agnes put her head round the door. She too had drunk a little more than was good for her.

'Anything I can do to help?' she asked cheerfully. 'I can peel a spud with the best of them!'

Jane ignored her.

'No thanks, Ag,' said Stan hastily. 'It won't be long now, I'm just coming. Ask George to pour you a drink – he knows where it is.'

'Well, if you're sure, dear.'

Jane flinched at the endearment, but did not move until she heard the door close.

Stan now changed his tune and began to wheedle. 'Look, love, I know how you feel about her—'

'Obviously you *don't* or you would never have invited her here!'

'But couldn't you put up with her just this once?' he begged. 'She *is* George's wife, and if Julia can forgive and forget, surely you can. You're supposed to be a Christian.'

Jane ignored this last jibe and said, 'Julia can do what she likes. That's her lookout. I don't have to like Agnes and I don't have to make her welcome here.'

Stan struggled with his rising temper. 'Look, just serve us up a bit of bloody dinner. That's all I ask and I swear I won't bring her here again. Never. Not never again!'

'It's no good, Stan,' declared Jane. 'I won't speak to her and that's flat!'

'Well, don't then. Just smile or—'

'*Smile?* I will not smile at her!'

'Look, Jane, for Christ's sake,' he cried, 'cut out all this bloody cackle and just give us the food.'

She eyed him stonily. 'There's not enough for four.'

'Make it go round. You can if you want to.'

Jane shook her head stubbornly but then abruptly her face crumpled and she began to cry. Stan tried to put an arm round her but she pushed him away.

'You should never have done this to me, Stan!' she sobbed. 'I'll serve your damned dinner but I won't eat with her. Not a mouthful – and if she doesn't like it, she can lump it.'

He groaned. 'Don't talk like that and stop crying, for God's sake. Do you want them to know something's up?'

'Oh, Stan, you great stupid *oaf*!' cried Jane, rubbing at her eyes. 'Do you think they don't know something's up? Oh, just leave me alone, Stan. Get out of here and let me get on with it.'

'You're a good girl, Jane; you're a real pal.'

'Oh no, I'm not, Stan,' she told him. 'I'm no pal of yours after what you're doing to me. Just get out of my kitchen before I say something I'll regret.'

Left to herself, Jane opened the oven door and slammed it violently several times to let her feelings be known. Then she rattled the pans and clashed the plates together, muttering vindictively as she did so. She sniffed, cried and blew her nose and all the time the sounds of cheerful chatter came from the dining-room and she imagined them all drinking merrily together.

Suddenly George came out with a small sherry in his hand. 'I told her you're not much of a drinker,' he said, 'but Agnes says just try a sip of sherry. She says it'll perk you up a bit, you know.'

'I don't want to be perked up, thank you, George,' she told him.

'Oh . . . well, I'll leave it there in case you change your mind.'

'I won't change my mind, George, thank you very much.'

'Oh come on, Jane,' he pleaded. 'Let bygones be bygones, won't you? It's all in the past and we all make mistakes.'

'Mistakes? Huh!' She turned on him fiercely. 'I liked Hettie – you know that, George. She was a thoroughly nice woman – a sight *too* nice, maybe! Now let me get on with the dinner.' She snatched up the sherry and threw it into the sink, and after a moment's silence, George went back into the dining-room where Jane heard him say, 'I think we ought to go, Stan.'

And Stan, foolish Stan, said he 'wouldn't hear of it'. So the cheerful chatter began again and Jane heard Stan offer Agnes 'a top-up'. She stood in the middle of the kitchen and wondered how she would feel if they had a maid and Stan got her pregnant and then kept her and the child at another home. She remembered Hettie, who had never willingly done anyone any harm and had loved George and had trusted him.

For nearly ten minutes she stood there thinking, then with a set face she went into the dining-room and laid a third place before carrying in three plates and setting them on the table. No one spoke for a moment until Agnes, ignoring the missing fourth place, cried, 'Ooh, Jane, it smells delicious! You have got a very clever wife, Stanley Coulsden! Hasn't he, George?'

'Jane's certainly a very good cook,' George muttered nervously.

The three of them sat down, Jane carried in the food and they looked at it apprehensively. The lamb had been hacked into large, uneven chunks and the potatoes looked like small rocks. The cabbage was obviously burnt and so were the carrots. The watery gravy looked more like washing-up water.

Still standing, Jane began to serve the food on to the plates, slopping the vegetables and meat indiscriminately so that it looked as unappetising as possible. At first George, Stan and Agnes attempted to continue their light-hearted banter but finally they faltered into silence, chilled by Jane's obvious malevolence. When they had all been served there was a deathly hush. Two bright spots of colour burned in Agnes's cheeks as she looked fixedly at her plate, while George looked at Stan and Stan stared with unfocusing eyes at a point above Agnes's head. No one knew what to say.

Jane walked out of the room and up the stairs. While Agnes and George were urging Stan to go after her, they heard her come down again and then the front door slammed loudly.

'Bloody hell!' exclaimed Stan.

They all looked at each other.

'She'll come round,' said George. 'Well, let's tuck in, shall we?'

'She'll be back,' stated Agnes.

But as Stanley Coulsden stabbed at a piece of potato he was not at all sure.

CHAPTER FIFTEEN

Winifred mashed a spoonful of potatoes with a spoonful of boiled fish and the baby on her lap waved her arms and gurgled.

'Look at her,' cried Julia, enchanted. 'She knows that's her dinner, bless her. Is that your dinner, Amy? Oh, you are a lucky girl!'

'I should move back a bit if I were you,' Winifred warned. 'She spits it all over the place; she's a real messy eater, this one. The others weren't, so I just don't understand it. There now, here we go, my pet. Open wide.' She popped a spoonful of the creamy mixture into her youngest child's open mouth. 'Who's a hungry girlie, then?' she asked. 'Who's going to eat up all her dinner, eh?'

After watching the performance repeated several times, Julia found it advisable to move back even further out of range. Jane had taken the other girls for a walk along the sea-front and this gave Winifred and Julia a chance to discuss the current family crisis.

'So where's Aunt Jane living now?' Julia asked. 'I thought she was still here with you.'

Winifred shook her head. 'She stayed with us for three weeks, but by that time she and Ernie were getting on each other's nerves and I think she found the kids a bit much too. Then she and Ernie had words and suddenly a week ago she announced she'd got herself a job, cleaning for this rich woman who lives in Priory Road. It's an enormous house, apparently, and she's got one room right up in the attic. Can you imagine it? Ernie's furious; he thinks she's mad.'

'What about Uncle Stan? What does he think?'

'He won't talk about it. I do wish you'd go and speak to her, Ju. She might listen to you.'

Julia was indignant. 'You leave me out of it, Win! Honestly, I wouldn't know what to say. Perhaps she'll get fed up with it and go home of her own accord.'

'I wish she would but I doubt it . . . Oh Amy! Naughty girl! Stop that.' She broke off to scrape fish and potato from the blue-checked tablecloth. 'Come on now – only a few more spoonsful.'

'So is this Aunt Jane's day off?' Julia asked.

'Yes. She has Sunday mornings free because they're all at church, and Thursday afternoons. She gets two shillings and sixpence a week and her board, with breakfast and a good dinner in the evening.'

Julia whistled. 'I can't imagine it,' she said. 'What does she actually do? Is it heavy work?'

'Bit of everything from what I can hear: beating carpets, polishing brass, mending the linen – all that sort of thing. Oh, come on, Amy – open wide.'

'Poor Uncle Stan!' Julia shook her head. 'He's probably cursing himself, but I suppose after all these years he thought it would be all right. Agnes and Papa were a bit shamefaced at the time, but now I think Ag's gloating a bit. Pa just says, "That's Stan's worry." '

'Well, of course, it serves him right,' said Winifred. 'He should have known better – he knows how strict Aunt Jane is about that sort of thing. This Mr Perry, he's a magistrate or something, I think. Or maybe a judge. I'm not sure.'

'Mr Perry? Who's Mr Perry?'

'The people Aunt Jane works for. There, all gone! Who's a good girl, then, eh?' She wiped Amy's face with her apron and dumped her unceremoniously in Julia's lap. 'Go to your Auntie Julia,' she told her offspring, 'while I make a pot of tea – and then you tell me about the big romance, Ju.'

Julia blushed. 'It's not a romance,' she protested. 'I just went to a dance with him. Well no, not really – we all went – me, Emily and the boys, but I did dance with Leo.'

'Ding-dong, ding-dong!' cried Winifred. 'Do I hear wedding bells in a few years' time?'

Julia's colour deepened delightedly. 'No, you do *not!*' she insisted. 'But I *do* like him a lot, Win, and I wish he wasn't a cousin. *Can* you marry your cousin?'

'Don't ask me,' said Winifred. 'It seems odd to think of my "baby brother" marrying anyone, but I suppose they thought like that when I married Ernie, although I was nearer to him in age than you are to Leo.'

'Well, Ernest was your cousin,' said Julia hopefully.

'Half-cousin,' Winifred reminded her. 'He's a Brett and only Uncle Stan's stepson, remember. Anyway, where was this dance you all went to?'

'At the Drill Hall. I rode on the crossbar of Leo's bike and
Emily went on Ben's. We laughed so much I nearly fell off and
then a policeman stopped us because Leo's head-lamp wasn't
working properly. I thought we were going to be arrested!'

She laughed again and jiggled Amy up and down on her lap. If
only she could have a child – Leo's child – she thought wistfully.
She would ask nothing more from life than to marry Leo and raise
a brood of children.

As Winifred spooned tea into the pot she glanced at Julia out of
the corner of her eye and hoped she would soon get over the
schoolgirl crush on Leo. It had come to her ears that a young
woman teacher of the same school where Leo now taught had
caught his eye. A certain Victoria Brooking, to be exact. Winifred
didn't want Julia to break her heart and she said casually, 'I
wouldn't recommend Leo as a husband to any girl. He's so
dreadfully selfish and he—'

'Selfish! Oh, Win, that's not true,' cried Julia, rushing to his
defence. 'Leo's not selfish and even if he *was*, I'd still think he
would make a good husband. Lots of men are selfish, so are lots
of women.'

Winifred shrugged. 'Ben's a much better bet,' she said, but
Julia dismissed the idea.

'Ben's sweet,' she told her cousin, 'but he's so young. I know
he's a year older than me, but sometimes I feel like his big sister.
Emily's potty about him, of course.' She sighed. 'I like Leo, Ben
likes me, Em likes Ben. It's so complicated! You are lucky, Win.
You and Ernie just fell in love with each other and it was so
simple.'

'It was nothing of the kind,' remarked Winifred. 'We were both
in the war, remember, and either of us could have been killed.
There was nothing simple about *that*.'

'Well no, I suppose not.' Julia hesitated. 'I suppose you haven't
got a photograph I could have, one of Leo when he was a boy?'

'I could probably find one sometime,' said Winifred, 'but I
don't have anything handy. Ah, is that Aunt Jane back already?'

There were footsteps along the side of the house, but the back
door opened to admit Ernest and a friend whom Julia recognised
with pleasant surprise.

'Ian Cornwell!' she cried.

'Good Lord! It's the runaway!' Ian exclaimed. 'I didn't expect
to see you here.'

'Bad penny,' laughed Ernest. 'She's always turning up. How are you, Ju? Isn't she beautiful, Ian?'

'Oh stop it, Ernie!' cried Julia, embarrassed by his teasing.

Ernest threw himself into the only comfortable chair and said, 'We saw Ma toiling along the sea-front, but we crossed over smartish to the other side of the road before she saw us. Both the kids had toffee apples. I thought she was supposed to be on her beam ends?'

'I gave her some money, Ernie,' said Winifred defensively. 'Just a little bit. I knew she'd want to treat them and she can't afford it.'

Ernest slapped his forehead. 'What a wife!' he exclaimed in mock despair. 'What a spendthrift! Toffee apples. Am I made of money? Never get married, Ian! Take a word of advice from one who knows the full horror of it.'

Winifred grinned at him. 'You love it,' she said, 'you know you do. You'd be lost without me and the kids. But why are we talking about you? I haven't seen Ian for ages. What have you been doing all this time, Ian? Going up in the world, to judge by that smart suit.'

'And he's wearing a tie,' said Ernie. 'Don't miss the tie, you ladies. A collar and a tie on a Thursday afternoon! Going up in the world is right. He's going to be a famous doctor like his father.'

While they all talked Julia studied Ian, amazed that he had changed so little since their eventful last meeting in Rye several years earlier. He looked more self-assured and the formal suit added distinction to his slim figure. The bright ginger hair was smoothed down and he had a centre parting. He really was a very attractive man, she thought – but not as attractive as Leo! Not by half.

'So could you take out my adenoids?' asked Winifred. 'Or my appendix?'

Ian laughed. 'I'm afraid not,' he confessed. 'I'd have to recommend my father for that job. But I *could* set your leg if you broke it, or diagnose yellow jaundice if you were suffering from it.'

'Diagnose it?' Julia laughed. 'But could you *cure* it? I mean, anyone can diagnose yellow jaundice. If you're yellow and you're not a Chinaman, that's what you've got. It's curing the jaundice that's the hard part and that's what doctors are supposed to be for!'

Ernest glanced slyly at Julia. 'Could you mend a broken heart, Ian? Our young Julia is lusting after a certain Leo Coulsden—'

'Ernest!' she cried, feeling her face burn. 'You hateful pig! I am *not*. Win, tell him to stop it.'

'Lucky Leo,' said Ian quickly, but Julia was too mortified by the clumsy joke to appreciate his compliment.

'Leo and I are just cousins,' she insisted, 'but because we enjoy each other's company, Ernie jumps to conclusions. I do not lust after him. It's your nasty mind, Ernie.' She choked back her indignation and added with an effort, 'I don't lust after anyone.'

'Well, he lusts after you, then,' said Ernie, ignoring Winifred's warning look.

Julia's eyes widened with shock. 'Does he?' she gasped. 'Does he honestly? Ernie, are you serious?'

'Of course he's not serious,' interposed Winifred hastily. 'Stop teasing her, Ernie, and take your daughter up to her cot. She'll sleep for an hour or so if we're lucky.' She turned to Ian. 'A cup of tea, Ian? I've only just made a pot and you're very welcome. There's some currant bread—'

'I'd love to accept but I daren't,' he told her as an unrepentant Ernest went upstairs. 'I've already explained to Ernest I have to get back to Appledore – my grandmother is expecting me.'

Julia collected her thoughts. 'I'm so sorry about your grandfather,' she said. 'I read about his death in the local paper. I wanted to go to the funeral, but I was at school and they wouldn't give me time off because I wasn't a relative.'

Ian's eyes darkened. 'It must have been pretty awful,' he said, 'and it's a wonder my grandmother survived the shock. He was sitting in his chair in the garden reading the *Chronicle* and Grandmother was just carrying out a plate of sandwiches. When she saw his newspaper fall to the ground, she thought he'd dozed off. Then he just toppled off the seat, unconscious. He died four days later without regaining consciousness. Poor Grandmother! We visit her as often as we can, but now South View is too big for her although she won't hear of leaving. Henry worked so hard on the garden, she says, and wouldn't want her to leave it.'

Upstairs they could hear Amy begin to wail as she was tucked into her cot. Ian stood up. 'If you won't think me terribly rude, I'll have to go,' he said. 'I came into Hastings to get the car repaired—'

'Car?' cried Winifred. 'You've got a *car* and never mentioned it? Oh, you *are* going up in the world! A car! We must see it. We could have gone for a spin if we'd known!'

She rushed through the passage and out of the front door, while Julia looked at Ian.

'It's a Jowett,' he explained. 'It was Grandfather's. If you are ready to go back to Rye, I could offer you a lift.'

'Ian! Oh, how marvellous! Yes, please!' cried Julia. 'I've only ever been in Uncle Jack's car – that's Win's father. I was going back on the train, but the car will be much more fun.'

As Ernest reappeared, she told him of her invitation to travel back to Rye by car. 'Good idea,' he said heartily. 'That way we get rid of you sooner. No, no, I'm only kidding, Ju! You take everything so seriously. Of course we shan't mind!'

For the next five minutes Winifred and Julia marvelled over the car, then Julia and Ian climbed in and after exchanging farewells set off in the direction of Rye. They drove in silence for a while. Julia turned back as they reached the top of the hill in order to catch a last glimpse of the sea, then settled back to enjoy the ride.

'Pushed anyone in the river lately?' Ian asked and she burst out laughing.

'I was hoping you wouldn't ask,' she said. 'Yes, I do it all the time; it's a sort of hobby.'

'I'm sorry,' he apologised, 'I'm only teasing you. It was a long time ago, now.'

'I never did thank you for rescuing poor Agnes,' she said. 'When I look back—'

'There's no need to thank me,' Ian assured her. 'I'm sorry I mentioned it. It was meant to be a joke but not a very good one, I'm afraid.'

'But I want to talk about it,' she insisted. 'It's something I've been wanting to say ever since I was old enough to understand how awful it would have been for me – and Agnes of course – if you hadn't been there. Can you imagine? Poor Agnes drowned and me having to live with it for the rest of my life!'

He made no comment as they negotiated the traffic in Ore, but as they drove into the country again Julia said, 'The funny thing is, we get along quite well now. All four of us.'

'I'm so glad,' he said, smiling.

'I try not to believe that my mother would disapprove of me liking Agnes and of the four of us living together like a family. Do you think it's wrong of me?'

'No,' he answered without even pausing to consider the question. 'It's not wrong at all. I think above all your mother would want you to be happy.'

'But would she want me to love Agnes or even Emily – my father's child by another woman? It does worry me sometimes.'

'She couldn't blame Emily for being born,' said Ian. 'Nobody could.'

Julia glanced at him gratefully. 'That's what I tell myself, because I'm sure my mother was a very kind person. I wish I could remember her but I can't. Over the years I've even forgotten how it felt when she held me. I used to be able to remember that – a sort of close, warm feeling of being protected. And her voice. I could remember her voice.'

'How old were you when she died?'

'Two.' Julia sighed. 'It's not very old. I know what she looks like, but only from photographs. I can't remember *seeing* her. Just the voice and being held in her arms. It's not much and even that's slipping away. I feel terribly disloyal sometimes, wondering what she would think or say if she could see me.'

'She'd probably say, "Be happy, Julia." Isn't that what you would say if you were in her shoes? If you were her, would you want your child to be unhappy?'

Julia was silent and he continued, 'It was a long time ago, Julia, and you can't live in the past. At least, you shouldn't. There's so much you can't know. Maybe if your mother could see that Agnes is doing her best to make a home for you and your father, and that Agnes is sorry about what happened, she might well forgive her for what she did. Agnes was wrong, I know, but we all make mistakes and if we're really sorry, then we shouldn't have to be punished for the rest of our lives.'

'I know,' said Julia, 'and I want to think you're right. But if I let myself believe you, is that just because it will make my life easier? If I believe that my mother approves, then I need not feel guilty or disloyal?'

Ian shook his head. 'I think you should believe me because what I say is logical and sensible and will allow you to relax and enjoy your life. Your mother gave you life – don't you think she'd want you to make good use of it?'

Julia fell silent again, considering what he had said as the dark green Jowett carried them through Icklesham and up the hill into Winchelsea.

'I'm going to let myself believe you,' she said at last with a shaky laugh which did not disguise her emotion. 'You've talked to me like a Dutch uncle, Ian, and I'm very grateful.'

'I've never been called a Dutch uncle before!' he grinned.

'It's a compliment,' she told him. 'I don't know why I've told you all my problems, but I'm glad I did. You've helped me a great deal – more than you know, probably.'

He smiled. 'I'm pleased. Everyone needs someone to talk to now and again.'

'Even you?'

'Oh yes, even me,' he told her. 'I'm not really very wise.'

'You seem so.'

Ian shrugged. 'Maybe we can all see other people's problems more clearly than we see our own.'

She looked at him earnestly. 'If ever I could help you by listening, I would. Will you remember that?'

'I will,' he laughed, 'and thank you.'

They drove in companionable silence for a while, enjoying the passing countryside.

'Oh goodness! We'll be in Rye soon,' exclaimed Julia, 'and I've talked most of the way from Hastings. I feel awful. You'll wish you hadn't offered me a lift. What awful company I must have been!'

'Julia Lady!' said Ian. 'Do stop talking like that. Of course you weren't awful company. We can't be jolly all the time. Everyone has worries and it helps to let off steam. I enjoyed your company and I'm glad you accepted the lift.'

'Well, thank heavens! But do tell me something about yourself before we get there. I'd like to feel you managed to get a few words in!'

'About myself? Oh dear, let me think.'

'Quick, Ian,' she cried with mock urgency, 'we're passing the harbour road! Tell me something. Anything. How old are you? Where do you come from? What do you like for breakfast? Anything, but hurry!'

'I was born at a very young age—' he began.

'Ian! Seriously.'

He laughed.

'All right then. I'm pretty ancient – twenty-nine in fact—'

'That's not old. Go on. Quickly!'

'We live in Highgate, near the woods—'

'And?'

'And what?'

'For breakfast?'

'Orange juice, boiled egg and toast with black cherry jam and a pot of tea.'

'I'll remember that,' she told him. 'What you like for breakfast – in case you ever come to stay. Oh dear, we're home and I hardly know anything about you. But thank you so much, Ian . . . for all your help. It's been a lovely ride and it's a very nice car. I'm sorry if I didn't say all the right things about it, but I don't know much about cars. I suppose I should have asked things about the gear-box, whatever that is, or the mileage?'

'It's just a car,' Ian said. 'Five wheels, one at each corner and one to steer it by. Cars aren't nearly as interesting as people.'

There was a long pause while Julia looked at the mahogany dashboard and Ian looked at her. Suddenly he said, 'Lucky Leo!'

Julia covered her face with her hands. 'Oh don't! That was just Ernie being silly. He only says it to embarrass me.'

Gently he pulled her hands away from her face. 'I met Leo once,' he said, 'and he seems very nice. You don't have to pretend not to like him.'

'You've met him? But where?'

'He and Ben came over with their father, to visit Win and Ernie.'

'Oh. And you liked him?'

'Yes, I did. He's a teacher, isn't he?'

'Yes.' She sighed. 'Actually, I do like him rather a lot – but I like Ben too. We have a lot of fun, the four of us.'

'I envy you,' he said. 'I'm an only child; I had a sister, but she died when she was one and I was seven.'

Julia hesitated. She wanted to invite him to join them one day, but the others might object. He was older than they were and might put a damper on their high spirits. Leo enjoyed being the oldest among them and she didn't want to put Leo's nose out of joint.

Ian seemed suddenly thoughtful. 'I don't suppose,' he said, 'that you'd come and have dinner with us? It would cheer up my grandmother to have someone else to talk to and we'd try not to bore you.'

'Come to South View? Oh, I'd love to,' cried Julia. 'I'll ask Agnes, but I'm sure it will be all right. When shall I come?'

He smiled, delighted by her obvious eagerness. 'Tomorrow

evening, about six? I'll fetch you and bring you back of course. Should I ask Agnes too?'

'No, there's no need. After all, you're twenty-nine and she'll think you a very responsible person. Oh dear, I didn't mean it to sound that way, as though I think you're old. I'm saying all the wrong things, but you know what I mean.'

'I know. And I did understand what you meant.'

He got out and went round the car to open the door for her. 'I'll look forward to it,' he told her.

*

That evening Julia spent nearly an hour trying to decide what to wear for dinner with the Cornwells. Ian had not given her any idea how formally his grandmother dined in the evening and therefore she went through her entire wardrobe. Under Emily's critical eyes, she tried on everything she possessed but nothing was suitable. She looked at Emily in despair and then both girls gazed at the pile of dresses, skirts and blouses which lay across the bed. 'Absolutely nothing!' cried Julia. 'What shall I do, Em?'

'You could try mine, Ju,' suggested Emily, but Julia gave an exasperated groan.

'They're too young,' she exclaimed. 'and they wouldn't fit. I'm much taller than you – but thanks anyway. Oh Em, this is terrible! What *am* I going to do?'

'Perhaps you shouldn't go,' said Emily, who was feeling very envious. 'You could say you're ill.'

'But I *want* to go!'

'Perhaps Ma's got something she'd lend you,' Emily began, but Julia groaned again and rolled her eyes despairingly. Agnes was hardly a fashion plate, at least not in Julia's eyes. Moreover she was altogether the wrong generation.

'Her clothes wouldn't fit me either,' she said hastily, not wishing to offend Emily. 'I really need to buy something new. Something grown-up. I don't want to look like a schoolgirl.'

'Why not?' asked Emily. 'His grandmother probably likes schoolgirls and no one else is going to be there except Ian and he's too old to count. I don't know why you're worrying so.'

Julia gave her a withering look. 'That's because you're not fifteen and you've never been invited to dinner by someone you hardly know. If I'm going to be a guest in someone's house, I want to look right. It's important. I wonder if Papa would buy me a new dress. Shall I ask him, Em? Do you think I dare?'

'Yes, I think you dare,' said Emily. 'Ask him if we can both have a new dress. Tell him it's really important.'

'I can't ask for two new dresses,' Julia protested. 'He's not rolling in money. I'll ask him for me, and then in a week or so when he's forgotten, you can ask him for you.' She clasped her hands dramatically. 'Oh, Papa, *please* say yes. Please do!'

However, George said 'No' and that was the end of it. So when Ian arrived the next evening Julia was wearing her best blue *crêpe-de-Chine* with the dropped waistline and a rope of crystal beads which Agnes had lent her. She had resigned herself to being a disappointment to Ian's grandmother, but in fact Helen Cornwell's welcome was all she could have wished.

'Goodness me, Ian, this is never young Julia Coulsden. Why, my dear girl, you've grown up since we last met.'

Julia offered her hand, but the old lady kissed her warmly on the cheek and then stood back to admire her visitor from all angles.

'So tall and your hair is bobbed! What a transformation! How old are you now, dear? *Seventeen*, is it?' she said kindly, knowing Julia would feel flattered to be thought older. 'Where do the years go? I ask myself that every time Christmas comes round. Really, Ian, it was very naughty of you not to tell me you were bringing home a young lady. Julia, my dear, come in and sit by the fire and make yourself comfortable. I know it's not really autumn, but poor Henry did so love to see a bit of fire. Just a log or two. He liked to *hear* it too.'

'A few flames and a bit of a crackle,' Ian said, 'that's what he always called it.'

Julia murmured something non-committal as Ian helped her off with her coat. It was marvellous – they were both treating her like an adult and Mrs Cornwell thought she was seventeen! No one seemed to object to the blue *crêpe-de-Chine* and suddenly it didn't matter at all that Papa had said 'No' to the idea of a new dress.

'Now then,' said Ian, reappearing from the hall a moment later, 'What about a drink? Grandmother? Julia? We've a medium sherry or a dry.'

They both looked at Julia, who had never had a sherry in her life. Medium or dry? The latter sounded a contradiction in terms.

'I'll have medium,' she decided.

Soon they were sitting by the fire sipping drinks. Julia thought it was a most sophisticated beginning to the evening and imagined pleasurably how it would all sound when she recounted it to the others. Surely Leo would be impressed and would stop treating her as a child? Surely he would see her in a new light – no longer one of the girls but a young woman who had actually been invited by Ian's grandmother to call her 'Helen' instead of 'Mrs Cornwell'.

'Perhaps, dear,' Helen was saying, 'you could come and see me again. You don't have to wait until my grandson invites you. He doesn't come down very often, I'm afraid. His visits are few and far between, but he's so busy with his studies.'

'I'd love to come again,' said Julia.

'I could show you the garden, then,' said Helen. 'It's too dark now and anyway, the evenings get quite misty. There's often a mist on the marsh. I don't know if it's the flat ground or all the dykes, but it's quite a feature of the landscape. Of course, we're high up here and so we don't always get it.'

'But we can see it,' said Ian. 'We can look out over it. It's like a wispy grey carpet spread out over the fields . . . but why are we telling you this, Julia?' He laughed. 'I forget that you lived here yourself when your grandmother was alive. Doesn't it seem strange – or sad – to come back and see it with new tenants, new furniture, different colour schemes?'

'Oh dear,' said Helen. 'I'd never thought of it like that. And I keep going on about all the changes Henry made in the garden.'

'It doesn't matter at all,' began Julia.

'Oh, but Ian's right. It must be very sad for you.'

'Not sad,' said Julia. 'Strange? Well, perhaps a bit strange and yet as we drove up it looked exactly the same. The outside hasn't changed at all. I could almost imagine Mama Sarah was still here and that she would open the door and – and . . .' She frowned slightly, avoiding their eyes suddenly. 'Yes, you're right. It is a bit sad, but in a nice way. Do you know what I mean?'

'I think so,' said Helen, leaning across to pat her knee. 'Some memories are worth the sadness, aren't they? Better to be sad and remember than to lose someone from your life altogether. I think I feel the same way about Henry. And that's why I don't want to move. I can remember him here at South View, but if I move he'll be gone.'

Her voice faltered and she glanced up at Ian who was standing beside her.

He patted her shoulder and she said, 'Oh dear! I'm going to get myself all upset if I go on about poor Henry. I think I'll pop out and take a look at the dinner. I thought a roast, dear? Most people enjoy a traditional dinner, and I know Ian loves a nice piece of sirloin. I keep meaning to get a woman in to do the cooking – my daughter-in-law tells me I should – but I never get round to it and now that I'm on my own it fills up an hour or two, thinking about the meal and preparing everything. I have a woman for the rough work but there . . .'

She looked round vaguely, losing her train of thought, and Julia said, 'I love beef. A roast will be lovely.'

'Oh, the beef! Yes, I thought so, too.' She held up a hand and Ian, smiling, pulled her gently to her feet.

When she had retired to the kitchen he grinned. 'She likes you,' he said. 'I hope you will visit her again.'

'Of course I will.'

'Another sherry?'

'No thank you. I'd better not.'

'Grandmother was right. You do look very nice and that blue dress suits you.'

'Thank you.' It was on the tip of her tongue to tell him about the difficult decision, her father's refusal to buy her something new and the fact that the beads belonged to Agnes. But she stopped herself just in time. Adults surely did not discuss such details. She tried to think of something topical which she could mention in a casual way – politics, perhaps? But she knew very little about the subject and would only show her ignorance.

Ian had sat down in Helen's chair and was staring into the fire. 'Appledore is a very pretty village,' she said to him at last. 'Have you had time to explore it?'

'I've wandered through.'

'They say the church is a fine example of – of architecture,' she finished vaguely, 'and there's a smithy. Mama Sarah used to take me there to watch them working. It was so noisy, I remember, but very interesting. This fire basket was made there.'

'Was it? I must remember to tell my grandmother.' He poured himself another glass of sherry and then sat on the floor beside Julia.

'What will you do when you leave school?' he asked her.

'I don't know. Isn't it dreadful? If only I were a boy, I could join the crew of *Silver Lady*. Agnes thinks we should study millinery or something equally ladylike!' She laughed. 'She does so want us to be "a credit" to them. Poor Papa! Fancy being a fisherman and having two daughters. He must envy Uncle Jack having Ben and Leo.'

'Ah! The lustful Leo!'

'Ian!' She protested. 'Don't start that again. I think I might study shorthand and typing and work for a solicitor.'

'That would be very ladylike,' he agreed. 'What about nursing, like your cousin Winifred? Then you could come to London to study at my hospital and we could see more of each other.'

Julia shook her head. 'I don't think I'd be any good,' she said. 'I don't like the sight of blood and I'd most likely faint.'

Helen came to the door then and asked, 'Do you like horse-radish, Julia?'

'Horseradish?'

'To go with the beef.'

'Oh – I've never tried it. We always have mustard.'

'Then I recommend it,' said Ian. 'Grandmother makes it with cream.'

'Henry always grew horseradish,' Helen told her. 'Wherever we lived, even when we were in India. He couldn't bear mustard with beef.'

'I'd like to try it,' said Julia.

'It's a bit naughty to grow, mind,' laughed Helen. 'It tries to take over the garden and you have to watch it like a hawk. Well then, about ten minutes, I think, and I should be ready.

'Can I help you at all?' Julia asked.

'No, no, dear, certainly not. You're our guest tonight. Ian always helps me and carries the heavy dishes into the dining-room. I can't trust my wrists these days; they're not very strong and I did drop one tureen. Such a pity. It spoilt the set, you see.' She looked round, frowning. 'Now what did I want in here?'

'You came in to ask Julia about the horseradish,' Ian reminded her.

'Oh yes. Oh, that's fine then.' She gave Julia a wink. 'He's very domesticated, dear,' she confided in a stage whisper. 'I know he's my grandson, but I must be fair and he's very good to me and so helpful about the place.'

Ian groaned. 'She'll be telling you next that I can mend a fuse,' he told Julia.

'Well, you *can* mend a fuse, dear,' said Helen fondly. 'I'm only telling Julia how helpful you are.'

When she had gone out again Julia smiled. 'I didn't know you could mend a fuse,' she mocked.

'Good Lord, yes!' he laughed. 'Blindfolded and with one hand tied behind my back! You mustn't mind – I think she's trying to get me married off. She's dying for a great-grandson she can name Henry.'

'And have you . . . I mean, is there someone in your life, or shouldn't I ask?'

'You may ask and no, there's no one – at least no one Grand-mother has met.' He gave a slight shrug. 'There are plenty of nurses at the hospital – we all get along quite well, but mostly we go out in a group. There are half-a-dozen of us, you know, and we fool around together. Go boating, to the zoo and so on, whenever we get off-duty at the same time. It's not easy. Sometimes it means swapping duty times and the girls have to live in the nurses' quarters where they're very strict about hours.'

'It's funny,' said Julia, 'but I can't imagine you being a doctor. Are you going to be a surgeon like your father?'

'I'm not sure. I think I'd rather be a GP. You get to know your patients and you must feel like part of the community. With my father's job, it's a constant stream of new faces.'

'Didn't your grandfather want your father to go into the Army?' asked Julia. 'That's quite usual, isn't it? We've got a girl at school whose family have been Army men for generations. Your grand-father was a colonel, wasn't he?'

'That's right – and *his* father was a major, but it didn't go back further than that. My father hated all the moving around when he was a young boy, and then he was sent to boarding school and hated that, too. So he decided to go into medicine.'

'You must be a very brainy family,' said Julia enviously. 'Poor Leo is the bright boy of the Coulsden family, but I don't think it's easy to be the odd one out. Uncle Jack would have liked him to go into the boatyard as well as Ben.'

'Does Ben like the work?'

'Oh yes, he loves it! Boats are his life, I think, and he's got a way with wood – a sort of feel for it. Aunt Cicely says he's never really happy unless he's knee-deep in wood shavings.'

They chatted pleasantly until Helen called them into the dining-room for home-made vegetable soup, beef with veget-ables and a trifle made with macaroons. Julia began to relax and soon forgot her earlier shyness. The conversation flowed easily – any gaps were quickly filled by Helen, who was never at a loss – and by the time the meal ended she felt that the three of them were old friends.

Just after ten o'clock, Ian took her home, but not before Helen had fixed a tentative date three weeks ahead for Julia's next visit. Back in Rye, they parked the car and stood for a moment on the doorstep, both equally reluctant to end the evening.

'Well, thank you for a nice evening,' said Julia. 'I'm looking forward to going to South View again, but I'm sorry you won't be there.'

'Not as sorry as I am,' he assured her. 'It's been great fun.'

She looked up at him. The street-lamp behind him cast a shadow over his face and she couldn't read the expression in his eyes.

'Take care of yourself in London,' she said lightly. 'Don't get into too much mischief with all those nurses!'

'I'll try – if you promise to keep the lustful Leo at arm's length.' His words were teasing, but she knew they were meant seriously.

'I'll try,' she told him.

'I'd like to kiss you good night,' he said. 'Would it be proper, do you think?'

Julia's pulse raced. A good-night kiss! Even Leo had never given her a real good-night kiss. Would she be disloyal to Leo if she allowed Ian to kiss her? A small and sinful inner voice whispered that he would never know.

'I think so,' she replied.

Gently he took her in his arms and his lips brushed hers so lightly that it was all over before she had a chance to enjoy it.

'Good night, Julia Lady,' he said.

'Good night, Doctor Cornwell!'

Laughing, he let his arms fall to his sides. At that moment they heard the window above them creak open on its hinges.

'Is that you, Ju?' came Emily's voice from the darkened window.

'Of course it is!' Julia looked at Ian. 'I'll have to go,' she said. 'I'll see you again.'

She tried to keep her voice calm, but inside her heart was light as air. She, Julia Lady Coulsden, was no longer a child. Ian Cornwell had kissed her! Somehow, she thought, she must let Leo know that Ju the awkward schoolgirl had gone for ever and her place had been taken by an experienced woman named Julia.

CHAPTER SIXTEEN

Cicely stood back to take a critical look at her arrangement of dried grasses and peacock feathers which she had set in the round brass pot. She was not at all satisfied with the results, mainly because the rich colour of the container tended to overpower the muted colours of grass and thistles, although the feathers had enough green and blue in them to withstand the comparison. She sighed, wishing she had used the copper vase instead, but then it would have been necessary to alter the outline and that would detract from the feathers Mrs Hook-Brayne had so generously given her.

At the thought of Mrs Hook-Brayne Cicely felt a warm glow of triumph. She could now – thanks to the flower-arranging class – count among her friends a woman with a hyphenated surname whose husband worked somewhere in the City. Cicely didn't like to ask Mrs Hook-Brayne point-blank exactly what he did in London, so she assumed he was a stockbroker. When the last committee meeting had been held in Mrs Hook-Brayne's home on Rye Hill, Cicely had admired the peacock feathers used in one of her floral arrangements and this morning Mrs Hook-Brayne had called on her way to Winchelsea to make her a present of five such feathers. True, they were not quite as large or as fine as Mrs Hook-Brayne's own, but Cicely understood the need for her friend to retain superiority in the matter and was genuinely grateful not only for the feathers, but for the thought behind the gift.

Yes, the brass colour was wrong, but it was too late now. She had neither the time nor inclination to start all over again. And why bother anyway, she thought resignedly. Jack would not recognise a successful floral arrangement if it fell on him from a great height! He was a peasant where flowers were concerned. If only Winifred were still at home, she at least would have commented kindly on the outcome of her mother's efforts, but Winifred was tied down with a houseful of children. Cicely shook her head at the speed with which her daughter's family was growing.

Producing them just like rabbits, she considered. Didn't the silly girl know anything about the new ideas on limiting a family? Cicely had tried more than once to drop a hint or two, but Winifred had only said, 'The more the merrier!' Was she quite mad? They had no money except Ernie's share of the catch and although that was reasonable for a man of his age with a *small* family, it was *not* enough for a man with a family growing as quickly as theirs. She wondered why children were such a worry long after they ought to be off one's hands.

Leo was another one who gave her sleepless nights. A few days earlier she had found a letter in his room from a woman called Florence. From the tone of the letter he had obviously known her for some years and now she was telling him her marriage was over and asking him to meet her again in London. So it seemed her son had been involved with a married woman, who was now about to be divorced and was offering to resume the friendship! Cicely didn't know what to do. She could only confront him by admitting that she had read the letter, which she had found underneath his shirts in the chest of drawers. She had not yet told Jack of her discovery; she knew he would rush at the problem like a bull in a china shop and the ensuing inevitable quarrel would solve nothing and might drive Leo out. Jack, she had always maintained, did not understand their elder son because Leo was intellectual and Jack was practical. But she had delayed telling her husband about it for another reason – he would almost certainly gloat; he would say that colleges and such places bred new-fangled ideas of morality and that someone as weak as Leo would be bound to succumb to temptations. She imagined she would get very little support from her husband if she did decide to confront Leo.

Carefully, she carried the floral arrangement through into the hall and set it on the table. In the dim hallway the clash of colours was less obvious, she noted with relief. She would mention the arrangement to Mrs Hook-Brayne next time they met and she might even . . .

At that moment she heard voices and two shadows appeared against the coloured glass window of the front door. Oh no! Not Jack back already! It was barely ten o'clock and she never expected him home until lunch-time at one or one-thirty. She hurried forward to open the door, but Jack had found his key by now and it swung violently open so that she had to step back to avoid being hit in the face as he burst in followed by Ernest. Jack looked angry and Ernest was obviously flustered.

'That bloody stupid fool!' cried Jack. 'He's only broken his bloody arm, that's all! Broke his arm!'

'*And* sprained an ankle *and* cut his head open,' added Ernest. 'Seven stitches he had to have in that cut!'

'Who?' cried Cicely. 'Who's broken his arm? Not Ben? Has there been an accident?'

'No, not Ben,' said Ernest.

'Not Leo!' she screamed, a hand to her heart. 'Leo's had an accident! It's Leo, isn't it?'

'It's *not* Leo, for Christ's sake!' roared Jack. 'It's bloody Stan, that's who.'

'Broke his right arm,' repeated Ernest, 'and cut his head open as he fell.'

'Fell where? How?'

'Down the bloody stairs,' cried Jack. 'Drunk! That's how – blind drunk! Tried to get up to bed, I suppose, and fell backwards down the stairs. It's a wonder he didn't break his bloody neck – and serve him right if he had. As I said to Ernie here, what am I supposed to do? I haven't got time to play nursemaid. How long's it going to take to get his arm right? It could be months. I could kill him, I don't mind telling you. *He* gets blind drunk and *we're* supposed to rush round and pick up the bloody pieces!'

Cicely decided not to remind him that she disliked swearing in the house and had frequently asked him to keep his bad language for the boatyard, where presumably it was appreciated. It took a further five minutes before she had the complete picture of what had happened. It seemed that Stanley had spent the evening on a gigantic 'pub crawl' with a few other fishermen. He had returned home very much the worse for drink (almost paralytic, according to an eyewitness) and his friends had left him being sick over the front step. The rest was a matter of inspired guesswork, since Stanley could remember nothing at all after his ninth pint of strong beer.

'I found him at the foot of the stairs next morning,' Ernest told Cicely. 'At first I thought he was dead – he wasn't moving, hardly breathing. His arm was all bent and there was dried blood all around his head. I rushed round to the nearest doctor but he was out and his wife said to get him up to the hospital, so we put him on one of the fish-carts and me and a few mates pushed him up the hill. They said at the hospital he'd got concussion and was unconscious. Well, we know he was that!'

'When was all this?' asked Cicely, wondering if any of the sordid details would ever reach the ears of Mrs Hook-Brayne and deciding that, if they did, she would never forgive Stanley.

'Day before yesterday,' said Ernest. 'Then I had to hang about at the hospital most of yesterday while they were fixing him up, and then in the evening they let him out. I had to take him back to his place because we've got no spare room – not even a bed. Winifred went round this morning, but she's got her hands full with the kids. So I came over here to let you know.'

'In case,' said Jack sarcastically, 'we have any bright ideas. Well, I've got one but I'd swing for it: I'd like to throttle the silly sod with my own bare hands!'

'Does George know?' asked Cicely.

'He's out in the bay,' her husband told her. 'I saw him go out early in the morning. And that's where Stan should be, bloody fishing, not sitting around crippled because he can't hold his beer.'

Cicely pulled herself up to her full height. 'Well, don't look at me because *I'm* not going over there,' she said firmly. 'So before anyone suggests it, the answer is "No". Let Jane look after him – she's his wife, not me.'

'But she's left him,' said Ernest. 'You know she has; that's the whole point.'

'Then she can jolly well go back to him. No, Jack, I mean it. Stan is his own worst enemy and if Jane left him it was his own stupid fault. He knew how she felt about Agnes and he was plain daft to think he could surprise her into thinking any other way. But she *is* his wife, and if anyone ought to be there looking after him, it's her. Nobody else. You'll have to go and see her, Ernest, and try to persuade her.'

Ernest shook his head vehemently. 'Oh no! Not me. I'm not good at words.'

'Winifred, then.'

'She's tried,' said Ernie. 'But Ma wouldn't listen.'

'Well, what in heaven's name *are* we to do?' exclaimed Cicely irritably. 'We've all got our own lives to lead. He's a damned nuisance; he may be your brother, Jack, but he's fast becoming a liability. How on earth can he manage with a sprained ankle and a broken arm? Can he walk? Have they given him a crutch or a walking-stick? Can he cook? What's he going to eat? Oh really, Jack, it's too bad!'

Her husband raised his eyebrows. 'Well, don't blame me, Cis, I'm only—'

'And *don't* call me Cis!' she snapped.

'Then just don't blame me,' Jack repeated. 'I'm only passing on the news – *I* didn't push him down the stairs.'

'I know!' cried Cicely, suddenly inspired. 'Let Julia ask her – she could persuade Jane if anyone could. Jane's always had a soft spot for her. Yes, that's the obvious answer. Julia can talk to her. The whole situation is too ridiculous – Jane carrying on as some glorified housekeeper at her age!'

Having persuaded Julia to visit Jane and see what she could do, Jack and Ernest took her back to Hastings in the car, where they told Stan what they proposed before setting out again.

They dropped Julia outside the wrought-iron gate in Priory Road with a flurry of last-minute advice and instructions and then drove off, promising to return in twenty minutes to collect her. Nervously, she walked up to the door and knocked. To her surprise, it was Jane herself who answered it: Jane in a plain black dress.

'Aunt Jane, I need to talk to you,' said Julia. 'Can we talk here or should I—'

'Mrs Coulsden! Who is it?'

A very overweight woman in a bright print dress had appeared at the top of the stairs.

'Mrs Coulsden! Are you deaf, woman?' she demanded. 'I asked you who it was.'

'Oh Mrs Perry, it's my niece Julia,' Jane stammered. 'She wants to talk to me.'

The woman began to walk down the stairs. 'Not another one – it's about that no-good husband of yours, I suppose?'

She reached the hallway and looked at Julia with disapproval written all over her face. 'Well, I suppose you had better come in, but I'm not at all pleased by these intrusions. I employ Mrs Coulsden to do my housework, not to gossip with members of her family.' She put up a plump, beringed hand to pat her immaculate hair.

'I'm sorry,' said Jane. 'It will only take a minute or two, I promise you. I didn't know she was coming.'

The woman pursed her lips and gave Julia another unfriendly stare. 'Very well. Five minutes, then. You had better take your niece through into the kitchen; I don't want you standing around in my hall.'

When they reached the kitchen Julia stared round at the old-fashioned decor and out-of-date equipment. It was very different from the rest of the house and it was obvious that the owner did not consider it at all necessary to waste money improving the servants' area.

'Oh, what an awful woman!' Julia whispered. 'Aunt Jane, you *can't* like working here. You just *can't*. It's so utterly depressing and she's a—'

'Ssh!' cried Jane in alarm. 'She'll hear you.'

'I'm sorry, Aunt Jane, but she's horrible. She made me feel like something the cat brought in! Is she always like that?'

Her aunt shrugged wearily. 'Some days she's a bit nicer. She suffers a lot from her digestion and—'

'She eats too much,' said Julia, 'that's why. She's enormous! Oh, it's dreadful; you can't possibly stay here. Well, I don't know what to say to you really, but they all insisted that I come. Uncle Jack and Ernie, that is. And Aunt Cicely, of course. Look, Aunt Jane, they think I should talk you into going home because Uncle Stan needs you, although I don't mean to try very hard. But do you really like it here? Honestly and truly?'

Jane stared at her, anguished, then sat down suddenly and leaned her elbows on the large scrubbed table. She hid her face in her hands and for a while said nothing.

'Aunt Jane! Say something, *please!*' begged Julia. 'She's only letting me stay five minutes, remember? Are you really happy here? If you are, then I won't interfere. But if you went because of Agnes, then I feel somehow to blame because it's my mother you were defending and that was so kind of you. Really brave. Only now that Agnes and I get along, it doesn't seem right for you to be stuck here without a home of your own.'

'I do have my own room,' said Jane. 'It's quite pleasant, not like this kitchen. It's in the attic and gets the sun in the late afternoon.'

'Well, that's nice.' Julia felt out of her depth. 'Look, all I have to say is this, and if you want to ignore it, go ahead. But Uncle Stan is miserable without you and he really needs you, not just because of his fall. He was wrong to bring Agnes to see you and Agnes was wrong to do what she did with my father. Maybe my poor mother was wrong to end her life; I don't know about that, I'm not wise enough. But you've done nothing wrong and yet you're the one who's got no home. You're working yourself to death for that horrible fat pig of a woman and you're not getting any younger.

What will happen to you when you're old, or if Mrs Thing gets tired of you? I don't see why you should be the loser in all this.'

Jane shrugged helplessly. 'I don't know,' she said, 'but I would never ask to go back, never in a million years! My pride wouldn't let me.'

'But you don't have to,' urged Julia. 'That's the whole point. If you like, you could say that fate has played into your hands. You could say you're going back only because Uncle Stan needs you. You don't have to pretend to like Agnes or forgive her or any of those things. Go back on the understanding that she never gets invited to your house again – Uncle Stan would never risk another row like that. He knows he made a mistake. You could give him another chance. It would be so much nicer for Win's children, too, if their grandparents were together. I know they miss you, and you can only see them for short periods. We all miss you. Please, Aunt Jane, will you think about it?'

There were footsteps in the passage and the door opened.

'That's seven minutes by my reckoning,' stated Mrs Perry. 'I think I've been fair, but I would now prefer it if—'

'I'm going,' Julia told her. 'I'm sorry, Aunt Jane, if I've kept you from your work.'

'That's all right,' said Jane.

Mrs Perry raised her eyebrows. 'I think it's for *me* to say if it's all right or not,' she said. 'I am your employer and it's *my* time you are wasting.'

'You gave us five minutes,' protested Julia.

'You took seven,' Mrs Perry reminded her, 'and now it's eight minutes and you are still in my kitchen, and still arguing.' She turned to Jane, her face flushed with anger. 'I don't care to be answered back by a chit of a girl in my own kitchen. Get rid of her at once.'

'No one needs to get rid of me,' said Julia coldly. 'I'm going and very glad to do so. If you must know, I'm trying to persuade my aunt—'

'*Julia!*' cried Jane. 'You'd better go.'

Mrs Perry pointed to the door. 'Get out!' she said to Julia, positively quivering with rage. 'Get out of my house, you nasty bad-mannered girl! If my husband was here you wouldn't dare to stand arguing with me like this.'

'Julia!' pleaded Jane, looking desperately from one to the other. 'Julia, please go! Mrs Perry, I'm sorry. I—'

'Don't apologise to her,' exclaimed Julia indignantly. 'She's the one without any manners. All this stupid fuss over two or three minutes of her precious time! It's pathetic! Oh, don't worry, I'm going. You can stay here and kow-tow to her if you like, but I can't think why. You stood up to Uncle Stan about Agnes and yet you let this dreadful fat woman — Yes, Mrs Perry, maybe you were right. Maybe I *am* rude and bad-mannered, but really I don't care what you think of me.'

'How dare you!' screamed Mrs Perry. 'Get out of my house this instant! Do you hear me? I don't have to put up with this rudeness from you.'

Julia wanted to hit the pink, fleshy face. 'And my aunt doesn't have to put up with you,' she shouted. 'She has a husband to go to, and a home of her own and a family.' She turned to Jane, who was white and trembling. 'They're coming back for me,' she said. 'Uncle Jack and Ernest; in about ten minutes. You could come too.'

Jane wavered. 'Perhaps I will. I think – yes, I will.' She turned to her employer. 'My niece is right,' she stammered, 'and I shouldn't be here. I don't belong here. But I'm sorry about everything and she shouldn't have been so rude, but maybe she's right.'

'You can't go,' cried Mrs Perry, aghast at the suddenness of her employee's change of heart. 'Not just like that!'

'I *can*,' said Jane. 'Yes, I'll go and pack my suitcase. Tell them to wait for me, Julia.'

As she moved towards the door, Mrs Perry called, 'You can't just walk out. I warn you – I shan't pay you for this week if you go now. Unless you stay to work out your notice, I shan't pay you a penny. I mean it!'

Jane stopped in her flight towards the stairs. 'I accept that,' she said quietly. 'I'm not prepared to work out my notice, so I forfeit my week's pay. I'm not arguing with you and I'm sorry if my leaving puts you in a spot.'

'In a spot! That's an understatement if ever I heard one. It's *very* inconvenient. *Very* inconsiderate! I thought you were a responsible person. The vicar who recommended you . . . I shall have something to say to him about this, I can tell you!' But Jane had already passed into the hall and they heard her running up the stairs.

Mrs Perry, her immediate anger subsiding, turned to Julia. 'The vicar asked me to give her a chance and assured me she was a respectable, hard-working woman.'

'She is,' said Julia. She too was rather subdued. The row, flaring so quickly and moving so decisively, had shocked her more than she realised.

'But then to throw my kindness back in my face . . .' cried Mrs Perry. 'I shall tell the Reverend Garnett exactly what I think of his respectable hard-working woman.'

'She's needed at home,' said Julia. 'It's not just you – it's her husband.'

'Oh, I've heard all about that from her daughter. Fell down the stairs, she told me. Probably drunk, I said to myself. Some people are no better than animals! I don't know what my husband is going to say when he comes home. She should have worked a week's notice; that was the agreement.'

'She has forfeited a week's wages instead,' Julia reminded her.

'That's not the point.'

'I think I'd better go,' said Julia. 'I'll wait outside.'

Mrs Perry followed her to the door and suddenly said, 'I have a glandular problem. My body absorbs a lot of fluid.'

Julia knew she was thinking about her insult. 'I'm sorry,' she said. 'I shouldn't have said that about you being fat. I lost my temper.'

Mrs Perry neither accepted nor rejected the apology. She merely held open the front door and Julia walked past her and down the steps.

'The Reverend Garnett will be hearing from me!' Mrs Perry called after her and Julia could only nod.

Uncle Jack and Ernest were waiting by the car which was parked further along the road.

'She's coming,' said Julia, somewhat subdued. 'There's been a bit of a row, but she's coming. And she's going to go back home.'

'Well, thank Christ for that!' exclaimed Jack. 'What happened exactly?'

Julia began to explain, but before she was half-way through the account Jane appeared and Ernest ran to take the bulging suitcase from her. Minutes later they were driving home and Stanley's immediate problems were over.

*

19 December 1925

It will soon be Christmas, although it's never been the same since

Mama Sarah died and we don't go to South View. We are all going to Uncle Jack's for Christmas Day (at least the Rye part of the family. Aunt J. and Uncle S. and Win's family will stay in Hastings), but on Boxing Day we shall be at our own homes – recovering, Papa says! I am the only one not looking forward to it, because Leo has asked if he can bring a young lady to stay for three days and Aunt Cicely said 'Yes'. How shall I get through the days? I feel so ill with misery. He cannot have any idea. Only Emily understands. Her name (Leo's girl friend) is Victoria. She's English, but her parents are in South Africa and she has no relatives here. She teaches at Leo's school and I now wonder how long they have been friendly without him giving the slightest hint to me. When I asked him about her, he said, 'Green-eyed monster' and I know that's true, but I can't help it. I've waited so long to be old enough for him and now that I nearly am (anyway, Ian kissed me) he finds this awful Victoria person. He calls her Vicky. I simply don't want to see her or speak to her. I'm afraid I'll pull her hair or scratch her eyes out and make a fool of myself. If only Aunt Cicely knew what she has done to me by saying 'Yes', she would never forgive herself, I know. I've knitted him a scarf, but now I don't know whether to give it to him or not. *Oh Leo*, I thought you were beginning to *love* me? Perhaps you do. Perhaps she is not special to you. I wish I knew.

VICKY. I don't know her other name and I don't want to.

I went to dinner at South View last night, but had to cycle because no Ian. It was a nice evening, just the two of us. She showed me photographs of Ian and his parents and talked about him a lot. They seem a very devoted family – not like us, always squabbling. I wish I could invite Ian to come for Christmas to make Leo *jealous*. But would it? I mentioned that Ian kissed me and all he said was, 'Good, isn't it?' sometimes I think I hate Leo, but mostly I know I love him. Perhaps if Aunt Cicely knew I loved her son she would find an excuse not to have Vicky over, but I don't dare tell her.

Uncle Stan's ankle is better, but his arm has not healed up properly. He also has a bald patch where they shaved his head to put in the stitches, but the hair is growing in now and Aunt Jane seems glad to be at home again. People are funny. *Oh Leo, I love you.* Perhaps I should write him a letter, but he might show it to other people. Emily is so happy because Ben is taking notice of her at last. I think he realises now that I am Leo's for ever. They went to the cinema and he paid for her ticket and bought her some chocolates. We cycled out (me and Em) to Winchelsea Beach to see the cottage where she lived with Agnes before Papa married her. It is derelict and she went all gloomy and tried to cry, but I knew she was only putting it on for my benefit.

A new boat was launched last week, with all the usual fuss. I wore my new grey and white dress with my white shoes, but I wasn't in the newspaper photograph. I asked Uncle Jack if I could christen the boat, but the new owner's wife wanted to do it so I couldn't, but I'm sure I could have made a better speech. She kept saying Um and Er. I shall make a point of sitting at the opposite end of the table to Vicky at Christmas. Leo can't expect me to be nice to her even if it is the season of goodwill. I don't think I will give Leo the scarf. It won't be appreciated. Perhaps I should give it to Frank Bligh. They are always hard-up. I could mention that I had given Frank a present when Leo was around. *Leo, I hate you.* (I don't really, but it would be easier if I could. Hating a person seems easier than loving them. I wonder why.)

*

Christmas Day was a great success. Everyone was agreed on that, even Julia, who – much to her surprise – had found Vicky extremely good company. The newcomer, a tall gawky girl, was not as pretty as Julia had feared, but she was certainly not plain. It seemed to Julia that Vicky's feeling for Leo was stronger than his for her. He treated her almost as a sister, occasionally tugging her soft brown hair, pretending to step on her rather large feet and generally teasing her in a boyish way. Julia had expected them to behave as if they were in love, or about to fall in love, which they most certainly did not. Once or twice Julia fancied that Vicky's eyes were on him when the limelight was on somebody else, but on these few occasions she felt an unexpected sympathy with her, as though the fact that they both admired Leo created a bond between them.

On Christmas morning Julia and Emily helped Cicely prepare the large quantities of food required and then when Agnes and George arrived just before one o'clock, everyone had a sherry. After this Cicely escaped into the kitchen to finish supervising the lunch.

Julia and Emily had great fun pretending to be waitresses, wearing frilly paper aprons and caps, then they all sat down to enjoy the traditional Christmas turkey with all the trimmings, followed by plum pudding with brandy sauce and mince pies. Leo, Emily and Jack found sixpences in the pudding and Ben pretended to swallow one, coughing and spluttering to great effect.

Mottoes and jokes were exchanged and then Vicky offered to read everyone's palm, inventing hilarious futures for all of them. The daylight was beginning to fade when at last lunch was over and volunteers were called for to assist with the washing-up. The waitresses were excused this ordeal because Cicely said they had done their share, so the two girls went into the front room and tried to play the piano.

By the time the washing-up was completed and the crockery and cutlery put away, it was too dark to go for a walk. Jack and George settled themselves in the dining-room with a small keg of beer and a store of reminiscences, while the women and children crowded into the front room to play the usual games and sing all their favourite songs. Julia was feeling uncomfortably full and slightly light-headed from the sherry, but at seven o'clock cold beef sandwiches appeared on the dining-room table, alongside a whole home-cured ham, bread and butter and pickles and a beautiful Christmas cake covered with nuts and cherries. The men dragged themselves away from the beer and eating began all over again.

Just before midnight, George, Agnes and Emily walked home. Only Julia remained, as she felt too ill to do more than stagger up the stairs to the second spare bedroom which was filled with lumber but still boasted a single bed. Cicely quickly made it up for her and Vicky offered one of her two pillows. Julia, unprepared for an overnight stay, fell asleep wearing only her slip and it was long after midnight when she woke. Her stomach rumbled ominously and she sat up feeling queasy and frightened. She hated bilious attacks. It rarely happened that her digestive system rebelled, so she was never prepared for the discomfort of retching or the upward rush of sour, half-digested food. When at last she acknowledged to herself that she *was* going to be sick, she rushed along the dim passage and into the bathroom with a hand held to her mouth. Within seconds she was crouching over the lavatory pan, heaving and moaning, while a fine, cold perspiration broke out on her skin.

'Oh, poor Julia!'

It was Vicky who stood beside her. Julia groaned and the other girl put a reassuring arm across her shoulders; then she found and washed out a toothbrush tumbler and filled it with clean water. After Julia had rinsed out her mouth, Vicky helped her back to the spare room where she sat on the side of her bed shivering.

'Pop back between the sheets,' Vicky advised. 'You don't want to catch cold.'

'I feel terrible,' whispered Julia. 'Why was I such a pig? It was that plum pudding. I had three helpings. *Three!* It serves me right!' She allowed herself to be coaxed back into bed, but sat up with her arms clasped around her knees.

'Shall I stay for a while?' Vicky asked. 'You look as though you need some company.'

Julia nodded gratefully, beginning to recover from the shock of being taken ill. The rest of the house remained silent, so she guessed she had not disturbed anyone else. She wiped her forehead with the sheet and smiled faintly. 'It was good of you to come and see if I was all right. I'm sorry if I woke you up but I had to run. It was urgent!'

'I wasn't asleep,' said Vicky. 'Just lying awake, thinking.'

'About Leo?'

'Yes.'

'He's my favourite cousin,' Julia said cautiously. 'He's nice, isn't he?'

Surprisingly, Vicky hesitated before agreeing.

'You do like him, don't you?' Julia persisted. 'I thought you and he were . . . well, I thought you were his girl friend. Aren't you?'

Vicky lowered her eyes hastily, but not before Julia saw what she thought was pain.

'I'm very fond of him,' she told Julia, 'but that's not the same thing at all. I don't think he feels much for me.'

'Have you asked him?'

Vicky shook her head. 'I don't need to,' she said, 'because I know he only looks on me as one of his colleagues – someone he gets along with well, but that's all. At one time I must admit, he did seem quite keen, but more recently he changed towards me and won't talk about it, except to say it's better if we remain "just friends".'

Julia expected to feel a glow of triumph that this outsider was not going to try to take Leo from her; instead she felt nothing but sympathy.

Vicky went on, 'He won't say why, but he has changed – I can feel it. He hasn't kissed me – not even today, though he had plenty of chances when it wouldn't have seemed out of place with all this mistletoe around and the Christmas spirit. But let's talk about you. Have *you* got a young man? I'm sure you must have!'

Julia heard herself say, 'I've always loved Leo, but I think I'm just a cousin to him.'

'He's very attractive to women. That's the whole trouble.'

'Is it? Why is that bad?'

'It's not bad exactly, but it's so easy for him to make a woman fall in love with him. At least, that's how I see it, but I may be wrong.'

Julia leaned back against the pillow and stared up at the ceiling. 'No, you're not wrong,' she said at last. 'I think that's exactly it. I've loved him ever since I was too young to hide it from him. I thought when I was young that all I had to do was tell him I loved him and he'd be pleased and love me back.'

Vicky laughed softly. 'That's much too simple,' she said. 'People and their emotions are very complicated.'

'Do you love him?' Julia asked. 'Would you marry him if he asked you?'

'Oh yes, I think I would but he won't ask me. And if I married him I don't think we'd be happy together – not for long. It would be so one-sided. Would you marry him, Julia?'

'I'm his cousin,' she said, 'but I would if I could. I didn't think about marriage at the beginning – just about being loved. Not in bed, I don't mean that,' she added hastily. 'I mean knowing he thought so highly of me that he'd die for me if necessary. Not that I wanted him to die, of course I didn't, but just to know he would because he loved me more than anything else in the world.'

'We're so foolish,' said Vicky with a rueful smile. 'We wear our hearts on our sleeves and we should learn not to do that. Mind you, I don't think it would make much difference to Leo.' She laughed. 'Just imagine, he's only a few yards away at the end of the passage. How flattered he would be if he could see us earnestly discussing him! I'm afraid, though, that Leo is not the marrying kind.'

Julia was surprised. 'Isn't he? Really?'

'I don't think so. Time will tell of course, but I don't think love is very important in his life. He's a very good teacher, but he also has charm – that's one of the ingredients of success and Leo is well aware of it. But I'm not saying any of this to detract from him. I love him – there, I've said it and I didn't mean to – but I love him the way he *is*. I don't pretend to myself that one day he'll marry me and we'll settle down and have a family, because I don't think Leo wants that at all. I wish he did, but then he wouldn't be the same

Leo and I think his independent spirit is one of the things I find most attractive.'

Vicky had grown serious throughout her little speech and now, seeing Julia's expression, she forced a light laugh. 'Don't look so downcast, I'm not infallible. I may be quite wrong about him.'

'I don't know,' said Julia slowly. 'He had another girl friend once—'

'He's had lots of girl friends!'

'Oh, has he? I thought there was ...' She hesitated, torn between her promise to Leo and the desire to share her knowledge of him. 'There was someone in his life—'

'Oh, you mean the wife of one of his tutors. Florence, her name was.'

Julia gasped. 'You know! He told you?'

'Was it supposed to be a secret?' asked Vicky.

Julia swallowed, her heart heavy. She felt suddenly dull and uninspired. All those shared intimacies that she had valued so highly as proof of their closeness had obviously meant nothing to Leo.

Vicky was looking at her. 'Julia? Have I upset you? I could kick myself! I really didn't mean it to come out like that. I had no idea ...' She gave a despairing shake of the head. 'Honestly, Julia, I *am* sorry. I'm so wrapped up in my own heartache I didn't give enough thought to yours.'

'It doesn't matter,' said Julia with a sigh.

'But of course it matters. Life's hard enough and loving people is the hardest part of it. Also the best part, of course, when it's mutual.'

'I can't imagine ever loving anyone else,' Julia told her. 'He's been in my life as long as I can remember.'

'Strange, isn't it, that we both adore Leo and yet Ben is probably worth two of his brother?'

'*Ben?*'

'He's very genuine, don't you think, and deep.'

'Is he? I've never thought about him much except that he's good fun. Emily's crazy about him though and he takes her to the pictures sometimes.'

'She's probably wiser than you or me,' said Vicky. 'But I shouldn't keep you talking – you've been sick and you ought to be asleep now.'

Julia nodded and slid down into the bed. Vicky tucked her in and said, 'Good night' and as she turned away Julia put out a restraining hand.

'Vicky, thank you for being so kind,' she said. 'I was all set to hate you, but I'm glad I don't.'

'Because of Leo, you mean? I think we're both in the same boat.'

'What will we do without him?'

Vicky hesitated. 'What does anyone do? I suppose we suffer and then recover and get on with the rest of our lives.'

'You make it sound quite easy,' Julia protested.

'I don't really want to think about it,' admitted Vicky. 'Try to get back to sleep now. Everything looks worse at night, you know, and tomorrow we shall feel happier.'

'Good night, Vicky.'

'Good night.'

Julia dozed and woke and dozed again. It felt strange to be sleeping alone, without Emily tossing restlessly in the next bed. It was so quiet that small sounds carried from outside – an owl hooting, a dog barking, tree branches creaking and occasional footsteps or sounds of traffic on the road. Between dozing she tried to convince herself that Vicky's assessment of Leo was wrong and that *she* was a better judge of his character. She had wondered earlier about their relationship and had tortured herself with visions of him creeping along the passage to Vicky's room. But now she knew that Vicky was not Leo's girl friend and the thought gave her some comfort. And yet, she argued, if Leo was not going to marry *her* because she was his cousin, she hoped he would marry Vicky – so long as that would make them both happy. She felt wise beyond her years and generous to a fault. Tomorrow night she would tell Emily that she was going to give up Leo and the way would be clear for Vicky. She rather liked the unselfish role in which she had cast herself and fell asleep feeling almost happy.

*

Next morning, at ten o'clock, they were finishing a belated breakfast of eggs and bacon, the Boxing Day treat they had eaten for as long as Julia could remember. She did not feel up to eating much, her appetite impaired by the previous day's excesses, but Vicky was her usual bright self. Ben was also in high spirits, but Jack had a hangover and could only manage toast and marmalade. Leo, always a late riser, was still asleep as Cicely had insisted they allow him to wake in his own time. Cicely was just saying that she thought the previous day had gone very well when there was a knock at the front door.

'See who it is, Ben,' she asked. 'I expect it's someone for your father. People have no consideration,' she went on as Ben pushed back his chair. 'They think that if you own a boatyard you're at everyone's beck and call twenty-four hours a day. I remember someone came round on the morning of Hettie's funeral – someone who knew! – and wanted a repair done *then* and *there*. I couldn't credit it was happening. "It will only take an hour or two," he said, "and it's urgent." "I don't care how urgent it is," I said. "We've a death in the family and I'll thank you to show some respect." It's really incredible how inconsiderate . . . who was it, Ben?'

He stood in the doorway looking rather awkward. 'It's someone for Leo – a woman.'

'For Leo?' Cicely half rose in her chair, then sat down again. 'Well, don't leave her in the hall, Ben, bring her in. And give Leo a call.'

'She won't come in,' he told her. 'I have asked her, but she's standing on the doorstep.'

'Oh. Do we know her?'

'I don't.'

Cicely paled suddenly. She stood up and threw her napkin on to the table. 'I'll see her,' she said. 'You carry on with your breakfast.'

'I'll call Leo,' said Ben.

'No!' cried Cicely. 'Not yet! You finish your breakfast, Ben.'

He stared at her. 'I have finished it.'

Everyone was staring at Cicely who, despite her apprehension, was trying to appear calm.

'Eat something else then,' she snapped and went out of the room, closing the door firmly behind her.

The woman who stood on the doorstep was pale and obviously agitated. Her smooth dark hair framed a beautiful face with a sweetly curving mouth and large grey eyes under long dark lashes. She was slimly built and dressed fashionably, but with good taste. Cicely noted a good complexion heightened by a small mole high up on her left cheekbone. Leo was a good judge of women, she thought incongruously, and judged her to be in her thirties.

'I'm sorry to trouble you,' the woman began in a low voice, 'and I know it's early – and Boxing Day – but I simply must see him.'

Cicely's heart sank. Oh Leo, what have you done?

'I'm afraid he's sleeping late,' she said. 'We're just finishing our breakfast. Have you eaten yet?'

'Eaten?'

'Have you had any breakfast? Would you care to join—'

'Oh no! No, thank you. I don't want to be any trouble. I just want to see him. I just . . .' She swallowed hard and Cicely caught a glint of tears.

'Come in and wait and I'll wake him,' she suggested, but the woman shook her head fiercely.

'No, I can't,' she said. 'I promised I wouldn't.'

'Promised you wouldn't what?'

'Wouldn't come to the house,' she whispered. 'But it doesn't matter – I'll wait just here, but do *please* tell him.'

'Well!' Cicely was both affronted and afraid. 'If you insist. What name shall I say?' She knew it, of course, she thought wearily. This was undoubtedly Florence, the letter writer.

'Just say that Florence Parker would like to see him.'

'Very well.'

Cicely went upstairs with a sense of dread. 'Boxing Day, nineteen-twenty-five,' she muttered sardonically. 'Wonderful!' Now the whole holiday would be ruined and all her hard work to no purpose. Florence Parker! Where on earth had she sprung from at such a time? And why did she need to see Leo so urgently? 'Don't let her be with child,' she prayed. 'Just don't let her be with child. I can stand anything but that.'

Knocking on Leo's door, she went in without waiting for an answer. He lay on his back, fast asleep with one hand dangling over the side of the bed, his long fingers just touching the bedside rug. She stood for a moment looking down at the handsome face, so young and carefree in sleep. Soon that peace would be shattered, she thought regretfully, and he would open his eyes to all his problems. 'Oh Leo. You fool!' she whispered, then bent down to shake him gently. He was always a heavy sleeper, even as a boy. She remembered trying to wake him on a cold winter's morning. He was late for school so many times and poor Ben, the loyal younger brother, had waited for him and been late also and had shared the punishments without complaint.

'Leo! Wake up! There's someone to see you – a young lady.'

He opened his eyes, smiled and rolled over and Cicely shook him again.

'Leo! Wake up, I said. There's a visitor for you.'

'I'm not seeing anyone,' he mumbled. 'I've gone away.'

'Leo! This is serious. For heaven's sake, Leo! Florence Parker is on the doorstep and not looking at all happy.'

'*What!*' He sat up abruptly and stared wildly at his mother. 'Florence? Here? Oh hell! How could she? On the doorstep?'

'She refused to come in – says she promised not to. What's going on, Leo?'

'Nothing,' he snapped, wide awake. 'She's no right to come here.' He threw back the bedclothes. 'Where's my dressing-gown, dammit?'

'Leo? You can't go down in your dressing-gown.'

'I can and I will. Look, leave me to it, will you, there's a dear.'

'No, Leo!' cried Cicely. 'I will *not* leave you to it. I want to know what's going on. Who is she? I think I'm entitled to know. Stop rushing about like a mad thing and – Leo! Come back here!'

But he had rushed out of the room, slamming the door behind him.

Florence heard footsteps and turned as the door swung open once more.

'Leo!' she gasped. 'Oh my darling, don't be angry. I had to see you; I couldn't bear it.'

He stood two steps above her looking down and she thought she would die with love for him. He wore a dark blue woollen dressing-gown and held the collar close around his neck to keep out the December air.

'Of course I'm angry,' he hissed. 'What the hell do you mean by coming here – after all I've said?' He looked anxiously around to see if they were being observed. A family on the way to church eyed them curiously as they walked past on the opposite side of the road.

'Aren't you going to invite me in now I'm here?' she asked him, her eyes pleading. 'I *must* talk to you, Leo.'

'Oh God, Florence, I could kill you for this!' was the ungracious reply as he ran his fingers through his hair and tried to collect his wits. He was never at his best first thing in the morning; his brain seemed to work less efficiently.

Florence stood mute, waiting for his answer. She looked cold and tired, he thought with a rush of compassion, but then he hardened his heart. He had told her never to come to his home. He had promised to see her again in London and had fully intended to do so.

'I waited for your letter,' she began. 'You didn't write, Leo. You knew how much it meant to me, but still you didn't write. I didn't know what to think.'

'I'm sorry,' he replied. 'I'm a swine, I know. You keep telling me.'

'I don't mean to,' she said, 'but you have to admit your behaviour—'

'No, I don't!' he answered sharply. 'I don't have to admit anything. And you're hardly in a position to tell me how to behave. You turn up uninvited on Boxing Day and embarrass me in front of my family.'

'But I have to speak to you,' she repeated. 'Just talk to me, here and now, if I'm not allowed into your home. Oh Leo, why are you like this? You make me feel as though I'm pestering you.'

'Your words, not mine,' he commented. 'Oh, this is impossible! I suppose you'll have to come inside. Now, don't start an argument. You've put me on the spot and you know it. My mother will be out again if we stand here like this, Florence. For God's sake, are you coming in or not?'

He held open the door and she stepped inside. Then he led her into the morning room and pointed to a chair. She shook her head, but he snapped, 'Oh sit down, for heaven's sake! Look, Flo, I'm sorry if I was short with you but I've only just woken up. How would you feel if I'd landed on *your* doorstep?' He thrust his hands into his pockets and then, looking down, noticed that his feet were bare. 'I shall catch pneumonia,' he said. 'I'll have to go and dress.'

She half rose from the chair. 'Oh, don't go, Leo!'

'I shan't be gone long and no one's going to bite you. If anyone comes in, just say, "Good morning" and, "Yes, I'd like a cup of tea". It's quite simple!'

'There's no need to be sarcastic,' she answered. 'You're making this so hard for me. If only you'd written – if you'd only kept your promise – I wouldn't have come.'

'Oh, so it's all my fault?'

'Well, isn't it, Leo?'

He turned on his heel without replying. As he went out of the room, she heard him speak to someone and then a young girl came in.

'I'm Julia,' she said. 'Leo says to ask if you would like a cup of tea or anything?'

'I would, yes. Thank you.'

The girl's brief smile had held no warmth and Florence thought wearily, 'They will all hate me, but I don't care. If it's the price I pay for Leo . . .'

She looked round at the room, which was well-furnished and decorated with holly and a Christmas tree. The signs of yesterday's revelry were everywhere – nutshells, wrapping-paper and string, a box of figs still unopened and a pile of pencils. Parlour games, she thought wistfully. Those family Christmases seemed a long time ago. Closing her eyes, she whispered, 'Leo, *please*. Don't turn me down!' She opened them again and forced herself to concentrate on the room rather than on the situation in which she found herself. Her gaze took in the wide chairs upholstered in dark blue velvet and the gleaming mahogany table. There were pictures on the wall and an arrangement of dried flowers and peacock feathers. 'They will hate me,' she murmured, 'but nothing matters.'

Julia came in again, handed her a cup of tea and offered the sugar bowl. Florence took two spoonsful and nodded her thanks, not trusting herself to speak as the girl went out. Julia. The name seemed familiar . . . one of his cousins. The tea was stronger than she liked, but she sipped it gratefully while her thoughts strayed back.

Leo had come into her life quite inauspiciously, appearing at one of her husband's evening 'get-togethers' for the students on his course. She had been impressed by his undeniable good looks and his cool manner. For one so young he had enormous confidence where women were concerned, and she was surprised and flattered when he began to seek her out at the various college events which they both happened to attend. Three months later, she was dismayed to find herself falling hopelessly in love with him and surprised when he insisted that he returned her feelings. He urged her constantly to tell her husband how they felt about each other but she resisted as long as she could, aware of the difference in their ages and certain the relationship could not last. By the time he left the college, he had persuaded her to ask for a divorce and her husband had finally agreed to bring proceedings. She took a room in London which Leo found and where he promised to join her, but in fact he had only visited her there on one occasion. Now, finding herself in this impossible situation, she had decided to take matters into her own hands. She sighed tremulously, aware how dreary the affair would sound to an outsider who could never know the extent of her love for Leo. His shabby treatment of her she generously attributed to his youth. Her distraught family had called her a fool and worse, but had said they would stand by her. Now it was up to Leo . . .

Before Florence had finished her tea he was back wearing grey flannels and a tartan pullover over a white shirt. His hair was uncombed, his face unwashed and he looked so young and vulnerable that her heart went out to him and she felt only compassion for him. But she would make it all up to him, she vowed. They would forget this unfortunate beginning and be so happy! She put down the cup and saucer and stood up.

'My uncle wants to offer you a job,' she blurted out. 'It's in Wiltshire. He owns a fairly large prep school for boys and he's looking for a new master for the summer term. He'll pay you ten pounds a year more than you're getting now.'

Leo was thunderstruck. This was the last thing he had expected and he stared at her as his mind whirled.

'I didn't know you had an uncle,' he said. 'On your mother's side, is he?'

'Does it matter?'

'No. Look, Flo, you don't have to stand up.'

'I would rather.' She tried to read what he was thinking. He was surprised obviously, but was he *pleasantly* surprised? She rushed on, 'Ten pounds isn't a great deal, but next year it will be another ten and then if a vacancy for a house master comes up – I mean, *when* it comes up – he will give you first consideration.'

'Will he now?' Leo stared at her and she saw a gleam in his eyes. 'I must say that's awfully decent of him. What a jolly old uncle he is!'

She felt her face burn and bit back a sharp retort to the sarcasm which she knew by now was a defensive mechanism. He felt threatened and she understood that.

'Uncle Edward will want you to apply in the usual way,' she said, 'and he'll send you an application form, but if you apply you will definitely get the job.'

'I see.'

Florence waited breathlessly; it was a marvellous opportunity and he knew it.

Leo picked up a piece of wrapping paper, screwed it into a ball and threw it into the hearth. 'There has to be a catch, Flo,' he said carefully. 'What is it?'

She tried to answer him but fear robbed her of breath and she felt a choking sensation in her throat. After a struggle she managed to say, 'I want you to marry me, Leo. I love you and I want us to be happy together, the way we planned.'

Abruptly she sat down in the chair she had vacated moments earlier. There was a dark mist in front of her eyes and she thought she was going to faint. 'That's all I want, Leo,' she told him, 'for us to be happy. My uncle and my parents – they are all willing to help us and it would be a wonderful chance to make a fresh start.'

'Are you all right?' he asked. 'Do you feel ill or something?'

'No, I'm fine. Really I am.' She stood up and went over to him, taking his hands in hers. 'You know how I feel about you, Leo. I love you so much it hurts me and I swear I'll make you happy. It will work out for us. No one will know us in Wiltshire. No one will know about the divorce. You can't let me down now, Leo. It's all been so awful – the divorce proceedings and everything – it was all so ugly and I was so alone. You can never know what I've been through, but it was all for you. You told me to do it and I did. Now this is our chance, Leo.'

He made no answer as she lifted his hands and kissed them, then looked up into his eyes hoping for a spark of kindness, for anything except this prolonged silence. But he was staring over her head, his face expressionless.

'Leo! For pity's sake, answer me!' she begged. 'Can't you imagine how I feel, having to come here like this and *beg* you to marry me? All I want is for us to be happy.'

'I need time—' he began.

'No!' she shouted, dropping his hands as though they hurt her. 'No more shilly-shallying! I have come for your answer, Leo, and I must have it now. You didn't join me in London – you promised to, but you didn't come so I've had to come to you. I don't despise myself because I love you and I'm not ashamed to tell you that I do or that I want to make you happy. We can get married and you can start the new job.' She clutched his hands again. 'You might well be a house master within three years, Leo! One of the present staff is due to retire four years from now, but his health is unlikely to last and my uncle is sure the vacancy will come up in three years' time. You could wait for ever, Leo, and not get a chance like this again!'

Suddenly she knew, with a surge of hope, that he was seriously considering what she was saying and had stopped being angry with her for her unwelcome appearance at his home. One step forward, she told herself. One step at a time.

Leo nodded. 'It would be good,' he said. 'House master before I'm thirty. Good God!'

He laughed delightedly and she held her breath. 'Well, I never!' he exclaimed. His tone had softened, there was a hint of eagerness and his eyes shone with excitement. 'Fancy old uncle turning up trumps!'

'I'm the catch, remember?' she said shakily, taking the risk.

'A very beautiful catch.' The words came easily with his practised charm.

Florence knew it was charm; she also knew he was almost certainly going to take the bait. The job was the bait and she would not . . . *could* not pretend otherwise, but she was beyond caring. All she wanted was Leo. She wanted him to marry her for love, but that would never happen because he did not love her enough and would never love any woman enough. But Florence convinced herself she had enough love for them both. 'Say yes, Leo,' she prayed, 'and then we can start to make plans.'

'Three rungs up the ladder in one step!' he cried. 'It sounds too good to be true!'

'But it is true,' she said. 'Tell me you'll take it, Leo.'

'I'll take it,' he said. 'By God, I will! And I get a beautiful wife as well? What a bonus!'

Suddenly, with growing enthusiasm, he lifted her off the ground and kissed her. 'My God! It's all happening so fast!' he exclaimed. 'Wiltshire – what's Wiltshire like?'

'Beautiful,' she said. 'Like you, Leo!'

He kissed her again. 'And your uncle? What's the old boy like?'

'He has no children of his own,' she told him slyly.

'Better and better!'

She marvelled at the transformation, although she knew him capable of such sudden swings of mood. Leo was young, selfish, shallow and ambitious, but she didn't care what his faults were. She had known him a long time and she loved him in spite of his faults.

'Tell me you love me,' she whispered.

'I love you, my funny Florence. Of course I love you!'

'Are you going to propose?' She tried to sound casual and amused, but she wanted desperately to hear the words.

'Am I going to propose?' he laughed. 'I suppose I'd better.' He held out his arms. 'Florence Parker, will you be my ever-loving wife, to love and to cherish and all the rest of it?'

'I will!'

He hugged her again and then, releasing her, cried, 'We'll tell them now! Would you like that?'

'Oh Leo, I don't know . . .' she stammered. 'Do we have to? Right now?'

'Right now! Why not? While they're still chomping away at their toast and marmalade. Come on. No, come *on*, Flo. We'll tell them now before I change my mind.'

Everyone at the dining-table looked up in alarm as the door burst open and Leo appeared, dragging Florence behind him. He shut his eyes and said loudly, 'I thought you'd like to know that Florence and I are going to be married!'

*

28 December 1925

Leo and Florence are getting married a week today. I thought I would die when he told us and Vicky was also upset. I had to take her back to Hilders Cliff with me to get her out of the house and we all three went for a walk and talked about it (Emily as well) and at least *I* am sort of reconciled. I think in my heart I knew he would never be mine. Poor Vicky went back to Hastings later in the day. I don't think she was really reconciled, but after she had gone I wrote to her and tried to explain that there will be other men in her life (and mine, I hope) and that time will heal the scar. What a terrible end to the year. Poor Em was so mad that she had missed all the excitement (well, most of it).

They are going to live in Wiltshire, so I shan't see him very often. They can't marry in church, so have to go to a Register Office. Poor Leo! Aunt Cicely and Uncle Jack were furious at first and said she was too old for him and that a divorced woman was a scandal in the family, but now they pretend to be pleased. Ben is not very happy, but Em thinks he's jealous of all the attention Leo is getting and Florence is very beautiful. The more I think about Leo, the less I admire him for what he must have done and that makes it easier for me. I'm sorry for Florence, although she seems very happy, but when she's forty Leo will only be twenty-nine!

This morning Agnes had a bad turn. She couldn't stop coughing and there was blood on her handkerchief. Papa wants her to go to the doctor, but she always says it is just bronchitis and she used to have it as a girl. I don't think I believe her, but she's a grown woman and there's nothing much I can do.

Chick Bird keeps hanging around the house and he pushed a note to Emily through the letter-box, but Papa found it and tore it up so we don't know what it said – Em is furious with him (Papa, not Chick). Papa said he doesn't want Emily having anything to do with Eunice's son because she's a thief, but I think he's got a guilty conscience. So does Em.

Ian is coming down to South View for the New Year and I'm invited to stay the night and see in the New Year. At first Papa said 'No', but Agnes made him change his mind. I wonder, if she had not fallen in love with Papa, if Agnes and my mother could ever have been friends? I have to believe so.

I shall wear my new dress to South View. Ian is talking about going to Australia. Poor Helen will miss him if he does.

I wonder if Leo and Florence will be happy together? I have to hope so for Leo's sake. She *is* old compared with him, but sometimes it can work out.

I'm going to find a job to help take my mind off Leo. Anyway, I am bored at home and Em is leaving school at Easter and I don't want her to find a job before me. Papa likes to pretend it isn't necessary, but Agnes drops large hints all the time about the idle rich and anyway I do so much work in the house I might as well be working for wages. Mrs Mack knows someone who runs a guest house and she is going to ask if they need any help. Also Uncle Jack wants someone to do the books at the boatyard, but Papa is not keen on the idea and anyway arithmetic is not my best subject. Still, I ought to be grateful for the chance with so many people out of work. I suppose I *am* grateful I don't have to scrub floors or work in a factory. Agnes says I don't know what hard work is and goes on about when she worked on the nets as though it was something to boast about. Why do people go on about the past? I could learn to type and work in an office, but it sounds boring. I must do something. I suggested joining the crew of *Silver Lady* but it was only a joke. They don't allow women on the boats. I wonder what 1926 will bring to all of us. Something good I hope. Must stop now. It's nearly midnight and Em is grumbling about the light because she can't get to sleep. I wonder what was in that note from Chick? Shall ask him if I see him again.

CHAPTER SEVENTEEN

Leo's wedding to Florence came and went and the family settled down once more into their normal routine, but their peaceful existence was shortly to be disturbed by none other than Chick Bird.

On the night of March 22, Chick made his way through the deserted streets, his hands thrust deep into his pockets and his cap set on his head at a jaunty angle. His boots clattered on the pavement and he whistled nervously and tunelessly under his breath. When he was within a hundred yards of the Coulsdens' house he stopped whistling and placed his feet less noisily. It was eleven o'clock and he judged it likely that by this time the girls should be in bed. With any luck the parents would also have retired, for the tide was an early one and George Coulsden would have to be up at first light.

When Chick reached the house he glanced up and down the road to make sure he was unobserved, then felt in his pocket for one of the small pebbles he had brought and tossed it with unerring aim at the window of the girls' bedroom. Grinning, he imagined their startled reaction and allowed a moment or two for them to wake in alarm and whisper together before following the first pebble with a second one. Two more pebbles were needed before a pale oval appeared at the window and then disappeared again.

'Oh come on!' he muttered impatiently. 'Are you deaf or something?'

Two faces now appeared and were again withdrawn.

'Christ Almighty!' he muttered, deliberately selecting the largest pebble. Let them think he'd break the glass, he reasoned as he threw it with greater force than before.

The window opened abruptly. 'Stop that, d'you hear?'

He recognised Julia Coulsden by her pale hair. To them he was only a silhouette, for he had placed himself in front of the flaring gas-light.

'Is that you, Chick Bird?' hissed Julia. 'Because if so you're to go away and stop pestering or I'll wake my father and he'll be down there like a shot and then you'll know it!'

Chick was delighted to learn that George Coulsden was asleep and suspected that Julia had intended him to know. He was just fourteen, but in the last two years he had grown heavier, and physically he had crossed the road into manhood. At five foot seven he would grow no taller, but already his body had developed a more adult way of moving and he favoured the slightly swaggering gait of some of the older fishermen. He had already had some sexual experience and that fact, in his eyes at least, compensated for his lack of years. At fourteen Chick Bird considered himself a man and Emily was the woman he had selected for his partner.

He now told himself that his earlier inexpert gropings with a much older girl had all been part of his policy. He needed to impress Emily with his knowledge and convince her that in terms of experience he was far older than *her*. If he had judged rightly, Emily was untried in the ways of sex and he had decided that tonight was the night to demonstrate some of the facts of life. He hoped she would be willing, although he could not be sure since she had not answered his letter, but possibly she had not received it. He had signed it '!' in an effort to confuse her parents if they should chance upon the carefully worded missive and had had the foresight to write in capital letters, laborious though this was, in order to retain his anonymity. He was very proud of the letter which was in fact a love poem which had taken him hours to compose.

> This letter comes from a boy
> Who loves you very dearly
> Please do not yourself annoy
> But take it very cheery.

Chick could not see how any woman could fail to be moved by such an offering.

Now he cupped his hands to his mouth and called, 'I want the other one, not you!'

'Well, honestly!'

As Julia withdrew, Chick shivered inside his heavy blue Guernsey, but not with cold although the March wind had a distinct nip of frost to it and Hilders Cliff was exposed to its full force as it raced in from the sea barely two miles distant. He shivered with anticipation, for it did not for one moment occur to him that he would not lure Emily Coulsden out of the house.

Suddenly Emily was at the window and the sight of her pale curls sent a thrill through him.

'Chick Bird! You've got a cheek,' she hissed. 'Do you know the time? You'll cop it if they catch you down there at this hour!'

He moved closer, his movements nonchalant, until he was directly under the window. 'D'you get my letter?' he asked.

'Pa tore it up.'

'Come on down and I'll tell you what was in it. You want to know, don't you?'

'Maybe.'

'Just for five minutes,' he wheedled. 'That's all. Five minutes and I'll tell you. It was a poem.'

'A poem!' She ducked inside again and he heard her repeating the information to Julia.

'Come on down, Emily Coulsden,' he thought, 'and I'll tell you about the letter and I'll start your education! So George Coulsden tore up the letter after all that effort! Right, Georgie Porgie, I'll settle your hash; I'll have your daughter if it's the last thing I do. Not tonight, but soon . . . She's old enough and willing. I'll teach you to tear up my letter!'

Above him Julia's head appeared once more. 'She's coming down but only for five minutes. If I hear anyone else about, I'll give you the tip-off.'

He nodded. 'Very helpful, I'm sure,' he muttered, going hot and cold at the thought that Emily was on her way down. He hoped she wasn't bothering to get dressed; the new-fangled brassières were a damned nuisance – *if* she wore one – and he fancied her straight from the bed. He was not disappointed, for Emily had slippers on her feet and a coat over her nightdress. Before she could say a word he had pulled her into his arms and landed a clumsy kiss on her mouth. Then he pushed her roughly against the wall of the house and slid his hands inside her coat. Under the flannelette nightdress her body was firm and warm.

'Chick Bird!' she gasped, taken by surprise. 'You've got a nerve! Take your hands off me!'

Chick blessed his past experience with Sally Noakes. 'No' always means 'Yes', he had learned that much at least. His hands moved up to feel her breasts, then down and round to press her buttocks. Everything felt as good or better than he had imagined. If Emily's mother had felt like this all those years ago, he could sympathise with George Coulsden.

'Chick Bird!' Emily protested, wriggling with affected disapproval. 'Who said you could touch me? You said you'd tell me about the letter.' Her protests entirely lacked conviction. 'Chick Bird, what are you doing? Not there! Stop that, d'you hear?'

Suddenly he released her and stepped away. Emily leaned back against the wall, her chest heaving as she pulled the coat firmly around her. Her eyes were large, she looked utterly desirable and Chick struggled to remember his plan. He had thought it all out so carefully, had rehearsed it so many times during the long wakeful nights. Give her a quick taste of joys to come and then hold back! Don't give too much away too soon. Let her wonder and think about it and then she'd come begging for it – that was the plan. If he rushed her now and she didn't take to it, he'd have a hell of a job to persuade her to try again. He had great plans for the spring when the weather was warmer. March was hardly the ideal time to go courting, but he would put the cold months to good use and prepare the ground for future adventures. Ever since the chance meeting at Camber Castle, he had had Emily's name carved on his tree.

He watched her face now, pale in the gas-light, saw the excitement in her eyes and knew with a sense of triumph that she wanted him to touch her again. But he wouldn't! Today he had felt her through the nightdress. Next time maybe he would feel the flesh itself.

'I'll tell you the poem,' he said quickly to take his mind off his own longings.

She listened distractedly and then asked him to repeat it. 'It's really lovely,' she said when he had finished. 'My Pa was a pig to tear it up. Could you write it again?'

' 'Course I could,' he assured her. 'Anything for you.'

'Really? Anything?'

He nodded.

'Say it again, then I can learn it and tell Ju.'

Chick began to repeat the poem, but before he was half-way through she was tugging him towards the half-open front door and he faltered in mid-sentence.

'Hang on!' he said hoarsely. 'What are you up to?'

'I'm freezing out here,' she told him. 'Why can't we stand in the hall?'

'In the hall? No bloody fear!'

'Scared, are you?'

'No, but I'm not daft either.'

'Just for a few minutes,' she whispered, 'where no one can see us. We could *do things* in the hall!'

'But . . .' His carefully rehearsed plans seemed to be going slightly wrong and he struggled to recall the correct order of things.

'Oh come on, Chick,' Emily begged. 'What you did was lovely but out here in the street – well, anyone could come along. Just for five minutes. We won't close the door, if you like, then if anyone wakes up . . .'

The idea sent a cold shiver through him. He certainly did not want to be discovered fondling George Coulsden's youngest daughter in the hallway.

'Just for two minutes then,' he compromised. 'No more.'

Inside, away from the cold night wind, Emily permitted him to repeat his explorations. She then took off the coat and allowed him greater freedom. When ten minutes later she lifted her nightdress – to please him, as she put it – Chick Bird took his chance and his carefully laid plan suffered instant obsolescence.

When Emily finally returned to her bed, Julia was horrified to learn what had taken place. Emily, unabashed, gave her a detailed account of most of the intimacies and seemed to have thoroughly enjoyed herself.

'But you'll have a baby now,' she said. 'And how can he marry you? He's only fourteen and they'll go mad when they know. Why on earth did you let him, Em? And how did you know what to do?'

'Don't ask me!' giggled Emily, undeterred. 'I just did. It was easy. I mean he did it, not me; I just let him do it.'

'But how did *he* know?' protested Julia. 'Chick only just left school, he's only a boy!'

'He certainly is *not*!' Emily assured her. 'He's a man, Ju. Look, don't keep asking me questions. I've told you everything already. I may not have a baby – you don't have a baby every time.'

'How do you know? *I* thought you did.'

Emily laughed kindly. 'Well, you don't.' She felt delightfully warm and relaxed and comfortably superior to Julia for the first time in her life. She, Emily, knew all about it and had actually done it *and* had a poem composed for her. Julia was prettier and everyone had left her money in their wills and she had had a fishing boat named after her (or was it the other way round? Emily wasn't sure) but she, Emily Coulsden, had discovered what grown-ups did with each other and she liked it.

'I'm seeing him again,' she said. 'He's coming again to-morrow.' She giggled at the unintended pun.

'What's the joke?' asked Julia.

'Coming again. Get it? Like he did tonight.'

'I don't think it's very funny,' said Julia, her voice tight with disapproval. 'And you won't think it's funny when you suddenly have a baby.'

'I won't *suddenly* have one. It takes nine months.'

'Well, in nine months' time then.'

'Look,' said Emily, 'I won't. He told me I wouldn't, because he knew what to do.'

'Like what?'

'Like he didn't . . oh well, you'll find out when you do it. Why should I have to tell you everything?' She drew a deep, shuddering sigh. 'I just wish it was tomorrow night,' she said wistfully.

Julia was silent. Emily saw her lying rigidly in her bed with legs straight and arms by her sides and knew how mortified she was. Her exalted kiss from Ian Cornwell was of no further consequence. Fifteen-year-old Julia had been pipped to the post by the younger Emily, with a boy of just fourteen! Emily grinned up into the darkness. In spite of her acknowledged fondness for her half-sister, she could not resist gloating at this about-turn in their fortunes.

'Are you going to marry him then?' Julia asked. 'Do you love him?'

'I don't know. I suppose so.' Impulsively she leaned across and patted Julia's shoulder. 'Please don't be huffy, Ju. It's all so much fun and you'll do it soon – then we'll both know and we can talk about it and have a good laugh. Look, I needn't have told you but I did. We always share, don't we? You'd have told me, wouldn't you?'

'I don't know,' Julia mumbled. 'I thought it was all supposed to be romantic and with someone you're in love with, but it doesn't seem to have been like that.'

'But it was *fun*,' said Emily. 'Good fun!' She slid further down into bed and pulled the blanket up round her neck. 'I think that poem was good, don't you? "This letter comes from a boy, Who loves you very dearly—"'

'But he hardly knows you,' interposed Julia.

Emily ignored the remark and went on, ' "Please do not yourself annoy—" '

'How could you annoy yourself?' asked Julia, secretly envious. Now that Leo had left a void in her life she wondered whether she could persuade Ian Cornwell to kiss her again. And perhaps he could write poetry.

' "But take it very cheery",' Emily finished. 'Fancy Chick Bird being able to write poems just like that. He's going to write it down for me.'

'What's the point? You know it by heart already.'

'You're jealous.'

'I am *not*!'

'Of course you are. You're trying to put me off him.'

'Why should I? I don't want him.'

'Just as well. It's me he likes, not you.'

'You're welcome,' said Julia. 'Anyway, he's got funny eyes. You said so yourself.'

'I *like* his eyes.'

'Good job somebody does.'

'Jealous! Jealous!'

'Shut up, stupid!' Julia sat bolt upright. 'The trouble with you is that you take after your mother!' she shouted.

Emily threw back the bedclothes and knelt on her bed, glaring furiously across the striped rug which separated them.

'What if I do?' she hissed. 'You take after Pa and he's not so marvellous!'

'I do not.' Julia clutched at the only available straw in her efforts to salvage her self-respect. 'I take after Mama Sarah. I'm a Gooding, not a Coulsden, *thank goodness!*'

'You're not a Gooding,' Emily taunted. 'You're a goody-goody. Too scared to find out what it's all about. Prissy, that's what you are. A prim old maid, that's how you'll end up. A prissy, prim old maid!'

'At least I won't have a baby on the wrong side of the blanket!'

'So what if I do?' cried Emily recklessly. 'I like kids. Anyway, what's so marvellous about the *right* side of the blanket? I was wrong side, remember, and it hasn't done me any harm. *I'm* the one who's enjoying myself. *You're* the one who's all twisted up and spiteful.'

'But my father looked after you and Agnes,' Julia reminded her. 'How is a boy of fourteen going to support you and a baby?'

'He won't be fourteen for ever, will he? People do get older, you know. Every year they get one year older and by the time the kid's born he'll be getting on—'

Julia could hardly contain her triumph. 'Oh, then you *are* going to have one!' she crowed. 'I thought he was so clever and he knew what to do and—'

The door opened suddenly and they froze to see George standing there, scowling.

'What the hell's going on?' he demanded.

'Nothing,' they said simultaneously.

'It's a bloody loud nothing,' he grumbled. 'Pipe down, the pair of you and let's get some sleep. You've woken Ag and she's kicking up hell's delight. Just pack it in and go to sleep.'

'We were only—' Emily ventured rashly.

'I said to pack it in!' he roared. 'One more word and I'll tan the hides off you!'

Agnes called out something the girls did not catch and he withdrew, closing the door carefully behind him.

After a decent interval to allow him to go back to sleep, Emily said, 'Ju! I'm sorry.'

But Julia did not answer, so Emily shrugged and returned to her memories. Mrs Charles Bird – it had a pleasant ring to it!

*

Alf Bittens was known as 'Bitty' to his few friends and many enemies. He was a tall loose-limbed man who had once been striking in an uncouth way, with fierce eyes that glittered and a large mouth. He had worked always 'with an eye to the main chance' and, having run away from home, found his niche in the world of the fairground at the age of fifteen. There he quickly became accomplished in the art of cheating customers at the various stalls he had run. His intelligence was very slightly below average but his native cunning sustained him, helping him to evade the police on occasions when he found this necessary. Lying came easily to him – as did swearing, drinking, fighting and womanising. He was also lazy.

Ellen – who had been married to him for thirty-one years – hated him from the depths of her being and had stayed with him so long only because she was afraid to leave. Several times she had left him, but each time he had found her, beaten her and taken her back to the dilapidated shack they called home. Tucked into the lower slopes of the hill behind Pett Level, the shack was stiflingly hot in summer and damp and cold in winter. A heavy snowfall in the winter of 1913 had forced in part of the roof and Bitty had never bothered to repair it. They lived therefore in one room, in what would have been squalor had Ellen not scrubbed the bare wooden floor, washed the threadbare curtains and blackleaded the cracked and inefficient stove until her arms and back ached and her thoughts were murderous. She envied her sister ¨Alice, who had married Sam Bligh – a good-natured, respectable, hard-working man. Alice had a decent husband, a decent home and, until the war, a son. She also had a grandson. Ellen, ten years her sister's junior, had nobody and nothing. Except Bitty! Now, at the age of fifty-two, his large mouth had slackened; his eyes glittered only for money with which to drink or gamble; his loose-limbed body had become a shambling shell, but in spite of his heavy drinking his health gave Ellen no cause for concern, which saddened her. She had prayed nightly and earnestly that he would drink himself to an early death, but so far her prayers had gone unheeded. On 12 April she and Bitty were engaged in putting up the keddle nets by which means they earned a meagre living. Bitty was never the sole breadwinner – far from it, she reflected spitefully. When he was sleeping off one of his more intense drinking bouts she frequently brought the horse and cart down to the beach herself and gathered in the fish with the help of willing neighbours who would then earn a share of the profits. Bitty earned money in more devious ways, she knew, though she never saw any of it. The prospect of his discovery and subsequent arrest one day was one of her more delightful fantasies.

Erecting the system of poles and nets at the beginning of each season was one of the few tasks for which Bitty's presence could be relied upon and that was only because the work could not be done by one person. Today they worked together, digging the holes into which the 16-foot poles would be inserted. To dig to a depth of 3 feet in wet sand the two diggers must work fast and expertly, but Ellen and Bitty worked as a twosome in body only, for their minds were not on the job in hand. Bitty's mind was on opening time at the pub on the hill, on the dice he would throw there and the sums of money he would lay out. His pocket bulged with pound notes – proceeds of last night's illicit meeting in the bay two miles off Fairlight. Since Dessin's death, trade with the French had been greatly reduced and Bitty cursed the day he had taken the young French-speaking Belgian into his confidence. At the time it had looked like a smart move and he did not deny the lad was keen, but Bitty knew the young man had never trusted him fully. Dessin's suspicions had been well-founded. His death had frightened away the French, although now they occasionally traded again, but the language was once more a barrier and Bitty frequently regretted Dessin's death if only on that account.

Ellen straightened her back as the last pole of the range went in. A 'range' was a row of poles at right-angles to the beach, extending out to a sufficient distance so that when the tide came in the sea would cover it. Beyond the range an incomplete circle of poles – called a bythe – extended even further. When the nets were hung in position and the tide came in, the fish would either become entangled in the range nets or else turn seaward to be trapped in the bythe. She glanced back to see that the horse and cart had not moved on. The horse was an ancient mare which cost next to nothing to feed, since Bitty tethered it wherever he could find free grazing, secure in the knowledge that it was not worth stealing. The animal would be easily recognised and few would try to steal it since Bitty could still swing a hefty punch and, when sober, his aim was very sure. The cart contained the remainder of the 90 poles and hundreds of yards of keddle net. Later, when the keddle was in operation, the cart would still be needed to collect and transport the fish.

Further along the beach Ellen saw another stand and reflected bitterly that as usual their own was last to go up. If she had not nagged incessantly for the past five days, poles and nets would still be in the lean-to shed. The season for keddle-net fishing did not extend beyond the summer and Ellen knew that their particular form of fishing was already under way around the bay wherever there were sandy beaches. Families paid for the right to erect the keddle nets by hiring an area of the shore known as a stand; it was a hard way to earn a living and during the season their lives revolved around twice-daily trips to the beach to take the mackerel from the nets and organise their despatch to Billingsgate. If a squall blew up, the nets would have to be taken down and then put up again when it was over. Ellen hated the work, but she hated Bitty more. Each day was an exhausting struggle against frustration and barely concealed rage and her nights were spent in luxurious thoughts of eventual revenge.

Ellen's hatred stemmed not only from Bitty's brutish behaviour to her over the years, nor from his excessive drinking bouts Neither did she hate him solely for his meanness with money or for his idle feckless ways. She hated him for two words he had uttered – for once fully sober – when she was in despair over her inability to produce a child. He had called her a 'barren bitch' and the deep hurt she suffered then had coloured the rest of her life a despairing grey. The words had shamed her in her own eyes and try as she would, she could never see herself as anything else. Humiliation was a heavy burden and hate a lighter one. Hate was positive and gave her something tangible to cling to throughout the long wretched years during which she changed from a loving, hopeful woman into a vindictive drudge. She could not know that none of the many women with whom Bitty had shared a bed had produced a child.

Bitty and Ellen worked in complete silence. After so many years they had nothing to say to each other – nothing that dare be said – for Ellen did not seek a confrontation and Bitty was too lazy to provoke one. When at last all the poles had been installed, he spoke: 'Get the cart.' Ellen trudged back across the wet sand, her boots – a pair of Bitty's cast-offs – sodden, the hem of her serge skirt flapping wetly around her legs. As she led the horse towards the bythe a man approached them; he wore waders and an oilskin smock but he was a stranger to her.

He raised his hat politely and said, 'Morning to you, ma'am.'

Ellen, surprised at the civility, nodded without returning his smile. When she saw him confer with Bitty, intuition told her that what he said was for no other ears. Deliberately she wandered nearer, pretending to be preoccupied with the progress of the horse and cart. She caught a few words – 'cave . . . tide . . . after next' and something that sounded like 'great'. She also noticed that they faced towards Fairlight Cliff as they spoke, as though the subject of their whispered talk might lie in that direction. Her suspicions were only fully aroused, however, when the two men moved out of earshot and she saw money being exchanged. Was this man the source of her husband's gambling stakes? From what she had heard, the sums involved in his dice games far exceeded anything he might conceivably earn from the daily mackerel catch. Hope surged suddenly like a tiny flicker of warmth in her cold heart. Then and there she made up her mind to discover more of Bitty' secret and, when she had done so, to decide how best to put the knowledge to her own good. From that moment on the thought uppermost in her mind was Bitty's downfall.

CHAPTER EIGHTEEN

Miss Fookes's friend – a Mrs Formby – ran a guest house called 'Trelees'. It was situated half-way up Rye Hill on the left side and was approached along a narrow lane. There were six bedrooms, four double and two single, some of which were shaded by tall firs. The panelled dining-room could seat ten people comfortably at five tables and there was a sunny lounge with three sofas and four easy chairs.

Mrs Formby ran the guest house successfully, but Julia soon came to the conclusion that she did so more by good luck than good management. She was a tall, thin, elegant woman who wore several ropes of beads at the same time and fluttered from one minor crisis to the next. Fortunately she had a reliable staff: Cook had been with her for eight years and Millicent for six. Millicent, a plump-faced woman in her early twenties, waited on tables and the heavy work was done by a daily woman.

Julia's job was not well-defined, although she always made the beds and laid the tables. Apart from these main areas of work, she was called upon to do a variety of tasks from mending torn or frayed linen to polishing furniture or doing last-minute shopping – which entailed a journey down into the town by bicycle, taking a short cut across the railway crossing in Rope Walk.

On the fourth of May, Julia was busy in the dining-room when Mrs Formby came in, one hand fingering her beads in her usual state of agitation, her nervousness strangely at odds with her regal appearance.

'I don't know what the country is coming to,' she began. 'Would you believe my books have not arrived? I sent a postal order more than a week ago, for four pounds ten, so where are the books? I've been all the way to the station myself and all I can get out of that wretched little man is that they haven't come. I said to him, "Really, if they cannot deliver a few books on time it's a pretty sad state of affairs." I shall write to Foyles first thing after breakfast tomorrow and tell them not to expect further custom from me.'

'It's probably the strike,' said Julia, smoothing creases from the tablecloth and beginning to set out the cutlery for the evening meal. 'It's very bad in London, according to the wireless.'

'Strike?' said Mrs Formby. 'It's the miners who are on strike, not the bookshops. Foyles has never been on strike. It's quite ridiculous. If . . . That fork's not clean. Here, give it to me, child.'

Her habit of referring to Julia as 'child' was irritating. Nearly sixteen and employed for the first time in her life, Julia felt very grown up; she watched resignedly as Mrs Formby ran a fingernail between the prongs of the fork and then handed it back.

'It's not Foyles that's on strike, it's the trains,' she explained. 'They said on the wireless that the railways are on strike and everyone in London is having to walk to work or else try to get a lift in somebody's motor. They say on the wireless that the gas workers are out and so are the electricity workers.'

Mrs Formby rearranged the small vase of fresh flowers that stood in the centre of the table. 'The wireless!' she said scornfully. 'I don't believe everything I hear on the wireless and neither should you if you have any sense. I still can't see what it's got to do with my books. Are the menus ready?'

'I don't know,' said Julia.

'Don't know? Well, you *should* know! I certainly haven't had time to do them, having to trail all that way into town for my books. If Cook hasn't attended to it, then you'd better see to it – unless perhaps Millicent has done them.'

'She's not back yet,' Julia told her. 'It's her afternoon off.'

'Oh, that wretched girl!'

'Shall I do them?' asked Julia hopefully, preferring the menus to setting the table.

Mrs Formby hesitated. 'I suppose so . . . although really your handwriting leaves much to be desired. No, child, I'd better do them myself. Now, what are we having? Lamb chops, I believe, or grilled plaice. Oh!' She clapped a hand to her mouth. 'Did anyone go to the Fishmarket? I meant to ask Millicent to call in on her way back, but did I?'

She stared at Julia, stricken with doubt.

'I don't know,' said Julia. 'Perhaps I could bicycle down and fetch some from—'

'Could you? Yes, I suppose you could, but then the tables won't get laid and there are the menus to see to. Oh, it's all the fault of that wretched bookshop. If I hadn't had to go out—' She stopped in mid-sentence and sat down heavily. 'Strike, indeed! I'd give them strike,' she muttered. 'I'd give that Mr Clark a piece of my mind.'

'It's Cook,' said Julia.

'What's Cook?'

'I mean it's Mr Cook, not Mr Clark, who's to blame for the strike. Mr Cook is the leader of the miners.'

Julia's employer looked at her with narrowed eyes. 'You seem to know a great deal about it. Good heavens, child, you're not a socialist, are you?'

Julia laughed. 'I'm not anything,' she confessed. 'I just listen to the wireless a lot and Papa is always going on about it.'

'Well, thank goodness! Strike, indeed. It surely should be possible, strike or no strike, to send down a few books from London to Rye. How far is it? Thirty miles?' A new thought struck her. 'Good heavens, we have a couple coming down today from North London, I believe it is. They've booked in for a week – Samson their name is, or maybe it's Salmon, something like that. I wonder how they'll get down here if the trains are on strike. Perhaps the coach.'

'The buses are on strike too,' said Julia, hiding her amusement at Mrs Formby's obvious dismay. 'Everyone's on strike. It's general. They say on the wireless—'

'Stop!' Mrs Formby held up a bony hand. 'Don't mention the wireless to me again. Or the strike! I don't want to hear another word about it. This conversation is getting us nowhere. Show me that cruet. I thought as much – yesterday's mustard and no salt! Check all the cruets, child, when you've finished laying the table, and then ask Cook what fish she wants and cycle down and get it.'

'But Mrs Formby, I'm due to finish at six!'

'Well, you won't, will you? It's your own fault; you waste time in chit-chat. You're all the same. If I've told Millicent once, I've told her a thousand times.'

'But I'm going out,' Julia protested. 'I'm expected for dinner at seven-thirty and I have to cycle to Appledore!'

Mrs Formby shrugged her shoulders. 'You should have thought of that earlier on and got on with your work more quickly. Oh, and the menus – do the menus and watch the spelling.'

'But I thought *you* were—'

'Don't think, child, act! Actions speak louder than words or thoughts, come to that matter. Cook will tell you what we're having, although I'm sure it's lamb because I picked some mint this morning. Guests do so appreciate fresh herbs.' She frowned anxiously. 'I do wonder about the Samsons, or it might be Salmon. Perhaps they will be able to hire a car? I think perhaps I should telephone Foyles if they are still open and make sure that my postal order has arrived safely. Is the Post Office on strike, I wonder?'

She hurried out before Julia could answer and did not see her stick out her tongue. 'Stupid old cow!' muttered Julia crossly.

With so many extra jobs to do she would never reach South View on time. And all, she thought wearily, for thirteen shillings a week. She began to feel a certain sympathy with Mr Cook and his striking miners!

*

Helen Cornwell opened the door with a look of great relief.

'I wondered what had happened to you, dear,' she said as she helped Julia out of her jacket. The bicycle was propped outside in the porch. 'I thought, how on earth can I get in touch with you if you don't turn up? I would never know if you'd had an accident.'

'It was Mrs Formby,' Julia told her. 'She kept me late.'

Helen tutted. 'She's always keeping you late and it's not good enough. People take advantage of the young, but I always say they can get just as tired as we older ones. You can outgrow your strength, you see.' She led the way into the drawing-room and settled Julia beside the small fire. 'It's a bit extravagant, I know, having a fire in May, and it's not really cold but I do so like to see a few flames. They're so cheering, aren't they?' She poured a sherry for Julia and refreshed her own, then sat down in the chair on the other side of the fire. 'Your health, Julia,' she said.

'Cheers!' said Julia. Being fussed over was such a treat, she thought, and Ian's grandmother was so sweet. In many ways she had filled for Julia the empty space left by Mama Sarah. Julia suspected that she in turn had made the loss of Helen's husband more tolerable by her visits and letters. It was certainly a relationship which grew closer with each month and which both valued more than they realised.

Now Julia said, 'I thought Ian would be here?'

'So did I, dear,' replied Helen. 'That's my exciting news: Ian is driving a bus! Isn't that splendid?'

'A bus?' Julia looked at her blankly.

'A bus, dear. The strike, you know?'

Light dawned. 'Oh, the strike!' cried Julia. 'Goodness! Is he really?'

Helen's eyes sparkled. 'He volunteered – isn't that splendid of him! Just like him. His father rang me, not at all pleased, but I told him to stop fussing and let the boy follow the dictates of his conscience. Can you imagine Ian driving a bus? I can't, but I'd give anything to see him.' She chuckled and took a sip of sherry. 'A state of emergency has been declared, so that shows you it's serious. I wonder how it will end? We're so protected down here from all the nastiness that goes on in the world. Don't you feel that, Julia?'

'I've never thought about it,' she admitted, 'but maybe you're right.'

'No newspaper today,' Helen continued. 'It seems so odd.'

Julia nodded, successfully hiding her disappointment that Ian would not be with them. Ever since the beginning of Emily's involvement with Chick Bird (which was flourishing) she had hoped to persuade Ian to take a little more interest in her as a woman. On the few occasions when he came down to South View she was always invited to dinner and when he took her home he kissed her, but he never made any move further than that and Julia still had no way of knowing how deeply he felt for her – if, indeed, he felt anything. Was she merely a pleasant companion?

Emily, who was meeting Chick frequently, always returned flushed and excited and willing to confide intimate details whenever Julia was in the mood to listen, but this she was finding increasingly hard to do. She was jealous and to herself she admitted it. She wanted to be initiated into the mysteries of love – *not*, she told herself, in the coarse manner which Emily indicated when she described some of their grapplings – but in a romantic, soulful way. She wanted to share a beautiful voyage of discovery – at least that was how she imagined it – and felt she could do that with Ian if only he would give her a sign. Was he shy, she wondered? If so, should she make the first move? Emily insisted that she should, and promised her all manner of sensuous delights if only she would 'take the plunge', as she put it. The trouble was that the way Emily described it did not inspire Julia. Only her flushed cheeks and light step reassured Julia that being in love would be wonderful. Of course she had been in love before, with Leo, but that had been so one-sided that now it was over she was half-inclined to discount it. Mutual attraction was what she now hoped for and Ian seemed the most likely partner with whom to explore the mystery.

'Perhaps he'll drive down later,' she suggested hopefully. 'When he's finished driving the bus?'

Helen looked doubtful. 'Maybe, dear,' she said, 'but never mind. We'll have a cosy evening on our own if he doesn't manage it. There's a nice piece of sirloin in the oven and I've made a Yorkshire – I'll go and pop it in if you'll excuse me a minute. Put on the wireless and we'll listen to the news. I don't know what's going on in the outside world without *The Times*.'

'I wish you'd let me do something useful,' Julia began, but Helen waved a dismissive hand.

'Certainly not, dear,' she said firmly. 'You've been busy all day. You're a working girl while I'm a lady of leisure.' She laughed. 'It isn't worth cooking a joint for myself, so I'm glad to have the company and someone to cook for. I miss that, you know – Henry did so enjoy his food. No, you sit there and relax. There's nothing else to do, anyway.'

After a leisurely meal they sat talking, comfortably at ease with each other; inevitably the conversation turned to Ian.

'He's such a quiet boy,' Helen mused. 'I do worry about him sometimes. Well, not quiet, perhaps that's the wrong word, but calm. He rarely gets ruffled, although he did sound excited when he rang about his bus driving. That's tickled him, I could tell. But he has an air of self-possession . . .'

'A bedside manner,' laughed Julia. 'Just right for a doctor!'

'I suppose so, dear. Yes, you're probably right. He seems so self-assured and yet he isn't really; he's very shy underneath. Do you find him shy, Julia?'

Julia knew immediately that the question was not as simple as it sounded and that Helen wanted to have her opinion of her grandson.

'Not really,' she said. 'Not shy exactly.'

'The two of you seem to get along well?'

'Yes, we do. He teases me sometimes in a nice way.'

'Does he, dear?' Helen seemed surprised. 'Fancy that!'

Suddenly it occurred to Julia that she might have a possible ally in Helen. 'I'm very fond of him,' she confided, 'but I don't know how he feels about me.'

'Oh Julia, he's fond of you too,' Helen assured her. 'At least,

I'm sure he is. He certainly talks about you a great deal, but he's very wrapped up in his work. He's very dedicated and truly wants to relieve suffering in the world. He's always wanted to be a doctor – oh, from way back when he was a boy of eleven or twelve, I think. They lived next door to a family of girls – three, I think there were – and when they were younger they would play nurses and hospitals and suchlike and poor old Ian would be called in to be the patient. I used to watch them sometimes when I visited; he'd have a bandage round his head and would lie on the grass with the three girls fussing over him. He never said much, he was quiet even then. But I suppose he got tired of being the patient and they let him be the doctor. Strange, isn't it, how such things can shape our lives? I sometimes wonder what he would have been if he hadn't got a taste for medicine.'

'A teacher, perhaps,' said Julia. 'Like Leo.' She could mention Leo now in a casual voice. He was no longer *her* Leo.

'Perhaps,' Helen hesitated. 'I sometimes wonder . . . he's twenty-nine, you know, and there's no sign of wedding bells. His mother says he seems to prefer going out with a group of people, but I do wish he'd find a nice girl and settle down. His mother does, too; she's so afraid he *will* go abroad.'

'Abroad?' Julia was surprised Ian had actually decided to go. 'Is he really thinking of going abroad?'

Helen sighed. 'Apparently he is. His mother wrote to me last week – Australia, I think she said. It's such a long way.'

'Is he really going to Australia? But for how long? You don't mean he wants to emigrate?'

'No dear, just for a change – for the experience. Just for a year or two. They want qualified people in Australia, you see. But really, we would never see him. You can't pop home from Australia, can you? It's not like Europe.'

'No.' Julia realised with a pang just how much she would miss Ian if he went away. 'Oh, I hope he doesn't.'

Helen smiled. 'I don't think he would go if he had a nice lady friend,' she said innocently. 'He's just restless and really, the way this poor old country is going, it's no wonder the young men are looking further afield. My great fear is – although I dare not voice it to his poor mother – that he will like it in Australia and won't come back at all!' They were both silent, thinking about the awful prospect of Ian's departure from their lives. To Julia, the thought of his possible absence over a prolonged period cast a gloom over the evening, but at least she understood now what Helen was trying to convey. If she established herself as Ian's girl friend, he might give up the idea of going to Australia and Helen would no doubt applaud the match. Probably Ian's parents would, also. She wondered what they were like and for the first time began to consider Ian as a future husband and not merely as the man who had given her her first kiss.

'Twenty-nine isn't old, of course, I didn't mean that,' said Helen anxiously, 'but a lot of young men are engaged by then, especially if they have a promising career ahead of them. I could understand it if he was unemployed.'

'Perhaps he's not the marrying kind,' suggested Julia.

His grandmother's eyes widened in alarm. 'Oh, don't even *say* such a thing,' she cried. 'Everyone needs a partner. Life can be very hard and it must be much harder if you're alone. Ian's not the solitary kind, he enjoys company. He just doesn't seem to find anyone special.' She shrugged. 'But listen to me, rattling on and on about Ian. He wouldn't thank me, I know, but we are speaking in confidence, aren't we, dear? And I'm not going to last for ever and I would like to see him settled before I go. I used to say that to Henry, but he only laughed at me. 'We've got years yet,' he used to tell me. Poor Henry! A gipsy woman once told me I would live to be ninety, but I don't think I want to. I'd like a few more years while my health's still good, but when that goes there's not a lot left to enjoy, is there?'

'You shouldn't be talking like that,' Julia protested. Talk of death distressed her. 'What's the good of planning for your great-grandchildren if you don't mean to be around!'

Helen laughed. 'Well! I'd never thought of it like that, but you're quite right. Is it a mournful subject? Perhaps it is to the young, but as you get older you see it quite differently. I remember my mother, just before she died. We knew her hours were numbered and I was so upset. I've never forgotten what she said to me: "I look at it this way, Helen," she told me. "I've been to a party and I've enjoyed it. Now I'm very tired and I want to go home." Life is the party, you see, and when it's over . . .' She smiled and shrugged.

Impulsively, Julia crossed to the old lady and bent to kiss the top of her head. 'Don't go home just yet,' she said. 'I'm at the party, too, and I should miss you.'

Ten o'clock came round all too quickly, and Ian had not arrived.

'I'd better not wait any longer,' said Julia. 'Papa still gets cross if I'm too late; it's a dark road and he worries about me.'

'I should think so,' said Helen. 'I don't think Ian will come now. He would have telephoned. That was the arrangement, you see – he said if he was coming he would telephone, and he hasn't. I hope you're not too disappointed.'

'Of course not.' But actually she was very disappointed; she had been looking forward to seeing Ian in his new role as prospective husband. If only she could feel towards Ian as she had towards Leo!

Helen accompanied her into the hall and was just reaching for the front-door latch when suddenly she swayed and put a hand to her head.

'Helen? Are you all right?'

The old lady turned unseeing eyes in Julia's direction. 'I don't know . . .' she whispered. 'I feel so . . . Julia, I must sit down.'

With a thumping heart, Julia seized her arm and led her to the nearest chair, which stood beside the hall table.

'What is it, Helen?' she asked fearfully. Their conversation earlier flooded back into her mind with dreadful clarity.

Helen's face was hidden in her hands. 'It's nothing, dear,' she said, but her voice shook slightly. 'Just a funny turn, a dizzy spell. Nothing to worry about.'

'Can I get you anything? A drink of water?'

'No, thank you – wait, maybe I should. Perhaps a few sips of cold water. If you would, dear?'

Julia rushed into the kitchen and returned with a glass of water. She watched nervously as Helen sipped at it; the old lady looked very pale and despite her protestations to the contrary, was obviously rather upset.

'It was a dizzy spell, dear, that's all. Probably indigestion. Too many roast potatoes, I expect, but I do enjoy them.'

'But have you had a dizzy spell before this?' Julia asked. 'Does it just go away and are you all right then? Should I get the doctor?'

'No, no, there's nothing wrong with me,' Helen insisted. 'I feel better now. It was just the suddenness of it which gave me a bit of a fright. I felt a kind of blackness sweep over me – rather like a faint. Yes, that's all it was, I'm sure – a bit of a faint. I have to expect something at my age.' She managed a weak smile. 'Don't look so worried, dear. I tell you it's all right.'

Julia was thinking rapidly. She could not leave Helen with an easy conscience. If she offered to stay the night she could cycle to work in the morning, but how could she let her father know what she was doing?

'I could telephone to Uncle Jack,' she suggested aloud. 'Ben would take round a message. Would you like me to stay the night?'

Helen paused for a second or two before insisting that she was quite recovered and there would be no need.

'Well, I don't know,' said Julia uncertainly. 'Let me help you back into the drawing-room and then we'll decide. You may feel funny again, later on, and I don't like to think of you being all alone.'

As soon as Helen rose to her feet, however, Julia saw that she was not at all recovered and very shaken. The old lady leaned heavily on her for support and moved slowly and carefully.

'It's knocked all the stuffing out of me,' she admitted. 'My legs feel like jelly. Oh dear, how silly of me to go and have a turn like that! But I'll be all right in a moment or two, you'll see.' She sank gratefully into her chair beside the fire and smiled up at Julia.

At that moment they both jumped as the telephone rang in the hall. 'Julia, do answer it for me, there's a dear. I expect it's Ian.'

Her assumption was correct and when the operator had connected them, his familiar voice crackled over the line reassuringly. Briefly Julia explained what had happened, despite Helen's protests that there was no need to alarm him. For his part, Ian explained that he had just finished his 'spell of duty' and was about to drive down. There were a lot of private motors on the road, he warned, because of the bus strike, so the journey might take longer than usual but he *was* coming down and he accepted Julia's offer to stay overnight.

'Just in case,' he told her. 'And it's awfully good of you.'

'It's no trouble at all,' said Julia. 'Should I telephone for the doctor?'

'Not yet,' he decided. 'If she has another turn then telephone immediately, but it is getting late and they won't want to turn out unless it's really urgent. Get her up to bed, Julia, I think that will be best. And you sleep in the spare room – it's always made up ready for me. I'll make do on the sofa with a blanket and some cushions. But don't stay up, because I don't know how long I'll be . . . and Julia, do try not to worry.'

'I'll try,' she promised.

She passed on his messages and Helen agreed to go straight to bed; when she was settled down to sleep Julia sat on the bed in Ian's room. She had phoned her uncle but Ben had taken the call, and had offered to go round to Hilders Cliff to explain her absence. As she looked at the heavy flannelette nightgown which Helen had lent her, she stifled an attack of giggles. It was old-fashioned and voluminous and not at all romantic. Fate was often unkind, she thought. Here she was about to spend the night under the same roof as Ian and her own pretty nightdress was at home. Still, she would not see him until the morning (unless Helen needed them in the night) and by then she could be wearing her own clothes again. She undressed, pulled on the nightdress and after a quiet laugh at her reflection in the long oval mirror, scrambled into bed, suddenly overcome with exhaustion. Her working day at Trelees started at 7 am and she rarely finished at six o'clock which was officially the end or her ten-hour-day – one hour being allowed for a break in the middle of the day.

Before she slept she gave some serious thought to the prospect of Australia. Suppose she *did* marry Ian and he *still* wanted to go abroad? What was Australia like, she wondered. Fragments of past geography lessons floated into her mind – Brisbane, Adelaide and Canberra. They were the towns. And Sydney, of course. Then there were sheep and aborigines and hot geysers . . . or was that New Zealand? She knew there were kangeroos and gum trees and the bush. Julia sighed. Suppose Ian asked her to marry him and go to Australia – what should she say? Did she want to leave all that was familiar to her, all her family and friends, and spend seven weeks crossing half the world just to share a lot of wide-open spaces with strange animals and even stranger people? Not that everyone in Australia was an aborigine, she knew that. But the white settlers had all been convicts – or most of them. She began to wish she had paid more attention to Mr Pegg's geography lessons. Making a resolution to ask for a book on Australia next time she went to the library, Julia drifted into an uneasy sleep.

She woke with a start, aware before she opened her eyes that someone else was in the room.

'Helen? Is that you? Are you ill?'

'It's me, Ian.'

Julia sat up. 'What on earth . . .' she began and then, remembering Helen's nightdress, hastily slid back under the sheets.

'The blanket,' he whispered. 'It's in the chest by the window. I didn't mean to wake you, but since you are awake can I have a bit of light? I can't see a thing.'

'Yes, of course.'

She blinked as the gas flared and Ian turned towards her. 'It was very kind of you to stay,' he said, keeping his voice low for Helen's bedroom was next door. 'Were there any problems after you spoke to me?'

'No.' She decided it was ridiculous to conduct a conversation lying down; it made *her* feel like the invalid. Reluctantly she sat up as Ian perched on the end of the bed.

'I've had such a day,' he began, eager to share his experience with someone. 'Quite extraordinary! I've never seen the Londoners so buoyant. It was quite incredible!'

'Buoyant?' Julia echoed. 'What have they got to be buoyant about?'

Ian laughed and looked suddenly much younger than his twenty-nine years – more like an excited schoolboy recounting an adventure, Julia thought.

'Why, the strike, of course! The atmosphere's fantastic. Everyone is so good-humoured and tolerant about it all; everyone willing to help everyone else. There are thousands of people on the streets, walking to work, and the Government has organised a fleet of motors to unload food at the docks. They obviously knew what was coming. The Army are dashing about in their steel helmets—'

'The Army? Is there fighting, then?'

'Not that I saw, but I believe there has been trouble in some towns. Clashes with the police and all that sort of thing.'

Julia's alarm gave way to amusement. 'You enjoyed it!' she challenged him. 'It's just a game to you. Go on, admit it!'

'Oh, I do,' he laughed. 'Most willingly. Just imagine me driving a bus from Kensington High Street to Euston Road, all through Park Lane and Knightsbridge. There are armoured cars, too, escorting the food convoys. They say Cook is delighted with the solidarity of the workers, but the Government's equally thrilled with the response of the public.'

'But the public *are* the workers, aren't they?'

'Not *those* workers,' said Ian. 'I mean all of *us* – students, undergraduates, professional men.' He shook his head in amazement. 'It's just like the wartime spirit when everyone unites against a common foe.'

'The foe are the strikers, then?'

'Of course!'

'The fishermen aren't on strike,' she said, frowning slightly as she tried to establish for herself the rights and wrongs of it all.

'The docks are.'

'I'm not on strike, but *I'm* a worker.'

Ian laughed again. 'Don't look so serious,' he said. 'It's only a strike – it will all blow over and people will forget about it. I can't solve the problem; I'm just having a bit of a lark, that's all. The buses won't run if no one volunteers to drive them and it might be very urgent for someone to get from A to B by bus. Poor people don't own motors and only a few of the trains are running. We can't sit by and let poor old London grind to a halt, can we?'

'I suppose not.'

They fell silent, the topic abruptly superseded by their awareness of their nearness to one another and the fact that Julia was in bed.

'It seems funny,' said Ian slowly, 'seeing you in my bed.'

Another silence followed.

'It seems funny,' added Julia, 'seeing you sitting on the end of *my* bed! It's like Goldilocks and the three bears. I wake up to find Father Bear—'

"Wasn't Goldilocks supposed to run away?' he asked lightly.

'I will if you want me to.' But as soon as the words were uttered, Julia regretted them; it sounded as though *he* might want her to go but that she preferred to stay. Her cheeks flamed suddenly. Almost at once she chided herself, remembering how buoyantly Emily had been behaving over the past few months. How Emily would laugh if she could see the two of them, staring nervously across a yard of bed in the middle of the night, in complete privacy. And Ian was *years* older than that wretched Chick Bird!

'I don't want you to run away,' said Ian. 'But I wouldn't keep you against your will.'

'Oh.'

He smiled. 'What does "Oh" mean?'

'Just "Oh".' She swallowed. 'Or maybe it means "Oh I see".'

'*Do* you see?'

'No,' she whispered and was at once furious with herself. If he was hoping for some encouragement then she was disappointing

him. She searched for something suitable to say – not too provocative but not too reserved either. Prissy – that's what Emily had
called her. *Was* she prissy?

'I like you being here,' she said desperately. 'It's just this stupid
nightdress. At least, I don't mean it's stupid. It was kind of Helen
but it's miles too big and . . . I feel rather silly,' she ended lamely.

'Take if off, then,' he suggested.

'Oh!'

'You keep on saying "Oh".'

'I'm sorry.' She was panic-stricken. Now she had gone too far –
and so had he. He had misunderstood her comments about the
nightdress. She lifted her hands to the buttons at the neck of the
gown, unfastened three of them and then let her hands fall to her
lap. 'It's no good,' she whispered. 'My fingers won't work
properly, my hands are shaking.'

He leaned forward and kissed the tip of her nose. 'Mine aren't,'
he whispered. 'They're as steady as a rock. Shall I undo them?'

'No!' she cried.

Her throat was dry, but anger against herself was mounting.
Emily had said it was fun and now she would find out for herself.
Ian regarded her with an expression Julia found hard to analyse.
Was it humour, or compassion? Certainly it was not lust. Yet lust,
Emily had told her, was what it was all about.

He kissed her forehead and then her lips – lightly, almost
playfully – and she felt a kind of exhilaration as his fingers
wrestled with the small pearl buttons. Julia was not sure whether
to be glad or sorry that there were so many. When they were all
unfastened, he leaned down to kiss that part of her throat which
he had exposed.

'You are very beautiful, Julia,' he said. 'Did you know that?'

'Yes.'

'And very desirable.'

'Yes.' She found it difficult to breathe. 'So are you,' she told
him. 'Desirable, I mean. Not beautiful.'

It might have sounded foolish, but if it did Ian gave no sign. He
spoke gently, without any sign of passion, yet all the time his gaze
was so direct. Julia felt helpless and yet protected. Whatever
occurred, it would be the right thing to happen, she told herself.
She was no longer capable of taking control. What happened,
happened. It seemed that Helen's fainting spell and the General
Strike had together conspired to bring this situation about. Ian

wanted her – or so she believed. Helen wanted Ian to want her.
Did *she* want him? Julia supposed so. She felt at once light-
headed and deadly serious. Her life was taking a new course and
yet she could only sit and wait. Fate had set the stage and written
the script; she and Ian were merely the players.

'I want you, Julia,' he said, 'but I don't want to take advantage of
you. You're so sweet, so young. Do you hear me, Julia? Do you
understand what I'm saying?'

She nodded, unable to speak.

'I didn't expect this to happen,' he told her. 'I don't suppose you
did either, but it seems to *be* happening. I want you so desperately,
Julia, yet I know I shouldn't ask. It's not fair to you. Tell me you
feel the same way – tell me you love me.'

Julia stared at him in wonderment that this man whom fate had
deemed her partner should be so gentle, so considerate.

'I think I love you,' she stammered. 'I think I do.'

'I know I love you, Julia Lady Coulsden,' he said. 'Here, take
my hands.'

She allowed herself to be pulled out of the bed, to stand beside
him on the striped rug. Carefully he pulled off the offending
nightdress and she shivered as he stepped back to look at her,
folding her arms over her breasts as though to hide them. Ian
looked at her for a long minute, then began to take off his own
clothes. Julia had never seen a naked man before. He stood with
his feet together and arms outstretched sideways. Then he lifted
his arms above his head and lowered them again. He turned
slowly around and when he faced her again he smiled.

'Just a man,' he said gently. 'There's no mystery. We're almost
the same. But not quite.'

As though hypnotised, Julia raised her own hands above her
head, lowered them and clasped them over her chest, then turned
round to face him. 'Just a woman,' she said.

'Not just a woman,' he commented. 'You're Julia Lady and that
makes you special.'

It did not feel at all odd, Julia marvelled, to be standing opposite
Ian Cornwell, in the room in South View which had once been her
own when Mama Sarah was alive. She wondered fleetingly if
Mama Sarah would have approved, but found she did not care.

'I feel drunk,' she said simply.

'It's the moment,' he said, his face serious. 'Come here.'

She moved towards him and he held her close. Behind them

the gas-jet spluttered. 'Shall I put it out?' he asked. 'Would you like to be in the dark? Would it be easier?'

'I think so.' Surely that choked voice was not her own. She swallowed, never taking her eyes from him. He *was* beautiful, she thought – the lean back and small buttocks, the long straight legs – and he was almost hairless. Most of the men she knew were dark and their arms were dark with hairs. Ian's bright ginger hair showed under the light as he reached up to turn off the gas, but the rest of his body was smooth and pale. She could still see him, after the room was plunged into darkness.

He took her gently and without hurry when she could no longer bear the agony of waiting. She knew that he came, for his body arched above her in a kind of frenzy which she could not match. Her own body flared briefly, then it was all over . . . a hint of future ecstasies, nothing more, but Julia was content. She had not failed him. It had happened and it had worked the way it should. The passionate need that Emily described would be hers one day and meanwhile she was content to wait.

'I love you,' she told him. 'I love you, Ian. Was it everything you hoped? Was it the first time? No, don't answer that. It's not important. It was the first time for me.'

'I love you, Julia Lady.' His voice was languid as he lay beside her on his back, breathing rapidly, sated. 'You were beautiful.'

'I want it to be always you,' she told him. 'No one else. *Ever!*'

'I know.' He rolled over and took her into his arms. 'Do you think you would ever consider marrying me, Julia?'

She heard the mockery in his tone but knew it was false. He wanted an answer. 'I'm sure I would,' she said. 'Would you ever consider asking me to marry you?'

'Julia Lady Coulsden, I formally request the pleasure of your hand in marriage. What do you say?'

'I say "Yes".'

'Oh, my beautiful Lady! My beautiful Julia Lady, I adore you.'

They clung together in the darkness. 'I'll make you happy, Ian. I swear I will.'

'And I'll make you the happiest woman in the world. Oh God!' He propped himself up on one elbow and stared down at her. 'I wish I could see your face!'

'Put on the light again.'

'No – we should sleep.'

'We never will, Ian.'

'I'm starving,' he said, 'and I've just realised I haven't eaten all day. That wretched bus! I was so carried away. Should we go downstairs and explore the pantry? Grandmother won't mind. Are you hungry?'

'No, but I'll eat something to keep you company.' She laughed. 'A midnight dorm feast. It's what they have in boarding schools, according to the books I've read.'

'Come on, then. Put on the awful nightdress again. I shall still love you.'

She heard him fumbling with the matches and then there was light. 'Oh, it's you!' she exclaimed. 'I wondered who it was!'

'Julia! I'm surprised at you.'

She was surprised at herself; she had solved the mystery of making love and had promised to marry Ian Cornwell. Her heart was very full. As they reached the bedroom door she hung back. 'Just say it once more,' she begged him. 'That you love me, I mean.'

'I love you,' he said. 'I will always love you . . . but I'm starving!'

As she followed him down the stairs she thought, 'We have the miners to thank for this,' and began to laugh. She couldn't stop laughing and Helen woke up and called out to find out what was happening. They told her that Ian had proposed and Julia had accepted and she was absolutely delighted. If she guessed from their shining eyes that anything else had occurred, she kept it to herself and, leaving them to their midnight feast, went happily back to sleep.

CHAPTER NINETEEN

As soon as Julia opened the front door, she knew that there was something wrong and her heart sank. Ian had insisted that he would ask George Coulsden for his daughter's hand in marriage formally. He would like to buy her an engagement ring on her sixteenth birthday and he hoped George would agree to let her marry at seventeen – if not, then eighteen at the very latest. Breathless with excitement, Julia had agreed to everything. A formal request for her hand in marriage! Emily would be green with envy.

Julia had clung to Ian when he left to go back to London and what Helen called his 'silly old bus', but she had not tried to persuade him to stay. She wanted time to herself so as to become accustomed to the sudden change in her life. She was no longer a girl, just out of school. Nor was she merely a member of Mrs Formby's staff at Trelees. She was Julia Coulsden, Ian's fiancée, and she could start sewing for her trousseau; she could stare in shop windows, assessing the varying merits of bed-linen and tableware; she could choose a ring, dream of her wedding-gown, decide with Ian where they were to live. If she met her old school-friends she could mention her engagement in the most casual way, pretending that she thought they had already heard about it. Mrs Ian Cornwell!

She had floated through her day at Trelees, astonishing everyone with her sunny smiles and willing ways, but had kept her secret. She had decided to ask her father if Ian could visit them the following weekend for dinner and, if pressed, intended to say only that he wished to discuss something important. If pressed further, she would tell them he wanted to marry her. Emily, of course, she would tell immediately.

The house was very quiet. The wireless was silent and there was no chatter. No one called out, 'Is that you, Ju?' – a question which always irritated her, since she returned home regularly about the same time and Emily, who worked in the baker's below the Landgate, was always in ahead of her. In the kitchen she found Agnes at the table, hunched over a mug of tea. Her eyes were red and her expression was sullen.

'Ag? What's up?' Julia asked, with a premonition of disaster. 'Is it Papa?' She took in at a glance the unwashed breakfast things, several pieces of broken plate still scattered over the floor and the fact that Agnes still wore her dressing-gown.

'Are you ill?' she enquired. Another thought struck her. 'Did you get my message? Ben said he would let you know – about me staying at . . .'

Agnes was shaking her head. 'Your bloody father!' she said at last. 'I'll swing for him one of these days.'

'Papa? What's he done? What's happened?' Her mind raced. 'Oh no! He's never left you!'

'I wish to God he had.'

'But *why?*' cried Julia. Disappointment filled her. Whatever it was she could not now tell them about Ian and all her plans were ruined. Tears of self-pity pricked her eyes and for a moment she could not speak but turned away and began to unbutton her jacket. When she had hung it in the hall she stood there for a moment, trying to control her anger at this setback. If Agnes was swearing, then no one was dead or even ill. Whatever it was, it couldn't be *that* bad.

She went back into the kitchen.

'Well, what is it?' she demanded. 'You'll have to tell me eventually, so why not now?'

Agnes sighed noisily but made no answer and Julia's voice rose: 'I said, what is going on? Are you deaf or something? And where's Emily?'

'Bloody good question,' said Agnes. 'She's buggered off and it's all your Pa's fault!' She put down the mug and her expression hardened. Having started the tale, she warmed to the telling. Julia sat down opposite her and prepared herself for the worst.

'She's buggered off with Chick Bird,' Agnes said, 'who has put her in the family way – *and* it's been going on for months under our very noses. I suppose *you* knew,' she added accusingly. 'You two are as thick as bloody thieves!'

Taken by surprise, Julia was tempted to pretend ignorance of the affair, but before she could decide whether or not Agnes would see through the lie, her stepmother had rushed on.

'A boy of that age! What right has he got to put anyone in the club? He's only just left school. He's a kid! He can't bring up a family; he's too young to even get married.'

'He's nearly fifteen,' Julia ventured unwisely, 'and he is earning.'

Agnes pounced. 'Ah, so you *do* know about it! I thought you two would have your heads together. Well, I hope you're satisfied, Julia Coulsden. Now you see what your deceitful ways have led to, don't you? Em's pregnant and she's gone off with Eunice's son. Oh yes, that's what's getting up your father's nose! Of all people, it had to be Eunice's son. After all these years, it's so bloody unfair. I bet she put him up to it, wicked bitch! She's caused us nothing but trouble, that one. It was her that wrote to your Ma all those years ago; it must have been. It was her that made your Ma kill herself.'

'No, it wasn't,' said Julia levelly. 'It was you and Papa. If you hadn't done anything, Eunice couldn't have sent the letter. *And* she had reason to hate you and Papa – you got her the sack, between you.'

Agnes's jaw dropped open with shock. 'How—' she gasped. 'Who told you that?'

'Does it matter?'

Agnes' voice rose to a shriek. 'Of course it bloody matters!'

'It was Chick Bird.'

Agnes recovered herself quickly. 'And you believed him? A nice thing, I must say. To believe that of your own father on the say-so of a spiteful kid.'

'You know it's true,' said Julia calmly. 'I found the silver. I was only five at the time and I didn't understand, but I spoke to Mrs Mack years ago. She told me she had tackled Papa and he had as good as admitted it.'

Agnes closed her eyes to hide her defeat and Julia waited. At that moment she revelled in Agnes's obvious distress, hating Agnes and her father – even Emily – for wrecking her happiness. Now not only was she unable to share her good news, but the good news itself was soured – for the news of Emily's pregnancy brought home to Julia for the first time the realisation that she might well be pregnant also. Could it happen on the first love-making? She wasn't sure. It hadn't happened to Emily – or had it? Frantically she began to work out how long ago it was when Emily had invited Chick into the hall. It was January, no February, March, April, May . . .

'When's the baby due?' she asked.

'What's that got to do with it?' Agnes demanded. 'I mean, what the hell does it matter *when*? The fact is she's having a baby and she's not fifteen yet. It's probably against the law. I don't know. Christ Almighty, an illegitimate child! It'll be all over the town.'

'At least,' said Julia spitefully, 'you were older when you had yours.' Immediately she regretted the words for Agnes's face crumpled up and she began to cry helplessly. 'I'm sorry,' said Julia. 'I shouldn't have said that.'

'Oh, you're *sorry*!' cried Agnes between sobs. 'Everybody's *sorry*. Emily was *sorry*. Your father was *sorry*. It doesn't help, being sorry. It's all a stupid bloody mess and all anyone can say is they're *sorry*. Well, I'm sorry too but—'

'Would you like another cup of tea?'

'No, I wouldn't. I've drunk enough tea to float a battleship. I'd like a sherry, a *large* sherry.' She raised her tear-stained face. 'I'd like a bloody large sherry. Better still, bring the bottle.'

When Julia brought it, she gulped down the first drink and then blew her nose. 'Don't you want one?' she asked.

Julia shook her head. She was wondering where Chick and Emily had gone. Maybe to Chick's home, she thought.

'They live on Winchelsea Beach,' she told Agnes. 'The Birds.'

'Well, of course they do,' said Agnes wearily. 'I'm willing to bet that's where they've gone, but your Pa refuses to go after them. I've begged him, but he won't budge.'

'He's scared,' said Julia, 'because of that business over the silver. He's scared that Eunice will go to the police.'

'She would too,' said Agnes. 'She's a real trouble-maker.'

Julia's eyes blazed. 'A trouble-maker? Aren't you forgetting you made her look like a thief? You lost her her good name. If I was Eunice, *I'd* want to make trouble.'

She wondered why Eunice *hadn't* gone to the police, but then realised that as far as Eunice knew there was no corroboration for her story. Eunice didn't know that the silver had been found, nor was she aware of Mrs Mack's involvement. If she ever *did* know . . . Julia groaned. It was all so sordid and this was supposed to be her happiest day. Or one of them. She hoped her wedding day would be the happiest.

'So,' she said, 'what's going to happen now?'

'Ask your Pa.'

'Don't you know?'

'Nobody tells me anything.' Agnes poured a second large sherry and Julia resigned herself to the fact that her stepmother would soon be drunk. Still, she had stopped crying and Julia was thankful for small mercies.

'Aren't you going to get dressed?' she asked.

'No.'

'Or wash up?'

'No.' Agnes looked at her blearily. 'I'm not doing anything more for this bloody family. I get more kicks than ha'pence here and I'm sick of it all. I shall never forgive Em, never! After all I've done for her. Worn my fingers to the bone, and this is how she repays me. Ungrateful little so-and-so! And as for your father, rot his bones! What I wouldn't like to do to him is nobody's business. The best years of my life, that's what I've given to this bloody family.'

Julia stood up. 'I'm going out,! she said.

'Where?' cried Agnes. Her eyes, Julia noticed, had the vague unfocused look that was the result of too much alcohol. 'Where are you going?' Her head rolled slightly. 'Everybody's going somewhere and I'm stuck here . . .'

'Where's Papa?'

'What?' She frowned, trying to concentrate.

'I said, where's Papa? Where's he gone?'

'Where do you think he's gone?' cried Agnes. 'He's either on *Silver* bloody *Lady* or he's down at the Pipemakers'. Take your pick. Julia! Come back here, I don't want you to go.'

But Julia slammed the door behind her and left Agnes to the sherry.

*

Julia rode first to the Fishmarket. The tide was ebbing fast and *Silver Lady* had gone. She could imagine her father stamping around the boat in a foul temper, watched cautiously by Frank Bligh and the rest of the crew who would be wondering what had happened to put the skipper in such a rage. Glad that he was safely at sea, she called in at the baker's shop where Emily worked, where you could buy 'a penny gut-full' – two layers of pastry filled with yesterday's stale cake. Emily was not there, so she rode out to Rye Harbour; there she left her bicycle and tramped the rest of the mile-and-a-half over rough shingle and fields, climbing over a variety of fences and other obstacles. She

passed the lifeboat house where the *Mark Stanford* waited. Julia
had watched several practice launches and had never ceased to
marvel at the strength and will-power of her crew. Now, however,
the lifeboat house was closed and shuttered and Julia, busy with
more urgent problems, did not give it a second glance.

She saw Emily before she reached the Birds' cottage – she was
standing at the water's edge where shingle gave way to sand,
throwing pebbles into the sea.

'Em! It's me!'

Emily turned as Julia ran towards her and held out her arms,
and a moment later they hugged each other as though they had
not met for a long time.

'I suppose you've heard,' said Emily. 'About the row, I mean?'

'Yes, I've just been home.'

'What did Ma say?'

'She's on the sherry but she's not at all pleased!'

'She said some terrible things,' declared Emily with a defiant
toss of her fair curls. 'I shall never forgive her. Chick's Ma says I
can live with them and when we're old enough we can get
married. I don't care what Ma says, or Pa either. I shall never go
back; I hate them both!'

'Oh Em, what will I do without you?' cried Julia. 'I shall miss
you. I wish this wasn't happening. I can't believe it. Yesterday
everything was the same as it always was and now it's all changed.'

'It can't be helped. Pa called me a trollop.' Emily sat down and
Julia did likewise. There was a cool breeze blowing off the sea and
they leaned together for warmth.

'He said I was no better than Ma and she threw a plate at him. It
missed, of course – she never could throw straight! Pa told her to
pick up the bits but she wouldn't.'

'What I don't understand,' said Julia, 'is how they found out.
Did you tell them?'

Emily giggled. 'He caught us at it – on *Silver Lady* of all places. I
think he could have forgiven us if it had been somewhere else.
"On my own effing boat!" he kept shouting. Poor Chick! I thought
he'd die of fright at first, but then they started fighting and Pa
began to breathe funny and I thought he was going to have a heart
attack, so I begged Chick to leave him be. I went home with Pa
and Chick came home here. Of course Ma had a fit when she
heard and they said I was never to see him again. Not ever. So I
told them about the kid; it seemed a good idea at the time.'

Julia sighed heavily. 'Poor old Em,' she said. 'I'm really sorry I wasn't there. It would have been one more on your side.'

'Doesn't matter,' said Emily. 'I don't care about the row. It's quite fun living with Chick's folks and Eunice seems to like me. I should have thought she'd hate me because of Ma.'

Julia struggled with her curiosity, but not for long. 'Where do you sleep!' she asked. 'With Chick? I suppose you might as well.' She felt slightly piqued. Just as she was gaining a fiancée, Emily was gaining a double bed.

'With Chick? No fear! Eunice – she said I can call her that – is very strict. Chick says she was pretty mad when he told her and clouted him round the ear, but Tommy just laughed; he doesn't care about anything. You know, he's really easy-going. Chick thinks the world of his Pa. I wish I did – mine, I mean.'

'You used to love him,' said Julia. 'I used to be very jealous.'

'You? It was me that was jealous of you. His 'silver lady'! He was always on about you. Ma used to get hopping mad and so did I.' She laughed wryly. 'Then I'd be extra loving to Luke Bligh when he called in. He was a nice man. I used to wish Ma would marry him and then I could have a pa around all the time. I prayed every night for a week that she'd marry him and then Pa turned up and was nice to me and I felt guilty inside. Funny what you remember, isn't it? Always the little things. I remember once how Pa took me to this fair and won me a necklace. Glass, I suppose, but I thought it was diamonds. I was so sure Ma would be jealous that I buried it in the vegetable patch. When I wanted to dig it up again I couldn't remember where I'd buried it; I couldn't help crying, so I had to pretend I'd fallen over. I wish we'd been real sisters, Ju, don't you?'

Julia considered, her head on one side. 'Would it have made much difference?' she asked.

Emily shrugged and they fell silent. The beach was deserted, but a few seagulls curled mournfully overhead and the fishing fleet lay to the west of the bay.

'When's the baby due?' asked Julia, putting an arm round Emily's shoulder.

'It isn't,' said Emily. 'I just made that up so they'd let us go on seeing each other. It seemed like a good idea, but it went a bit wrong.' She giggled nervously. 'Don't look at me like that, Ju. I just thought it was a good idea.'

'Not having one? But . . .' Words, which rarely failed her,

did so now.

'Perhaps I shouldn't have,' said Emily. 'But after I'd said it they carried on so I was scared to tell them the truth.'

'But Chick – does he think you are?'

' 'Course not.'

'Emily! You really are the limit, you are!' Julia was shocked. 'And I've been feeling sorry for you all this time and . . . honestly, Em! How *could* you?'

'Well, I might have been, we've done it often enough. Don't keep looking at me like that, Ju. I'll tell them in time, when they've calmed down. I'll just say it was a false alarm. That will cheer them up and make them feel better.'

'Em, honestly!'

Emily stood up and began to throw pebbles into the sea again. 'Your trouble, Ju, is that you're such an innocent,' she began loftily. 'You don't understand these things and you take everything so seriously. One of these days—'

Julia stood too and grabbed hold of her half-sister. 'Shut up, Em,' she said and gave her a little shake. 'Shut up and listen! I've got some news – some marvellous news – and I was only not telling you because I was so sorry for you and everything. Now I'm not sorry and you can jolly well listen to me for a change.'

They faced each other, Emily taken aback but curious, Julia smiling and triumphant. 'I'm going to marry Ian Cornwell,' she cried, 'and I *do* understand "those things" *and* I liked it and we might be going to Australia. I told you everything changed yesterday – for you as well as for me.'

'Getting married?' said Em, stunned by the news.

Julia nodded, eyes shining.

'To Ian Cornwell?'

'Yes.'

'Hell's bells, Ju!'

Once more they flung their arms around each other, then broke away but, holding hands still, regarded each other at arm's length.

'As you so rightly put it,' repeated Julia. 'Hell's bells!'

*

14 May 1926

The strike was over after only nine days. Everyone has gone back to work. They have taken Ian's bus away from him, thank goodness, so now I am hoping he will come down to dinner and ask formally for my hand. I did tell Papa he had proposed and of course he said I was too young to know my own mind, but Ag said it would be a good match and he should be thankful that one of his daughters had her head screwed on straight!

Emily is going to write them a letter to tell them the baby was a mistake, but she still wants to live with the Birds. It won't go down very well, but I am getting used to being on my own and certainly have more space in the bedroom. All Em's things are now in two tea-chests. Pa put them there in a rage, soon after it happened.

Poor Helen had another dizzy spell and fell and hurt her back. She has to stay in bed for a few weeks and she has a nurse who lives in. It must be costing a lot of money, but Ian's father is paying for it. I'm longing to meet his parents. Agnes's cough seems much worse and Pa is on to her to go to the doctor. I think she is scared to go, but she is getting very thin. She said her mother's sister died of TB and that means it may be in the family.

I had an invitation from Aunt Cicely to a preview of pictures and sculpture in the Drill Hall on Saturday next. It's for charity (I forget which one) and it's organised by Mrs Hook-Brayne and her brother is going to open it. He's a famous artist who paints the West Country and she and Aunt Cicely and another woman are doing all the flower arrangements. I'm hoping Ian will be down so we can go together. I just want to be seen with him. I do wish we had a telephone. I keep on to Papa. Lots of people have them now and it's terrible that Ian can't get in touch with me. I keep remembering that night and it is simply my happiest memory. I have seen a beautiful ring in the High Street, but I don't know how much money Ian can afford. He's still very hard up while he's doing his hospital year, although he finishes in July and my birthday is on the 18th. It's a gold band with three opals in a row over the top. I look at it whenever I go past and am terrified that someone else will buy it. I just pray they don't.

All Win's children have the mumps, so I am staying away.

I nearly forgot. Poor Mrs Mack died last week. I went to the funeral, although I knew I would be miserable. I thought she would like to see me there – if dead people can see anything. I don't know whether to hope they can or not. I don't know whether my mother would have liked to see me and Ian making love, but perhaps she wouldn't mind if she saw how happy I was.

GOODNIGHT, IAN. I LOVE YOU, DARLING

*

Coulsdens' yard was not exactly a hive of activity when Julia arrived. Tommy Bird was sitting on an upturned dinghy holding a mug of tea and Jack stood beside him with one foot resting on the boat's keel, drinking from a similar mug. Frank Bligh was talking to them, his feet slightly apart, his hands thrust into his pockets. All three looked up as Julia arrived, picking her way among the wood shavings and sawdust that had settled in most of the depressions. Here and there scanty grass survived and a rough path of cinders led down to the empty slipway.

'Hey up, Julia,' Jack greeted her cheerfully. 'Drop of tea, love? We could squeeze out another cup.'

She shook her head, greeting them all with a smile as Ben emerged from the boat shed with a newly painted board which he propped up against the side of the shed to dry.

'For Sale,' read Julia, curious. 'What's that for?'

'Fred Leggett's boat,' Jack told her. 'He's giving up. Bloody sad day!'

'Giving up?' cried Julia. 'But why? He's not very old, is he?'

Ben shook his head. 'It's not his age,' he explained. 'It's just that he can't keep going any longer. Poor old Fred; he can't afford to pay his crew and can't sail her single-handed.'

Tommy sighed. 'We saw it coming months ago,' he said, 'but poor devil, he wouldn't face up to it. Christ, when I told Eunice she wouldn't believe me. He's fished out of Rye as long as I can remember. My age, he is, or a bit over. Poor old sod!'

'But what's he going to do?' asked Julia.

Jack shrugged. 'Look for something else,' he said. 'His wife's father's got a bit of a smallholding and he's talking about helping out there. Making out he's looking forward to it, but no way! Fred's a fisherman through and through; never settle to anything else, Fred won't.'

Julia sat down on the upturned boat next to Tommy. 'I suppose he'll make a bit of money out of the boat.' she said.

'*If* he can find a buyer.'

'Oh, poor Fred.'

'He won't be the first,' said Tommy. 'Things are going from bad to worse and the bloody strike didn't help. No coal coming into Rye – and no timber. So no harbour dues. Nothing to unload, so no work. No boats so no repairs. Nothing! I'd give 'em strike, I would! There's folk down here would jump at the chance of a job and them strikers got work and wouldn't bloody do it. I don't understand, I really don't.'

There was a brief silence and then Jack, seeing their despondency, made an effort to change the subject. 'So what brings the Gooding girl to our humble boatyard?' he teased and they all laughed as the colour rose in Julia's cheeks.

Frank said quickly, 'Whatever it is, I'm glad,' and she flashed him a grateful look. She was surprised to realise that he had grown up over the last year or two and was very different from the gawky boy who had exhausted himself in the Regatta race against Jean Dessin. She recalled the way he had tricked her into a kiss and smiled suddenly.

'Penny for them,' he offered, eyeing her intently, but she shook her head. She wondered what he thought about poor Jean's death and whether he believed that her father was guilty. If so, then surely he would hardly continue working for him. She wanted to convince him of her father's innocence, but here in front of Tommy and her uncle it was quite impossible.

'How are your grandparents?' she asked him.

'They're both fine.'

Jack said, 'They've had a tough row to hoe and they're good people. First Luke, then Jean.'

Julia looked appealingly at Frank who smiled briefly. Then Jack suddenly reached out his hand and pulled her to her feet. 'So,' he said, 'this young lady has got herself engaged. Isn't that right, Ju?'

Immediately Julia was aware of a change in Frank Bligh's manner and a quick glance at his face confirmed this. His jaw had tightened and his eyes were dark with shock.

'What d'you think about that, then?' Jack asked, unaware that he was treading on dangerous ground. He surveyed his niece proudly. 'Got herself engaged to a doctor,' he said, 'and it's off to Australia as soon as they're wed!'

'Well, I'm not sure about the Australia bit,' Julia hedged. 'That's where Ian wants to go, but—'

Tommy grinned. 'Why then, you'll have to go with him if you're wed. Can't let the old man go off on his own, can you? You've got to keep your eye on him.' He chuckled at the look on Julia's face. 'Don't trust a man further than you can throw him,' he told her.

'That's sound advice, that is. My old gran passed that on to my ma and I'm passing it on to you. Isn't that right, Mr Coulsden?'

Jack grinned. 'I reckon so, Ju. You keep an eye on him.'

Ignoring their good-natured banter, Julia allowed herself another look at Frank and was disturbed by what she saw. His expression was inscrutable, as though he dared not allow his feelings to show. But why, she wondered? Had he heard something bad about Ian? She could not believe it, but something certainly had upset him. Her eyes met his in a mute appeal, but he lowered his gaze.

'I must get back,' he said suddenly and without another word, turned and walked quickly towards the gate.

'Frank!' Julia called, but he gave no sign that he had heard. She looked at her uncle and from him to Ben and then Tommy. 'What have I said?' she asked.

'Search me!' said Jack.

Impulsively, she ran after Frank, who had reached the gate and gained the path as she called to him to wait.

'Frank, please!' She put a hand on his arm to delay him and he swung round, his eyes blazing with an emotion she did not recognise.

'Frank, what have I done or said? Frank, I'm sorry, but I truly don't know.'

He swallowed hard. 'If you don't know,' he said, 'then . . . oh hell, Julia!'

They stared at each other helplessly. 'Won't you wish me luck, Frank?' she asked tremulously, but the anguish in his eyes answered for him.

'I'm sorry . . .' she faltered, but he turned on his heel without another word and strode off along the path towards the Fish-market leaving her at the mercy of her emotions, confused and tearful and longing to call him back.

*

Julia had to wait another week before Ian came to dinner. Once it had been arranged she was on tenterhooks, determined that everything should be perfect. She complained bitterly to her father about his so-called best suit and begged him to buy a new one which, she assured him earnestly, would also serve at her wedding. When he refused, she tried to persuade Agnes to use her influence, but Agnes pointed out sharply that times were bad and there was no money to spare for anything but necessities. Julia sulked for a whole day, then she found something else to worry about. It was Agnes's habit to serve the meals on each plate so that everyone's share was allotted before the plates reached the table. Julia informed her that at South View the food was served at the table from separate dishes and that the diners helped themselves to what they wanted.

'Bit hard on the last one,' commented Agnes, clattering soapy spoons on to the draining-board. 'I mean, you might find the others had taken the lot.'

Julia began to dry the cutlery. 'But they don't, Ag,' she said. 'Everyone takes a fair share of what's there.'

'I thought you said they took what they wanted?'

'They do, but—'

'So – your Pa likes potatoes. If he takes what he wants there won't be much left, I can assure you. He'd eat potatoes until they came out of his ears!'

'Look,' said Julia with exaggerated patience, as though to a small child. 'If I like potatoes I might take quite a lot, but there's probably someone who *doesn't* like potatoes as much, so he takes a lot less but he might like carrots so he takes more of those. It evens itself out.'

'You mean it *might* even itself out,' argued Agnes. 'Suppose this "he" *does* like potatoes and *doesn't* like carrots. Then what? Your Pa and this "he" person take all the potatoes and we're stuck with the carrots. I'm not mad about carrots. Are you?'

'No,' Julia admitted reluctantly, 'but there will be peas, won't there?'

'Probably.'

'Then I'll have peas.'

'Just peas?'

'Peas and chicken and stuffing and—'

'Your Pa likes stuffing. And "he" might like it. Suppose they've taken all the stuffing?'

Julia looked at her. 'You're doing it on purpose,' she said accusingly. 'Just to be awkward. Yes you are!'

'I'm not,' said Agnes, who was doing just that. 'I'm just saying that if it all depends on everyone taking equal shares, then why not put it on the plates like we always do and save the washing-up?'

'Because that's not how they do it,' cried Julia.

'Who's they? Posh people?'

'Yes.'

'Well, we're not posh so why pretend we are?'

'Because—' Julia bit her lip, not wanting to admit that she wanted to impress Ian. Then she had a flash of inspiration.

'Anyway,' she said triumphantly, 'it's ladies first, so you and I will be served first and we can take small helpings of everything—'

'I thought you said we all take as much as we want, so why do we have to take *small* helpings? Anyway, we haven't got any vegetable dishes.'

Struggling to keep her face straight, Agnes kept her head averted as she scoured burnt custard from the bottom of a saucepan.

Julia threw down the teacloth.

'You *are* being awkward,' she cried. 'You don't *want* it to be a success. You're jealous, Ag, just because he comes from a good family where they do things properly.'

'How do you know it's a good family?'

Agnes's amusement gave way to irritation, for there was a good deal of truth in what Julia said. She was mortified that her own daughter had run off with a Bird while Hettie's daughter was to marry into the professional class. Julia was going up the social ladder while Emily was going down.

'How do I know?' cried Julia angrily. 'I know because they don't keep rowing or having affairs and because they don't rant and come home drunk! They're polite to each other and they have nice manners and they go to places.'

'What sort of places?'

'Art galleries, theatres and . . . I don't know. They just live different lives. Look at us! Look at the Coulsdens. We're always squabbling. Mama Sarah was the only one; she came from a good family.'

'She was an old cow,' said Agnes, bitter memories flooding back.

'She was not!' said Julia. 'She was a Gooding.'

Agnes wiped the sink round to remove the grease, then turned and wagged a finger at Julia.

'You could have done a lot worse,' she warned. 'The Coulsdens may not be posh but they're honest, hard-working folk. We earn what we get, we don't get it handed down to us from our rich relations. Having it handed to you on a plate is nothing to boast about. You think we're not good enough for your precious Ian, is

that it? Oh, don't deny it, it's written all over your face. Well, I'll
be impressed with your fancy boy friend *when* he earns a bit more
money instead of poncing about in his grandfather's car.'

'He doesn't ponce!' cried Julia. 'And why shouldn't he drive it?
Wouldn't you accept a car if your grandmother gave you one? I
know I would. And he will be earning more very soon. He finishes
his hospital year in July and he'll be getting another appointment
then.'

'*If* he gets a job,' said Agnes. 'Jobs are hard to come by at
present, or maybe you haven't noticed. There are thousands
unemployed.'

'Not doctors. They're not unemployed.'

'We'll see then,' said Agnes. 'Are you going to finish that
wiping-up or is such humble work beneath you? You watch you
don't get too big for your boots, Julia *Lady* Coulsden.'

She marched out of the kitchen leaving Julia fuming. However,
she dared not goad Agnes too far and they both knew it. Without
Agnes's co-operation the dinner would be disastrous. She picked
up the teacloth and finished the wiping-up. Then she went in
search of her stepmother.

'Look, Ag,' she said, 'I've bought those two tureens for my
bottom drawer – the cream ones with little flowers round the
edge. You could use those and then I could wrap them up and put
them away again.'

By this time Agnes had recovered from her ill-temper and was
immediately tempted. Although she would never admit it, she too
wanted to impress their guest and had already bought an expensive new tablecloth on the 'never-never' from the draper's in the
High Street, which she would pay off at sixpence a week.

'All right,' she conceded, after a suitable pause to signify her
reluctance. 'We'll use them if it makes you happy.

Julia positively beamed with relief. It did.

*

On the appointed hour of the appointed evening the front door-
bell rang and Julia flew to open it. Ian stood there looking more
handsome than ever before and she flung herself into his arms,
almost crushing the large bunch of flowers he was carrying.

'Oh Ian, darling!' she whispered. 'I thought never to see you
again. It's been so long! Oh, what lovely flowers.'

'For Agnes,' he whispered with a conspiratorial wink. 'Must

get well in with mother-in-law!'

Agnes, presented with the flowers, was quite overcome and stammered her thanks. No one had ever given her flowers before. She fingered the delicate blue irises reverently and hurried ahead of them to show George.

With a wildly beating heart, Julia led Ian into the drawing-room where George, a glass of beer in one hand, rose to shake hands with the visitor.

'Nice to see you again,' he said.

'And you, sir.'

'Good drive down?'

'Yes. I came through Farningham. There's some beautiful country.'

'Is there? Oh, good.'

Everyone stood awkwardly, Agnes clutching her flowers, Julia holding Ian's arm. She had rehearsed the scene in her imagination and had tried to suggest to her father a line of behaviour suitable to such an important occasion. The silence lengthened and Agnes said hastily, 'Well, I'll put these flowers in water,' and made her escape.

'The weather's being kind to us,' Ian commented.

George nodded. 'It is. Yes.'

Julia caught George's eye and indicated the bottle of sherry and whisky which stood with a selection of glasses on a tray on the table by the window.

'Drink, Ian?' asked George. 'Sherry, whisky or a beer? And do sit down.'

He put his glass down on the mantelpiece, but Julia nudged Ian.

'Ahem, sir—' Ian began. 'Mr Coulsden, that is, I would like to ask for . . .' He took a deep breath and Julia squeezed his arm encouragingly. 'I am very fond of your daughter, sir, and – I'm in love with her, I mean – and I would like your permission to marry her.'

George, who had been carefully primed by Julia, promptly forgot his 'lines'.

'Marry her,' he echoed. 'Yes, well, why not?' Then he caught Julia's eye and saw the beseeching look. Frowning, he tried to remember what else she had considered it necessary for him to say. 'Yes, why not,' he repeated, playing for time. 'She's a good girl, but she is only fifteen, you know, and that's—'

'Sir, I know,' Ian broke in eagerly. 'We would expect to be engaged for at least eighteen months – two years even – but we'd like to get engaged now.' He smiled at Julia, whose heart sang. It wasn't going exactly according to plan, but Ian was with her and she knew George and Agnes had agreed to the engagement. She was too thrilled to worry too much about the details.

'Why not?' said George. 'Can't see any harm!' He laughed to show that this was a joke on his part. Then Ian laughed and Julia released his arm and whispered in her father's ear.

'Oh yes!' said George. 'And I hope you'll both be very happy.'

'Thank you, Papa,' said Julia demurely, determined to get her own part of the script correct. 'I love Ian very much and I'll do all I can to make him a good wife.'

Ian smiled and took her hand and they both smiled at George. Two pairs of shining eyes being more than he could cope with, he reached for his glass and emptied it in one gulp.

'Right,' he said dutifully. 'Now we've got all that nonsense over with, let's have a drink.'

By comparison with the preliminaries, the meal went very well and Julia could find nothing to complain about. Not that she wanted to, for two glasses of sherry on an empty stomach had gone to her head and she knew she was giggling too much and making foolish remarks. However, it seemed unimportant. All that mattered was that Ian, her future husband, was sitting across the table looking at her adoringly and everyone seemed to be pleased. Her only regret was that Emily was not with them to share the celebrations. Emily's letter had not yet materialised and she was still unmentionable so far as George and Agnes were concerned. Towards the end of the meal the conversation turned to London and Ian said he hoped that before too long Julia would come and stay at his home in order to get to know his parents.

'We'll take in a show,' he said. '*Rose Marie* has had rave reviews. My aunt has seen it twice already and according to her it beats *No, No, Nanette* into a cocked hat.'

'Does it really?' said Agnes. 'I expect they're all dying to meet Julia, you being an only child. What is it they say, not losing a son but gaining a daughter. We're gaining a son. Well, a son-in-law.'

George leaned forward and pointed a finger at Julia. 'This one,' he told Ian, 'knows how to behave herself, if you get my drift. She's a good girl. Lady by name and Lady by nature, that's Julia and I want her to stay that way.'

Ian blushed very faintly, warming the pale tones of his skin beneath the bright ginger hair. Julia nearly choked on a piece of apple pie as she avoided his eye.

'Now George, there's no need to—' began Agnes.

'I know what's needed, Ag,' said George, 'and I don't need you to tell me. After what's been going on around here, I think I *do* need to spell it out. It's for Julia's own good if we know we can trust her and that Ian's not going to take advantage—'

'*Papa!*' cried Julia. 'You can trust Ian, of course you can. And me. Please don't go on about it.'

George ignored her. 'I've got another girl, you know,' he told Ian. 'She's not been—'

'George!' This time it was Agnes who protested. 'That's enough said. Ian doesn't want to hear about Emily and you've no right! That's family business, not for strangers.'

Her face was red and she was breathing fast. Julia searched frantically for something to say to avert what looked like possible disaster.

But it was Ian who spoke. 'I understand, sir. You can trust Julia and me.' Impulsively he held out his hand across the table, but when George reached out to shake it he knocked over the gravy boat. A congealing brown mess crept across Agnes's new table-cloth and she jumped up angrily.

'George Coulsden! You clumsy oaf, now look what you've done!'

Ian's blush deepened. 'I'm terribly sorry, it was really my fault,' he stammered.

'Get a cloth, Ju, quickly,' cried Agnes – but at that moment a burst of coughing seized her and she began to gasp for air, doubled-up, her eyes bulging.

'A drink of water!' cried Julia.

However, Agnes knew what was coming. She had hidden the extent of her illness for a long time now and knew she must reach the privacy of the bathroom. Usually she locked herself in, but on this occasion there was no time. When Julia followed her a moment later with a glass of water, the bright red frothy blood from her diseased lungs was everywhere. Dr Jamieson was called and insisted that she be admitted at once to the new hospital at the top of Rye Hill. After a week she was transferred to the sana-torium at Midhurst where they did all they could to prolong her life, but she died on Julia's sixteenth birthday.

*

My very dearest Julia,

Thank you for your sweet letter. I am so sorry to hear the sad news about Agnes, although not altogether surprised. When we visited her last weekend I could see she would not live long, but did not say anything to you for fear of depressing you further. I know you were fond of her and whatever had happened in the past, she did her best to make a home for you. I appreciate that you would like me to attend the funeral, but my mother's health is still rather precarious and you will understand that I cannot leave her just now. The attack was so sudden and very puzzling, but no doubt the doctors will soon diagnose the cause.

I have missed you too, my sweet Julia. The week has dragged by and only your letters keep me going. As soon as I can, I will come down again and we will choose a ring. Of course I had not forgotten. How could I?

I'm very pleased you manage to find time to visit South View. Grandmother so looks forward to your visits. Thank goodness she now seems quite recovered; she did not like that nurse at all!

Now Julia, please do not be upset but I must tell you that I may have to go down to Devon for a few weeks. My mother's oldest friend lives in Exeter and has offered mother a period of convalescence there when she is well enough to travel. Father is much too busy to accompany her, so it will have to be me. I shall try to see you before I go, but if not will write to you as often as I can. You know I will be thinking of you constantly. When we return, we will arrange your long delayed trip to London to meet my parents.

Darling, I know this is a sad time for you, and my being so far away makes it all worse, but it is only a matter of time before we are together again. Then we have all our lives ahead of us and once we are married I swear I will never let you out of my sight! *Never*. I love you, my sweet, adorable Julia. You *must* believe me and try to be happy. I can't bear you to be so wretched.

Your ever loving Ian

CHAPTER TWENTY

Frank sat on the bank of the military canal, his bicycle beside him on the grass. He leaned back against an elm tree, his eyes fixed on the road that zig-zagged its course across the marsh between Rye and Appledore. At twenty, he was still five-foot nine, but more heavily built and with powerful shoulders. The summer sun had bleached his dark hair in streaks and the dark brown of his eyes was softened by his tanned skin. He wore the usual fisherman's rig – shapeless serge trousers in dark blue, a faded dark blue sweater knitted by Alice in the Guernsey style and an ancient cap perched on the back of his head; this had once been Luke's but was now out of fashion among the young men, having a stiffened peak and ear-flaps permanently buttoned on top. His boots were entirely lacking in polish and the smell of fish lingered faintly in his clothes. He did have a Sunday rig, but today was Saturday and it had not occurred to him that a change was called for. He wasn't interested in what he wore.

While he waited he whittled a stick with a penknife and thought about his father, Luke, who had died in the war. Alice had shown him some of the letters Luke had sent home; they were brief, scrawled and misspelt, but they all ended with the same words: 'Tell young Frank to watch himself.' Frank knew what he meant. The six words were all he had of his father. The letters had been written to the whole family and addressed to Mr and Mrs S. Bligh, but the six words at the end were for Frank alone. He had tried hard to build his philosophy of life around the simple phrase, interpreting the injunction as a warning – a warning to be cautious, an encouragement perhaps to be aware of the value of life and not use it recklessly.

In a way that he could not begin to understand, Frank was living two lives – his own and his father's. He tried to take Luke's place in the family and liked to imagine that now Sam and Alice regarded him more as a son than a grandson. He took life seriously and had no time for the company of foolish young men who drank too much and spent their hard-earned money on women. Having made up his mind years ago what he wanted from life, he had planned to that purpose, working long and hard and saving whatever he could. He would have a wife and family to support.

He watched the vehicles that passed him. The motorised van from the Hygienic Laundry, a horse-drawn coal cart, a furniture removal van and several private motors. There were plenty of cyclists including a club of twenty or more, women and men, who swept past, complete with haversacks and the new brightly coloured shorts. They waved and Frank grinned back. He could never see the point in that; a bicycle was useful to get around on, but cycling for pleasure? His own working week was so arduous that it never occurred to him that people engaged in sedentary work, locked away in stuffy offices all week, were glad to escape into the fresh air and take some exercise. He often wondered what he and his father would have done together if Luke had lived. After his death Frank had pestered his grandparents for information about the young Luke. *What did he like to do?* He did what he was told. *Who were his friends?* He liked the Simmons boy, but he drowned. *What was he like?* He was a good lad and you'd do well to take a leaf out of his book.

Alice, perpetually harassed, answered his questions briefly, but Sam was a little more forthcoming. It seemed that Luke had tried hard at school and was very good at sums, but not much of a one for writing. He liked to make things out of wood. He enjoyed helping out at Coulsdens' yard. He used to hang around with a group of lads, one of whom was Billy Simmons who had fallen into the Strand Quay at low tide and drowned in the mud before anyone could get him out. He was generous with what bit of money he had and always remembered birthdays; always bought a card and a bit of chocolate or a few flowers. Luke's wife had given him a son and then she had died. For a time, when Frank was old enough to think about it, he wondered if Luke blamed *him*, but he had never plucked up the courage to ask and Luke had shown no resentment towards him.

He squinted suddenly, shading his eyes from the sun as a familiar figure cycled into view. Jumping to his feet, he scrambled down the grassy bank on to the road. As Julia drew nearer he sprang out into the middle of the road and held his arms wide, forcing her to stop.

'Frank Bligh!' she smiled. 'What are you doing here?' She climbed off the machine and wheeled it to the side of the road.

'Waiting for you.' he said.

'For me? But how did you know I'd be here?'

'A little bird told me.' He thrust his hands into his pockets. 'I'm sorry about poor old Agnes. I didn't get a chance to say so at the funeral.'

'It was good of you to come,' said Julia. 'There were more people than I expected. I suppose over the years people forget – or else when you die they forgive you. Even Aunt Jane cried; I was surprised. It's a funny thing, Frank, but I miss Agnes dreadfully. After hating her for all these years, now I miss her. It was all over so quickly – she must have been so ill and none of us realised. Poor Emily blames herself for that business with Chick – upsetting them about the baby – oh, I forgot, you probably don't know about that?'

'I heard. These things get round.'

'I suppose so.' She shrugged helplessly. 'You can't go back and put things right, but at least Em told Agnes the truth when we visited her in the sanatorium.' She laughed faintly at the memory. 'Agnes said that when she was better she'd box her ears.' She swallowed. 'Poor Agnes, she had a tough life. I know she did wrong by my mother, but she paid for it I suppose.'

'I reckon we all do.'

'I spoilt her wedding, you know,' Julia told him. 'I interrupted the service and shouted out "Wanton woman" or something like that. I try not to think about it.'

'That doesn't sound like you,' Frank grinned.

'It wasn't really, it was Leo. He put me up to it.' She shook her head. 'All seems years ago now.'

'I didn't see your gentleman friend at the funeral,' said Frank casually.

'No.' He saw her expression change.

'I thought he'd be there.'

'He wanted to come, but his mother was taken ill,' said Julia defensively.

'Oh. What's the matter with her?'

'They're not sure yet.'

He nodded.

'But she really was ill,' repeated Julia.

'Did I say she wasn't?'

'No.'

'Well, don't fret,' comforted Frank. 'He'll be down again soon.'

'Yes. I'm on my way to South View to see his grandmother.'

Frank grinned. 'I know. Useful, that little bird of mine.'

She was intrigued. 'Who did tell you?'

'Aha! That would be telling. Does it really matter?'

'No, but why did you come?'

He shrugged. 'It's Saturday and I've got a few hours off and I thought to myself – what would I most like to do?' He paused.

'And?'

'And I thought I'd most like to clap eyes on Julia Coulsden, for whom I once half killed myself trying to win a rowing race.'

After a moment's reflection, a broad smile lit up Julia's face.

'You mean the Regatta!' she cried. 'Oh, wasn't that fun? I've never forgotten it. You did come second, though. You were awfully good to come second.'

'Your Uncle Jack gave me the money, but I did it for you. I must have been mad.'

'Mad?'

'Well, now you're going to marry someone else. Still, you did kiss me.'

Julia laughed again. 'You tricked me into that kiss, I remember. You said, "The winner always gets a kiss;" and then I realised afterwards you hadn't won!'

'I got what I wanted though.'

'Did you?'

'I got the kiss!'

'Oh.' She looked at him uncertainly. Why on earth was Frank Bligh flirting with her? 'Is this a leg-pull?' she asked.

'No.'

'Well, why then?'

'Why what?'

He was being very unhelpful, thought Julia. 'Why did you come out all this way to stop me and to remind me about the race and . . .' She stopped, confused.

'And the kiss,' he prompted.

'Yes. Why did you?'

'I told you just now. It was what I most wanted to do: to see you.'

'Even though you know I'm engaged?'

'You're not wearing his ring yet.'

Instinctively Julia hid her bare left hand. 'That's because we haven't had time,' she said. 'With his mother being ill, but we will choose it next time he comes down.'

'That's it, then,' he told her. 'When you're wearing his ring it will be too late.'

'Too late for what?'

'To tell you you're making a mistake. I thought I'd better come along and tell you today, to give you time to get used to the idea.'

'Frank Bligh!' stammered Julia. 'You have the nerve of the devil! I have *not* made a mistake.' For the moment, surprise tempered her anger. 'I'll have you know, Frank Bligh, that Ian and I are perfectly suited and terribly happy and madly in love . . . and everything we should be,' she ended lamely. 'So I'll thank you to mind your own business and not come chasing miles after me to tell me I've made a mistake.'

'I'm doing you a favour,' he said, apparently unperturbed by her reaction.

'And I say you're not!' she cried furiously. 'You're annoying me for no good reason and I certainly don't know why. I've never done you any harm, so I don't see why you have to try to upset me.'

'I don't want you to marry the wrong man,' he said reasonably. 'Ian is not the right man for you. I am.'

'*You!*' She was so angry she spluttered incoherently and this allowed him to continue.

'I suppose I should have told you earlier, but you only seemed like a schoolgirl. Doesn't your father think you're too young to get married? Just sixteen?'

Julia drew herself up to her full height and stepped astride her bicycle.

'I am not too young to get engaged,' she said haughtily, 'and I shall be marrying Ian when I'm seventeen-and-a-half. That is final. So I'll thank you to stay away from me, Frank Bligh, and stop annoying me.'

'I'm not annoying you,' he said. 'You've let yourself get annoyed. I've simply told you something for your own good.'

'It is *not* for my own good!' retorted Julia. 'It is not at all for my own good for you to wait until I'm engaged to someone and then come along and say it ought to be you, but you never got round to telling me.'

He looked at her steadily and she glared back at him. Then he said quietly, 'I'll have another kiss before you go, then.'

'You will not,' cried Julia furiously. 'Get out of my way, Frank! I don't want to talk to you any more.'

'After you've kissed me.'

'No.'

'You'll have to stay here, then.' He put a restraining hand on the handlebars of her bike and she knew he was quite capable of carrying out his threat.

'Look, I'm engaged to Ian,' she said helplessly. 'How can I go around kissing other men?'

'Who's to know except you and me?'

'Frank, please be sensible,' she pleaded. 'This is all so silly; I hardly know you.'

'We could soon put that right. This is a start.'

Julia glanced up and down the road, wondering how to extricate herself from the awkward situation. She imagined stopping the next vehicle and saying 'This man is pestering me' but it would sound rather ridiculous and might get Frank into trouble which was the last thing she wanted. Frank Bligh was a nice enough man. He worked for her father who spoke well of him, and he had come to Agnes's funeral. For some obscure reason, Julia had been inordinately grateful to all those who attended. Ian's absence had hurt her more than she knew. Now she glanced at Frank from the corner of her eye and saw the determined set of his jaw and the steely glint in the dark eyes.

'If I kiss you,' she began, ' – and it's only *if*, mind – will you promise not to do this again?'

'No, I won't.'

'Frank!'

'Look, Julia,' he said, 'I made up my mind to marry you a long time ago—'

'But that's ridiculous,' she protested. 'We were children then. I was only about nine.'

'Not then,' said Frank. 'Not at the Regatta. It was one evening when you'd all been for a picnic and I rowed you back across the river – you and Emily and the Coulsden boys.'

'Good heavens!' she said faintly.

'I admit I made a mistake,' said Frank. '*I* knew it would be you and me and I suppose I thought *you'd* know too. Now suddenly you've got yourself engaged to the wrong man. What do you expect me to do?'

'Well, I don't know,' said Julia with a shrug. 'I suppose you must look around for someone else.'

'That won't do,' he said with a firm shake of his head. 'It's got to be you.'

'Well, I'm sorry,' said Julia, 'but I am in love with Ian Cornwell and I do intend to marry him. If you must know, I shall be going to meet his parents as soon as his mother is better.'

'And has come back from her holiday.'

Julia's eyes widened. 'You do know a lot,' she said. 'I suppose my father's been talking to you. Or Em. Was it Em?'

'It was a little bird, like I said,' Frank laughed. Julia was suddenly aware of the intense look in his dark eyes and knew that his laughter hid a very real affection for her. No, she corrected herself, it was not affection but desire. This knowledge disturbed her and she tried to put the idea from her. 'Look here,' he said, 'I daresay you can't *agree* to kiss me but if I didn't give you any choice—' and he stepped forward suddenly and kissed her briefly on the mouth. Then he put his arms round her and kissed her again, slowly and with a hint of passion. When he released her he said lightly, 'Now if your conscience pricks you, you can tell the boy friend I took you by surprise. You can tell him you didn't enjoy it.' He grinned. 'You can tell him any story you like; he can't blame you.'

Julia swallowed. Several biting comments surfaced in her mind but she uttered none of them. Her heart was racing and she made an effort to appear calm, taking several deep breaths before answering.

'Please, Frank,' she said slowly. 'I shan't tell Ian because it might upset him, but please promise me you won't do that again.'

'But I can't, because I will!'

It seemed to Julia that the only way to convince him of the depth of her feeling for Ian would be to tell him they had been lovers, but dare she do that? No one else knew and it had only happened on that one occasion. She was sure Frank would reject her if he knew, but equally Ian might reproach her for divulging such a secret. Reluctantly she decided against telling him.

'Then I'm sorry,' she said with a sigh, 'because you'll only make yourself miserable for nothing. I'm Ian's girl, Frank. You're a very decent man and I've always thought well of you, and what you say about your feelings for me . . .' she shrugged '. . . but I'm promised to someone else. I'm not the only pebble on the beach and there are plenty of nice girls.'

'You're the only pebble on my beach, Julia,' said Frank, then he turned abruptly away and she watched speechlessly as he strode towards his own bicycle. Looking at him, she thought he moved with a powerful animal grace and for a moment compared him very favourably with Ian's light, almost feminine body. Feeling disloyal, she hastily dismissed the comparison as Frank pulled his machine from the grass and swung his leg over it.

'Be seeing you!' he told her and cycled off towards Rye without a backward glance.

As his figure dwindled in the distance Julia continued to watch him, feeling a sense of physical loss which disturbed her.

'Frank Bligh,' she whispered, 'you shouldn't have come here. You shouldn't have said all that.' Yet in her heart she was glad that he had.

*

A week later Ian was in Exeter staying with his mother and her friend, and had volunteered to exercise the Cornwells' large Basset hound which went by the unlikely name of Towzer. The dog had been christened by Donald Cornwell in one of his more humorous moments. Only child of Helen and Henry, Donald had married Dorothy Scott and their marriage had been reasonably happy. He was a mild and humorous man with little liking for the cut and thrust of human relationships. In his profession he was required to make important decisions every day of the week, with lives often at stake. At home he found it much more enjoyable to allow his wife to make most of the decisions. Naming the dog was one of the few things which Dorothy had left to him, and after four pink gins 'Towzer' had seemed to Donald a very sound name.

As soon as the door closed behind Ian and Towzer, Dorothy pulled her chair near to the table and prepared to tell Ivy, her closest friend, why she did not intend to allow Ian to marry a fisherman's daughter.

'I can't tell you the nights I've tossed and turned,' she began. 'I've been so ill with the worry of it all that I just had to get away. I had to talk to someone with a little sense and some understanding of what's right and what's wrong. Dear old D.J. is never going to understand in a million years why this match has to be discouraged.'

Ivy nodded. It always impressed her when Dorothy referred to her eminent surgeon husband as 'dear old D.J.'. She had known Dorothy since – as children – they lived next door to each other and shared the same desk at the local school in Honiton. Ivy had married a local butcher. Dorothy had gone to London to be a nurse and there had met and married Donald John Cornwell, one of the most promising students at Guy's Hospital.

Ivy said now, 'You have only the boy's welfare at heart, Dot, I know that.'

Dorothy clasped her hands nervously. 'I can't seem to convince D.J. of that; I wish I could. I feel so alone with this problem, but D.J. just can't see it. He says, "Let the boy make his own decisions; he's old enough to know his own mind; he's got to live with her" and all that sort of thing. But *is* Ian old enough to know his own mind, Ivy? I'm not at all sure he knows what he's doing. I think he's just rushed into it impulsively without any thought at all. A fisherman's daughter, for Heaven's sake! I hate to say it, Ivy, but I lay much of the blame on Helen's doorstep.'

'Your mother-in-law, you mean?'

'Yes, I'm afraid so. This wretched Julia turned up at their house years ago after some sort of family row. Ran away from home, if you please. That's the sort of girl she is!'

'Oh dear!' Ivy, who was knitting, dropped a stitch and Dorothy waited impatiently until she had retrieved it before continuing.

'Then somehow Ian met her again, years later, and invited her back to Helen's. I do wish he would stay in London at the weekends, but he likes Appledore and now Helen's on her own, I can see that she's lonely and welcomes his visits. But the girl visits her, too, and so they keep meeting. That's really how it all started and that's why I say blame Helen. She encourages the girl, encourages the match, too. The way she wrote to me, she's obviously very taken with Julia, says she is very striking to look at and has a sweet disposition, but that's not the point. There are plenty of young women just as nice and just as striking but from better backgrounds.'

Ivy looked up and nodded encouragement.

'I've never met her, Ivy, and between you and me I don't think I want to; I don't want to be influenced by her. She may be as charming as Helen says, I'm not disputing that. All I am saying is that if Ian has a career ahead of him as a doctor he's going to need a different kind of wife.'

'Hmm.'

'What does "hmm" mean, Ivy?' cried Dorothy. 'Don't you agree with me? It's not only for Ian's sake, it's for the girl's as well. She's going to be right out of her depth.'

'I daresay you're right,' Ivy said cautiously, 'but don't you think perhaps you ought to meet her? Should you not give the girl a chance?'

'No, it's quite out of the question.' Dorothy took a deep breath. 'Look Ivy, there's something else which I'm only telling you in the strictest confidence. I haven't even told poor old D.J.'

Ivy stared into Dorothy's eyes. 'I won't breathe a word,' she assured her friend.

'Well, I know someone down there in Rye. A friend of a friend, shall we say, without mentioning any names. But she's written out of the highest motives, I'm sure, to warn me about the *family*. My dear, they are quite beyond the pale! Now I do know it's not the girl's fault, but you will see what I mean when I say that she has quite the wrong background to be my son's wife.'

'How do you mean – beyond the pale? In what way?'

'I mean their behaviour, Ivy. Her mother *killed* herself!'

Ivy stopped knitting, shocked. 'Oh dear, how very dreadful,' she said.

'Because of another woman who had an illegitimate child!'

'Oh, my dear! No!'

'I'm afraid so. You do see what I mean, Ivy? And that's not the end of it. Apparently the husband married the woman with the child and then *she* had an affair and they say – although I have to admit this is only a rumour – that he murdered the other man!'

'Murdered him? Who? The father?'

'Yes, it would seem that Julia's father killed the other man. Mind you, I did say this last part was never proved, but there was a body – he was drowned – and the inquest brought in a verdict of death by misadventure.'

Ivy frowned. 'What does that mean exactly? Misadventure?'

'I'm not absolutely sure, but I think it means they are not positive it was pure accident and there may have been other circumstances involved.'

Ivy picked up her knitting and put it down again. 'Poor Dorothy,' she sympathised. 'I do see what you mean. What a ghastly mess! That poor girl – one has to feel sorry for her. Really, you can't blame her.'

'Well, of course I *don't*,' said Dorothy, 'but Ian is my only child and we've both got such high hopes for him. I just cannot stand by and let him make a mistake like this.'

'Does he know you are aware of this Julie's background?'

'Not Julie – Julia. No, he doesn't. But Ivy, *he* must know and he obviously doesn't care. He's madly in love . . . or thinks he is. Honestly, I have been almost out of my mind with worry ever since I heard. No wonder I've had palpitations and this awful panic feeling. I had to get away quickly because Ian, poor lamb, is so keen for me to meet the wretched girl and I really cannot face her. I just can't. So I pretended to be worse than I was and wrote to you. Then I had the brainwave of bringing Ian with me – to keep them apart. I'm so terrified—'

'Terrified?'

'That something will happen between them. You know what I mean.'

Ivy looked rather blank and Dorothy lowered her voice. 'A *baby*!' she said.

'Oh no, Dot!'

'Well, it's always possible.'

'You don't think they . . .'

Dorothy sighed. 'I don't know. Young people are so different these days. All the old ideas have gone and anything goes now, it seems.'

'Oh Dorothy, not your Ian. He wouldn't, I'm sure. Not that.'

'I hope you're right, Ivy, but . . . oh, he's back. Not a word now! Remember, we've been talking about gardening.'

'Gardening? Oh, yes. Of course.'

Ivy kept her eyes fixed on her knitting, but Dorothy looked up with a bright smile as Ian came into the room.

'Had a nice walk, dear?' she asked. 'I was just telling Ivy about the garden at South View. Henry did wonders with it, but it's too much for Helen now.'

*

The crab-apple tree was loaded with fruit. Small hard yellow apples, turned bright red by the sun, glowed amongst the leaves like decorations on a Christmas tree. Cicely stood below with a large basket, while Ben attempted to shake down the fruit. Crab-apple jelly was one of Cicely's successes and she usually spiced some of the fruit whole. Her one attempt to make crab-apple wine had failed, so she now concentrated on those products she did best. Sometimes she marvelled at the fact that she managed to fit in these domestic jobs, since the demands on her time had increased over the years. She now spent one morning a week as a voluntary worker at the hospital and played bridge on three mornings a week with a dedicated group of friends. She also organised privately an annual outing for the children of the town's unemployed fishermen. Now that business was greatly depleted, her husband spent more and more time with his brother Stanley in Hastings, but Cicely was not at all dismayed by his protracted absences. When he was home he was morose and irritable, as though she were somehow personally to blame for the decline in the fishing industry. She felt at times as though Jack resented her ability to find satisfying ways to fill her days now that his own were so empty. He had resisted her attempts to include him in her activities and she admitted, though only to herself, that they had less and less in common. Their home was virtually the only thing they shared. She liked to believe that Mrs Hook-Brayne was her closest friend, but the truth was that Cicely did not make friends easily although she could claim a large number of people as acquaintances.

As Ben paused in his shaking, she moved in to gather up the fallen fruit, ducking under the laden boughs.

'It's a bumper crop,' she told her son. 'I've never seen so many; it's a wonder some of the boughs haven't snapped. Look, do give me a hand, Ben, or it will take me all the evening. It doesn't matter if some of them are blemished. I shall sort through them later.'

Together they gathered up the apples and dropped them into the basket.

'I shall be out on Thursday night,' Ben told her. 'We're going to Dungeness, fishing.'

'All night, do you mean?'

'Yes. We'll go about nine, be back some time the next morning.'

'Who's "we"?'

'Me and Frank. Why do you ask?'

'I merely wondered if you'd invite Julia, that's all – the poor girl looks so miserable! I said to her, "Being in love is supposed to make a woman *bloom*." She said that she blooms when she's with Ian, but he's still in Devon. Living for his letters, poor child. I can remember when Winifred was doing just the same, eating her heart out waiting to hear from Ernest. I seem to—' Suddenly she jerked back her hand. 'Ugh! There was a wasp on that one. Do be careful, Ben. As I was saying, I thought it might take Julia's mind off her troubles. It can't be much fun for her, stuck in that house all on her own now that Em and Agnes are both gone. George isn't much company for her, that's for sure. Worse than your father, I should think!'

Ben straightened up and flicked an apple over the hedge into the next garden.

'Ben! Must you? No one would think you're a grown man. But do invite Julia on the fishing trip. It would be a bit of excitement for her.'

'I can't take one girl along,' he argued, foreseeing various difficulties.

'Well, invite Vicky, then,' suggested Cicely. 'She and Julia get on well together; they could keep each other company.'

Ben began to look a little more interested in the scheme. He had taken Vicky out once or twice since the disastrous Christmas and had found her pleasant company.

'I'll have to see what Frank thinks,' he said. 'I can't suddenly produce two women like rabbits out of a hat; he's expecting it will be just the two of us.'

'Oh well, do what you think best,' said Cicely, losing interest. 'I only thought it would be nice for Julia; she doesn't look at all her usual self these days.'

*

Julia's first instinct was to turn down Ben's invitation, but when she knew that Vicky would be there she wavered and then finally accepted. Ben did not mention that Frank would be going until after she had said 'Yes', at which stage it would have been impossible to back out without explaining what had occurred between her and Frank on the road to Appledore. Her mood was uncertain too. She longed to see Ian with a desperation that was ruining her appetite and sapping her energy, yet she suppressed a great anger at his prolonged absence. His daily letters were not always as reassuring as they might have been. One paragraph of his Tuesday letter had imprinted itself on her memory with painful clarity:

. . . Aunt Ivy (an *honorary* Aunt) understands how much I am missing you and is doing her best to console me by inviting friends round to dinner to cheer me up. Saturday it was a retired couple (he was something in the Foreign Office) and last night Ivy's younger sister Ella, widow of a bank manager, and her daughter Virginia – a rather homely young woman, but very witty. I must admit she kept us all in fits of laughter throughout the meal, which gave me terrible hiccups . . .

Julia was haunted by the cheerful vision of *her* beloved Ian sharing jokes with the daughter of a bank manager. The fact that the girl was 'homely' did nothing to reassure her. The rest of the letter contained everything she wanted to hear, but she could not rid herself of the feeling that it was not quite decent of Ian to be having so much fun while she herself was lonely, distraught and ill. Well, maybe ill was too strong a word, but certainly she felt out of sorts and lethargic. Once Ian held her in his arms again, she knew she would feel better. Virginia? She hated the name. Witty? She wondered if Ian liked his women witty and tried to think of something humorous she might say when they next met. Homely? Since when had being homely deterred a man, she asked herself bitterly. Her own mother, Hettie, had been homely and she had married George, the most handsome of the Coulsden boys. A bank manager's daughter surely would be rich, well-educated, well-dressed. Julia ground her teeth. If Ian *had* to spend a happy evening in the girl's company, surely he could have had the sense to keep it to himself. Of course she didn't mistrust him and of course she wasn't jealous. And no, she didn't want him to be miserable but *she* was. She was miserable, lonely, out of sorts and had been sick. Only once, though, she reminded herself. And anyone could be sick – people were lovesick all the time.

If she had had any remaining doubts about the wisdom of accepting Ben's invitation, Ian's Thursday letter removed them. In it he informed her that they would be returning to London at the weekend and that his mother had invited Virginia to travel back with them and stay for a week or so, as 'the poor girl has never been to London.' He went on: 'Mother is so much better and looking forward to meeting you. She suggests you come up while Virginia is with us, and we will book to see *Rose Marie*. We shall be together again at last, my dearest Julia. I am so longing for everyone to meet you . . .'

Julia's secret fears leaped into the open and she crumpled the letter into a tight ball and hurled it across the bedroom. Now she knew exactly what was happening, but Ian would never believe her. She knew it as surely as though Ian's mother had shouted her intentions to her from the wilds of Exeter. The sophisticated Virginia and the fisherman's daughter would be side by side, so that Mrs Cornwell's precious son could make his own comparisons. It took her only a few moments to unravel the horrid plot. She hated Dorothy Cornwell. She hated Virginia. She hated Ian for being so blind, so innocent. How could he let them play out such a charade and not see what was happening?

Simmering with fury, she paced up and down the small room, wondering how best to fight back. If she accused his mother, Ian would defend her. Mother and son were very close and Ian would think Julia jealous and hysterical. No, if Mrs Cornwell was being subtle and underhanded, Julia decided to play her at her own game. With trembling hands, she took out a sheet of notepaper and reached for her pen.

'Dearest Ian', she wrote, 'I am so pleased that your mother has recovered from her mystery ailment . . .' Pausing, she reluctantly crossed out 'mystery ailment' as being too sarcastic and substituted 'attack of whatever-it-was', then continued:

I can't wait to see you all (and Towzer, of course) but especially you, my own sweet Ian. It has been such a long time that we've been apart. I shall count the days until you hold me in your arms again. Ivy sounds very kind and Virginia great fun. I look forward to meeting them all, your father too. Also *Rose Marie*. I have been very lonely without you, but my Aunt Cicely has done her best to cheer me up. She has talked Ben into taking me fishing at Dungeness tonight. We shall go about nine o'clock and sleep on the beach in a little tent thing called a bivouac. Not just me and Ben, of course. Vicky is coming with us and also Frank Bligh who works as crew on *Silver Lady*. They are not very witty, but I'm sure we shall have a lot of fun. I didn't really want to go, but Aunt Cicely said [this next part was pure fiction] that you were obviously enjoying yourself in Exeter and would want me to be having fun too. She is very sensible about such things. So think of the four of us on the deserted beach in the middle of the night, fishing for codling . . . or whatever! Frank is going to lend me a rod and Ben will lend one to Vicky. I think it will be a bit of an adventure.

Anyway, darling, do take care of yourself. Longing to see you again.

Yours for ever, Julia

She added a row of kisses, then threw down the pen and burst into tears. When finally she stopped crying she addressed the envelope, stuck on a stamp and went out to post it.

*

They went in Jack's car, crammed in with their luggage and in a
mood of growing excitement. Frank and Ben sat in front, with the
two girls in the back. The tin containing the bait – lively, wriggling
lugworms dug from the beach that morning – was stowed at
Frank's feet, since both Vicky and Julia declined to have it anywhere near them.

'I shan't be able to bait my hook,' Vicky confided as they drove
through Appledore and out on to the marshes. 'Ben will have to
do it for me.'

'He will,' said Julia. 'He's a good sort, Ben is.'

She was glad that Ben and Vicky seemed interested in one
another and wondered hopefully if they might marry one day,
although she did not speak of it. They discussed Leo's baby, a
girl, but there was not too much to say for the christening had
been a small local affair in Wiltshire and none of the family had
attended.

'They sent a photograph,' said Julia, 'but all babies look the
same really. At least, they do to me. Leo says she sleeps a lot and is
putting on weight.'

Vicky asked her about her engagement to Ian and was vaguely
surprised by the lack of enthusiasm in Julia's answers. She wanted
to ask if anything was wrong, but decided she had no right to invite
confidences so held her tongue.

The moonlight was very bright, fortunately, although they had
come prepared with torches. They struggled on the steeply shelv-
ing shingle with their blankets, rolled mattresses and pillows, for
the girls were definitely not prepared to 'rough it' as Ben had
suggested. Their footsteps seemed deafeningly loud in the
silence of the deserted beach and the sound of the sea was very
close. When they had finally unloaded the car, Julia and Vicky
offered to organise the 'camp' while Ben and Frank prepared the
four fishing rods.

'I'm starving already,' Vicky confessed, 'and we haven't even
started! I'm glad we don't have to wait until we catch something
before we can eat. Might be a long, hungry night!'

Julia laughed. 'They're bound to catch something,' she said.
'The sea bed shelves very steeply here and the fish come in very
close. It will probably be sole for breakfast, or maybe a cod steak
or codling.'

They sorted out the bedding and weighted it all down with
large pebbles – for there was a breeze blowing off the land – and

then set off with one of the torches in search of driftwood for the fire.

'We shall need a lot of wood,' said Julia, 'if we want to keep it going all night, but if it goes out while we're asleep I daresay someone will light it again. We'll have to act all helpless and let the boys be gallant and do it for us!'

'There's a mass of dried seaweed over here,' called Vicky. 'Will that burn, do you think?'

'We can try,' said Julia. 'Let's just take anything that looks burnable.'

'I must say,' said Vicky, 'that the prospect of a few flames is rather appealing. It's so creepy, isn't it? I keep thinking there could be other people out there in the shadows, watching us.'

'Don't!' cried Julia. 'I wasn't going to say anything in case I made you nervous. Now you're doing it to me! Are you any good at lighting fires?'

'Not very.'

However, they surprised themselves for within ten minutes they had a blazing fire going which gave them comforting and reassuring warmth as well as holding back the surrounding darkness.

Ben called to Vicky to take the rod he had baited for her and as she left the comfort of the fire, Frank took her place. He crouched beside it, rubbing his hands.

'It's parky out there,' he told Julia. 'I reckon you've got the best job.'

'I'm going to cook the sausages,' she said, 'and we've a mass of cold potatoes and onion to fry up. How come you're not fishing? Given up already?'

'No,' he grinned at her and the firelight emphasised the angles of his face. 'I've propped up the rod and there'll be a fish waiting when I go back!'

Julia busied herself with the two large frying pans and without speaking Frank helped her to wedge them securely over the flames. She separated two pounds of Ashbee's best pork sausages and arranged them in one pan with a lump of dripping.

Frank looked at the tongs she was using and laughed. 'Everything bar the kitchen sink, by the look of it,' he said. 'You'll be telling me next that you've brought a tablecloth and solid silver cutlery!'

'Well, I haven't,' she retorted. 'I've just brought what I thought we'd need. Of course if *you* want to take over the cooking you can. I suppose you'd use a bent twig and a prayer?'

'A few curses, more likely!'

Julia was aware that he was watching her and in her nervousness she dropped the tongs into the fire and Frank had to pull them out for her.

'Poor Agnes's best tongs,' said Julia. 'She was very proud of all her kitchen things. Her "utensils", she used to call them. I expect I've scorched the handle, but it's too dark to see properly.'

There was a long pause and then Frank remarked, 'Seems my luck's changing.'

'Is it? How's that?' asked Julia, knowing full well what he meant.

'Well, you and me spending the night together!'

'Frank Bligh!' she protested. 'It's not at all like that and you know it.'

'I do and you do,' he agreed. 'But does the boy friend know it? Doesn't he mind?'

'He won't know until it's too late,' said Julia with a toss of her head. 'My letter won't arrive until the day after tomorrow.'

'Ah!' He nodded, pursing his lips. 'So he might have objected if he'd had time?'

'Maybe – but he has no right to.' Julia's anger was still there, but well suppressed. 'He's going out for walks with a young woman, a friend of someone.'

'Is he now?'

'Yes, he is.' She tried to speak lightly.

'Would you have come otherwise?'

Julia hesitated, then shrugged. 'I don't know, but I don't think so.'

'You're better off with me. Don't envy her,' he said.

'How's that then?'

'Because *I'd* never do that to you.'

She believed him. Savagely she pushed the sausages around in the pan until they began to sizzle, then emptied the dish of potatoes and onion into the other pan. Sighing heavily, she took another sideways glance at Frank as he sat back with his hands round his knees.

'I heard something,' he said, wisely changing the subject, 'but it was only a whisper, mind – about Jean's drowning.'

Julia stared up at him, the cooking momentarily forgotten.

'About Jean? Who told you? What was the whisper?'

He held up a warning hand. 'Don't count your chickens!' he warned. 'I said it was a whisper. My great aunt Ellen – that's my grandma's sister – she's married to a chap called Bitty. A nasty piece of work; really evil, he is.'

'So what about him?'

'Give the spuds a stir and I'll tell you,' he grinned. 'We didn't haul two women out here just to eat burnt spuds.'

She gave them a perfunctory stir. 'Go on, Frank.'

'Well, it seems he and Jean and another man used to do a bit of smuggling on the side and the night Jean drowned there was something going on a mile or so off Fairlight. Bitty drinks a lot and when he's drunk he can't keep his mouth shut; he talks about it then, but he'd always deny it, wouldn't he, and there's no proof.'

'How d'you know all this?' breathed Julia.

'Aunt Ellen told it to my grandma in confidence. She'd like to tell the police, but if they couldn't prove it he would go back and take it out on her – most likely kill her. He's beaten her up before now – put her into hospital with stitches in her face. She's too scared to leave him.'

Julia's eyes were large in the firelight. 'It's such a long time ago,' she said. 'I don't suppose there would be any clues or anything. Oh, poor Jean! How awful for him. It's bad enough to have an accident, but to be *killed*! Isn't there any way we could find out?'

'I could try to knock it out of him,' suggested Frank.

'*Knock* it out of him? You mean *fight* him?' Julia was horrified.

'It's the only way. I'll have a try if you want. I'd like to even the score for Jean.'

Her throat was dry. 'I don't know . . .' she stammered. 'I don't want you to have to fight anyone, but – oh, let me think about it, Frank.'

Nodding, he asked, 'Did you think your father had killed Jean?'

'I didn't know what to think,' she answered carefully. 'In fact I tried not to think about it in case the police took him away. Yet I know how angry he was, so I always thought he could have done it without meaning to. He's a very strong man.' She thought for a few minutes. 'What's this Bitty man like?'

'Tall, a bit on the hefty side, but gone to seed. Too much drink. Flabby and not very fit, I'd say. Why, are you scared I'll get hurt?'

'Yes, I am. He might kill *you*!'

'Not on your life! You look very pretty tonight.'

'Oh!' The abrupt change of subject flustered her.

'Ian's a fool if he's playing around with—'

Julia broke in quickly. 'He's not playing around, I only said he was going for walks.'

Sudden squeals of excitement from Vicky interrupted them and sent them both crunching over the shingle to admire the large plaice she had caught.

'It's a fluker!' called Ben, using the local name for a particularly large plaice without much flesh on it.

"A couple of pounds, Ben says,' Vicky told them breathlessly. 'There was a humming sound as the line went spinning out and it's so difficult to see anything. The moonlight's reflecting off the water and it's hard to see what's happening. Oh, my very first fish! I was petrified. I thought I'd lose it again.'

She threw her arms around Ben's neck and kissed him. 'Thanks for your help, Ben. I never could have landed it on my own!'

He winked at Frank. 'Don't you wish you'd helped Julia to land a fish?' he asked.

'Who needs a fish?' cried Frank and before Julia could dodge away, his arms were fast around her and he had kissed her.

Vicky laughed. 'That's cheating, Frank,' she exclaimed.

'No, it's not! That's payment in advance for when I *do* help her land one. Right now we're busy with supper, so you two can get on with your fishing.'

And he dragged Julia back to the privacy of the fire. The sausages, spitting cheerfully, were duly turned and the potatoes and onions were given a good stir.

"I suppose I shouldn't say so," said Julia, 'but it's beginning to smell rather good. At least I can cook,' she added enigmatically.

'What can't you do?' he asked.

Julia was surprised. He was much shrewder than she had expected.

'I can't be the daughter of a bank manager,' she said bitterly.

She waited in vain for him to ask what she meant by the cryptic comment, but he threw himself full-length beside the fire with his hands propping his head. She fought down a desire to tell him all her doubts and fears about Ian's mother and the 'witty' Virginia.

Instead she said, 'He wants to go to Australia.'

'You'll have to learn to stand on your head, then.'

She laughed.

'What's he going to do out there? Shear sheep or something?'

'No, of course not. He's a doctor – people get ill in Australia, the same as they do here.'

'You amaze me.'

Julia tried to imagine him fighting Bitty and her stomach turned over. 'Don't fight that man,' she begged. 'There's no reason why you should. Suppose I tell my father and let him decide what to do? He might think it best to go to the police.'

Frank shook his head. 'Bitty'd guess it was Aunt Ellen who had spilled the beans and then she'd cop it. No, my way is the only way we'll get a confession, but even then it would have to be in front of witnesses. Bit of a long shot, I'm afraid.'

'Perhaps it would be better not to rake it all up again,' sighed Julia. 'Oh dear, I don't know. Why is life so difficult? I've got plenty of problems already and I just don't need any more.'

'Problems?' he said. 'What problems have *you* got? You're going to marry a handsome young doctor who's madly in love with you. I don't see any problems there.'

She looked at him soberly. 'Nothing is ever as simple as that. For a start there are his parents . . .' she hesitated.

'Lots of people have parents,' he said. He sat up, picked up a handful of pebbles and tossed them over his shoulder into the darkness.

'His parents . . .' She hesitated again, staring into the flames, not meeting his eyes. 'They're a different kind of people.'

'I thought you'd never met them?'

'I haven't but – I've got this feeling that . . .' She looked up fearfully. 'I don't think they approve of me,' she said. 'I have a terrible feeling that they won't like me. They think I'm not good enough for him.'

After a moment Frank said, 'You're marrying him, not his folks.'

'I know but . . . his father's a famous surgeon. I expect they live in a big house and lead a different sort of life.'

'Your Ian's not a famous surgeon, though, and you'll be in Australia so what does it matter about his parents?'

'But I don't want to *go* to Australia,' she burst out. 'I want to stay here.'

'Right here on the beach?'

'No! In England, I mean.'

'Perhaps you should marry a local man instead,' he suggested. 'I know someone who might be persuaded to make an honest woman of you.'

Alarm swept over her as the words 'honest woman' reminded her of her sickness. 'What d'you mean by that?' she demanded sharply, anger masking her fear.

'Perhaps you should marry me,' he said with an attempt at lightness. 'I'm a very obliging sort. Twist my arm and I'd marry you tomorrow.'

Julia relaxed a little. 'You're very persistent,' she told him. 'And it is sweet of you, but I want to marry Ian. The trouble is that there's this wretched Virginia.'

'Don't tell me! She's the daughter of a bank manager.'

'Yes she is, damn her!' She sat hunched over the fire and by its light Frank read the misery in her eyes. He moved to sit beside her and put a comforting arm round her shoulders.

'Look,' he said, 'you're a lovely girl and if Ian can't see that you're worth ten of Virginia – well, he doesn't deserve you. So stop worrying about it. It'll work out.'

'I wish I thought so.'

'Of course it will.'

'But you don't really want it to.'

'No, I don't.' He rested his head against her shoulder. 'I want it to be me, but I also want you to be happy.'

'You see!' she cried triumphantly. 'I told you life wasn't simple.'

'So you did. Oh, Julia!' He lifted his head. 'I love you, that's all I know. I always will. If you marry your Ian, then that's the end of it and I'll come to the wedding and wish you luck. But if you don't, just remember *I'm* here and *I* want you.' His voice was low. 'I could make you happy and I will if only you let me. Oh, hell and damnation! I'm making a blasted speech! Forget it.'

He stood up, put his hands to his mouth and shouted, 'Hey! You two! Supper's ready.' He turned to Julia. 'It is, isn't it?'

'Just about.'

They sat companionably in the glow of the fire eating the sausages and potatoes. Julia wished that Ian was with them and then reluctantly found herself wondering if he would enjoy the adventure. But of course he would, she told herself loyally. Would Virginia? Did the daughters of bank managers sit around on the beach late at night, eating sausages and slightly burnt potatoes?

Perhaps they did. Perhaps she was prejudiced. Vicky was obviously at ease and she was a teacher. Julia had a great respect for schoolteachers. She remembered her geography master, who could be distracted from a dull lesson by discreet questions about the coming of the railways, a subject on which he was something of an expert. And dear old Miss Standing, who acted out the poetry she read to them – and poor Miss Stobart, whose fiancé had been killed in the war.

'Do you like being a teacher?' she asked Vicky.

'Yes, I do,' Vicky replied. 'It's very satisfying. Not much money, but I suppose we get our rewards in other ways. I've never really thought of doing anything else. Ever since my parents gave me a toy blackboard and easel.' She laughed. 'I used to line up my dolls and teddy bears and teach them the alphabet.'

'I'd like to be in your class,' said Ben.

'He'd play you up,' warned Julia. 'He was terrible at school, so was Leo.'

Ben said hopefully, 'Maybe I could stay behind after school?'

'Maybe,' said Vicky.

'How are we going to wash up?' Julia asked as she put the last forkful into her mouth.

'Scour the plates with sand,' said Frank, 'then wash them off in the sea. Just turn them up on the beach and they'll be dry by the morning. I hope you two girls will be warm enough. If not, we'll share the bivvy and keep you warm.'

'What a *kind* offer,' laughed Vicky. 'How very generous!' She patted her stomach. 'That was delicious. Thanks to the cooks!'

'Your turn in the morning,' Frank reminded her.

They caught four more fish that night – a fairly large cod and three more plaice – and afterwards they made cocoa and sat round the fire talking until well into the early hours of the morning. Then Frank and Ben erected the makeshift bivouac for the girls, with poles and a couple of tarpaulins, while Julia and Vicky collected more driftwood – some to bank up the fire and some ready for the morning.

The girls laid a mattress in the 'bivvy' and covered themselves with blankets. Outside, on the far side of the fire, Frank and Ben wrapped themselves in blankets and after some good-natured back-chat, finally they all slept.

*

Julia woke first, blinking in the strange light, then recalled instantly where she was. Beside her Vicky slept heavily, one arm hiding her face.

Feeling a now familiar queasiness Julia sat up cautiously. She had slept soundly, lulled by the muffled splash of the waves against the steep shore, a sound which had haunted her uneasy dreams. In her first waking moments she struggled to recapture the last dream – a confused fantasy of flying over the sea, looking down on it from a great height; Leo was there, his face stern, his arms folded across his chest; there was a strange, tall woman dressed in black and Agnes was there too, sitting up in her bed in the sanatorium and looking exactly as Julia had last seen her. For a moment she tried to unravel the dream's meaning. Was the woman in black Ian's mother perhaps? And why was Leo looking so grim? And where was Ian in the dream? Resentfully she thought that since he couldn't be with her in reality, the least he could do was to inhabit her dreams and make her nights happy.

Her stomach rolled ominously and she gritted her teeth. She could not spoil everything by being ill. Would any of the others feel sick, she wondered? Perhaps it was food poisoning. She took a few deep breaths to calm her nerves, for already the tight knot of panic was forming deep inside her. Deciding to walk in the fresh air, she wriggled to the entrance of the little shelter. Pulling on her shoes (they had all slept in their clothes) and being careful not to disturb Vicky, she crawled out on to the beach. The fire had gone out and the men still slept, huddled and shapeless within their rolled blankets. Ben breathed noisily but Frank was silent. For a moment she stood gazing down at them, then looked around her. It was very early, perhaps an hour or two after dawn, and overhead the sky was streaked with high, trailing clouds tinted warmly by the hidden sun. A low band of white mist hung over the sea and the air was very still.

Julia turned westward and began to walk, shivering a little in the clammy early morning air. It would be a fine day, she forecast. The beach was mysterious in the half-light and the sea calm and quiet, the wavelets merely slapping against the shore. She walked with long firm strides, trying not to think about her uneasy stomach. As she went she picked up scraps of driftwood to supplement the supply they had laid in the night before, but the thought of lighting it and cooking the fish made her heave and she covered her mouth with a trembling hand and tramped doggedly on. She would *not* give in to this ridiculous weakness. She had never been ill in her life, she reminded herself sternly, and did not intend to start now. But was being pregnant an excuse for being ill, or a reason? Was it necessary or could she control the workings of her body? And anyway, she was *not* pregnant; she would not even consider the possibility. Her eyes narrowed suddenly as a thought occurred to her. If she *was*, would it turn the opinion of Ian's parents in her favour – the prospect of a grandchild? Probably not, she concluded despairingly. More likely to turn them against her. They would no doubt think she had seduced their precious son! She swore under her breath, then whispered, 'Ian Cornwell, where are you when I need you? Why aren't you here with your arms around me, telling me not to be afraid? I *need* you, don't you understand? Don't you care?'

She swore again – the worst words she could think of – threw down the wood and clutched her stomach. Then she ran down the sloping shingle towards the water and fell on her knees, crying and vomiting at the same time. Fumbling for a handkerchief, she wiped her mouth and sat back on her heels, shaken but already feeling better. She rubbed at her eyes and then, finding a clean corner, blew her nose. She felt insignificant and unattractive and suddenly she wanted Agnes or Mrs Mack, or even her grandmother, to pat her head and tell her she was a good girl.

'Although I'm not,' she whispered. 'I'm no better than anyone else. Mama Sarah was wrong. There's nothing special about the Gooding girls and they're certainly not good – at least, this one isn't!'

Julia forced herself to face the facts. She had been so scornful of people like Agnes – and Emily when she had pretended to be pregnant. Now everyone would point the finger at *her* and if Ian married her it would be a hurried shamefaced affair and not the most wonderful day of her life. Suddenly she became aware that someone was watching her and turned sharply to find Frank standing a few yards behind her. His expression was grim and her heart sank.

'What's up?' he asked brusquely.

'Nothing,' she hedged.

'Are you ill?'

'No. At least, I might be. I don't think so.'

She knew her confusion was painfully obvious and turned back to stare out into the mist. Briefly she envied Agnes, out there in

the vast beyond where nothing could touch her. Presumably
Agnes had gone through all this when she was expecting Emily.
Julia felt a rush of tenderness towards her stepmother.

'I wish I'd been nicer to Agnes,' she whispered, her voice
choked as fresh tears rolled down her face. She averted her face
quickly, but not before Frank had seen her glistening cheeks. He
came to stand in front of her and, reaching down to take her
hands, pulled her to her feet.

'Stop it,' he said. 'Tears don't help. Here – it's a bit grubby but
it'll do.' He handed her a large handkerchief.

'It must have been the sausages,' said Julia.

'Maybe.'

A quick look at his face told her that he guessed there might be
another reason and the knowledge of what that meant was hurting
him.

'I was collecting wood,' she said, pointing to the scattered
evidence. 'Perhaps we should light the fire again?'

'There's plenty of time. D'you think you're in the family way?'

Shock rendered her speechless for a moment.

'Could you be?' he persisted ruthlessly.

'Do we . . . look, it's really nothing to—'

'Yes or no?'

Julia took a deep breath. 'Since you insist on knowing, then yes,
I could be,' she told him with a hint of defiance in her voice, 'but I
hope I'm not.'

'Why's that, then?'

'It makes it all seem . . .' She shrugged, searching for the right
word. 'So mean. I don't want it to be like this.' She looked at him
with unspoken appeal in her eyes. 'You always think that being in
love will be so wonderful, but it's not. It's doubts and fears and
misunderstanding each other. Everything's going wrong.'

She waited for his comment but he said nothing, just put his
arms round her and hugged her gently with a few reassuring pats
on the back for good measure. He did not kiss her.

'Cheer up!' he said. 'It happens all the time and it's not the end
of the world.'

Releasing her, he stepped back suddenly and she felt herself
blush under his scrutiny.

'You look awful,' he said. 'If you *are* and if he backs out, I'll be
here.'

'He wouldn't back out—'

'That's all right then, but if he does, remember—'

'He won't, Frank; he's a good person. He'll be upset and obviously it will upset everyone, but he won't back out. I'm sure of that.'

'You don't look very sure.'

'I am sure. Certain sure,' she insisted.

'Then why look so gloomy? You'll be married to the man you love and you'll have the young 'un.'

'That's right.'

'But!' He smiled for the first time. 'If he doesn't make an honest woman of you, I will. No, wait,' as she was about to speak, 'I'll give you until a month from today. You sort things out between the two of you over the next few weeks. If it's him, that's my hard luck. If it's not, come and tell me and we'll get wed. No one else will know it's not mine, and the rest of them will be!'

She tried to smile, but her face felt stiff and cold. 'Frank, I don't know what to say,' she began.

'Oh, Christ! No speeches, please,' he said. 'Come on, I've had my say and I don't need an answer. It's understood between us, right?'

'Right . . . and thank you, Frank.'

'My pleasure, ma'am.' He grinned. 'Now, give us a smile, Julia. It'll all come out in the wash, as my gran says, and she's right. You'll look back in five years' time and wonder why you got so upset.'

'Five years!'

'Well, two then.'

Julia laughed shakily. 'You are a dear, Frank,' she told him.

'No, I'm not. I'm a very selfish man. I want you and if this is the only way I can get you . . .' He shrugged. 'Well, that's fine with me. I hope he does back out.' He grinned. 'I hope his dragon of a mother talks him into marrying the bank manager's daughter.'

'Oh, don't say such things! Please, Frank!'

He held out his hand. 'Come on, let's walk a bit further and then we'll pick up the wood on the way back.'

She nodded and took his hand, and as they walked the mist cleared from the water and the sun came out from behind the cloud.

CHAPTER TWENTY-ONE

Jack sat at the table in the front room and surveyed the accumulation of papers and bills with a feeling of utter hopelessness. There was no way left to him to deny the seriousness of the situation. Coulsdens' yard was through.

'Through!' he muttered. 'We're bloody well done for, Jacko. After all these years. Oh, Jesus Christ! It's bloody all over, my son. But how? *How?*'

He picked up a piece of paper at random. Rates outstanding; threatening court action. He picked up a handful of bills and invoices. Old Brett owed Coulsdens £185, but Jacko knew he hadn't got it; probably he hadn't even got the five, let alone the rest. So he wouldn't pay. Sammy Stevens had paid only half of the £52 he owed. Not much chance of any more there. Nobody had any money. Even his own brother, George, owed him £70. He might get that, if the lazy sod would stop drinking long enough to take the boat out and earn himself a few bob. Jack didn't envy George's crew, but then his own workforce had dwindled and he owed the remaining men four weeks' wages. He looked up uneasily as Cicely came into the room with a cup of tea.

'Still doing accounts?' she asked in some surprise.

He nodded a 'Thank you' as he took the tea. In a fancy tea-cup, he noticed. If he had told her once, he had told her a thousand times that he preferred tea in a large mug. Two swallows and this cup would be empty, but Cicely did not think it 'nice' to serve tea in a mug. That sort of thing was all right in the yard but not in the house – that was her argument. Now he was too depressed to care one way or the other.

'Might not have to do them much longer,' he remarked.

'I should hope not. You've been at it since just after eight.'

'I don't mean today, Cis, I mean *ever*.'

'Ever?' Her expression was blank.

'There won't be many more accounts,' he said. 'There's no more work.'

'No more work, Jack? Oh, don't talk so silly!'

At least he had caught her interest, he thought. Lately her mind had been so full of her various activities that conversation between them had necessarily been reduced to a minimum.

'I'm not talking silly, love. I'm trying to tell you how things are.'

Still Cicely did not understand the full significance of what he was trying to tell her.

'Don't worry so, dear,' she said. 'Things will pick up, they always do. We've had these slack times before, you know we have. It's not the first time and it won't be the last.'

'Cis, I'm telling you,' he said heavily, 'but you never listen. There won't *be* any more slack times because we aren't going to survive this one. I'm sorry, love, but there's no way out as far as I can see and you have to know some time.'

He saw her stiffen and read the alarm in her eyes. 'There's always a way out,' she said. 'Always, Jack. You can't mean it – you're just trying to frighten me.'

He shook his head. 'Sit down, love, before you fall down,' he said and guided her unresponsive body to a chair by the table. She watched him silently, her eyes dull with shock.

'Listen, Cis—'

'I do wish you'd call me Cicely,' she said automatically. 'You know how I hate "Cis".'

Jack ignored her. 'Listen,' he said again. 'We have to face facts and the facts are that although I'm owed money I can't get hold of it – and even if I could it wouldn't be enough.' He held up the rates demand. 'They're going to take me to court,' he said. 'Ned's owed four weeks' money and he'll have to go because there's nothing else for him to do if he stays. There's barely enough for me and Ben. I'm sorry, but that's the hard truth. This is the slump to end all slumps, the whole country's in a mess and God knows how we'll get out of it. *If* we ever do.' He shook his head. 'Coulsdens are finished,' he said. 'Washed-up. It's true.'

Cicely continued to stare at him as the enormity of what he was saying finally registered in her brain.

'But what about Benjamin? Does *he* know?' she asked. 'What does he say?'

'Can't say nothing, can he?' said Jack. 'But he must know how things are going, he's not blind or daft. I shall have to tell him, but he won't be surprised. I can't tell you how sorry I am, but I don't know what else I can do. I've done my best all these years. Thank

God the old couple aren't alive to see this day; it's enough to make them turn in their graves.'

'The end of Coulsdens,' said Cicely, dazed. 'It can't be! I can't believe it. There must be something we can do. You can't just take a cup of tea and tell me we're finished. You've never said anything before, never even hinted.'

'Oh yes, I have, Cis, but you only hear what you want to hear. It goes in one ear and out the other. You've always been the same – head in the clouds.'

For once Cicely did not rise to the bait but stared at the litter of papers and appeared not to hear.

'Couldn't Stanley help?' she asked at last.

'How can he? He's had to lay up one of his boats and he's got nothing. I don't know how they make ends meet.'

'But what will we *do*?' cried Cicely. 'We can't go on the dole.'

'Why not? There's plenty more out of work. I reckon we'll have to – and be damned glad of it, too. What's the alternative, Cis? Starve? Is that what you want?'

'Of course not. Oh, but Jack, I couldn't bear the dole, I really couldn't. What would everyone think? All my friends! Oh no, Jack. I couldn't bear it. You mustn't let it happen. There must be *something* we can do. Some way out of the mess. There *must* be!'

With a despairing gesture Jack pushed all the bills towards her. 'Right then,' he said. 'There's the bill from the chandler's; he's waiting for just on two hundred. Timber merchant, upward of six hundred. Rates. Wages. How are you going to pay them? Eh? Are you going to sell the family heirlooms?'

'Don't be flippant, Jack,' said Cicely sharply. 'We haven't got any heirlooms and you know it.'

'Then *you* tell *me* how you're going to pay all these bills.'

A long silence fell between them as Cicely picked up one invoice after another and studied them intently.

'George, then,' she suggested. 'Can't *he* help?'

'Oh God, Cis, you know what a state he's in! Be reasonable.'

Her eyes gleamed suddenly. 'What about Julia's money?' she demanded.

'Julia's?'

'Yes.' Cicely eyed her husband excitedly. 'She's got money, Jack. Hettie left her money in trust and so did your mother.'

'Oh no, Cicely.' He shook his head emphatically. 'No, I couldn't. That's hers, she'll need it.'

'Not if she's going to marry a doctor and go to Australia. She could invest it in the yard.'

'She never would. And George would never allow it. No, Cis, it was a good try but it just isn't possible. Anyway, the money's tied up until she's older. I'm sure it is. No, we couldn't ask – and anyway, what would we do with it?'

'Pay these bills.'

'And then what?'

'Carry on as before.'

'Cis, there's no work! *No work*. Why the hell can't you understand what I'm telling you?'

She looked defeated, her face muscles sagged and her shoulders drooped resignedly. 'I've got a little jewellery,' she offered. 'You're welcome to that, Jack, if it's any help.'

'No, no, you keep it,' he told her. 'You may never get any more and it wouldn't make much difference. I shall sell the car. That can go.' He sighed heavily.

'Oh Jack, not the car! I know what that means to you.'

'It doesn't matter,' he said. 'I'd rather go without it and know I've paid some of my bills. Don't want it all round the town that we've cheated our creditors. I don't want fingers pointed.'

The prospect plunged Cicely into an even greater despair. 'Perhaps Benjamin will think of something,' she suggested without conviction.

'Don't count on it, love. Even Ben can't work miracles. And that's all that can save us now – a bloody miracle!'

'I wish you wouldn't swear, Jack,' she rebuked him.

'I wish I didn't bloody well *have* to,' he shouted and, with a sweep of his arm, sent the bills fluttering from the table on to the floor.

*

The dreaded invitation from Ian's mother arrived at last. In fact it was from both his parents, but in Julia's mind his father had ceased to matter. She felt sure it was his mother who was the danger, the one most likely to thwart her plans to marry Ian. It was a printed invitation on a deckle-edged card and that in itself made her nervous. Obviously it was going to be a formal occasion. No doubt deliberate, she thought, and intended to make her feel out of her depth – which it certainly would do. The most formal occasions she had ever attended were the visits to Helen at South

View, but they were no comparison. Evening dress would almost certainly be worn and Julia did not possess anything suitable. There was no point in asking her father for money for a new dress because Julia knew it would not be forthcoming.

In desperation, she cycled out to the Birds' home and consulted with Emily, who could not lend her anything but did suggest that she might borrow something from Aunt Cicely and shorten it just for the occasion. On reflection, Julia approached Vicky instead and her letter was answered promptly by an invitation to 'come to Hastings and choose something'. Full of gratitude, she took the train the very next day and spent an enjoyable hour considering Vicky's adequate wardrobe, finally selecting a short green crêpe. The dress suited her perfectly and the colour complemented her silvery blonde hair. She imagined herself astonishing the Cornwells with her dazzling appearance and revelled in the thought that Virginia could not look any better. She was not vain but she knew that she was beautiful, although the knowledge did not greatly excite her – except, that is, in the present situation where she felt that her looks might be at least one point in her favour.

Vicky was a little taller than Julia, but Vicky's mother offered to raise the hem an inch or so for her. That done, they had a cheerful meal and Julia went home with rising hopes that the event might not, after all, be the disaster she had at first anticipated.

The great day came and she travelled to London on a late afternoon train, the dress in a small suitcase with her night wear and toiletries. She would have Sunday breakfast with the family, then Ian would drive her back to Rye and stay with her until Monday morning. The proposed visit to the theatre had been conveniently forgotten and the 'stay' had been shortened from the original long weekend to an overnight visit. Julia regarded these departures from the earlier plan as indicative of the Cornwells' waning interest in Ian's fiancée, but as she stared out of the train window, she vowed to put aside such ungenerous thoughts and to concentrate on the fact that she would be with her beloved Ian again. Whatever might go wrong, whatever might be said to upset her, she would remain calm because when it was all over she, Julia, would leave with Ian for Sussex and Virginia would be left behind. In that respect at least, Julia felt that she held the trump card. If only Helen had been invited, she thought wistfully; then she would have had another ally.

The train drew into Charing Cross with a squeal of brakes and a rush of steam and Julia leaned out of the window to look for Ian. She was searching for a man standing alone and almost missed him. In spite of all her good intentions, she gave a gasp of dismay as she saw that he was standing with a young woman and they were both waving cheerfully.

'No, Ian, *no!*' she cried silently. 'How could you bring her with you? How could you ruin our meeting?' But even as she forced a smile and waved back, her thumping heart had steadied and she knew exactly how she could turn the situation to her own advantage. She could let Virginia see with her own eyes the ecstatic way two lovers greeted each other.

As soon as the train stopped, she jumped down on to the platform, set down her suitcase and flung wide her arms as Ian hurried towards her. He looked more desirable than ever with his bright blue eyes and the distinctive red hair. Her heart gave a lurch and all her doubts were dispelled as he reached her. Their arms went round each other as he lifted her off the platform, kissed her and swung her round and kissed her again.

'Oh darling!' cried Julia. 'My dearest, adorable Ian! Oh—' She flashed a quick smile at Virginia. 'Isn't he the most wonderful man? Aren't I the luckiest girl?' Before Virginia could answer, Julia flung her arms round Ian's neck and clung to him, kissing him repeatedly so that he had no choice but to respond. When at last she thought the demonstration sufficient she released Ian, who looked slightly flustered, and turned her attention to his companion.

'Oh, you must be Virginia,' she said. 'Ian mentioned you in his last letter.' She seized Virginia's hand and shook it briefly before turning back to Ian. 'Oh darling, thank you for those marvellous letters. You must have been up all night writing them. Poor man!' She laughed towards Virginia. 'He ought to have writer's cramp by now. Pages and pages!'

Ian picked up her case. 'Virginia insisted on coming to meet you,' he said. 'I didn't think you'd mind.'

'Mind?' Julia laughed. 'Of course I don't mind. I'm just so thrilled to be in London. Nothing could spoil it for me.'

'Not even Virginia,' she thought, seeing by Virginia's face that she had, correctly, interpreted the suggestion that her presence *might* have done so. Ian understood it too and hastily led them towards the ticket barrier, with Julia clinging to his left arm and

Virginia walking on his right, separated from him by Julia's suitcase.

Virginia was not exactly 'homely' as Ian had suggested in his letter. She had beautiful dark hair, fashionably waved and falling forward over a high forehead. Her eyes were brown and her brows heavy. Her mouth was large and her nose rather short, but the effect was pleasantly frank and open. She was not beautiful but she knew how to make the best of herself and her clothes could not be faulted.

Julia had seen jealousy in the other girl's eyes. So, she thought, Virginia could very easily fall in love with Ian if she had not already done so. Forewarned is forearmed and suddenly Julia's doubts melted away. She could and would hold on to her fiancé; she would see to it that his mother's little plan misfired. Going back in the car, she monopolised the conversation with a vivacious account of what she described as her 'beach party' and could see that Virginia was impressed and Ian was jealous. So far, so good!

'Vicky caught this marvellous fluker,' she told them.

'Fluker?' said Ian. 'What on earth is a fluker?'

Julia laughed. 'It's the local name for a very large plaice. The very small ones are known as friers. We have our own language, you see. They spear flounders down at the harbour and they're "eye-ballers". The tiny stuff that comes up in the nets, that's "stalker bait". They're too small to sell, so we use them as bait for lobsters and crabs.'

'How quaint,' commented Virginia.

'Yes, we are,' Julia agreed. 'We're terribly quaint!'

There was a moment's silence. 'It all sounds great fun,' said Virginia.

'It is,' Julia assured her. 'Honestly, Virginia, if you've never been to a beach party you must make the effort. Sleeping under the stars with the waves splashing on to the beach! Oh Ian, I know what we'll do. We'll organise one next time you come down. Just the five of us. The others are such marvellous company.'

When she paused, breathless, Virginia said, 'It sounds marvellous, but wasn't it cold?'

Julia laughed once more. 'Well, I suppose it might be to a town mouse, but we're country mice and we're used to it. Don't worry, Ian, we'll give you an extra blanket or else you can snuggle up to me!'

Before anyone could react to this broad hint, she turned to

Virginia. 'You've been for lots of exciting walks, I hear,' she said, managing to make the walks sound as unexciting as possible. 'What fun. I'm dying to meet Towzer; Ian went on and on about him.'

'He's a lovely dog,' said Virginia eagerly. 'He—'

'Oh Ian, I forgot to tell you, Helen sends her love.' Julia turned to Virginia again. 'Ian's grandmother is like a mother to me. We get on so well. She was the first person to hear about our engagement and she was so delighted, wasn't she, Ian?'

'Yes, she was. She—'

'I'm so looking forward to meeting Ian's father, if he's anything like Ian's grandmother,' Julia went on. 'Do you have a man in your life, Virginia? I'm sure you must have.'

'Well, not exactly,' Virginia stammered. 'At least, there was someone, a boy I grew up with—'

'Oh Ian, remind me to tell you something about my father,' Julia interrupted. 'I won't bore Virginia with all the details, but it was something Frank told me. I'll tell you when I've finally got you all to myself . . .'

She maintained this aggressive flow of conversation until by the time they pulled up in front of the house, she was mentally exhausted and her throat was dry.

*

It was Donald Cornwell who met them at the door.

'My dears, you're back very soon.' He took one look at Julia and was immediately enslaved. Good God! The girl was an absolute corker. Poor old Virginia couldn't hold a candle to this one.

'There was not too much traffic,' said Ian. 'Father, I'd like you to meet Julia. Julia, this is my father.'

'Very pleased to meet you, m'dear,' he cried. 'Well, what a cracker Ian's chosen for his wife. Always knew the boy had a good eye, but my word! She's quite lovely, Ian, quite lovely!'

Julia's spirits soared at the prospect of another ally and she gave him a dazzling smile of gratitude. Donald Cornwell was fifty-one, a tall man, heavily built and with the beginnings of a paunch. His large square face was fringed with white hair and he was rapidly going bald. He sported a small white moustache, his cheeks were very pink and his eyes a faded blue. He did not conform in any way to Julia's idea of an eminent surgeon, looking to her more like a cheerful child. Brought up in an Army family,

Donald Cornwell had adopted many of his father's expressions. In fact, he had modelled himself on his father in a subconscious effort to compensate for the anguish he had caused him by declining a military career. Patients found his appearance disconcerting, but fortunately his bedside manner was entirely reassuring.

'I'm very pleased to meet you at last,' said Julia. 'I've been so looking forward to it.'

'Have you now? Well, that's splendid. Come along in and meet Dorothy. She's pottering about somewhere. A great potterer, my wife. Ah! Here's Towzer come to say "Hullo". Towzer's not backward at coming forward, are you, old chap?'

Julia knelt to pat the dog, who also seemed pleased to see her. 'Towzer,' she said. 'What a lovely old-fashioned name.'

Donald's smile expanded. 'Aha! You're a young woman of discernment, isn't she, Ian? Towzer was my choice. I thought it had a certain ring to it. It's quite unusual, you know; you won't meet many Towzers around.' He stood with his hands on his hips looking down at the dog and the sleek silvery head bent over it. 'Say "How do you do," then, Towzer. Where are your manners?'

To Julia's surprise the dog barked twice and she stood up, laughing, just as Ian's mother came out of a door to the right of them.

'Mother,' said Ian, 'this is Julia.'

Julia's hand was taken in a firm but brief grasp and their eyes met in mutual appraisal. Dorothy was four years younger than her husband and as many inches shorter. She was very plump, yet she did not look fat for the flesh was distributed quite evenly over her frame. Her bust was large above a neat waist, her brown hair was waved in the current fashion and suited her well enough. She wore an expensive though simple grey dress and no make-up, her jewellery consisting of several large rings and a long rope of pearls.

'How do you do, Mrs Cornwell,' said Julia. 'I've been looking forward to meeting you.'

'I'm sure we have all been looking forward to it, haven't we, D.J.?'

'Good Lord, we certainly have. And what a lovely girl our Ian's chosen. Do the Cornwells credit, eh?'

'I'm sure we shall all enjoy your visit,' said Ian's mother. 'Did you have a good journey? The trains can be very crowded at this time of the year.'

'It wasn't too bad,' replied Julia.

'Good! Travelling can be very exhausting,' said Dorothy. 'Well now, suppose I show Julia up to her room? I expect you'll want to freshen up. Ian and Virginia were in the middle of a game of tennis, so I expect they will want to finish it. Ian is very keen on the game and we have just had a court laid out. Do you play, Julia?'

'No, she doesn't,' Ian broke in. 'And actually, I don't think we mind about not finishing the game, do we?'

He turned to Virginia, who hesitated long enough for Dorothy to say, 'Oh Ian, don't be so selfish! I'm sure Virginia wants to.'

Virginia smiled at Ian. 'I was winning, remember, two sets to one, and I—'

Donald intervened. 'Of course you don't mind; it's only a game and I'm sure Ian wants to spend a few minutes on his own with his lovely Julia after all these weeks.'

'In the bedroom?' said Dorothy. 'Really, D.J. – Julia is going up to her bedroom now. There will be plenty of opportunity for them to be on their own later.' She smiled at Julia. 'You'll have to forgive my husband; he's an incurable romantic, I'm afraid.'

'I like incurable romantics,' said Julia with a bright smile. 'I am one myself and of course I'd love to have Ian to myself for a few minutes.' She gave him a challenging look. 'Why doesn't Ian show me to my room? That solves the problem, doesn't it?'

'Capital idea!' cried Donald before Ian could answer for himself. 'Off you go then, and when you come down I'll be waiting to offer Julia a glass of our best sherry. You do drink sherry, I suppose?'

'Sometimes,' said Julia. 'Thank you, Mr Cornwell, I'd like that.'

'Splendid! A sherry it shall be, then. Now Ian, don't keep her away from me too long!'

Sensing Dorothy's disapproval, Julia did not risk a glance in her direction but smiled at him and followed Ian upstairs. When the door was safely closed, Ian threw the suitcase on to the bed and turned to take Julia into his arms. They kissed passionately for a moment and then stood back to look at each other.

'Julia! Oh darling, you look so beautiful. They're knocked sideways by you. Did you see Father's face? He adores you – and so do I!' They embraced again.

'It's been so long,' Julia complained. 'I almost forgot what you looked like. You'll have to have a photograph taken for me—'

'We could have one taken together—'

'Oh Ian, I love you!'

He said hesitantly, 'I'm sorry about Virginia. Mother suggested she should come and she seemed so keen.'

'It doesn't matter now. Does your mother like me, do you think?'

'Oh yes,' he replied, his tone rather lacking conviction, 'I'm sure she does. She's not so . . . well, she doesn't show her feelings the way Father does, but I'm sure she likes you. You do look terrific.'

'As terrific as Virginia?' The words slipped out and it was too late to take them back.

'Virginia? Who's Virginia?'

They both laughed. 'Who *is* she exactly?' Julia asked as she flipped open the locks on her suitcase and began to unpack.

'She's the daughter of a friend of Ivy's. I thought I told you when I wrote.'

'Oh, thank you for all those lovely letters.' Julia picked up a pair of shoes and put them in the bottom of the wardrobe.

'Who's Frank Bligh?' asked Ian.

'Frank? Oh, he works for my father. He lives with his grand-parents at Rye Harbour; his father Luke died in the war. I've known him for ages.'

Ian sat down on the bed. 'You've never mentioned him before. I was consumed with jealousy.'

'I was jealous of Virginia. Oh darling, why are we so silly?' She flung her arms around him and kissed him. 'Look, we won't talk about them any more. We'll have a lovely evening and then—'

'Julia,' he said hesitantly.

'Yes?'

'About that night . . .' he lowered his voice, 'when we made love. For goodness' sake don't say anything about it – you know how parents are.'

Julia hesitated. This might be a good time to tell him of her fears, she reflected, but then again it might not. It could send him into a panic and ruin the visit before it had properly started.

'No, of course I won't,' she assured him. She would tell him on the drive home, she decided. That was a much better idea.

'Well, I'll go on down,' he said, 'and you join us when you've finished unpacking and so on. And Julia . . .' he took her hand, 'do be nice to Virginia, won't you. She's not a threat to us or anything like that and she is an awfully decent sort of girl.'

'She's keen on you, Ian. I can tell.'

'Maybe this Frank Bligh is keen on you. I'd be surprised if he wasn't. Does it make any difference to us?'

'No.' She sighed deeply. 'I'm sorry. I just get frightened, that's all. It's all so wonderful, Ian, and I don't want it to go wrong.'

'How could it?'

'I don't know. It just could.' But in fact she could think of two reasons: he could fall for that 'awfully decent' Virginia, or he could turn against her when he learned that she might be expecting his child.

Ian grinned. 'You don't get rid of me that easily,' he told her. 'I'm your official fiancé, remember? We'll soon be buying you a ring and then I shall expect you to dazzle all the Franks—'

'And all the Virginias!'

He kissed her again. 'Everyone,' he said. 'They will all know you're mine!'

'Ian, when will we get married, d'you think?'

'Married?' His face changed. 'Oh, I don't know. There's no hurry, is there? Mother thinks you are too young to get engaged, so for heaven's sake don't talk about marriage yet.'

'But between ourselves, how long?'

'I suppose a year or two.'

'Oh!'

'What's the matter? Don't you agree? Darling, it's not my decision, it's *our* decision. When would you think?'

'Six months?'

'*Six months!*' His jaw dropped. 'But that's . . . Julia, you're not serious surely? You won't even be seventeen in six months' time.'

'So?'

'So . . . darling, I have to get established in my work first. We have to save up for our home.'

'But if you're going to Australia next year—'

'Look Julia, we have to be sensible. If I go to Australia, it would have to be for a year at least, possibly two. Say eighteen months anyway. As soon as I get back—'

'You mean I'm to get engaged and then not see you for eighteen months?' She was horrified. 'Ian, what on earth are you saying? I thought we would both go. I thought we would be married first and then both go to Australia.'

'But Mother thinks you're too young and she is right. It—'

Julia's face was grim. 'I see.' She held up a hand peremptorily. 'Don't tell me any more. Your mother! I see it all now. She's trying to separate us, just as I knew she would.'

He tried to interrupt but she went on rashly, 'She has obviously been working on you while we've been apart. Having decided against me, she's putting up all these reasons for delaying everything. And Virginia has been invited along to demonstrate that you're making a mistake.' Her voice rose. 'I suppose Virginia is not too young? I suppose *she's* just the right age for a quick engagement and off to Australia!'

'Hush, Julia! Keep your voice down!' cried Ian. 'Let me get a word in.'

Julia regarded him breathlessly. Her heart pounded against her ribs and she knew she was trembling. She felt as cold as ice. The visit was turning out to be every bit as bad as she had expected. Maybe worse! She had not been in the house five minutes and here she was quarrelling with Ian.

'Darling, please listen to me. Calm down, Julia, please! There's nothing to get upset about. Will you listen to me?'

She nodded reluctantly.

'I admit Mother is doubtful, *but* only because you're young and she thinks you may not know your own mind. She means that kindly – that you may not have had any other boy friends and—'

'Have you had any other girl friends?' cried Julia. 'You said you hadn't.'

'No, that's true, but I am a good bit older than you and I have met more people. She wants us to be happy and she thinks we shouldn't rush into anything. It *is* sensible, darling. Do be fair. Don't get yourself all upset about nothing. I expect if your mother was alive she would say the same thing.'

'No, she wouldn't,' declared Julia. She looked desperately round the neat bedroom with its heavy silk curtains and matching bedspread, polished wooden floor, thick fluffy rugs . . . and hated it all. Downstairs there were three strangers, two of them waiting for her to make a fool of herself and so prove she was an unsuitable match for their son.

'I want to go home,' she said. 'I'm not welcome here and I want to catch the next train home. You needn't take me but I mean to go home.' She refused to cry but her heart was aching with anger, misery and fear.

'Darling!' It was Ian's turn to be horrified. 'Don't say such terrible things. You *are* wanted here. I want you. You're so quick to get on the defensive. No one's against you, darling. Not even Mother. She only wants what's best. Like all mothers with their sons, she tends to be a bit possessive and inclined to worry.'

'What's so special about sons?' Julia demanded. 'Aren't mothers possessive and worried about their daughters?'

'Of course. I only meant – well, I was talking about my Mother and she's only got me.'

'She wants you to marry Virginia.'

'She does *not!*'

'Let's ask her.'

'Julia!'

Feeling she had frightened him, some of her courage returned. 'I didn't mean that,' she said. 'It's all right. I'm not going to make a scene.'

'And you won't go home, Julia? Please, darling! Let's forget this silly squabble and start again. I promise you Mother has nothing against you, so don't take anything she says too personally. Look, I'll tell you something else if you promise to keep it a secret from them. Promise?'

Julia nodded.

'Well, they were both upset that I had proposed to you before they had even met you. They felt hurt and I suppose it was a bit thoughtless of us. Of me, rather. I should have introduced you and then when they got to know you and like you—'

'If they ever did!'

'Julia!'

'I'm sorry. Go on.'

'I should have broken it to them gently. They do have a point, Julia, but I'm to blame and I accept that. I got so carried away that night – it was all so wonderful – but I should have waited. Just for a few more weeks.'

Julia looked at him, subdued. 'Poor you,' she said. 'Were they very angry?'

'Not angry exactly, but very hurt and upset. Mother cried.' He sighed. 'They came round eventually of course and wanted to meet you. And here you are.'

'And it's all going wrong.'

'But only if we let it. I want us to be so happy they will be convinced that we're right for each other.'

'And that I'm not too young to know my own mind.'

'Something like that, yes.'

'And you really do still love me?'

'Of course I do. I've thought about you all these weeks and dreamed about seeing you again. I just want us to be together and to be happy.'

Julia looked straight into his eyes. 'Ian, if I wanted to marry you, desperately, for any reason and your Mother was dead against it, what would you do?'

'I'd marry you.'

'Are you sure?'

'Of course I am. What a funny question!'

'Not really.'

'Why ever should you be desperate to marry me? I've told you we'll get a ring soon, next week I hope. I just don't . . .'

Julia felt sorry for him, standing beside her with sagging shoulders. He really had no idea how easily she could shatter his composure with just a few words and throw the entire household into a state of confusion. She wondered why she was protecting him; she had lived with the fear for the past two weeks, yet he was talking about *her* being too young. When she considered what a sheltered life he had led, as compared with her own stormy passage, she wanted to laugh. Suddenly she could no longer let the possibility of a child be her responsibility. The child – if there was one, and it seemed likely – was his responsibility as much as hers. She would tell him now.

'Ian,' she began, but at that moment there was a tap on the door.

'Come in!' she called.

Donald put his head round the door. 'Ah, unpacking, are you? Jolly good show! Just thought I'd tell you, Julia – your sherry's getting cold! Can't have a lovely girl like you drinking cold sherry.' He laughed and they laughed with him.

Julia felt a rush of affection for Ian's father. He liked her, he wanted her company. Well, he should have it. Her news would keep. She felt strengthened, somehow, and less vulnerable because of her decision to tell Ian about the child.

'Give me two minutes,' she told him with a smile, 'and I'll be right down.'

*

Much later the same night Alf Bittens left the pub at the bottom of
Chick Hill and stared round him vaguely, blinking his eyes and
swaying slightly. He had drunk more than usual, but that was
because young what's-his-name was buying – Luke's boy from
the harbour. 'More' was four whiskies over his usual Saturday
night's intake of about six pints and two doubles. On that amount
he was always drunk but not too drunk to know his way home.
Tonight he wandered a bit.

Which way was he facing? Where was the sun? Or was it the
moon? He tried to raise his head, but was seized by a sudden
attack of giddiness and had to hold on to the rail beside the pub
yard to steady himself.

A good lad, Luke's boy. Pity he had to go early, they were
getting on fine. He took a few steps and belched loudly. Pity about
Luke getting himself killed in the war. Staring round, he
muttered, 'Too many bleeding clouds.' When his head swam
again, he reached for the rail, missed it and found himself on all
fours. His hands and knees were smarting and he swore, but
made no effort to get up. It was closing time and other people
were spilling out of the pub into the darkness with much laughter
and noisy farewells. A group passing paused to stare at him – the
men mocking, the women 'clucking' disdainfully.

'What you doing down there, Bitty?' cried one of the men and
made an attempt to help him to his feet. 'You'd best get along
home.'

Bitty shook himself free and muttered, 'Bugger off!'

'Well!' cried one of the women. 'That's the thanks you get for
trying to do him a good turn. Leave him be, Will. He don't
deserve a helping hand. God help Ellen, that's all I can say, living
with a pig like that!'

They went on their way and when they had gone Bitty managed
to pull himself to his feet. Pity the lad had gone home early –
they'd had a bit of a laugh, one way and another. Pity about Luke.
Pity about . . . He belched again and his head began to throb.
More people passed him; some ignored him, others called out a
brief, 'Night, Bitty.' He didn't answer any of them, because he
had no energy to spare for anything except remaining upright. He
tried to see if his hands were bleeding, but it was too dark. His
knees were sore, but they had been protected by the thickness of

his trousers. Pity about the boy. And Luke. Getting himself killed like that. It was the Germans, the Germans that killed him. In the war . . .

He managed a few steps and then, finding a convenient low wall, sat on it, breathing heavily. Eventually there were no more passers-by and no more 'Good nights'. The lights downstairs in the pub went out; upstairs they went on. Considering these facts carefully, he concluded they were going to bed and was overcome by a strong desire to be in his own bed. The point was, which way was it? It was back the way he had come. Surely? He squinted along the road.

'This way, Bitty.'

The voice came from behind him and he turned round clumsily. 'What's that?' he muttered.

'Over here.'

'Oh?'

'Come on, Bitty!'

'Come on?' he muttered. 'What's up now?'

The wall ran parallel to the road and at right-angles to it a rough hedge ran towards the bench. Bitty stood up and stared in the direction of the voice. Was it Luke's boy? But he'd gone home a while since.

'Who's there?' he called.

There was no answer, and with a weary shake of his head, Bitty began to stumble towards the voice, his feet slithering on the thin layer of shingle that topped the sun-baked soil.

'Who's there?' he called again.

Nobody appeared out of the darkness to greet him as he lurched further from the road and nearer to the sea. Soon he was on the beach and then the sound of his footsteps was deadened by the soft dark sand of the Level.

Without any warning, someone jumped on him and sent him flying to the ground where he lay for a moment, winded by the fall. Then that someone was astride his back and his arms were pinioned behind him in a hard grip.

'What happened to Jean Dessin?" hissed a voice close to his ear. 'Who killed him? Was it you?'

'No! No!'

Relentlessly the hand forced down his face again, but by this time he was beginning to collect his wits. The need to survive had a sobering influence upon his muddled head. With a sudden effort he threw himself sideways and his attacker, taken by surprise, fell off cursing. Bitty was kneeling on the sand now and his temper was rising. Anger and his natural cunning rallied to his aid and he was ready for the next move. As his assailant leaped on him he lowered his head and butted the man in the stomach. Hearing a gasp, he experienced a glow of triumph. This did not last long, however, for the figure had disappeared in the darkness and suddenly all was silent.

'Where's the bugger gone?' he muttered.

As though in answer to his question, an arm encircled his neck and he was forced down into the sand once more, but managed to throw off his attacker. He swung a wild but heavy punch at the elusive form and felt it connect with a head. There was a thud and Bitty decided it was time to go. He staggered to his feet and swayed precariously, but almost immediately his right ankle was clasped and he was thrown off-balance again. A ferocious blow caught him on the side of the head and dazed him and before he could recover, he found he was being dragged towards the water.

'No!' he muttered. 'No, you don't!'

But they were almost at the water's edge before he could reverse the forward rush towards what he imagined was certain death. The bugger was going to drown him!

Lunging forward, he caught an arm and then the two of them were wrestling backwards and forwards, thrashing about in the shallow water. Bitty grunted and swore and grew more sober with every second. He began to realise that if he could hold out long enough, time was on his side. He was a powerful man and frequently boasted that he had rarely been beaten in a fight. Not that he had ever fought in the dark before! After landing a few useful blows, he was just beginning to congratulate himself that he had the upper hand when he was tripped. He lost his balance and fell full-length into the water and knew in that instant that he was lost.

Frank dragged him to his knees and hit him again.

'Now tell me. Everything!' he demanded. "About Jean Dessin. Because I think *you* killed him and if so, I'm going to kill you, d'you hear? I'm going to drown you the way you drowned him.'

'I didn't—'

'But if I'm wrong and you *didn't* kill him, then you'd better prove it and fast!' He held Bitty's head under the water as long as he dared, then jerked him up, gasping. With a desperate heave, he pulled the prostrate form into deeper water and Bitty gave a scream of fear.

'No! No! Don't. It wasn't me. I swear it!'

'Then who?'

'I don't know. I swear I don't – argh!'

For a second time Frank forced Bitty's head under the water, glancing round fearfully as he did so in case they had been overheard. He could taste the blood that trickled from a gash under his left eye and one of his back teeth was loose. His jaw ached from one of Bitty's more successful blows, but he didn't think it was broken. He was astonished that anyone as drunk as Bitty could have looked after himself so well. Now, however, *he* had the upper hand and meant to make the most of it. For a full five minutes, they thrashed about in the cool water until Frank had extracted a full account of what Bitty claimed had happened on that fateful night.

The story was that Bitty and Jean had rowed out in *Silver Lady*'s dinghy to meet a similar dinghy from a French fishing smack – the *Cheval de Mer* – which was bringing them brandy, stolen perfume and tobacco. After the contraband had been stowed in their boat, Bitty handed over the money and when the Frenchman checked it he declared it short. Jean accused Bitty of keeping back part of the money which they had both contributed and the Frenchman demanded the return of some of his goods. In the ensuing struggle, Jean went overboard and the Frenchman, in trying to help him, accidentally hit him with the oar.

'I swear it!' cried Bitty. 'It was an accident. Then what could we do? Tell the police?'

'The Frenchman's name,' said Frank. 'What was it?'

'He never told us. We never told him ours either.'

Frank felt a deathly weariness sweep over him and he tugged Bitty to his knees.

'Listen to me,' said Frank heavily, 'and remember – I know and I can go to the police. You've got twenty-four hours to lose yourself. Ellen will be better off without you. D'you hear me? Lose yourself. For good! Sling your hook and don't come back. I mean it, Bitty! Because if I hear that you're still around, I shall go to the police and *they* may not believe you. I'm sure they'd love to nail something on you, Bitty. You see, *I'm* giving you the benefit of the doubt, which is more than they will. D'you understand me?'

'Yes, yes.' Bitty staggered to his feet. 'For Christ's sake! You bloody near killed me.'

'Think yourself lucky I didn't,' replied Frank, 'because Jean Dessin was a mate of mine. How he ever got mixed up with your sort, I'll never know. If I thought for one minute that you meant to kill him, *you'd* be out there now, floating in the sea, face downward. This is not a nice place for you to be now, Bitty, so take my advice and get out while the going's good – because if ever I set eyes on you again, you'll live to regret it.'

He strode away along the beach in the direction of Rye, leaving Bitty to squelch homeward for the last time.

*

Early on Sunday morning Julia wrote earnestly in her diary.

19 August 1926

Not such an ordeal as I expected, thank goodness. Ian's father is such a dear. I know we are going to be good friends. I am not so sure about Mrs Cornwell, but I tried to see things from her point of view after what Ian said about them being upset at not meeting me first, before the engagement. Virginia wore a grey dress which must have cost pounds, with beautiful embroidery and in a very delicate material, georgette I think it was, but I know by the way everyone looked at me that I outshone her and without being too unkind (I hope) I was glad. I'm sorry if she has fallen for Ian, but I met him first and we are engaged and she has no right to have designs on him, which I'm sure she does.

Donald sat at the head of the table with me on his right and Ian on his left, while Virginia sat next to Ian and then there was Mrs Cornwell next to me. It's a round table, otherwise I don't know how we'd have sat. There were so many knives and forks (twice as many as at Helen's) and lots of courses but not much of each. I suppose she was trying to impress me or maybe just show me how I will be expected to entertain if I marry Ian. Why did I say 'if'? She is making me unsure. Is that part of her plan?

We had soup, some sort of fish in a jelly (ugh!), lamb in a circle with bones sticking up and 'hats' on them (don't ask me why, but at least it did look pretty and Ian told me later it was called 'crown of lamb'), apricot fool (delicious), cheese and biscuits (I know it was Brie because we'd had it at Helen's, so I could sound intelligent about it), and coffee. If I hadn't been so on edge after my talk with Ian, I would have enjoyed it more, but it wasn't too bad. Virginia *is* witty, I have to admit; she tells things in a very funny way and everyone laughed a lot except me, and I tried not to but after two glasses of wine (oh yes, we had wine with dinner and port after), I found myself laughing too and who cares? Donald is also very amusing at times and he uses such extraordinary words I want to laugh at him even when he's not trying to be funny. Mrs C. kept dropping hints about people who were friends who had married too young or started their families too soon. I could have killed her. I *could* have made nasty comments, but I didn't want to let Ian down and I felt I should try for his sake so they can't tell him he's made a mistake.

I wanted to say casually, 'Oh, by the way, I've missed my "month-lies" a couple of times.' Just to see their faces, but you can't do things like that. At least, I couldn't for Ian's sake.

Ian's father kept touching my arm and I saw Mrs C. give him a few nasty looks, but he drank rather a lot and took no notice. Although Virginia was next to Ian they weren't very close (it's a biggish table) and he couldn't see her without turning sideways, but he *could* see me right opposite. I had put on a bit of rouge (not much) and had pencilled my brows. I know I was looking my best, so I was glad that Virginia could see me full-face. I have to have something in my favour.

When they started to discuss politics (the General Strike, of course) I said that politics bored me almost as much as knitting and to my surprise they all found that witty and laughed. Even Virginia. In the evening before I changed for dinner, we all played tennis (except Mrs C. who said she had a headache, but I didn't believe her), and I think I could easily get the hang of it. They talked about Wimbledon and Suzanne Lenglen (just so that Mrs C. could boast she had seen her play) and someone called Cobham who flew to South Africa (never heard of him but I didn't say so) and airships because Mr C. had had a short flight on one (can't remember why) and was terribly airsick, poor man. Virginia went on a bit about all the novels and plays she has read, but I could see she was only showing off so I pretended to be interested. I told them again about the beach party and Mrs C. looked down her nose a bit but didn't say much. I kept wishing Helen could have been there to be on my side. Then Ian's mother began asking me about my family, and as I couldn't tell lies, I had to answer and I was angry and made everything sound worse than it was, so she kept saying, 'Oh, you poor dear!' but Mr C., bless him, kept saying 'By Jove!' and then said, 'What a jolly exciting life you lead, Julia! You

make me feel like a real old fuddy-duddy.' I could have kissed him.
He winked at me a lot and kept patting my arm. Ian winked at me
several times and I was sorry Virginia couldn't see him doing it. The
more I looked at Ian, the more I loved him. Please God, let everything
turn out all right for us. He is such a dear, good man and he is all I
want.

*

On the way back to Rye they had been driving for half an hour
before Julia plucked up courage to tell Ian what was troubling her.

'Ian,' she began, 'I'm a bit unhappy about something. Well, not
unhappy. It's not a sad thing, exactly, but it is scary.'

'Cough it up, then,' Ian said cheerfully, braking rather sharply
and swerving to avoid running down a small flock of ducks
waddling across the lane. 'I'm all ears, as they say.'

'It's about that night,' she said. She had planned to come right
out and state boldly what was wrong, but now the moment had
arrived it was proving more difficult than she had expected.

'You don't regret it, do you?' he asked quickly. 'Because I
don't.'

'No, no. I don't regret it. At least, I don't think I do. It all
depends.'

'On what?'

Julia searched for her vanished courage but still it eluded her.

'Oh, on you and if you regret it,' she answered.

He glanced at her. 'But I've just said I don't.'

'I know . . . Ian, why don't you park the car for a few minutes?
The views are so lovely and we could stretch our legs.'

'I'd rather not, darling. We were late leaving and Helen will be
expecting us. I expect she's dying to hear all about the visit.'

Julia took a deep breath and closed her eyes.

'Ian, I may be going to have a baby.'

The car swerved again, but this time there were no ducks. Ian
steered on to the grass verge and stopped the engine.

'Oh, my God!' he said without looking at her. He covered his
face with his hands. 'My God, Julia. You *can't* be!'

Julia's heart sank but she stammered, 'I may not be, but I think
I am. I've missed and I keep feeling sick. Don't be upset, Ian.
Please!'

Still he did not look at her. He was silent for a long time and
then he exploded, 'Just that one time! It's so damned unfair.'

She felt a great coldness sweep over her. 'But if it is . . .' she began.

He turned wild eyes to hers. 'It can't be. Dammit, Julia, you must be wrong. Have you been to a doctor? Did he say it might be? What did he say?'

Frozen-faced, she explained that she was only interpreting the usual signs. 'I'd be due again in four days' time,' she told him. 'If it doesn't happen then, I suppose I'll have to go to the doctor. Oh darling, please don't be like this. Say something to comfort me, I'm so afraid.'

'Oh God, Julia, how do you think *I* feel? I just can't believe it. It mustn't happen, it must be a mistake.'

'It might be,' she said but without any conviction.

With an effort he put an arm around her shoulders. 'I'm sorry, Julia. It was such a shock. Forgive me! You must have been very worried. But you can see how disastrous it would be for us, can't you? I can't afford a wife, let alone a baby. God, if my mother gets wind of this!' His alarm increased. 'Does anybody else know? Have you told anyone else? Your father?'

'No one,' she lied, thinking guiltily of Frank Bligh. 'My father's still in a state of shock after Agnes's death. He just keeps drinking and blaming himself for not being a better husband. I couldn't tell him.'

'It would ruin everything. And then they'd know – my parents, I mean – about that night at Helen's. They'd be so upset.'

'Your father would understand,' said Julia dully. His reaction was all she had feared.

'Mother wouldn't let him understand! Hell and damnation! What are we to do?'

'I thought you might *want* me to have your child,' said Julia. 'If you really love me, that is.'

'That's not fair,' he said, his face flushed with indignation. 'Of course I love you, you know I do. But that doesn't mean I want you to get yourself with child.'

Her guilt flared into resentment. 'I didn't get myself with child!' she cried. 'You got me with child – or rather, we did it between us. *If* you remember!'

He was at once contrite. 'I'm truly sorry. Of course you're right. That was stupid of me. Cruel of me. Forgive me, darling!'

She huddled closer, longing for reassurance. 'Ian, if it is a baby, can't we make up our minds to be pleased about it? Whatever the problems? Couldn't we—'

He swung away from her suddenly and withdrew his arm. 'You were only fifteen!' he gasped. 'Is that legal, Julia? Oh God! If it's not and it gets out – my career! Mother will never forgive me if there's a scandal! She's so strict about these things.'

'Ian!' she begged. 'Don't look at me that way. I'm not suddenly a monster or something. I'm the girl you're going to marry and I may be expecting your child. Or our child. That's all I am; I haven't committed a crime.'

He groaned. 'Try telling my mother that,' he said.

Julia put her arm round *his* shoulders and hugged him awkwardly. 'Look,' she suggested, 'why don't we get married quickly, maybe without telling anyone. We'll all go to Australia, if you like and—'

'No, no! That's no good. Let me think, Julia. You've sprung it on me and I need time.'

'I didn't spring it on you,' she said. 'I told you. Whenever I told you it would have been a shock. Did you want me to wait a few months so that it *showed*?' After a long miserable silence, she went on: 'If you must know, Ian, I think you're being beastly. All you're concerned about is yourself. *Your* parents. *Your* prospects. What about *me*? Don't you think I'm upset and afraid? Do you think *I* wanted it to happen like this?'

'Oh for God's sake, Julia, give me some time!' he cried. 'I need to think things out clearly.' He shook his head wearily. 'What an end to the weekend!'

'It wasn't a weekend,' she snapped. 'It was barely twenty-four hours. Obviously they changed their minds about putting up with me for a whole weekend.'

Ignoring the implication, Ian got out without a word and cranked the engine into life. Then he drove back on to the road and they travelled without speaking for a few miles.

'I'm taking you home,' said Ian, 'and I'm not stopping to speak to your father. I shall be at Helen's until tomorrow morning, then I shall go straight back to London. Not because I don't want to see you again, or because I'm angry or upset, but because I need time to think. At least you'll grant me that much, I hope? I have a lot of responsibilities to consider if we do decide to get married.'

'Oh, Ian! If only we—'

'I said *if* we do. I don't know yet. What I do know is that I can't face long arguments about this. I need to be calm and to think carefully. When can you tell me for sure?'

'Four or five days,' she said. 'Should I go to the doctor?'

'No. Yes. I don't know, Julia. You can decide on that.'

'Oh, thank you,' she muttered bitterly. 'When will I see you again, then? I need to be near you. You should want to be near me. Don't you even care about your own baby? Your own son or daughter? Can't you think of it nicely just for a few moments?'

Her voice shook and he said, 'Oh Julia!' and pulled over again on to the side of the road. He put his arms round her and kissed her.

'Forgive me,' he said. 'I'm a brute. A selfish brute! I will think kindly about it if it is a baby and not a mistake. You look as though it's certain, but there are other reasons why you could be late. Let's wait and see. Let's not talk about it any more until we know for certain. I'll work out something, darling, so don't worry. Smile for me, Julia, please. That's much better. I'm sorry, darling. You're absolutely right. I'm an unfeeling brute.'

'I didn't say that,' she protested. 'You did.'

'Well, I am.' He kissed her. 'You just try not to worry and I'll work things out in my mind – what's best for both of us. And you let me know when you have definite news, then we'll talk again. How's that?'

'That's fine, Ian.'

'So no more snapping my head off?'

'I wasn't.'

'Somebody was.' He laughed. 'All forgiven, eh?'

'Yes.'

'And you won't tell anyone? You promise.'

'I promise.'

And there for the time being the matter rested.

CHAPTER TWENTY-TWO

Ellen hummed cheerfully as she worked. Bitty had been gone for four days now and showed no sign of returning. He had told her he was going back to the fairgrounds, but she had not believed him. Now she was allowing herself to hope. The tide was ebbing and the catch was a good one, but she had help; she worked swiftly and efficiently, as did the others: eighteen-year-old Danny and Steve – Bitty's twin nephews – their parents Dave and Maud Bittens and Bitty's uncle Reg, nearing eighty but still very fit. There was plenty to do and it was always a race against the tide.

If anyone wondered where Bitty was, no one asked and Ellen offered no explanation. Because the catch was good, she drove the horse and cart through the middle of the shoal, pulling the draw net which was guided by the two boys. Dave and Reg used their round skim nets to scoop more fish from either side of the cart while Maud, her skirts tucked up, waded in two feet of water pulling the wildly flapping mackerel from the upright nets and dropping them into a basket which floated beside her and was steadied from time to time. Already one cart-load of fish had been emptied on to the sand and the twins' younger sister was sorting it into boxes.

As Frank approached the girl looked up, caught sight of him and waved. 'Hullo, Frank.'

He smiled. 'Hullo, Tiddler.'

'I'm not! I'm nearly eleven!'

'Sprat, then.'

Frank shouted to Ellen and she relinquished the horse's reins to Maud and waded back on to the sand.

'What brings you here?' she asked him.

He moved out of earshot of the girl and Ellen followed.

'I wanted a word,' he said.

'About what?'

'Your old man.'

'He's gone, I hope.'

'I know. I gave him his marching orders. Do you mind? Will you be all right on your own?'

'You did?' She peered at his face. 'What happened to your face? Fall under a steamroller?'

'Something like that.'

'It was Bitty, wasn't it?'

'Yes. Do you want to hear about it? You don't need to.'

Ellen hesitated. She thought it might be more prudent not to know, but her curiosity won. 'Tell,' she said.

Briefly Frank described the events of the previous Saturday night and she listened impassively. When he had finished she asked, 'Do you believe him?'

'That it was an accident? I think so. He needed Jean for the language. It must have helped, him speaking French.'

'He was a mean bastard.'

Frank knew she meant Bitty and nodded.

'Could the police touch him, then?' she asked. 'Supposing they found him, that is.'

'I doubt it. All hearsay, isn't it, and it was a long time ago. There's no proof, is there, and they'd never find the Frenchman . . .' He scuffed the sand with the toe of his boot. 'I want to tell someone else,' he said. 'I want to tell Julia Coulsden. The police suspected her father because of that other trouble. She's never been sure and I'd like to tell her.'

Ellen shrugged. 'Can't make no difference now,' she said.

'She might want to tell her father and then it might get round; you know how these things do.'

She shrugged again. 'No skin off my back,' she said. 'Does Alice know?'

'No. I wanted to talk to you first.'

'You're a good lad, Frank . . . and thanks. About Bitty, I mean. If I never set eyes on him again, it'll be too soon.'

'What about his family?' Frank jerked his head in the direction of the group now only knee-deep in water. 'They'll probably get to hear.'

'They won't say nothing, will they? A dead man and smuggling. They'll keep quiet if they've got any sense! There was never much love lost. They're a decent lot and he was the black sheep, as they say. Only his mother could see any good in him. Mothers do, don't they? Broke her heart when he ran off, I'm told, but she's long since dead and buried.'

'I must go.'

'Right. Bye, then!'

He turned to go and she called out, 'What's so special about this Julia then?'

Frank looked round slowly. 'Everything,' he replied.

Ellen nodded and saw the look in Frank's eyes which warned her not to pry further. 'If it's any consolation,' she told him, 'Bitty looked twice as bad as you.'

Frank smiled briefly. 'I should bloody well hope so!' he exclaimed. 'I half-drowned him, too.'

'I'd like to have been there.'

'Next time,' he grinned.

For a moment she stood watching him stride away. 'So, Alf Bittens,' she muttered, 'you got your come-uppance at last. And not before time!'

She nodded with satisfaction and returned to her work with a faint smile on her face and a sudden lightening of her heart.

*

When Julia arrived home she found the house empty and un-washed pots and pans in the kitchen sink. She sighed. Where was her father? At the Pipemakers' perhaps, or with Stanley in Hastings. It seemed unlikely that he had taken out *Silver Lady*; that would be expecting too much. She went to the window and looked down to the Fishmarket where she saw the boat in its usual mooring. As she stood gazing down on the familiar scene, she had a vision of her mother standing where she now was, looking out across the same view. They had told Julia of her birth day, and Cicely had filled in the details for her. She knew how she had come before the expected date, when everyone was away or difficult to contact; how her father and uncle had got themselves blind drunk and had come to the next morning to find the baby safely delivered; how Cicely had taken Hettie's place at the launch of *Silver Lady* and had given such a splendid speech. And Hettie had stood at the same window, looking for George.

Agnes, too, had stood there, screened by the net curtain which gave them a little protection from prying eyes. No doubt her feet had rested upon the same patch of polished wood floor when she was watching for her husband . . . or Jean, her lover. Now Julia stood there with the silent house around her and strained her eyes for a glimpse of her father or maybe Frank. Someone was working on *Silver Lady*, but the figure was too small to be her bulky father.

Probably Frank, she thought and let her mind wander.

Suppose Ian refused to marry her? What would she do? How could she take up Frank's offer of marriage when she did not love him? He did not deserve that, although he had insisted that he wanted her 'by hook or by crook'. 'Frank Bligh.' She said his name aloud and tried to consider him without comparison with her beloved Ian. He would make someone a good husband, she did not doubt that. He came from a good, honest, hard-working family; he did not have a reputation for drunkenness or womanising; he did not make lewd remarks or improper suggestions; he spoke his mind with no reserve and she knew he was trustworthy. He had been generous too – he had offered to bring up another man's child as his own, which was more than most men would do. Had she lived, his mother could have been proud of her son. But could she, Julia, live with a man she did not love? Yes, of course she could. It happened all the time, she agreed, but did *she* want that? Did she want a lifetime spent with the wrong man?

On the other hand, suppose she married Ian and then he died? Would she marry Frank if he was still single? It occurred to her that he was a very attractive man and many women would jump at the chance to become Mrs Frank Bligh. Recalling Frank's lips on hers, she remembered she had not found them unpleasant. Presumably he had had other women; he was twenty, with normal male appetites. She wondered who they were, those who had shared his lovemaking, and was surprised to experience a feeling of jealousy towards the nameless women. What had he said? That he had waited for her to grow up. She was touched.

'Mrs Frank Bligh,' Julia said again.

He was down on the boat, no doubt repairing the nets or touching up the paintwork. How was he managing as crew on a boat that so rarely put to sea? Julia felt a wave of anger towards her father.

Suddenly a familiar figure came into sight and her Aunt Cicely was ringing the front door-bell. Julia went into the hall to let her in and was surprised to see her aunt in a state of slight disarray with her hair straggling beneath a cloche hat that did not match her coat. Her eyes were red and her face puffy.

'Julia, child! I must talk to you,' she began, without even a 'Hullo'. She followed Julia into the kitchen, twisting her hands nervously in great agitation.

'Whatever—' began Julia, but her aunt interrupted her.

'No, child, let me talk,' she insisted. 'Let me say it all before my courage fails or I shall start to cry again. Oh, if your uncle knew I was here he'd be so angry. He doesn't want me to ask you, but I must; it's the only way out for us.'

'Ask me what?' enquired Julia, mystified and apprehensive.

'About the money, Julia.'

'Look, Aunt Cicely, do at least sit down.'

'What? No, no. I won't, I can't stop long. Julia, this is the most dreadful day of my whole life. The most dreadful! I know you have money and Jack says it's all tied up. I don't know about that, nor how much it is, but I must tell you that without help we are finished. Coulsdens is finished!'

'Finished? But what on earth . . . ? How?' gasped Julia. 'I'm sorry, but I don't understand.'

'I'm trying to *tell* you,' cried Cicely. 'The yard is broke. Quite broke. Bankrupt – at least, we will be before long. I had no idea things were so bad. I swear I didn't. Poor Jack didn't want me to worry, but now I'm quite beside myself. Can you imagine it? The scandal will kill me, I know it! I'm just not reared for this sort of thing. And the bills, Julia. We can't pay them. Or the wages. Do you see? I said to Jack that you might help and he wouldn't consider it. He says you need your money and of course you do, but if we could just borrow some of it – if it could be arranged legally – then we could pay you back when things get better. A loan just to tide us over, only if you say "No", you mustn't let Jack know I asked. If it's "Yes", then he'll have to know but – oh Julia! Where will it all end? Jack says there's always the dole or we could sell the yard, but who would buy it with no work coming in? It's all so terrible, so very terrible, like a nightmare. Can you imagine how I feel? And Jack, too. And poor Ben. Where's his future now?'

She begun to cry as Julia, stunned by the news, sat down beside the table staring up at her aunt, her mind racing.

'You mean the money I have in trust?' she asked. 'But can I have it yet? I'm only sixteen.'

'There must be ways and means,' cried Cicely. 'The solicitor would know.' She dabbed her eyes and blew her nose fiercely. 'If you go to him and explain, I'm sure something could be done.'

'I could talk to him,' said Julia, 'and see what he advises, but I can't promise anything. I'll see what Papa says. Does he know about all this?'

'Not that I'm coming here to ask you for a loan. Jack doesn't know either, you see. Oh, can you imagine? In a small town like this. Everyone will know and I shan't be able to face anyone. All my friends! Whatever will they think?'

Julia was silent, thinking. She had not given the matter much thought until recently, but it had occurred to her that if she had to bring up a child single-handed, the money would be very useful. If she lent it all to her uncle she would then have problems of her own, but she could hardly explain that to her distraught aunt.

'Please don't cry,' she said. 'I'll make you a cup of tea—'

'No! I daren't stop. I told Jack I was popping out for some minced beef. Oh Julia, please do what you can to help us. I can't bear it if—'

'I suppose Uncle Stan can't help?'

'No, he's in a poor way, too. It's the times we live in. The whole country's in a mess and the fishing industry is suffering like everyone else. Don't ask me to explain how it happens because I just don't know. One minute you own a successful boatyard and the next you find yourself without two halfpennies to rub together.'

Julia stood up. 'Aunt Cicely, if I should be unable to help you . . .'

Cicely gripped the back of the chair and her knuckles were white. 'God knows, Julia, I don't!' She drew a long shuddering breath. 'Jack's selling the car, you know, to pay the men. It was either the men's wages or the bills. What a terrible choice! But the men have families and you have to be loyal to your work people. That's what Jack says. But owing money – can you imagine how people will talk?'

'What does Ben say?' asked Julia.

'Not much. I suppose he knew it was coming – if he didn't, he must have been blind. I did wonder if your father might agree to sell *Silver Lady* and throw in his lot with us. Jack could find him work. But Jack says there's no market now for a boat like that. Who'd want to buy a fishing boat in the middle of a depression? But I must go. Do please let me know what you decide, Julia. As soon as you can. I think you're our only hope.'

Julia closed the door behind her aunt and shook her head slowly. She thought, 'What a time to have an illegitimate baby!' and did not know whether to laugh or cry.

*

Eight days later as Emily and Julia walked on the beach, Julia broke the news that she was definitely pregnant. The doctor had been quite certain. All the signs were there, he said, and the baby could be expected early in February 1927. He advised her to inform her own father and to marry the child's father as soon as possible.

'Just like that?' said Emily.

'More or less.'

'Oh, you poor thing! At least, you're probably not. I mean, your Ian is sure to marry you and you'll be Mrs Ian Cornwell. I shall be green with envy. Not that I'm not happy with my Chick, but you'll be married and have a baby before I've even got started!'

'*If* he marries me!' Julia tried to sound light-hearted.

'Of course he will, Ju. You know he will. Who are you kidding? I bet it'll be a spanking wedding, too. Do you want a bridesmaid? Oh, I suppose it'll be Winnie's lot. Who's going to pay for it all? Oh, I wish Ma was still alive; she loved weddings. She'd have been tickled pink, wouldn't she? When are you going to tell Ian?'

'That's really what I've come about,' said Julia. 'I wanted to read you the letter and see what you think of it. I spent all the evening struggling to get it just right.'

They sat down on one of the wooden groynes that ran down into the sea, intersecting the beach at regular intervals, and Julia drew the letter from her pocket.

'I'll read it slowly,' she said, 'and you stop me if you think it doesn't sound right. I started off with "My dear Ian".'

' "My dear Ian"?' cried Emily. 'That's not very romantic, is it? Why not "My most adored Ian" – or just "My beloved"? That's very romantic.'

'But I don't want to be too romantic or lovey-dovey just in case he says "No",' Julia explained. 'Then I should feel worse. I thought I should be a bit formal and . . . business-like.'

Emily looked doubtful about the wisdom of this policy, but made no comment and Julia continued.

' "You asked me to let you know the doctor's verdict as soon as possible. He says I am going to have a baby next February. There is no real doubt in his mind, but I have to go back in three weeks for another test of some kind—" '

'A test?' said Emily. 'What sort of test?'

'I don't know,' Julia confessed. 'He didn't say and I didn't like to ask . . . in case it was painful and then I'd be worrying about it.'

'Oh Ju, you poor old thing, but do go on.' She broke into a sudden grin. 'Hey, I've just realised that I shall be an auntie. Or rather a half-auntie. Golly! It makes me feel terribly old. Sorry, Ju! Go on, I'm listening.'

'Where was I? Oh yes. "—test of some kind. I think we must accept his opinion –" '

'That's nice.'

' "—and make plans. I know you will be upset but so am I, of course. I shall not tell my father until I hear from you, as he is not in good health." '

'Isn't he?' asked Emily. 'What's wrong with him?'

Julia looked a trifle sheepish. 'Well, nothing really but I can't very well say I can't sober him up long enough to hold a sensible conversation!'

'Is he as bad as that?'

'I'm afraid so. He's just given up. He doesn't care about anything.'

'Poor old Pa! I wish I could help.'

'I don't think any of us can.'

Emily sighed. 'Well then, go on with the letter.'

' "Do please come down, Ian, as soon as you can, so that we can talk. I hope you will agree to an early wedding—" '

'*Very* early,' grinned Emily. 'Fancy you and him and you not telling me! You are mean, Ju. I told you about me and Chick.'

'That was a bit different,' said Julia defensively. 'Anyway, you'd moved out by the time it happened.'

'You could still wear white,' said Emily. 'No one would know – as long as you hurry it up. You still look exactly the same. Oh, sorry! Go on.'

' "If you are afraid to tell your parents, I will come up to London again and be with you when you break the news. I know it won't be easy for you. I ought to feel bitter that this has happened, but I try to think that it is our child I am carrying and every baby has a right to be loved by its parents—" '

'Oh, that's lovely, Ju! I like that. It's true, too.'

' "Please think it over carefully, Ian, and write and tell me your feelings—" '

'You ought to make that "write *soon* and tell me your feelings",' Emily suggested.

'Yes, maybe you're right.'

Julia took a pencil from her pocket and added the required word before continuing: ' "Do remember, Ian, that we love each other and that having a baby should make us love each other more and not less." ' She looked at Emily. 'It should, shouldn't it?' she whispered and Emily nodded.

' "Goodbye for now, my sweet Ian. Your loving Julia." '

'Very nice letter,' said Emily. 'No man could resist it.'

'I hope you're right, Em.'

'What will you do if he says "No"?'

Julia had decided not to tell anyone of Frank Bligh's offer of marriage. 'I don't know,' she said. 'I'll face that when the time comes.'

'It won't,' said Em. 'I'm sure it won't. He loves you and he's not exactly poor. Golly! D'you realise that by this time next month you could be walking down the aisle!'

Julia sighed as she folded the letter. 'Do you remember your mother's wedding?' she asked.

'A bit,' Emily giggled. 'I know you put a spanner in the works, Julia Coulsden! Ma was hopping mad and she kept blaming Pa. "She's your bloody daughter," she kept saying. Quite a charming scene!'

'That wretched Leo,' said Julia, 'and yet I thought he was so wonderful. I was sure I was going to marry him. And now he's married a divorced woman and they've got a child. Isn't life strange, Em? I was really shocked when I knew and then I thought you'd done the same thing and you hadn't and I have.'

Emily stared out to sea. 'Do you really love him?' she asked. '*Really*, I mean. I don't know if I *really* love Chick. I was *in love* with him at the beginning but now we live together and I see him every day, he seems a bit ordinary and I don't like the way he gobbles his food and licks his knife – and Eunice keeps on at him to change his socks! Even his laugh gets on my nerves now and then. I used to love that laugh. I still like him a lot, we have great fun together and I expect I'll marry him, but is that really love?' She turned to look at Julia.

'I don't know,' Julia replied. 'I'm not an expert.'

'I mean, suppose I met someone else and I was *in love* with him and then I left Chick to marry this other man and afterwards I found out he snored and kept me short of housekeeping and didn't like kids or something. Would that still be a sort of love, or does it all just disappear? Did Ma still love Pa when she died? It didn't look much like it. How could she if she loved Jean Dessin?'

'I don't know,' Julia repeated soberly. 'I wish I did.'

'Perhaps it's just a trick to make us get married,' suggested Emily.

'But who's playing it?'

Emily shrugged. 'Don't ask me.'

'Does Eunice love Tommy, do you think?'

'They get along. They don't squabble very often. She nags a bit, but not much.'

'Well, maybe that's all there is to it,' said Julia. 'People fall in love and then they get married and have children . . .'

'They do love the children,' said Emily. 'Usually.'

'Yes, I think they do.' Julia sighed. 'Perhaps we all think we're going to be happy and it will be different for us . . .' She stood up suddenly. 'Emily! This is too depressing. Here am I, about to get married to my lovely Ian and we're talking as though it's a disaster! Perhaps it's what you make it. Oh come on. It will be dark soon and I want to make a shepherd's pie. If I don't cook, Pa won't eat. Sometimes he won't eat even if I do. He's quite hopeless without Agnes and I think if I weren't there he would starve to death. He really doesn't care any more. It's so sad, Em. Drink and sleep – that's his life now.'

Emily looked startled. 'What will happen to him when you're married?' she asked.

Julia gave a deep sigh. 'That's something else I don't know,' she said.

Emily put her arm around her and squeezed her. 'Don't worry, Ju. We'll work something out. But first things first: you marry your Ian.'

'I'm trying to,' laughed Julia. 'I'm really trying!'

*

For the first time in years the Coulsden family sat down together, in Jack's and Cicely's front room. Stanley sat in an armchair, with Jane perched on the arm of it. Ernest was beside them in a high-backed chair, feeling as uncomfortable as he looked. Julia sat on a cushion on the floor in front of Ernest, and Ben sat astride another of the high-backed chairs, his arms resting on the back. George was in an armchair and Jack and Cicely on the small sofa. Emily had been invited at Julia's insistence, although Cicely had not felt it necessary to include her; she sat on the arm of George's chair. Winifred had chosen to stay at home with the children, for which most of the family were grateful. When at last everyone was more or less settled, Jack cleared his throat.

'Thanks for coming,' he said. 'It seemed like a good idea at the time. Now I don't know.' With all eyes upon him he suddenly dried up and Cicely, who had offered to do the talking, gave him a frosty look.

'What I mean to say is,' he rushed on, 'that things are bad and

it's nobody's fault, but they are, and if anyone's got any bright
ideas now's the time to give them an airing!'

It appeared that nobody had any ideas and there was an awkward silence, broken when Cicely said scathingly, 'Shouldn't you
give a slightly clearer picture of our own predicament, Jack?'

'We're skint,' said Jack.

One or two grins were quickly erased as Cicely's gaze was fixed
on each face in turn.

'What Jack means,' enlarged Cicely, 'is that the boatyard is on
the point of bankruptcy with unpaid bills, no work coming in and
no money to pay for materials even if there was. If we don't get an
immediate loan from somewhere we shall have to close down.
Coulsdens' yard will be finished.'

'Have you tried the bank?' asked Stanley. He knew they had,
but as the senior member of the family felt it necessary to make
some contribution to the discussion.

Jack nodded. 'No dice,' he said.

'What Jack means—' Cicely began, but Jack interrupted her.

'They know what I mean,' he said. 'I don't need a bloody
interpreter.'

'Won't they lend you anything?' Ernest enquired.

'Not a bean. I've paid off the men by selling the car. I've shot my
bolt and that's it!'

'Well,' said Stanley, 'it won't come as a surprise to anyone to
hear that we're not much better off. We've only the one boat now,
and as George knows, there's not much money to be made fishing
with prices so low. Two of my mates have thrown in the sponge
over the last two months. Old Buller Bates has gone into his
father-in-law's sweet-shop—'

'Good God!' muttered George, roused momentarily.

'And the Doyles have done a moonlight. Packed all the gear
they could in the boat and pushed off. I helped them, so I know.
I've known them all my life and I cried my bloody eyes out, I don't
mind telling you.'

'You wonder who's going next,' said Jane.

'*We're* going next!' cried Jack. 'That's what this meeting's all
about. So Stan's got no spare cash? Fair enough; I didn't think he
had. What about you, George?'

George appeared lost in thought. He was leaning back with his
eyes closed.

'Pa!' Emily nudged him.

'What?' George lifted his head sluggishly.

'Uncle Jack's talking to you.'

'I asked,' repeated Jack with an attempt at levity, 'if you had any bright ideas? Or any cash? Filthy lucre? Green-backs? Have you got a sackful of tenners hidden away anywhere?'

There were a few smiles and everyone looked at George. 'No,' he said, 'I've got nothing.'

'Perhaps you could try working,' said Cicely spitefully. 'At least if we have nothing it's not because we're bone idle.'

'Cis!' cried Jack. 'Enough of that kind of talk. Let's keep this friendly.'

'Pa's not up to it at the moment,' said Emily. No one answered her and she glanced at Julia for support.

'Papa's just lost his wife,' Julia said. 'It takes people different ways.'

'I should think—' began Cicely.

Jack broke in hastily. 'Well anyway, that's another "No". Ben's obviously in with us. Ernest? Anything tucked away for a rainy day?'

Ernest shook his head. 'With kids?' he asked. 'You can't mean it. I'm sorry. Mind you, I have to say it, since this is honesty time, that if I did have any it would go on the kids. They take some clothing and it's all second-hand.'

Jack nodded. 'I know, lad,' he said. 'I wasn't expecting anything, just giving everyone a crack of the whip. Seems we're all in the same mess. It's a right mess.'

Emily said, 'Well, I'm sorry I've nothing except me wages and a few stale cakes half-price on a Saturday night!'

They all laughed except George. Then Cicely gave Julia a meaningful look.

'I've been to see the solicitor,' began Julia. 'I asked him about my money – that Mother and Mama Sarah left me. Mr Dawson thinks it's probably about a thousand pounds—'

There were a few gasps of surprise.

'— but he has to check up on some of the shares and things and he doesn't know if any of it can be released while I'm only sixteen. He's promised to write to me when he has all the facts.'

Cicely did her best to look surprised at these revelations and Julia continued, 'I explained about the yard and everything and he did say that he didn't think it would be enough to do any more than pay off the debts and . . .' She hesitated.

'And what, child?' prompted Cicely.

'And he thought that with the present situation I would be taking an awful risk. As one of the trustees he would not be very happy about authorising it, but he said he couldn't refuse if I insisted.'

'Mr Dawson's right,' said Ben. 'I don't think we should ask Julia to do it. That's all she's got in the world.'

Cicely cried, 'It's a sight more than the rest of us, Ben.'

'I didn't say I wouldn't lend it,' said Julia. 'And I didn't say I would. I'm just telling you where we are and what Mr Dawson said. After all, we don't know yet whether it would be legally possible. *Would* the thousand pounds be enough to save Coulsdens?'

Jack shook his head. 'I doubt it.'

Cicely snorted impatiently. 'But the bank might look at us more favourably if we could come up with some of the money we need. They might double it by way of a loan. I don't know. I'm only saying they might.'

Emily, aware of Julia's personal problems, said, 'Well, I think Julia ought to keep her money. She might need it one day.'

'No one asked your opinion,' snapped Cicely. 'You're not even a proper member of the family.'

'She is!' cried Julia.

George opened his eyes. 'She bloody well is,' he cried. 'You watch your tongue, Cis. You always were a spiteful bitch!'

Everyone began to look anxious. 'Now, now,' said Jane. 'I'm sure Cicely didn't mean it. We're all a bit upset, but let's not start to bicker.'

Cicely turned on her. 'Well, *you're* a fine one to talk, Jane Coulsden, after all the fuss you made over Agnes and her—' She bit back the word 'bastard' just in time.

'That was years ago,' soothed Stanley, "and all forgotten now. Anyway, she didn't hold any grudge against the child – only her mother.'

'Is that supposed to make it any better?' Emily cried. 'Ma's only been dead a few weeks and already you're having a go.'

'Please!' said Julia. 'If everyone's going to quarrel, then I'm not staying. It's supposed to be a family conference because things are tough. Squabbling won't help any of us.'

'Ju's right,' said Ben. 'Let's get back to business. Either we can solve the problems or we can't. I just want to know, one way or the other.'

'Have you got any ideas?' Stanley asked him.

'Yes, I have. I suggest Uncle George sells his boat – since he's obviously not going to sea again – and comes into the business with us.'

'Bloody marvellous!' said George bitterly. 'Thanks a lot, Ben.

Nice to know who your friends are.'

'Who said he's not going to sea again?' demanded Emily.

Julia looked at her father. 'Are you?' she said quietly. When he did not answer she went on, 'I think Ben may have a point. Maybe Pa doesn't want to fish any more. Maybe he would like to go into the boatyard. It's a fair question.'

'Well, I don't like the way he asked it,' said Emily with a stubborn tightening of her lips. 'He could at least be civil.'

'I'm sorry,' said Ben.

'Pa?' prompted Julia.

'I don't know,' he said heavily. 'I'd have to think about it.'

'What I was thinking,' said Ben, 'was if Pa, Uncle George and I worked in the yard we'd have no other wages to pay out – then if things are sticky for a bit we can tighten our own belts whereas you can't ask your men to do that.'

'But what would you do if there's no work coming in?' asked Ernest.

'Put a new boat on the stocks.'

'Who for? Who'd buy it?'

Ben's expression hardened. 'God knows!' he said. 'Sod it!'

'The point is,' said Stanley, 'whether it's worth trying to raise money if there's nothing to do with it when you've got it. There's something in what Ben says. If we raise money just to pay off debts, we're still broke at the end of it and where do we go from there? If people are going to invest in the firm they have to have a reasonable chance of getting back their stake money and eventually making a profit. Otherwise it's throwing good money after bad.'

The ensuing silence was uncomfortably prolonged.

Jane was longing for a cup of tea. Cicely was considering making one, but was afraid to leave the conference in case she missed anything. George was wondering how soon they could decently bring the meeting to a close and repair to the Pipemakers'.

Emily said suddenly, 'I could make us all a cup of tea if Aunt Cicely doesn't mind. Then you lot could go on talking.'

'I'll give you a hand,' offered Julia, turning to Cicely. 'Would you like us to do that?'

'Oh yes, Julia, please dear. That would be a good idea.'

The two girls took the opportunity to escape into the kitchen where two large trays were already set out with the best white china on white lace cloths. A clean teacloth covered two plates of cakes, one of butterfly cakes and the other of raspberry buns.

'D'you think she's counted them?' asked Emily as Julia filled the kettle.

'Probably.'

'Oh, pity!' She picked up a cup and examined it admiringly. 'When I'm married I shall try to get some really nice china like this.' She looked round the large kitchen with interest. 'And I shall get some nice pots and pans. What on earth's this?'

'A lemon squeezer.'

Emily giggled. 'Oh no, that's too funny!' she said. 'But tell me quickly, Ju – any letter from you-know-who?'

'Not yet.'

'Oh Ju! *No!*' Her jaw dropped. 'How long is it since you sent the letter?'

'Eight days.'

'*Ju!*'

'I know. I don't know what to think.'

'I've been thinking,' Emily said carefully. 'There are things you can do. The girl at the shop, her sister was expecting and she'd only had the first one five months before so she kept jumping off chairs and having very hot baths. It loosens the baby so you . . . lose it.'

'Oh dear,' said Julia. 'Did it work?'

'No,' Emily admitted, 'but it does sometimes. You could try it. Or,' she went on, 'you could have it adopted as soon as it's born. By somebody who couldn't have any children of their own, some-body who'd give it a really good home.'

Julia looked stricken. 'But *I* want to give it a good home,' she whispered. 'I don't want to give it away. I couldn't.'

'Then you hang on to your money,' Emily urged. 'Honestly, Ju, you'd be mad to part with it. I wouldn't. It's not your fault they're in a mess.'

'It's not theirs, either.' Julia spooned tea from the caddy into the teapots. 'I feel sorry for Uncle Jack. He's always been very good to me and they gave me a home when Mama Sarah died. I was happy with them. In a way I had a proper family for the first time; a whole family. I feel I owe them something and I'd like to help. If I do marry Ian I could offer them some of the money, if he agreed . . .' She shrugged. 'But then would it be fair to Ian if we were hard-up and with a baby?'

'You hang on to it all,' advised Emily. 'It's not being selfish, Ju, honestly it isn't. Whether or not you marry Ian, you have to think of the baby. The baby deserves to come first, surely?'

'But I can't tell them about the baby, not yet anyway. Ian would never forgive me. If we're going to get married and then pretend it happened afterwards – well, I can't tell everyone now.'

The kettle began to whistle and she poured boiling water into the two teapots, one white china, the other silver.

'A silver teapot!' breathed Emily, impressed.

'I think it's just plated,' said Julia. 'It was Mama Sarah's. I remember thinking how grand it was when I was a child.'

'Julia . . .'

She looked up, aware of the subtle change in Emily's voice.

'Julia, how would it be if *we* adopted your baby. Me and Chick.'

Julia's eyes widened in surprise. 'You and Chick? But *why*, for goodness' sake?'

Emily swallowed. 'I don't think I'll ever have any children,' she said, her voice low. 'I've been trying for ages. We're still . . . you know . . . but nothing happens.'

'But Em! Why try now? You're so young.'

'We want to get married and they'd have to let us if I was expecting.'

'But they wouldn't let you,' Julia protested, 'just in order to adopt someone else's baby. It wouldn't work like that.'

'I'm so terribly jealous,' Emily whispered. 'I almost hated you, in my heart, when I first knew. I'm so sorry.'

'It doesn't matter at all.' Julia threw her arms round her half-sister and hugged her. 'Look, you probably will have a baby. It's early days yet, isn't it? But if you don't, then you can share mine – come round and bath it and take it for walks and everything. Oh, Em, don't look so sad. Perhaps nature knows best and is making you wait another year or so.'

'If nature knows best, why are you having one?'

'Oh Lord, I don't know.' She laughed shakily. 'I sometimes think I don't know anything about anything. I go from one muddle to the next. Oh cheer up, Em. Let's look on the bright side. I'll marry Ian and you'll have a baby before too long. It could all turn out right if we believe hard enough.'

'You want to take a bet on it?' Emily sniffed.

Julia laughed. 'Not really. But come on, let's take the tea in and see where they've got to in our absence.'

'I don't see where they *can* get to,' said Emily.

Her assessment of the situation was entirely accurate. By the time the 'conference' broke up nearly two hours later, nothing at all had been agreed and all the basic problems remained apparently insoluble.

CHAPTER TWENTY-THREE

Alice was banging saucepans and clattering cutlery, which was a sure sign that she had something of importance to say and that it would not be particularly pleasing to hear. Sam listened nervously for about six minutes and then his courage failed him. He got up from the table intending to make his escape, but Alice was too quick.

'No, you don't, Sam Bligh!' she said, whirling to face her husband and grandson. 'I have something to say and I want you to hear it.'

Sam sank down again, muttering something about having another slice of toast. In fact, he was still hungry, but the suggestion was primarily intended as a delaying tactic.

'There's no more bread,' she snapped. 'You've just eaten the end crust, remember?'

'Ah! So I have.' He winked nervously as Frank, who glanced up at his grandmother.

'Out with it, then,' he told her. 'As if I didn't know!'

Alice wiped her soapy hands on her apron and tucked up a stray wisp of hair before settling her hands firmly on her hips.

'I've two things to say to you, Frank,' she stated. 'When are you going to find another job, and what's going on between you and the Coulsden girl? And I want straight answers, mind. No beating about the bush.'

'Do I ever?

Sam said, 'He never does, Alice. Give him his due.'

Alice fixed Frank with her dark button eyes as he drew in his breath and let it out again in a tuneless whistle. 'I haven't lost my job yet,' he said, 'So why should I be looking for another one?'

'Because the one you've got doesn't earn you any money!' answered Alice. 'That's why! It's weeks now since that boat left its moorings.'

'I'm not skipper,' said Frank. 'It's not up to me. I don't decide when it sails.'

'But is it ever going to?' demanded Alice. 'That's what I'd like to know. How are we supposed to live, if there's no money coming in? Another week or two and we'll need to be buying coal.'

'It's not the boy's fault, Alice,' Sam put in. 'Be fair, he works hard enough when he gets the chance. You can't blame Frank.'

'I'm not *blaming* anyone,' said Alice. 'I'm asking him what he's going to do about it. I know it's not his fault. I know George Coulsden's lost his wife and is drinking himself into the ground, but that doesn't help us. All right, I'm sorry for the man, but other folk have to earn a living and if he's not going to give Frank the chance to earn a few bob, then the boy had best look elsewhere. That's all I'm saying.'

'I keep hoping he'll snap out of it,' Frank told him. 'I like working for him and God knows where I'd get another job – not on another boat, that's for sure. I can go on the dole, if that's what you want, like some of the others.'

'I don't want that,' said Alice, 'but beggars can't be choosers, and we'll have to get some money from somewhere. The ferrying's not bringing in much.'

Sam nodded in agreement. 'Soon there'll be no more holiday-makers and it'll be the end of that bit of extra. We shall be down to the regulars then and there's few enough of them, as you know.'

'I do know,' said Frank. 'I just keep hoping Mr Coulsden will pull himself together. I can't take the boat out on my own.'

'Maybe I could come along?' suggested Sam.

Alice rounded on him. 'You'll do no such thing, Sam Bligh! You're not up to it with your legs and you know it. The slightest swell would have you over. You took a tumble yesterday and the ground wasn't even moving.' She turned to Frank. 'He's too unsteady on his legs,' she insisted. 'Now don't you go taking him on any boats. You promise me?'

'I never said I would,' said Frank. 'Stop fretting.'

'If I was a few years younger—' Sam began.

'Well, you're not,' interrupted Alice, 'and you're not setting foot on any boat with those legs of yours, so that's that settled!' She turned back to Frank. 'And if you want my advice, you'll get yourself up to Mr Coulsden and ask him to his face what he means to do. Tell him if he's not going to sea you'll have to be looking elsewhere. Tell him straight out.'

'Your grandmother's right,' said Sam. 'It might be best in the long run.'

Frank shrugged. 'It's fine by me. He can only say "No".' He

levered himself up out of the chair.

'Hang on!' cried Alice. 'We haven't talked about the Coulsden girl yet. I hear she came to the beach with you when you went to Dungeness. How come?'

'What d'you mean "How come"?' retorted Frank. 'She was invited by her cousin; nothing to do with me.'

Alice regarded him keenly through narrowed eyes. She knew him to be straight as a die. 'You said it was to be just you and Ben.'

'It was, but then he invited Julia and this girl Vicky.'

'Vicky? Vicky who?'

'I don't know.' He shrugged. 'I told you Ben invited them both. It was news to me.'

She looked slightly mollified. 'Well, I don't know. Two men and two girls – there's bound to be talk and I heard she was engaged to a doctor.'

'She is.'

'Well, then. There you are!'

'I don't follow,' he said innocently.

Alice's tone hardened. 'Now don't you take that attitude with me,' she told him. 'I've known you all your life and you don't fool me, Frank. There's more to this than meets the eye, I know it here.' She tapped her head.

Frank said nothing.

'He's told you,' put in Sam. 'The girl's spoken for. What more do you want him to say?'

'I want the truth,' said Alice, 'that's all.' She continued to stare at Frank, who avoided her eyes.

'This Vicky,' said Sam hopefully. 'Is she a nice girl, Frank?'

'Very nice.'

'There you are, Alice!'

'I want the truth, Frank,' Alice insisted.

'The truth?' said Frank. He drummed his fingers on the table and Sam looked apprehensive. 'All right, then. I'd like to marry Julia Coulsden, but she's engaged to someone else, so there's an end to it.'

Sam looked startled, Alice triumphant. 'I knew it!' she breathed. She sat down heavily in the third chair and leaned across the table.

'Have you asked her?'

'Yes.'

'And she turned you down?'

'Yes, she did,' said Frank. 'Turned me down flat. Satisfied?'

'Well!' said Alice, momentarily lost for words. She and Sam exchanged looks of relief.

'Well,' he repeated, 'it's for the best, Frank. She's out of your class.'

Frank looked from one to the other. 'I still want to marry her,' he stated, 'and if she changes her mind I will.' He stood up. 'Now, that's your two questions answered.'

At that moment there was a knock at the back door and when Alice answered it she found Julia on the doorstep. She was so shocked she could only stammer, 'It's her!'

Sam cried agitatedly, 'Well, ask her in, Alice. Remember your manners, woman!'

Julia came in, instantly aware of the obviously charged atmosphere and puzzled by it.

Frank and Sam stood up. 'Where did you spring from?' asked Frank.

'I cycled,' she told him breathlessly. 'I have a message from Papa. He's taking *Silver Lady* out.' She hesitated awkwardly. 'He's had a bit to drink, I'm afraid, but he's determined to go and sent me to fetch you.'

'Just the two of us?' Frank was collecting oilskins and sea-boots as he spoke.

'Ben's agreed to go, too,' Julia told him. 'I just called on him.'

'I'd best be on my way then,' said Frank, but he made no move to go. He was eager for work and eager to escape his grandmother's questions, but reluctant to leave without Julia.

'I'll cycle back with you,' he suggested.

'You let her be,' Alice told him. 'The poor girl's out of breath enough already and you'll cycle quicker on your own. Miss Coulsden might like a nice cup of tea. Sit yourself down, miss.'

Julia hesitated, with a look of appeal at Frank, but Sam intervened. 'You get along, Frank. Miss Coulsden will be quite safe with us. She can take her time, then, and cycle back at her own pace.' He smiled at Julia. 'You'll take a cup of tea with us, won't you?'

She nodded. 'But Frank . . .' she said with some embarrassment, 'Papa is in a funny mood. We had a bit of a family conference yesterday and something was said – you know, about his drinking and not taking the boat out. I think it got to him and . . .'

She sighed and Frank nodded. 'Don't worry,' he told her. 'I'll see to things. He'll be all right.'

When Frank had gone Julia sat down at the kitchen table. The ride had exhausted her and she *was* glad to rest, but she felt very nervous as two pairs of eyes regarded her curiously. She hoped her anxiety did not show in her eyes.

'I was sorry to hear about your stepmother,' said Alice. 'Taken it bad, has he?'

'I'm afraid so.'

Julia wondered desperately how much – if anything – they knew about her relationship with Frank. She thought it unlikely that he would have told them anything.

Sam smiled. 'It takes people different ways,' he said. 'My grandma turned real funny when my grandpa went; it turned her head, you know. She got all suspicious, even of her own family. Locked herself in the house, she did and wouldn't let no one in. I remember my poor old mother had a right game with her. Mind you, she was ninety-three – and do you know, she died exactly a year later. To the very day! A year after my grandpa. It's on the stone, in the churchyard. What about that for a coincidence, then?'

'That's amazing,' agreed Julia, grateful for a safe topic of conversation.

Alice said, 'But Miss Coulsden's father—'

'Oh, please call me Julia.'

'Miss Coulsden's father,' Alice repeated as though Julia had not spoken, 'hasn't gone funny in the head. He's just drinking a bit heavy, like. To drown his sorrows, I expect. He'll get over it in time.'

'I don't know about that,' said Julia. 'He's not eating and he looks terrible. He says he eats while I'm at work, but I'm sure he doesn't.'

'You go to work then?' asked Sam.

'Oh yes,' explained Julia. 'I work for a Mrs Formby. She runs a guest house. I do various things – lay tables, sweep, dust, some of the shopping, write menus . . . whatever needs doing, really.'

'Is it hard work?' Alice asked as she poured tea into a mug and added milk. 'I'm afraid we've no sugar until I get to the shop.'

'I don't mind it without sugar,' Julia assured her. 'No, it's not hard work, but it's a long day.'

'You look a bit peaky,' commented Alice.

Julia felt her face burning and prayed that Alice did not notice. 'I – I'm a bit worried at the moment,' she said. 'Family troubles. Things are very bad at present.'

'They're bad for all of us,' said Sam. 'Never known them

worse. Never!' He shook his head. 'We were just saying to the boy – to Frank – that if your father was giving up fishing he'd be hard put to find another job. You came knocking on the door that very moment.' He sighed. 'No, times are bad, they certainly are. Can't remember a time like it and that's going back a few years.'

Alice smiled at Julia. 'I hear you've got yourself engaged?'

'Oh . . . yes,' Julia stammered. 'I have. His name's Ian Cornwell and he's a doctor. His grandparents took South View at Appledore after my grandmother died. That's how we met.'

'It's a small world,' said Sam.

'Yes.' She sipped her tea, not looking at either of them.

'And the parents?' Alice insisted. 'Pleased, are they?'

'Yes, of course.' Julia hesitated. 'They think I'm a bit young to get married, but I don't feel too young. I'd like to be married quite soon.'

'Oh?' said Alice.

'She knows', thought Julia, 'or else she's suspicious.'

'Because Ian wants to spend a few years in Australia,' she explained. 'There's a lot of opportunity out there and I don't want us to be separated for such a long time.'

'No, you wouldn't, would you!' said Alice sympathetically.

Sam laughed. 'We got married in a bit of a rush like,' he confided. 'Like a lot of—'

'Sam Bligh!' cried Alice, her voice steely. 'That's no way to talk to Miss Coulsden. She doesn't want to know about when we got married.'

'I was only saying—'

'Well, don't! We were much too young,' said Alice, 'and it's even worse for young folk today, with no jobs and no money. I wonder sometimes where it's all going to end. He's a doctor, your young man, then?'

'Yes, he's qualified and just completed his hospital year and now he'll be looking for a post,' explained Julia.

'So you want to go to Australia, do you?' said Sam.

'Not really,' said Julia. 'I'm afraid I'm a home bird, but if Ian wants to go then I'd like to be with him.'

'Of course you would,' said Sam. 'Stands to reason.'

Julia was drinking her tea as quickly as she could, eager to be on her way and free of the probing questions.

'Well,' said Alice with a smile, 'let us know when to expect the wedding bells and we'll come and throw some rice. And don't fret about your pa – there's not much you can do for him. We all have to work out our own salvation. As Sam always says, there's no law as says life's got to be easy. It never is; you have to take the rough with the smooth.'

Julia swallowed the last mouthful of tea, put down her cup and stood up. 'Thank you for the tea, but I ought to be going,' she said. 'I've promised to pop over and see Ian's grandmother. It was nice meeting you again after all these years.'

Alice frowned. 'When did we meet last?' she asked.

'At the Regatta,' Julia told them. 'Frank came second in the ship's boat race and Uncle Jack gave him ten shillings.'

'Good heavens!' said Alice. 'That was years ago! Where has the time gone? I'm sure I don't know.'

She and Sam stood in the doorway and watched Julia remount her bicycle and ride off along the track with a quick wave of the hand.

Sam shook his head. 'So that's the girl our boy wants to marry. He knows how to pick 'em, I'll say that for him. She's certainly a beauty.'

'She's a Gooding,' said Alice shortly. 'She's also pregnant.'

*

By nine o'clock that evening Rye Bay was shrouded in a thick fog that came from nowhere quite unexpectedly, rolling silently over the calm sea. The crews already at anchor cursed mildly and took little further notice except to post a lookout in the normal way.

There were four Rye boats, seven from Dungeness and two from Hastings; also – further out and keeping a respectful distance – half-a-dozen French vessels. *Silver Lady* was somewhere in the middle of the fleet; Stanley's boat was still ashore on the Hastings stade. The dense fog muffled the normal sounds of flapping sail and swelling sea and occasionally a voice whispered eerily in the gloom as one lookout called to another across the intervening water.

On board *Silver Lady* George, recovered from his previous night's drinking, dozed on an old mattress in the empty net room. Frank, on lookout, had positioned himself in the bows of the boat and Ben had just made a jug of hot cocoa to which he had added a good measure of rum. The fog made the air cold and clammy and Frank shivered as he took the welcome drink into his eagerly cupped hands.

'Thanks, Ben. How's your uncle?'

'He's fine, silly old sod!' said Ben.

'At least he ate something.'

'Cold gooseberry pie!' Ben grimaced. 'Still, it was all we could rustle up at such short notice.'

'Good of you to come out,' said Frank.

'I was glad of something to do.'

'Not much on at the yard?'

'Nothing at all. It's a real facer.'

There was a faint shout from another boat to the south of them and both men peered ahead, immediately alert. Almost immediately a red Very flare went up.

'I'm damned if I can see anything,' said Ben, straining his eyes to peer into the grey murk.

'I can hear something!' cried Frank. 'An engine—'

'Christ Almighty!' shouted Ben as suddenly, out of the gloom ahead, the high bows of a huge tramp loomed over them. Before either man could utter another word it had rammed them with a sickening crash of splintering wood and grinding metal. Ben was thrown backwards on to the deck by the shuddering impact and Frank went overboard with a despairing cry and vanished into the dark water. Below deck George was hurled against the bulwark with a force that knocked all the breath out of him. The Belgian merchantman, steaming ahead with a full cargo of coal, ploughed on through the centre of the fishing fleet and struck three more vessels, badly damaging two of them. She enmeshed herself in *Silver Lady*'s nets and within minutes the little fishing boat had heeled over and was being dragged under the water, the nets sheared as the stricken vessel plunged steeply to the sea-bed, leaving a gurgling swirl of bubbles to rise to the surface. The merchantman stopped her engines, but it was too late. *Silver Lady* had gone and all that remained were a few broken spars floating in a patch of oil.

*

Unaware of the tragedy, Julia spent a pleasant evening with Helen and left just after 11 pm to cycle home. Minutes later Helen answered the telephone to receive the news from Cicely.

'Oh God, that poor girl!' she whispered as she hung up. 'That poor dear girl!'

Julia was surprised but not unduly alarmed to find a police constable standing outside the door of her house. For a moment she thought it no more than a coincidence – that he just happened to be there. In fact Constable Barnes, comparatively new to the Force, felt extremely aggrieved. Not only was he averse to being the bearer of sad news, he was also missing all the excitement. The rest of the local police, with the exception of the sergeant, were among the crowd waiting on the beaches of Camber and Winchelsea.

Julia leaned her bicycle against the wall and fumbled in her pocket for the front-door key.

'Miss Coulsden? Miss Julia Coulsden?'

She turned. 'Yes?'

'I'm afraid I have some bad news for you,' he said. 'May we go inside?'

Julia stood rooted to the spot, panic flaring within her.

'Not Ian?' she whispered faintly.

'No, Miss,' he said, indicating the door. 'Should we go in first? I think it would be—'

'*Who?*' cried Julia. Thoughts of her mother's suicide and the recent revelation about the boatyard leapt into her mind. 'Not Uncle Jack! Oh not—'

'No, miss.'

She stared at him blankly. 'Then what's happened? What is it?'

'I really think . . .'

She let out a thin moan of impotent fear. 'Tell me! Tell me!' she cried.

'It's about your father, Miss,' he said desperately. 'Please open the door. Give me the key.'

Slowly she handed it to him. 'My father? But . . .'

The door swung open and Constable Barnes stepped inside. There was a letter on the mat which he handed to her. He found the hall light and lit it and she followed him indoors, her face chalk-white in the glare of the gas-light.

'There's been – a bit of an accident,' he said. 'A collision at sea. I'm afraid your father's boat was lost and—'

Julia looked at him carefully. He was tall but very young, with small, pale eyes. There was a large spot on his chin and his Adam's apple seemed too big for his rather scrawney neck. She felt sorry for him; his eyes were so very pale and his neck so painfully thin.

'What did you say?' she asked as a wave of faintness swept over her. 'About Papa?'

'I'm afraid he went down with the boat, Miss.'

'Oh no,' she said, with great calmness. 'No.' She shook her head.

'I'm afraid it's true, Miss. I'm very sorry, Miss.'

He looked vaguely familiar.

'Aren't you Ronald Barnes?' she asked inconsequentially, refusing to accept what he had told her.

'No, Miss. I'm his brother Andrew.'

'Oh.'

His words refused to go away. What had he told her? 'He went down with the boat, Miss.' Papa had 'gone down'? Papa had *drowned*?

Julia put a trembling hand to her lips. 'And is he really dead? Papa?'

'Yes, Miss. Your aunt wants you to wait here; she's coming round as soon as she gets back from the hospital.'

'Oh God!' She began to cry and he guided her on to the nearest chair.

The meaning of his words filtered slowly into Julia's dazed mind. 'The hospital?' she repeated dully.

'Your cousin, Miss. Benjamin Coulsden received a head injury, but is comfortable.'

'Oh God.' she sobbed. 'Papa! Don't be dead. Please don't be dead!' The young constable averted his eyes from her grief. He was very inexperienced.

Julia covered her face and sobbed. 'Dear Papa! Oh my poor, dearest Papa! I love you, do you hear me? I love you, Papa. Oh, *please* don't be dead!'

'The third member of the crew . . .' said the constable nervously.

She looked up sharply. 'Frank?' She jumped to her feet. 'He's not—? Oh no, he can't be! Not Frank?'

'We don't know yet, Miss. We hope not.' We hope not . . . We hope not . . . Hope not . . . The dreadful words echoed in the darkness of her despair. 'The third member of the crew'. How cold and detached that sounded, not like a real person at all. A member of the crew. She looked at the constable through tear-stained eyes.

'He's not a member of the crew,' she told him. 'He's Frank. Frank Bligh.'

'Beg pardon, Miss?' He frowned, puzzled. 'I understood he was a member of *Silver Lady*'s crew.'

'His name's Frank,' she said again.

Frank Bligh . . . Not just a member of a boat's crew but a

warm-hearted, generous man. A man with a deep capacity for love. A man who loved and respected her. Who cared about her happiness. She tried to conjure up his image, but his face eluded her. All she could summon was his personality – his quiet controlled manner, his directness and lack of pretence. She heard his voice, low and intense; she remembered his cool resourcefulness, the humour and the power of the man. And was all that gone, too? Frank *and* her father, taken from her by the same cruel trick of fate.

The constable put out a hand and patted her shoulder.

'Don't take on so, Miss,' he implored. 'Your aunt will be along soon. She said about ten—ah! Perhaps this is her now.'

Hurrying footsteps on the cobbles brought Cicely to the still-open front door and Julia ran into her arms, sobbing frantically.

Cicely glanced enquiringly at the constable. 'Any more news?' she asked. 'Were there any more casualities?'

'Not that I've heard of, ma'am,' he told her. 'I've not been down to the beach, but the lifeboat must have returned by now. The coastguards at Winchelsea Beach have been in touch with the Dungeness station and the Dunge men are supposed to be safe, though two men have minor injuries. I don't know about the Hastings boat.'

'Let's hope there are no more,' cried Cicely. 'Dear God! What a tragedy! I can't believe it. I don't know how such a thing could *happen*.'

'Is your son all right, ma'am?'

'He will be. He was fully conscious and I spoke to him for a few minutes. He says Frank Bligh saved his life.' She turned her attention to the sobbing girl. 'Julia? Do you hear what I'm saying? Frank Bligh saved Ben's life. Ben was unconscious and Frank swam around until he found him. They reached Frank first and wanted to pull him out, but he refused. He just stayed in the water until he found Ben. Then somehow they lost track of him. But we mustn't give up hope.'

Julia nodded dumbly and Cicely handed her a handkerchief. 'Come on,' she said briskly. 'You must stop crying. Just while I walk you home to our place. Yes, you must. The fresh air and the walk will do you good. When we get you to bed with some hot milk and brandy, you can cry all you like.' She turned to the policeman. "We shall be all right now, constable, and thank you. It's never a pleasant job, I'm afraid, breaking bad news.'

'Just doing my duty, ma'am. If you're sure, then.' He smiled uncertainly at Julia. 'And I'm really sorry about your father, Miss.'

Julia nodded and the young constable left the house. Together Cicely and Julia began to walk along the High Street, but half-way down Monastery Hill Julia stopped suddenly and pulled free of her aunt's encircling arm.

'Where's Uncle Jack?' she asked.

'He's gone to Camber with everyone else. He'll bring us news, don't you worry.'

'I want to go with him,' exclaimed Julia. 'I want to go to Camber. I want to *be* there.'

Cicely put her arm round Julia's waist. 'Julia, my dear,' she said gently. 'George is dead. You must face up to it. There can be no good news about your father. Ben says he was below deck and he couldn't possibly—'

'I know that,' cried Julia. 'I know about Papa. It's Frank; I want to know about Frank.'

'But you *will* know,' Cicely insisted. 'Jack will bring us the news.'

'I want to *be* there,' Julia repeated. 'I must. I just feel I must be there. It may be the last thing I can do for him – just to *be* there, waiting for news. Please, Aunt Cicely. I want to go to Camber.'

Cicely argued vainly for five minutes or more, but eventually she was forced to give in, albeit ungraciously. 'Well, if you're going I shall have to come too,' she grumbled. 'I can't let you wander about on the beach on your own after the shock you've had.' She sighed.

After a prolonged search they found someone willing to take them. It had finally occurred to Cicely that possibly the activity on the beach might take Julia's mind off her bereavement and help to dull or delay the pain of her loss. Also, since she herself could not reasonably return to the hospital since Benjamin was not seriously hurt, she might as well be with Jack.

They finally arrived on the beach at Jury's Gap just after midnight and found a silent crowd gathered there, all eyes towards the sea, their faces ghostly in the dim glow of a dozen or more hurricane lamps. The mist had thickened and with the coming of darkness only the edge of the sea was visible. Sounds carried eerily in the grey air as small knots of people talked together in hushed voices. The coastguards were in evidence, moving purposefully along the shoreline, their binoculars trained on the softly breaking waves. 'Watching,' thought Julia with a shudder, 'for the first sighting of a body.' A sighting which would mean the premature end of Frank Bligh's young life.

Cicely kept an arm linked through Julia's as they threaded their way amongst the waiting people, looking for Jack Coulsden's familiar figure. Julia wondered how many times this pathetic scene had been enacted over the years along this same stretch of beach. The silent shocked relatives, waiting, hoping against hope, their eyes wide with fear or closed in prayer. Mothers, fathers, wives and sweethearts, their happiness at the mercy of the sea, drawn together by mutual dread and a wild but stubborn hope.

Jack, who was talking to Tommy Bird, turned at Cicely's greeting and put an arm round each of them. Julia felt a deep sob rise within her. Her uncle's solid presence made her dead father lack substance. As she struggled with her tears, she wondered how they could say their last good-byes to him if his body lay at the bottom of the sea, trapped within the hold of *Silver Lady*. Poor Papa, she thought. He had been so proud of his beautiful boat and now it had taken him to his grave.

Jack released Cicely and put both arms round Julia, bending to kiss the top of her head. 'I'm sorry, love,' he told her huskily. 'I'm so bloody sorry. I can't tell you—'

She nodded, shaken with helpless tears of misery. Jack and Stanley, she thought – so like her father and yet unlike him. Sprung from the same roots, borne on the same tides. Three brothers, their lives dominated by shared blood and a shared dependence on the sea. Being held in Jack's arms brought home to her the realisation that her father's arms would never again surround her in that rough bear-hug that she remembered from childhood – the strong arms that had protected, or tried to protect her, from the rest of the world.

'Is there any more news of Frank?' asked Cicely.

'No. The lifeboat's gone out again. It's a bloody pea-souper out there.'

'Couldn't one of the other boats have picked him up?'

'We just don't know, love. Anything's possible and we just have to go on hoping.' He lowered his voice. 'You shouldn't have brought Julia.'

'She insisted,' protested Cicely, 'and I couldn't dissuade her.'

Suppressing her tears, Julia straightened up as Tommy Bird said, 'I'm sorry about your pa, Julia. It's a damned shame!'

'Yes,' she whispered. 'Thank you.'

'Chick's somewhere around,' he told her. 'Eunice wouldn't let

Emily come.' Julia nodded as Ratty Hall came up to them.

'Bloody bad business,' he said to Jack. 'Sorry to hear about your brother.' He caught sight of Julia. 'I'm sorry, Miss,' he said. 'Can't hardly believe it. How did it happen, that's what I'd like to know? Must've been going at a hell of a lick, those Belgians. Got to have been. There's no getting round that.' He shook his head. 'He was a good man, your pa.'

'Yes,' said Julia.

'And young Bligh. I saw his grandparents just now.' He turned to look for them, peering short-sightedly into the darkness. 'They don't deserve this,' he added. 'First their son. Now their grandson. It's a stinking shame.'

Julia looked up at Cicely. 'I'd like to have a word with Mr and Mrs Bligh,' she said. 'I won't be a minute.'

She found them standing together with some of the men who acted as launchers for the lifeboat. Another woman stood with them, whom Julia did not recognise.

'Miss Coulsden!' cried Alice. 'What are you doing down here?' She held herself very straight and her jaw was set in a hard line. Only the panic in her eyes gave a clue to her agony of mind.

'I wanted to come,' Julia said. 'I wanted to know about Frank.'

'Your father's gone,' said Sam. 'What a terrible thing! I just can't tell you how shocked we were when we heard.'

'I can't believe it yet,' said Julia. 'It seems no time at all since your Frank was cycling off and I was thinking, thank goodness Papa's made the effort, even if he was—' It seemed disloyal to say 'drunk'. 'I was so glad Frank and Ben would be keeping an eye on him.' She shook her head. 'I'm sorry about Frank,' she said. 'I mean, not knowing. There must be hope; all the time there's no news, there's still hope.'

Sam shrugged. 'Hope's all we've got left now,' he muttered.

'Kids!' Alice burst out. 'They're nothing but a heartache. You do your best, you break your back for them and then . . .' she shrugged helplessly. 'You lose them; first his father, now Frank.'

Sam patted her arm. 'Now, Alice, we don't know for sure. Give it the benefit of the doubt. If we hear, well, that's time enough to say he's gone. But not until then, do you hear me?'

Julia looked at Alice. 'Uncle Jack says he saved Ben's life. That was very brave, just like Frank. You can be very proud of him.'

'Proud?' cried Alice. 'I don't want to be proud. I don't want a dead hero. I want my grandson.'

'Now, Alice!' cried Sam. 'That's no way to speak.' He turned to Julia. 'She doesn't mean it,' he whispered. 'She's that upset.'

'Of course,' said Julia. 'I understand.'

'What's the point of it all?' Alice demanded. 'That's what I want to know.'

'I don't know,' Julia replied. 'First my mother, then my father. And Agnes.'

The woman standing beside Alice turned to Julia. 'You're Miss Coulsden, then?'

'Yes.'

'I'm Ellen,' she said. 'I suppose you heard?'

'About what?' Julia asked.

'Your father. That he didn't do in that Dessin boy.' She explained briefly what she knew of Frank's fight with Bitty and the outcome.

Julia's head reeled. So many shocks in one evening!

'I didn't know,' she replied faintly, then she swayed and Alice caught her as she fell and they laid her on the sand.

'Poor kid!' said Ellen.

'You should've kept quiet,' Alice told her. 'Don't you think she's had enough for one day, with her father gone?'

'I never thought.' Ellen was contrite.

'You never do,' commented Alice. 'That's always been your trouble!'

A small crowd gathered rapidly and when Julia opened her eyes she found herself the focus of a dozen pairs of eyes. Weakly she struggled to sit up.

Alice whispered, 'You should take better care of yourself, love. You shouldn't have come, the way you are.'

Julia flashed her a frightened look and Alice thought, 'Good job it wasn't Frank's child!' and then wondered if perhaps it *was*. She knelt clumsily beside Julia and put an arm round her. 'Lean back on me,' she urged. 'Don't try to get up just yet; take it easy.'

Overcome by a terrible weariness, Julia let her head fall on to Alice's shoulder. Someone took off a coat and they draped it over her solicitously.

'I wish . . .' she began dazedly and her lips trembled.

'Wish what?' asked Alice.

'I wish it was Frank,' said Julia in a choked voice. 'I wish I could have said "Yes". I wish I could have made him happy. I've made a terrible mistake and now it's too late.'

'Hush! Hush!' murmured Alice. 'Don't talk that way. Least said, soonest mended.'

'Oh, Frank!' sobbed Julia.

Alice put her arms round Julia, rocking her soothingly. 'There, there. Don't take on so. These things happen. God knows why, but they do. We all just muddle through, best we can. Things'll work out somehow.'

Just then there was a shout from the direction of the road, voices were raised excitedly and the crowd around them melted away as there was a concerted rush towards the new arrivals.

'He's safe!' shouted someone. 'The Bligh boy – he's safe.'

'Oh God!' cried Alice. 'Please let it be true!'

Julia struggled to her feet with Alice's help and together they stumbled over the sand and met Tommy running back.

'He's on his way!' he shouted. 'He was picked up by a Hastings boat, but they were holed so they made for home as fast as they could. The message has just reached the coastguards. He's safe and well, thanks be to God. Safe and well!'

The mood of the crowd changed dramatically from one of brooding dread to wild triumph. They rejoiced in the knowledge that they had cheated the sea of one of its victims. Everywhere men grinned and thumped each other on the back. Women embraced, many weeping openly with tears of relief. Alice's and Sam's joy was everyone's joy. A ragged cheer went up and then another.

Julia hung back, watching the excited throng as further details of the rescue were passed on. It was enough for her that he was safe. Frank Bligh, the man she should have married, was alive and well. Her father was dead. And she must marry Ian because she carried his child. She knew now that she loved Frank and that she had made a terrible mistake. But there was no way out. She would marry Ian and they would go to Australia and she would never see Frank again. What was worse, in the circumstances she dare not tell him of her feelings. That would be intolerable; she must keep the bitter knowledge of her folly to herself. She drew a deep, shuddering sigh and straightened her drooping shoulders, reminding herself that she had responsibilities, that somehow she and Ian must make a loving home for the child.

'I'll try,' she whispered. 'I swear I'll try!'

But as she made her way up the beach to join her aunt and uncle, her heart was as heavy as lead.

CHAPTER TWENTY-FOUR

Mrs Formby, writing out the day's menus, kept a watchful eye on Julia Coulsden. The poor girl looked positively ill – and no wonder with her father dying in that dreadful way so soon after her stepmother's death . . . and the boat lost as well. She had urged her to take a few more days' rest, but Julia insisted that it helped to have something with which to occupy her mind. There were no funeral arrangements to be made, but it seemed there would be a memorial service at some stage. With a start of annoyance Mrs Formby saw that she had written 'peas' instead of 'pears'. She sighed heavily and reached for an ink rubber, chiding herself for not concentrating.

Julia was arranging flowers in the small glass vases which served as centrepieces for the tables. She seemed preoccupied and worked hastily, spilling water on the table. Out of the kindness of her heart, Mrs Formby forbore to comment. Indeed, she even pretended not to notice when Julia mopped it up with one of the spare table napkins.

'These wretched menus!' exclaimed Mrs Formby. 'They really are such a trial to me. I know I could have them typed, but I do pride myself that a daily handwritten menu adds a touch of class in a world where everything is becoming mass-produced. There is something very cold and unattractive about a typewritten menu, don't you agree?'

'Yes, Mrs Formby, I do.' Julia glanced up, answered dutifully and resumed her work.

'Did you sleep last night, child?'

'Not very well,' Julia admitted.

'You look very tired. It's the strain, I expect. Strain and shock. It does things to the system, you see.' She fingered a rope of blue glass beads. 'The body is a very delicate instrument, you know, and it's not designed to be shocked and strained. Have you seen your doctor, since the . . . since the accident? You really must look after yourself, child, now that you have no parents.'

'I've seen him, Mrs Formby. He's given me a tonic.'

'Good! I'm glad.' She glanced at the clock and tutted. 'Wherever has Millicent got to? Look at the time! I'm afraid I shall have to talk to her. She gets later and later. Oh, do leave those flowers, child – they look quite good enough – and start laying the tables. And I must ask Cook if she spoke to the butcher about that minced beef he sent us. Full of fat! It was quite disgraceful.'

She stood up, smoothing her long neck gently with an upward motion of her fingers and hoping thereby to help delay the onset of age and its accompanying wrinkles. Mrs Formby spent a lot of money on buying numerous skin creams and considered her elegant neck to be one of her few remaining assets; she was forty-seven, but many people thought her much younger. She stroked her neck and watched Julia as she rummaged in the deep drawer of the mahogany sideboard for the cutlery. She did *hope* that Julia was not going to Australia, just when she was becoming useful as a member of the staff. Willing girls who were also hardworking and punctual were not easy to find or keep. Mrs Formby paid as little as she dared and consequently her 'girls' came and went with depressing regularity. She sighed noisily, missing Julia's normally cheerful conversation. The poor girl had hardly spoken since her father's death, and then only to answer questions. Sighing again, she went along to the kitchen to tackle Cook on the matter of the beef.

Mrs Formby could not know that the cause of Julia's preoccupation was the letter she had received from Ian, the contents of which had shocked her deeply. She had read it with a growing sense of disbelief and the feeling of humiliation it engendered refused to leave her. As she set knife to the right and fork to the left, the words of the letter echoed and re-echoed in her brain in a wild and ugly tumult. Julia knew the dreadful letter by heart:

Dear Julia,

Thank you for your letter. I won't pretend it wasn't a terrible shock to hear that you are definitely expecting a baby. I am so glad you wrote to me promptly. Now, my dear Julia, you must realise that to take on the responsibility of a child now would place me under an intolerable strain just as I am about to begin my career. You are a sensible girl and will understand what I am saying. I love you, of course, but this could ruin all our plans for the future and I want to urge you *most emphatically* to reconsider. Later on we will start a family, but right now it is out of the question.

I want you to be very discreet and go to the address at the end of
this letter. Do not mention my name, but as soon as you tell him
yours, he will do whatever is necessary. I hope I do not need to
impress on you the fact that this is to be a secret. *No one* must know
about it. The man will be doing me a personal favour and I cannot
expose him to any risk. The penalties are severe, as I'm sure you will
appreciate. The money for the operation is also enclosed. It is the
money my grandmother gave me for my birthday and I had ear-
marked it for an engagement ring. Never mind. First things first and
we will talk about all that later on.

I have not told my parents about this problem, as I do not wish to
alarm them or cause them any distress. Please, PLEASE, if you love
me at all, tell no one. Your father would never understand that what I
am suggesting is for the best and he could make trouble for us.

Don't be afraid, Julia. It will all be over very quickly and I promise
we will never speak of it again. It will be just you and me, Julia, with
our love and a wonderful future. Trust me to know what is the right
thing to do. I love you and we will soon be together again. Write to me
when it is all over. I will keep my fingers crossed for you. Be a brave
girl.

                                                  Your loving Ian.

The address was in Brighton and Julia had memorised that, also.
Now she carried in a trayful of glasses and water jugs, setting
them carefully in their correct places. The monotony of her work
soothed her jangled nerves and left her free to pursue her
thoughts, which were chaotic in the extreme. Ian, *her* Ian, who
had loved her and wanted to marry her, was now coolly directing
her towards an illegal and possibly dangerous operation to remove the child. He was protecting himself in every way, instruct-
ing her to maintain strict secrecy, but was expecting her to
undergo the whole sordid business alone. Then she was to write
and tell him it had been done and all would be forgiven and
forgotten. It was unbelievable! She had read the letter over and
over again, but nowhere had she discovered a phrase or word that
offered any comfort or indicated a real regard or even concern for
her feelings.

Julia had thrown the letter and the money on to the floor, but so
far she had not shed a single tear. Betrayed, disillusioned, she felt
utterly degraded by the hateful suggestion he was putting forward
as the way out of their difficulties. Ian did not want the child, *their*

child, and he was prepared to go to great and terrible lengths to be rid of it.

By now he would know of her father's death, for it was in all the national papers and had been mentioned on the wireless. No doubt, she thought bitterly, he would be relieved that George no longer posed a threat and would be unable to take up the cudgels on his daughter's behalf. Ian must know that she was in a state of shock and grief, but he had made no attempt to contact her. He had not driven down to be with her, or to offer to take her back to his own home. Helen had sent a letter at once, assuring her that soon Ian would be coming down. Sadly, Julia knew better.

After reading the letter, Julia had experienced a frightening surge of anger and a fierce desire to inflict on Ian as much pain as he had inflicted on her. She imagined herself arriving at his home and throwing his letter and the money into Mrs Cornwell's lap. Or posting it to them in a large brown envelope. She even considered taking it to the police – let them take legal proceedings against Ian and his 'friend'! Imagination running riot, she visualised their names and photographs splashed all over the front pages of the newspapers and crowds of women jostling at the steps of the court to jeer at them as they were hustled up the steps by the police. For an hour or more nothing she could devise was too terrible for the man who had taken her body so lovingly and promised such joy, but her anger eventually burned itself out to be replaced by a deep sense of sorrow. Sorrow for the child whose father could so lightly consign it to a premature death before it had even seen the daylight or filled its lungs with air. Regret for Ian who, proving himself so selfish, surely must have experienced a loss of self-respect and the knowledge that in Julia's eyes his once bright image was thus shattered beyond repair.

How could he possibly think they could live together or continue to love one another as before? Their chance of happiness, she knew, was irrevocably lost in the carefully penned words of the letter.

'Hullo, Ju.' Millicent's cheerful greeting broke into her thoughts. 'How's tricks?'

Julia greeted her and smiled. 'Mrs F's out for your blood,' she warned. 'She says you're late.'

'She should pay me proper wages, mean old skinflint!'

Millicent took off her jacket and hat and went out to hang them on the hall-stand. When she came into the dining-room again, she took a clean apron from the sideboard and fastened it in place.

'I saw that Bligh chap in the town,' she said. 'He was coming out of the newsagents. Frank Bligh, the one that saved your cousin's life. Ever so handsome, isn't he? I could really fancy him! I expect he'll have all the girls after him now he's famous.'

'I expect so,' agreed Julia. Her hands trembled and the salt with which she was refilling the cruets went on to the carpet.

'Hey, watch it! You'll have her ladyship after you! No, leave it. I'll do it.'

Julia was grateful for the girl's brash manner. Millicent had not once referred to George's death, but had continued to chatter inconsequentially, just as she always did. Mrs Formby condemned her conversation as 'a lot of nothing' but Julia found it reassuring in her present state of mind. Having pinned on her starched white cap, Millicent snatched the brush and pan from Julia's hands, swept up the salt and threw it under the edge of the carpet.

'What the eye don't see, the heart don't grieve over,' she declared cheerfully. 'Have those people in number 4 gone home? The Knights?'

'I don't really know,' said Julia. 'I haven't seen them around today.'

'Hope not,' said Millicent. 'They don't half tip well – must be loaded! Yes, I quite fancied that Frank. He's got this simmering look, sort of brooding. D'you know what I mean?'

Julia nodded and sat down suddenly, her head swimming. She had eaten very little in the four days since her father's death, the combined shock of the tragedy and her own personal dilemma having robbed her of any appetite.

'You all right, Ju?'

She nodded weakly.

'You ought to go home,' Millicent insisted. 'You should never have come in.'

Mrs Formby came back into the dining-room in time to overhear Millicent's remark. 'Just what I've been telling her,' she said tartly. 'But no one listens to me. What's the matter, child? Are you unwell?'

'I do feel a bit odd,' admitted Julia.

Mrs Formby glanced at the clock. 'Well, you'd better go home,' she said. 'It's not six yet, but we'll let that pass. You certainly do look very pale. Tell your aunt I sent you home early because I was worried about you. Will you be all right on your own? Should I call a taxi?'

'No, no!' said Julia. 'I'll manage, thank you.'

She did not tell Mrs Formby that despite Aunt Cicely and Uncle Jack's offer of a home, she had returned to the house on Hilders Cliff where she was supposedly looking after herself. There, in the familiar surroundings of her own home, she believed she could best deal with the problems whose number and complexity threatened to overwhelm her.

Later, as she let herself in at the front door, a small spark of courage glowed in her heart. She stood in the passage and closed the door behind her, letting the heavy silence of the empty house settle over her like a shroud. It was Saturday. She would give herself until Monday morning at nine o'clock to decide what to do. Then she would do it! A faint smile of satisfaction touched her lips at the thought that she had taken that one small step forward. All her life stretched before her and what she decided now would make or break it. She would not ask for advice; she would consider her options and make a decision. Then she would have no one but herself to blame if she made the wrong choice.

'Julia Coulsden,' she whispered, 'stop feeling sorry for yourself and *do* something.'

Her stomach churned hollowly. Starving herself would not help matters, she knew, so she would force down some food, however unwelcome it might be. She drew a deep breath and made her way to the kitchen.

*

On Monday morning, at seven minutes to nine o'clock, Julia rang the bell at the office of Dawson & Clark, the family solicitors situated near the Ypres Tower. She had not slept at all the previous night but had sat in the kitchen wrapped in a blanket, making and drinking endless cups of tea to keep herself awake. She acknowledged that she had reached the lowest point in her whole life and that if she allowed herself to collapse under the crushing blows life had recently dealt her she might never rise again. There was always the way out that her mother had taken, but for Julia – with her unborn child to consider – that could never be a possibility. Although the child was one of the factors contributing to her despair, it was also one of the incentives for finding the very best course of action. In the quietness of the night, Julia struggled with her conscience, trying to achieve complete self-honesty. She must now face up to her shortcomings, she told herself, and admit to her mistakes. She was determined to emerge wiser and less vulnerable from this close examination of her life.

After only a little heart-searching, she admitted her share of responsibility for the child. She could not blame Ian for her own willing co-operation and their love-making had been a mutual joy. What she could and did blame him for was his unwillingness to accept the consequences and his refusal to consider keeping the baby and giving it a home and parents. Perhaps in time she would feel less bitterly towards him and would be able to see his betrayal as cowardice and immaturity. *Perhaps.* She was not at all sure that she would ever find it in her heart to forgive him, but she did not dwell too long on that problem. No doubt he would marry Virginia and she would give him other children. Julia tried to imagine meeting him in a few years' time when the scars of her own child's rejection had healed, but the picture did not inspire her. After much thought and many abortive attempts, she finally composed a letter to him.

Dear Ian,

    I am enclosing the money you sent me, which I shall not be needing as I intend to keep our baby. I am dreadfully upset by your letter, as surely you must have known I would be. I have read it many times, trying to find some way to believe that you really do still love me as you insist, but how can I believe that you do? Surely if you cared for me you would not expect me to do such a terrible thing and take such a dreadful risk all on my own. That is so unkind, Ian, and so unlike the man I thought I knew and loved. I think you are scared and sooner or later you will be sorry that you sent me such a letter.

    Please don't come near me or even write to me, as I do not want to see you ever again. I don't know how you will live with yourself, but for your sake I hope you find a way. I am trying not to be bitter and angry, but you have hurt me so much.

    Despite your instructions to me to tell no one about all this, I shall confide in Helen – not to cause you any trouble, but because she will want to know why you and I have parted and I will not lie to her. I will, however, swear her to secrecy.

    I will do my best to give the baby a happy home, so you need not worry about that side of it. Perhaps I should thank God that I have found out in time just how shallow your feelings for me really are.

I don't know how to end this letter, except to say that perhaps we were not meant for each other. Better to find out now for both our sakes.

Good-bye. Julia

It was not the perfect letter, but Julia hoped it covered most of what needed to be said. Pushing it into an envelope, she wrote the address and then found a stamp which she stuck on. For a while she sat with the letter in her hands, looking at the name she had written. 'Ian Cornwell,' she whispered. 'I thought I loved you.'

Then she propped the letter against the teapot and began to consider the rest of her problems.

*

Mr Clark, the new junior partner, opened the door to Julia at once and showed her into the small waiting-room which was full of dark furniture and smelt strongly of wax polish and mildew. The lower half of the window on to the street was curtained with ancient lace which hung down several inches below the sill. There was a wooden form along one wall and a small gate-legged table which bore a selection of *The Field* and *Punch*.

'Mr Dawson, was it, that you wanted to see?'

Mr Clark had cut himself shaving and still had a small tuft of cotton wool adhering to his chin.

'Yes, please. I'm Miss Coulsden.'

'Yes, I know. Of course I recognised you immediately,' said Mr Clark. 'I was so sorry – that is, we all were – to hear of . . . to hear the sad news of your father's fatal accident.'

'Thank you,' said Julia.

'Such a tragedy. Such a waste of a life. There will be an enquiry, I hear, and so there should be. It's a wonder there were no more fatalities. I know nothing can bring him back, but someone was responsible for a grave error of judgement and the guilty person should pay the price. Or it might have been rank carelessness, perhaps, Either way, a man is dead.'

Julia nodded. 'What time will Mr Dawson be here?' she asked. 'Does he start at nine?'

'Oh yes, most certainly. At least, he should do. Officially we all start at 9 am, but Mr Dawson *is* the senior partner and he is due to retire at the end of November. Seventy-three is a good age. I think at seventy-three one is entitled to be a few minutes late at the office. Maybe even five minutes.' He smiled.

'I wonder if I could use your telephone,' asked Julia, 'to call Mrs Formby where I work? Just to let her know I shall be late. She sent me home early on Saturday because I wasn't feeling very well.'

'By all means. Come along into my office.'

He led the way into another room, smelling exactly the same as the waiting-room but boasting an ancient leather-topped desk on which the telephone rubbed shoulders with a vase of bronze chrysanthemums. The operator had just made the connection for her when Mr Dawson arrived, and Julia could hear the buzz of whispered conversation between him and Mr Clark as she explained the position to Mrs Formby and promised to be at work as soon as possible. When she had hung up, Mr Dawson shook hands with her, offered commiserations on the death of her father and then led her into his own office, an altogether larger and more sumptuous room with the added luxury of a fine grandfather clock in one corner and a large aspidistra on a stand in the window.

As soon as Julia was comfortably seated, Mr Dawson rang for a Miss Petty who was instructed to bring a pot of tea for two and some oatmeal biscuits.

'I find an oatmeal biscuit first thing in the morning very beneficial to my digestion,' he told her, 'even though I have had a full breakfast. My wife insists upon it. But then breakfast is so early, you see, because since we bought a bungalow ready for my retirement, I have forty minutes' travel which is so tiresome, but there we are – we all have a cross to bear. But you remember that: an oatmeal biscuit and a cup of tea about an hour and a half after breakfast. Ah, thank you, Miss Petty.'

Julia waited patiently until he had poured the tea and her own cup was set on the desk in front of her. Mr Dawson told her about the problems of moving house and establishing a new garden at his time of life, but explained that with the arthritis in his legs stairs were increasingly difficult and would soon be out of the question. Julia nodded politely and continued to wait. He had grown old so suddenly, she thought. The merest fringe of hair remained round his head, his face had wrinkled into pink folds around his small nose and the collar of his white shirt looked much too big for him.

As soon as the solicitor paused to break off a piece of oatmeal biscuit, Julia began her 'speech'.

'Mr Dawson,' she said firmly, 'I am expecting a child by a man to—' The shock made him choke on his biscuit and she counted slowly to ten as she waited impatiently for him to recover.

'Miss Coulsden!' he began, but Julia rushed on before her new-found courage failed her.

'By a young man to whom I was engaged to be married. That engagement is now at an end.' This had sounded dignified when she drafted it out in the early hours of the morning. Now she thought it sounded pompous and promptly abandoned her carefully prepared sentences. 'Look, Mr Dawson, I have plenty of problems,' she told him, 'and I've worked out in my own mind the best way to deal with them. I'd like you to hear me through and *then* tell me what you think about my ideas. I can't promise to take your advice, but at least I will listen to it.'

'I see,' he said nervously. 'Very well then, but—'

'Please, Mr Dawson,' said Julia. 'I won't go all round the houses, just keep to facts.' She took a deep breath. 'Fact one, I am expecting a child who must be provided for. Fact two, my Uncle Jack is on the verge of bankruptcy—'

'I know. Yes, indeed. That's very sad—'

'Fact three, my father has just died.'

'Oh dear, yes. I—'

'Mr Dawson, *please!*' cried Julia. 'I have been up all night and I'm desperately tired and when I leave here I have to go to work. Please let me finish. As you know, I have some money left in trust for me by my mother and my grandmother. There will also be my half of the insurance money on *Silver Lady*. Emily will get the other half. Thank goodness Papa continued to pay the premiums. Now I'm going to suggest to my Uncle Jack and his son Ben that I go into partnership with them in the boatyard by investing my capital. Before you tell me that there is no future for the boatyard, may I explain that the accident which drowned Papa also damaged several other boats and some of that repair work – probably a large proportion of it – will be brought to Coulsdens. In fact there is probably enough work to keep the yard going for six months, maybe longer. By that time I think we may be over the worst and Coulsdens will I hope be on the way to better times.' She crossed her fingers and held them up.

Mr Dawson blinked furiously. 'Miss Coulsden, I—'

'There is one other thing,' she went on. 'With the loss of *Silver*

Lady Frank Bligh has lost his job, so I shall insist that he be taken on at the boatyard if he wishes. I'm sure my uncle will have no objection; there will be too much work for Uncle Jack and Ben to handle on their own. They may well also take back Ratty Hall and Tommy Bird, but that will be up to them.'

'But you . . . and the child?'

'I'm not quite sure,' said Julia carefully. 'I shall keep my job at Trelees until the baby is born, but I shall have to ask for a small rise so that I can pay the rent of the house.'

The solicitor leaned back in his chair, took off his spectacles and polished them vigorously. 'Well,' he said, as at last he replaced them. 'You seem to have – I must say you . . .' He waved his plump hands helplessly.

'I have thought it out carefully,' said Julia, 'and I think it will work. At least it has a very good chance. The point is, can I have the money which was left in trust for me? If not, the whole plan fails. If the money is tied up until I come of age—'

'No, no,' Mr Dawson interrupted. 'At least, yes *and* no. It is tied up, but there are certain clauses which I advised should be included at the time. I don't think it should prove too difficult to release the money, but I should of course want to discuss the matter with your bank manager and your uncle before finally committing myself. As trustee, you see, I must be wholly convinced that the plan is in your best interests.'

'It would be,' said Julia. 'I should have an income from the boatyard. I might also do the firm's book work and earn a small wage. It will work, Mr Dawson; it *has* to!'

She smiled at him and the determination in her eyes brought a lump in his throat. Suddenly he removed his spectacles for the second time, so that he could dab at his eyes with a handkerchief.

'Forgive me,' he said, 'I'm a sentimental old fool, but I can see much of your grandmother in you. She was a very fine woman, your grandmother, and if I may say so, a very beautiful one. Hard for you to imagine, I expect, but there was something about her – apart from her looks, I mean. She could be very intractable, of course, but . . .' he sighed. 'Well, it was always a pleasure to talk business with her; she had a shrewd head on her shoulders, even as a young woman. She was a little older than me, but I'll confess her visits to the office were always a very great pleasure for me. For all of us, in fact. I think we were all half in love with her, if the truth be known.' He laughed a little wistfully.

'But I digress, forgive me. What was I saying? Oh yes, she would have been very proud of you.' He cleared his throat. 'Well, the only problem we have not discussed – if I may make so bold – is the . . . child. The father should legally make financial contribution to the—'

'*No!*' Julia interrupted. 'I won't take a penny from him.'

Mr Dawson clasped his hands on the desk in front of him and regarded them closely. 'The father is not, I take it, prepared to marry you . . . um . . . in the circumstances? It's not uncommon for—'

'No!'

The solicitor lowered his voice. 'But an unmarried mother – it's not an easy life, you know and it can be very lonely. Perhaps if I wrote to him . . . ?'

'I have just written to him,' said Julia. 'Marrying the baby's father is quite out of the question, but I don't want to explain my reasons.'

'You are so very young . . .' he said. 'Perhaps if you took your Aunt Cicely into your confidence . . .'

'No.'

He sighed deeply. 'You may change your mind as the time draws nearer,' he said hopefully. 'If you do, just contact me and I will write to the young man in question.'

'Mr Dawson,' said Julia, 'I don't want his money. I don't want to marry him. And there's an end to it.'

'If you say so, though I am duty bound to point out the various options open to you.'

'I do say so.' Julia stood up. 'If I marry – and it's quite possible I will – I shall want my husband to share my holding in Coulsdens. Do you see what I mean? To have a half-share with me.'

The solicitor blinked again. 'You really have done a great deal of thinking, Miss Coulsden,' he said. 'Of course I understand. But – well, if you are not going to marry the child's father . . .' He shrugged.

Julia smiled. 'Another man loves me,' she said.

Mr Dawson's astonishment was almost comical. 'Good heavens!' he stammered. 'Another man!'

'Yes, a very fine man. I hope he will ask me to marry him. I think he will, but nothing is ever certain, is it?'

'No . . . No, it isn't. Well, I don't know what to say. You

certainly *are* like your grandmother! My goodness me, yes!'

'Well, I must get along to my work now,' Julia said. 'Please write to my uncle and tell him what I'm proposing; and let me know if there are any objections.'

'He will be delighted, I should imagine,' Mr Dawson assured her. 'For myself, I must say it seems to offer a most happy solution for the Coulsden family. Your father would have approved, I think.'

'I don't know,' said Julia. 'He might well have preferred me to build a new boat, but that may come later on. For the moment I think my solution is the best all round.' She held out her hand. 'Don't worry about me,' she told him.

'I shall try not to do so,' he replied. 'But you must take care of yourself. Eat properly – good nourishing food.'

'I know,' she said, 'and an oatmeal biscuit! I'll try to remember. And thank you, Mr Dawson. I knew I could rely on you. Oh, I nearly forgot.' She took a letter from her handbag and handed it to him. 'The envelope is unsealed,' she told him. 'Please read it, then as soon as possible enclose a cheque and send it to Eunice Bird.'

'But what—' he began.

'You'll understand when you read it,' Julia told him. 'My father did Eunice a great wrong and I want her to know that I, at least, regret what he did. The small sum of money is by way of compensation. I think Papa owes her that much and I hope she will accept it.'

'A great wrong?' he repeated, puzzled. 'And you knew about it?'

'Not at the time,' she explained, 'and then when I did find out I didn't know what to do. But now that Papa is dead I can try to make amends. Now I really must go.'

When she had gone, Mr Dawson reached for another biscuit and poured himself a second cup of tea while he began to read the letter.

'Well, I'll be damned!' he muttered. 'That slip of a girl!' He shook his head. 'She's a Gooding, all right,' he said and laughed. 'Sarah would be well pleased!'

*

The following day Julia arrived home from work and let herself into the house. Taking off her jacket, she began wearily to unpack the groceries she had bought. A knock took her to the front door, where she found Frank.

'Can I come in?' he asked. 'Are you on your own?'

'Yes, I am.' She opened the door wide. 'I've just got back from Trelees. Thank goodness it's easing off a bit up there. The season's just about over.'

He followed her into the kitchen.

'Sit down,' said Julia. 'I'll make you a cup of tea.'

'No, thanks.'

She shrugged tiredly.

'You all right?' he asked. 'You look a bit pale.'

'I'm tired, that's all.'

'Still being sick?' She nodded.

'I'm sorry about your pa,' said Frank. 'I'm not much good at words, but I am sorry.'

'Thank you, Frank. I have to thank you, too, for saving Ben's life.'

He grinned. 'It was nothing.'

'It was *not* nothing!' she protested. 'It was extremely brave. I'm very glad you were picked up; I nearly died a thousand deaths when they said you were missing.' She looked at the scar under his eye. 'Was that . . .?'

'No. That was something else.'

'I see. Aren't you going to sit down?' she asked.

'No. I'll stand up and grow good.'

'Frank . . .' she began.

'Is he going to marry you?' he asked with his customary bluntness.

She swallowed. 'No, he's not.'

'Why's that, then?'

She could see the effort he was making, not to allow himself to hope too early, and she turned away, nervous now that the moment had come. 'He wanted me to get rid of the baby,' she said, slowly turning back to face him. 'He sent me the money, but I couldn't agree to that. It's my baby, too, and I didn't want to . . . well, I want to have it. So I've made some arrangements—'

'Have you told him? Does he know what you've decided?'

'Yes. Originally he wanted to marry me after the baby had gone, but I suddenly knew that he didn't love me, that he couldn't possibly love me. Which was wonderful.'

He frowned. 'What do you mean?' he asked.

Julia tried to explain. 'It was wonderful to know that he didn't really love me, because by then I had already discovered that I was in love with someone else. I realised that evening when Papa died – waiting at the beach for news of you.' She took his roughened hands in her own smooth ones. 'I suddenly imagined how I would feel if you never came back – if you had drowned. I felt so empty and lost and I knew that if I was free to make a choice I would choose you. But I was carrying Ian's child and if he'd wanted it, I would have had to marry him.'

'Send the money back,' he said. 'We don't want his money.'

'I have, Frank,' she said softly. 'I love you and I respect you and—'

'And do I still want you?'

'Do you?'

He looked at her. 'Yes, I reckon I do. More than anything else in the world.'

'Oh, Frank!'

He pulled her towards him and kissed her with passion and then again with restraint.

'Tell the young 'un,' he said, 'that he's got himself a new pa!'

She laughed tremulously. 'Does that mean you're going to make an honest woman of me?'

'Aren't you convinced yet?' he demanded with mock exasperation. 'Miss Coulsden, I love you. I want to marry you as soon as possible and I think two for the price of one is a real bargain!'

For a moment he held her close in his arms and Julia felt, not a wild exhilaration but a warm contentment.

'Frank, I'll make you as happy as I know how,' she whispered, her eyes shining. 'I swear you will never regret it.'

'That goes for me, too,' he grinned. 'Can you cook?'

'Fair to middling, but I'll practise a lot.'

'Your pa,' he said. 'Do you think he'd approve?'

'I think he would be very pleased. I love you, Frank.'

'I love you.' He shook his head in wonderment. 'Julia Lady Coulsden is going to be my wife.'

'I hope your grandparents won't be too upset.'

'They'll love you if you let them.'

'Of course I will.'

'Do I have to speak to your Uncle Jack? Ask his permission?'

'I don't know. I suppose so.'

'Christ! What a palaver it all is,' said Frank, amused. His expression softened. 'God, Julia, I want you so much, right now

. . .' He hesitated. 'But I can wait,' he assured her. 'Not for long, but I can wait. We'd better get round to see your uncle and then the vicar.'

'What, now?' she stammered. '*Today?*'

'Why not? I want everyone to know as soon as possible. What have you got in the cupboard?' he asked. 'Eggs? Bacon?'

'Yes.'

'Good! We'll eat when we get back. Come on, I'll help you with your jacket.'

He held it while she slipped her arms into the sleeves and then, before she could turn to face him, he closed his arms gently around her and pressed his face into her hair.

'Swear you won't change your mind,' he whispered. 'Not ever?'

'I swear it,' said Julia. He relaxed his grip and she turned round to face him. 'Please God we will be together always,' she said and they clung together, their brimming hearts too full for words.

CHAPTER TWENTY-FIVE

The sun shone on the fourteenth of June 1931. It shone on the small crowd gathered beside the river in Coulsdens' boatyard to see the launch of Frank's new boat, *The Spirit of Rye*, which waited on the slipway. The immediate family stood beside the vessel, dwarfed by her black hull, their faces upturned to watch the bottle of champagne which Julia held in her right hand. With her left hand she clung to her hat, which was threatened by the brisk wind that blew up from the sea and stole the warmth from the sun. Frank held the hand of four-year-old Georgina, and beside him Jack had their two-year-old son Luke in his arms. Georgina was Ian's child, named after Julia's father; Luke was Frank's first child, named after his father. As Julia's dress was blown taut against her body, only Frank knew that she was carrying his second child.

Cicely watched critically, remembering the launching she had graced when Julia was born, recalling the moving speech she had made on that occasion. She *knew* Julia would not perform the ceremony as well and took some consolation in the thought.

The photographer was shouting to everyone to keep quite still and look towards the boat. *The Spirit of Rye* belonged jointly to the owners of the boatyard. Frank would be the skipper and the profits would be shared out appropriately. He had not enjoyed boat-building and finally Julia had overcome her fears and suggested that he return to fishing as soon as the yard could finance a new boat.

Jack, much heavier now in his fifty-second year, watched with one hand shading his eyes as Julia swung back the bottle.

'I name this boat *The Spirit of Rye*,' she cried, 'and may God bless her and all who sail in her!'

Crash! As the champagne splashed down, the group standing below hastily pushed back. Jack pointed to the boat. 'What d'you think of that, young Luke?' he asked. 'You'll go fishing in that boat when you're a big boy. You'll help you pa, won't you? Be his right-hand man, eh? How would you like that?'

The boy, who was the image of his mother, blinked large serious eyes and waved a chubby hand. Everyone was clapping and there were scattered cheers. Jack turned to Frank. 'Pity Stanley and Jane couldn't be here,' he said, 'but Jane wouldn't leave him.'

Stanley had recently suffered a mild stroke which had left his right leg very weak and affected his eyesight. Jane cared for him devotedly.

'God!' said Jack – half to himself, half to Ben who also stood beside him with his arm round Vicky. 'Seems only yesterday we were all here, cheering the launching of *Silver Lady*. The old lady was still alive then and so was poor old George.' He forgot that Agnes had been there too, like a spectre at the feast. 'How long ago was that, then? Bloody years!'

Cicely sent him the same disapproving look which Sarah would have given him so many years earlier, but she made no comment. The last five years has been a struggle and the strain was telling on her looks. She was too thin now, but her health gave no cause for complaint, for which she was grateful. Her auburn hair had lost some of its glow, but it was still thick and glossy and occasionally commented upon by members of her flower-arranging group.

The band struck up a rousing sea shanty and more photographs were being taken.

Over on the other side of the crowd, Winifred stood with Ernest and the children; Emily and her husband Chick were with them, Emily radiant with her first and long-awaited pregnancy. Ernest was talking to Tommy Bird, who was looking very prosperous having won a small prize in the Irish Sweepstake two years earlier.

Vicky appeared beside Cicely and slipped an arm through hers. She had been married to Ben for two and a half years and their first child was expected in October.

'It's a pity Leo couldn't have come,' she said. 'He would have enjoyed it.'

'He was invited,' said Cicely shortly. 'Leo is a law unto himself, I'm afraid. It's out of sight, out of mind with him. That's his trouble; he has no real feeling for the family.'

Nobody noticed the handsome red-haired man who stood at the back of the crowd, his eyes fixed on Julia Bligh. He saw the laughter in her eyes as she christened the boat and he watched her climb down from the improvised dais, escorted by her husband who hugged her cheerfully and with obvious affection and pride. Julia kissed him and then turned to pick up a small boy in her arms and hug him, but almost immediately the little arms were turned towards Frank who took the boy from his wife.

The red-headed man moved from the back of the crowd in order to get a better view and saw a girl with red-gold hair take Julia by the hand and Julia bend to hug and kiss her. That must be his daughter, thought Ian. He was seeing his daughter for the first time and she was already four years old. He experienced a deep sense of loss and closed his eyes. As Helen had told him, the young Blighs were a very happy, very united family and she had warned him to stay away. However Ian, who was just back from Australia, had insisted on seeing for himself that Julia was well and happy. He had been very successful in Australia, considering his youth, and intended to settle there. He had not married and thought it unlikely that he ever would. Medicine was his whole life.

Suddenly the band stopped playing and there was a splash as the boat slid into the water. This was greeted by more cheers, more photographs and another tune from the musicians. Ian watched until most of the excitement seemed to be over. He wanted to tear himself away, but found he was unable to do so. There was a general exodus as those invited to the celebration lunch made a move in the direction of the George Hotel. People tucked themselves into the available cars and the children squeezed in to sit on their laps with much good-humoured banter.

Somehow the boatyard emptied and Ian found himself alone – except for Julia and Frank, who stood together by the last car. He saw Frank speak to Julia and she turned and looked at Ian. She shook her head, but Frank gave her a little push and reluctantly she crossed the grass. He thought she had never looked so beautiful. Motherhood suited her, he thought. She moved without hurry and her smile was fragile. She wore a fitted, calf-length dress in a fine print of red and white with a white collar and a brimmed hat. When she reached him she held out a hand; it was cool, he noticed, and her handshake was firm.

'I didn't know you were here,' she said levelly. 'I'm so sorry. Frank saw you and thought I should say "Hullo".'

'That was very kind of him.' Ian's throat was dry.

'You look well,' said Julia. 'Helen tells me you like Australia.'

'Yes, it's a beautiful country. The land of opportunity, as they say.'

'And you've made your home there.'

'Yes. I doubt if I shall ever live in England again permanently. This is a special visit because my grandmother is in such poor health, as you know. She says you call regularly and she adores seeing the children. It's very kind of you.'

'Not at all. It's my pleasure. She knows that Georgina is your daughter, of course.'

He nodded. 'You were right to tell her. She always wanted a grandchild – although she has kept the secret well. My parents don't know.'

There was a long pause. Ian had so much he longed to say, but Julia merely wondered how soon she could politely rejoin Frank.

'I'm glad the boatyard is such a success,' Ian said. 'Congratulations to all concerned!'

'We've had a long struggle,' Julia told him, 'and it wasn't easy. It was ironic really – a strange twist of fate. Coulsdens were on the point of bankruptcy when Papa died. The insurance on *Silver Lady* helped to put the boatyard back on its feet – that and the repair work which came in from the other boats damaged in the collision. Add to that the money my mother and Mama Sarah left me – well, the rest is history. We survived the first twelve months and have never looked back. It's astonishing that a terrible tragedy at sea should bring about something good.'

'An ill wind,' said Ian.

'I suppose so. It's almost as though my father gave his life for the family. I like to think he'd be glad if he knew – that he didn't die in vain.'

He laughed gently. 'You were always a worrier,' he said. 'I remember you telling me how guilty you felt about making friends with Agnes . . . that first day in the car.'

'That was a long time ago,' she smiled.

There was another awkward pause and Ian wanted to say, 'I'm sorry!' or 'Forgive me.'

She glanced towards Frank. 'Did you see your daughter?' she asked Ian. 'I expect that's why you came.'

He searched her eyes for a glimmer of the love she had once felt for him, but saw only indifference and . . . was it pity?

'I saw her,' he said. 'Yes, she's a lovely girl.'

'We love our little red-head,' she told him. 'We have a son, too.'

'Yes, I know. Helen writes to me. She says you're very happy—'

'Oh yes, I am. I hope you are too.'

Ian looked at her and she saw the regret in his eyes. 'Do you?' he asked, his voice low.

'Of course I do,' she said, surprised.

'I don't think I shall ever marry,' he told her. 'I think I've thrown away my chance of happiness, but I have my work, and that must suffice. It gives me great satisfaction.'

'Helen tells me you are highly respected. I'm so glad for you.'

Suddenly Ian took hold of her hand and whispered, 'Will you tell me I'm forgiven? *Please*, Julia!'

She said gently, 'You are forgiven, Ian. Of course you are. That's all in the past now and I am so very happy and very lucky. We love each other, you see. You don't have to feel guilty for what happened.'

'But I do,' he said.

Julia smiled. 'Now who is the worrier?' she asked. Then still smiling, she withdrew her hand from his. 'Well, Ian, you'll have to excuse me. They won't start lunch without us.'

He clasped the slim cool hand in his for the last time and said, 'Goodbye, Julia.'

'Goodbye, Ian. Be happy.'

With a brief smile she turned and walked back to Frank, who immediately put an arm round her possessively and helped her into the waiting car. After they had driven away Ian took a last look round the deserted yard and down to the water where the new boat rocked at her moorings, the splashes of champagne already drying on her hull. He gazed past the boat to the flat marshland that stretched towards the sea and then glanced back to the red-roofed houses which clung to the rising ground that was the town. *The Spirit of Rye*, he thought, and the Coulsden family. They were indivisible and Julia Coulsden, now Julia Bligh, was where she belonged, among her own people, in her own world. Everything had turned out for the best – for Julia if not for him. A little of the burden of guilt lifted from his narrow shoulders as he walked slowly back to his motor and prepared to drive away from the memories.

In the dining-room of the George Hotel a cheer went up as Frank and Julia arrived and the celebrations began in earnest. Outside the June sunshine lay over the little town and below the cliffs the silver ribbon that was the river wound its way across the marsh to join the sea.